A HOST
OF FURIOUS
FANCIES

A HOST OF FURIOUS FANCIES

Mercedes Lackey
Rosemary Edghill

A HOST OF FURIOUS FANCIES

A Baen Book

Baen Publishing Enterprises
P.O. Box 1403
Riverdale, NY 10471
www.baen.com

ISBN: 978-1-4516-3800-4

Cover art by Eric Williams

First Baen printing, September 2012

Distributed by Simon & Schuster
1230 Avenue of the Americas
New York, NY 10020

Library of Congress Cataloging-in-Publication Data

Lackey, Mercedes.
  [Beyond world's end]
 A host of furious fancies / by Mercedes Lackey and Rosemary Edghill.
    p. cm.
  ISBN 978-1-4516-3800-4 (pbk.)
 1. Banyon, Eric (Fictitious character)--Fiction. 2. Bards and bardism--Fiction. 3. Musicians--Fiction. 4. Wizards--Fiction. 5. Manhattan (New York, N.Y.)--Fiction. I. Edghill, Rosemary. II. Lackey, Mercedes. Spirits white as lightning. III. Title.
  PS3562.A246B49 2012
  813'.54--dc23
                            2012022387

Printed in the United States of America

10 9 8 7 6 5 4 3 2 1

CONTENTS

❖❖

BEYOND WORLD'S END

"By a knight of ghosts and shadows
I summoned am to tourney
Ten leagues beyond the wide world's end
Methinks it is no journey."

—Tom O' Bedlam (traditional)

ONE:
THE PARTING OF FRIENDS

❖

"Are you sure you really want to do this?" Beth asked Eric for roughly the five hundredth time in the past month.

As a long-time stranger to big cities, it was hard for Eric to believe that there was anywhere in New York City where she could have been heard without shouting, but this strange little tree-shaded court was somehow as quiet as a desert canyon miles outside of Los Angeles—and just about as hot. It was September, but there was no hint of fall in the air, and the leaves on the slender maples growing in their squares of earth allocated in the sidewalk were still green. Today was one of the shimmering-hot days that persisted well into October here, and the stone of the buildings surrounding them seemed to hold and reflect back every degree of heat. The buildings also shut most of the traffic noise out, making a private oasis in the heart of the city. Beth and Kory—and their motorcycles-cum-elvensteeds—were the only creatures on the street besides Eric.

Eric looked up at the old apartment building that was going to be his home for the next year or so, and nodded.

"I'm sure," he replied firmly. "Things couldn't go on the way they have been—and none of us wanted them to." Then he grinned. "Besides, you aren't going to be that far away by Underhill standards. And I'm a fully functional Bard now, remember? I can come visit you any time I want to—or any time you guys are getting stir-crazy."

Beth looked as if she might want to argue that point for a moment; then, instead of saying anything, she just sighed.

"You certainly aren't the same Eric Banyon anymore," she admitted. "You not only have feck, but you know what machine to buy your clues from," she said, grinning proudly.

"And I brought my own roll of quarters to put in the machine," Eric shot back, grinning.

Earlier this morning, the three of them had packed up the last of their stuff from the friend's place they'd been crashing at between Faire weekends. The Sterling Forest RenFaire ran every year from July to September at a site about an hour north of New York City. There was even a Nexus there, Elfhame Everforest, the only one on the East Coast, tucked away in the State Park that surrounded the Fairesite.

The three of them had been working the Faire together, just like old times. Only this time it was a farewell performance, and they'd all known it. It had added a certain sweetness to the music. But all good things must come to an end.

He put down his two bags to hug her. "No worries, pretty lady. I'll be fine. The kids at Juilliard are already calling me 'old man,' and taking bets on who's going to win the confrontations between me and the administration. Odds are in my favor, by the way." Classes started on Monday, but he'd already been up to the school several times, for Registration and Orientation. It hadn't changed much in all the years he'd been away—schools had a lot in common with Underhill in that respect.

Beth traded places with Kory, who was not at all ashamed to bestow as hearty a hug on Eric as Beth had. "You do know the way Underhill, if you need to come," Korendil appealed. There was an unspoken plea in the elf's emerald-green eyes. "Do not allow pride to keep you from seeking your friends if you need help."

Eric shook his shaggy head; haircuts had not been a priority either Underhill or at the Faire, and he didn't want to do anything about the length of his mane just yet. "Believe me, Elfhame Everforest is the first place I'll head for if I get into trouble," he promised. "Now, you two—go! If you don't make some tracks, you won't reach Sterling Forest before sunset, elvensteeds or no elvensteeds, and this is going to be your last RenFaire gig before the baby comes. I think I can manage to move my last two bags into an apartment without help—and take care of myself once I've settled in."

They'd been staying with Bonnie and Kit up in Inwood—a comic book writer and a Witch that Beth knew from years ago—while Eric and Beth made the many purchases necessary to turn a rented apartment into a home—*and* waited the several weeks for delivery of the furniture! Eric wasn't displeased to have the transition time: living Underhill for an extended period made returning to the World Above a distinct shock. And no place else, in Underhill or the World Above, was quite like New York City. It made even the Chaos Lands seem quiet.

Beth paused to hug him once more. "You know, I think you can," she admitted, looking just a little tearful. "And maybe that's the scariest part of all. You don't need us anymore."

There wasn't any reply he could make to that statement—there was enough truth in it to sting—so Eric didn't bother to try. Instead, he picked up his bags and moved away from the curb, walking backwards, as Kory and Beth mounted their sleek, exotic motorcycles.

A third bike already resided in the tiny parking lot behind the building, and Eric had no fear that anyone was going to steal it. For one thing, they wouldn't be able to find a starter or a place to hotwire it. For another, *she* wouldn't let them. Lady Day was an elvensteed, and could take any form she chose. Eric didn't really ride her, she carried him; he could go to sleep while riding her and she would get him safely to his destination no matter what the conditions were. She could take any shape he wanted her to—he'd heard that there were even elves in other Elfhames that had elvensteeds the shape of racing cars, though frankly Eric would believe *that* when he saw it.

His mind was already running ahead, into his future here. He preferred her as a motorcycle, and Lady Day preferred to take that form, but as soon as the weather turned, she was going to have to take on the form of a little econobox car, unless he intended to take the subway across town to Juilliard. She wasn't looking forward to that, and frankly, neither was he, but that was the price he paid for returning to Juilliard—East Coast winters.

Maybe I can have her clone a Kia, a Neon or a sporty little Isuzu 4x4 instead. That wouldn't be too out-of-keeping with my cover story, Eric thought hopefully. It had been so long since he'd had to worry about money at all that he wasn't too sure he remembered the gory details. *I can always say I put the bike in storage for the winter. Nobody at Juilliard is likely to know enough about cars to wonder how I can keep a maintenance hog fuelled and running!*

Eric paused at the front door of the building for a last look back. Beth and Kory had donned their helmets, and "started" the bikes, thus making further conversation a moot point. The elvensteeds not only knew enough to counterfeit the roar of powerful motorcycle engines, they seemed to enjoy doing so. The two riders, anonymous now in their matching helmets and leathers, pulled neat little reversal moves that got them going in the right direction on the street with an appropriate amount of tire spin and smoke. They waved, and Eric tucked one bag under his arm and freed up a hand to wave back. He kept waving as they roared out of sight.

That didn't take long in the city; they were out of sight as soon as they turned the corner. He evened his load again, and walked soberly up to the door of the building.

Home. Sweet home? Well, home is what you make it, I guess. This is as good as any. And a lot better than some. Good thing I'm not on a starving student's budget.

He could have had any apartment in any building in the city, of course: as an adult student, Eric didn't have the same residence restrictions that the minors and first-year students did at Juilliard, and a fellow with a safety-deposit box full of gold Krugerrands could pretty much afford whatever he wanted. But he'd gone out walking one day when he and Beth and Kory first arrived here, and found the old building as if he'd been drawn to it. It'd had a name once—most old New York apartment buildings were named—but time had eroded the carving above the door, until all that remained was a florid "G" and a barely legible "ouse." Something-house. Maybe Gargoyle House, for when Eric had looked up—he was enough of an out-of-towner to do that frequently—he had been surprised to see the hunched winged forms of classic medieval gargoyles perched on the building's four corners. New York was rich in such hidden sculpture, he knew. Art for birds, someone had once called it.

There'd been a discreet sign in the building manager's window—the only "For Rent" sign he could remember seeing anywhere, actually—and the building itself had attracted him. There were three apartments available. One was a corner apartment on the top floor, and when he saw that there was a gargoyle perched right outside the living-room window, he'd been sold.

That had been the good part. The bad part was the age of the building. Old buildings had old building problems. Still, it had a lot more heart to it than some of those high-rise condos that were going up everywhere. And a place like this would be a lot easier to explain if anyone ever asked.

For a wonder, the building manager—her name was Toni Hernandez, a middle-aged Latina woman—had been ready to show him around right then. The building was of about the same vintage as the Gunfight at the OK Corral, which meant that the ceilings were high and the bathrooms were ancient—which meant very cool lion-footed bathtubs, but teeny sinks and plumbing he wasn't altogether sure about. The kitchen cabinets and counters looked like originals from when the building was new, and forget central air—if he wanted to be cool during the summer and early fall, he'd have to buy a window AC, and hope the wiring could stand it. He was going to have to swelter for the rest of this year, though—by the time he could get a window unit delivered and installed at this time of year, snow would already be falling.

As for the heating, it was all by ancient steam pipes, and those didn't function until the super decided it was cold enough—and Eric knew all about the way steam pipes sang and banged at night.

He'd probably need to supplement the radiators with space heaters, given how far away his apartment was from the basement boilers, anyway.

He'd been assured that the wiring was modern, though—and looking the apartment over, seeing all new cover plates and plenty of grounded outlets, Eric had felt fairly sure he wasn't being lied to. If the wiring was modern enough to accept the load of a computer, a microwave, and an air conditioner, he felt he could put up with steam heat and ancient plumbing. He'd accepted the top-floor apartment on the spot, and the rest had been mere formality.

The building might be old, but it had some nifty modern amenities where it really counted, and considering its West Side location, Eric was surprised that the building hadn't gone condo a long time ago. A security system mounted discreetly in an etched brass plate beside the door had a code for every tenant—and with ten digits, it would take a long time for someone to hit a correct one at random.

He punched it in now—a little slow, but he'd taken care to pick a string of numbers fairly easy to remember—and walked in through the front door. The coolness of the lobby was welcome after the heat outside, and as he usually did, he paused to admire the foyer—very Art Nouveau, and all of it original. Even the opulent brass faces of the mailboxes were vintage. Of course, that meant that the elevator was pretty vintage too—hydraulic, and in mint condition, but very slow. Ms. Hernandez told him that when the building had been built, people had been afraid of fast elevators. So it rose gently and serenely at a less-than-walking pace, but hey, if he was in a hurry, he could always use the stairs.

The elevator took its time in arriving on the top floor, but that wasn't bad either. He wasn't as frisky as he'd been when he first came to school at Juilliard, himself. He liked the folding bronze safety-gate; it reminded him of an old hotel he'd once stayed in that actually had an elevator attendant, little red uniform and all. Fortunately the building didn't come with a doorman, like some of the posh places along Park Avenue did. He didn't think he could quite handle that.

The long elevator ride up to the 10th floor gave Eric time to think and to probe his feelings as if they were a newly filled tooth. Did it hurt, Beth and Kory going off like that and leaving him behind? Should he reconsider?

Nope. It doesn't really hurt, it just feels different. It stopped hurting a long time ago. And the decision isn't really new. It's old.

He remembered the day Beth had first told him she was pregnant. She and Kory had looked so happy—Beth wanted a large family, and elves were crazy about children anyway—but all Eric had felt was fear, as though he'd made a disastrous mistake in fathering this child. It had been Beth who'd gently broken it to him that she already knew what Eric had only that moment discovered: that while he'd been growing into his magic, she and Kory had been growing into a couple. Without him.

Only not really. After what we've been through together, we'll be friends forever. Only it's a different kind of friendship now. In some ways it's better.

Better, because it lacked the element of sexual anxiety that had flavored the earliest days of his relationship with Beth . . . and Kory. This was something strong and deep that didn't need sex to fuel it, something that would last as long as the pillars of Underhill.

The elevator creaked to a halt on the top floor, jarring him out of his reverie, and Eric opened the safety gate and the door. His apartment was a corner apartment, which had been another selling point. Its location meant that there would be less noise from fellow tenants, and no noise from the elevator itself, as well as a cooling cross-breeze on most days. He still wasn't used to how *noisy* this city was—even in the middle of Central Park you could hear the sirens and the traffic noises.

New York, New York, it's a wonderful town. The Bronx is up and the Battery's down. And the city never sleeps.

Like the lobby, the hallway decor had somehow survived being "modernized"; it was original, and for a wonder, no one had ripped off the vintage *paté verine*[1] light-fixtures. Then again, maybe that was why the owners had put in the security system in the first place.

---

[1]Glass-paste

Architecture thieves were only one of the problems of life in the Big City.

The only concession to the modern world was in the carpet running the length of the hall; it was standard grey-beige industrial stuff, but it didn't clash with the Art Nouveau wallpaper and frosted-glass fixtures, not all of which were lights. There were cameras in some of those wall fixtures, and smoke and heat detectors too, and sprinklers in the ceiling—everything the heart could desire from a safety and security standpoint. Another selling point, not that a fully trained Bard had much to fear from human thugs. Magical attacks were another matter, but frankly, Eric wasn't expecting many of those.

At the end of the hall was his door. No hollow-core flimsy barricade or scary metal portal this, but a solid slab of oakwood, polished deep brown with the passing of years, with brass lockplates and doorknob that gleamed brightly against the old wood. Here was the building's second concession to the modern age—there were two key-operated deadbolts plus the door key, and a final key pad on which once more to enter his ten-digit code. If he didn't enter it, or keyed it wrong and didn't correct himself when it beeped at him, the system would alert Ms. Hernandez—she'd check the cameras and maybe call the cops.

I wonder why this place has got so much security? Or maybe this is normal for New York? After all, I have been away for a while. . . .

Like about 20—no, closer to 30—years. Though he'd spent a lot of that time Underhill, where time flowed more slowly than it did in the World Above. That was one of the reasons he'd been willing to risk coming back so openly. Anybody who was still looking after this long would be looking for a guy in his forties—not a sassy young dude still in his twenties.

He negotiated the three key-locks—here was a moment of fumbling with the ring of unfamiliar keys (Eric hadn't carried keys in years, and had kept losing them for the first few weeks)—punched in his code, and watched while the light went from red to green. Then he was inside and locking the door of his new home behind him. Beth's friends said it would soon become second nature, but for now it was an effort to remember the actions involved.

At last he turned away from the door and looked around with a sudden feeling of hesitancy. Even with as much work as Beth and Kory had already done while he'd been getting squared away with Juilliard, there was a lot still to unpack and arrange, and most of it was brand-new untouched-by-human-hands stuff. This was the first time in his life he'd had this many *things*.

Immediately before him was the living room, a huge space (so Bonnie had said) by New York standards. A new leather couch and matching recliner in the sort of oxblood brown that reminded him of Old English clubs sat cozily in front of the fireplace—this place was retro enough to have fireplaces, (with terrific white-marble mantels, though he didn't think the fireplace still worked). To the right of the sofa and behind it were the tall sash windows, and if he looked up, Eric could just see the back of the gargoyle on the corner of the roof. Against the blank wall was his new rack system and a television and laser-disk player. In the corner farthest from the windows was his desk—light cherry, from Levinger's—which mostly held a brand-new computer with a music keyboard and speakers as well as the usual techie stuff.

Sheepskins covered the worn wooden parquet floor, and the glazed-chintz curtains in an archival William Morris pattern—mostly deep greens, with a hint of orange—that Beth had picked out were pulled open to display the view. There were flowers in a blue glass vase on the mantlepiece—moonlilies, so that was Kory's touch; they didn't grow anywhere but Underhill, and a daily little touch of magic would keep them alive forever. The heat made the apartment seem stuffy, and Eric moved around opening windows. Though there was a six week wait for delivery of an air conditioner, he'd been able to pick up a couple of wall fans. He lifted them into the kitchen and bedroom windows now and switched them on. A cooling breeze began to waft through the apartment, and Eric sighed with relief. He could manage to be pretty comfortable, so long as he didn't get into any heavy lifting.

Eric still had a faint feeling of trespassing when he moved around the place. It looked like an apartment belonging to a moderately (okay, let's admit it: more than moderately) prosperous classical flautist—at least, until you got to the CD collection, which was currently still in boxes waiting to be unpacked. He'd had one heck of a time putting that together, and the look on the clerk's face at Plastic Meltdown over in the East Village when he kept coming up to the counter with another stack of disks had been worth every penny. Thanks to a little help, both magical and non, Eric Banyon had an A-1 credit rating and an AmEx Platinum card to prove it. Thanks to the Krugerrands in his safe deposit box, he even had a way to pay the humongous bill that was going to arrive!

Beside the empty bookshelves—more light cherry from Levinger's—were boxes of books, also waiting to be shelved. He'd had almost as much fun in the Strand as he had in the record store. More, in a way, because he kept straying over to the children's sections, picking up volumes he'd read as a kid and wanted to get reacquainted with. This place was as unlike his L.A. apartment as possible—and just as unlike the house he'd shared with Beth and Kory in San Francisco. That had been due to calculated effort on all their parts. He was starting over, in a sense, and he should start fresh.

Beth had stocked the kitchen, so he wasn't going to starve, and she hadn't loaded it down with equipment he didn't know how to use and food he didn't know how to cook. Mostly microwave stuff, he suspected, to go with the mother-of-all-microwaves sitting in silent splendor on the white-marble kitchen counter.

It was too quiet, suddenly, and he walked over to the rack and turned on WQXR, the local classical station. Stravinsky's *Pulcinella Suite* filled the room; not his first choice, but not bad, and more to the point, not reeking of Omens and Portents. He'd had about enough of those for a while.

He took his bags into the bedroom and once again was confronted by newness. The bedroom was small, only 14x14, with just enough room for a double bed with a bookcase headboard. The bed, covered with a thick, red, silk-covered goosedown comforter—another of Kory's touches, Eric suspected, because elves liked color and weren't shy about using it—was a classier version of one of those adjustable beds you saw on late-night TV commercials. He hadn't wanted a waterbed; that would have come with too many memories of Beth and Kory attached. The headboard had built-in lamps and his new alarm clock (retro-Deco to match the building) nestled cozily in a nook that would be difficult to reach if he wasn't awake. On top of the matching bureau was a smaller television, and one of those nifty-keen Bose Wave radio/CD players. The curtains were the same glowing red silk as the comforter. There was another sheepskin rug—dark brown this time—on the floor in front of the bed; it reminded Eric slightly of a large flat dog.

He carried his bags over to the walk-in closet and opened it. It was the old-fashioned kind with drawers in the back and several tiers of shelves reaching all the way up to the ceiling, and it was full of bags of brand new clothing that he hadn't yet opened. Eric slowly unpacked his bags and hung the only things he owned that had any wear on them on polished cedar hangers at the back. The clothing was nothing if not flamboyant; Faire garb, all of it, and all of it made by magic. That was Kory's forté: he could produce clothing at the drop of a pointed ear. It wasn't likely that Eric would need any of this at any time soon, but he wanted to have it around. A link to his past—to the Faires and Underhill—to the only part of his life that Eric thought of as real.

Everything else in the apartment had come by way of the efforts of Eric's mentor, who was as skillful at producing gold as Kory was at producing clothing—and as Beth was at knowing where to shop. Thanks to Master Mage Dharinel's work, Eric was not going to have to worry about where his money was coming from for a very long time, if ever. The rest of his tenure at Juilliard was already paid for in advance. His rent was paid up for the next year in advance. Utilities, phone, cable, ditto—all handled out of an escrow account administered by a "friend of the family" down in Wall Street some-where, just so Eric wouldn't have to worry about them. And in addition to everything else, Eric had a bank account again, besides that excellent credit rating and the emergency stash of Krugerrands.

As for the inevitable IRS agents (if nothing worse)—well, he'd found a way to handle them. They'd stopped in DC before coming up here; Eric had set up shop outside the agency, put out his hat, and played his flute until he found one agent that was susceptible. A little Bardic magic, a sob story about being out of work in Mexico for the last couple of years, a tale of winning an unspecified lottery outside the States, and an expressed eagerness to pay his rightful share of taxes (and a check for the amount the nice agent deemed appropriate), and his record with the IRS was as clean and shiny as Lady Day. He could use his own social security number without being afraid it would red-flag every Federal computer from here to Ultima Thule . . . in fact, his entire record was so clean and shiny that anyone checking on him might suspect he was in the Federal Witness Protection Program. Eric's name, his real name, was on the mailbox, the apartment lease, the utilities, in the phone book, and on the driver's license and bank and credit cards in his wallet. He wasn't hiding, he wasn't Underhill, and he didn't have to start thinking of ways to escape whenever he saw a cop or someone in a too-perfect suit. *I'm a person again,* he thought with wonder. *I'm real. Whatever I do will go with me; I can't shed my past like a snake with an old skin.*

He went back into the living room and sat in his new chair, the glossy leather chilly through the back of his damp shirt. He listened to the Moonlight Sonata wafting in courtesy of the radio station. It all felt—odd. Very odd. Not luxurious, no—strangely enough, although this was luxury by all common standards, it did not match the level of sumptuousness Underhill, or even the standards of comfort Kory had established in their old San Francisco townhouse. But it was all Eric's, chosen to please only his taste and no one else's, and it was real and solid, not something conjured up out of energy and thin air like goods of elvish making.

It might have felt restrictive after the bootless freedom of the past few years, but somehow it didn't. It felt solid and comfortable and good. And when the Krugerrands ran out, and the account that covered his rent and utilities expired, he'd have to have a job to pay for all of this.

Not that he had any doubt that he'd be able to do that when the time came. He was probably one of the few people, if not the only person, who ever quit Juilliard and then returned to finish what he'd started.

Returned to finish . . . that had been a recurring theme lately. It wasn't the first time the thought had crossed his mind over time—but the first time, it hadn't been his thought at all.

"You have unfinished business."

When he closed his eyes he could hear that stern voice saying those words even over the strains of Beethoven in the here-and-now. He didn't have to think about it; the scene played out behind his eyes without effort, as clearly as if it had happened yesterday.

Underhill. He'd been Underhill, at Elfhame Misthold, and he hadn't known what day, week, or even month it was. Time moved strangely Underhill; light came and went, but there was no telling if it was the end of a day or if the Queen of the Hill had decided she was tired of light and wanted some darkness for a change. Beth—Beth needed not to be Above, in the mortal world, where there were law-enforcement people who thought she was responsible for some very unfortunate occurrences. And she was—but not in the way that they thought.

Besides, as the elves with the ability to See into the future had said at the time, at some point Real Soon Bethie was going to show up preggers, even more reason not to go back into the World Above. So he and Kory were living Underhill with her, and in that strange timeless land Eric had thrown himself into his music—which meant his magic—fully and completely for the first time in his life.

After the Loma Prieta almost-disaster, the Nightflyers, and the absolute proof to everybody involved of the madness of allowing a half-trained Bard to run around leaking magic and going off unexpectedly, he'd had little choice. It hadn't been ambition that had driven him, it had been desperation. Beth was slipping away from him more every day, and he knew it. Things were changing in his life, even in the timeless world of Underhill, and he didn't like it. Maybe he'd thought that being a real Bard, one with full control of his powers like the old Druidic Bards,—Merlin, Taliesen, Gwion—would lure Beth back and put him on an even footing with Korendil, Elven Knight of Elfhame Sun-Descending. Heck, Kory didn't have all that much magic by elven standards, surely Eric could catch up!

But before long, the music and magic stopped being a crutch, or a means to an end, and became the end itself.

One day—a day much like any other, here—he had finished playing and put his flute down, waiting for Dharinel to give him the usual critique. Dharinel was a Magus Major and one of the most powerful of Elven Bards in any Elfhame, anywhere, and there was always a critique. Either Eric's control over the magic energy was not firm enough, or it was too grasping, and he didn't let it flow. He went too slowly, or too fast. There was always something wrong, and Dharinel was always correct when he pointed those things out.

It had all felt right when he played, completely and utterly right, but it had felt right in the past, too. But this time when he stopped, Dharinel said nothing for a very long time. The perfumed mists of Underhill drifted past them both, and the birds that had stilled out of politeness while Eric played resumed their song. There was no sunshine, of course: there was no sun Underhill, only a perpetual twilight, except when the Prince or the Queen deemed it appropriate to deepen the twilight to something like true night, so that the fireflies, Fae Lights, and Faerie Illuminations could enliven the darkness. Eric held his breath and wondered what he had done wrong this time. Was it that horrible?

Finally Dharinel had let out his breath and opened his jewel-toned eyes. "I have nothing more to teach you," he said in his controlled, utterly perfect voice.

Eric had shaken his head. "What?" he blurted. "Was I that bad?"

"You were that good," Dharinel corrected. "I have nothing more to teach you. The rest will come with maturity and practice, and it is a pity that you are not of the Blood, for you would be a force to reckon with in a hundred years or so." He had actually smiled then; a thin smile, but the expression so seldom crossed Dharinel's sardonic lips that Eric had nearly fallen off his bench. "As it is, in a mere handful of mortal years, you will be a force to reckon with in the mortal world. And that is where you must go now. You have unfinished business there."

The moment Dharinel said those words, all of the vague discontent that had been in Eric's heart attained an object. Once music had become his All again, he had been able to come to terms with the fact that Beth and Kory were an Item and he had been slowly eased out of that side of their relationship. They would always be friends, the three of them, but—Kory and Beth were a pair, and he wasn't part of that structure anymore. He'd allowed it to happen without trying to fight. And once those last pieces of the puzzle had fallen into place, like the tumblers in a lock, he'd known what he should do.

Besides, Beth had a lot of Things she needed to deal with. She and Kory wanted kids, and while Eric liked kids in the abstract, he wasn't ready to play daddy right now, even though he'd fathered the child she was carrying. It had seemed like a good solution at the time—call it a kind of parting gift. Kory and his cousins were very pleased with the idea of raising a baby-Bard from scratch in Underhill where she could be properly taught. Though Eric knew that Beth wanted more children—and with Kory—an elf couldn't father a child on a mortal woman without a lot of high-powered— and very dangerous—magical intervention. Halfling births could be arranged in a number of ways, but most of them involved stealing life-energy from another source to allow the woman to conceive— and that meant wholesale slaughter of the innocents who donated that energy. There were rumors that there were gentler ways, but no one in Misthold was really certain what was involved, actually, though Kory had the elven librarians searching the most ancient records and sending to the other hames for hints of the ancient Seleighe quickening magics.

But unlike Eric, Beth really didn't have much choice about staying in Underhill. Those very unpleasant people from the "alphabet agencies" were still looking for Beth. This was bad. It meant that Beth Kentraine could never live in the real world again, unless she concocted a whole new identity or moved to another country where no one would ask her about her past. She could visit—with care and constant vigilance—but she couldn't live in the States anymore. And babies and the Faire circuit didn't coexist well, at the best of times. . . .

And if the two of them didn't have enough problems, there's the fact that if Beth spends long enough in Underhill, she CAN'T come out, ever. She'll die. And before that happens, even if she does find some way to live Outside, she gets older. And Kory . . . doesn't. Or not fast enough, anyway. He's young by Sidhe standards. He has centuries ahead of him. Bethie has less than a century. There are spells that can slow her aging, but they'd tie her and Kory together for the rest of their lives—and shorten his. And even if she were willing to take that kind of responsibility, she won't even let Dharinel try anything like that while she feels responsible for me!

It all had come together in that moment. Eric wanted his life back—his life in the World Above. There were things he needed to finish, like his degree, if only to prove to himself that he could. And he just didn't like Underhill all that much, to tell the truth. He had at first. He'd enjoyed the timelessness, the tranquility. But after a while, what was sweet had become cloying, what was tranquil seemed stale, and a growing restlessness brought it home to him that nothing ever changed here.

"You're right," he'd told his mentor. "I have unfinished business. And I don't belong here." He'd looked around, for a moment. "Maybe no mortal belongs here—"

"Unless they're sorely wounded in heart or soul, lad," Dharinel said softly, so softly Eric had to strain to hear him. "Only then, when mortal sunlight brings pain, not gladness, can they bide happily with us. Or if they're so heart-bound to one of the Blood that losing the sun of the mortal lands seems no kind of sacrifice to make."

Eric opened his eyes in the here-and-now and sighed. Well, if anyone qualified as "wounded in the heart or soul," it was Beth. Hell, she still couldn't even sleep at night unless someone had her sandwiched between him and the wall—except when she was Underhill. Living at Kit and Bonnie's during the week, doing the Sterling Forest RenFaire on weekends, was one of the rare situations when she relaxed outside of Underhill—it would be next to impossible for a government goon to insert himself into the organization of Rennies. Rennies all knew each other, or knew people who knew each other, and the habits and mannerisms of a Rennie were something it would take a long time for a government agent to master. Not to mention the esoteric skill-sets it took to get hired on at the Faires in the first place! Beth could feel safe there, and at night, surrounded by other campers (and guarded by her and Kory's elvensteeds) it would be pretty hard for anyone to get at them. Impossible to do it quietly.

Unless you're a ninja, and I don't think they take government contracts. At least I hope they don't.

The three of them had already planned the trip to the Sterling Forest Faire before Eric had made his decision—he'd just expanded the trip to include his reentry into the human race. It hadn't been easy, but the biggest hurdle had actually been getting an audition to reapply at Juilliard in the first place. Convincing Beth that this was something he had to do had been child's play. Kory hadn't objected at all, largely because Dharinel, who was his superior as well as his Elder, had made it quite clear in his quiet but implacable way that this was something he felt Eric had to do.

After that it was just a matter of lining up the ducks, and shooting them down. And here he was.

He shook his head, levering himself up out of the chair with a sigh. He had a lot to unpack, so he might as well get to it. He could always brood later. There'd be a lot of time for it. And it wouldn't get much cooler even if he waited: the stone and concrete of the city held heat for hours after the sun set, unlike both L.A. and San Francisco, where temperatures tended to drop sharply once the sun went down. Since his apartment was near the Hudson River he could expect a drop of at least a few degrees tonight, but not really enough to count on. Still, there were only three or four more weeks of this hot weather at the very most, and he could always conjure up some cool if he really needed it.

Say . . . there's an idea. He rubbed his sweaty forehead, and then went into the bedroom for his flute.

Music was a handy tool for focusing his Bardic magic, but in most situations it wasn't absolutely necessary. Still, Eric enjoyed the game of fitting the music to the spell. And here in the World Above, where magic didn't fill the ambient air as it did in Underhill, it was nice to have a bit of a framework to work within.

He fitted the pieces of the flute together and blew an exploratory trill before segueing into "Troika," one of the five pieces that made up Moussorsky's *Pictures at an Exhibition.* A troika was a three-horse Russian sleigh, and you could almost hear the sleigh-bells and the cadence of the horses' pacing feet in the bounce of the main theme. Eric closed his eyes, imagining the crunch of hooves on snow, the clear cold bite of the wintery air—

But not too much. We just want to make it a little cooler in here, not turn the place into an icebox. . . .

As a pleasant chill rolled through the apartment, Eric opened his eyes. He could see a faint shimmer of magic over the windows, where the parameters of the spell he had set turned the air from hot to cold as it passed through the window. In a few moments, the muggy cloyingness of the air was gone. The spell would fade away naturally after a few hours in order to avoid being too disruptive; after all, he could set it again any time he needed to. Eric walked back out into the living room, flute in hand.

Now for a little urban renewal.

He started with the CD collection, although the first things he unpacked didn't go into the storage cabinets, they went on the machine, and when he was done, he had a stack of thirty empty jewel boxes piled beside it.

He set the changer on "shuffle," and let it rip, sinking back down in his chair and thinking amusedly that this was one mix no radio station on the planet would ever match. *Hey, it's K-Banyon radio, all Celtic, all the time!*

Then again, maybe there was one station that could match his CD-shuffle. WYRD, a little station somewhere in the middle of nowhere in North Carolina or Georgia or someplace like that, was allegedly programmed by elves. All he knew was the one or two times he'd accidentally picked it up, it had played things he was only thinking about, as if the DJ were reading his mind. And supposedly, you could count on it to give you omens of what was going to happen to you.

No thank you. And I certainly hope and pray my CD player doesn't start doing so.

Well, he had some pretty esoteric platters in his Celtica-mix today; stuff he hadn't known was back in production, stuff he hadn't known was in production in the first place. Strange little labels he'd never heard of, and some that were clearly self-produced.

"We don't get a lot of call for this—" The clerk had said that over and over, in a bewildered voice, as Eric brought out disk after disk that wasn't in his computer. Finally one of the assistant managers had taken pity on the poor kid and sent him off to help a Gen-Xer find the latest Smashing Pumpkins CD.

"Our owner has a hobby," the assistant manager explained, as he patiently entered the prices and stock numbers manually. "He's independently wealthy; as long as the store breaks even, he doesn't care. His hobby is to make sure that no matter what someone's musical taste is, he'll always find fabulous surprises here. You should see the mail he gets—catalogues from individual artists, even. So—a lot of stuff may sit around for a year or more before anyone buys it. He doesn't care; he knows that someday someone is going to want it, be amazed and thrilled that it's here, and keep coming back to see what else shows up. That's why the store's called 'Plastic Meltdown.' He expects credit cards to go into overload when the right people walk through the door."

Eric just grinned. "Well, I know I'm going to put my plastic through a workout here on a regular basis. Does this happen often?"

"Often enough," the middle-aged fellow said, with a wink. "Yesterday it was someone who collects movie scores—she was funny, kept saying, 'My God! My God!' until I thought the Big Guy was going to show up to find out why she was calling on Him. Today it's you. Tomorrow, probably no one unusual, but next week, maybe an opera buff. The heavy hitters are usually from out of town; the rest of us know we don't have to blow all our savings at once."

If that was a subtle inquiry, Eric didn't answer it quite as the fellow expected. "I just took the plunge on a CD player—I resisted for a long, long time; now that I'm a convert, I put the vinyl in storage and gave away the tapes, and I'm replacing everything with CDs. And picking up stuff I didn't know was around."

The clerk coughed, but didn't comment; it was a Centurion AmEx card on the register.

He probably sees a lot of heavy rollers in here.

"Win the lottery?" the clerk asked instead, as the total on the register continued to mount.

Eric grinned, since that was his original cover story. "Actually," he said, "yes, I did. Low enough it paid out all at once, high enough to let me do what I've wanted to for a long time."

The clerk stared at him for a moment as if to see if he was joking, then said, almost reverently, "Does any of that luck rub off?"

Eric chuckled. "Not that I've ever heard of. You know luck—you always get it when you don't need it. I was pretty happy where I was—playing for tourists down in Mexico. Climate was good, cheap to live down there, and the tourists were pretty pleased to discover people who spoke English, so they always tipped well. But—when I didn't need luck, there it was. And if things don't work out here like I hope, I'll probably go back."

"Why would anyone leave Mexico for New York?" the clerk shook his head wonderingly as he passed the AmEx through the reader and waited for the approval to come through.

"Because the coast of Mexico doesn't have Juilliard, and I want to find out if I'm a musician or only a busker," Eric told him as the approval came across the wire and the receipt scrolled out. The clerk nodded, and might have said something more, except at that moment four more customers appeared behind Eric, and all of them looked in a hurry to check out and leave. So Eric took his bulging bags and got out of their way before they started giving the clerk a hard time.

He opened his eyes and sank a little deeper into the chair, acutely aware of the silence beneath the music coming from the speakers. For the first time in a long time—a very long time, going back to even before his last girl dumped him, just before he met Kory and got really involved with Beth—there were no other sounds of occupation around him. The walls and floors of the building were very thick—which would be a blessing on the whole, but right now it prevented him from hearing the sounds other tenants made, noises that might have let him feel less alone and isolated. The only sounds within this apartment came from him. There would be no quiet clatter of Beth puttering about, or of Kory experimenting with modern human foods in the kitchen—

On the other hand, that isn't altogether bad. The kitchen won't have to be hosed down at least once a week. I'll never forget the day he discovered microwave popcorn. . . .

But the place felt like a museum—a stage set, with no life in it. He sighed. *Maybe I ought to get a cat. Or a couple of finches. Anything to sound as if there's something home besides me.* He couldn't remember what the lease said about pets; he'd have to look it up.

But a cat would mean more responsibilities, and having to remember to feed it and change the litter and be here to play with it. How much time would he have to give a pet, anyway? Even if the lease said he could have one (he hadn't read it that closely), he'd better be careful about what kind of companion he chose. He'd be in classes and rehearsals all the time, and studying when he wasn't at the school. It would be cruel to have a pet that needed a lot of attention.

A dog would be out of the question. So would a parrot or any other bird bigger than a pair of budgies. With enough toys and each other, a couple of budgies would be all right left alone all day, and so would the right temperament of cat. *If I got an adult cat from the pound, or even rescued one off the street. . . .*

Maybe a tabletop waterfall and some environmental disks might be the better answer. Or canaries? Eric sighed, remembering the birds of Underhill. Now *that* was one thing he *would* miss about the place.

I wonder if Dharinel would let me sneak a couple of those Underhill larks out here? I could leave the cage open so if they got bored or hungry they could go back home. . . .

He watched the clouds pass outside the window, and let his thoughts drift with the music. And at some point he must have actually fallen asleep, because he suddenly woke with a start, to find that the sky outside his window had gone from silvery to indigo, there was a crick in his neck, the environmental spell had faded, and his mouth was dry. *Sunset! I didn't think I was that tired; I must have been working harder than I thought.* By now the Faire was over for the day, and Beth and Kory were—what? Probably gathering with old friends and new around someone's fire, passing around bowls of stew, trading gossip. The Faire circuit really was a world unto itself, upon which the real world seldom intruded until Monday rolled around again.

He got up, stiffly, and wandered into the kitchen to get something to drink.

Beth had loved the apartment's kitchen, which meant, he supposed, that it was laid out well. There were too many cupboards for his few pots and dishes, though Beth had seen to it that the pantry was filled with things that were easy to cook, even for someone of his limited skills. The cabinets were newer than the building, but not by much: cream-colored metal with black Bakelite Deco motifs, and the floor was those tidy octagonal tiles that no building outside of New York seemed to have. But the stove was modern enough, and so was the refrigerator, and at some time in the past one of the cabinets next to the sink had been sacrificed to permit the installation of a dishwasher, which was a good thing, since Eric never liked to wash dishes. The countertop and splashboards were of white marble that matched the cabinets, and it all looked very unused and perfect, like an illustration in *House Beautiful* from 1920.

Yeah, well, I'll try making an omelet tomorrow, and fix that in a hurry. If I don't slash my hand open chopping onions, I'll drop at least two eggs on the floor and leave bits of potato all over the top of the stove.

He opened the fridge and was confronted with a vast array of crystalline water bottles of various shapes and labels, with a few lone bottles of juices, root beer, cherry, and cream soda providing a little color among the colorless army. There'd be no one to drink it all but him, and suddenly Eric was struck with a sense of loss that brought a lump to his throat.

Kory had obviously, personally—lovingly—stocked the fridge.

Elves couldn't handle caffeine. It was as destructively addictive for them as cocaine was for humans, and worse: it acted on them like horse tranquilizers, sending them into a euphoric, oblivious state they called "Dreaming." Kory would no more have put cola or tea into a fridge than Eric would have stocked one with heroin and crank.

Bless Kory! Nothing wrong with yuppie-water. And until I get a filter on it, I'm not sure I want to trust what comes out of the kitchen tap. Kory's "allergy" had done Eric a favor. The pipes in old buildings frequently added a liberal helping of rust—if not lead from the pipe solder—to the drinking water. *I've killed enough brain cells on my own, I don't need to lose any more!* Eric snagged the first bottle that came to hand, twisted off the top, and took a long swig of water as he wandered back to the living room.

As he settled back into his chair, Eric suddenly had enough of the CD player. He shut it off with the remote control, and silence rushed in so abruptly it felt as if his ears had popped.

He waited, straining to hear what, if anything, the building contained. By now people should be coming home from work or school; they should be taking baths, fixing dinner, turning on TVs for the evening news. And there were some sounds, faint and far-off, as if from another building, but they certainly weren't intrusive. In fact, he had to really concentrate to hear them at all.

He shivered, stood up and started to pace, then stopped himself and sat down quickly on the sofa, putting the water down on the floor and reaching for the flute case that lay on a small table in front of the sofa. Suddenly he wanted the silence filled again—but not by someone else's music.

For a while he simply played whatever was most familiar, a mix of the tunes he'd used to play when he busked alone. One thing he knew he didn't want to do, and that was to play the things he and Beth and Kory performed together.

But as his fingers warmed up and the notes came as easily as breathing, an idea came to him.

He didn't necessarily have to stay alone. He was a magician, and although he had to be very careful not to meddle, there were things he could do for himself without casting a *geas*. Why not use Bardic magic to hunt out a friend here in this building?

There was no good reason why he shouldn't do just that—now. He had the control; he knew what not to do as well as what to do. Instead of the old sledge-hammer process of using brute force to get something done, his touch these days was the equivalent of a neurosurgeon with a hair-thin laser beam. All he had to do was to send out a call for someone who also needed a friend like him— simply speeding up the inevitable, because sooner or later he'd run into people in the building who had similar interests anyway.

If he did this right, whoever came would hear his music despite the excellent sound-deadening qualities of the building. He—or she—would recognize it for live music, become curious, and follow it to the source. He shouldn't get too specific, though. And he should keep the need on the lighter side of friendship. *Otherwise I could end up with a case of Fatal Attraction. Oh, no; no thank you! We'll keep this casual and innocent. Just the same kind of good times and good fun I had with some of my Faire buddies.* He knew what that felt like; friends you could count on, but who gave you the space you needed. He'd taken it for granted: first, on the Faire circuit, and then Underhill, but now that he'd shut himself out of both worlds, he realized how much he'd unconsciously depended on them.

He set his thoughts in the right pattern, breathed softly into the flute, and set the magic free on the wings of the song.

Three times to repeat the song; that was what Dharinel had taught him. Once to make the pattern, twice to set the pattern, three times to bind the pattern. For really heavy work, he'd repeat his melody nine times—or, more rarely, five—but this wasn't heavy work. There was nothing riding on whether or not anyone "heard" his call, there would be no grave consequences if no one answered. He had been careful in being so completely species-nonspecific that it was even remotely possible that something from Underhill might answer the call. He didn't think any of the Sidhe lived in New York City—they lived in Los Angeles and San Francisco, but so much more of New York was man-made than either of the other cities, layers and layers of infrastructure descending as far below the surface as the skyscrapers stretched above, that he doubted they could stand it. He hadn't even specified "in the building," only "nearby"—and for Sidhe or other Underhill creatures, "nearby" could be quite some distance away.

Not that he wasn't being cautious; the other half of his "call" was very specific. Nothing would "hear" him that didn't have what Dharinel called "good intentions." These were not the kind of "good intentions" that the road to Hell was allegedly paved with—more like a healthy set of ethics and morals. Nothing would hear or respond to Eric's music that would harm him, willingly or accidentally.

It was no longer a difficult proposition to hold all those components of his magic in his mind—but it was rather like being a skillful juggler. It required intense concentration, and he kept his eyes closed to maintain that concentration right up to and through the final note.

And as the last breath of that note faded, Eric heard a quiet tapping, just loud enough to catch his attention.

But not from the door. From the window.

Surprised, he opened his eyes, wondering if the wind had blown some bit of debris up against the frame of the open window that was making the tapping sound. But he knew there were no trees that close to his windows. Maybe a pigeon? That was possible. If the last tenant had been feeding them. . . .

What the hey, there's bread in the kitchen.

He walked over to the window to see, still thinking of pigeons, so it was with a profound shock that his eyes met another pair of eyes on the other side of the frame—dark, wide, and set in a fanged grey face beneath a pair of waving, batlike wings. And just to confirm that it was no accident, beside the face was a claw-like hand with a single talon extended, tapping once again on the frame.

TWO:
A CALLING-ON SONG

If this had happened a couple of years ago, before Eric had the unique experience of having an Elven Knight appear in his apartment and scare the crap out of him, been worshipped by Nightflyers, chased by Unseleighe Elves and become a Bard, he probably would have put an Eric-shaped hole in the door on his way out. By now though, he had seen so many arcane and outré critters that having a monster staring at him from his fire escape, wanting to come into his apartment, was not going to frighten him. It was a surprise, even something of a shock, but it didn't frighten him.

If it had happened the last time he was in the World Above he might still have come at it with either a baseball bat or a sword. He hadn't known how to protect himself, not really, and his grasp of magic had been rudimentary at best. He had tended to assume that anything he didn't already recognize—or which hadn't been properly introduced by someone or something he already knew— was dangerous. And that wasn't an unreasonable way to operate, given all he'd been through. Paranoia was not a bad thing, in the appropriate degree.

But that was then. Now he had the responsibility that magical ability brought. He didn't act without thinking. He observed and thought before he did something. He had enough power and the control over it to protect himself for a limited time against almost anything. And he had the ability to call reinforcements quickly, which was even more important. All these factors gave him a level of calm he wouldn't have had before, but his time Underhill had made some deep-laid changes in Eric's psyche, had made him realize that his mind could work faster than his body, and that there generally was time to take in and process information before doing something, because acting without thought usually led to doing something that might prove to be very stupid.

So he had taken in a lot of information with his first glance at the visitor outside his window. It wasn't as large as shock had first made it appear; only half the size of a human, though that didn't mean it couldn't be dangerous. Still, there were other considerations as well.

First of all, he had noted the eyes; there was no anger or aggression in them. Granted, a professional killer would probably look just as calm before he killed you, but at the moment, Eric couldn't think of any enemy he'd made Underhill that would have the motivation to send an assassin after him.

Second, the creature was just sitting there tapping on the window frame. And even if the window had been closed, from the look of it, if it wanted to get in to attack him, a sheet of glass wasn't going to stop it.

Third, it appeared to want to be invited in, rather than just walking in through the open window. Now, all vampire mythology to the contrary, most nasty critters could cross a mortal's threshold without any problem; he hadn't had time to set up the heavy-duty wards that would stop it. So there was a very high probability that this thing—whatever it was—was friendly. That it had, in fact, answered his call. So what if it wasn't necessarily the kind of drinking-buddy he'd assumed he would get? After all, he hadn't specified species—just someone he'd like to know, and who'd like to know him.

So, after the first jolt of atavistic fear, Eric carefully put down his flute and walked slowly over to the window. The thing grinned at him as it saw that he was going to let it in, and he noticed a few more things about it.

One, except for its big dark eyes, the creature was a uniform, textured grey, all over, just like granite. Right down to the soot smudges and patches of lichen.

Two, the gargoyle that perched on his corner of the building just outside his window was gone. Or to be perfectly accurate, it wasn't where it had been. It was on the fire escape outside his window, bat-wings, fangs, ape-like arms, and all.

"Hi," he said, extending his hand cautiously (the creature did have some formidable talons, after all). "My name's Eric Banyon—"

"Sieur Eric, Knight and Bard to the court of the Queen of Elfhame Misthold, don't you mean?" the creature asked, in a thick accent that was part Bronx, part Irish, and all cheerful, raising what would have been an eyebrow if it had any hair on its uniformly granite-colored exterior. It took his hand in its for a firm but not overly aggressive handshake, and stepped through the window. Its hand was surprisingly warm and dry, though rough and hard as granite.

"Or is it that you aren't much of a one for titles and all?" It didn't wait for an answer. "I ain't, so that'd be all right with me. Greystone, at your service. Glad you whistled, Eric me fine laddy-buck. I was trying to figure out how I could do my job without you noticing that I was moving. Or gone; sometimes, y'see, I got to leave, and I figured you'd catch on that I wasn't there pretty quick."

The gargoyle released his hand, and Eric blinked. "Job?" he said carefully, then woke to his duties as a host. "Please, would you like to sit down? Can I get you anything? A drink? It's pretty hot out there." *So what do I offer a gargoyle to drink? I'd think they'd get kind of tired of water.*

"Yes and yes, and me thanks t'you." Greystone plopped himself down on the floor and stretched his wings luxuriously. "Water— more of yon yuppie-water, if you please. Take the acid taste of the smog-wash out of me mouth."

Just goes to show I shouldn't jump to conclusions. Eric fetched two more bottles of a different (and more expensive) variety of water. The best he could offer would be nothing compared to the waters of Underhill, after all, and any gargoyle he met would be more than familiar with Underhill, after all. At least it ought to be.

Greystone accepted his offering with a grin and an appreciative smack of the lips as he drank about a third of the bottle in a single gulp.

"Ah!" he said with enthusiasm, while Eric took a seat on the couch. "Now that's more like it! Clean, clear—you wouldn't believe what city rainwater tastes like these days."

He drank again and put his bottle down on the floor beside him. "Well, Eric Banyon, and did you think you'd come to live in this grand building all by accident? Not hardly. Yon cold-spell was an amusing little conceit, but I'll admit I didn't think you'd have the balls to make a calling-on song; that took some brains and some moxie, I'm here to tell you."

Eric took a careful sip from his own bottle before replying. He had the feeling that he needed to phrase his questions carefully. "You say I didn't get this apartment by accident?"

The gargoyle nodded.

"So why did I end up here?"

"The building chose you, lad, what do you think?" Greystone nodded wisely. "That's the long and the short of it. No one comes here that Guardian House doesn't want; that's the way it was built. It felt you enter the city, and it made its own calling-on song to bring you here. That's why you went for a walk, and that's why you found the building and saw the sign. The building manager just serves the building's needs. When it has a vacancy, Ms. Hernandez waits until someone shows up who can see the *For Rent* sign—not everyone can, but you've probably guessed that by now. That's why it's called Guardian House. One of the reasons."

A building that picks its own tenants? Boy, that's a new one! "Why choose me?" Eric persisted. He wasn't alarmed; he was quite certain that if there had been anything ill-omened about this place, Kory would have sensed it. And the name—Guardian House—sounded as if it were a force for Good, at least. "Is it because of the magic?"

Dharinel had warned him it would make him visible to all kinds of creatures that didn't have the time of day for an ordinary mortal, but Eric had already had a taste of what that was like.

"A bit." Now Greystone seemed to be picking his words carefully. "Most people who live here aren't witches, sorcerers, or even mages—not the way you are, me lad—they're just people with a very singular talent for living, and certain gifts to be nurtured. Most of 'em are artists, but not necessarily the way most people think of artists. Oh, there is a fair crop of painters, writers, musicians and dancers, but there are others who do things like—like putting exactly the right people together. Or who can make computers do things that'd bug your eyes out. Or who've got the gift of healing the mind and body together. The city needs people like that, and this building— this House—needs them too. They make things and people around them happy, and the House lives on that happiness. It's a living thing, not just a bunch of plaster and stone, and happiness is food and drink to it. So it shelters the special people it finds and protects them in exchange for their happiness—it's like that arrangement with the little fish and the seaflower."

"The clownfish and the anemone?" Eric hazarded, out of his memories of some half-forgotten *National Geographic* special, and Greystone nodded.

"What about the people who live here who are mages. Do they know about the House? About you?"

"Only four of them do. Ms. Hernandez's one, of course. And, no disrespect intended, boyo, but each one of the four of 'em could blow you into powder and not have to think about it."

Greystone waited to see what Eric's reaction was, but Eric just shrugged. It was hardly news to him that there were other magicians out there who were much more powerful than he was. What surprised him was that four of them lived in the same building, as mages tended to be as touchy and egotistical as . . . well, as professional musicians.

The gargoyle seemed satisfied with Eric's response, for he continued. "As for the other four, they know about me, of course, since I—well, we, me an' the lads—are their security system." The gargoyle smiled smugly. "And sometimes guard dogs. Stuff they need to worry about won't even show up on a camera, like as not, but we'll sniff it out before it ever gets within a block of here."

"Why?" Eric asked. "I mean—why do they need you?"

He realized as soon as he asked the question that he really didn't have any right to know the answer, but Greystone didn't act upset. He laid one finger along his nose and leveled his gaze at Eric.

"I'm telling you all this for your protection, lad. Maybe those four can blow you into powder, but you're streets ahead of the rest in the House. The four—well, they take care of things Out There, in the city. One's a real cop, the rest, well, you wouldn't know they were special. But when bad things happen out there, bad magical things, sometimes they need to get taken care of, and the four of them do that. That's the real reason the House was built, grown, whatever you like—to shelter the Guardians. There've been as few as one and as many as nine here at once. And that's why we're here, me and the lads, to watch while they're sleeping. But the four of us can't stop everything, and sometimes when bad things come looking for a fight, they don't much care who's in the way, or take the time to sort out the Guardians from the bystanders."

Ain't that the living truth. Eric thought over the possible implications. "So something coming after one of them might mistake me for the right target?" he hazarded. There had to be a reason Greystone was telling him all this.

"Might. Not likely, but might. So you get to know about the House, and about me." Greystone grinned. "You did a calling-on for a friend, you know. I hadn't figured on letting you know about all this so soon, but I couldn't pass up such an open invitation."

Eric grinned back; he liked the feisty little fellow! In fact, he couldn't think of a better answer to his call. "Do the four mages you mentioned know about me yet?"

"Ms. Hernandez, of course. The other three will figure it out in the next couple of days if she doesn't tell them first," Greystone said complacently. "Now don't you go get cocky now that you know about them, mind! They're not here to babysit you—you're expected to defend yourself against anything you get yourself into. That's only fair—they've got a deal more to worry about than you, any day of the week."

"Oh, believe me, I've learned my lesson!" Eric assured the gargoyle hastily, with a shudder as he thought of some of the things he'd done out of ignorance in the not-so-distant past. *And if I never see another Nightflyer again, it will be just fine with me!* "At least, I hope I have."

"You did all right with your calling-on song," Greystone assured him kindly. "Just keep thinking cautious and conservative, and you'll be all right." He grinned again. "Anything else you want to know?"

He wanted to know who the other three mages were, but he had the feeling that Greystone wouldn't tell him. "You're a sort of magical security system—how do I know if there's trouble around?" Eric finally asked.

"I'll tell you," the gargoyle informed him. "You'll hear me in your head. I'll tell you what the danger is, and give you my best guess on what to do to avoid it. After that, you're on your own. If you don't do what I tell you to, that's your problem, and you handle it."

"Fair enough," Eric acknowledged. They both finished their drinks in friendly silence, then Eric slam-dunked the empties into the trash basket near the kitchen door. "Can you be a security system and hang out with me at the same time?"

"Sure," Greystone replied firmly. "I have to be able to do that— multi-tasking, you mortals call it. Sometimes I sit out there and read a book, if it isn't raining. Ms. Hernandez lets me borrow hers. And P— One of the others gave me one of those little FM ear radios. I used to use a set of headphones until some smart-ass photographer took a picture of me wearing them and it got into the paper, but that little one hardly shows."

Just what I was hoping to hear! "In that case," Eric said, as the gargoyle watched him with a look of expectant anticipation. "How about popcorn and a movie?"

Greystone had good—and sophisticated—taste for someone who sat on the edge of a roof all day every day. After a quick scan of the movies Eric had bought to go with the new DVD player, he chose *Bullets Over Broadway*. "I have to tell you, laddybuck, sometimes it's downright frustrating sitting out there, listening to a line or two from this or that, and not able to even catch all the dialogue." Greystone shook his head sadly as Eric unwrapped the DVD and loaded it. "I can't tell you the number of times I've sat up there and thought about flying down to a window and taking my chances on being spotted."

"Well, if you get bored at night, even if I'm asleep, just come in the window and channel-surf or load a tape or something; I'll leave the window unlocked," Eric promised him. "I guess you'll take care of any burglars that happen by."

Greystone sighed happily. "Somehow we're never bothered with that sort of thing," he said innocently. "Blessed if I know why. But you're sure it won't wake you?" he asked, anxiously. "I've got good hearing, I won't play it above a whisper, I promise."

"It won't wake me," Eric assured him. "Honest. My last roommate never slept to speak of, and he used to run the tube or the stereo all night long. He was pretty considerate about volume, but some of his friends weren't, and they'd drop by any time they felt like it. I learned to sleep through entire parties."

"Ah, the Sidhe are not always thoughtful guests, now, are they," Greystone observed shrewdly, then turned his attention to the screen.

When the movie was over, Eric's sides hurt from laughing. Since it was his choice next, he put in a copy of *Riverdance*, which had Greystone tapping his talons in time to the music almost immediately.

"You could do that," Greystone said when it was over. "You could play with that group, right this moment. You're good enough. Why don't you? Why are you wasting another couple of years going to school when you don't need to?"

Eric was no longer surprised that Greystone knew so much about him. A telepathic gargoyle would be an entire intelligence network all by himself.

"Because I have a couple of things to prove to myself," Eric told him, as he sat on the floor beside the DVD player and ejected the disk. He cocked his head to one side as he watched to see Greystone's reaction.

"One of them is the laying of old ghosts. Another is that I have to prove to myself that I have the discipline to make it through to a degree; that I have the patience to put up with teachers who are going to put me through the wringer just because they can. I have to know that I can do something alone, without help from anyone else. And there are things I can learn in classes that I'll never learn on my own. The piece of paper I'll get doesn't mean a damn insofar as my passing auditions; it's what it will mean to me that matters."

He hadn't explained any of this to Beth or Kory; Kory wouldn't have understood, and probably Beth wouldn't have, either. Kory would point out that he could study with the finest of Underhill Bards if what he wanted was to learn about music and discipline—hadn't he survived Dharinel's teaching? Beth, who never had graduated from college, had the contempt for the sheepskin that many who drop out or never make it through often have. In Beth's case, Eric was fairly certain it was because she had seen so many overeducated idiots pass through the television studios she worked at. She had a point, but every time Eric had tried to argue the counter-point, he'd had to give it up before he lost his temper with her. Or she with him—Beth had a tongue that could strip wallpaper at 600 yards, and the temper that went with it. *And her not even a redhead. . . .*

"In a way, you need to prove you're a man, eh?" the gargoyle observed shrewdly, and Eric had to laugh. Going back to Juilliard was a far cry from John Wayne heroics.

"Yeah, you could say that. This is kind of my manhood ordeal." He made a face. "And part of it is going to be an ordeal, all right. I'm going to have to keep slapping myself down to keep from using magic to deal with some of those bastards in there that call themselves teachers. Why is it that the teaching profession attracts so many insecure sadists? But I won't do it. That would be cheating—and hundreds of people who don't have magic manage, after all. I just have to remember that my way won't count in there, figure out what they want, and give it to them."

"I don't know. Sounds like knuckling under to me." Greystone examined his talons carefully, not looking at Eric.

"Sometimes you have to knuckle under," Eric replied without heat, though such an implied slur would have had him in a rage as recently as a couple of years ago. "That's life in the mortal world; it's a food chain, and you can't always be top predator." And, a part of him acknowledged, he wouldn't *want* to be top predator. You gave up as much as you got if you became King of the Hill—Above or Below—and there were some things Eric wouldn't give up, no matter what price he was offered for them.

"I suppose." The gargoyle sighed. "Makes me glad I have a simple job, one with no compromises involved."

"And there are plenty who'd envy you," Eric told him honestly, and yawned. "Well, I'm for bed. Knock yourself out: watch or listen to whatever you like, just shut the window behind you when you leave, okay?" He got up, and offered his hand to Greystone, saying in his best Humphrey Bogart voice, "Louis, I have the feeling this is the beginning of a beautiful friendship."

Greystone shook his hand and, to Eric's delight, then saluted with his bottle of water and responded (in a better imitation), "Here's lookin' at you, kid."

Eric went off to his bed and fell easily and quickly asleep, with the reassuring sounds of British comedy and the gargoyle's low chuckle murmuring through the apartment to keep him company.

In the morning, it all could have been a dream. The disks Greystone had used had been put neatly away, and the gargoyle was back in place, looking like an ordinary stone gargoyle. But as Eric entered the living room, the gargoyle moved just enough to look over his shoulder and wink.

Eric laughed, and waved back. Greystone returned his gaze to the street below.

With that reassurance, Eric sauntered into his warm, pleasant kitchen, and sat down at his own tiny kitchen table. Memories of other kitchens, other wakings, filled his thoughts. *I never used to get up this early,* he thought, noting that the time was only nine A.M. *But then again, I used to drink or smoke myself into oblivion most every night, too. That tends to make for late risings.*

He poured and devoured a bowl of cereal absentmindedly, and considered what he was going to do for the day. It was Sunday, his last day of complete freedom. Tomorrow he'd begin classes and all the rest. While he didn't expect to have a great deal of trouble with actual playing, there would be things like music theory and composition, orchestration, and other technical subjects where his natural gifts wouldn't carry him. *Homework! My god, I'm going to have to deal with homework again!*

At least this time around the drudgery of homework would be lessened by the computer set up on the desk in the living room. Pointing and clicking, and even typing, were all things he could manage on his own, and there were classes at Juilliard in using the same composition software and MIDI interfaces he'd had installed on his box. Then again, the tech he'd hired to install his rig had sworn to him that the MIDI software wasn't all that hard to learn, so maybe he could play around with it himself. That would take up a bit of his time.

And then there was the not-unattractive possibility that he might find some female company somewhere along the way, which would also take up some more of his time. . . .

I guess I've gotten over Beth pretty painlessly, he realized with a pang of surprise.

Then again, he'd have to be careful about letting new people into his life. There were holes in his carefully-patched-together cover story that would be pretty hard to maintain against someone who was getting close to him.

Complications, complications. Oh, well. I guess the first thing I'd better do is go down and 'fess up to the building manager that I've penetrated her little disguise.

Though if he was going to do that, he'd better fix himself up to look more like a responsible, respectably cautious mage and less like a Gen-X slacker who couldn't be bothered to shave.

An hour later, shaved, chestnut hair thoroughly brushed and pulled back with an elastic tie ornamented with a silver plaque inscribed with Celtic knotwork, and wearing a perfectly proper outfit of jeans, a good collarless shirt, and a moleskin vest, Eric Banyon presented himself at Apartment 1-A on the first floor. There was a small hand-lettered label that said 'Hernandez-Manager' over the bell. After a brief interval, she answered his ring.

Ms. Hernandez didn't look like a mage. She was a Latina woman with skin the color of buckwheat honey; an older woman who wore a harried lifestyle and a score of responsibilities like an invisible cloak. She was dressed in jeans and a pink Henley, and her blue-black hair was pulled back in a tail.

Her eyes showed a flash of annoyance—quickly hidden—when she saw who was at her door, and Eric knew what was going through her mind. She probably figured that he was going to complain about one of the many features of the apartment that she couldn't do anything about, because you simply had to accept a few problems when you lived in a building that was this old.

He held up his hand in the universal gesture of peace. "I'm not here to hassle you about anything, Ms. Hernandez," he said quickly. "I just wanted you to know that I've met my neighbor, Mr. Greystone. He was kind enough to spend some time watching movies with me last night, and he told me that you sometimes loan him books. He told me to say hello to you."

For a moment she stared at him without comprehension, as if his words had taken her by such complete surprise that her mind had gone blank. Then her eyes widened, and she opened the door further. "Please, Mr. Banyon, come in," she said formally, gesturing to him to move past her. "I'd like to talk to you about that, and see how you're settling in here."

He took the invitation, and she shut the door behind him. Her hallway was the mirror image of his, and so was the living room, though the apartment looked as if it had a dining room as well, and probably three bedrooms instead of one. By New York City standards, it was palatial, and any place else it would cost a fortune to get this much space. Most of the people Eric had known from student days here lived in about two hundred square feet of room, and considered themselves lucky if they didn't have to share it with a roommate.

Her living room was pleasantly furnished in the usual mishmash of furniture that most people who didn't buy "suites" out of department stores owned. Her color scheme was a mix of golden yellows and browns, and she had a couple of bright rugs on the polished wooden floors. He wondered soberly just what Ms. Hernandez did to earn this place. *If the House rewards these Guardians commensurately with risk—yikes!* Guarding a city the size of New York? He wasn't certain he'd have what it took. *I wouldn't want to get her mad at me!*

"The kids're out at a movie, so we'll have some privacy. I'll put on the kettle and make us up a nice pot of peppermint tea. I don't do coffee in the morning any more. Makes me jittery. I hope you don't mind."

"Not a bit," Eric said, following her into the apartment with a smile. He'd met Toni's two boys—Raoul and Paquito—briefly when he'd signed the lease. They were eight and ten, and seemed—from Eric's limited experience with that age group—to be perfectly normal kids, if a bit more polite than the average run.

She gestured, and Eric seated himself at the table tucked into one corner of the kitchen. Evidence of Toni's boys was everywhere, from the action-figures tucked onto the shelves along with the dishes, to the promotional glasses for the latest *Star Wars* movie in the drainer.

"Please, sit down, Mr. Banyon," Toni Hernandez told him, moving over to the sink to fill the teakettle.

"Call me Eric; I'd rather," he replied. "Mr. Banyon is still my father to me, and I don't think I've turned into him yet."

"Fair enough. And I'm Toni. Well then, Eric," Toni Hernandez said, looking into his eyes intently. "Either you have managed to get hold of a name and a fact and put them together with extraordinary skill, or you must have been a bit startled last night. Which is it?"

"Startled," Eric smiled. "It isn't every day that a gargoyle comes to call—but it was my fault, if fault there be. I did invite anyone who might be a friend to come over and say hello."

"Interesting—so that was you, playing?" She smiled. "I don't think we need to play word games, then, or beat around the bush.

You're obviously a mage, and a better one than most of the people in the House who dabble in the Art. You got Greystone to reveal his nature to you by cooperation rather than coercion, so he may know more about you than he's told me. I heard you playing, recognized what you were doing, and admired the careful crafting—and if I hadn't been busy at the time, I would probably have followed the invitation. I knew that it couldn't be a trap or a trick, but it didn't occur to me that it might be the new tenant who was setting the spell."

Eric spread his hands, grinning despite himself at her praise of his magic. "Consider the invitation still open—on weekends, anyway. During the week I have to be a conscientious student."

She made a face. "I wish you could talk my kids into that attitude. All right then—I knew the House wanted you the moment you came in, but it wants a lot of people that aren't the kind to get visits from Greystone. So what are you, besides a music student at Juilliard? You aren't Wiccan, I know that much."

Eric considered his words carefully. "Are you aware of the powers once attributed to Bards?"

"Like that Welsh guy, Taliesen?" she asked. "Magic through music? That what you do? How the heck did you find someone to teach you that? Not at Juilliard, I'll bet."

He smiled crookedly, answering her questions with others—a habit he'd picked up from the elves. "Wouldn't True Bards confine themselves to a single student at a time? And wouldn't any of the old True Bards tell you that no bard can ever afford to stop learning?"

"Touché. Perhaps I ought to be asking, then, why a True Bard is incarcerating himself in Gotham." She raised an eyebrow. "Except that the answer is obvious; Juilliard is here. So I'll try a different angle—is that the only reason you're here? Is there something going on I should know about?"

Eric recalled what Greystone had told him about the four Guardians "fixing" things that needed to be fixed around the city. She was probably thinking that Bard Eric represented someone with a problem that could easily get out of hand, given what some of the ancient legends said about bardic mischievousness.

"Juilliard is the only reason I'm here," he promised. "Or at least, it's the only reason I know about. I am not aware that there's about to be a War of the Trees played out in Central Park, or that the Fair Folk are about to start Wild Hunts through the East Village, if that will set your mind at rest."

She heaved a sigh of relief. "In that case, the interrogation is over, Eric. Here in the House we respect people's pasts, so whatever you choose to tell me you can do so socially. And in return for your forthrightness, I'll tell you that the fallout shelter in the basement is proof against magical fallout as well; if Greystone sounds a warning, you aren't certain of your own protections, and you haven't time to get out of the free-fire zone, head for the basement. Punch three, six, and nine all at the same time on the elevator and it becomes an express to the basement."

She held up a warning finger, and he noticed that there was no polish on the well-kept nail. "Be careful not to try it outside of an emergency, though, and keep your knees flexed. It's a jury-rigged override on a very old system, and although it does work, the stop is abrupt enough to drop you to the floor. Fred rigged it—he's the fellow who had the building manager's job before me, and he's the one who installed the regular security system. I know the override works, I've used it and the shelter."

Which means that she lived here before she was a Guardian. Interesting. I wonder if her kids know what she is? I'd think she'd have to tell them, but maybe somehow she's managing to keep it secret from them.

Then again—these were kids. Even if she thought she was running a double life, she probably wasn't.

The kettle was boiling now, and Toni poured the tea into the pot, bringing it over to the table to steep. She took down two hand-thrown stoneware mugs from the cabinet above the sink and brought them over as well.

"Adam made me these. He's one of the artists who lives in the building—a potter. He's got a lot of stuff at Mad Monk, down on Sixth and Nineteenth. If you need any dishes or anything like that, he's got a special rate for tenants."

"Thanks," Eric said. From the look of the mugs, he already had a few of Adam's creations in his own cupboards. Beth had insisted on the hand-thrown pottery, saying that fine china was too soulless—and too easy to break.

When the tea had steeped, Toni poured both mugs full and added a liberal dollop of wild honey to her own. Eric picked up his cup and inhaled the fragrance. *Fresh mint, no matter what the box said. I wonder if it grows wild anywhere around here? There's a lot of wild herbs and plants growing in empty lots here, if you know what you're looking for.*

"Do you ever worry about your kids, I mean, living here in the city?" Eric found himself asking. *Gods, where did THAT come from?*

Toni checked in the middle of raising her own cup. "All the time, *mi hermano.* I worry about them following in my footsteps—and I worry about them not. Drugs, gangs, stray meteors—life is just one big anxiety-filled minefield when you're a parent," she said, with a rueful note of amusement in her voice. "But I wouldn't have it any other way. I only wish their father had lived to see them grow up. I think he'd be proud of them."

Eric nodded, his thoughts turning to the other things he'd come to ask her about. "I'm wondering—Greystone said there were three more of you in the building? Would it be a good idea if I threw a little private housewarming for the four of you? And anyone you want to bring along, of course. That might be the best way for all of us to get a look at each other." *And for everybody to get the chance to interrogate me at once.*

She pondered that for a moment. "It wouldn't be a bad idea," she said slowly. "Maybe it should be just the five of us and Greystone. Believe me, I know these apartments like the back of my hand, and six people will more than fill up your living room. How's next Saturday night for you?"

It sounded good to Eric—he'd need a break after the brutal first week of classes.

"Sure. I'll get the usual party stuff—ah, except for one thing." He flushed, a little embarrassed, but not too embarrassed to insist on it.

"No alcohol. I don't do it anymore, and I don't like having it around me."

"No problem. As it happens, none of us drink, other than the old honey-and-whiskey thing for a sore throat." Toni looked oddly relieved, and explained why in the next sentence. "The House doesn't like druggies and drunks, and it seriously doesn't like addicts of any kind. The House doesn't make mistakes, but people change, especially here. I've had the unpleasant duty of finding reasons to evict some of the tenants in the past who thought that artists had to debauch themselves in order to be artists."

Eric winced, since he had come rather too close to that line himself a time or two. Looking back on it now, he'd been on a collision course with oblivion before he'd stumbled into Kory. *All the freedom in the world, and no place to go but down.* "Right then, I'll see you all Saturday night?" He swigged down the last of his now-cool tea and stood.

Toni Hernandez smiled, and held out her hand and shook his. Her grip was warm and quite firm. "Once you meet them, I think you're going to find that you fit in here quite well, Eric. Even if you actually turn out to be an elf or something."

Eric managed not to wince. "See you Saturday, then."

❖❖ ❖❖ ❖❖

Over the course of the week he found that he had cause, more than once, to look forward to that party on Saturday. Fitting back into the student life was much harder than he'd expected.

His alarm clock jarred him awake at seven A.M. Monday morning. It was set to an all news, all the time station, and a woman who sounded far too perky for this hour of the morning was chattering on about tie-ups at various bridges and tunnels. Eric staggered out of bed, groping for the "Off" switch.

A cold shower jolted him awake, but his brain didn't seem to want to take the hint and join the rest of his body. He dragged a comb through his hair and tied it back with a strip of rawhide, then grabbed the first things out of his closet—chambray shirt, feather-weight suede vest in a deep rich burgundy, and well-broken-in jeans.

Not bad, if I do say so myself, he decided, glancing into the mirror.

His stomach was too jumpy for breakfast to seem like much of a good idea, so he grabbed a handful of granola bars and stuffed them into his messenger bag for later. Fortunately he'd made most of his preparations the night before, so his course schedule and the paperwork he'd need for today was already stowed away, along with his flute in its case. With one last look around the apartment—amazing how much it had started looking like home in just a few short days—he headed for the street.

The hot weather had broken overnight—though according to his friends uptown, it would be back a time or two before autumn really came to stay—and the morning was bright and cool, a perfect early fall day. He hesitated about taking Lady Day over to the school, but then decided against it: the only easy-to-find parking around Lincoln Center was paid parking in garages, since most of the students couldn't afford to keep cars in the city, and public transportation made it really unnecessary. He'd been in the subway a few times since his arrival, and there was a stop only a few blocks away. That would do for now.

The subway station was hot—the trains were air conditioned to the point of pneumonia, but the platforms weren't—but as he passed through the turnstile, Eric was surprised to hear the sound of music echoing off the walls: a busker setting up his pitch to take advantage of the early-morning commuter traffic.

Can't beat the acoustics, Eric thought, looking around for the source of the music. He saw a tall, regal young woman, her hair dyed a surreal cherry-black, playing an electric violin. Its silvery surface gleamed with rainbow iridescence in the florescent lighting of the platform. Her case was open at her feet, and there was already a tidy accumulation of coins and bills—even a few subway tokens. He caught her eye and grinned, giving her a thumbs up. She smiled back and nodded without missing a beat: he recognized Copeland's *Variations on a Theme from Appalachian Spring.*

For a moment Eric thought about joining her for a little impromptu jam session, but decided against it: he'd heard that street musicians had to have a license to perform in New York, and that was something he hadn't gotten around to finding out about just yet. He dug in his pocket and tossed a handful of change into her fiddle-case. With the practice of long experience, the violinist brought her music to an end just as the train pulled into the station and her appreciative audience began moving toward the open doors. Eric joined them.

In a few short stops he reached his destination: Lincoln Center. The Center was essentially the Juilliard campus: the school itself was a tall building tucked off in a corner behind Lincoln Center. Though when evening came this would be one of the busiest parts of the city, there were few people in the plaza at this hour of the morning. Familiar with the layout from previous visits, Eric found his way to his classroom without difficulty.

The halls were filled with students, some new, some returning. Juilliard wasn't "just" a music school. It offered programs in Drama and Dance as well. The dancers were easy to spot, most of them already in leotards and soft shoes from early-morning practice, with their dance-bags slung over one shoulder. A number of the other students were carrying—or towing—instrument cases.

He found the auditorium without difficulty. There were several of his fellow students waiting around outside. One of them—a short blond kid who looked like he should still be in grade-school, waved.

"Hi. You must be 'Pappy' Banyon." He grinned, relishing the joke. "I'm Jeremy Mitchell. Oboe. You know what they say about double-reed players."

"Hi," Eric said, holding out his free hand. "Pleased to meet you. Back when dinosaurs ruled the earth, they always used to say the pressure on the brain'd drive you crazy. Glad to hear it's still true."

"Some things never change," Jeremy agreed happily. "I'm a musical prodigy—but then, hey, aren't we all? This is Lydia," he added, pulling a redheaded girl forward. "Lydia Ashborn, meet the legendary Eric Banyon."

"Hi," Lydia said, blushing heavily. If he hadn't met her here, Eric would have been sure she was one of the drama students. She had the looks for it—flaming red hair, ivory skin, and the most amazing eyes Eric had seen outside of Underhill, a deep violet color.

"With Banyon here, Rector won't have any time to pick on you," Jeremy promised her. "He's supposed to be a real monster—likes to keep his students from getting too stuck on themselves, from what I hear."

"I know the type," Eric said. "Ashborn. Isn't—"

"Yeah," Lydia said too quickly, looking even more uncomfortable than before. Marco Ashborn was a world-class violinist, and Lydia was obviously his daughter. And equally obviously would rather be anywhere but here.

"But it isn't your fault," Jeremy said. "Nobody's going to hold it against you. *We* won't, anyway. Right, Banyon?"

"Right," Eric said, because it seemed to be expected of him. For all his upstart sassiness, Jeremy seemed to be fond of Lydia and doing his best to put her at ease. It couldn't be easy coming here as the child of a star of the music world. Talk about performance pressure. . . .

At least that was one thing I never had to face: parents who were expecting me to follow in their golden footsteps.

Just then the bell rang. "Time to face the lions," Jeremy said cryptically. "C'mon. Let's sit together."

Before long, Eric knew exactly what Jeremy had meant, and was grateful for the warning.

Professor Rector taught History of Music. He was new since Eric had last studied here, and seemed to be one of those professors who believed in teaching through intimidation. That meant that somebody in the class had to be the scapegoat, and after meeting the sixteen-year-old Lydia, Eric was just as glad it was him. Before the hour was over, he'd already had his fill of sardonic comments about unusual aspects of the work of this or that obscure composer aimed directly at him and ending with, "but I don't imagine that you encountered any requests for his work in the subway, Mr. Banyon."

It was obvious that his history had preceded him, and if there'd been anyone at the school who didn't know that he'd left Juilliard years before and gone out to make his living as a street-busker, they all certainly knew by the end of the first class.

Eric kept his temper, although the constant gibes really began to grate after the fourth time. When Mr. Rector actually phrased his comment as a question, Eric answered it when he could, and when he could not, he admitted it. Otherwise, he ignored the constant stream of barbs—at least that was something at which he had plenty of practice, thanks in no small part to having studied under Dharinel. Dharinel didn't like *anybody,* least of all half-trained ragamuffin scapegrace dragged-up-anyhow human Bards foisted on him by his liege-lord. When it came to hitting nerves, Dharinel had all the accuracy of a surgical laser, and had taken just as much malicious enjoyment in getting a reaction out of Eric as Professor Rector did.

Probably Rector thought Eric was a pushover, and some of the students might, too—but the ones who weren't getting off on seeing Eric constantly slapped down were beginning to see just what a sadistic bastard the man was without having to become a target themselves. So in a way, Eric was giving them a useful lesson in maintaining dignity in the face of adversity. And that was certainly a vital survival skill in the world of music.

I've faced off with bastards who could kill the populations of entire cities, and who got a kick out of the kind of torture that leaves lifelong scars. I can handle a little harassment. And besides, it's still the first week. Maybe he'll get tired of it. It's possible.

Fortunately, none of his other professors were as confrontational as Rector, nor did they seem to want to waste class time busting his chops, and by the end of the day, Eric had figured out a way to take the wind out of Rector's sails if he ever needed to. He'd bought a very nice microcassette recorder with a good microphone in order to tape all of his lectures in addition to taking his own spoken notes. When he got home that evening, he sat down to transcribe his notes—including every word of Professor Rector's lecture, inappropriate gibes and all.

When he was done, he labelled the tape and put it aside—from now on he was going to save every golden word of Rector's lectures, and if the man tried to drive Eric out of Juilliard by any monkey business with Eric's grades, he'd find out in a hurry that Eric Banyon wasn't the pushover he'd thought. Those tapes would be in the hands of the president of Juilliard—along with a neatly typed transcript with the important parts highlighted—within hours, and the good professor would have a hard time explaining away what would look like a really unhealthy negative fixation on a student.

Microcassettes were wonderful things.

But Eric didn't think he'd ever have to use that weapon. He'd eaten lunch with Jeremy and Lydia, and Jeremy seemed to be a clearing-house for every scrap of gossip on the Juilliard campus. He'd told Eric that Professor Rector didn't have tenure—and as a result, Rector didn't have any real power in the Juilliard hierarchy.

So Eric didn't waste any energy fretting over one more bully. Energy and time were two things he didn't have enough of to waste; there was an awful lot to learn, and the structured classes—with their structured expectations—were more of a drain on his energy than he'd thought they'd be. Students were expected to do three things in the course of their studies: learn, perform—and compose original works.

When it came to composition, he'd always worked on pure inspiration and impulse; now he had to learn music theory and be able to explain why certain things worked or didn't. It was a lot like mathematics, and left his head aching with the amount he was trying to comprehend. And this was only the first week, the overviews of what students would be expected to master in the weeks ahead.

It was only when it came to performance that Eric was completely at ease. The years of playing at RenFaires and on the street had taught him how to improvise endlessly on common themes, and playing before the Sidhe—the toughest audience on either side of the Hill—had polished his performances. All of that showed, even when he was playing classical or contemporary music, and so Eric was quickly recruited, not only for the main orchestra, but for the chamber group and a trio.

He wouldn't take any more ensemble groups after that, in spite of the fact that he was repeatedly asked to, and the fact that many of the Advanced Certificate students were carrying a lot more. He was older than they were. He needed a life away from music; he was too old to be able to dedicate himself obsessively the way some of the younger kids could, playing in half a dozen chamber groups besides their regular work. Granted, some of it paid—and that was another reason not to take potential work away from people who needed the money more than he did.

He reflected with some irony that, as with mainstream religion, it was easy enough to dedicate your life to music before you discovered sex—but afterwards, it was a different proposition. The way the kids threw themselves into everything—they had an intensity he'd lost somewhere along the path to growing up. He didn't regret his loss—change was normal everywhere but Underhill—but sometimes he envied the passion the younger students seemed always to carry at their fingertips.

By Friday, Eric had less idea than before if he was going to come out of this experience as a really brilliant musician (as opposed to a Bard) or merely a competent one, like the normal run of Juilliard graduates. If he didn't add magic to the music he played, just how good a flute player was he going to be, anyway? He was way too old to be a prodigy now, but had the years of actual playing been enough to make up for lack of formal schooling?

It was not a question that caused him to lose any sleep—as Greystone had pointed out, he could get a decent-paying professional gig just as he stood, and he could even go back to the Faire circuit with time in between spent Underhill—but it was a question that he pondered in the few moments not devoted to his coursework. Did he really want to be another James Galway? Eric didn't think so—being a True Bard *and* having the high profile of a celebrity musician could be a dangerous combination.

But being very good didn't necessarily mean you had to be very famous. There was always studio work, for instance, if he wanted to stay in one place. And there were a lot more recording studios in New York than most people thought.

The weekend arrived, and he spent Saturday afternoon happily shopping for his party, taking Lady Day rather far afield to obtain some of the things he wanted. After all of the celebrations Underhill and in the house in San Francisco, he had the feeling he would never again be content with potato chips and dip, a platter of cheddar and jack, and boxed crackers, and he was rather proud of the spread he assembled.

I know I don't really have to try to overawe these guys, even if I could, but heck, it sure would be nice if they liked me. Greystone's cool, and I like Toni—and I guess I can judge the rest of them by the company they keep, at least more or less—but it never hurts to make a good impression. And besides, after a week like that one, I'm entitled to a little celebration.

By the time his guests began to arrive, he'd finished arranging the food in the living room and kitchen—not at all bad for a lone bachelor, he congratulated himself. There was something here for every taste—he figured that between him and Greystone, there wouldn't be any leftovers, either. There were two plates of the sushi rolls he'd grown to love on the West Coast; a cheese platter containing brie and neufchatel and other strange or strong cheeses; lox and cream cheese and bagels from the corner deli; a cold hors d'oeuvres tray from Balducci's, with shrimp and miniature quiches and spinach rolls and stuffed mushrooms; fresh-baked, thinly sliced, miniature loaves of bread for the cheese and the handmade Amish jams and jellies he'd found down at the 14th Street Farmers' Market.

Remembering what Toni Hernandez had said, for drinks he had gourmet teas and coffee, his vast assortment of designer waters, Classic Coke, plain seltzer, and a couple of oddball soft drinks. He could hardly wait for his guests to arrive.

Eric found himself going to the mirror nervously, over and over. He'd dressed carefully, in a mix of the clothing Kory had kenned for him and more mundane garb. Tucked into a pair of black suede trousers from a leather store was a deep burgundy silk shirt straight from Underhill, and the pants were tucked into his Faire boots with the burgundy leather pattern laid into the side. Under a side-laced, black suede vest he wore his sword belt without the sword, and wondered if any of the four would notice that omission.

Greystone slipped in the window as he was going to the mirror

for the fourth time. "You look simply fah-bulous, kiddo," the
gargoyle said, with a wink. "Settle down, you'll like these people, and
they'll like you. You've already made points with them, just by being
low-key."

"I wish you'd told me more about them," Eric fretted. "At least
what they look like! I mean, I'm never comfortable meeting people
cold, and you're hitting me with three total strangers! I don't even
know how many are men and how many are women—"

"Well, they won't be strangers for long, now, will they?"
Greystone countered, scarfing up a plateful of food and a bottle of
water. "Toni an' me, we didn't want you forming any opinions in
advance. Have some sushi and relax."

"As if I could," Eric grumbled *sotto voce,* and just then the door
buzzer sounded. He opened it to let in the four "senior mages" of the
House.

And as Greystone had said, maybe it was a good thing that he
hadn't been told anything about these people, because he couldn't
have picked out four more normal folks if he'd tried.

"Everyone, this is Eric Banyon," Toni said, as they all moved
inside and Eric shut the door. "Eric, this is Jimmie Youngblood—
that's short for 'Jemima,' and she'll kill you if you use it. Jimmie is
with NYPD Detective Division."

Even in her street clothes, Jimmie looked like a female cop; Eric
had come to be able to recognize the commonalities with other
LEOs[2] he'd met. She didn't have to look tough, it was simply a part
of her. In point of fact, if you only looked at the surface and not at
the way she moved and the carefully wary way in which she was
always checking her surroundings, you'd have said she looked
frail—but she wasn't thin, she was whipcord and muscle. It was
difficult to identify a nationality for her; she had thick, lustrous
straight black hair, very dark eyes, a bronzy complexion under a
good, even tan, and cheekbones a model would kill for, though the
rest of her face was too strong to be called "pretty." *Maybe some
Cherokee in there?* Eric thought.

---

[2]Law Enforcement Officers

"Good to meet you, Eric," Jimmie said formally, shaking his hand firmly. She raised an eyebrow, glancing at his waist. "Nice belt, but isn't there something missing?" she asked with a glint of a smile in her amber eyes.

"Now it's my turn to make an introduction. This is Paul Kern: computer nerd by day, gaming addict by night."

"Eric," Paul said, shaking his hand with a grin. Paul was a tall elegant black man who carried himself with the grace of a dancer. Most of the computer nerds Eric had known had moved as if they weren't sure where to put their hands and feet, but Paul moved like a cat turned into a human. Eric noted that his eyes had already flicked to the computer in the corner and back to Eric's face in the brief instant of their introduction. "You get in trouble with that system of yours, give a shout," he said with a grin. His voice held a faint trace of a British/Islands accent.

"I will, if you won't mind," Eric replied fervidly. "What I know about computers would fit in a greeting card."

Paul laughed. "Now I make the last introduction—this is José Ramirez, who leads a triple life to my double one. He's the super— which is less work than you'd think, since the House's systems tend to cooperate rather than break down at the drop of a power surge— he's our fourth Guardian, and when he's not fixing faucets, he's raising African Grey parrots who are probably more intelligent than most of our tenants." There was general laughter at the last remark, which had the flavor of a family joke.

"Pleased to meet you, Eric." Like the others, José had a firm, warm handshake. His bronze skin and strong square features made him attractive—if not as model-handsome as Paul—and he reminded Eric slightly of a darker Charles Bronson. "If you are ever considering a parrot as a companion, please let me know. I can help you decide whether or not you will have the time, and if so, which breed would suit you best." He grinned. "I'm afraid, like most bird people, my conversation tends to begin and end with my little ones."

"So?" Toni put in, gesturing with a piece of sushi. "That's not much different from any other person with an all-consuming avocation. Or a parent, for that matter, but I promise I'll leave Raoul and Paquito out of the conversation tonight. José is night-shift supervisor for any extraordinary problems here at the House; I'm day-shift. We cover for each other if a problem takes one of us outside."

All of them found places in the living room; Eric took the kitchen chair, Toni and José shared the sofa, Paul got the chair and Jimmie stood leaning against the wall where she could watch all of them. As usual, Greystone sat on the floor, since his wings tended to get in the way of using furniture.

Eric had a million questions he wanted to ask, but he didn't get a chance to, for Jimmie, who'd gone and gotten her own plate of food, got her question to him in first.

"So, Banyon—just where did you learn your stuff?" she asked, direct and to the point. "And how come your clothes have magic all over them?"

He'd intended to tell them anything they wanted to know, but he hadn't planned on telling them about Kory and Company quite yet; he'd hoped to warm up to the subject.

"Ah—" he hesitated, then tried to look apologetic. "I'm not sure just how much you people are going to believe."

Granted, Greystone already knew about Underhill, but from his conversations with the gargoyle, Eric had been led to believe that these people had yet to encounter anything like the Sidhe. He'd gotten the impression that their problems had all dealt with the consequences of powerful, untrained amateurs dabbling in magic, or powerful, trained magicians doing very nasty things.

"Hey, they believe in living gargoyles," Greystone said (now around a mouthful of bagel). "How much harder to believe in can your pointy-eared friends be?"

"Pointy-eared friends?" Paul raised both eyebrows. "Somehow I don't think Greystone's referring to Vulcans."

"He's not," Eric said faintly, then gave up and blurted it all out. "Elves. *Seleighe Sidhe.* The Fair Folk. I learned my magic from them."

At first, the four Guardians looked at him as if they thought he was joking. Then they looked at each other, questioningly. Finally, they looked at Greystone, who nodded emphatically.

"Cross my heart, folks," the gargoyle said, making the appropriate motion. "He's not putting you on. I'd never seen a Sidhe before his buddy Korendil showed up to help move him in, but I'd heard about them. No kidding; under the glamourie that made him look human, there wasn't a doubt. I knew what Korendil was the first moment I saw him."

So much for disguises, Eric thought. He'd have to remember to mention to Kory that his Seeming spell wasn't as seamless as it might be.

"Elves." Jimmie pondered that for a moment. "Well, that's not the sort of thing you expect to hear about in the Big Apple, and I've never met anyone before who could say he'd seen elves, but—well, we've seen weirder things than elves, I guess. So, okay. Elves." She sounded as if she were pronouncing a judicial verdict. Luckily, it seemed to be in Eric's favor.

"My impression is that there's too much Cold Iron around this town for elves to be anything but uncomfortable here," Eric put in, hesitantly. *At least, without a Nexus closer than the one at Elfhame Everforest.* "Kory can stand it only because he wore silk from neck to toes while he was here with me, and because he's been conditioning himself to handle it. I've heard that Sidhe can manage to build up a resistance to what they call Death Metal—kind of like you or I developing a tolerance for snake venom. Most of them, though—at best, they'd be uncomfortable all the time, and at worst, in terrible pain, depending on how sensitive to Cold Iron they were, and how much experience they'd had being around it."

There were more questions about Eric's friends, as his four guests batted the idea around until they got comfortable with it. He was rather surprised that it took them as little time as it did, but then, they were trained professionals.

"If elves taught you magic and took you Underhill, how did you get away from them?" Paul asked pointedly. "All the legends I've heard indicate they tend to grab musicians and keep you prisoner for extended periods of time. Thomas the Rhymer, Tam Lin, Taliesen—" He shrugged, breaking off what promised to be a lengthy catalogue of examples.

"It's a long story," Eric admitted. "Basically, you can't believe everything you read. I wasn't their prisoner. I was an honored guest. And—well, the whole story involves elves in Los Angeles, and elves in San Francisco, some of them Seleighe and some of them Unseleighe, and—it's a long story."

"We have food, drink, and it's Saturday night," José said, settling down on the couch as if he was prepared to stay for as long as it took. "So, stranger among us—tell us the story. As you are a Bard, it should at least be entertaining."

Since Eric couldn't think of any reason why he shouldn't tell these people the truth, he did, starting all the way back at the Grove of Elfhame Sun-Descending at the L.A. Fairesite.

"Once upon a time—a very long time ago (more or less)—there was this traveling musician named Eric Banyon. . . ." he began.

And the story did take a very long time to tell, but not as long as he had thought it would, since other than the Sidhe themselves and the existence of Underhill, the four Guardians were quite familiar with magic, nodes, Groves, and other arcanities, including power-mad Black Magicians. And while they were hardly a group of conspiracy nuts, they were also more than familiar with some of the military, governmental and quasi-governmental projects involving psychics that were floating around the espionage underworld—including many that were supposed to be secret.

To Eric's surprise, they even knew about Nightflyers, those terrifying, life-devouring creatures from the Chaos Lands Underhill, and were about as fond of them as Eric was.

"Not my chosen dancing partners," Jimmie said with a shudder. "Not that you really get a choice once they show up. Well, Eric, you just verified your story for us. We knew something about the business in San Francisco—not everything, of course, but nothing you told us conflicts with what we already knew, and most of it dovetails very nicely. You couldn't have done that if you'd been making it all up."

Eric felt himself relax inside. Jimmie Youngblood seemed to be the one in charge of vetting newcomers for the group, and even on such short acquaintance, Eric found himself valuing her good opinion.

"That thing with Project Cassandra's something I don't ever want to have to go through again," Eric told them soberly. He thought of Warden Blair, the madman responsible for hurting Bethie and hundreds of others so horribly. "It would have been so easy for everything to go terribly wrong—as it was, well, people got hurt, and people got killed, and I can't help thinking it was my fault that they did. If I'd realized what was happening sooner—if I'd figured out a better way to handle the situation—"

Jimmie patted his hand and the others murmured sympathetically, but none of them said the kinds of things others had said—about how it wasn't his fault, and that he'd done the best he could. He was grateful for that. Platitudes didn't help, not when he remembered how many people had been hurt or even killed.

"Every time you have a situation, you always think it could have gone better," Jimmie sighed. "And you know what? It probably could have. My partner always says you can only try to keep it from eating at you so bad that you can't learn from it. He might even be right." She grinned faintly.

"So, what about this guy that taught you about being a True Bard?" Paul said, quickly changing the subject to something less painful. "How'd that happen? I thought you said that most of the older elves didn't much like humans."

Explaining Dharinel—which meant trying to explain a little about Underhill—was harder than explaining the last several years of his life, and by the time they were done with their questions, Eric felt like a wrung-out—but content—dishrag. It was nearly four in the morning, all the food was gone, and most of the drink, but he didn't have that dissatisfied feeling that usually came when he'd been raked over the coals. It felt more as if these were four people who really wanted to be friends, but needed to find out everything they could about him and didn't have a lot of time to do so.

That impression was reinforced when Toni called a halt to the "party."

"That's enough. You're tired, we're tired, and we all know for certain that you're all right. Next time, I promise it will be your turn, Eric," she said, for they had all quickly gone to a first-name basis, even Jimmie. "None of us will ask any questions, and you can put *us* through the wringer."

"I'll help," Greystone offered, grinning wickedly, and Jimmie groaned. "Oh, no. *Not* the Jell-O shooters story! If you turn it into another 'Truth or Dare' game, I swear I'll wring your neck," she threatened.

"Who? Me?" Greystone spread his wings and managed to look as innocent as it was possible for a gargoyle to look—which wasn't very.

"Meanwhile, we all need sleep—well, except José," Toni continued, ignoring both of them, and setting a good example by getting out of her seat. "Thank you, Eric; we know what we needed to know. You've got a lot of power, but you're also responsible and mature. We don't have to worry about you getting all of us into trouble by doing something stupid, and we don't have to worry about you messing up something we have going by blundering into it. I think you're going to be a welcome addition to the House."

"Absolutely," Paul seconded, as they all got up, stretched, and took their leave. It was all accomplished smoothly and efficiently; so much so that they were out the door almost before Eric was ready to say good night.

He shut the door behind them and turned to face the suddenly empty apartment. Well, almost empty.

"You made a good impression, kiddo, like I said you would," Greystone told him. "And they're a tough house to play for, y'know what I mean?"

"They aren't planning on recruiting me, are they?" Eric asked, a little anxiously. "I mean, all that about being a welcome addition to the House—I'm not up to taking on other people's problems, you know. I have my hands full with my own!" He knew it sounded a little selfish, but it was the plain truth. He hadn't done so well on his last outing as a would-be Worldsaver that he wanted to repeat the experience.

"Naw. If you were going to be a Guardian . . . believe me, you'd'a known a long time ago, laddybuck. Or your elf buddies would've, and pointed you our way a lot sooner. No, they folks're just glad you're smart enough not to attract trouble, and skilled enough to duck anything that comes here. Wish I could say the same about some people that've moved in. I could tell you stories. . . . And—I will, but not tonight. Get some shut-eye, kid," Greystone said severely. "You're about to go up with the blinds."

"Yeah, thanks. I will." Eric felt exhaustion drop over his shoulders like a too-heavy cloak, and stumbled into the bedroom, barely noticing that Greystone was courteously picking up the party detritus. He managed to get undressed and make it as far as his bed, and all he remembered of the rest of the night was a deep and dreamless sleep.

THREE:
ON THE SEACOAST
OF BOHEMIA

I can do this. The woman walking down the expensively-carpeted hallway that led from the express elevator to the penthouse board-room gave no hint that there was anything amiss. From her Manolo Blahnik pumps to her fashionably disheveled ash-blond hair, Ria Llewellyn looked as if she belonged here.

Once she had. The world of mega-corporate high finance had been her element, and she had moved through it as naturally as a shark moved through water. Until the Accident.

Oh, Christ, Ria. Tell the truth, if only to yourself. Before Beth Kentraine hit you over the head with a Fender guitar and the backlash from your loving father's magic scrubbed your brain like a copper pot.

Almost against her will, she remembered. It all began with the Nexus, the rent in the fabric of Reality that let the power from the World Beyond seep over into this one, to be tapped by the Sidhe and others with similar magics. Only a human Bard could create a Nexus, for Creative Magic was the human power. Elves could imitate, copy, refine on the original. But they could not create something as unique, as powerful as a Nexus.

Since before she was born, Perenor had plotted to steal the Nexus of Elfhame Sun-Descending near Los Angeles and bring it under his direct control. He'd created LlewellCo to do that. He'd created Ria to run it, to deal with the daily grind that elves had so little taste for. And after years of plotting, he'd managed to buy the Fairegrove where the Nexus was—in order to destroy it, bulldoze the great trees that anchored the Nexus in the World. The warriors and mages of the Sidhe Court were powerless against him, lost ages before to Dreaming and despair. It should have been easy.

But at the eleventh hour, the Sidhe had found an unlikely champion. A human Bard, living in ignorance of his true nature and his great power: Eric Banyon, street-busker and Rennie. Perenor had ordered Ria to destroy him, but she'd thought she'd found a better way. She'd englamoured him, taken him and hidden him away, with her.

And it had worked, for almost long enough. But then he'd awakened to the danger—come into his birthright of power, driven by dire necessity and danger to his dearest friends. He'd awakened the High Court, stolen back the Nexus from Ria's control to move it to Griffith Park, high above the city, a place where bulldozers and urban development could never come. To protect it and him, Eric's ally and lover, the human Witch, Beth Kentraine, had gathered those humans together who had not quite forgotten the Old Knowledge, and offered battle.

Ria remembered driving like a madwoman in her Porsche, up the twisting mountain roads that led to the park. The sun had been high—a glorious bright L.A. day, the last she was to see for quite some time. Even then she'd thought there would be some way to end the war without bloodshed. With the power of the Nexus at her command, Ria could have sent the surviving Sidhe of Elfhame Sun-Descending across the Veil, to the Faerie Lands beyond. She'd thought that Perenor had agreed to that. But conciliation had never been her father's way. He'd intended to kill them all, in repayment for an eons-old insult.

She remembered the hot smell of summer grass, remembered how glorious Perenor had looked in his armor the color of blued steel, remembered the music that had filled the air, the Celtic rock of Kentraine's group Spiral Dance. Since that day she'd never been able to listen to Celtic music, though she'd once loved it. The memories were too terrifying, too painful—as if she'd been given a glimpse of Paradise, only to have it ripped away before she could reach it. Most of all, she remembered her first sight of the Court in all its glory, gathered around the musicians and the Bard on that sunny hillside. In all her life, she'd never seen any Sidhe other than Perenor. How beautiful they had all been in their silks and armor! Something glorious, out of the oldest dream of strength and beauty there was. In that moment she had hated them, for being something she, by the curse of her half-human blood, could never be.

But she had never meant to kill them.

But Perenor had. By what right? they had asked him. She remembered the defiant words he had shouted in return:

"By the right of the strong over the weak, Eldenor. Of the master over the slave—the right of one who was unjustly banished, cast from his place among you, and has dreamed of the moment when all of you shall lie lifeless in pools of your own blood—"

In that moment, a moment far too late, she had truly understood her father for what he was—a monster, without love or charity, compassion or honor. He had reached out to her, stripping away all her carefully constructed shields and defenses with no more than a thought, making her nothing more than a tool of his madness, a wellspring of Power for him to draw upon in the fight. Imprisoned by his magic, she had been forced to watch as day became night, as the sunlit hillside became a shadowy glen filled with billowing black fog, as the Seleighe Sidhe had clashed with nightmare monsters of Perenor's summoning.

They had died to music, to the clashing of blades and the wild howl of guitars, to the hammering of drums and of sword-blows. The black ground had gone red with blood, and the screams of the dying had melded with the frenzied song of the Bard's flute. The day would have been lost in that moment, save that Terenil, Prince of

Elfhame Sun-Descending, had shaken off his despair and challenged Perenor directly.

And all Ria could do was scream silently within her own mind, fighting uselessly against what Perenor had made of her.

She had not seen Terenil die, though die he had. Before that moment, the Witch Kentraine had realized the truth, and had struck her own blow against Perenor and his nightmare allies.

Ria remembered that last moment: Kentraine standing over her, her Fender guitar raised like a club. She had willed the girl not to flinch, to do what had to be done to stop the madness and slaughter. And Kentraine had—striking with all her strength, smashing her guitar down on Ria's head, shattering the magical link Perenor had forged, saving them all. Saving the Nexus, and the Sidhe foothold in this world.

Ria had only learned the details of the end of the battle long afterward—how the dying Terenil had slain Perenor with his last breath, how Eric had reached beyond himself to pierce the Veil and anchor the new Nexus in a place beyond harm, how when Korendil would have slain her, Elizabet and Kayla, healers who had been drawn into the conflict on the very morning of the war, had claimed her life in payment for their help.

Together the two, Healer and Apprentice, had brought her back on the long slow journey from the edge of death, piecing back together Ria's shattered body, mind, and soul. She owed them a debt she could never repay.

Even when she was well at last, it would have been so much easier just to slink away and hide herself forever. As Perenor's heir at law, everything they had built together was hers. She never needed to work another day in her life if she didn't want to.

But when she'd tried to offer Elizabet money, the Healer wouldn't accept it. *"You'll repay me best by taking up your life again, Ria. I don't Heal people so that they can hide from their lives. You have responsibilities in the world. Go see to them."*

So now she was here.

But that was old news, and Ria preferred not to dwell on the past. Perenor was dead, his bid to claim the power of Elfhame Sun-Descending a failure, thanks to a Witch, a Bard, and an elven knight. She'd never figured out by what twisted mercy the three of them had spared her to claw her way back to memory and sanity once more. She tried not to think about it.

Ria had other things to think about.

She reached the end of the corridor, and the uniformed LlewellCo security guard opened it for her.

There was an audible hush as she entered the boardroom. Nine men and three women were gathered around the gleaming oak table. A breathtaking view of Los Angeles and the Valley was visible through the enormous windows that filled one wall of the room, but most of those at the table were sitting with their backs to the view. An oil portrait of Ria—done in Early Hagiography, she'd never liked it—hung over the head of the table. She'd been wearing black when it was painted, but today she wore red. Phoenix red, the color of rebirth.

She shut the door behind her.

"Good afternoon, gentlemen. Ladies. I hope I'm not late?" she asked with a warrior's smile.

Several of the people sitting around the table glanced from Ria to the portrait as if confirming her identity. Ria smiled inwardly. She didn't look a day older than she had when it was painted. One last advantage of her elven-Blood heritage—she wouldn't age as fast as mortalkind, though she didn't share the elves' immortality. In the mortal world, especially in these rarified corporate circles, her prolonged youthfulness would be taken for the work of an excellent plastic surgeon, nothing more.

Jonathan Sterling had gotten smoothly to his feet as she entered—of all those in the room, he was the only one who had been expecting her arrival here today—and stood aside as Ria took his place at the head of the table. The seat at her right was unoccupied— *how had he managed that feat of choreography?* a small part of her mind wondered idly—and he settled into it, trusted courtier to a grand prince. Only a shadow of a smile marred his perfect corporate mask, and you would have to know him very well to be able to see it. An answering flicker of amusement in her own green eyes, Ria took her seat.

She let her gaze sweep slowly up and down the table, taking careful note of who flinched, who looked angry, who looked relieved—and there were one or two—and who couldn't meet her gaze at all.

"I understand that there was some doubt about the extent of my recovery," she said dryly. "Thank you for your concern. Now, if you will all direct your attention to point one on the agenda. . . ."

For the next three hours Ria worked them unmercifully, probing for signs of timidity and unsoundness in LlewellCo's interim rulers. It was primarily a display of power, proving that no matter how long she'd been a bed-ridden basket case, she was back now, and as much to be feared as ever. It was easy enough to know what buttons to push: their minds fairly shouted out their deepest fears and reservations, allowing her to leaf through their eddying surfaces like the pages of a high-fashion magazine. Only Jonathan, beside her, was a still pool of well-organized calm.

There had been lapses and attempted coups, of course. She'd hired the cleverest and most ambitious corporate sharks, and one had to expect a little feeding frenzy now and then. Baker and Hardesty, in particular, had taken advantage of her absence to do things they knew she wouldn't approve of, and that Jonathan would be hard-pressed to discover. Several of the companies they'd bought had been bleeding money for years, with precious little to show for it.

"So we're all agreed on breaking off the courtship of TriMark Pharmaceuticals?" Ria said, looking Sabrina Baker right in the eye.

"Of course, Ms. Llewellyn," Baker said. She put up a good facade, but the TriMark deal had been all Baker's idea, and everyone here knew it. Most of them didn't know that TriMark was substantially funded by certain South American investors, but Baker did, and if she didn't, she should have.

"And the leveraged remortgaging of our Far East assets?" she added, turning to Colin Hardesty.

"Well, with the Asian dollar going soft . . . yes," Hardesty said, capitulating all at once. Ria hadn't quite made up her mind whether he was stupid or just subtle, but what was plain was that he'd over-reached himself mightily with this deal. And now he and everyone else here knew it.

"Good," Ria purred. "I imagine this concludes all our current business. I'd like to move our next meeting forward a bit, so that I can get an update on your other projects. So shall we say two weeks from today? I'll have my secretary prepare you a memo."

She did not smile now. Smiling was a sign of conciliation, and she had no need of that. There wasn't any argument—she hadn't thought there would be—and her staff quickly gathered up their papers and left the room. Ria stayed behind, watching the long blue shadows stretch over the L.A. Basin and savoring the moment.

Jonathan remained behind.

"I thought for sure you were going to can Baker and Hardesty," he said.

She smiled then, a genuine smile without edge or malice. "So did they. They know that I know, and they know I let them off just this once." Her expression turned grim. This was not the whole war, just a minor battle in it. Today's victory settled very little. "And from this second on, they are going to be so careful how they operate that if I get run over by a bus the moment I walk out of here, the two of them would still wait a year before making any moves, just so they could be certain I was dead." She heard an echo of her father in her own voice, and steeled herself against flinching. Perenor was a part of her—her blood, her bone—and once she would have exulted in that. Now it was only a fact, and one that sometimes made her tired.

Jonathan chuckled. He'd been the one stuck with riding herd on them over the last several years, after all. "And they aren't clever enough to hide their activities from that suite of computer hackers you insisted I hire. And I know they know that."

"Which puts you safely in the driver's seat for about a year if anything happens to me." Ria shrugged. "If you can't get firm control of LlewellCo by then, you aren't ever going to." She owed Jonathan the truth, and Ria had always valued honesty over kindness. In her world, kindness had always been a feint, a prelude to war.

"And if I don't, I'm not the person to handle it in the first place," Jonathan answered. "Which, by the way, I'd rather not, unless you're going to be around to pick up the reins again."

Ria looked at him quizzically. It was almost an admission of weakness, and Jonathan Sterling was anything but a weakling. If he had been, he could not have survived to rise in the company she had built at her father's orders, much less managed to keep control of it in the aftermath of her . . . injury. All her life, she'd never depended on anyone in quite the way she depended on Jonathan. Theirs was not a romantic relationship—he was quite comfortably married, and she'd never seen any reason to change that—but it was a partnership that was stronger than any bond formed of bodies. He had always been her trusted aide, but the relationship she had forged in the arrogant assumption of her own invincibility had changed when she had come to truly need him. He had given her unswerving loyalty and trust; even in her weakness, he had given as a gift what she could no longer demand, and that gift had changed both of them. In another age, Jonathan would have been squire to her knight, trusted vassal to her prince, a relationship to endure beyond all testing. She'd trusted him, and had been given his trust in return. In the last six months she'd learned more about his family from a few oblique remarks than she'd learned in all the years he'd been her assistant.

"I don't like the feeling of the hounds nipping at my heels," he explained simply.

"And you'd rather be married to your wife than your work. I can't blame you there," she added.

"You would have, once," he replied.

Ria shrugged, getting to her feet. "Now I just envy you, sometimes," Ria said.

She walked to the window to stare out over the Valley. The sunset light painted the scene before her in tones of fire and gold, the light bouncing off the inversion layer that hung over the metroplex. She'd told him the truth. She received truth in return.

"There's something you'll want to know," he said, and something in his voice kept her from turning back, kept her gazing out over the city. Her unacknowledged kingdom, bought with blood.

"Eric Banyon's surfaced. I waited until I had definite word from the PI I hired for you that it was the same Eric Banyon you wanted, but there's no doubt. He's in New York, enrolled at Juilliard. After all this time, the Feds aren't looking for him any more; I checked that too. I suppose he figured that."

Eric! She forced herself to relax, and when she spoke her voice was even, neutral. "And?"

"No sign of his friends. He's there alone."

Jonathan, her trusted champion, knowing what she wanted to know and making certain to tell her those things first. Money could not buy such care. Fear could not command it.

So Eric was back at Juilliard. She had as complete a file on him as money could buy. She knew he'd been a child prodigy, knew he'd dropped out of Juilliard on his 18th birthday to make his living on the street and at RenFaires, a rootless rebel, as shy as a wild hawk. The Eric she'd known would never have gone back to the scene of his failure . . . much less abandoned his friends.

But had he? Or had they abandoned him?

Perhaps the truth was somewhere in between.

She'd traced the three of them as far as San Francisco, but there they'd vanished. She'd assumed that meant they'd gone to Underhill—the elves would always welcome a Bard, and Korendil and Eric between them could have sponsored the Kentraine bitch—but why had he come back?

Did she dare go and ask him? His enrollment at Juilliard argued that he'd be easy to find. He must feel safe if he'd been willing to go there. But of course the years in Underhill would have been as good as a disguise.

"Does our set of New York interests need a shaking up as well?" she asked. *No. Leave it. He's the past. Let him stay there.*

But Jonathan came to her side, silently holding out a slim leather pilot's wallet. She took it, seeing the sheaf of paper inside from the travel agency LlewellCo used. Plane tickets. A hotel reservation.

"I think you'll just have time to pack and catch the red-eye," Jonathan said. "Your schedule's there. There's a board meeting scheduled for LlewellCo East the day after tomorrow, which should just give you time to get over jet lag."

He handed her another folder, this one legal-pad-sized and thick. "This is the PI report and contact information. You'll have time to read it on the plane. The reports on our East Coast holdings are there, too. Have a good trip."

She might have kissed him then, but such gestures had never been a part of what was between them. Instead she turned away from the window and favored him with a cool Sphinx-like smile.

"Thank you, Jonathan. You always know just what I need."

His answering smile was only in his eyes. "It's good to have you back. And now . . . your car is waiting, and I've just got time to return a few calls before I hit the freeway."

The old yellow-brick building occupied most of a city block, and dated back to the days when there'd been factories in Manhattan. It faced the East River, in an area that was sporadically gentrifying. But no matter how many new glass office buildings studded Hudson Street and Second Avenue, old dinosaurs like the riverside warehouse remained, legacies of the past of The City That Works.

And as always, they adapted to circumstances.

The logo in gold on the front door said THRESHOLD LABS, as did the sign over the loading dock doors. It was a cryptic declaration that might mean almost anything. Whatever Threshold did, it was clear that the company—and its employees—valued their privacy.

For good reason.

Despite its functional, down-at-heel exterior, serious money had been expended on the interior of the building. The three floors had been remodelled and subdivided into offices, Cray sequencers and the power lines to feed them brought in, microwaves and centrifuges, air scrubbers and clean rooms and serious water purification systems installed, as well as a number of modifications below-street that would never have passed any New York building inspection, no matter how well-bribed the inspector. The small clandestine lab three floors below the street was bisected by a wall of triple-sealed glass, and could only be entered through an airlock by technicians in full clean suits. The lab was kept at negative pressure, so that in case its seals were broken, the air would flow in, not out. On the other side of the glass was a window-less office. It, too, was dark, but there was someone there, sitting behind the desk with a guitar in her lap, fingers soundlessly stroking the strings. She was working late as usual, mulling over the last run of tests. It wasn't as if she had someplace else to go, after all.

She looked up as the timer cycled the lights in the lab down to sleep-time levels. The sudden darkness in the room beyond turned the thick glass into a mirror, mercilessly reflecting the office's occupant. She met her own gaze unflinchingly, a woman who prided herself on having shed all her illusions.

She'd had plenty of help in doing so. If she hated what she saw at 31, she also knew that wishing wouldn't change it.

Romantic loners of any sex should be tall and slender and dressed in black. Jeanette Campbell was short and sloppily plump, with thin fine mouse-brown hair dragged back in an unforgiving ponytail, persistent acne, and short stubby fingers that struggled to fit around the neck of a guitar. She was a loner through both arrogance and fate—verbal and opinionated, she had always been the sort of person who, when teased, lashed back viciously, taking no prisoners.

By the time she reached high school, Jeanette was a full-blown social pariah. Through pride, she rejected the few tentative overtures that were made to her—it was very clear to her that those willing to be kind to her branded themselves worthless by the gesture. She'd yearned for romantic isolationism while longing to be popular. She'd dressed in studs and leather, knowing she made herself look ridiculous, but still somehow unable to give up the gesture. She was desperately unhappy and worse: bright and insightful enough to know she had woven the tapestry of her sorrows strand by strand through the long years that separated third grade from high school freshman, but unable to find her way out of the web. She would not bow down to the pretty and popular whatever it cost her. She would never admit that their opinion mattered.

High school was hell, but by then Jeanette had calluses on her soul as well as her fingers. She concentrated on her classes and her part-time job, intent merely upon getting things over with: so fixed upon the destination that she discounted the journey.

Then something happened. Halfway through her senior year, Jeanette slowly became aware of something that had never been true before.

Nobody cared.

Nobody slimed her locker, tripped her in the halls, stole her homework, made crank calls to her house. Nobody mocked her in classes, pasted stupid bumper stickers on her guitar case, cut in front of her in lines, or stole her lunch. She could read any book she liked, in public, without being afraid it would be snatched from her hands and ruined.

Nobody cared about her at all.

It took her a long time to believe it could be true, and longer to trust her good fortune. She'd spent more than half her life in a war she'd known she could never win. Nobody had ever told her that it wouldn't go on forever. And one day, when she wasn't looking, it had just stopped. The enemy had declared peace and gotten out.

She didn't know what to do about it. At first the relief had been so great that she didn't care about anything else. And when the truth finally sank in, it made room for an anger as devastating as grief.

That's it? You ruin my life, all of you, and then you just walk away? You don't even pretend it never happened. You just FORGET IT?

Well, I can't forget it.

She tried. But all that left her was the realization that she had nothing at all to say to her former tormentors. The only connection she'd had with her classmates was being their scapegoat, and now she didn't even have that. They had shaped her more than she had ever understood and left her to cope with the result. Freed of constant peer pressures, Jeanette sought new pressure as instinctively as the flower seeks the sun. She drifted into things that appalled her, but she couldn't summon up the interest in her own actions to stop. She couldn't even take refuge in a romantic self-image. She'd always longed to—she dressed the part—but it required a level of self-delusion that Jeanette Campbell had never had. She was not and could never be the thing she loved most.

Unless she found the answer.

That there *was* an answer was something she'd never questioned. She'd read all the books, the ones that told her the human mind had powers which, if she could only unlock them, could transform her life. She'd started studying the mind then, reading the classics in the field. The brain was a biological machine. It could be reprogrammed with the right tools.

She'd grown up at the tail end of the period that considered drugs recreational, and for a while she'd thought that was the answer—the right chemical cocktail could do what she wanted and needed it to, unlock the hidden powers of her mind and make them available. A few semesters at the community college had given her the rest of the tools she needed to pursue what she thought of as her Research, and as soon as she had the basic tools for her quest, she'd dropped out. She already knew that legitimate research wouldn't divulge what she sought. For one thing, it frowned on human experimentation.

And she had experimented—first on herself, then on others—a combination of loneliness and rage pushing her down the easy road from science geek to outlaw chemist. Bills had to be paid, and research took money. But she knew the answer was there, somewhere. If she only had the courage and the discipline to find it.

The answer was in the hallucinogens. She'd always known that, from the first time she'd dropped acid. But LSD alone wasn't enough. It was too diffuse, too variable, too soft. She'd added mescaline, crystal meth, cocaine, trying to come up with the right cocktail that would let her push through all the barriers and claim the lightning for her own. She'd known she was on the right track, but every time she had a compound she was ready to try, it failed somewhere along the way. Sometimes people died, but she hadn't cared. She worked frantically, desperately, knowing her time was running out, because life on the street just wasn't safe, and when you were supplying illegal drugs, the working conditions and your co-workers left a lot to be desired. Sooner or later somebody would sell her out, and she'd go down.

But in her own strange way, Jeanette was heroic. Inevitable arrest and imprisonment didn't faze her. Finding the key was all that mattered.

Then Robert Lintel came, and that changed everything.

She'd been in the back room of a garage somewhere in New Jersey, cooking up a batch of methamphetamine in a makeshift kitchen. She'd had to move three times in the past month because of the Feds, and the last time she'd lost her whole lab. If the Sinner Saints—the bikers who were her protection and distribution network—hadn't tipped her off, she would have lost more than her lab, but her product was pure and consistent, and they knew that if she went down she'd sell out as many of them as she could.

Won't live to see thirty if I do, but I don't think that matters, do you, Jeannie?

Of course, they might kill her themselves to keep that from happening. Even without the psychic powers she coveted, Jeanette could tell that. She could almost hear Road Hog thinking that, when he set her up out here in the middle of nowhere. But the Saints were greedy, and already had a deal in place for this current batch. She was safe at least until it was done, and maybe longer if the heat died down.

When the door of the garage opened, she looked up, irritated, thinking it was Road Hog or Hooker coming back to chivvy her along. But it was someone she'd never seen before, a well-manicured man in an expensive dark grey suit, walking in like he owned the place.

Her hand had crept toward the gun in her knapsack—people in her profession always went armed—but she hesitated for a crucial second, because the room was full of acetone and ether and the muzzle flash from a shot would send the whole lab up like the Fourth of July.

And he'd smiled at her, like there was something that he wanted. Her hand closed over the gun, and she pulled it into her lap, behind the desk where he couldn't see, but she didn't fire.

"Jeanette Campbell? Hi. My name is Robert Lintel. I've got a business proposition for you."

With those inane words he'd changed her life. So that now she could look in a mirror, and not flinch quite so hard.

The lights in her office flared to full merciless brightness, and Jeanette blinked and squinted up at the figure in the doorway, laying her guitar aside.

"Hey, Campbell. What are you doing sitting here in the dark?"

There was an edge to Robert's voice, but there always was. He'd rescued her years ago, but it was for reasons even more selfish than her own, if that were possible.

While she wanted the powers that were hers by right—and God help anyone who stood in her way once she had them—Robert wanted Ultimate Power. She wanted the power for herself, Robert wanted to control the powerful people. He saw himself in charge of a group of perfect psychic spies, assassins, and saboteurs, whose work was undetectable . . . and whose skills were for sale to the highest bidder, though he never said that.

He didn't have to. Jeanette, better than anyone else, knew how his mind worked. Hadn't he sought her out back there in Jersey because he'd gotten to see the research notes she'd left behind in the lab the Feds had seized, and knew she could be a means to his ends?

Just so.

There was no love lost between predators.

"Thinking," Jeanette answered sullenly. She gestured toward the primate cages waiting on the other side of the glass. The experimental animals were only one of the things here that shouldn't be. When she'd been a street chemist, she had to make do with what she could get, with random customers as her experimental subjects. These days things were much more satisfactory: absolute immunity from the law, pure chemicals to work with, the best apparatus, and an unlimited budget.

But no human subjects.

"It's too dangerous," he'd said, and for years she'd accepted that. There'd been too much else to do—first, catching up on all the schooling she'd sluffed off, then re-documenting and refining her previous research, as what good was a breakthrough you couldn't replicate at will?

She'd made do with primates—chimps siphoned to Threshold from other projects or bought on the black market. On paper—and more or less in fact—Threshold was a small pharmaceutical research company. Most of its employees were engaged in legitimate research into the neurochemistry of the brain. Few of them even suspected the existence of the Black Labs that occupied the cellars of the building, the place where Jeanette Campbell did research that went far beyond simple cures for ADD, narcolepsy, clinical depression, bipolar disorder, and the like. Some of the hundreds of primates shipped to Threshold every year even went to the careful legitimate experiments of the people in the labs upstairs, but more of them went to the Black Labs.

The brain structure of a chimpanzee was similar to that of human beings, and some of them even knew sign language. Jeanette wasn't interested in talking to them, but language use modified the deep structure of the brain and gave her a benchmark by which to measure the effects of her drugs.

She had three consistent results from her drug protocols to date: dead chimps, crazy chimps, and superficially unaffected chimps. She'd lost count of the number of brains she'd centrifuged, looking for results and reasons. But she was getting closer. That was all that mattered.

"Thinking," Robert echoed scornfully. "You want to get up off your dead ass and do a little more than think? Beirkoff told me you were going to be ready for another trial today."

Beirkoff was Jeanette's personal assistant—somebody had to do the record-keeping gruntwork who was in on Threshold's big secret—but she'd always known he geeked for Robert. It was how the world worked.

"Yeah, well, I am ready," she said, getting up and putting her guitar down. The reflection in the glass mocked her like an evil angel, showing her the hated reality so far from her dreams. "Beirkoff should have the chimps prepped. I can shoot them up and leave the cameras running, then check them out in the morning. It's better to do this sort of thing at night, anyway."

No need to put into words the nebulous feeling, not even a hunch, that something about the drugs would just work better in the small hours of the night when most people were asleep. Once upon a time she'd fancied herself a magician, but in the years since then Jeanette had put both magic and superstition behind her. She worked entirely with what was, abandoning dreams.

"What's your hurry, anyway?" she asked incuriously.

"I'm not paying you to sit around playing that damned guitar," Robert said grudgingly, and Jeanette smiled inside, though she allowed no vestige of that expression to reach her face. In fact, Robert *was* paying her to sit around playing that dammed guitar, and whatever else she wanted to do with her time. Her work was as much inspiration as anything else—and the accidental discoveries along the way had proved her worth. She'd come up with a compound that induced abject terror in its subject and one that destroyed the sleep centers. Both killed the subject in anywhere from 24 hours to a week, but Robert had liked them, even though they'd never be mentioned in Threshold's quarterly report to its parent company. He'd taken them off somewhere and never told her what he'd done with them, but Jeanette knew those discoveries were what had bought her a free pass for the foreseeable future.

"I'm going to go down and inject them now. Want to watch?" she said.

Robert gestured, indicating she should precede him. It was one of the few things she actually liked about Robert. He wasn't squeamish.

She walked out of her office and down the grey-carpeted corridor to the room that held the airlock that would let her into the primate lab. She didn't bother with a clean suit—the whole fantasy of biological contamination was just a useful fiction for any of Threshold's legitimate employees who might stumble accidentaly onto her work area. No one but Robert and Beirkoff really knew what it was she did here, and neither one had the brains to follow her science. Secrecy was power. She remembered that from her magical days.

When she walked in, the full-spectrum lights brightened slowly to their daytime levels, washing every corner of the main floor in pitiless illumination, illuminating the row of cages so brightly that their contents seemed like unliving mannequins. The room was warm, and smelled strongly of ozone, ammonia, and fermenting fruit. She looked up, and saw the blinking red lights of the cameras. They'd record every move that anyone made in this room from half a dozen angles, no matter the light level, and store the images in digital computer memory for instant retrieval, so that later Robert and Jeanette could scrutinize and speculate about every squeal and twitch of the subjects. The oldest files were purged on a six-month rotation, leaving no trace of themselves behind. Robert ran a clean operation.

Her subjects were in the five cages along the wall, brought in from the larger primate lab at the other end of the building. Beirkoff had sedated each of them an hour ago, so that now they were torpid and manageable, but most of the sedative had already been processed, so that chemical residue wouldn't screw up her study.

Satisfied that everything was in readiness, she went over to the big refrigerator at the end of the room—past the stainless-steel exam table with its drains and shackles—and punched a nine-digit code into its locking key pad.

The light at the top of the pad turned from red to green, and Jeanette opened the door. Inside, it looked like any other lab refrigerator, with anonymous bottles and bundles neatly stacked and labeled on the shelves. She pulled out the jar she wanted. It was half full of a sparkling white powder, as pure and anonymous as salt. "Threshold 6/157" was written on the label. Sixth year of trials, test 157.

From the cupboard beside the refrigerator she took a fresh bottle of distilled water, and mixed and measured until she had a seven percent solution of T-6/157. She filled five disposable syringes with the liquid, and then advanced on her subjects.

She'd had a lot of time to get good at wrestling primates in the last six years. Pop open the cage door, make sure the damned thing wasn't lying doggo, find a vein, drop her load, snap the cage door shut again. The chimps' bodies were warm and flaccid in sleep, their muscles relaxed. It was over in less than five minutes, the subjects twitching and restless, rousing to wakefulness under the tonic effect of the injection. The temporary restlessness would pass—T-6/157 was a minute variation on a previous recipe, and she knew the spectrum of effects almost by heart—and the subjects would fall into a brief coma. In about fifteen minutes the compound would begin to take effect, though most of the subjects continued to sleep for several hours. The effects would pass completely within twelve hours. Then they could review the tapes and start again.

"What are you waiting for? Brass bands?" she snapped. This was the part that always got her down, when she injected the drug and nothing happened. She knew she couldn't expect anything to happen right away, but it still depressed her.

Robert had already turned away. As he reached the door, he tapped the switch, and the lights went back to nighttime levels. Jeanette followed him back into the hallway, in the dark.

The sound of the bedside telephone woke her. Jeanette groped for it in the dark, but at her first flailings the night-lights went on, motion sensors activating a strip of illumination all the way around the floor. With that to guide her, she grabbed the telephone. The clock on the bedside said 4:07.

"Get down here. Now," Robert said.

The cab ride down from Central Park West—the posh uptown apartment had been Robert's idea, not hers—took about twenty minutes at this time of night, but it was plenty of time for Jeanette to think. Obviously, something had happened—fire? —break-in? At any rate, something big enough that Beirkoff had freaked and phoned Robert—which was as it should be. Threshold was Robert's baby. He was the CEO, and she (on the books at least) a lowly researcher. She even had a tiny office upstairs, with a window looking out over the river, and attended the monthly staff meetings that were a part of

Threshold's legitimate side. But her real work was here, down in the Black Labs, alone and unconnected to the rest of the company.

But in that case, why had Robert phoned her?

She came in through the night entrance, using her passcard, and Beirkoff met her at the doorway. His eyes glittered with excitement and she realized that whatever was going on here, it was really huge. Big enough to get Beirkoff excited, anyway, and most of the time the technician approached his job with all the verve of someone working the counter at McDonald's.

Sometimes Jeanette wondered where Robert found all these people. Beirkoff didn't seem to have any life outside Threshold. The security staff were hardcase mercs like she'd never seen working the sunny side of the law. Dr. Ramchandra, who handled the medical side of the Black Ops project, smiled a lot, but from living outside the law Jeanette knew a stone cold spook when she saw one. And she wouldn't have the first idea about how to pull a crew like this together.

Either Robert had a lot of backing, or a complex secret life, or maybe both.

"Mr. Lintel says you should meet him downstairs—" Beirkoff began.

An unfamiliar emotion filled her—hope—and she pushed past him and headed for the executive elevator. She had to present her passkey again, but once she had, the elevator descended into the secret world beneath the street, the one that most of Threshold didn't even suspect was there. Robert was waiting for her in her office, looking as immaculately corporate as ever.

"Tell me," she said, when she saw his face.

"Look for yourself." His eyes were shining with the same light that was in her own: the glow of pure triumph. He turned off the lights, and in the darkness it was easy to see through the wall of glass into the small lab.

"Nobody's gone in there yet. I gave orders," Robert said. His voice was hoarse with sheer stupefied emotion. "Nobody's gone in there since you left, four hours ago."

For a moment she didn't understand what she was seeing. At last her eyes and brain worked together to tell her what she saw.

This was what success looked like.

The room was a mess. Drawers and cabinets had been torn open, their contents strewn around like a fall of strange snow. The wheeled cages were scattered around the room, as if someone had been shaking them, and blood, urine, and chimp feces were spattered everywhere. But most of all, there were only four cages, and four hours ago there had been five.

Four. Yes. She was sure of it.

There was movement in the corner of the room—since no one had gone into the room, the lights were still nighttime dim—and she saw it was the fifth chimp. He was moving slowly, as if he were ill.

"How did he get out of his cage?" she asked aloud. *And where's the cage?*

"Keep looking," Robert said, his voice filled with unholy glee.

She turned her attention to the other cages. One was empty, its bright yellow plastic security seal still intact. In two of the others, the animals were obviously dead, having ripped themselves to pieces with their own teeth and nails. She'd seen that side effect often enough.

But in the fifth . . .

Its occupant was an older female chimp, obviously once somebody's pampered pet until she had grown too inconvenient. Her body was smeared with red, and for a moment Jeanette mistook it for blood, until her disbelieving mind finally admitted what she saw.

Strawberries. Raspberries. And Godiva chocolate-covered cherries. She knew they were Godiva cherries because the distinctive gold-foil box was still in the cage.

How? cried half her mind, and: *It worked!* said the other half.

She looked at Robert, her eyes alight.

"It was T-6/157," she said.

"Yes," Robert said simply. "It does seem to have been."

"We'll have to arrange for more trials—find out what happened—maybe direct injection into the neurocortex. I'll review the surveillance images—we'll have to prep some more chimps—" she said, almost babbling.

"No need. I told Beirkoff to put the rest of the chimps down, anyway."

All she could do was stare at him, stunned by the enormity of her success. Robert smiled, as pleased by that as by the nearness of his ultimate goal.

"Campbell. We aren't going to learn anything from a bunch of monkeys that can't answer our questions, now, are we?" Robert asked, almost playfully.

"Human trials." She felt a thrill of excitement course through her. There was an exhilaration at watching a drug take possession of a person that all the lab animals and private funding in the world couldn't match. Finding volunteers for this sort of experiment was difficult, but there were ways. Expensive. Unethical. But ways. "I'll tell Beirkoff to get the Large Primate Containment set up. I'll need at least half a dozen subjects to start with."

"But not volunteers," Robert said, as if reading her mind. "Not yet. But that's nothing for you to worry about. I'll have your lab rats for you by tomorrow night. This is New York. You can find them on every street corner."

FOUR:
THE DARK CARNIVAL

He had been born a Lord of the Bright Court when mortalkind was still painting itself blue on a small island off the coast of Europe, and for uncounted years of Man's time what the mortals did had not mattered to him. Among his own kind, Aerune mac Audelaine was a high prince, a Lord of the Sidhe, and his rank and birth had insulated him from the petty squabbles that others of his race liked to fall into, spending eons on a vendetta in retaliation for some petty slight. Strong emotion was the bane of the near-immortal Sidhe, tied as they were so closely to place and kindred. Instead of great wars that could tear Underhill apart and doom them all, their energy was spent on small battles and long-running spitefulness.

Aerune, even as a youth, rejected this code of cool serenity. Passion drew him as the flame drew the moth. Grand hatreds, nurtured in secret, had sustained him from his earliest memories, leading him inevitably to declare his allegiance to the Great Queen Morrigan, ruler of the Unseleighe Sidhe. He was her courtier and most trusted lieutenant—but in secret. For centuries Aerune was as trusted a guest at the Bright Court as the Dark, until that shadow-game began to pall, and he withdrew from them both to follow his own inclinations. Still he ignored the race of Men, whose antics so amused the other Sidhe.

And I would have left them to their sordid lives forever, were it not for Aerete. Aerete the Beautiful, my love . . .

She had been barely a woman when Aerune had known her: golden as the day, a child of the Bright Court, filled only with love. She had spent that love upon the mortalkind, healing their wounds, listening to their woes, ruling over them as their Queen.

It was she who had opposed him, standing alone before him when Aerune would have taken his Wild Hunt among the tribes under her protection. She had stood unafraid in the path of the Unseleighe *rade,* her child's face stern, telling him that he and his folk must ride another way.

He might have cut her down, bespelled her, done a thousand things to remove this obstacle from his path, for Aerune cared for nothing living. But something in her stern innocence had stopped him, and he had turned the Hunt aside.

Afterward, he had sought her out. She knew him by reputation, but had accepted him into her hall as a guest. She had spoken to him of the humans, the lastborn of Danu, and had tried to show him the good in them, the spark of magic that they shared with Danu's firstborn, the Sidhe. Aerune felt his dark heart open to her like a flower to the sun. He begged her to come away with him to the World Beyond.

"But how can I abandon my human children, Lord Aerune? They are so innocent, so helpless. Their lives are but a brief span compared to ours. Stay with me, and offer them your guidance as well."

He had not stayed, but he had come to her often, always hoping to persuade her to come away with him. And perhaps, Aerune told himself, he would have succeeded in time.

But time was not granted to them.

War came out of the East. At first Aerune paid no attention to it. Mortalkind's battles were the echo of the Sidhe wars, eternal and unchanging. They could not matter to him.

Or so he thought.

Aerete tried to make peace between the two tribes. It was hard, for the newcomers had the secret of a strange metal far stronger than the flint and bronze weapons of her people, and their losses had been heavy. Aerune had urged her to fight, counselling that only their victory would end the threat. He had not meant for Aerete to take the field beside her war-captain, using her magic against their iron blades.

Iron. It was iron that had killed his love, a spear thrown to strike her in her chariot, piercing the elvensilver armor that she wore. She had cried out for his aid. . . .

And Aerune had come, with all the hosts of Darkness at his side. But he had come too late.

He cradled her dying burning body in his arms, there on that bloodsoaked human battlefield. And as she died, all there was of kindness and mercy died with him. When he left the battlefield that day, all that lived upon it were the ravens of Morrigan. There were no survivors, and no victors. Only his pain, his loss, remained. He would have vengeance upon everything that had conspired to take his Aerete from him.

He began by seeking to crush the Bright Lords who were his kind's natural enemies—those who had let his golden darling go among Men to find her death. His campaign against them had blossomed secretly, silently, over the course of centuries.

It had failed at last, beyond any hope of success, and finally Aerune turned his attention to the world of Men. Men who, in what seemed only a moment of his inattention, had gone from weapons of bronze and stone to weapons of smith-forged iron—deathmetal, fatal to all who drew their life force from magic. These he could kill, if he was careful, but no matter how many he killed there were always more to take their place. They called him Arawn, Lord of Death—but even as they cowered in terror from his Hunt, they fought back in a thousand other ways, breeding like the vermin they were, challenging the Sidhe in their Groves and high places.

His kindred fought back, of course, trying to retain their pride of place. But Men had magic of their own, and the love of powers far greater than Seleighe and Unseleighe alike. With love and iron, mortal Man bound and banished its elder brothers, the Sidhe, until at last the Courts fled the Old World entirely, searching for a place where they could take up the Old Ways unmolested. And Aerune fled with them, wrapped in his hatred and pride.

But Man—arrogant, presumptuous Man—followed the Sidhe even across the Great Water, destroying the ties the Bright Court forged with the mortalfolk of this new land. Destroying the mortalfolk as well, in a slaughter that would have gladdened Aerune's heart if it had only been his own work. At last elvenkind was banished into the shadows of this world, its foothold a tenuous one, its vast empire shrunken to a handful of *hames*.

From his stronghold Aerune had watched all this, too bitter in his wrath even to ride forth as he had once done. The natives of this new land sensed his presence, and avoided his place, but when Mortals followed the Sidhe across the sea, many of them disregarded the warnings of their brown-skinned cousins, and flocked to settle in the place that Aerune had made his own. Aerune tolerated them. There was much to learn before he could work their doom. Cautiously, Aerune sought allies, but even in this extremity, the Sidhe had battled one another, as if seeking to do the humans' work for them.

He had watched from his tower as the Seleighe Sidhe of Elfhame Sun-Descending had destroyed Lord Perenor and saved themselves from the Dreaming. He had watched as the Sun-Descending elves had summoned great sorceries and forged a new Nexus that would allow them to flourish safely forever in the lands of the Uttermost West, forging a strong alliance with Elfhame Misthold. They thought themselves safe. They would not swear fealty to him now.

And so, like any good general, he had turned his efforts elsewhere—to the iron-haunted city that had grown up in the World Above. To the world of Men, Men who were kin to those who had slain Bright Aerete.

Underhill was a place composed of all places and none, Chaos Lands given form and substance by magic alone, in which the hames glowed like abhorrent stars, welding all Underhill together into one vast tapestry. The Seleighe Sidhe were the bright threads in this weaving, the Unseleighe were its shadows, and once—long ago— that balance had satisfied him. But within Aerune's memory, Elfhame Everforest, with its Nexus so near the heart of the Lands of Men, had grown stronger as well, and the Dark Sidhe could foresee a time when the Bright Lords' weaving would bind the shadows in an unbreakable net, and the Bright Lords would bow their necks and their pride to a yoke forged by mortal Man.

Aerune planned accordingly.

If he could not defeat his Bright Kindred directly in Underhill, nor bring them beneath his banner, then a flanking attack was needed. Aerune turned his attention once more to the Lands of Men.

Aerete, Aerete . . . if you could see what they have become, surely you would renounce them as well!

Cold Iron was their weapon, and in their hands, it could slay Seleighe and Unseleighe alike. But if the Sidhe of Elfhame Fairgrove could learn to tolerate Cold Iron, why shouldn't he and his be able to do likewise? On his dark throne, Aerune dreamed of a mortal army under his command, bearing the Cold Iron that could allow him to wrest the Nexuses from the control of the Bright Lords and plunge all of Underhill into endless night; a first step before he turned his human armies on their mortal brethren, sweeping aside everything that stood in the way of vengeance, his Dark Queen's rule of all the lands, mortal and Sidhe.

But to summon such an army, he needed a foothold in the World of Iron. He needed a Nexus under his control, one that would allow his followers—boggles and boghans, his bane-sidhes, water-horses, nixies, and the like—to move freely in the world of Men. Without that power source, even opening a Portal between the worlds would drain him, and so he moved cautiously, searching for the perfect time, the perfect spot. And in the concrete canyons of Manhattan, he had found it.

Take this city, and with it such souls as these mortals possess. I shall humble them in the strength of their fortresses, until not one stone remains set upon another.

And at last he was through with waiting. It was time to act. And so, in the sanctity of his greatest stronghold, Aerune began the weaving of his webs.

The place in which Aerune held his Court would have been beautiful to mortal eyes, if any had lived to see it . . . a forest of dark silver, with leaves of shadow. He sat upon a throne forged of darker shadow yet, his hellhounds lolling at his feet, his Court surrounding him, a host of insubstantial wraiths and bound servitors, all of whom owed him fealty, just as he owed it to the Morrigan. From the base of his throne stretched a pool of black mirror, in which Aerune often watched the antics of his future subjects, into which he sent dreams to guide them. Even the happiest mortal carried within himself a spark of darkness, the phantom of Death whose dark wings would one day enfold him, and it was from that phantom and that fear that Aerune forged the chains that bound mortals unknowingly to his service.

Just as the joy of the Bright Lords had created a human land of magic and imagination around their grove, so did Aerune's dreams create a darkness in the World Above his palace—a vast dark iron city that the mortalkind had crafted out of blood and betrayal and the dreams he had sent them, filled with pain and sorrow and suffering enough to glut even a rapacious Unseleighe lord. There was even a place in its heart filled with great trees such as his followers needed to anchor themselves—Central Park, the mortalkind called it.

And so, at last, Aerune made his first move upon the chessboard of war.

He sent for the least of his servants, the redcap, Urla.

"My lord?"

Urla seemed to coalesce out of the mist of the grove itself. The redcap was one of the Lesser Sidhe, shaped by the nightmares of generations of men. It was small, barely the size of a child, but with a distorted, misshapen form . . . and very long arms. It wore a laborer's smock and ragged pants, but upon its head there was a soft cap of bright scarlet, as bright as the blood of men.

It approached the Shadow Throne nervously, bowing low and

grovelling as it judged its lord's mood. One of the hellhounds raised its massive shaggy head and growled, red eyes glowing. Aerune silenced the beast with a gesture. Today he had need of Urla, for of all his servants, Urla was one of the few who could move with relative freedom in the World Above, for the redcap preyed upon men, stealing their strength to replenish its own. So long as the blood in which Urla soaked its cap remained fresh, it had the strength of those it had slain.

"Do you love me, Urla?" Aerune asked gently.

The redcap winced, and grovelled more deeply, inching its way toward Aerune's feet. "More than death. More than darkness, Great Lord. All my strength, all my power, are yours."

This was nothing more than the truth, and Aerune accepted it as such.

"Then you are mine, to do with as I choose. And so I choose to send you back to the world of Men. Hunt this city for me. Slay whom you will, hunt whom you will, saving only that you choose those souls who will not be missed in the World of Men. But find me the power to open the door between the worlds once more.

"Find for me . . . a Bard."

Why did I ever decide to do this? Eric asked himself again. He ran his hand down the side of his slacks to dry it, and then transferred his flute to that hand and repeated the gesture. He was wearing the standard "school uniform" for recitals—white shirt, black pants, dress shoes, and tie. His long chestnut hair was pulled back in a length of black velvet ribbon. His feet hurt, and his collar felt as if it were strangling him. *Look at me. I'm sweating like a novice.*

He'd already been out there once before tonight, but that had been with the chamber orchestra, and there'd been safety in numbers. But now it was time for his chamber group, and there were only seven of them. The other six members of his group—Jeremy, Lydia, two French horns, a violin, and a cello—were standing nearby, waiting to go on when the previous group finished playing. He took what consolation he could from the fact that they all looked as if facing a firing squad would be preferable—even Jeremy, who normally carried ironic detachment to new heights. And Lydia looked as if she were about to faint.

"Hey," Eric said gently, reaching out to gain her attention. "Relax. It's just another performance."

She turned toward him, her scared violet eyes huge. The three of them had become friends in the last several weeks, though Eric's need to keep his other life under wraps, and the crushing weight of rehearsal and course work, had kept them from becoming as close as they might otherwise have done. While a part of Eric regretted that, mostly he was grateful. He wasn't ready right now for any more of what Toni Hernandez had called "hostages to fortune."

But right now, it looked as if Lydia could use a friendly hand. Her red hair was pulled back into a tightly scraped bun and her pale-gold freckles stood out against her skin like a dusting of golden pollen on the surface of skimmed milk. Lydia had real talent, but even in the short time he'd known her, Eric was afraid that the Juilliard pressure cooker would destroy any love she had for the music . . . assuming Marco Ashborn hadn't done that already. Lydia was a technically flawless musician, but with her it was *all* technique, no heart.

"It's a *performance*," she said in a low trembling voice. "People will be watching. Important people. Father's friends."

"So what?" Eric said cheerfully. "Our friends will be there too."

Lydia blinked as his words penetrated. Each student got a limited number of tickets to hand out to recital performances, and empty seats could be filled by Juilliard students on a stand-by basis 15 minutes before the performance. Eric had given his passes to Toni, José, and his other friends from Guardian House, including Caity, a children's book writer (with no magical gift outside her stories, so far as Eric could tell) whom he'd met while doing laundry in the basement of the House. He wasn't sure if they'd be able to attend—Jimmie had the usual last-minute crises that came with an LEO's job, and Toni might run into something that kept her at the House.

He'd only wished there was some way for Greystone to attend as well. At least the performance was being taped, and he could play it for his gargoyle friend later.

Lydia hesitated, about to say something, but just then there was a wash of applause from the other side of the curtain. The previous group was finishing, and it was time for them to go on.

"It will be fine," Eric said coaxingly. "No matter what happens."

He could see that the girl didn't believe him. If there had been time, he might have used magic to calm her and give her some of the confidence he felt, but the other musicians were moving past them, making way for them on the stage, and he knew better than to meddle with another musician's concentration just before they played. Lydia would be fine once she got on stage—Eric knew that from experience—but he also knew that no matter how well she played, it wouldn't be good enough . . . for her, or her father.

Then he had no more time to consider anyone else's problems, because the septet was moving out onto the stage.

He always forgot how hot the house lights were, dazzling his sight even as they pressed down on him like a heavy hand. The small Lincoln Center auditorium was full—he could tell from the sound, even though he couldn't see the audience—and in the first row sat their instructors, clipboards in hand, preparing to grade the performances of their students.

Oh, sure. No pressure, right? Just a big chunk of your final grade and no way to gloss over any missed notes.

And, of course, the fact that, since he was sitting First Chair, the others were looking to him to set the tempo and carry them along.

Their first piece was a sprightly Mozart contradance—fast, but not too fast, with a French horn solo in the middle that Lisa choked on half the time, even in yesterday's dress rehearsal. Eric waited for the others to take their places, gathered them in with his eyes, and smiled encouragingly.

It's just like leading troops into battle. Act confident, and they'll be confident.

Then he raised the silver flute to his lips, nodding to set the tempo, and blew the first note.

The little trio he'd formed with Kory and Beth, Beth's group Spiral Dance, and the pickup jams at RenFaires were no kind of preparation for working with a real ensemble. It called for discipline as well as spirit, cooperation as well as feeling—all characteristics that Eric had grown used to thinking of himself as lacking. But if the difficulties were greater, the rewards were greater as well—the complex surge of melody filled him like a storm of light, the passion and discipline of the others creating an ocean that bore him up like a windjammer upon its surface, its master and victim all in one.

There is nothing better than this, Eric thought, in the last moment in which words were possible, before he surrendered to the music and simply *was.*

Their first piece ended—there was applause—and he led them through the second, a sprightly rondo that called for fast fingering on everybody's part, five separate threads of melody weaving into a glorious braid of sound. Moments later—too soon—it was over, and he and the others were coming to the edge of the stage to take their bows. Lisa had hit every note perfectly, the horn's golden mellowness soaring over the brightness of the flutes and the deep echos from cello and bassoon. Jeremy had regained his usual bland expression, and even Lydia looked radiant.

"It was good, wasn't it? It was good," she said, as soon as they were off.

"It was okay," Eric said, smiling back at her. And best of all, it was a part of himself that he could share with those who could not share any other part of his life—this music was a matter of skill and craft, not magic, though the discipline he'd learned in those long lessons with Dharinel certainly helped here.

In fact, I don't think I could have gotten this far without it. You've got to want it, and work for it, to be able to do it. The first time I was here it wasn't my idea at all—it was Mom and Dad, wanting to add "prodigy" to their list of my Trophy Child accomplishments. But this time it's my idea. My success.

"Are you coming to the dorm party?" Jeremy asked.

"Sure." Eric paused to consult the program tucked into his pocket. "I've got a solo after this, then the reception, then I'm there."

"I'll see you, then," Jeremy said, turning away to go look for his bassoon case. "Good luck."

The others had already wandered off, still giddy with the high that came with performance. Eric smiled. No matter how often you performed, it was always a rush to find yourself off the stage alive and in one piece, and these kids didn't have a lot of experience with performing yet.

"These kids." Boy, does that make me feel old!

There were times when the gulf of years—only a handful by the calendar, but far more in terms of experience—made Eric feel like he came from an entirely different planet than his classmates. Sometimes he just felt like grabbing them and shaking them, telling them to value what they already had, to see how precious it was. The mood, fortunately, always passed. If there was one thing he'd learned from his time Underhill and his experience with the elves, it was that you couldn't pass on wisdom just by talking about it. Wisdom came only from experience.

He hung around backstage while two more groups went on, doing his best to stay out of their way. There was a woodwind trio—the clarinetist faltered badly at the beginning and they had to start over—and a baroque group whose members were already getting outside gigs, they were that good. The wail of the shaum and dronepipe sent shivery hackles up his spine—not Bardcraft, but close, close. . . .

But it was time to focus inward, because his next performance was only minutes away. The evening had started with the full chamber orchestra, moving slowly toward smaller and smaller groups as the stagehands cleared away the stands and chairs during breaks. The soloists traditionally closed out the evening. In the high-stakes world of classical music, they were the heavy horses that everyone was waiting to see, the next Galway or Weisberg.

Tonight there were three of them, including Eric. And the whimsical gods of misfortune had placed him last.

Professor Rector was out there laying for him, Eric knew. Tonight wasn't only a solo for him. It was his first Juilliard performance of his own composition, "Variations on 'Planxty Brown.'" He'd picked the tune not only for its lively melody, but because it had no associations with Bardic Magic or elves or anything else uncanny.

The other two soloists—one piano, one violin—acquitted themselves honorably (as Dharinel might have phrased it), and then—too soon!—it was Eric's turn to step out on the stage again.

He was sure he'd sweated all the way through his shirt, sure the audience could see his nervousness and uncertainty. Some of them, probably, still remembered his last memorable solo appearance on this stage, when he'd unwittingly summoned Nightflyers with his nascent Bardic Gift.

Oh, THERE'S a cheery thought!

For a heartbeat he was filled with panic, and for just that moment he was tempted to call up the magic again—under control this time—to exert just a tiny bit of influence on the professors grading and critiquing his performance. It would be so easy. . . .

No. I came back to do this on my own terms. No magic, no Gift but the music I was born with. I know I'm a good Bard. I'm here to see if I'm a good musician, too.

He lifted the flute to his lips and began to play.

It wasn't as powerful an energy surge as playing with an ensemble. That was like driving a team of wild horses, a swelling power that came from many hearts and minds all working as one. This was more like flying, soaring over the earth on the wings the music lent him. As always, his anxiety vanished with the first note, and he carried his audience with him through all the intricate variations of the old dance tune. And perhaps because it was music made for dancing, he felt his audience caught up in his rhythm, toes tapping and heads nodding to the music.

He brought the piece to an end with a flourish, and there was that one moment of silence as he lowered the flute that was the true tribute every musician looks for.

Then the applause began, and Eric stepped forward to take his bow. The house lights came up, and for the first time he could see the people he'd been playing for all night.

He looked down at the front rows—still bowing—looking for Rector and the other professors. He could just imagine the sour look on Rector's face—he'd been good, and he knew it, and so did they. He was smart enough not to catch Rector's eye—the man looked to be in a towering snit, and his mood wouldn't be improved by knowing Eric had seen it—and glanced around the rest of the house as he straightened.

And froze.

Ria Llewellyn was there. Second row aisle, the critics' seats.

She was wearing something in pale blue, looked just the way she always had, the ice princess who had turned his world inside-out. Only years of professional experience kept him moving, and smiling, and got him off the stage.

Ria! How did she get here?

Backstage was full—friends and relatives coming back to congratulate the musicians, stagehands, other performers. Several of them tried to stop him, to congratulate him, but Eric tore through them, looking for the stairs that led down into the house, his flute still clutched in his hand. By the time he reached them, the audience was getting to its feet, preparing to leave.

He didn't see Ria.

He shoved through the concertgoers, fighting his way up the center aisle like a spawning salmon. He reached the street ahead of most of the audience, but he didn't see Ria anywhere.

The biting chill of late autumn cut through the damp cotton shirt he was wearing, bringing him back to himself. Even if she had been here, he'd never find her now.

And face it, Banyon. You could have been imagining things. And the only question that leaves is—why would you imagine Ria Llewellyn coming to Juilliard?

The Sherry-Netherland was the grande dame of New York hotels . . . expensive, tasteful, and with better security than the White House. It kept secrets better than the White House did, too, even with the Joint Chiefs thrown in. If you wanted to vanish in style in Manhattan, you booked rooms at the Sherry-Netherland.

LlewellCo kept a permanent suite here to pamper its out-of-town execs and to provide a perk for visiting guests. It had probably been occupied when Jonathan booked her flight. It wasn't now.

Ria didn't care. She'd had a long day with a killer ending.

Damn the boy! she thought furiously, and then, with grudging honesty: *No. That isn't right. He's no boy. He's a man, now—and how does that make you feel, Ria-girl?*

She didn't know. That was the worst. Not the loss of command of her emotions, but the turbulent swirl that didn't even let her know clearly what they were.

She walked into the bathroom, shedding pieces of her ice-blue satin dinner suit as she went. She kicked off her Ferragamo pumps and tossed her jewelled Judith Leiber handbag onto a chair, standing before the bathroom mirror wearing only a silk slip and enough pale-gold South Sea Island pearls to finance a startup company on the Internet. The bathtub beckoned invitingly—water hot enough to scald away her sins, and bath salts from a little shop down on Chambers Street that blended them to her personal specifications. She turned the taps on full, then, too keyed up to simply stand there, walked back out to her bedroom to pace.

The papers from this morning's meeting were still strewn across the bed, as if she'd have the discipline to look at them any time soon. She felt a faint pang of guilt, knowing that she'd dealt with the New York people a bit high-handedly. She'd pay for that later—if there was one thing years of corporate infighting had taught her, it was that while friends came and went, enemies accumulated. She was sure she'd made more than a few enemies today.

But she hadn't been able to give the meeting her full attention, because more than half her concentration had been on the contents of that folder Jonathan had given her, and on the lunch appointment she'd made to interview the private investigator that she'd hired as soon as she'd started reading the report. She'd taken the woman to Le Cirque to overawe her, but the woman hadn't been overawed, and Ria had liked that about her at once.

Claire MacLaren was an uncompromising woman in her fifties, prosaic as bread. She made no effort to hide either her age or the fact that her figure had long since lost, if it had ever possessed it, the whippet slenderness of youth. She resembled the Miss Marple sort of detective, grey-haired and kindly, her strong Scots bones and pale blue eyes showing her heritage, even without the faint flavor of the

Hebrides still in her voice, and was, very simply, the very best at what she did.

"I'm pleased to have the opportunity to speak with you personally on this matter, Ms. Llewellyn," she'd said, after they were both seated and the waiter had taken their drink orders. Ria had ordered white wine. Claire had unabashedly ordered Scotch.

All around them the hubbub of Le Cirque's lunchtime clientele eddied and flowed, providing perfect privacy for their conversation. Mechanical eavesdroppers would be foiled by the background noise, and magical ones would be baffled by the sheer numbers of minds all thinking at once. Even Ria, whose gift was very small, had some trouble shutting them all out. But even with her shields in place, Ria could easily sense the unease radiating from the woman seated opposite her at the table.

"I find it's always best to do this sort of thing personally," Ria said. "There are always some things that don't make it into a report. Things too . . . tenuous? to commit to paper."

"Oh, I wrote it all down," Claire assured her strongly. "Everything I could find. And that wasn't enough—considering. There's the matter of the money, for one thing."

"Money?" Ria said, momentarily at a loss. She knew Jonathan had already paid Claire MacLaren's exorbitant fee in full.

"Money doesn't just appear out of nowhere," Claire said. "And that young man has quite a lot of it. Where'd it come from, is what I'd dearly love to know."

"Oh, that," Ria answered.

She kept a show of interest on her face, but in fact, the source of Eric's money didn't concern her very much at all. A full elven mage could ken and replicate anything—rubies, diamonds, Krugerrands, bearer bonds. She couldn't work that magic, and neither could Eric, but all that meant was that someone Underhill had set Eric Banyon up with a serious stake and the means to finish his studies Here Above.

Why?

That was the question that had occupied her throughout the meal, as she'd fenced with Claire and finally thrown a small glamour over her to quiet Claire's worries that Eric Banyon was being financed by drug lords, industrial espionage, or worse. It had nagged at her through the round of afternoon meetings with various LlewellCo East department heads. She'd been supposed to have dinner with one of them, but had cancelled at the last minute. That was good luck of a sort. If she hadn't, she wouldn't have given in to the impulse to drive past Juilliard and seen the notices of a student concert to be held that evening. She wouldn't have looked at the list of the soloists and seen Eric's name. She wouldn't have gone inside—gaining a seat by a minor enchantment—and seen Eric soloing up on the stage, performing with a surety, a grace, and an art that he had never had before.

The bathtub was full, and she walked back into the bathroom, shedding the last of her clothes, and turning off the taps. She picked up the bottle of bath salts and shook in a generous helping, watching the crystals dissolve and stain the water a rich living green.

She sank into the water, wincing at the temperature. But the heat did its work, leaching away the nervous energy that filled her, calming her.

Eric is back, and he has Underhill backing. And why is he back? Because he's finished with everything he needed to learn Underhill— that much was clear from tonight. You saw that performance. The old Eric couldn't manage to play "Baa Baa Black Sheep" without some magic leaking. This Eric has as much control and discipline as any Elven Bard I've ever seen.

She closed her eyes, trying to surrender to the spell of the water. In a lot of ways, an Eric in control of his magic was the scariest thing she'd encountered since she'd reentered the world after her coma.

First of all, who taught him? And most of all, who sent him back?

She knew that most of the Seleighe Sidhe didn't blame her for Perenor's attempt to grab the Nexus back in Los Angeles. She'd changed sides at the last minute, at great cost to herself, and that counted for a lot with their kind.

But what if Eric's teacher were one of the few who did bear a grudge against her—either because of her past actions or because of her halfblood ancestry? What if Eric had come into the world as a kind of secret agent, intending to lure her out?

What if, for that matter, Eric held a grudge of his own? She'd tried to kill his friends, after all. Most people tended to take that personally.

She sighed, sinking deeper into the water and inhaling the fragrant steam. She had no idea what Eric was feeling right now, and that disturbed her more than she could express. She hadn't been able to read anything in his face but shock when he spotted her, and after that . . .

She'd panicked, plain and simple. Proof (as if she'd wanted any) that her feelings for the man were too strong to lightly dismiss. There was unfinished business there, and like it or not, one way or another, it was going to be finished. *Before the turn of the year,* she thought, with an undependable flash of Foresight, and shivered.

The bathwater had grown cold while she'd sat musing, and now Ria got to her feet, swirling her long ash-blond hair up into a towel and wrapping herself in another of the voluminous Turkish towels the hotel provided.

It was just too bad the problem wasn't on Eric's side, she thought, rubbing herself dry until her fair skin was pink and tingled. If Eric hated her, it wouldn't matter. Ria had been hated by experts. It made little difference in her life.

The trouble was the fact that *she* wanted *him.* Still. Again. Not as a pet, as she had before, a graceful subservient boy who could amuse her while she used his magic for her own ends. No, if it were that, if her own desires were that simple, it would be an inconvenience, but not a problem.

The problem—the real problem, the insurmountable one—was that seeing him tonight on that stage, assured and totally in control, Ria had realized that Eric Banyon would never again be anybody's pet. Not a boy, not a toy. He was a man now, with a man's will and determination. Her equal, and more.

And everything in Ria's half-Blood Perenor-nurtured soul rebelled against the thought of accepting anyone on equal terms. Conciliation was weakness. Cooperation was only a trap. Only the strongest had any right to survive, and Ria knew that if she matched her power and her tricks against the Eric she had seen tonight, she might very well lose the battle.

And the worst was, she had no heart for such a fight. Unless he truly was here hunting her, he was no threat to her, and unlike Perenor, Ria had never had any taste for empty cruelty. She was ruthless. That was her nature. But viciousness had never been a part of her spirit, and if it had, that part of her was purged long since. So she had no quarrel with Eric Banyon, True Bard of Underhill, and if he were in truth sent here as her foe, mercy would be impossible. For either of them.

I can't be his pet. He won't be mine. Where does that leave us? *Where does that leave ME?*

FIVE:
GOBLIN FRUIT

✢✢

It was cold out here under the highway tonight, but Daniel Carradine tried to ignore it. There was money to be made, and the need to make it. Bobby wanted his money, and Daniel wanted his White Lady, the demanding mistress for whom Daniel had given up everything else.

Not that there'd been all that much. When home was a decaying Pennsylvania steel town and a father who couldn't accept that times had changed, even the underside of the West Side Highway on a freezing December night was better.

The wind came whistling in off the Hudson, cold as memories. If he'd been able to fix before he came out, Daniel wouldn't have minded the cold, he knew, but Bobby didn't sell on credit. *Still*, Daniel told himself hopefully, *it might be a good night*. He was seventeen, and looked younger, and that was good. It was what the marks liked, the guys who came cruising down here with their Mercedes and their Jags, looking for what Daniel and the others were selling. Goblin fruit, like in the Rossetti poem, where no matter how much you ate, you were always hungry for more.

A friend of his—Tony—went by, and he smiled and waved. Bobby had come across for Tony before he left the flop tonight—it was obvious in the way Tony strutted, as if he were living in a warm world where the river wind didn't blow—and for a moment Daniel felt a pang of envy that was shocking in its violence. He quashed the emotion firmly. There was no point. Nothing came free. That was the first lesson growing up in Cartersville had taught him. There was a price for everything, even freedom. And if the only freedom he could buy with the only thing he owned—his body—was the freedom of a derelict flop down in the Bowery that he shared with half a dozen other rentboys, then he'd take it.

A car cruised by—slowly, on the prowl—and Daniel smiled hopefully, arching his back and shaking his head so that a lock of bleached-blond hair fell down over his eyes. But the car moved on, and Daniel hunched back into himself again, seeking what comfort he could.

He wanted to get this over with and go find Bobby. He really did.

From a few feet away, beneath the body of a burnt-out and abandoned car, Urla watched its victim. The redcap had been about to rush out, but the cruising car had stopped it. The Great Lord had said there must be no witnesses, and Aerune's command sat upon Urla like a *geas*.

He had also said that Urla must take no one who would be missed, and Urla knew that nobody would miss this one. Still young and strong, and filled with such self-hatred and despair that the redcap was nearly drunk with it, all laced through with a yearning, a fiery craving for something that was not food or drink or sex. Urla dismissed its own curiosity. It did not matter what the boy hungered for, for he did not hunger as much as Urla did for the bright warmth of the untasted years, the unspent years the boy would have had if Urla had not come hunting here tonight.

Another car passed, then two more, and each time the boy was assessed and refused. His fear was stronger now, and Urla licked its lips in anticipation. Soon, soon. . . .

At last the boy stumbled away from the pillar by which he

stood and began shuffling up the street, his steps uncoordinated. He shivered, wrapping his thin jacket tighter around his starved body as if the thin cotton had the power to grant him the warmth he lacked. In a few moments more he would pass directly before Urla's hiding place.

But the redcap's anticipated feast was not to be. Another great black chariot turned down the street, its night lamps pinning the boy in their beams. Urla saw its prey stop, hopeful once more, as the car drew level with him, and the door opened. The boy stepped forward, and a mortal—tall, tall, with the stink of Cold Iron about him—rose up out of the car and grabbed Urla's prey, dragging him into the car as he began, too late, to struggle and cry.

The door shut. The chariot moved away, more quickly now, belching foul gasses that made Urla cough.

No! They will not have him! He is mine!

Snarling its disappointment, the redcap wrapped itself in shadows and began to trot after the black chariot that had taken its prey.

"I said no alkies, goddammit! Which word don't you goons understand?"

The tall dark man with the sleepy eyes blinked at her. Jeanette wished she could kick him, but she didn't dare, quite. She took a deep breath and tried again, marshalling her hard-won and inadequate social skills.

"Look, Elkanah." Was the name on the tag first, last, or even his? Not her problem. "Most of these people are fine. But you see that one in the corner?"

Jeanette gestured toward the monitor in the Security Room. It showed the space they called Large Primate Containment—a euphemism for the Black Labs and holding cells set up for human experimentation. Just now it was dressed to look like a police holding cell—an environment she was sure all of her guests were more than familiar with. Junkies, rentboys, and hookers, the lot of them, and that was fine with her.

Except for the man in the corner, the one in the tattered

vomit-stained trenchcoat, his face long-unshaven and caved in upon missing teeth and malnutrition. The others gave him a wide berth, and she could imagine why. He probably stank to high heaven.

"That guy is a juicehead. I can't use him. His liver's already shot to hell—drugs process through the liver, *Elkanah,* did you know that? Alcohol's *legal*—by the time a juicehead gets to the street he's already a walking corpse; all his insides pickled and shot to hell. I told you guys when you went out: no alkies, no crazy street people. Junkies and whores, that's what I told you to get."

The man in the uniform of Threshold Special Security blinked down at her, as impassive as a cigar-store Indian, and for a moment Jeanette didn't think he'd heard her. Didn't any of Robert's hard-boys speak English, for God's sweet sake?

"So what do you want me to do with him, Ms. Campbell?" Elkanah finally said. His voice was slow and deep and thoughtful, and despite her fury, Jeanette did not for one moment make the mistake of thinking he was stupid. Stupid people did not rise to key positions in Threshold's Black Ops.

She took a deep breath.

"I don't care what you do with him. Throw him in the East River for all I care. But get rid of him before lights out, because if he's still there tomorrow when my Judas Goat goes in to offer these losers a trip out of this world, I am going to be seriously pissed. And when I'm pissed, Robert Lintel is pissed. Are we communicating?"

"Yes, Ms. Campbell. I'm sorry about the confusion."

He wasn't sorry and there'd been no confusion. Jeanette knew that perfectly well. But she'd won, and that was all that mattered.

"Okay," she said. "I'll be in my office if anyone needs me."

She turned away and walked quickly out of Security before this Elkanah person could guess how scared she was. When she'd been running with the Sinner Saints, she could have eaten corporation rent-muscle like Elkanah for breakfast, but it had been years since she'd had to face off anything but chimps and wimp lab technicians, and, unlike riding a Harley, some skills didn't stay with you forever.

Security and personnel were Robert's problem. They always had been. She supplied the science. He supplied the money and muscle. That was the deal. So why did she have to do everything around Threshold herself?

She reached the safety of her own private lab and closed the airlock behind her gratefully, irritation and a feeling of narrow escape both fading as she surveyed her private kingdom. Nobody would bother her in here. Nobody would dare.

The room had been cleansed of all traces of the chimps' occupation, though they were still looking for the one that had vanished. The two that had died instantly had been autopsied, and she'd found about what she'd expected: massive stroke and brain hemorrhage, the inevitable side effect of chemical Russian roulette.

The other two—the ones that had manifested the bizarre powers— had also died, but several hours later and of something that looked surprisingly like starvation, though how the old female could have died of starvation with all she'd eaten was an interesting question. She was the one who'd survived the longest, and Jeanette was looking forward to seeing those autopsy results, but right now both bodies were in freezers awaiting their turn. Ramchandra had better work fast, because in a day or so those chimps were going to have a lot of company.

Jeanette fully expected that the people Robert had gotten for her off the New York streets would die of the drug the same way the chimps had. That was what lab trials were for—to find out what killed them and to try to refine the next batch even more. She'd obviously found the right button to push, the one she'd been looking for ever since she was a teenager.

Now all I have to do is keep their heads from exploding. A few more hours alone would clean her test subjects out of whatever they'd been using, then another of Robert's goons would be thrown in with them, the packets of T-6/157 in his pockets looking like any other sample of party dust. He'd say he needed to get rid of it before the police searched him, and if Jeanette knew junkies, they wouldn't ask too many questions when there was free dust on offer. They'd suck the stuff right down, and then . . .

Then she'd finally start getting some answers.

✤✤ ✤✤ ✤✤

Hell couldn't be worse than this, Daniel thought. And to think, he'd thought his luck had changed when that limo had pulled up.

He could still feel the shock of anger, almost of betrayal, when the big man had seized him and dragged him into the limo. He and his buddy had tried to make it look like they were vice cops ringing him in on a solicitation bust, but Daniel had been through that mill more than a few times since he'd gotten to New York, and he'd never seen a vice cop that rode around in the back of a fancy car— or that put a hood over your head so you couldn't see where you were when they dragged you out of it.

That was weird, and for a while he'd tried to console himself with the fantasy that they were just two kinks looking for a wiggy party, but he couldn't make himself believe it. He'd never seen a co-ed holding tank, for one thing, and no matter how much this place might look like the Tombs, it just didn't smell right. And it was way too quiet. In prison there was always somebody screaming, somebody crying, somebody jonesing for a fix that wasn't going to come any time soon.

That would be him, in a couple of hours. He needed his White Lady, his beautiful lady who made the world all soft and sweet. He didn't know about the other eight people stuck in here with him, and he didn't care. Life on the street was rough enough without caring about other people, and Daniel had jettisoned his emotional baggage early.

They fed him a couple of times, and once the lights went down low and he'd slept a little, but by the second day he was too sick to care about his breakfast. A lot of the others were just as bad off, and when one of them started screaming and wouldn't stop, two guys in black almost-a-cop uniforms had come in and dragged her away pretty quickly. The rest of them sat, huddled in silent misery, waiting for the torture to end.

No lawyers, no bondsmen, no arraignment. This isn't any bullpen I've ever been in. But I ain't gonna be the one to say it. They're probably watching everything. Whoever they are.

The word must have gone out to make up the numbers after the woman disappeared, because a little while after dinner—he'd forced himself to eat, but thrown up again almost instantly—they brought in someone new.

He was dressed better than they were, but still street. Daniel's internal radar prickled instantly. He was pretty sure he knew what this guy was, and he was only hoping that the rest of his guess was right as well. The guy was holding. He could smell it. Nobody had searched Daniel when they brought him in. Why should they search any of the others?

He waited until the lights went out, when everyone was curled up in their bunks. There were twelve bunks—four sets of three tiers each—for nine people, which meant that nearly everyone could have his pick of places to sleep. The New Guy took what was left—a bottom bunk, of course, since anyone with brains wanted a top one.

Daniel made sure he had the top bunk on the New Guy's tier. It wasn't his to begin with, but he got to it first and stared down the woman who'd been sleeping there. She just shook her head bitterly and went to find another bed.

"Hey," Daniel called softly. "Hey, New Guy?"

"That's me." The voice came out of the darkness, pleased and mellow and unafraid. "You got a name, pilgrim?"

"Danny-boy." It was what Daniel answered to on the street, as if keeping the name he had been called at home a secret could somehow lend him armor against the cruelty of the streets.

"Well, Danny-boy, you can call me Keith."

"Hey, Keith." Daniel's voice was ragged with relief. He knew the moves of this dance, and knew he'd been right. The man was holding, and Daniel meant to cut himself a slice of that pie.

"Now Danny-boy, I got me a problem that maybe you could help me with. I was checking you out earlier, when I came in. You look like an intelligent kind of a guy."

"Yeah, that's me." He wasn't entirely successful at keeping the bitterness out of his voice. If he'd been really smart, would he have ended up here?

"Well, I've got this inventory. And I kind of need to hold a fire sale, as it were."

Daniel dropped down out of the top bunk, quick as a cat, and squatted beside the bottom bunk. Keith was resting on one elbow—looking toward him, though it was hard to see that in the darkness. A gold ring in the shape of a phoenix glinted in one ear, the brightest thing Daniel could see.

He's holding. And he needs to get rid of the stuff before the cops figure that out. Daniel held out his hand.

Keith dropped the small white packet into it. "There's plenty for everyone," he said in his mellow voice, as the other inhabitants of the holding tank began converging on him with a slow tidal movement.

Daniel backed away, defending his prize. In one pocket, along with other odds and ends, was a chopped off bit of soda straw. He tore open the small glassine packet—carefully, oh so carefully—and dipped the straw end into the white powder. It wasn't as good as spiking a vein, but it would do, oh, yes. He snorted hard, pulling the powder up into his sinuses, and from there, straight to the bloodstream. He didn't know what Keith had offered him—coke, horse, one of the new supposed-to-be-legal concoctions—and right now he was too far gone in need to care. Just a little something to quiet the dragon trying to gnaw its way out of his bones.

He felt it come on almost instantly: a velvet-wrapped pile driver that made his heart race, even while it wrapped him in soft clouds of not-caring. He blinked, forced himself to look up, and saw Keith handing out packets to everyone.

"Hey," Daniel croaked. "Save me some for later." The white tide was rising, carrying him off to a place where nothing hurt and no one was cruel.

"Don't worry, Danny-boy." He heard Keith's slow rich voice as from a great distance. "This stuff, nobody ever needs two."

And the heaven and hell of it was, Daniel heard him. Heard him and didn't care.

Five minutes after the last of the meat had gone on the nod, Keith stood up and stretched. The floor of the cell was covered with unconscious junkies. He shivered, looking down at them.

Whatever this stuff was, he was sure as hell glad *he* hadn't sniffed any of it.

He looked up at the main security camera in the ceiling.

"Hey. What are you guys waiting for? An engraved invitation?" he demanded.

There was no response, but a few minutes later the lights came up in the corridor outside, and technicians in white lab coats wheeling gurneys appeared. The one in the lead opened the cell door, and Keith stepped outside hastily, as if whatever had sent the eight people in the cell off to dreamland might be catching.

"Everything go all right?" Beirkoff asked.

"Fine as frog hair. What the hell was that stuff, anyway?"

Beirkoff smiled, and the lights turned the lenses of his tinted glasses silver. "Hey, you know the drill. I could tell you, but then I'd have to kill you."

Keith growled wordlessly under his breath, and stalked off to report.

Jeanette had slaved the security cameras to her desktop PC. She could have been down in the security room, where all eight holding cells were being monitored on visual and audio as well as by a whole spectrum of other devices, but she didn't want to share this moment with some wage slave of a technician. She could see all she needed to from here, anyway. By tapping a few buttons, she could watch as her unconscious subjects were transported to separate holding cells, implanted with transceivers that would monitor their heart and brainwaves. As soon as the pickups were live, she killed the picture and brought up the telemetry. Slow rolling delta waves billowed across her screen like the waves of an ancient ocean.

What are you feeling? she asked the silent screen. *Where are you?*

But the answers, she knew, would have to wait. Until the awakening.

Beneath the edge of the desk, her hands tightened into fists. *Give it to me,* she demanded silently. *Give me something I can use!*

Outside the building, wrapped in a darkness of its own weaving,

Urla watched the metal door through which the car had gone. Day had come and gone while the redcap waited. When the sun rode high in the sky, Urla retreated to the friendly darkness of the city's sewers, killing rats to amuse itself while it waited. Their tiny deaths were only an appetizer, though, one that left the redcap restless and unsatisfied. Urla hungered for its stolen prey, taken by the men in the black night-wagon, the one that had burned with such painful inner fire.

There were others like that one in the grimy yellow building, and Urla comforted itself with fantasies of a gluttonous feeding, one that might slake even the redcap's eternal hunger, for there were many within the yellow building filled with terror and such a burning despair that it made Urla's mouth water. When night came again it took up its watching post once more, though by now it had lost all hope that the prey it had tracked here would emerge once more.

Its tiny mind had been occupied for several hours with the question of whether it would be better to abandon its waiting and go once more in search of the Bard its dark master had commanded it to find, but instinct told it that this place contained many secrets, and secrets were always good to know.

The moon rose high and began to set. And then, just before the sky began to lighten and Urla must once more choose whether to retreat into the sewers again or to admit its failure, something happened. The prey-creatures' lives burned in Urla's consciousness like bright candles, but suddenly several of them simply . . . went out.

Urla crawled forth from its concealment beneath a parked car, leathery brow wrinkling in puzzlement. They had been there a moment before, and now they were not there. It did not sense the tang of death, and sleep alone could not render prey invisible to a redcap's hunger. Urla crept closer to the strange building, wondering.

The riptide of fury that followed the strange quenching was enough to send the redcap sprawling stunned in the middle of the street, visible to any who might look. After the first shock, Urla dragged itself to concealment again, shaking its head as if to ward off the effects of a mighty blow. The rage still keened through its senses—an unhinged fury worthy of a mighty Unseleighe lord, black and all-devouring.

It had to know more.

Forcing itself forward against the tempest of madness, Urla began searching for ways to enter the building.

She'd ordered someone to go out for pizza—one good thing about New York, you could get takeout at any hour—and most of a deluxe pie now sat on the corner of Jeanette's desk, cold and forgotten. Styrofoam cups, half full of cold coffee, studded every available surface within reach. Across the screen the readouts scrolled, changing only slightly from moment to moment.

The first effects of the drug should be wearing off now, Jeanette thought. It had been four hours, and her psychoactive cocktail was layered, like a fine perfume, to deliver its effects in calculated stages. So at least some of those loser-freaks should be coming around by now. Jeanette ground her teeth in impatience. They couldn't all just die on her!

Suddenly two of the readouts . . . vanished. Jeanette stared at the screen, galvanized to alertness by the impossibility of it. A moment later she heard the faint hooting of the situation alarm sounding through the building. She pushed herself to her feet and ran.

"What is it?" she shouted, flinging open the Monitor Room door. The technician turned toward her, white-faced and scared. GALLIARD, her nametag said.

"I was watching them every moment," the tech babbled. "Every moment! They didn't go anywhere, they couldn't have, I locked them in myself—"

The denials made no sense until Jeanette looked at the screens. Eight were live. Six showed sleeping subjects, lying on the floors of their padded cells.

Two cells were empty—as in, nobody home.

Well, Galliard, you're going to wish you'd chosen another career when I get done with you.

"Where the hell are they?" Jeanette asked in dangerously reasonable tones. She took a step toward the cringing girl.

A scream from the monitors stopped her. The subjects were awake, going from a comatose sleep to full consciousness in instants. She watched, spellbound, as first one, then another, of her test cases began throwing himself about his cell, violently seeking escape, battering and tearing at the padded walls until streaks and flowers of blood appeared.

After a timeless moment, Jeanette realized that the technician was staring at her, waiting for her to give orders. Jeanette reached out and turned the master audio control on the console to "Off." It didn't totally shut out the screams, audible even through the sound-proofing, but it did make it easier to think as she mulled over what to do next.

Sedate them? No, with the dose in their systems, that would be a quick ticket to the boneyard, and even if they were doomed, she didn't want to kill them so quickly. Restrain them? Gazing down at the gyrating madmen, Jeanette wasn't sure there was enough money in the world to pay anyone to enter one of those cells. One of the madmen—the display at the bottom said his name was Nelson—cheated of any other outlet for his rage, had turned his fury on himself. He'd gouged out both his eyes and clawed his skin to bleeding ribbons, and was still tearing at himself, howling in a deep voice as he drooled blood from a mouth from which he'd torn his own tongue.

Galliard was still staring at her, eyes wide and scared.

"Go find Mr. Lintel. Tell him two of the subjects have escaped. Tell him to find them," Jeanette ordered. That should keep both Robert and this bimbette busy!

Galliard scuttled out. Jeanette settled down in the vacated chair to watch the show.

Urla was inside the building now, crawling through the ventilation system unseen, making slow progress against the invisible headwind of madness that buffeted it. The presence of Cold Iron was a palpable weight against its bones, but unlike others of the Seleighe kin, the redcap was not affected by its poison. It winced as the first mind was joined by one, two, three others, until the four of them raged in a torment that was almost Power—the rage of a demon lord. What was it the mortals did here to cause such anguish? Urla desperately wished to learn their secret, for it would make the redcap's kind a rich banquet. Some there were among the Unseleighe Court who fed on emotion as Urla fed on lives, and did it own the secret of such cosmic despair, it could trade it to them to its advantage.

But then something happened that thrust all thought of self-interest from the redcap's mind. For the last of the mortals prisoned here awoke, and the uprush of true Power nearly blinded his Sidhe senses. Here was the power of Bard or Elven mage trapped in mortal flesh—a wellspring of such Power as the dark lord Aerune had sent him to find. It was here, somehow here where it had not been a moment before, in mortals who had not possessed it before this instant.

Daniel Carradine awoke with a sudden start, shivering and sweating, his strongest emotion a cheated anger that whatever it was that Keith had supplied, it hadn't taken the edge off his need. The long-unslaked craving, stronger than he had ever known it, filled him now like a wild thing desperate to be free.

His Lady . . . his beautiful White Lady . . . . Somehow Daniel could sense her somewhere near, somehow certain that this was Truth, and not some withdrawal-fuelled hallucination. His hunger was strong enough to tear down walls, to see into all the hidden places of the world as if they were made of glass. He knew she was here, knew that all he had to do was reach out for her, and he could have her.

Daniel reached. The first attempt brought pain, enough almost to blot out the fire in his bones, but it also carried a teasing promise of certainty. If he could only try a little harder . . .

He reached out again, whimpering as he did it, his whole body shaking and drenched in a greasy sweat. The pain flared again, blinding him, but behind it he felt a strange cool flexing of senses he'd never known before, and abruptly there was a hard roundness in his hand—the object of his desire, summoned to him through all the walls and barriers that separated them. In his surprise, he dropped it, and then crawled frantically across the padded floor after it until he'd grabbed it in both hands.

He looked down at the stoppered jar half filled with glistening white powder. He didn't need to open it to know what it was. His Lady. The White Lady. Pure, pharmaceutical-grade heroin.

He could have taken her that way, opened the bottle and snorted its contents or spilled it across his tongue, but now Daniel knew he didn't need to. The rest of what he needed to make everything perfect was out there. All he had to do was imagine it, and its location appeared in his mind. Then all he had to do was . . . reach. This time, when his hand was filled, he clutched the bottle tightly, chuckling with success. Here—and here—and here. *And wilderness is paradise enow,*[3] he quoted out of some half-full store of memory.

He broke the seal on the pint of distilled water, and slopped a little into the Pyrex beaker. The powder dissolved into the water easily, turning it a milky moonstone color. The rest of what he needed was here, summoned from the same place as the water and the beaker. He syringed the mixture up with the ease of long practice.

Now everything will be all right, he thought, tapping his arm to find a vein.

And it was, for those few moments before the massive overdose of uncut heroin—far more, far purer than any fix he'd ever known—carried Daniel down into the darkness and the safest place of all.

Ellie Borden woke suddenly out of a long confused dream. Her whole life the last few months had been a dream—a bad one—as she lost first her job, then her health insurance, then her apartment, ending up on the street doing whatever she could just to survive one more day.

It wasn't supposed to be like this. The automatic protest no longer held either fury or grief, only a weary resignation. She'd paid her taxes, obeyed the law, been kind. She was supposed to be safe,

---

[3] The *Rubaiyat*

protected by Society from cradle to grave. But that hadn't happened. All the social services' safety net that was supposed to be there to catch people like her had melted away the moment she needed it. The programs that were supposed to help had waiting lists months long, and Ellie didn't have months. She'd discovered that the halfway houses were not for people like her, that the only place that would take her in on that terrible day she'd gone home to find everything she owned piled on the curb in front of her former apartment was the street.

She'd quickly learned there were ways to take the edge off the pain, to gain the minimal money that would buy her a room in a flophouse she'd never have dared enter when she'd had a life, to buy her the things that would let her live with the sickness that was eating her life away, but the things she'd had to do to get them were best forgotten.

When she'd been arrested, it had almost been a relief, because you got medical care in prison, didn't you? Only that had turned out to be another grim joke like the rest of her so-called life, because all they'd done was dump her in a cell with a bunch of other street people and forget about her. She'd taken the packet from the dealer the way a starving man would take food, not caring what it was, half-hoping it would kill her if it would only end the pain.

But it hadn't.

She awoke in a strange room, not the holding cell, all by herself. The pain was gone. Gone! She felt better than she had in almost two years. The evil shadow that lived in her bones had vanished forever, she knew it. She felt reborn.

What have they done? she thought in slow-growing wonder. *What did they do to me?* She stared at her hands, marveled at the soft brown skin. No longer cracked, scarred, covered with sores. New again, reborn.

Just as she had been reborn.

Thank You, God, Ellie thought silently. *I won't forget this. I won't throw it away.*

One was dead, killed by his overreaching appetite, but the other remained, still connected somehow to the magic so very like that of Underhill. In the air ducts, Urla gnashed its teeth, hating the choice it must make, the choice of gluttony deferred.

This was not the answer that its dark master sought, the news of a human Bard who could form the Nexus Aerune sought to build, but it was news worth the bringing, regardless. The redcap abandoned its own hunt and turned back the way it had come, hurrying back to the door in the air that led into Underhill and the road that led to the Dark Court.

Jeanette glanced at the clock on the wall of her office. The digital readout said 11:36 in glaring red numbers—a 24-hour readout, so it was a little before noon of some damn day or other. She rubbed her eyes. She hadn't slept all night—she hadn't left the lab for two days—and the strain was beginning to tell on her.

It had been a busy morning, full of new discoveries. And mistakes, but those happened in any research program.

The first mistake she'd made had been in assuming that all six of the surviving test subjects would react the same way. Obviously they hadn't. The four that had gone psychotic had fixed everybody's attention on them until it was too late . . . sort of. And by the time they'd gone catatonic, what was going to happen, had happened.

For the thousandth time, she replayed the tape of Cell One on her computer screen. That had been a young white male, early 20s. Keith said he'd given his name as Danny-boy. She watched as Danny-boy awoke, agitated but obviously not as crazy as the berserkers. She watched him reach out and pluck things out of the air—a jar of white powder, a bottle of water, a beaker, a syringe. He'd teleported them all from her lab—she'd been able to tell by the inventory number engraved on the beaker, and the bar codes on the stock—but how had he gotten them through a locked door and a solid wall? And how had he known they were in her lab in the first place?

If we'd been watching, could we have stopped you? she wondered. She watched as he fixed, hands shaking with his addiction, and watched as he slumped a moment later, dead in a heartbeat from an overdose of pure heroin.

Stupid boy. Don't you know street drugs are stepped on six or seven times—if you're lucky—before they get to you? This was the pure stuff. You should have cut back the dose. You should have WAITED, you blockhead.

She sighed, and rubbed her tired eyes. Now, dammit, she had no way of knowing if her mix would have killed him without the heroin, and an autopsy probably wouldn't be able to sort it out either.

"Campbell?"

She looked up from the screen with an effort as Robert came into the office. If he'd spent as many sleepless hours as she had, it didn't show. He had an ulcer, too—she'd hacked into his personal files once out of idle curiosity—and that didn't show either. Robert Lintel was the original Teflon boy. His three-piece grey suit was immaculate, and he was wearing the particular smug expression that Jeanette liked least. But Robert always had only seen the possibilities in her work, the ultimate goal, and not the long process that led there.

"What?" she said sullenly, knowing that letting him see her mood was weakness, and weakness had always been the thing she defended herself hardest against showing.

"Hey, Campbell. *Smile.* We're almost there, you know. It worked!"

"Two missing—have you found them yet?—four crazy, and of the two qualified successes, one dead. Some success," she grumbled.

"We're looking for the two that vanished, but frankly, I think they went to the same place the chimp did. I had Elkanah dump the other four out on the street. They should be dead by now, or at Bellevue. Either way, not our problem." He walked into the room and stood over her desk, beaming down at her paternally.

"So that leaves—what's her name?—Borden? And her readings have gone back to normal. Whatever she had, it's gone," Jeanette said.

"But while she had it, it was enough to get her clean. I had Dr. Ramchandra give her a quick once-over. According to his interview with her, she'd been diagnosed with terminal cancer. But she doesn't have it now. In fact, she's in perfect health. What do you think of that?"

"I think you aren't paying me to find a cure for cancer," Jeanette answered, but Robert's smug smile only grew wider.

"That's right. But actually, I don't think you need to work on refining your formula any more. We know it works on ten percent of the population. We just have to find the ten percent it works on." He sat down in the chair opposite her desk, the big comfy leather one that only Robert ever sat in.

He was talking about mass trials.

"So where are you going to get enough people to put together a profile for that? Carradine and Borden both manifested Talent, but other than that, they have nothing in common. He was white. She's black. He was a teenager. She's in her thirties. They were both users, but we don't even know they were using the same things."

"Campbell, Campbell, Campbell. When are you ever going to learn to trust me? I have this all figured out." He leaned forward, and she caught a whiff of soap and expensive cologne.

"I want you to go into production with this. Whip me up a few kilos of Batch 157 and portion it out into single-dose packets—we'll call it something like T-Stroke. I'll put it out on the street—we'll sell it of course, but we'll undercut everything else—crank, Mexican brown, snow, the whole menu. They'll buy it, and you'll have your test pool—cheap, easy, and nothing for us to clean up after. We'll rope in the ones that survive, run them through the mill, and find the common thread. Once we have that profile, we can use it to find volunteer subjects."

Jeanette had always been serenely convinced that nothing could shock her, that she didn't care about all those faceless drones she shared the world with. But the butcher's bill Robert was proposing so guilelessly startled even her.

One out of the eight in the first group had survived. Statistically, that meant the odds were that if eighty people received T-6/157, seventy would die. And if you took those numbers out to the thousands of doses that Robert was recommending they spread across the streets of New York . . .

"There's going to be dead junkies stacked like cordwood on every street corner," Jeanette said slowly, trying to decide how that made her feel. She knew she ought to like the idea, but instead she felt curiously numb inside. How confident must Robert be, how eager for his results, to suggest a plan that held so much possibility of . . . unforeseen consequences.

But Robert didn't even seem to notice her lack of enthusiasm. He bored in, eyes glittering like a high-pressure salesman closing a big deal.

"And your point is? C'mon, Campbell, we're looking for results here, not scientific validation. If we generate the Survivor Profile, nobody's going to care how we got it."

"You're right," she said, knowing it was true. Who cared how a lot of junkies died, anyway, so long as the deaths couldn't be traced back to Threshold? She got to her feet, making Robert stand also. "Look, I've got to crash. Beirkoff knows the stuff to order to make up about ten keys of T-Stroke. I'll come back tonight and put it together."

"We could take care of that," Robert said, too casually. "The formula's in your lab notebook, isn't it?"

Jeanette smiled at him, the street predator that had been hidden beneath a veneer of years and good living suddenly stark and plain in her eyes. It wasn't that she didn't trust Robert—she didn't, that had never been an issue. But T-Stroke was an entirely bigger deal than the other compounds she'd handed over. She intended to keep control of it until she was satisfied.

Of what, she wasn't sure.

You're hoping you'll fit the Survivor Profile he'll come up with, don't you? The Survivors—Robert's new race of psionic hitmen. What're you going to do if you do, Campbell? What are you going to do if you don't?

"Aw, c'mon, Robert. You don't want a numb-nuts like Beirkoff to futz this up at the eleventh hour, do you? You don't want to be wondering if he got the formula exactly right and have to do it all again to be sure? Give me a couple of hours. It'll take him that long to get the stuff here anyway. You can call me when it comes in. And meanwhile, you gotta make up your mind what you want to do with the Survivor bitch you've already got."

She didn't wait for him to reply. She grabbed her coat and headed out the door before he'd quite rearranged his face into whatever expression he'd chosen. She knew he'd go looking for the formula. He always did. She knew that.

And she always left one ingredient out of her notes.

He knew that.

SIX:
TO CHAIN THE PHOENIX

✣

If it was *her, so what?*

Mechanically, Eric Banyon went through the motions at the après-concert Artists' Reception, standing around an overheated room with a glass of seltzer in his hand along with the other soloists, featured performers, and those who'd paid money to meet them and each other. Politically, it was the most important part of the show— at least if you were aiming for a paying gig in the hothouse incestuous world of classical music. There were many other job openings besides Featured Soloist or Touring Superstar—to name just one example, there were chairs in any number of orchestras, from the Boston Philharmonic to the Hudson Valley Symphony Orchestra, that always needed to be filled with the best, the brightest, and the most underpaid. Music scouts made careers out of tracking the progress of new young talent the same way other talent scouts cruised college athletics. Eric had already been approached about a few spots—Composer in Residence in an artists' retreat in someplace called Glastonbury, New York, various "sure-thing" grants from one program or another, even a booking agent who swore to him that Juilliard had nothing to teach Eric and it was time to look at professional gigs. *As if I haven't heard that song a lot lately, with all of its verses. . . .*

Eric had turned them all down politely. For one thing, none of his reasons for returning to Juilliard were about worldly fame and power—as a Bard, he already had more of both than most people could imagine. For another, he couldn't get Ria out of his mind enough to give any of them serious attention.

He was glad he hadn't been pressured into wearing a tie to the concert tonight. He'd already unbuttoned the neck of his tab-collared shirt—it was that or strangle in the tropical heat of the reception room. He hoped he looked raffishly artistic—it was one of the reasons he'd left his hair long. *Image isn't everything. It's the only thing. Or so they say.*

His flute in its case was slung over his shoulder; Eric didn't delude himself that everybody at Juilliard loved him, and a musician's instrument was an easy target for jealousy. Better to keep it with him than bespell it to keep it from sabotage and risk harming somebody unintentionally.

Once I never would have worried about that. Give me the power and I would have used it any time it benefited me, and de'il take the hindmost, as my old Irish grandma would have said. I guess this is maturity—taking the responsibility of protecting idiots from themselves.

I bet Ria wouldn't think twice about something like that. She'd say it was their own fault for messing with her in the first place.

He frowned. That had been true once. Was it true now? He gave up trying to ignore the inevitable and devoted some serious thought to the question of the hour. It wasn't impossible for Ria to have been here tonight. She wasn't either dead or in a coma—in fact, the last time he'd talked to Kayla and Elizabet (though between juggling Underhill and World Above time zones, he wasn't quite sure when that was), they'd said Ria was on her way to making a full recovery.

They also said she'd acquired a conscience and morals, but dammit, what does that MEAN in real-life terms? They said she was still Ria—memories, Gifts, and all—so it's not like she's been Touched *by An Angel or something sappy like that. She's still the same Ria I knew, and the Ria I knew was ruthless.*

But not vicious. She didn't care what happened to other people, but she didn't go out of her way to hurt them. Not like Perenor. Not that it mattered a lot if you happened to be the person who got in her way. . . .

All the while his brain kept turning over that unanswerable question, he smiled and made meaningless conversation with men and women in expensive clothes. Lovely concert, yes he was very pleased with his performance tonight, no he hadn't really made plans for what he'd do after he graduated. Round and round they circled, drawn to Eric by something they probably didn't even understand—the aura of Power that a fully trained Bard wore like an invisible cloak—though the other performers got their fair share of attention as well. It was a little like being in a shark tank—but Eric wasn't afraid of any of these particular sharks.

There's nothing they can do to me. None of them is pointing a gun at my head or offering to torture any of my friends. They're all just looking for some way to use me. Once upon a time that would have driven me crazy with righteous indignation. Now it just seems kind of sad.

He circled around behind the buffet. It was pretty well denuded by now—only some cheese and fruit remained—and the ice-sculpture centerpiece was so melted it was now impossible to tell what it had originally been. Eric reached out and placed his hand against it, savoring the coolness. You'd think they could just open the doors and let some December in, but apparently nobody'd thought of that.

"I'm not going to let you ruin your future over some silly girlish tantrum."

The voice was low and furious. Eric glanced up in surprise. Lydia Ashborn was standing backed into a corner by a tall man in a very expensive suit and an even more expensive haircut. Eric recognized Marco Ashborn, Lydia's father.

"Do you want to be a bit player all your life, just some faceless unknown musician without even a separate credit? You should have had a solo tonight, and you know it. Don't you want to record and tour in your own right? Why are you trying to piss it all away? Is this about me? Is that what this is all about, Lydia?"

Man, does it all have to be about you? The uprush of anger was automatic, stemming from still-unhealed scars. He'd been in Lydia's position once: a Trophy Child, treated as nothing more than a playing-piece on the parental chessboard. An accessory. A *thing*, not a person. And that was wrong on so many levels.

Eric saw the glitter of tears as Lydia ducked her head, and fought to control his anger. Discipline above all things, Dharinel had told him. A Bard's displeasure could wound. A Bard's anger could kill.

"Don't you look away from me, dammit!" he heard Marco hiss. Marco grabbed his daughter's arm roughly, and Eric saw Lydia's face go white with the pain.

That's enough.

Eric reached for the *stillness within* that Dharinel had created in him with all those long months of training, and composed his face into a simple harmless expression of hero worship as he walked over to the two of them.

"Hey, excuse me, but aren't you Marco Ashborn, the violinist?"

The burly man turned toward Eric, irritation warring with the game face that every public performer learns to assume at need.

"It's an honor to meet you, sir," Eric went on, blithely ignoring the emotional undercurrents swirling around Marco and Lydia. "I've enjoyed your work so much." That, at least, was true—though how much he'd ever like Marco's playing now that he knew what a goon the guy was in real life was an interesting question. "Lyd's certainly inherited your talent—I'm in some of her classes as well as her chamber music group." Eric held out his hand, still radiating peaceable obliviousness. "Eric Banyon."

Marco's face cleared. He recognized Eric, and more, he responded to Eric's calm confidence, his assumption of being someone whom the famous Marco Ashborn would want to know. It was the simplest sort of magic—and not really magic, because in its own way, it was true.

"I saw your performances tonight. Both of them. That solo was most impressive," Marco rumbled.

"Thank you, sir," Eric said. "I was pleased with our ensemble work. Lydia made me look good," he went on, deliberately misunderstanding the other man's words. "You must be very proud of her."

He could almost see the conflict between the desire to administer another put-down to his daughter and the instinct to appear praiseworthy chase themselves around Marco's face, but the older man, as Eric had expected, went with political expediency. You didn't get to where Marco was on talent alone. A career was built on a network of relationships. Prima donna attitude might make good news stories, but professionalism and tact built a career that lasted.

"Yes, I am," Marco said, gazing into Eric's eyes with deep sincerity. "I only wish her mother could have been here to see her."

Eric felt rather than saw Lydia dart an angry glance at her father, hating him for his hypocrisy. Eric sent out the tiniest tendril of Power, willing someone to appear who could end this deadlock before Marco could resume taking Lydia apart again.

"Marco—darling! I've been trying to get you alone all night. Hello, Eric—you were wonderful this evening. You must come and play for us some time soon. Now, this won't take a moment—" The tall grey-haired woman—Eric had spoken to her earlier, but didn't remember who she was—expertly claimed Marco for her own and led him off. As Eric had hoped, Marco was too much a manipulator to want to carry on abusing Lydia with witnesses present. That sort of emotional torture worked best when no one suspected it.

Well, I *suspect it.* For a moment he was tempted to cast a *geas* on Marco that would keep him from ever being cruel to Lydia again, but Dharinel had emphasized, over and over, that use of the Power was like a stone thrown into a still lake—ripples spread out from every action, and the smallest uses of Power could have the largest—and most unforeseen—consequences. Unless he was certain of what would happen, he'd better leave the matter alone—at least magically.

Eric glanced at Lydia, who favored him with an effortful smile before turning blindly away. He knew he hadn't done much to help, but at least he'd done something. And undoubtedly Marco Ashborn would be jetting off to some exotic foreign city soon to leave his daughter in peace.

For a while. But maybe a while will be enough.

After a few minutes more, Eric was able to make a graceful exit from the Artists' Reception and head over to the student party in the dorms. The celebration there was a lot noisier and a lot more honest—everybody was blowing off steam, filled with relief at having gotten through the all-important Winter Concert without absolute disaster.

There was a "No Alcohol" rule for the dorms, honored except by those few who simply had to break any rule just because it was there. But this party was proctored, and after the performance high of the concert, nobody really needed anything other than soda and fruit juice to get really rowdy anyway.

"Hey, Eric!" Jeremy shouted, waving. The young bassoonist was balanced on the end of the battered couch in the Student Lounge, his pale hair damp and standing up in spiky cowlicks. He looked like a goblin-child from a Victorian children's book.

Now where the hell did THAT simile spring from?

"Hey, Jer," Eric said, coming over. There was a big cooler beside the couch. Trust Jeremy to take up a strategic position by the refreshments. He was as savvy in his way as Kayla, Elisabet's young Healer-apprentice, was in hers.

"Have a drop of the pure," Jeremy said, lifting the lid of the cooler and pulling out a bottle of Glacéau.

It was spring water flavored with various fruit essences, and was a great favorite with the elves: Eric's refrigerator at Guardian House was full of it. Eric twisted the cap off and chugged the bottle, relishing the shock of cold. The reception had taken more out of him than he'd thought it would. He felt grimy, like a window so covered with smudged fingerprints that the light barely shone through.

Dharinel told me there'd be days like this. "Nothing comes without a price," he always said. Being a Bard makes you vulnerable to influences most people never even notice, while at the same time it gives you power most people can never imagine.

Jeremy handed him another bottle without even asking. "You looked better backstage before we played. So. How many propositions did you get?"

Eric stared at him blankly. *Do you mean that the way it sounds?* Jeremy was 17, but he was short and round-faced, and looked much younger. The boy's face twisted, and for a moment it wore a bleakly cynical expression that Eric had never seen before. "You know. The 'I could do so much for your career with just a little private tutoring' line?"

Funny. Isn't that the phrase Ria used once?

"Oh, you know," Eric said lightly. "The usual nebulous job offers. But nothing like that."

"You're lucky," Jeremy said, then looked guarded, as if he felt he'd ruined his Captain Cool image by saying too much.

If he'd been someone else, Eric would have urged Jeremy to tell him more, to report incidents like that to his Student Advisor. But Eric already knew that offers like that were rarely made openly. It was all interpretation and innuendo, impossible to prove. And the act of bringing the accusation could bring an end to a promising career before it even started.

"Yeah, well," Eric said. "Nobody rides for free. Isn't that what they say?" *Everything comes with a price. Too bad they don't always tell you what it is going in.*

"That's what they say," Jeremy said, obviously relieved that Eric wasn't going to go all over Adult and Role Model on him.

"Hey, Eric!" someone called. It was David, another of the soloists, calling him over to congratulate him on his playing. Eric turned away, the second bottle of Glacéau still in his hand.

He'd only meant to look in at the after-concert party, pick up his jacket, and then go on home. He didn't have any classes tomorrow, or even any rehearsals, but he did have a big assignment in Music Theory that had to get done Real Soon Now, and that meant making time for work instead of socializing.

But the next time he thought to look at a clock—watches didn't work well Underhill, and Eric had never been much for timebinding at the best of times—he realized it was after midnight and the party was starting to break up.

By the time he stepped out onto the street, Lincoln Center was deserted, the cafes and restaurants that abounded in this high living area mostly closed for the night. If someone wanted a set for New York After The Bomb Dropped, they couldn't pick a better place than right here, right now. Eric shivered, even in the dark-red leather jacket he wore, as he juggled his options. He had to get home somehow. It was too cold to walk, and he hated the subway. The Center was usually a good place to pick up a cab, but since the Mayor's new policy on medallion licenses, cabs were in short supply everywhere. He looked up and down the deserted street, and decided to chance it.

Putting his fingers to his lips, he whistled loudly and shrilly, a few bars of her signature tune forming in his head as he summoned his elvensteed to him. The tune was "God Bless The Child," a Billie Holiday song. He'd named Lady Day for The Lady of the White Camellias, and the song was his surest link to the elvensteed. He felt her acknowledge the call, and a few moments later—far too quickly for a vehicle that had been paying any attention at all to the posted speed limits—he heard the deep growl of Lady Day's engine and saw the gleam of her lights as she suddenly popped visible.

The elvensteed pulled to a stop in front of him and waited, engine thrumming. She looked almost smug, and so she should, having figured out all by herself how to get here while drawing the least attention to herself. If any mortal had enough Talent to manage to glimpse her as she drove by, he wouldn't have seen a riderless motorcycle—and if he had, well, people had a way of editing what they saw until it made sense.

Eric patted her gently on the gas-tank, and heard a ghostly whicker of amusement inside his mind. He climbed aboard, retrieving his helmet and gloves from the back of the saddle and putting them on. As he settled into the saddle, Eric realized that he'd been neglecting Lady Day these past few weeks, taking cabs and subways to school and even walking, and a good run was just what they both needed. A little magic would take care of the cold, and there was nothing on earth more sure-footed—or sure-wheeled—than an elvensteed.

"What do you say, girl? Want to go for a run?" He squeezed the throttle experimentally, and was rewarded with a wail of glee from the elvensteed's engine.

A few turns, and they were headed up Riverside Drive, going north. The enormous bulk of the George Washington Bridge towered above him, and for just a moment, riding through the night, Eric felt a flicker of temptation to just keep on going, let the road take him away from all pressures and responsibilities and everyone he knew. But the thought quickly vanished—not out of any artificial sense of other-imposed responsibility, but because he'd already done that dance in all its many variations. The footloose existence of the open road no longer held any enchantment for him.

I've already done that. It's part of the past, not who I am now. But the past doesn't go away neatly, does it? It's always there, like the key the music is written in.

All unbidden, an image of Ria as he'd seen her—or thought he'd seen her—at the concert tonight rose up in his mind, vivid as a Sending. Unlike the rest of his old life—the drinking, the drugs, the running away—she still had power over him. That was what had been nagging at him all evening, driving him to do everything but think his problem through. Like it or not, he and Ria Llewellyn had unfinished business.

But what? And how? And is all this—seeing her and the rest of it—just what Bethie's old therapist would have called "displaced anxiety"? Juilliard is rough—no secret about that—so maybe I'm just trying to come up with reasons to quit without having to blame myself for quitting.

It was a valid point, and Eric realized he needed somebody to talk it over with. Someone he could tell the whole story to, without editing out the magical parts—a sounding board of sorts. Right now he felt as if an invisible trapdoor had opened up beneath him and left him standing on air.

:Eric. Bard, do you hear?:

It was Kory's voice in his head, and if Eric had actually been driving a motorcycle rather than being a passenger aboard an elvensteed, Lady Day would have gone down and he would have been kissing asphalt.

:*Kory?*: Eric Sent back. :*Kory—what's wrong? Is it Bethie?*:

:*She is well, Eric. But come to us here. We must speak.*:

Unbidden, an image formed in his mind, and Eric knew where to go. Lady Day continued northward, much faster now that Eric had a true destination in mind.

Sterling Forest State Park was larger than just the few acres the Faire covered every year. The park was nestled in the gently-rolling Ramapo Mountains—known for centuries to be filled with haunted places and strange creatures, and for good reason. If he hadn't known that NYC was 90 minutes away, Eric wouldn't have been able to guess from the surroundings. He rode through the gates of the park, heading away from the long-gone Faire encampment—the Faire had already closed two months before—and a few moments later saw the pale flicker of a Portal open before him.

Kory and Beth were waiting for him just inside. At a quick glance, the place where they stood looked just like the park—grass, trees, dark sky above. But the air here was warm and perfumed, the trees were in full leaf and the grass was green and soft and lush. He could see clearly, even into the darkest shadows, and nothing in the mortal world had the rich perfection of the meadows and forests of Underhill.

Kory had shed the glamourie which protected him in the World Above. Now he appeared as himself—an elven knight and Magus Minor, with pointed ears and jewel-bright eyes, dressed in the silk and gold and baroque armor of a warrior of Faery, with a faint glowing nimbus of magic all around him.

Beth was dressed in elven-kenned clothing that was a mix of Earthly and Underhill styles in soft deep greens and russets. She was visibly pregnant now, though the baby wouldn't be born for some months yet—her cheeks were rounder, and in the magic-laden air of Underhill she glowed with the power of Life and Creation.

When she saw him she gave him a cocky "thumbs-up" salute, looking pleased.

"Looking good, Banyon."

Eric grinned back. Whatever the reason Kory had summoned him here, the trouble couldn't be as bad as all that if Beth was in such a mood. Of the three of them, Beth had always been the one to see the trouble from farthest away, the one who planned for the future, even when a future for any of them seemed most unlikely.

He glanced toward Kory, and his attention was almost immediately captured by the Sidhelord standing beside Kory—one whom Eric had, quite frankly, never expected to see again once he'd left the halls of Elfhame Misthold: Dharinel, Master Mage, Elven Bard, and Prince of the Sidhe. Dharinel looked about as happy as a wet cat.

Eric swung himself off Lady Day's saddle, pulled off his helmet, and bowed formally to his teacher—however much you could let slide in the World Above, in Underhill proper form and due courtesy were absolutely indispensable—before turning back to Kory and Beth. He'd said there was nothing wrong with Beth, which meant the baby was okay too, and Beth's cheeriness seemed to underscore that, but seeing Dharinel here, Eric desperately wanted to know why he'd been called.

"There is trouble in your city," Kory said, looking pretty troubled himself. "We have come to warn you."

"Warn me?" Eric risked a glance at Dharinel. *My city? New York?* Try as he might, he could not imagine his teacher caring whether or not Manhattan sunk into the ocean or flew off into space. There weren't any elves there, and Dharinel thought mortals were a waste of time. "About what?"

Beth started to answer, but Kory put a hand on her arm, silencing her.

"First you must know its history," Dharinel said, glaring in a way that warned Eric not to interrupt, no matter how impatient he got. "As you know, many centuries ago as mortals reckon time, the World Above and the World Under Hill lived together in harmony, until elvenkind was faced with a harsh necessity: either to seek new lands beyond the sunset, or to withdraw from the world altogether into the Fairy Lands Beyond.

"This necessity fell upon both Courts, the Dark and the Light, equally, for all that many believe that the Unseleighe Sidhe draw much of their form and power from mortalkind, being shaped in the image of your fears and hungers—" Dharinel didn't quite sneer, but Eric was used to that. The origin of the Dark Court, and the reasons for its difference from the Bright, was a topic of endless discussion among the elves, and Dharinel's theory was a common one.

"And so it was that the Sidhe, Seleighe and Unseleighe alike, came to the West, planting their Groves and shaping their Nexuses as they had in the Old World, gracing the tribes of Men with their puissance and their strength—in the case of the Bright Court—and shaping mortals in accordance with their own base nature—in the case of the Dark."

Eric fretted, trying not to let it show, but Dharinel would not be rushed, as he knew from bitter experience.

"But there were always places that all the Sidhe avoided, for good and sufficient reason. Places belonging to neither Court. In some of those places mortals have built great cities, where their own natures flourish without influence. Others, mortals had the good wit to avoid, until recent times. You have gone to such a place."

New York? Eric thought, even as he boggled at the thought of calling the city "recent"—the Dutch had first settled Manhattan back in the 1600s. Still, he supposed almost four centuries was recent by Underhill standards.

"Yet before you did so, another came here before you, and now, he seeks to take this mortal place and make it his own. This Unseleighe Prince is subtle and patient, and did we openly oppose his works, it might be . . . inconvenient."

"Inconvenient," Eric knew, meant that the network of treaties and promises that bound the Elfhames, and even the Dark and Light Courts, together in an unbreakable web of favors, customs, and obligations, would be severely strained by such interference, maybe even broken. And that would mean a war that nobody in either Court wanted.

"Elves are invading Manhattan?" Eric asked, just to make sure he had it clear. Beth snorted. Well, it did sound kind of funny when you said it out loud.

"One elf," Kory corrected, looking unhappy. "But he is very powerful, very old . . . and very Unseleighe."

"He wishes to build a Nexus there," Dharinel said shortly. "As you know, it requires great power to open a Gate between the Worlds. It is his way that he will seek others to provide it."

"Others like me," Eric said, and surprised a chilly smile on his old teacher's face.

"There are no others like you, Sieur Eric, and I trust that after all I have taught you, you would recognize the traps he would lay for you, and have the mother-wit to run for your life. Others will not, for our legend has become less than a nursery-tale for mortals in this time, and as you know from your own experience in the World Above, many will not believe the evidence of their own senses . . . until it is far too late. And so it has been decided in Council that in order to protect the mortals from the consequences of their own folly, you will carry this warning to the Guardians, and instruct them to take steps to save the mortals under their care from this threat."

"I— But— Wait—you know about the Guardians?" Eric floundered.

Again that look of amusement from Dharinel, as though he were greatly enjoying Eric's discomfiture. "Once we knew them quite well, Bard, though undoubtedly they will have forgotten over the years. Humankind has always had its defenders, paladins of the Light. Some are great warriors, whose exploits are known to all: Launcelot, Roland, Beowulf. Others work in secret, for the knowledge of the forces that they fight would do as much harm to the mortals they choose to protect as those forces themselves. Once we fought side-by-side, brothers on the field of battle. Now they fight alone. But we remember those days, even if they do not. Tell them what you must to arm them against this foe, and warn them well."

Eric sighed, knowing that babbling more questions would only irritate Dharinel when he was in a mood like this, and not get Eric anywhere. Neither Dharinel nor Kory had named the Unseleighe enemy that was causing all this trouble, but Eric knew that to do so in Underhill—and even in some places in the World Above—would be like shouting a warning of their intentions in the Unseleighe Lord's ear. And it wasn't as if Eric would be confusing his new enemy with some *other* Sidhe Lord trying to turn Manhattan into his own private fief.

"Do only that, send them fair warning, and nothing more," Dharinel warned. "Do not let yourself be drawn into the battle against this opponent. It might well be that this is the very thing he looks for to complete his plans, and that your involvement could spell disaster."

"I'll remember that, Master," Eric said.

Dharinel grimaced. "And you will follow your irresolute mortal heart despite anything I may say. I am finished here," he said abruptly. A moment later, he was gone.

Eric blinked at Kory. The young Sidhe smiled, and shrugged sheepishly—a human gesture he'd picked up from Eric—as if to say "you know how he is."

"C'mere, Banyon," Beth said, now that the three of them were alone. She enfolded him in a fierce hug. He could feel the baby pressed between them, a daughter that somehow belonged to all three of them at once.

"God, I've missed you!" she said, letting him go at last. "How are you?"

"I— Well," Eric said, and stopped. How to compress the last two months into a comprehensible tale? He wasn't sure how to bring up the topic of Ria to Beth, either, and he wasn't at all sure this was the right time, anyway. Beth had other things on her mind right now.

"How's the baby?" he asked instead.

"Impatient," Beth said with a grin. She took Eric's hand and placed it against her belly. He felt a flutter of movement against his hand, and stared at Beth, eyes wide.

"Yep, that's her," Beth said proudly.

Hello, little one, Eric Sent gently. He felt a flurry of unfocused response—happiness, eagerness, amusement—and withdrew his hand. Beth's eyes were shining.

"You see how she is," Beth said. "Just wait till she's born—we're going to throw the biggest party Underhill's ever seen!"

And she'll have Power. I can already tell that. And she'll grow up in a world where that kind of thing is understood and accepted. She'll never be an outsider, never have to wonder if she's going crazy because she can see and do things most humans can't.

"Be sure to send me an invitation," Eric said. The thought brought his mind around in a tight circle to the reason Dharinel had called him here. "But right now, this thing with Dharinel . . . it must be something pretty important for him to come all this way," Eric said. *And to care about what happened in the World Above at all.* Another threat, this time not a quarrel between the Sidhe that humans blundered into, but one of the Fair Folk seeking out humans to use them in some plot of his own.

"Yes," Kory said. "It is a matter that is not a new one, I fear. This Lord is very old, and very cunning, and has long blamed humankind for his own misfortunes. But if he seeks human allies now, it is a matter for great concern. But Master Dharinel is right in this, Eric: this must not become your fight. We think he seeks to work through human agents, and so it must be the Guardians' work to protect them. I know you must warn them—but once you have, won't you come back to Elfhame Everforest with us? Surely you have spent enough time in the World Above?"

"Hey, I haven't even gotten up to mid-terms yet," Eric said, trying to downpedal Kory's plea by turning it into a joke.

"Aw, he just doesn't want to leave his new girlfriend, whoever she is," Beth said. "What about it, Banyon? Had any hot dates lately?"

Of all the times for Bethie's erratic Sixth Sense to kick in! It's true there's a woman in my life . . . sort of. But not the way she thinks.

"Too busy studying," Eric said lightly, turning it into a joke once more. "But I've made some new friends. One of them's a gargoyle."

Beth stared at him for a moment before deciding he was serious. "Only you, Banyon!" she said. "A gargoyle? That's a new one on me."

"His name's Greystone. He's a friend of these Guardians. Did you know that my whole apartment building's, well, sort of the equivalent of an Elfhame, only for humans? Everybody who lives there is special in some way, and some of them are actually magicians. Like these Guardians."

"You learn something new every day," Beth said wryly. "But hey, no reason to stand around here like strangers waiting for a bus. Kory brought a picnic. Kick back for awhile and tell us all the news. We've missed you. Not that you were ever the world's best letter-writer, as I recall, and anyway, e-mail doesn't work that well Underhill."

"As if I could figure out how to use it," Eric groaned. "I can barely get the thing to spit out my classwork assignments."

He looked around. Lady Day was getting reacquainted with Beth and Kory's elvensteeds. Since the other two were Underhill most of the time, they'd reverted to their "natural" form as horses. Bethie's mount was a glorious palomino, with a silvery mane and tail and a coat like dark gold. Its mane and tail were braided with tiny silver bells, and Eric remembered the old tales that the Seleighe Court would braid bells into their horses' manes when they went out riding.

Kory's elvensteed was a little more startling—it had the form of a horse, but still retained the markings of its motorcycle form, maroon with black and silver lightning bolts along its sides. Both of them watched Eric with a certain amount of equine amusement.

When he looked back to the others, there was a blanket spread out on the grass, and Kory was kneeling beside a picnic hamper, unpacking savory dishes. The odor made Eric's mouth water—he'd been too nervous before the performance tonight to eat much, and his stomach was reminding him that he'd missed dinner, lunch, and midnight snack as well.

As Kory spread the feast before them, Eric helped Beth to sit down—the pregnancy made her a little awkward at things like that—and for awhile everything was like the best of the old times Underhill when the three of them had been happy together. But the present merriment only served to underscore how much things had changed, as well.

"And after the baby's born," Beth was saying, "we're kind of thinking of taking her around on the Faire circuit. Of course, that depends on . . . things," she finished awkwardly, glancing at Kory.

It wasn't hard for Eric to interpret that glance. Beth had talked about it with him in the time just after she'd first known she was pregnant. Beth wanted a large family, and she was hoping to have more children—*Kory's* children. But even full-blooded elven children were rare occurrences among the Sidhe; it was one of the reasons that the elves were so fond of human children, after all, and spent so much time among them. And children born to a human and a Sidhe were even rarer still. Eric feared that Beth had set her heart on something that was almost impossible, and the worst part of it all was that she knew it.

And being Beth, refused to believe that *anything* was impossible if you wanted it badly enough.

Kory took Beth's hand silently, looking wistful. There was an even greater problem that the young Sidhe lord faced than the problem of children. Korendil had centuries of life ahead of him— and Beth did not. Right now, it was easy for her to move back and forth between Underhill and the World Above, but eventually she would have to stay Underhill full-time, because humans who stayed in Underhill for too long didn't age . . . until they stepped once more into the World Above. Then, all the years they'd cheated by living in elven lands caught up with them instantly, killing them. So in a few decades—a short time by elven standards—Beth would no longer be able to do the Faire circuit without instantly aging. In fact, Beth wouldn't be able to come back to the World Above at all. But Kory loved the human lands . . . he'd hate to give up visiting them.

And he wouldn't want to visit them without his human lover.

As if he knew what Eric was thinking, Kory glanced hopefully at Eric. They both wanted children. Kory didn't want to lose Beth to death and age in an elven eyeblink. Both problems seemed equally insurmountable.

And the impossible was supposed to be his specialty.

A reputation is a terrible thing, Eric thought, looking back at Kory. *When nothing's ever been done before, how come everyone looks at me? But I'll find a way,* Eric decided, with sudden determination. *I'm supposed to be this great magical Bard. What good is that if you can't help the people you love?* And then, a wisp of inspiration: *I bet Ria would know about the children. . . .*

Eric forced a smile. He clasped Kory's shoulder companionably. "Don't worry so much about the future, Kor'. It gets here no matter what you do."

"Yeah," Beth said. "And *I'm* the one that's going to be having the baby. All you have to do is pace outside the delivery room door looking worried. And think of names for her."

"She will be a great warrior and Bard," Kory said seriously. "We should name her Maeve. Queen Maeve was a great warrior in the human lands of long ago."

Beth laughed, and the moment of sadness passed. "Maeve, it is, then. Who knows? Maybe someday Maeve Kentraine will have her own rock and roll band!"

At last it was time for Eric to go. Time in Underhill ran parallel to World Above time this close to a Gate, and though tomorrow— today, rather—was Saturday, Eric still had studying to do over the weekend. He ought to make time to check in with Jeremy to see how Lydia was doing, too.

He called Lady Day back from frolicking with the other elvensteeds, and reluctantly prepared to depart. He walked Kory a few steps away from Beth, who was gathering up the remains of their picnic and tucking them tidily back into the basket.

"I don't want you to worry about me—or anything," Eric told Kory. "I promise I'll stay out of this Sidhe Lord's way. And who knows what tomorrow may bring?"

"'Don't borrow trouble, they give so much of it away free'?" the Sidhe quoted wistfully. "A true saying, O Bard. But the future is where mortals live."

"'Never their minds on where they are, what they are doing,'" Eric misquoted, smiling. "Yeah. I heard all about that from Dharinel, lots and lots. But it's the way we are."

"And I would not change you," Kory said seriously. "Even if I could. Fare you well, Eric. Visit us again soon."

"I will," Eric promised, hugging Kory forcefully. Kory raised his hand in salute, stepping back. Beth blew him a kiss from where she knelt beside the picnic basket.

Eric swung his leg over Lady Day's saddle and reached for his helmet, settling it on his head. The elvensteed wheeled and turned back the way she'd come, taking Eric through the Portal and back into the park once more, into the sudden darkness and wintery chill.

It was nearly two in the morning when Eric arrived back at the apartment house, so it was no surprise that Toni Hernandez's first-floor front windows were dark, but what surprised Eric was the sense of *absence* he felt as he walked into the lobby, as if all the building's tenants—not just the Guardians—had packed up and left while he'd been gone.

That's ridiculous. After all, he'd seen a few lights on the upper floors as he came up the walk. Artists and writers tended to be a solitary, nocturnal bunch, given to working in odd scraps of time stolen from day jobs. So he knew that there were still people here. Had to be. It was just that . . .

It's just that this place feels like Sleeping Beauty's Castle, all of a sudden.

It had started to rain on the ride back—thick slow drops on the edge of becoming snow—and Eric rode Lady Day right into the courtyard, leaving the elvensteed to find her parking spot while he rushed inside. His leathers had turned most of the rain, but his dress slacks were soaked and his shoes were wet as well.

Impatient with the usual glacial pace of the elevator, Eric elected to take the stairs at top speed. He was panting and out of breath from his climb by the time he reached the top, but he'd shaken the fey humor that had possessed him in the lobby. No matter where his other friends in Guardian House were tonight, Eric knew someone who was always here and never slept.

"Greystone? Hey, buddy?" Eric called, flipping on the lights in his living room. He kicked off his shoes and tossed his jacket aside. It was still the same mess it had been when he'd left for the concert at four this afternoon: clothes, CDs, and empty bottles of designer water scattered around like the debris of a small whirlwind.

Housekeeping had never been Eric's strong suit, and he supposed if he was going to keep on living here he'd need to hire some kind of cleaning service, assuming he could find one that would pick up and put away his things . . . before he needed to hire an archaeologist to find the bedroom.

Maybe a house-brownie would like to live here and do the dishes. They're supposed to come if you put out a bowl of milk for them, but with my luck, I'd probably just end up feeding half the neighborhood cats.

Despite the season, he'd left the living room window open so that his gargoyle friend would know he was welcome to come and go as he pleased when Eric was out. "Hey? Greystone?" Eric called softly. The curtains billowed, and Eric heard the soft click of stone against iron as the gargoyle climbed down from its perch.

"Well, if it ain't O'Banyon," Greystone said, in his odd mixture of Irish and Bronx. "And how was the concert, laddybuck? Hmpf—you smell like you've been rolling in magic." The gargoyle wrinkled its nose and looked disapproving, much as if Eric had come home reeking with beer from the corner speakeasy.

"I took a little trip through the looking glass." Eric shrugged. "The concert went okay, but the ending was a real killer. I'll have the tapes in about a week and you can hear it then for yourself. At least I didn't screw up my solo, so Rector must be spitting nails; half the school saw me on stage and there's nothing he can do about it but give me a fair grade. And something really weird happened tonight—I saw Beth and Kory, and Master Dharinel asked me to pass on a message—and now that I get here, it looks like something really weird has happened here, too. Where is everyone? I kind of need to talk to Toni, but I'm not sure what I'm going to say."

As he spoke, Eric walked into the bedroom. He pulled off his slacks and shirt, and shrugged into one of Bethie's finds: a bathrobe of heavy cashmere. He began to feel warmer almost at once. From there he went into the kitchen and came back with two bottles of spring water. He offered one to his guest—Greystone was already crouched in his favorite spot in front of the TV—and flopped down on the couch, exhausted.

"What sort of a weird thing?" the gargoyle asked, ignoring the rest of Eric's speech.

"Two things, actually. First, I ran into an old friend of mine," Eric said. "Or else it was a really convincing hallucination. Either way I wanted to run it past some friends I could trust." *It's not that I think Ria's out to get me. It's just that I . . . well, I don't know. It's Ria. I never could think straight when I was around her the last time.*

A sudden tactile memory, vivid as a kiss, intruded in Eric's mind: Ria in bed, wearing nothing but a seductive smile, her blond hair fanned out against the red silk sheets as she reached for him. . . .

"Yeah, well. . . ." The gargoyle seemed oddly embarrassed. "Toni and the guys . . . they're going to be out for a while."

Eric looked at him, jolted out of the unbidden erotic reverie by the tone in Greystone's voice. "'Out.' Is this one of those things that Bard was not meant to know, or can you tell me something more? Dharinel sent me to warn them, so I'm wondering if this is tied up with that." *And did Dharinel pass on his warning too late?*

Greystone shrugged noncommittally. "Might be a false alarm. It just seems that Something's loose in the city, and they're out there trying to find out what. I've seen a lot of cases like this before. Sometimes you never do find out what spooked you. Other times, it's Gotterdammerung with a full orchestra." The gargoyle shrugged again, unable—or unwilling—to tell Eric anything more. "But tell me what your mentor said. Ms. Hernandez will want to hear it directly from you, but it can't hurt to tell me as well. And that way, I can tell her the minute she comes in. You might be asleep, you know."

"More than likely," Eric admitted with a yawn. Now that he was feeling more relaxed, the tension and stress of the earlier evening was catching up with him in the form of an urgent need for sleep. "Well . . ." Eric marshalled his thoughts. "You know how there are Good Elves and Bad Elves?" Unbidden, a scrap of one of his old movies came to the surface of his mind, Glinda the Good, in Oz, asking, *"Are you a Good Witch or a Bad Witch?"* "Well the short version is, it looks like one of the Bad Elves has the idea of moving into New York and setting up a Nexus here."

"Can't be done," Greystone said promptly. "Too much iron—

and everything else—here. New York goes down as far as it goes up—did you ever take a good look beneath the surface of the streets? There's a whole city under the city!"

Eric shook his head. "I know. That's why the closest Nexus is up in Elfhame Everforest in Rockland County. But what Dharinel told me is that this guy—he didn't give me a name, but I guess that doesn't really matter—really doesn't like anybody very much, elves or humans, and thinks he can use humans to take over the local territory. To top it off, he's supposed to be pretty powerful. So I'm supposed to tell Toni and the gang to be on the watch for something . . . er, unusually elvish."

"Hrumph. Been down to the Village lately?" Greystone snarked. "But what has this got to do with that old friend you said you ran into tonight? From what you've said, this Master Dharinel of yours doesn't exactly qualify as an old friend."

"Not quite," Eric said, grinning as he tried to imagine his mentor here in his living room hanging out with his new friends. "I don't think the two events are connected, but you never know." Although he doubted that Ria's presence in the city, even if she did mean harm, would be enough to set off the Guardians' alerts in the way that something obviously had. "I told you about a woman named Ria Llewellyn, right?"

"The half-Blood that kept that elf-lord from doing in all the Sun-Descending elves and ended up in a coma?" Greystone asked helpfully.

"That's the one, yeah." Suddenly he couldn't even keep his eyes open. He leaned his head against the back of the couch, half-mumbling with tiredness. "Only I saw her at the concert tonight, and I'm wondering—if I didn't imagine it all—what she was doing there. All her corporate stuff is out in L.A."

"I take it she isn't a music lover?" the gargoyle said drily.

"No. I mean yes—I used to play for her. But . . . I don't know." Eric sighed, and reached up to pull the tie out of his hair. He shook his head, making the long chestnut strands—his natural color, restored by the same elven magic that had once turned it black as a disguise—spill across his cheeks.

"Yes, you do," Greystone said unexpectedly. Eric opened his eyes and looked at his friend in surprise. "You're a Bard. You see into people's hearts. You know whether she's a threat or not."

"But what if I'm wrong?" There, at last, was the thing that had been bothering him all evening, brought out into the open. *What if I'm attracted to her for all the wrong reasons? What if I can't trust my own judgment? Leaving aside, for the moment, what HER reasons were for coming to the concert tonight. What if she's working WITH this Unseleighe guy?*

"Do you think she could fool you that easily?" Greystone asked.

Yes. No. Maybe. Dharinel once said that stage illusionism and true magic have this much in common—that the glamour only really works if the subject WANTS it to on some level.

I guess it's not really that I don't trust her. I guess, deep down inside, I don't trust myself. Maybe all this growing up makes me nervous. Maybe I'm looking for some way to pack in all this maturity and adulthood and go back to being what I was. Even if that isn't what I want on the surface, who knows what I want underneath? Caity's always saying "your mind is not your friend." Maybe this is what she means?

"No," Eric said with slow reluctance. "Not if I don't want to be fooled."

"You're a Bard now," Greystone pointed out unnecessarily. "That might not have been true the last time you two tangled, boyo, but it is now. 'Trust your feelings, Luke.'"

"So you think I should believe in myself?" Eric asked, yawning again. "Is that the answer, Master Greystone?"

"I think you should go to bed," Greystone said. "You look all in. You can tell me the rest of your troubles tomorrow. Because if there's one thing I *do* know about mortals, it's that they don't function well without sleep or food."

You can say that again, buddy. Eric got to his feet, conscious of how tired he was. Sleep sounded like the best idea anyone'd had in quite a while.

"Don't wait up," Eric said, stumbling toward the bedroom. He heard Greystone chuckle as he closed the bedroom door.

❖❖ ❖❖ ❖❖

He discovered that he was walking through a forest. No, not walking. Almost like swimming; pushing the branches out of his way and pulling his body along afterwards. The slippery black bark was cold and silky against his fingers, reminding him unpleasantly of polished bone. The association was so peculiar that he stopped, holding the branches away from his face as he tried to clear his thoughts. How had he gotten here, to this weirdwood, anyway?

I'm asleep, Eric realized. *Dreaming.*

With the ease of practice, he held himself in the lucid dreaming state, not intending to wake up until he found out what had summoned him here. Was this another warning message from Underhill? Half the elves he knew would have just sent him an e-mail, and Master Dharinel had already told him everything he was going to.

So this must be something else—one of those odd visions-cum-premonitions that Bards apparently got from time to time. But who was warning him . . . and about what?

Ria? But even as he thought the name, Eric realized this was none of her doing. Ria had always been more straightforward than this in her dealings with him. This was something else, and he'd better find out what. Feeling a great reluctance to do so, Eric forced himself to study his surroundings.

The bonewood he was in was lit with the sourceless silvery illumination that Eric associated with all things Underhill, but there the resemblance to the familiar Elfhame Misthold ended. Everything around him was in shades of silver—even the bark on the trees was not truly black, but the deep grey of tarnished silver. Swags of what looked like Spanish moss festooned their bare branches. Mist lay on the forest floor like a thick carpet, and in the distance the bone-trees faded to a pale grey in the hazy air before vanishing entirely.

There was no life in these woods. No birdsong, no small scuttling forest creatures, none of the playful life he associated with Underhill. Yet this *was* Underhill, his instincts told him, even if it was an Underhill much different than any he'd ever known.

This must be what Underhill would be like if the elves were all dead. But that can't be. Dharinel and Kory both told me that without the elves, there is no Underhill, just Chaos Lands, so some of the Seleighe Sidhe must be around here somewhere or this place wouldn't have any shape at all.

Cautiously, but with renewed determination, Eric forced himself onward through the dreaming wood. The sense of artifice—of being an actor moving across a well-dressed but artificial stage—was very strong, and Eric wondered once again what purpose had summoned him here. It wasn't that he was in the least worried about being able to defend himself. If things got hairy, he could just force himself to awaken. The dream had only as much power over him as he allowed it to have, but he did feel the need to find out why he was having it, especially coming as it did on the heels of Ria's appearance and Dharinel's warning.

It seemed as if he had walked for hours, when slowly Eric became aware that the character of the weirdwood had changed. He began to hear faint scuttlings behind him—they stopped each time he turned around—and now there were faint ghostly shapes flitting about at the edges of his vision: things with eyes that gleamed like faint red embers. And at last Eric realized why this place seemed so familiar to him.

"The sedge is withered by the lake/and no birds sing."

This was Keats' haunted wood, home of La Belle Dame Sans Merci. With a lagging sense of danger, Eric remembered that the Bright Court weren't the only elves inhabiting Underhill who might be sending him messages. The Unseleighe Sidhe had their home here, too . . . the Dark Court that had been the stuff of human nightmares ever since humankind had crawled out of the caves.

Okay. Fun's fun, but this isn't going anywhere I like. Time to wake up now, Eric told himself.

But he couldn't.

Jeanette Campbell came back to Threshold late that afternoon, and spent several hours in her private lab mixing up enough T-Stroke to waste a large percentage of the population of New York and the five boroughs. When it was finished, she trundled the cart and its several pounds of white powder—all neatly packed in large brown plastic pharmaceutical jars—to the Dirty Lab, where Threshold drones would have the unenviable labor of packaging it up in five-gram doses for the street. There was little need to bother with laboratory protocols or sterile conditions down in the Dirty Lab; it was used mostly for scutwork and mass production, and the people who administered the drugs Jeanette made weren't overly concerned with sanitary conditions or the safety of their users. By tonight, T-Stroke would be the new hot ride in everyone's pocket. By tomorrow morning, Robert would be able to start harvesting the Survivors.

And then they'd start getting an idea of how it worked.

Afterward, too keyed-up to sleep, and not willing to go back to her high-priced high-rise crackerbox, Jeanette went down to her office. Her guitar was waiting for her there in its shiny black case. She sat down in her chair, not bothering to turn up the lights, and took it out, running her fingers over the strings. Maybe a little time spent here would help her shake the headache she'd been running all day. Like many former users, Jeanette scrupulously avoided everything, even aspirin. She forced herself to concentrate on her instrument.

It was acoustic, strung with silver, just like the instruments in all the old legends. Once upon a time she'd thought that would make a difference. Now she knew that all she could reasonably expect from silver strings was a brighter sound and a little decoration. But maybe that was enough.

Music had always been her refuge. When the pain got too bad, when even thinking hurt, she could turn to the discipline of music and wipe it all away. She'd even transposed some old Celtic Harp pieces to guitar, and her fingers moved automatically into one now. Silvery rills of music filled the office, painting a vision of a future in which she could be happy and free, where the person she'd always wanted to be and the person she was would match. Where she wouldn't have to brace herself every time she caught sight of herself in the mirror.

If T-Stroke works . . . if we can figure out how to keep it from killing people . . . what happens then?

Would she take it? It was a long way from 16 to 31. She'd always thought her dreams hadn't changed, but that was before they'd come within reach. Now the thing she'd hoped for most was about to happen, and the thought both frightened and delighted her. The goal that had obsessed her for more than half her life—having Power, real power, invincible power—was almost in her hands. She'd done what she'd always dreamed of doing. She'd found it. She'd found the key to do what the fantasy novels she'd devoured as a teen only hinted at—a way to unlock the Talent that would set her apart from everyone else, make her special.

Give her revenge.

The music in her hands turned darker, mocking and warning at the same time. What revenge would ever be enough for all the disasters of her life? Where could she begin?

A sudden flood of light blinded her, and she pressed her hand against the strings, stifling the music into silence. Past and present jangled against each other, and she almost flinched before she remembered where she was. Jeanette had a lot of problems these days, but getting ambushed and beaten up wasn't one of them.

"I thought I'd find you here."

"It's customary to knock," she said icily. She winced at the light, squinting up through the glare to find Robert standing in the doorway of her office. She'd used to respect Robert in a way—he was so much more ruthless than she'd ever dared to be—but lately that respect had faded. She'd never really trusted him to protect her from prosecution the way he'd promised he would back at the beginning, but now she didn't even trust Robert Lintel to have his own best interests at heart. He was in danger of believing his own publicity, she realized with a flash of insight.

But he was still a dangerous man. And right now, he wanted something from her. She knew the look on his face, the one that told her he was going to try to talk her into something—but so close to her goal, Jeanette was feeling a little bit forgiving, and was pretty sure she'd agree to whatever he came up with. It was the easiest thing to do, and in her own peculiar fashion, Jeanette had always taken the easy way.

"They're packaging the stuff up now," she said before he spoke. She set her guitar back in its case. Robert always made fun of her music. There wasn't any power to be gained from music. Or so he thought.

But a protest song can start a riot. End a war . . . or start one. Great musicians live forever.

"That's great," Robert said warmly, oozing false charm from every pore. It must work on his bosses, whoever they were, but it'd never worked on her. And Robert was too self-obsessed to see that. "We'll be able to start distributing the stuff tonight, and have our next batch of subjects rounded up by the end of the week. I wanted to talk to you about developing protocols for the second round of tests, the ones on the Survivors."

"Sure." Jeanette grinned without mirth. "But don't you think it should wait until we have guinea-pigs to test it on? Anyway, I'm not sure what re-dosing the Survivors will do. Maybe it'll just kill them. In terms of practical applications you've got to remember that this stuff wears off fairly quickly. Twelve hours and it's out of the system—and from what we've seen with the chimps and the first round of people, the overt effects only last for an hour or two."

Robert smirked at her, sure he knew things she didn't.

"Well, that's just the thing. We could get started on that second round right now. We've still got that live one from the last round, and we've got plenty of T-Stroke. Why don't you shoot her up again and see what happens?"

The sadistic glee in his voice made her wince inwardly. Jeanette knew that all their human victims were going to be TTD—Tested to Destruction—and that none of them were going to be allowed to survive, but down deep inside somewhere she also thought that they should be treated with respect. Whether they'd chosen to be lab-rats or not, they were heroes. But Robert saw them as nothing more than toys.

And Robert liked breaking toys. She already knew that.

"She's the one who healed herself, right? Fat lot of good that is, for your purposes," Jeanette said grudgingly. She couldn't resist slipping the needle in, even if only a little. What if the only thing this stuff was actually good for was healing impossible-to-cure diseases? Not much power for Robert in that. *Too bad if that's true, party-boy.*

"Yeah. Ram says she had stomach cancer. I was thinking a higher dose might, I don't know—do something else," he said, too casually.

If there was anything Life had taught her, it was that trying to save anyone else only got you hurt. She'd sold folks down the river before. One more couldn't matter. Jeanette shrugged. "Worth a try, I suppose. And if her head explodes we can dump her somewhere like all the others. Okay. Tell Beirkoff to get her prepped and bring her down to my lab and we'll see what we can do. Oh, and Robert? Strap this one down real good, okay? I don't want to spend tomorrow cleaning the place up."

Robert grinned and saluted her from across the room, a faux-macho gesture he'd picked up from some movie or other. Jeanette grimaced—she'd always particularly detested it. But Robert didn't notice. He'd already gotten what he wanted.

After he left, she rummaged through her paper files until she found the one she was looking for: the intake report on Ellie Borden, the sole survivor of the first run of trials. The black hooker'd had the lowest body weight of any of the test subjects, and so the dose she'd gotten in the cells had been proportionately higher.

Was that the reason she'd survived? Would a small dose of T-Stroke kill, but a large one liberate the mind from its fetters?

We're going to get a chance to find out, aren't we? Jeanette thought with grim humor. Her headache was worse than it had been all day. *See? You're going to do someone else down. And it doesn't hurt at all, does it?*

They had to let her go. God had given her a second chance, and Ellie Borden didn't intend to waste it.

She knew she was in some kind of trouble. Her head was clear for the first time in many, many months, the disease wasn't hanging over her head like a flaming sword, and she knew that wherever this place was, she was not in the hands of the police.

Everyone she'd met here had treated her with distant kindness. A little while after she'd woken up whole and well, alone in that padded cell, a woman wearing a black uniform had come and escorted her to a bathroom with a shower, given her a rolled towel that contained a toothbrush and soap, and told her to wash. When she'd stripped, she found two disks glued to her skin—one under her ribs, another high on her back—but try as she might, she could not pick them free, and the guard had ordered her to get into the shower and stop wasting time. The water was hot, and beneath its stream Ellie had luxuriated in being clean, really clean, for the first time since she'd been turned out onto the streets.

She might still have been in the shower if the woman hadn't told her to come out. When she had, she'd found her clothing was gone, and she'd been given a set of blue surgical scrubs to wear, and a pair of soft slippers for her feet. The connection between these clothes and those given to prison inmates did not escape her.

"Where am I? Can you tell me that? I know this isn't the Tombs[4] . . . I need to get out of here. I promise I won't cause any trouble."

But the woman had only stared at her with hard-eyed pity, and refused to answer any of her questions.

After her shower was over, Ellie was taken down a long white corridor to yet a third cell. It was an improvement on the first two: it had a fold-out table, a chair bolted to the floor, a bunk, and a sink and toilet, like an upscale designer version of a prison cell. There were cameras in all four corners of the ceiling, and an overhead fluorescent light protected by a metal grid. The room had no windows, and she heard the heavy sound of multiple locks being thrown as the door closed behind the guard.

That was when she really began to be afraid. Because this place was like a prison, but it wasn't a real, official prison. And that meant that the people running it could just make people . . .

Disappear.

After awhile—not more than an hour, Ellie thought—an Indian

---

[4]The Manhattan Security Detention Facility

man in a white lab coat came in, accompanied by another guard and a trolley full of medical equipment.

"Where am I?" she'd asked them, hating the sound of terror she heard in her own voice. "I know this is . . . could you just tell me what you want? Please?"

"If you'll just cooperate, I'm sure all your questions will be answered later. This is just a routine medical examination, Ellie. We want to know how you're doing," the doctor answered. His voice was soothing, professional, but Ellie had taken a look at the sleepy-eyed guard standing behind the man in white and stopped asking. The guard was a tall bronze-skinned man, in the same black uniform the guard who had taken her to the shower had worn. The nametag on his shirt said ELKANAH—a Biblical name, a good name, but she didn't think Elkanah was a good man. He had a full equipment belt—nightstick, walkie-talkie, gun, pepper spray, handcuffs—and there was something about him that made Ellie submit to the doctor's examination in passive silence. It had been very thorough and puzzling to her, though she was drearily familiar with medical procedures from the time she'd started getting sick. The doctor removed the two silver disks—spraying the places they were stuck to her with something very cold first—and somehow that frightened her even more, as if she'd suddenly lost whatever value she might possess in these strangers' eyes.

Once the doctor was finished—he'd taken blood samples, hooked her up to an EEG and an EKG, and a few other things—he let her dress again.

"Someone will feed you soon."

The words were meant to be kindly, she knew. He hadn't had to say anything, after all. But they'd only made her feel even more like an animal in a cage. She hadn't been able to look at him when he left.

In a few minutes, another of the hard-faced guards had brought her a sandwich and coffee, obviously from a local deli. She'd taken one sip of the creamed and sweetened coffee but found it gaggingly bitter and poured it into the sink, using the cup for water instead. She'd thought she was too frightened to eat, but instead she was ravenous, finishing the sandwich in only a few bites and wishing there were more.

Then all there was to do was pray, huddled up on her bunk with the blanket wrapped around her shoulders, hoping against hope that what she feared so much wasn't the truth.

The sound of her cell door opening jarred Ellie awake—somehow, despite everything, she'd fallen asleep. What she saw in the doorway made her cringe back against the far wall. Elkanah was back, this time with a white guard who looked just as intimidating. They were wheeling a hospital gurney with them. Four thick leather straps were laid loosely across it.

"Please . . ." she heard herself whimper.

"Get on the table." The white guard spoke. His voice was harsh and indifferent. Ellie shook her head, too frightened by the sight of the straps to comply. "Do it," he said, a thread of irritation coloring his voice.

"Hey, Angel. You gotta understand people's limitations," Elkanah said. "Now, Miss," he went on, speaking to Ellie for the first time. "Nobody's going to hurt you. We have to take you somewhere. You have to get up here on this gurney. Can you do that?"

To Ellie's horror, she began to weep. She shook her head, trying to explain how afraid she was, how unfair it was that this should happen now, just when a miracle had turned her life around—had given her a life instead of the death she had expected.

Elkanah took no notice of her tears as he approached her. He pulled her gently to her feet and removed the blanket from her shoulders, then led her over to the gurney. Before she could react, he had scooped her up in his arms and laid her down on it, and the man he'd called Angel was buckling the straps across her legs.

She began hopelessly to struggle, but Elkanah held her shoulders down and stared into her eyes. "There is no point to this," he said firmly. "Do you understand?"

She'd turned her head away then, giving up, letting them do what they would. Uncontrollable shudders racked her as all four straps were buckled tight. The leather creaked as she breathed.

She knew better than to ask for mercy. The streets had taught her that much.

Once she was strapped down, the two men wheeled her quickly through a disorienting series of corridors, until she arrived at a brightly-lit room that smelled of chill and disinfectant. There were two people there waiting for her.

One was a white man in his forties. He wore an expensive three-piece grey suit and looked to Ellie like a lawyer, one of those irritable important people who had inhabited the fringes of her world in the days when she'd been a good citizen. He was frightening, but his companion scared her even more—a short dumpy woman with mouse-colored hair wearing a rumpled lab coat, sneakers, and jeans. She had the pasty complexion of someone who spent all their time locked away from the sun. The woman's eyes were the flat pale blue of the winter sky, and there was no humanity in them.

"Well, this is an improvement over chimps," the man in the suit said. His companion smiled thinly and ignored him.

"Hello, Ellie," she said. "I'm Jeanette Campbell. Do you know why you're here?"

"Oh, for God's sake, Campbell. You don't need to talk to her," the man snarled.

"Of course I do, Robert. That's the whole point of this, isn't it? Lab rats that can talk? If you want data from her, she's going to need a context."

Campbell turned back to Ellie, coming closer to the side of the gurney. Elkanah and Angel had backed away like respectful servants, going to stand beside the door.

"When you were brought in here, you had cancer, and you were addicted to something. What was it?"

"P-Percodan," Ellie managed to stammer. Her mouth felt dry as salt.

"Okay. Percodan's a good drug. Highly effective, highly addictive. But you haven't had any in about four days. How do you feel now?"

"I feel—oh, *please,* let me go! I haven't done anything!" Ellie pleaded, hating herself for begging when she already knew it would change nothing.

"But you *have* done something, Ellie. You've contributed to Science. You see, when you were first brought in, you were given an experimental drug. And now you don't have cancer any more. And you don't need Perc. And we want to know what happened to you. So we're going to give you some more of what we gave you before— intravenously this time. And I want you to tell me everything about what happens to you then."

"If I— If I do that, will you let me go? I won't tell anybody about this, I promise, oh, just let me go, please, let me out of here and I'll never tell, I *swear*—"

"Now, Ellie." Campbell's voice was remote, faintly chiding. "You know we aren't going to let you go. But you don't have any place to go anyway. That's why we picked you. If you cooperate you'll be well treated for the rest of your life. That's more than you could expect on the streets."

But I'm well now! I have my life back! Helplessly, Ellie began to struggle against the straps. Campbell reached into her pocket and produced a needle and a bottle of milky fluid. She swabbed down Ellie's arm with cool efficiency and began probing for a vein.

"How do you know you'll get the same effect with an injection?" Robert said.

"I don't." Campbell sounded almost amused. "What I do know is that this will work faster and more of the drug will reach the brain. And that's sort of the whole point here, wouldn't you say?"

The needle stabbed into Ellie's arm with a lancing pain that seemed to strike at the roots of her soul. Eyes tight shut, she could only moan in protest as Campbell gently squeezed the plunger home, injecting the drug directly into her bloodstream. She felt a rush of warmth so intense it was as if she'd been lowered into a hot bath, and when she tried to open her eyes again, she couldn't.

Once Ellie passed out from the drug, Jeanette glued contact pads to her temples. Their wires led to an electro-encephalograph—an EEG—and instantly the displays lit up, displaying the rhythms of deepest sleep, a sleep verging on coma.

"What do we do now?" Robert asked edgily. "Wait six hours for her to wake up?"

Jeanette leaned back against the counter, watching the green waves of Alpha, Beta, Gamma, and Delta roll across the EEG display behind Ellie's head. Something was happening there, down inside where she couldn't see.

"It should go faster this time," she said absently. "And I gave her twice the dose. What I want to know is, what's she going to be able to do when she wakes up?"

Less than fifteen minutes later, Ellie's eyes opened. She stared around herself wildly, as if she'd forgotten where she was.

"Ellie?" Jeanette leaned over her.

She saw Ellie's eyes widen, as if she were seeing things no one else could. Jeanette reached out to touch her forehead, and in that moment a *pulse*—Jeanette had no other word for the sensation— passed between them.

Jeanette recoiled, and suddenly realized that the nagging headache she'd been fighting since she got up this morning was gone as if it had never existed. "Robert," she said thoughtfully, "come over here. Touch Ellie."

"Why?" Robert said suspiciously.

"It's an experiment." *Because you've got an ulcer and I want to see what happens.*

He did as he was told, clasping her wrist above the strap, then jerking away as if he'd been burned. "What the hell?"

"I bet your ulcer isn't bothering you now," Jeanette said sweetly. Robert shot her a narrow look, not pleased.

"My headache's gone, too. It makes sense. Ellie, what do you feel?"

"Hurt," the woman moaned, in a tranced, petulant voice. "It hurts. I can't let it."

"First she heals herself. Now she can heal others," Robert said thoughtfully. His eyes were alight with a dangerous fervor. "We have to test this." He turned to the waiting guards. "Go find Dr. Ramchandra. Bring him here."

❈❈ ❈❈ ❈❈

He could not wake himself up—and worse, he'd lost all control over the dream. Helplessly, Eric's dream self pushed on through the forest, surrounded by slinking red-eyed shapes out of nightmare and the Chaos Lands. Where he was going   and what would happen when he got there—were questions he found himself unable to answer, and that powerlessness fed a sort of angry fear.

This isn't right. I'm dreaming and I know it. Why can't I wake up?

At last the unchanging forest of stark bonelike trees began to thin. Eric found himself drifting to a halt at the edge of a clearing. The open space ahead was perfectly round, and the bone trees that circled it gave it the appearance of some sort of temple. The floor of the clearing was carpeted with a silvery moss, as thick and smooth as an expensive carpet, and at one end of the clearing was the first artificial thing Eric had seen in this tulgy wood—the back of an enormous throne, its high back blocking the occupant (if any) from Eric's sight.

The strange throne was as black as the trees, and seemed at the same time to be both insubstantial and terribly solid, as if perhaps it were forged from something alive that hadn't finished growing yet. Eric knew now that this dream was a message, a warning—but of what? And from whom?

Or was it a trap that had somehow penetrated Guardian House's defenses instead? The fear he'd begun to feel when he lost control of the dream blossomed into outright panic. As he struggled to wake, the throne began to turn, slowly, so that in moments Eric would be brought face to face with its occupant. Somehow, Eric knew that would be a disaster of an even greater magnitude than his present situation, one that he must avert at all costs.

With all his strength he called upon the Bardic Gift within him, setting the bright humanity of his music against this ghostly moribund wood of silver and shadows. He built in his mind an image of his own safe bedroom in Guardian House, its walls garlanded with the invisible wards of familiarity and good wishes.

You have no power over me! I reject you! I dismiss you! Go AWAY!

It worked.

Eric struggled upright in his own familiar bed, gasping with relief. Not a trap, not a warning, it had been a particularly vivid nightmare, nothing more after all. He stared around at the walls of the familiar bedroom, imprinting its images on his mind, forcing himself to breathe deeply and slowly, banishing fright. It was still night outside. Despite the fact that he seemed to have spent hours in the dream-wood, he'd probably only been asleep for a few minutes.

Can't sleep after that. He flung back the covers and swung his legs out over the side of the bed. His feet sank into the fluffy flokati rug and he wriggled his toes appreciatively. He remembered that sometimes in the old days, Bethie'd had nightmares like this (though nothing, a small voice inside told him, could be quite like this), and when she had, they tended to come in chains that destroyed a whole night's sleep. Elizabet had always said that the best thing to do was make a clean break with the dreaming state— get up, move around, have a cup of tea, connect with the waking world—before trying to sleep again.

Tea sounded like a good idea right now. He wondered if Greystone were still in the living room. Maybe the gargoyle would like a cup as well.

Eric had left the curtains open when he went to bed, hoping that the morning sun would wake him before he slept the day away. As he headed for the kitchen, he glanced casually back that way, wondering if it was raining outside. There was an odd glow shining in; probably the reflection of one of the skyscrapers off the clouds. . . .

It wasn't.

He ran to the window and stared out, unable to believe what he was seeing. New York was gone.

No, not gone. Worse. Blasted to rubble, the twisted remains of the familiar Upper West Side buildings looking like the Judgment Day aftermath of nuclear war.

And out of their midst, a glowing tower, impossibly tall, rose in evil triumph over the ruined city. He felt a wrenching shock—

And then there was brightness, and Eric was struggling against something that wrapped him in inexorable, unbreakable bonds. . . .

Eric awoke again—this time for real. The sun was high in the sky—that was the light—and he was wrapped tightly in the sweat-soaked bedsheets that had wound around him during his nocturnal struggles.

A dream. It had all been a dream, the weirdwood forest and his first awakening. Still gasping with the dream-induced panic, Eric struggled free of his bedclothes and ran to the window. All was as it should be. Everything was normal—wintery trees and pale December sky. No devastation. No dark elven tower raised by Unseleighe power to rule over what was left of the New York skyline.

Unsteady with relief, he staggered back to the bed and sat down heavily, waiting for his heartbeat to slow from its frantic racing. The dream and its aftermath of false waking faded, its insistent nightmare reality becoming less urgent by the moment. He was safe. New York was safe.

But if Toni and the others saw—felt—anything like my dream, no wonder they're all out running around trying to round up the unusual suspects.

But had they? Did the dream—vision, premonition, whatever—have anything to do with whatever was alerting the Guardians? Or was it a message meant for him alone?

Of course, like Freud says, sometimes a cigar is just a cigar.

The joke fell flat, even in his own mind. Whatever it was that had happened to him, Eric couldn't afford to just shrug it off. In the world of elven magic that he lived in, such things were never just innocent nighttime fantasies ralphed up by the collective unconscious. They were warnings—even if the warning came muddled and coded in symbols he couldn't decipher just yet.

He'd have to pass on Dharinel's warning to one of the Guardians as soon as he could, and do his level best to convince the Guardians this was something really serious. Somehow Eric knew that *that* wasn't going to be a lot of fun.

The trouble was, the employees of Threshold were a generally healthy bunch. All Dr. Ram could come up with to test Ellie on were some mild allergies, a cold, a few strained muscles.

At Jeanette's insistence, they'd unstrapped Ellie's chest and legs and raised the back of the gurney up into a sitting position: Ellie could hardly escape, and her new powers seemed to have no aggressive capabilities. In the face of human pain—or even mild distress—Ellie could do nothing but react, healing the injured party as quickly as possible. She seemed entirely without the capacity of self-preservation, a totally vulnerable creature.

It'd be funny if it weren't so flaming annoying. I finally get a lab rat who CAN talk, and she won't say anything! If Ellie Borden had any insight into the process that had gifted her with these powers, she was doing a good job of keeping it to herself. In fact, the second dose of T-Stroke seemed to have reduced her to little more than an animal . . . an animal who could work miracles.

Robert was insistent that they find something that could really challenge Ellie, and they lucked out with one of the lab techs— Donaldson had spilled industrial solvent all over his arm the previous week. Fortunately he was at his desk, within easy reach, so Jeanette sent the two guards up to escort him down to the Lab. When Dr. Ram unbandaged his arm down there in the lab, the ulcerated skin was purple and weeping, an ugly sight. If Donaldson hadn't been such a Type-A control freak, he'd have been home on medical rest with an injury like that.

As soon as he'd come through the door Ellie had started to whimper and reach for him. Jeanette was fascinated. The girl reacted to the presence of the sufferers as if someone were jabbing her with a red-hot poker—as if, in fact, she felt their pain more keenly than they did.

There was a word for that, Jeanette knew. Empathy. But what Ellie had was light-years beyond healing touch. Whatever was wrong, she fixed it. When they brought Donaldson over to her, all Ellie had to do was touch him, not even near the injury, and within seconds the skin on his arm was pink and healed.

"What's all this?" The tech looked bewildered, staring from Ellie to the healthy new skin on his arm.

"Just an experiment in Healing Touch," Jeanette said quickly. Donaldson was a good soldier. He wouldn't ask questions. "You've been a great help. My department will get in touch with you later about filling out an incident report. It'd be great if you kept this to yourself until then, okay?" With an arm around his shoulders, she urged Donaldson from the lab and back into the arms of the Security who'd walk him back to his own turf. There'd be some gossip, she knew, but it wouldn't go far. Threshold's corporate culture didn't encourage idle gossip about its projects.

"This is great—great," Robert muttered, ignoring the byplay with Donaldson completely. "How much more can she do?"

"Do you want me to shoot someone so you can find out?" Jeanette asked, closing the door behind the tech.

She saw Robert start to agree, then catch himself. Yes, Robert would like that just fine, but Jeanette suspected it would play hell with employee loyalty.

Just then she had an idea.

"Does anybody know where Lawanda is? She ought to be here now. One of you guys," she said to the hovering Security. "Go get her."

Lawanda Dupre was Jeanette's personal charity case. She had terminal ovarian cancer, and had come to Threshold through one of Robert's other test programs—Jeanette didn't know where he'd found her and had never actually cared enough to ask. When the test had run its course, Robert was going to cut her loose, but something about the woman had struck a spark in the wasteland of Jeanette's soul, and she'd offered to continue running a private test program of her own with Lawanda, strictly under the radar. She was the one who'd come up with the idea of Lawanda working as a cleaning lady in the Black Labs, and Robert had no complaints of the arrangement.

Neither did Lawanda. Without the morphine, heroin, and methamphetamine cocktail Jeanette provided, she'd be lying somewhere in a welfare bed, dying in agony. With the twice-daily injection, she was still able to work. Robert thought the research might be a way to produce another kind of super-soldier: impervious to pain, oblivious to wounds. Jeanette didn't really care. Treating

Lawanda was one of the few things she did at Threshold that made her actually feel good about herself.

There was no denying that the drugs Jeanette gave her shortened the woman's life. But they improved its quality, and let her die with dignity. That was more important, though Jeanette knew the FDA would hardly agree.

After a short wait, Angel appeared, herding Lawanda before him. The woman moved at a painfully slow shuffle. She was in her early forties, and looked sixty. The injections could mask the symptoms, but all the drugs in the world couldn't cure the disease.

Ellie began to moan and keen before Lawanda had even gotten all the way into the room. Interesting. Jeanette knew that the cleaning woman was in very little pain—if any—but Ellie seemed to feel the presence of the cancer itself, not the pain of its victim.

"Did you want me for something, Dr. Campbell? It isn't time for my shot yet. You aren't going to stop those, are you?" Lawanda asked anxiously.

"No, Lawanda. Of course not. We just want to try something new in addition to the shot. It won't hurt, I promise you. I just want you to come over here and let Ellie touch you."

Lawanda Dupre laughed cynically. "You trying faith healing on me now, Doctuh Campbell?"

"Maybe." Jeanette smiled. "Just come over here."

Ellie strained against the restraints that still held her to the bed, reaching out toward Lawanda. The older woman approached her cautiously. "Sistah, what are you doing here?"

"Let me—just let me—please, it hurts so much," Ellie groaned. Her hand darted out, fastening over Lawanda's emaciated wrist like a clamp.

There was a sudden spark where the two women's flesh met, an ozone-like tang in the air. Lawanda's face had gone slack, as if in a sudden rush of ecstasy, while Ellie's was contorted like that of a saint seeing God. Everything but Lawanda had ceased to exist for Ellie. That much was plain. But what did that *mean*?

"Something's happening," Robert said in a low excited voice.

"No force, Sherlock," Jeanette muttered back. Whatever was

happening now, it was on a much greater scale than the previous healings. This time, Ellie's struggle was something Jeanette could almost see—a palpable force conjured into the little room.

Jeanette tore her gaze from the tableau of the two women and looked at the clock. The long red second hand swept magisterially around the dial. A minute passed. Ninety seconds. Longer than any of the previous healings.

There was a faint groan from the bed. Ellie fell back, limp, releasing Lawanda's hand. The cleaning woman staggered away from her, blinking in astonishment. Jeanette could see that Lawanda's eyes were clear, the yellow tint gone from the corneas. She looked years younger, and even stood straighter.

"Lord have mercy! I— What did she *do*, Dr. Campbell?"

"I don't know," Jeanette said slowly. Ellie had healed Lawanda— but how? Cellular degeneration at that level couldn't be reversed. This wasn't like the burn—not a case of speeding up what the body had the power to do anyway.

This was a genuine, bonafide miracle.

Or to put it another way, Jeanette had just seen magic. Real magic.

Robert made an impatient gesture, and Angel stepped forward again to usher Lawanda from the room. She went quietly, glancing back a few times at the woman on the bed.

Ellie still didn't move. Filled with a sudden awful suspicion, Jeanette moved over to the gurney. Gingerly, she reached out to touch the girl.

Ellie's skin was already cold to the touch, and the skin beneath the blue coverall lay slack over withered flesh. There was no pulse.

"She's dead." And oddly, the realization gave Jeanette a faint pang of guilt.

"Well, hell." There was only self-centered regret in Robert's voice.

SEVEN:
LIGHTNING IN A SIEVE

Aerune hated the Iron City, hated the World Above, hated the Mortal Kind, even as he planned to bend it and them to his will and his vengeance. His flesh crawled in the presence of the ferrous metal that the humans filled their world with, diminishing his powers considerably and making the use of magic an uncertain thing. But there were some prizes worth any amount of suffering, and the ability to own the Gift of a human Bard was one. Urla had told him that somewhere within this city mortals who lacked the Gift were given it. Now Aerune wanted to see for himself.

The cloak of silk and shadow that concealed him from mortal eyes also gave him some protection from the iron that clogged the very air, but he could not long remain here without dwindling away to a wraith. Some elven gifts, however, were not hampered by the world the mortals had fashioned for themselves. A darker shadow among the shadows, Aerune sifted through the minds within the building known as Threshold Labs.

Once he had the power to open his own Nexus, he could spend as much power as he needed to in shaping this city to his ends,

164

conjure serpents and nightmares to feed upon its populace. At the hem of his cloak, even now, a faceless chittering mob of his servitors waited to do his bidding.

At first he found only deception and fear, which pleased him, though the first minds he touched held only small malice. But though they knew little, they knew there were secrets to find, and so, patiently, Aerune sifted through their witless babble.

At last he found what he sought. A mind dark and fragrant with overreaching ambition and sublime cruelty: *Robertlintel.* Through this mind, Aerune learned of an elixir which could wake the dreaming spark of magic in mortal hearts, raise the Power that Urla had told him of and make mortals into living Nexuses. Aerune learned with approval and delight of *Robertlintel's* adventures in discovery—how the elixir had killed or maddened all but two upon whom it was tried, one of whom had died by his own hand, and yet this mortal lordling still persevered. He meant to spread his drug throughout the streets of this city, and harvest for his own any who displayed the Mage-gift.

But that cannot be. Such useful mortals are mine.

Drawing upon his power, Aerune summoned all those creatures of his Dark Court who had the power to walk these streets: the gaunts and boggins, the redcaps and phookas, trolls, goblins, Bane-Sidhe, all the dark fellowship of the Unseleighe Court, those creatures twined closer to mortal man than any lover, for Man was their prey.

"Go," Aerune said to his followers. "Follow those who go from this place with the Mage-elixir. Find those in whom the Power kindles brightly, and bring them to me, for they are mine. Feast as you will, slay whom you will, so long as you succeed in this one thing."

There was a swirling in the air as the infernal host Aerune had gathered about himself vanished to their task. The business of following a handful of men through a city of teeming millions was a simple one to creatures with powers such as they possessed. No one of the human lordling's minions would escape their hunters, nor would any to whom they gave the elixir be overlooked. Aerune turned his attention back to the curdled minds within the building's walls.

Robertlintel's alchemist now administered her elixir to the last survivor for the second time, and Aerune relished the victim's despair, as well as the more subtle bouquet of emotions in the mind of the alchemist. The power the elixir had woken was one of healing, and Aerune watched as, ignorant of the necessities of the gifts that had been woken so powerfully into life within her, *Ellieborden* let herself be sent down into death by the mortal lord and his minion.

Aerune smiled, reconciled to the discomfort of the Iron City by the sight of the triumph almost within his grasp. The children had broken their toy. That was good. Because like all children, they would soon want a new one. . . .

His day having been thoroughly spoiled for him by his unsettling nightmare and the prospect of explaining things to Toni Hernandez, Eric moped around the house until he realized that was what he was doing, then went for a walk. He tried Toni's door on the way out, but she was still out, or else not answering it.

When he hit the street, the cold was a shock, and he slitted his eyes against the light. The raw December day at least gave him something else to focus on besides the assignment still lying undone on his desk. The end of the semester was in two weeks, and the coursework was piling up with all the time he'd been spending on rehearsals. He was going to have a lot to keep him busy over the next fortnight.

And after that? His imagination shied away from the thought of the holidays like a skittish colt. For too many years, Christmas had been a cheap apartment and an expensive bottle: a holiday that everyone else but him seemed to celebrate with their families, whether biological or otherwise. Eric hadn't seen his own parents since the day he'd left home, and for years he hadn't felt any lack there. But the sense of unfinished business that had brought him back to Juilliard was tugging at him there, too, and he knew that sometime soon he was going to have to work up the courage to face the last of his personal demons. *One way or another.*

He still had the next month to get through first, though. Christmas . . . alone again. For a time, Kory and Beth had changed all that, though neither Christmas in hiding nor Christmas Underhill was anything like a Charles Dickens novel, the Sidhe having no concept of Christmas and very little of seasonal festivals. He *could* go back to Underhill for the holidays, but managing the temporal transitions back and forth from here to Underhill with any degree of temporal accuracy was often difficult; if he went to visit Beth and Kory in Elfhame Misthold over the holidays, he had no guarantee that he'd be back before Groundhog Day.

And this is something I've got to do on my own, or I might as well just chuck it now and go back to Underhill for good. That meant Christmas alone once more, and it was surprising how much it hurt. No wonder the suicide rate went up in December.

None of which solved his even more immediate problems. Seeing Ria at the Winter Concert seemed as if it had happened a million years ago, not last night, and somehow, she—or her doppelganger—didn't seem like quite so urgent a problem in the face of astral sojourns to the Night Lands, an invading elf-lord, and a bunch of wizards on Yellow Alert.

He rambled down familiar streets, past Korean groceries, Italian delis, boutiques and antique stores. The streets were full of his neighbors—as much as any place in New York could be said to be a neighborhood—and if the faces weren't familiar, the dogs were. Everybody in New York seemed to have dogs—he saw the woman with the three enormous German Shepherds (all bouncing around and tangling their leashes together), the professional dog-walker managing two Great Danes and half a dozen little fur-balls with ease and efficiency, and the man in the grey suit who walked his Himalayan cat twice a day. Eric stopped to greet her; she sniffed his fingers with ladylike disdain before continuing on her way.

New York is really like a village, I guess. A really big village with about twelve million people in it. A few thousand years ago there weren't that many people on the entire planet. There hasn't been a city this big and this complex since the time of Ancient Rome.

But Rome was long gone, and if he were a pessimist, Eric would think that New York was going the same way. In his dream, there'd been nothing left but ashes . . . and the goblin tower.

Don't think about that. It was a dream, nothing more.

The walk cleared his head, and after an hour or so he turned conscientiously back toward Guardian House. He decided to stop along the way to pick up a peace offering—though why he should feel the need to make peace with Toni was something he didn't really understand.

Maybe I feel guilty for adding one more thing to her workload? I know this Unseleighe Lord isn't my fault, but sometimes it seems that wherever I go, trouble follows.

He spotted a familiar sign on the street ahead, and turned toward it. Sanctuary. And a chance to warm up—he'd gotten thoroughly chilled on his ramble.

Bread Alone was one of Eric's favorite places in his new neighborhood. It had the look and feel of one of those old Lower East Side neighborhood bakeries from the turn of the century, the kind of place where you could stop in for coffee and a bagel and to catch up on neighborhood gossip, with a painted pressed-tin ceiling, black and white marble floor, and a few antique cast-iron tables and chairs nestled into the corners.

He'd just walked inside and taken a deep lungful of the warm heady vanilla-and-baking-bread smell when a familiar voice hailed him.

"Well, if it isn't the Pied Piper."

Eric turned toward the voice. Jimmie Youngblood was sitting at one of the tables, a large styrofoam container of coffee in front of her. She was off-duty, dressed casually in jeans and a black leather jacket worn over a plain white T-shirt. She waved him over, smiling.

"Haven't seen you since the party," she said when he'd sat down. "How are you settling in?"

"Some days are better than others," Eric admitted. "I never realized how much time and energy school can take up. It's different when you're a kid, I guess."

She studied him critically. Though her flawless bronze complexion was more forgiving than lighter skin might be, Eric could see that Jimmie was tired—bone tired.

"You're not much more than a kid yourself," she said. "Or are you using a little of that Bardic Magic to shave a few years off?"

"I'm older than I look," Eric admitted cheerfully. "At least inside. And I'm starting to think that's where it counts. If your body's twenty-five and your mind . . . isn't, the mind is what counts, I guess."

"Ain't it the truth," Jimmie admitted with a long sigh. "Double-shifts and all-nighters were a lot easier when I was twenty. Places like this . . . I come here to re-charge. Look around. Have you noticed that everyone's happy here?"

Eric looked around the tiny bakery. Jimmie was right. The girl behind the counter, the older man (probably her father) transferring pastries from the cooling racks to the case, the patrons waiting patiently for their orders to be filled, even the Gothamites seated at the other tables with morning papers and breakfast, all looked contented.

"Maybe it's the Christmas spirit?" he suggested.

Jimmie grimaced. "Christmas spirit is overrated. Take it from someone who's on the streets eight hours a day. No, this place is like this year round. It sounds kind of stupid and New Age, but this is a happy place."

"You're right," Eric said with surprise. He'd found places like this in the human world before, but they'd usually been places touched by at least a hint of Sidhe enchantment. He lowered his shields cautiously and took a peek, but found no trace of elven magic here, only the happy contentment of people honestly enjoying simple pleasures. "I guess that's one of the reasons I ended up here today."

"Rough week?" Jimmie said sympathetically. "I know you had that concert thing last night. How did that go?"

Eric thought back to the hot lights and the watchful audience, remembered the soaring feeling of *rightness* as he wrapped them all up in his music, the joy of playing with an ensemble of talented musicians. There was no way to put those feelings into words. It almost made up for the downer the reception had been.

"It was okay," he said with a bashful smile. "What really gets me, though, is how people can start out in music because it's something they love, and then forget why they did it. Something they loved just becomes a grind—a duty. It's like they twist all the joy out of it."

"Way of the world, my friend," Jimmie said. "When I started out on the Force— Look, I'm up for another round—let me get you some coffee and something to go on with. You look like you could use it." Before he could answer, she got to her feet and headed over to the counter.

I wonder what she was going to say? Eric thought. One thing that Beth—who'd been Wiccan for as long as Eric had known her—and the Elvenmage Dharinel both agreed on was that there were no coincidences, especially for those who were the least bit sensitive to magic. The more you attuned yourself to the invisible currents of Power that underlay everything, the more you moved in harmony with them. *And the more you end up in places like this, having coffee with your fellow magicians.* Though it was hard to remember that Jimmie—practical, down-to-earth, New York street cop that she was—was a magician as powerful as any in Underhill. A line from one of his favorite Gilbert and Sullivan operettas came back to him suddenly: *"Things aren't always what they seem/Skim milk masquerades as cream . . ."*

A few minutes later Jimmie was back, balancing two tall containers of coffee and a couple of Danishes wrapped in bakery paper. They were still warm from the oven.

"I got you decaf, because of what you said at the party about not drinking coffee much any more because the Sidhe can't tolerate it."

"You're right there," Eric said. "Before I met Kory, I couldn't even get up in the morning without that first cup, now I hardly ever touch the stuff. Caffeine in any form acts like the worst kind of drug for them—like a combination of cocaine and LSD. If you're ever having problems with a mad elf-lord, just pitch a can of Coke at him."

"I'll remember that," Jimmie said, sounding tiredly amused. "You never know; it might come up. But they roast and grind their own beans here. It's a special blend—you won't miss the caffeine. And Papa Lombardi only makes these pastries at Christmas. It'd be a crime to miss them."

She handed one to Eric. The golden crust was fragrant with almond and cinnamon, and when he bit into it, Eric could taste citrus and currants as well. His stomach awoke with a growl, reminding him he'd missed breakfast by several hours, and he had to restrain himself from wolfing the whole thing in a few bites. He set the pastry down and took a sip of the coffee. As Jimmie had promised, it was rich and fragrant. No sugar, but it didn't really need any.

"Oh, man," Eric said, around another mouthful of pastry. "This is heaven!"

"When you're out on the front lines, it's important to remember the little pleasures. Without them, sometimes we forget who we are," Jimmie said gravely.

"Do you have that problem often?" Eric asked. He hadn't meant to ask such a direct question—it seemed almost hostile—but Jimmie didn't seem to mind. She smiled gently.

"I've lost my way a few times," she said. "Even after I became a Guardian. I've seen too many good people go down into the belly of the beast and not come out again. Out here—on the streets—every day good people die, and bad people walk away smiling. And sometimes there's nothing you can do about it."

"Is that why you became a Guardian?" Eric asked.

"That's why I became a *cop*," Jimmie said, correcting him gently. "Being a Guardian came after—sort of a natural extension of the badge, don't you know? When I was a kid, I always wanted to grow up to be Batman. Well, sometimes I wanted to be the Green Hornet, but usually it was Batman. Fight crime and evil, always come out on top. It didn't hurt that my dad and my—my brother were both cops. I just sort of always knew this was where I'd end up. Not the Guardian part, of course."

"Do your folks still live around here?" Eric asked idly, still thinking about Christmas.

Jimmie sighed and shook her head. "Dad caught a bullet about fifteen years back. El—my brother, well, we kind of lost touch. A long time ago."

Even through his shields, Eric could feel the flare of raw pain when Jimmie talked about her brother. She'd said he'd been a cop, and she hadn't said he was dead. But a lot of things could happen, some of them worse than being dead.

"I'm sorry," Eric said, meaning it.

"Don't be. He made his choice, and I made mine. You can't undo the past. But I didn't mean to bring you down. When you walked in here, you looked like you'd lost your last friend."

"Not quite," Eric said. *More like I remembered how few of them there were.* "I had kind of a rough night, and so I went out for a walk this morning to try to clear my head. And from the look of things, I'm not the only one who had a rough night."

"Can't put anything over on you, can we, Banyon?" Jimmie asked with a rueful smile. "Actually I haven't been to bed yet—Toni and I were chasing around the city all night like Starsky and Hutch because of some stuff, and I'm back on shift in another few hours. I do hate working nights. City gets crazy then. It's like it turns into a whole 'nother place, you know?"

You don't know the half of it . . . or do you? Eric thought.

"What kind of stuff?" he asked aloud. "I got—well, I don't know if you want to talk about it here. But I was going to try to get ahold of Toni. There's some things I need to tell her. But she was out when I came downstairs."

"Probably up in East Harlem, seeing if the *santeros* know anything about what's going down. You don't have to worry about talking here, Eric. I told you. This is one of the Good Places. And nobody's going to overhear our conversation unless I want them to. Sort of one of the fringe benefits of being a Guardian," Jimmie said.

"Okay." He liked Jimmie a lot—and more, he trusted her judgment. When you spent a lot of time on the street and the RenFaire circuit, you got to develop an instinct that helped you tell the good cops from the bad. And Jimmie was definitely one of the good ones.

"So shoot. What's got you walking the streets on a day like this?"

"Well . . . ." He was stalling, and he knew it. But one of the things that Dharinel had drummed into him during his magical training was that words had power, and it almost seemed to Eric that by telling Jimmie the problem he'd be making it more real than it had to be.

"I've already told Greystone most of it. And, well, it's a lot of different things. Some really personal. Some I've been told to stay out of at all costs."

"Too bad that's the kind of advice that nobody ever takes," Jimmie said. She sipped her coffee, and for a moment her eyes were cold and far away, focused on some secret pain. He noticed that whenever she was thinking intently, her black eyes lightened almost to yellow. It was a startling effect. "The good people . . . they always try to help. And sometimes they get killed. But that's what *I'm* here for. If anybody takes a bullet, it should be me. I chose to put myself on the line, knowing the risks ahead of time." She took a deep breath, consciously shutting away the pain. "But that's old news. Anyway, it's one of the reasons I'm kind of touchy about civilians on the fire-line, if you hadn't noticed already. Good people, who just want to help. But it's my job to protect them—even to take a bullet if I have to. They never asked to be in the kinds of situations I run into. All they want to do is live their lives. And it's my job to make sure they can. I don't want any more deaths on my conscience."

Eric met her gaze squarely, thinking of his own dead. Of the people who hadn't gotten out of the way in time when the magic got loose. Or—worse—had been dragged into situations by people who didn't care who they hurt.

"Understood," Eric said. "I don't like it either." He shook his head.

"Yeah," Jimmie said, with a long sigh. "Looks like you know how it is. I lost a partner once, a long time ago. Because my gun was loaded with silver bullets and his wasn't. Because I knew what we were chasing and I couldn't find any way to tell him that it wasn't his fight. Never again! I guess that's one of the reasons why I never married—though the old joke about being married to my work has some truth in it. What about you, Eric Banyon? Any hostages to fortune?"

"I guess not." The answer sounded wrong, and he examined it. "I have—I mean, I'm going to have—a daughter. But she isn't really mine. She's Beth and Kory's. They just can't have one together, so it's more like—I mean, she'll be theirs, not mine."

"No one else?" Jimmie asked.

Ria. "No. At least, not that I know of. I mean, other than everyone. I'm not going to walk away from a problem just because nobody I know is involved."

"Good answer. Or a bad one. Some things you've just got to walk away from, Eric. It hurts, and you feel horrible, but if you got involved all you could do would be to make things worse."

Eric shook his head stubbornly. On one level, he knew what she said was true, but in reality he didn't know if he had the detachment to just walk away from people in trouble.

"I'm not sure I could ever do that," he said slowly.

"Then be glad you're not a cop, because we have to do it every day," Jimmie said fiercely. "But I didn't mean to lecture you. You look just about all in."

"Bad night," Eric said. "One of the worst, actually, but not really relevant to the business at hand." Once more he hesitated about conveying Dharinel's warning. He'd told Greystone. Surely that was enough?

Thinking like that is what gets people killed, Eric told himself roughly.

"Anyway, here's the deal. I talked to Greystone when I got home last night. He said you were having kind of a situation, but I didn't know about that until I got home from the concert. Before that, I got a warning from my friends that they wanted me to pass on to you."

"A warning?" Jimmie asked, suddenly alert. "For me by name?"

"No. For the Guardians. In general. Dh—my teacher seems to know a lot about you folks. Anyway, he said this was your kind of problem, something that you were equipped to handle. He didn't tell me much, but I'll give you all the help I can. Apparently, Manhattan Island is one of those places that Sidhe just don't go. Only last night I heard that an Unseleighe Lord—that's one of the Dark Sidhe, and pretty much bad juju all the way around—is planning to move in and take over here. They say he's going to try to open a Nexus to Underhill here in New York City. If he can do it, he'll have quite a lot of power to play with, and from everything I've heard the Unseleighe Sidhe tend to play pretty rough. My friends said I should warn the Guardians, let them handle it."

"That's what we're here for," Jimmie said with a sigh. She held her cup near her face, inhaling the steam. "And since you've been so open with me, I'll pass on a little information in return. The reason we were out last night is that a bunch of people are turning up dead—street people. More than usual, even in this weather, and all with something kind of . . . funny about them. Paul thinks it might be a case of serial possession, but it doesn't quite feel right for that. And then there was this kind of . . . blippy thing. Like somebody was powering up and then just . . . stopping. Kind of hard to figure out—not really like anything any of us has seen before, and if Paul can't pull a parallel out of his books or the Internet, it's got to be some kind of really exotic mojo. So we were trying to run down leads half the night, and coming up with nothing. This helps a lot. Now we know one of the things we should be looking for." She finished her coffee with a flourish and tucked the last bite of pastry into her mouth.

"The important thing from your point of view, I guess, is that my guy's going to be trying to get his hands on anyone with Power to draw on them to build the Nexus, and my teacher thinks that means he's going to be going after humans with the Gift, but from what you're saying, what you folks were following doesn't sound like Sidhe work. Even if he does have a way to find the Gifted, he'd have to drain—kill—thousands, maybe millions, of ordinary people to get enough power to open a Gate here, and I know it sounds awful to say, but that's just too much like gruntwork for their tastes. And . . . the other thing is, last night I ran into an old friend. Only I don't know for sure whether she was there or not—and if she *was* there, I'm not sure what she wants—or if she's tied up with him."

Briefly Eric sketched the details of Ria Llewellyn's appearance and disappearance from the concert, explaining that while it wasn't impossible for Ria to have been there—or for her appearance to have been a coincidence—he wasn't completely sure of what it might mean.

"It's just that she's, well—ruthless. And pretty self-involved. She isn't the type to count casualties if you get in her way."

"Sounds like a real executive type," Jimmie commented. "But not like the type who'd want to be a street soldier for someone else from all you've said about her. At least from what you say there isn't already a local Nexus, so she isn't likely to be out there trying to buy it up to bulldoze it. Not that anybody'd notice if she did. This is New York, after all, the land of Donald Trump and combat-strength urban renewal."

"Yeah. I'd kinda figured that out for myself." Eric thought about telling Jimmie about his dream, and hesitated. Just what could he say? He'd had a vision? A premonition? A guided tour of a place that he wasn't sure existed outside his own mind? He knew it had been a warning, but the Guardians were already on alert, and he'd passed on Dharinel's warning. They wouldn't be any more careful just because he told them he'd dreamed of a New York in ruins, presided over by a baleful elvish tower.

And Greystone hadn't sounded any warning when he'd had the dream. That was the main thing. So whatever had been the source of his dream, it hadn't come from outside Guardian House.

Or Greystone hadn't considered it a threat. . . .

"Well, I just thought I'd mention, and to let you know that if there was anything I could do to help out," Eric said hesitantly.

"No!" Jimmie said, too quickly. "I mean, you're a nice guy, Eric, and a helluva magician from what Greystone tells me, but you didn't come to New York to join the Guardians and fight evil. You know what they say about old age and treachery overcoming youth and skill? We've got a few tricks up our sleeve that'll probably come as quite a shock to somebody from the Old Country," she said, sounding just a bit pleased with herself.

"And most of all, if four Guardians need help, Eric, the people of New York are in more trouble than we thought. But I'll pass the word to the others," Jimmie said, smiling at him. "Maybe the two cases'll end up tying in together. Sometimes they do. But I hope not." She glanced down at her watch, and got to her feet in a hurry. "Aiee! Two o'clock already and I'm on duty at four—that leaves me just about enough time to get downtown and get suited up." She held out her hand, and Eric took it, standing as well. "I've enjoyed this, Eric. It isn't that often I can find somebody to talk to. You know how it is."

"Me, too," Eric said. "Meanwhile, I've got a paper to write, and I guess ought to be writing it. Thanks for the coffee. And the conversation."

"We'll do this again," Jimmie promised.

"It's a date," Eric answered warmly.

He walked the few blocks back to his apartment in a far better mood than he'd been in when he left it. Jimmie Youngblood was definitely a nice lady and a good cop, and Eric hoped he'd be able to see more of her. Not romantically—Jimmie'd made it clear she wasn't looking for anything like that—but as a friend. How many people were there, after all, that he could talk about the magical part of his life with and have them accept it so matter-of-factly? Not many, and you could take that to the bank.

The phone was ringing as he opened the door to his apartment, and Eric dived for it without thought.

"Hello? Hello?" *Just my luck this will be someone trying to sell me aluminum siding or* The New York Times. . . .

"Eric? This is Ria Llewellyn."

Pure surprise held him speechless for a moment. He had almost managed to convince himself that the Ria he'd seen last night had been a ghost, some kind of illusion, or at the very least a non-recurring phenomenon. But the rich sultry sound of her contralto was like a blast of concentrated yesterday, whirling him back to his mooncalf idyll—in her home, in her bed—when she had tried to turn him from a knight to a pawn, nothing more than a reservoir of Power to be tapped . . . just as Perenor had meant her to be.

Or maybe into something more?

"Hello, Ria," Eric said, his voice slightly cool.

In her own way she had cared for him, Eric knew. Fought for him, tried to protect him, turned on her father in the end. For him? Or for her own freedom?

"'Hello, Ria,'" she echoed, her voice languidly mocking. "After all this time, that's all you have to say? I admit, I'd expected more."

"I saw you at the concert last night," Eric said flatly, still too rattled to dissemble. He'd managed to pick up a number of the courtly arts with which the Elvenborn wiled away their time Underhill, but the whole business of saying one thing while meaning another—all in the most elliptical fashion—had eluded him completely, to Kory and even Beth's amusement.

"You were very good," Ria said. "That solo piece at the end—your own work?—was most impressive. And all done without magic. That somehow makes it even more exceptional."

"You didn't call me up just to congratulate me," Eric said, sinking down into the chair in front of the stereo with the phone cradled on his lap.

"No. Not really. I called to see if you'd be my guest for dinner this evening."

There was a long silence. When Ria spoke again, her voice in his ear was just a shade less confident.

"Eric?"

"I'm still here." He was thinking fast, trying to figure out what she *meant,* not just what she was telling him. In all of his experience with Ria, she'd never been absolutely underhanded. She might try to influence him, overshadow his power with her own, but she wouldn't lure him into a blatant trap. "Yeah, sure. I'd love to." *Almost as much as I'd love to know what you're really up to, lady.* "Just let me know the time and place."

Candlemas was the new hot restaurant in the Triangle District. What had formerly been the Meat-Packing District was gentrifying rapidly, high-priced boutiques and luxury condos driving out the artists, drug dealers, and fetish clubs that had flourished here in low-rent days. The restaurant and its five-star CIA[5]-trained chef had recently been anointed by Gotham's reigning foodies, and as a result, even on this raw Saturday night

---

[5]Culinary Institute of America, Hyde Park, New York

there were people lined up halfway down the block waiting for tables.

Eric had dressed carefully for this meeting. Fashion was, after all, just another form of warfare . . . and if this wasn't precisely a war, it bore more than a passing resemblance to that gentle art. Back before he really knew what either Power or Bardcraft were, Ria'd frightened him into lashing out at her—and that had terrified them both. She'd seen him as an enemy and driven him away. He hadn't seen her again until Beth had broken a guitar over her head at the final battle, destroying Perenor's access to her power and gaining the day for the Sun-Descending elves.

And now she was back, pushing her way into his life once more. Why?

Like the man says about the afterlife: sooner or later you will KNOW. So let's see what the lady has to say for herself.

Ria must have been approaching their "reunion" in much the same spirit—why else pick a place like this to meet? A venue more calculated to put the old Eric nicely off-balance could hardly have been better chosen.

Too bad I'm not the same guy she used to know. Eric grinned wolfishly. Beneath his duster-length topcoat he was wearing one of the suits Beth had helped him choose—wild silk, in a shade just this side of true black, paired with a collarless linen shirt in a deep rich cream. Instead of a tie, he wore a small elvenmade brooch at his throat: silver, set with a large, almost transparent opal. A clasp of the same design held his hair back from his face.

Once, Eric would have completely distrusted such an outfit, seeing it as somehow dishonest. Now he wore it as if it were second nature, knowing fashion for what it was: a tool, nothing more.

Which is great. But how am I going to get past that crowd at the door or find Ria once I do? I could be standing out here for hours.

As he hesitated on the curb—the weather was bad enough that he'd come in a cab instead of bringing Lady Day—a man in a chauffeur's uniform came up to him.

"Mr. Banyon?"

"That's me," Eric said a little warily.

"Ms. Llewellyn's compliments, sir. She asked me to tell you to go on in. She's already seated."

"Thanks," Eric said. *If she wants to overawe me with an ostentatious display of wealth and power . . . well, let's say I appreciate the show.*

The chauffeur retreated to the fender of a glorious vintage maroon and cream Rolls Royce Silver Ghost—a stand-out ride even by New York standards—and Eric made his way to the door of Candlemas. Getting inside was a bit like swimming upstream to spawn, but he finally made it. The next obstacle was the official greeter, a slender black man who advanced upon Eric with an openly disdainful expression.

"Good evening, sir. Welcome to Candlemas. Do you have a reservation?"

"I'm joining someone," Eric said. "Ria Llewellyn?"

The man's demeanor changed at once from arrogance to subservience, though the change was so subtle as to qualify as magery in its own right.

"Yes sir. Right this way. May I have someone take your coat?"

Eric handed the garment over, and received a discreet coat-check token in return, before following the maitre d' farther into the restaurant.

The interior of Candlemas made no concessions to currently-voguish Manhattan industrial chic. Whatever this space had been last month, it now gave the impression of being an out-take from a particularly decadent Tuscan chateau. The lighting was fashionably low, and the walls were hung with a pleated, amber-colored velvet a few shades lighter than the deep-pile carpet. Gilt medallions anchored the fabric, and light spilled out from behind them in sunburst patterns, drawing a faint shimmer from the deep nap of the fabric. The velvet walls softened the ambient noise to a muted background, like ocean surf. The tables on the service floor were swathed in a creamy brocade and set far enough apart to give the diners at least the illusion of privacy.

Around the edge of the room there were half a dozen recessed alcoves, like the private boxes at the opera. They were even curtained to give the diners more privacy. Somehow Eric wasn't surprised to be escorted toward one of them. Ria always traveled first class.

She was waiting for him at the table. Her eyes widened slightly as she saw him, and Eric smiled to himself. He might have been Underhill, but time hadn't stood still for him . . . though it seemed to have for Ria. She was still the woman he'd first spotted in a crowd in L.A.—pale blond hair, cat-green eyes, ruthless mouth. Whatever injuries she'd suffered from her coma weren't evident tonight, and Eric looked carefully, his shields warily in place against any magic—though the magic Ria was deploying was of a far older and more fascinating sort.

She was wearing a dark-green dress with an old-fashioned portrait neckline, with a necklace of cloudy green stones around her throat—jade?—that only served to accentuate the flawless whiteness of her skin.

Eric felt his throat close in a purely masculine acknowledgement of her beauty. She was as fair and fey as the unfading moonlillies that bloomed in Underhill.

"Satisfied?" she asked, and Eric only just stopped himself from blushing. The maitre d' seated him, giving him a moment to recover.

"You've . . . changed," Ria said, favoring him with a sphinx-like smile.

"This is my cue to say you haven't. But I know you've got a mirror. And I remember that you hate people being obvious," Eric said boldly.

"I'm easily bored," Ria admitted, with a throaty mock-seductive purr in her voice. If you could put what she had in a bottle, Eric decided, there wouldn't be any reason for anybody to ever be lonely again.

"So—without being obvious—it's good to see you. You're obviously well." He was surprised to find that, when he spoke them, the words were true. Seeing Ria again was like . . . was like having the answer to a question he'd been asking for a very long time. "You gave me quite a start when I saw you in the audience last night. If you'd called ahead, I would've gotten you tickets."

"You concealed it admirably. Your performance was wonderful. Shall we order? Or would you like a drink first?"

There was a glass of white wine in front of her, in one of those huge tulip-shaped glasses that restaurants used for everything from Chardonnay to frozen daiquiris. Eric shook his head.

"Just water for me, thanks. Evian if they have it."

Ria raised an eyebrow, but made no comment. She must have signalled somehow, because a hovering waitperson instantly appeared to take Eric's drink order and bestow upon both of them leather-backed menus only slightly smaller than the surface of a coffee table.

"Have you eaten here before?" he asked, scanning the menu. Candlemas seemed to run to Continental Fusion fare—Eric hesitated over the medallions of venison with kiwi and mango, smirking faintly. But what the heck—if people wanted to put stuff like that in their bodies, at least it was better than drugs.

"No. My assistant suggested the place. These days, my idea of dining out is usually takeout at my desk. And I don't get to New York that often."

But you're here now, Ria. Why?

"There are a lot of good restaurants here," Eric said noncommittally. He decided on the chicken in balsamic vinaigrette as being a safe choice, one that wouldn't offer too many surprises. Ria would be surprise enough this evening.

"Oh, I don't deny that New York has its attractions. Some of the best schools in the world are here, for example."

Eric sipped at his water. If this was Ria's opening gambit, it was an awfully mild one. They both already knew he was attending Juilliard.

"Yes. I didn't appreciate it much the last time, but I think formal training has a lot to offer, don't you?"

Her eyes widened slightly as she took his double meaning. When they'd last clashed, Ria was an accomplished sorceress, and Eric barely knew what magic was. Now he was a Bard . . . and Ria had always been a political animal, raised amid Perenor's plotting. He didn't know what contacts with the elves she still had . . . or wanted.

In fact, he decided, they'd both changed a great deal. And suddenly it was very important to Eric to know who Ria had become.

"So, Tell me everything. How are Kayla and Elizabet?"

"Well, when last I saw them," Ria said, accepting the change of subject smoothly. "Kayla will be going away to school, soon. She won't have to worry about tuition—I'll see to that—but neither Elizabet nor I feel that the child needs a free ride through life. And she can't earn her living as a Healer. The medical establishment doesn't take kindly to people working miracles without a license. And Healers need a lot of downtime in order to function without burning out, so it isn't likely she's going to go for an M.D."

"Computer programming, maybe? Or web-designer?" Eric suggested, thinking of Paul Kern. If anyone needed a flexible schedule, it was a Guardian. "Those are both professions with a lot of built-in privacy. I've got a friend who could suggest some good places to study."

"We may take you up on that. I know she wants to come to New York. Says the San Fernando Valley's too quiet for her tastes."

Eric laughed, thinking of the scrappy little punkette he'd met at the Dunkin Donuts the morning of the battle for Elfhame Sun-Descending. A greater contrast with the stately, dignified Elizabet could hardly be imagined, but Elizabet's apprentice had the true Healer's gift—as well as more street-smarts than anyone Eric had ever known, and a tongue that could strip paint off a wall at sixty paces.

Now it was Ria's turn to change the subject, and she did, asking Eric about his work at Juilliard. Eric answered readily enough—he had nothing to hide in that regard, at least from Ria, and the two of them continued sparring verbally all through the meal—appetizer, salad, entree, and dessert. Without being evasive, Ria didn't talk about anything that really mattered—Eric gathered that she was essentially making a tour of her holdings, reconsolidating her position as head of LlewellCo after a long absence. But that hardly explained her appearance at Juilliard . . . or her dinner invitation.

"I was surprised to see you surface after so long," she finally admitted over coffee. Ria's half-human heritage saved her from the poisonous effects of caffeine on her system, and Eric had surprised her once again by ordering coffee himself. The hit of the unaccustomed caffeine made his heart race, giving him a feeling as if he were riding Lady Day down a very long straightaway.

"No reason I shouldn't," Eric said. That much was true: the Feds had always really been after Bethie, not him or Kory, and besides, the Eric Banyon they were looking for would be older than he was by enough years to fool a casual inspection, even if there were anyone working the case who still remembered him.

Not that he was completely convinced they'd been legitimate Feds in the first place. . . . "And as I said, I had some business here."

"The music school."

The next obvious question would have been why Eric, with Bardcraft at his command, would even bother with something so mundane as a Juilliard degree, but Ria didn't ask it. She hadn't asked any hard questions at all over the course of dinner, Eric realized. It was as if it were enough, from her point of view, simply to be *in* view, displaying herself.

And it very nearly was. Eric had almost forgotten how downright *desirable* Ria was, in a way that had nothing (well, almost nothing) to do with sex. It was almost as if she were somehow *realer* than everyone else. She drew the eye to her automatically, like the focus of a painting.

But what the hell does she WANT?

If she wanted to kill him, they wouldn't be sitting here discussing mutual friends. If she wanted information, sooner or later she was going to have to ask some questions. If she wanted to *use* him in some way, well, those days were long past, and Eric was pretty sure that she knew it by now. But she hadn't made an excuse and left, so that wasn't it. She was still here, sitting across the table, regarding him with that steady gaze with a hint of challenge in it.

The waiter came with the check, and Ria pulled out her card to pay. Nothing as paltry as a platinum AmEx for Ria Llewellyn: what she placed on the server tray was an indigo-and-black Centurion AmEx. The user fees alone for the card were over ten thousand dollars a year, with all charges due in full at the end of each month.

Okay. Color me a little impressed. I knew back in L.A. that LlewellCo had money. I just didn't think it was quite this much. And you know what they say: money will get you through times of no magic better than magic will get you through times of no money. . . .

"So I'm a corporate expense?" Eric asked, glancing at the card.

"You might be," Ria answered enigmatically. The waiter returned with the charge slip in record time. Ria signed it, tucked her card back out of sight, and rose to her feet.

"I don't feel we've quite said all we have to say to each other, Eric. Why not come back to my hotel and we can continue this conversation? I promise, no harm will come to you."

That's what you said the last time, Eric thought, the ghosts of old memory stirring. Just then inspiration struck.

"I've got a better idea. Why don't you come back to *my* place?" he said, standing in his turn. "I'm sure you want to see it. And good burglars don't come cheap these days." *Especially once they got a look at the building's security system.*

If he'd expected to embarrass her, Eric was disappointed. She threw back her head and laughed—a full-throated, *joyous* laugh—and smiled at him, eyes sparkling.

"Quite right. I'm not sure what market price for housebreaking is these days, but I'm sure there isn't a line item in my budget to cover it. Lead on," she added, almost gaily, laying her hand on his arm.

The sensation of the contact sent a thrill of heat up his arm and straight to his groin. He'd better stop kidding himself now: Ria Llewellyn was still an enormously attractive woman, and she used that beauty like a weapon. Once he would have been felled by its effects like a clubbed seal. He still felt its pull, tempting him.

But things, as they'd both said over the course of the evening, had changed.

It was rising eleven when they left the restaurant. Ria's limousine waited patiently at the corner. When he spotted them, the chauffeur jumped out from behind the wheel to open the passenger door for them.

The luxury of Underhill was exotic, often strange beyond his imagination, and certainly beyond his achievement here in the World Above. Bardic magic and Elven magic fit together like gloved hands, touching, but separate. Eric could reweave the fabric of Reality, open gates between worlds. But much of Elven magic was species-specific, far beyond his ability and his understanding.

This was different.

The door of the car closed behind them with the solidity of a bank vault. Eric could smell the leather of the seats, the better-than-new-car scent of the fine materials, the engineering and craftsmanship that had gone into the car's construction. And there was nothing magical about it. All of it was a creation of human hands and minds. It was certainly the most decadent thing he'd experienced since he'd come back to human lands. The inside of the Rolls was almost like walking into a small room: there were fresh flowers in matching crystal vases on the cabin walls, a table, and a sleek bulkhead panelled in mahogany burl, from which jumpseats could be folded down. There was enough floor space for two people to lie full-length— though as he settled into the deep bench seat, Eric thought there was plenty of room here, too, for the kind of things Ria's presence made him think about.

Ria settled into her seat and leaned forward to tap at the black glass partition separating them from the driver as soon as Eric was settled. They'd picked up their coats at the door, though in Ria's case the coat was a deep-hooded evening cloak, lined in satin the color of the dawn. As she moved, it fell open. The movement did interesting things to that portrait neckline. The car moved off, sleek and powerful. Eric could feel the vibration of the engine in his bones.

"Shall I tell him the address, or would you like to?" Ria asked mischievously. "The intercom button is right there, in the wall."

Eric pressed the button and gave his address. The powerful car swept uptown through the rain-slicked streets.

The clouds had broken by the time they arrived at Guardian House, and the temperature had dropped several degrees, promising snow before morning, though at this time of year the flurries should melt by noon. Eric shivered as he got out of the car. He watched as Ria looked around, mentally assessing the desirability of the neighborhood with a cold realtor's gaze. Whatever answer she came up with, it seemed to please her.

"You've moved up in the world, Eric."

"Yeah, well, nothing ever stays the same. What about your car?"

She turned back to the chauffeur, still standing alertly beside the car. "He'll wait."

She turned back to Eric. He only hoped Ria wasn't going to be back on the street again in the next ten seconds. He had no real idea of how Guardian House would respond to one of the half-elven, especially one of Ria's ambiguous loyalties.

But isn't that what you brought her here to find out?

It was, of course, but it had just now occurred to him that anything that would rouse Greystone would probably land the Guardians in his lap as well, and with all they had to worry about right now, they probably wouldn't be grateful for the interruption. He wasn't looking forward to the explanations he'd have to make if it came to that. *Still, it's always easier to get forgiveness than permission.*

He tapped out the entry code on the front door and ushered Ria through the lobby.

She was silent on the ride up, but it didn't take Bardic magic to see that Ria was thinking furiously. Eric wondered if he'd ever know the real reason she'd wanted to track him down, and thought he wouldn't. They had one new thing in common, though. Each of them was having to adjust to a world they'd been away from for several years. He wondered if the new millennium was as much of a shock to Ria as it sometimes was to him.

"Very nice," Ria said, looking around the hushed and carpeted corridor that led to Eric's apartment. "No wonder Claire thought you must be some kind of Mafia drug lord."

"I like it," Eric said, refusing to take the bait she so temptingly dangled. He punched the keycode to unlock his door. "Enter freely and of your own will."

In the living room, Ria swirled off her cloak with a practiced gesture and laid it over the back of the couch, making Eric glad he'd gone to the trouble of cleaning the place up before he left. He was really going to have to see about that house-brownie, though.

"Here, let me hang that up for you," Eric said, picking it up. He walked through to the bedroom to hang up her cloak and his coat. The unmade bed, still rumpled from his nightmare, invited his thoughts down pathways he'd rather not take just now, thank you very much. He realized he was tense, waiting for Guardian House to sound an alarm, though surely if it had been going to, it would have done it already. Ria's presence didn't seem to even be a blip on its psychic radar.

Figures. If I can't figure out what she's up to, what chance does a building have?

He came back out to find Ria inspecting his CD collection.

"You must have bought out the store," she commented, turning to him.

"Pretty much," Eric agreed. "I've got to say, these things are a lot easier to store than vinyl."

"Cheaper to produce, too," Ria agreed. "And when the cost comes down, a lot of music that was marginal before has the chance to get out there and find its audience."

Trust Ria to find a way to think of everything in economic terms, Eric thought with an inward grin.

"I promised you coffee. Will espresso do? I've got one of those fancy machines. It was a housewarming present. It even works most of the time."

Ria smiled with what seemed like genuine warmth. "Then you're more technologically advanced than I am. If I didn't have Jonathan to make the coffee, I'd go into caffeine withdrawal."

She followed him into the tiny kitchen, where Eric navigated the intricacies of the bright-orange Italian espresso maker Caity had given him without too much difficulty. Ria's presence—her warmth, her perfume—were even more distracting in this small intimate space.

Is she coming on to me? Unbidden tactile memories rose up strongly in Eric's mind. He controlled his blush with an effort. *Or is she just trying to get me so aroused I'll stop thinking?* To cover his momentary confusion, he grabbed a tray from the shelf and arranged a box of assorted biscotti on a plate. When the espresso had brewed, he drew off two cups and carried the tray back out into the living room.

"So why don't you tell me what you're really doing here?" Eric said bluntly, once they were both seated. He didn't expect her to tell him, but his question should bring the answers to the surface of her mind for Greystone to read.

"You invited me," Ria pointed out, sipping her espresso. She nibbled delicately at a biscotti with sharp white teeth. "And frankly, isn't that question the least bit insulting? Next you'll be offering to leave the money on the dresser."

Eric grinned in spite of himself at her bold words. *The best defense is always a good attack.* "I don't think it's an unreasonable question, given who we both are," Eric responded. "We didn't part on the best of terms."

"That was my fault, I suppose," Ria said graciously. "I'm not the most trusting person in the world. And you frightened me. It doesn't hurt to admit that. My father has—had—many powerful enemies. I thought you might be one of them."

"But Perenor's dead."

Ria inclined her head. "But the elvenkind has long memories. I sought you out because I was certain it was only a matter of time before you did the same to me. I have no interest in taking up my late father's feuds . . . but I will defend myself."

Was that a warning or a threat?

"I haven't got any quarrel with you, Ria." As he said the words, Eric knew they were true. "I came back to finish at Juilliard. That's all. So I'm still asking: why are *you* here?"

She wasn't convinced—he could see that in her expression. But would he have been convinced if he was the one who'd been raised amid a Sidhe Lord's intrigues? Ria's entire existence, her magical training, had been shaped to one end, to make her into a living battery from which Perenor could draw power at will. That didn't make for a trusting nature.

"Tell me who trained you in Bardcraft. Tell me he didn't send you back into the world of Men to kill me," Ria said in a low intense voice.

"*Dharinel?*" Eric said in surprise. Dharinel disliked humans and despised the half-blood, it was true, but his contempt was meted out with a fine evenhandedness. It would be completely beneath his dignity as Magus Major and Elven Bard of Elfhame Misthold to acknowledge any particular human enough to want to destroy them.

Ria was about to reply when there was a scrabbling on the fire escape. She set down her cup quickly, and glanced from Eric to the window behind her.

The sash raised, and Greystone climbed down into the room. Ria got slowly to her feet, staring at the gargoyle.

"She's okay, boyo," Greystone said to Eric. "I admit I had me doubts about you bringing her here an' all, but 'tis copacetic. She's levelling with you, laddybuck."

Ria stared down at the squat, misshapen creature in speechless shock. It had a fanged doglike face and curling horns. Its arms were long and apelike, and its hindquarters like a satyr's, right down to the cloven hooves. Great bat wings lay against its back like furled umbrellas. And despite the fact that it lived and moved and talked, it seemed to be made of solid stone.

"So," she heard it say, "how'd your night out go? Or should I say going? Any o' that high-powered coffee left? It's a cold night out, and no mistake. I could use a wee bit of a jolt."

"Sure," Eric answered easily. "I'll get you a cup. Ria, this is Greystone. Greystone, meet Ria Llewellyn. I've told you about her."

With a distant part of her mind, Ria registered that Eric seemed to be on very good terms with this creature—and that he had brought her to it as a sort of test. She found it hard to be angry with Eric for showing such caution. She'd been wary herself.

She stood perfectly still as the gargoyle waddled up to her. Though if it could stand completely upright it might be as tall as she was, its crouched position made it several inches shorter.

"You've nothin' to fear from me, Blondie. As for meself, there's more things in heaven an' earth, as I'm sure you know," Greystone said, and winked at her.

"I'm finding that out," Ria said levelly.

Eric returned from the kitchen with a mug of espresso and handed it to Greystone. The gargoyle slurped it down with evident relish, then reached out a long simian arm to grab a handful of biscotti. The talons on its fingertips would have done credit to an eagle with their sharpness, for all that they seemed to be made of stone. It set the empty cup down on the table, and, still clutching the handful of cookies, headed for the window once more.

"Well, I've gotta be going. No rest for the wicked, an' all that. You kids behave yourselves, now." He favored both of them with one last toothy grin and made his exit, closing the window carefully behind him.

Eric was looking at her, obviously waiting for her reaction.

"Well," Ria finally managed. "I see you still have interesting friends."

Eric laughed. "I seem to have a knack for that."

Cautiously they both sat down once more.

"So . . ." Ria said finally, returning to the earlier conversation. "Master Dharinel trained you?"

"Even he had to admit that everybody was better off if I knew how to use what I had. But he didn't send me after you, Ria. I swear it. I don't think most of the elves really care one way or the other about you now that Perenor's dead."

"I hope you're right. But I do know that your friends blame me for a lot of what happened at Sun-Descending and the Fairegrove . . . Beth Kentraine, for example?"

She knew she was fishing now, but if Claire MacLaren's PI report hadn't mentioned talking gargoyles, it was even less likely to have included mention of elves and their friends. Beth Kentraine was not somebody she wanted to have appear unexpectedly in her life. From what Ria remembered, Kentraine had a fiery temper and a wicked right cross.

"Oh, you won't be seeing her. She and Kory mostly live

Underhill these days. It's not like they'd be dropping by unexpectedly. We're still close, but it's . . . not like it was."

When to scratch one of the three of you made the other two bleed, Ria finished silently. The way Eric spoke of them—as a couple—made Ria cheer inwardly. So little Bethie had thrown her lot in with the elven lover, had she? That was the best news Ria'd had in a long time.

"I suppose I ought to offer my condolences," Ria said politely. "Or . . . not?"

"Not," Eric said cheerfully. "Things just worked out the way they had to. The only thing is . . . I'd like to be able to think of some way to help them out. Because they want kids, and—with elves and humans—it's hard to arrange. I don't know if I ought to be asking you this, but . . . do you know anything that could help? Some kind of spell or magic, I mean. I mean, *you're* here."

Half-Blood children were incredibly rare occurrences between Sidhe and mortalkin. In most cases the unfortunate children were ostracized by their father's and mother's people both, so perhaps it was a blessing that such half-Blood children rarely inherited the immortality of their elven parent. Immortality had been the bribe Perenor had held out to his half-breed daughter, but lately Ria had come to wonder if he had meant to give it to her as a blessing . . . or as a curse? She shook her head slowly.

"Not in the way you mean, I think. Believe me, Eric. What Perenor did to create me is nothing your friends would ever want any part of," Ria said with quiet intensity. "It nearly killed my mother. It *did* drive her mad. And it cost the lives of several other people—he drained their essences to fuel his magic."

Eric sat back, a look of surprise and, oddly, pity on his face. "That's a helluva thing to have to live with. To know you're here only because a bunch of other people gave their lives—or had them taken away."

"Survivor's guilt, they call it," Ria said with a crooked smile. "It's not the only way, of course, just the quickest and easiest if you have no conscience and no scruples. If you'd like, though, I'll see what I can find about the other methods. I *am* uniquely placed for that kind of research." *And we'll see whether the high and mighty Beth Kentraine is willing to let bygones be bygones if I can offer her her heart's desire on a silver tray.*

"I'd like that," Eric said. "I'm sorry I was so hard on you before...."

"But you didn't trust me. And considering how we parted, you had every right not to. That wasn't one of my best calls, Eric. If I'd been thinking clearly, I would have realized it at the time. I should have trusted what I knew of you. If you were out to get someone, you wouldn't pretend to be their friend first."

She could tell by his expression that he knew she was telling him the truth. Truth-sense was one of the oldest of the Bardic gifts; she supposed she'd just been lucky he hadn't developed it the last time they'd met.

"Is that all we were? Friends?" Eric asked. "Funny, but I remember the relationship as being somewhat . . . warmer."

This is moving a little too fast for me. Ria got to her feet. "And it might be again. I won't lie to you, Eric. As a boy you were pretty. As a man you're devastating. But I think that right now it's time for me to go."

He looked disappointed—her pride was grateful for that—but got to his feet without complaint.

"I'll get your cape."

Eric walked her to the curb and the waiting Rolls. The chauffeur opened the passenger door and stood waiting like a well-oiled automaton.

Eric opened his mouth to speak, and Ria touched him lightly on the lips with her fingers. "I'll be in New York for several more days. There's no hurry. I hope we can see each other again. I'd like to get to know you."

And before Eric could assemble an answer to *that*, Ria had stepped into the car, and it was moving silently away.

❖ ❖ ❖

There was someone standing outside his apartment door when Eric got back upstairs.

"Toni?"

The Latina woman spun around when she heard him. "Blessed saints! Greystone said you were here, but I called and no one answered, so I came up."

Must be pretty important. She looks kind of worried.

"I was just walking a friend out. Do you want to come inside?"

"No. I mean, I'd like you to come outside. We've . . . found something, and none of us has seen anything like it before. Jimmie said— So I thought . . . you've had a certain amount of experience in this sort of thing, and I was hoping I could get you to come take a look. Maybe it's . . . what you were talking about."

Christ, I hope not! Eric thought fervently.

"Sure," Eric said. "Just let me get my coat and I'll be right with you. Do I have time to change?"

For the first time Toni seemed to notice what he was wearing. A slow smile crossed her face. "Sure. We wouldn't want to scare the Ungodly with your great beauty. Heavy date tonight, eh?"

"You might say," Eric said with a smile.

He dressed quickly in sweater, jeans, leather jacket and boots. He hesitated, then picked up his flute case and swung it over his shoulder. Toni hadn't said what she wanted him to look at, but if it was capable of spooking a Guardian, he wanted to go loaded for bear.

Toni's Toyota was waiting on the street—a side benefit of Guardianship seemed to be never lacking for a parking space—and in a few moments they were moving. Toni Hernandez drove like a New York cabbie, zipping into spaces almost before they opened, weaving through a deadly dance with the fleet of trucks that took over the New York streets after-hours. The traffic lightened as they headed east, and Eric realized they were going toward Central Park.

"Want to tell me what's going on?" Eric asked, catching his breath after one particularly spectacular maneuver. *She drives the way Bethie does—or did.*

"Not really. I think we'd rather see what you come up with on your own. Paul and Jimmie are already there."

The park was closed to street traffic at this time of night, and the gates were down across the road. Toni swerved into a parking space right outside and bounced out of the car before Eric had finished unbuckling his seat belt.

"I'm afraid it's a bit of a hike from here," she said. "Good thing you changed your shoes."

He felt it long before he reached the spot where Jimmie and Paul were standing. Jimmie Youngblood was in her uniform, looking shuttered and forbidding, hand on her gun, though her expression lightened with something like relief when she saw him. Paul looked like an escaped university professor, Norfolk tweed jacket with leather elbow patches and all. Eric almost expected him to pull out a pipe and light it.

The stench of magic was everywhere, a sort of palpable wrongness that made his hair stand on end. Eric's steps slowed as he approached the Guardians. Outside of a few burned patches on the grass there wasn't much to see with normal vision. Eric stopped where he was, closed his eyes, and looked again.

He could see it now. A sketchy shape in the air, as though the night was a different color here. He turned slowly around in a circle, trying to pin it down further. He felt a chill that had nothing to do with winter, and a crawling feeling along his spine.

"You already know this is magic, right?" he said at last, trying for a light tone in the midst of this incredible *wrongness*.

"Ah, but what *kind* of magic?" Paul asked, as if this were just some sort of academic exercise.

"I told you before how a lot of people've gone missing in the last couple of days, Eric," Jimmie said. "People you wouldn't ordinarily miss, except that so damn many of them are just dropping out of sight. Or turning up dead. What we need to know is, is this a part of that?"

Yes, there was death here, and pain, and darkness. Eric thought again of the bonewood and goblin tower of his dream.

"This feels like Unseleighe Sidhe," he said reluctantly. "Mind, I've never had any direct contact with them, but it's Sidhe magic, but twisted, so I suppose that's what it feels like. . . ." He hesitated before saying more. "And there's a lot of death here. Human death. Beyond that . . ." His voice trailed off again.

"So what you told me about really is happening," Jimmie said unhappily. "But why? And how, especially here? Don't the Dark Elves have to follow the same rules as the Light?"

"They've got the same limitations," Eric agreed. The taint of inside-out magic was starting to make his head hurt. "But I kind of think the Unseleighe Sidhe would like the City, if they could stand to be here."

"Can you tell what kind of working this is?" Jimmie asked urgently. "Its purpose?"

"It's a Gateway," Eric answered slowly. "It isn't finished. If nobody messes with it for a few days it'll probably fade away. But someone was here—an elf-mage or another human Bard—trying to open a Gateway between Underhill and the world."

He explained what he could about Nexuses—how they gave elvenkind a way to tap the power of Underhill that was life itself to them, how many of the Elven Court, especially the Lesser Sidhe, could not survive away from a Nexus, and that even the High Elves needed frequent access to one in order to replenish their magic. And that someone, apparently, was building one here.

"Well, that's something to go on with, anyway," Jimmie said when he was finished talking. She shook her head. "Now we just have to figure out what to do about it. I wonder what you bait Sidhe-traps with?"

"Power," Eric said bleakly. "At least in this case. Not your kind, though. That's at least partly learned, I'm guessing, and pretty well shielded. He isn't really interested in that. He wants the raw stuff, the innate Gift some people are born with and don't know they have."

"Well, that's a relief," Paul said dourly, then forced himself to smile. "At least we know more than we did before. Thanks for coming out on such short notice, Eric."

"Why don't you let me get rid of it for you?" Eric offered, reaching for his flute.

"No!" Paul and Jimmie spoke at once. There was real pain on

Jimmie's face—and more. Fear. He remembered their conversation at the bakery: *If anybody takes a bullet, it should be me.*

Was that what she was worrying about? Him?

Paul held up a hand. "No, that's okay Now that we know what it is, we can keep an eye on it. It's more important to stop who's doing it rather than scare them off."

If you think you can scare off the Unseleighe Sidhe, you haven't met many of them, Eric thought. "I still think I should—"

"C'mon, Eric. I'll drive you home," Toni said briskly, taking charge of the situation before it could degenerate into an argument. "Paul, you want a lift?"

"No," Paul said. "I think I'll stay out here a little while. You two go on ahead. Jimmie can drop me when she heads back to the station house."

"I still think I ought to do something about it," Eric said. Most people wouldn't notice anything out of the ordinary here, but anybody with any amount of Talent would have a natural aversion to the place. Or an attraction to it. . . .

"I'm not bringing any more civilians onto the fire-line. Do what your friends told you, Eric. Stay out of this one, for your own sake," Jimmie said urgently.

There was a world of pain—and bitter self-recrimination—in Jimmie's voice, and Toni was hovering over him as if she were about to pick him up and carry him. Reluctantly, Eric allowed himself to be led back to the car. He couldn't force his help on them if they didn't want to accept it, and Dharinel had all but ordered him to stay uninvolved. He let himself be led out of the park and deposited back on his own doorstep after another hair-raising ride in the Toyota.

But the sense of unfinished business, layered on top of the unsettling evening with Ria, made sleep particularly hard to find that night.

EIGHT:
THE CITY OF
DREADFUL NIGHT

Chesley Kurland did not believe in miracles, even though he was holding one in his hands right now. Free samples. Hell, he hadn't seen anything like that since the Sixties, and unlike most of the crowd on the streets these days, Chesley had been there for the Summer of Love and retained fond memories of it today. As dark and grey and unfriendly as the world had gotten, there were times when the memories were all that kept him going.

Chesley made his living as a free-lance mechanic. He could repair any kind of engine, the more complicated the better. Anything mechanical just talked to him, always had, the same way some people knew what horses wanted just by looking. He was a man of no fixed address, and currently lived in the back of an old Ford van parked in the back of Ralph's Niteowl Garage up in Inwood. Ralph paid him in cash, and Chesley liked to say that he was taking his retirement in installments, a line from an old book that he'd particularly liked.

Earlier this evening he'd been hanging out down at the old Peacock Coffeehouse on the edge of the Village, and this dude who looked like he'd wandered out of the last *Terminator* movie had made the scene, offering little bundles of joy to anyone with a sense of adventure. And if there was one thing Chesley still had, it was a sense of adventure.

The garage was fairly quiet as he walked across the floor. Despite the optimism of its name, there wasn't often enough work to occupy a full crew 24/7, and tonight was one of those times. He saw no one as he made his way to the van and climbed in through the back.

Most of all, he didn't see the dealer who had been offering free samples, and who now stood concealed in the shadows with another man beside him, both of them watching Chesley as he climbed into his mobile home.

Inside the van was everything Chesley needed in this world: a mattress to sleep on, his toolcase, his stashbox, and a towering blue glass bong. You could buy them on Main Street in the bad old days, Chesley remembered. What had happened to the world since he was a kid? It seemed as if all the joy were slowly draining away from everything, like somebody'd pulled out the plug in the Bathtub of the World. Well, in a few moments they'd see if modern chemistry was there to meet the challenge.

Sitting cross-legged on the floor, he prepared the bong for use with the ease of long practice. He filled the upper half of the pipe with bottled water and packed the bowl with pipe tobacco and slivers shaved from a block of Turkish Blonde. Over that, he sprinkled the contents of the little packet. The powder glistened brightly, like a fresh fall of Vermont snow. "T-Stroke." That was what the guy at the Peacock had called it. Well, the proof was in the smoking, he'd always said. When the mixture was smoldering brightly, Chesley picked up the mouthpiece and took a deep drag.

The iron all around him made his skin crawl and put him in a foul temper, but Aerune was not to be deterred from his quest. He had chosen to follow the chief of the underlings that bore the Bardmaking elixir himself, and watched as the humans succumbed to its lure one by one. Two so far tonight had not died immediately nor manifested the insensate fury that not even Aerune could shape to his own purposes. But he had not been quick enough to seize either of them, and so they had both been spirited away by his great enemy.

It had puzzled him for a short while why these men wasted their time giving their elixir to so many who would simply die, until he realized that he could see what they could not—the blue light, so feeble as to be nearly invisible, that crowned those who possessed gifts that could be aroused by the elixir. That faint flame burned above the head of the grey-haired mortal whom he had followed here, and Aerune was determined that the mortal men should not have this prize. To his elf-sight, the corners of the garage were not dark, and he could plainly see the two men lurking there. From Urla's thoughts, he recognized one of them as the man in the black chariot who had first stolen Urla's prey.

"There is your quarry, my fine hunter," Aerune said softly, his fingers brushing the redcap's head. "Take him as you will."

Just then there was a flash of the blue light invisible to mortals from within the van, and the sharp ears of the Unseleighe Sidhe heard a stifled cry.

Urla darted forward, its long arms swinging, lips spread in a toothy grin. It bounced toward its victim, its expression vacuous and innocent.

"What the hell? You— Kid— Get outta heeeere—!" one of the men shouted. Aerune turned away. There was a sound of gunfire. The man's words faded into a scream as Urla seized him.

Aerune hesitated at the door of the van. A modern car would not have given him nearly as much trouble, but the old van's panels were of heavy sheet steel, perilous to touch. He would have no more than a moment's grace, he knew, before the surviving mortal minion was upon him.

Aerune grasped the door handle and wrenched it from its hinges with inhuman strength. His gauntlets smoked as they touched Cold Iron, but they were dwarf-forged, and his skin did not burn. Within the fetid kennel lay the prize he sought—a skinny, unlovely mortal man, his face distorted with the ravages of age. The dark lord seized him, lips drawn back in a snarl of distaste, and flung the human over his shoulder. His elvensteed was waiting in the street outside. With one leap, Aerune gained the saddle and galloped away, toward the place he had chosen for his Nexus.

Michael knew he was in trouble. He and Keith had followed Geczerboy back to this chop shop from the coffeehouse where Keith had been doing his candyman imitation. The two guys who were there—waiting for tonight's shipment of Gone In Sixty Seconds, Michael had no doubt—had been easily persuaded to go in the closet and stay there, and the decks were clear for a sweet little snatch-and-grab. They'd been about to make their move when everything went wonky. Some kid wandered in from somewhere and made a beeline toward Keith.

Only it wasn't a kid. It was . . . something else. It'd bitten Keith's throat open with one chomp. It bathed in his blood, and it laughed, a high terrible sound like broken glass on a blackboard. Michael had emptied half his Glock into it with no effect, though he knew the Teflon-coated bullets hit it.

Then he saw the other guy.

Tall. Dark like Darth Vader was dark. Menace radiating off him like chill off a chunk of dry ice. And Michael had made a command decision, right then and there. He'd run for his life. Out the side door, up the hill onto Riverside, yelping at every shadow.

But he wasn't followed.

His hands shook as he got his Star-Tac open and dialled the private number they'd been given for emergencies.

"Boss? Boss! We've got a situation here—"

It was not much of a greenwood, but it was all these mortal drones deserved. Aerune reined in and dropped his burden ungently to the ground before vaulting down himself. A moment later he crouched on the turf beside the mortal.

The human creature twitched and muttered, still caught in a web of the elixir's spinning. Aerune could see the nimbus of power grow brighter around him as the tiny guttering spark of the human's innate magic grew and flowered under the effect of the draught he had imbibed.

Here is power indeed. Aerune basked in its presence as the mortal might bask in the warmth of a fire. It purged the Sidhe's cold bones of the ache of Cold Iron all around him, and fed Aerune's resolve with the siren song of power ripe for the taking.

It was a simple thing for one of the Dark Court to drain the vital essence of a mortal, though few of them had enough Power to make it worthwhile. This one was different. Aerune bent his head low and sealed the mortal's doom with a kiss. *Spin for me, little Singer. Weave the web of your race's doom.*

The veil between the worlds began to thin, and the lattice that would anchor Aerune's Nexus began to take shape on the midnight air. First the pattern must be completed, then the veil itself pierced, and then Aerune and his Court would be able to call up the power of Elfhame into the World of Iron with no more than a thought. The power poured through him from its mortal wellspring: intoxicating, vast. . . .

And then it stopped.

Aerune roared his displeasure, turning on the mortal in a fury. But the man was dead beneath his hands, his body wasted away, his skin and bones crackling like a handful of autumn leaves in Aerune's grip.

Dead. And of no more use to me, Aerune realized, choking back his rage. The mortal alchemist's elixir gave them access to their Power, he realized, but no way to replenish it from Underhill's eternal wellspring, and so they burned out quickly, their bodies feeding on their own life-force.

The ghost of the Gateway, less than a shimmer on the winter air even to Aerune's Sight, mocked him with its incompletion. *But there are others. They are mine of right, and I will have them. Aerete, beloved, soon they will repay your death in the last full measure!*

He whistled for his mount and was away again, in a clatter of hoofbeats so swift they sounded like one long drum roll.

Four of the containment cells in the underground warren at Threshold were full. It had been a busy—and potentially profitable—Saturday night, and Jeanette felt an excitement that had little to do with Robert's glorious future.

Her drug was working. Not as well as she'd hoped, but working. She'd tweaked the last batch a little, hoping to shorten the time the subjects spent unconscious, and that yielded a kind of sorting mechanism. Ninety percent of those who received T-Stroke still died, two-thirds of them instantly. The thirty percent of the Survivors that were going to manifest berserker rage came up out of the drug within minutes. But the ones who were going to manifest some kind of useful Talent slept for an hour or so, and Jeanette had decided that the deep sleep was necessary to allow the neural pathways for handling the Gift to be reconfigured without the interference of outside stimulus.

And we have four: telepathy, teleportation, psychokinesis, and I wonder what this one is going to be?

Intently, she watched the monitors for the containment cells. The telepath, Vicky Moon, had been the first to awaken, screaming at the voices inside her head and begging them to stop. Jeanette had her lightly sedated, and at least the screaming had stopped, though she doubted the voices had. The PK and the teleport—Plummer and Langford—were less trouble. Langford had gotten out of his cell four times before they figured out what he could do, but he hadn't been able to 'port far and the effort had left him exhausted. He was sleeping now; no action there.

Jeanette watched in fascination as Plummer played with the test objects in her cell, a set of child's building blocks. Lost in a world of her own imagination, the PK talent made the brightly-colored cubes swoop and dance through the air like a flock of strange butterflies, perfectly content.

The alarm began to beep as the fourth subject returned to consciousness, and Jeanette waited to see what he'd do, her mind wandering over the evening's harvest. Four, out of how many doses handed out in Soho and the East Village tonight? At least two hundred, and even assuming the sweepers missed half of them, there should be ten bodies down here in the cells, not four. She knew she'd been generalizing from pitifully inadequate data—was her viability rate closer to 5% than 10%?

Or were the others going . . . somewhere else?

Just then a scream riveted her attention on Cell Four, and Jeanette uttered a startled yelp of disbelief at what the monitors showed her.

There were *things* in the cell with Hancock. Coiling, horrible, impossible things. Things that glowed with their own light. Things that dripped blood. Things that moaned and mewed in the voices of tortured children, pressing up against the door and beginning to flow under it as if they had no bones.

Jeanette's heart hammered in terror, and for a moment all she could think of was flight. But wherever she ran, these things would find her, find her and hurt her, hurt her, *hurt* her. . . .

Unable to tear her eyes from the screen, Jeanette fumbled for the row of covered buttons, scrabbling blindly to release the safety cover. More of the *things* were sliding under the door now, creeping and slithering down the corridor, drooling blood and pus and other, less nameable fluids. They twittered like birds and mewed like kittens, and some of them were speaking words that in moments she was terrified she would begin to understand. *Please, God, I have to be right about this, please, please, please. . . .*

The guard at the end of the corridor saw them too. His eyes bulged with disbelieving terror, and he dragged at his sidearm, firing wildly and without effect into the mass of nightmare moving toward him as he screamed for mercy.

She found the button for Cell Four and stabbed down at it hard enough to break a nail. The display above it turned from green to red and began to flash; she could see it pulse out of the corner of her eye.

The guard in the corridor shot himself just before the first of the *things* reached him.

And then the gas with which Jeanette had flooded Hancock's cell did its work. Hancock slumped to the floor, unconscious, and all the nightmares began to fade away.

I was right. Oh, thank God, I was right. Jeanette blinked back tears, furious with her own weakness as the crippling terror receded. An illusionist, that was all. Some kind of mental projections, and a really sick mind behind them all.

She turned and picked up a handset on one of the other consoles. She needed to clear her throat several times before it would work. "Housekeeping. This is Campbell. I need you down on Level Three to pick up a body. And send Beirkoff down with some euphorics strong ones." *I want Hancock thinking about nothing but white fleecy clouds and little pink bunnies until the T-Stroke has worn off.*

"What are you doing here?" Robert demanded abruptly from behind her.

Jeanette spun her chair around with a strangled shriek, her nerves still raw from the brush with Hancock's mind.

"My job, Robert," she said in a harsh voice. "We've got three usables from tonight's trials. Cell Four's no good unless you want to drop him behind enemy lines to drive the bad guys mad. I'm wondering if my original model is off, though. There should be at least a dozen more Talents from tonight's sweep."

Robert grimaced in impatience. "That's what I'm trying to tell you, you stupid bitch. Michael just called in. There's someone— some*thing*—out there that's stealing our Talents."

His words dovetailed so neatly with her earlier thoughts that Jeanette was startled. "What? *How?" I barely know about this project— how can anyone else have figured it out so fast? Not to mention picking off the Survivors with that kind of accuracy.*

"I don't know and I don't care," Robert snarled. "What I do know is, we're going to catch the bastard and make him sorrier than he's ever been in his life. Come on."

Having touched one such Empowered life, Aerune knew the scent of his prey now. He whistled up his pack of red-eared, red-eyed hounds, and set them on the hunt. With each of the Crowned Ones he found and took, his wrath increased, for the power in each of them flickered and guttered in moments, its mortal vehicle consumed by the body's own fires before the work of building the Gateway to anchor the Nexus could be well begun. Each desiccated shell Aerune cast aside with the others, filled with a ravening lust for victory, now that victory seemed so close. The night had been long and its rewards meager. It was nearing dawn now, and in his diminished condition, the light of the sun was as much the Unseleighe Sidhe's enemy as Cold Iron was.

But there was time enough to take one more of the Crowned Ones tonight before retiring to plan his assault upon the stronghold from which that power flowed.

His hounds took the scent and began to give tongue. In the sleeping city around him, animals and even insects fled in terror, and the pent-up hounds of the mortals barked and howled in a frenzy of helpless terror at the presence of their ancient enemy. But no mortal could see him as he rode, unless he wished it.

Somewhere ahead, Aerune sensed several of the Crowned Ones gathered together, but saw only one. His prey sat alone upon a bench in one of the city's many open spaces, his head bowed in sleep or submission. Aerune whistled his dogs to his side, and dismounted from his elvensteed, dropping his cloak of confusion and shadow. He stepped forward. . . .

And all the world was filled with blinding light.

"Freeze, bastard! We've got you covered!" a mortal voice ordered.

Who dares to command the Lord of Death and Pain?

Oh, my God, Jeanette thought numbly.

Caught in the blaze of the handheld searchlights was something off the cover of one of the books she'd read in high school.

He was tall and slender, with skin as white as an Anne Rice vampire's. He was wearing some kind of medieval costume—black chain mail and plate armor that glinted like hematite, and his long black hair was held back by a silver circlet that plainly revealed a pair of long pointed ears. He looked like Frank Langella done up as a Vulcan in a really bad mood.

"Moon!" She pinched the arm of the handcuffed woman standing at her side. "Read his mind! Now!"

The girl whimpered. Jeanette slapped her, hard.

"Aerune. His name is Aerune. He's—" Moon broke off, moaning. "It hurts!"

"*Do it,* or I'll lock you in Bellevue and give you something to whine about!" Jeanette snarled. Moon cringed away from her anger. "The Lord of Death and Pain," she moaned.

"You!" Robert strode through the ring of armed men toward the . . . elf. Jeanette watched him in horror. Robert had been so convinced that it was the Feds who were hijacking their project that the stranger's exotic appearance didn't even slow him down. "Who are you, and just what the *hell* do you think you're doing here?"

The stranger—Aerune—drew himself up to his full height. His black cloak billowed in the wind.

"I am the Lord Aerune mac Audelaine of the Dark Court, and this man is mine. Contest with me at your peril, mortal lordling."

He turned his back on Robert, and reached for Hancock again.

Jeanette saw the glitter of the .45 in Robert's hand and stifled a cry of warning, though she wasn't completely sure who she wanted to warn. Robert jammed the barrel into Aerune's back, and even from where she was, Jeanette could see a curl of smoke rise up from Aerune's cloak, as if the pistol barrel were red-hot.

"It burns! It burns!" Moon cried, as Aerune whirled around with a roar, his face twisted in an inhuman mask of fury. He lashed out at Robert with a backhand blow.

"You will pay dearly for that insult!" he snarled in a voice like broken music. Robert jumped back, motioning his troops forward to deal with the intruder.

But Aerune wasn't there.

"Fan out! Find him!" Robert shouted, sounding too furious to be rattled. "I want him alive!"

You won't find him, Jeanette thought. "Moon," she said gently. "Moon, what happened? Can you tell me who he is? What he wants?"

The girl looked at her, and now there was something almost serene in her expression. "He's what you think he is, Jeanette. He's a lord of the Unseleighe Court. He wants all the Crowned Ones— us—the ones you call Survivors. He needs us. . . ." She sighed, her head lolling on her shoulders as if exhaustion had suddenly overwhelmed her. "He needs us to kill you all."

Jeanette led her over to the bench and let her sit down beside

Hancock. Moon curled up, instantly asleep. Her face looked haggard, and there were dark bruises of exhaustion beneath her eyes.

This one isn't going to last long either, Jeanette thought clinically. Something about T-Stroke worked like putting a penny in an old-fashioned fusebox: people could access their hidden potential, but it burned them right out within a matter of minutes. She was glad she'd brought Moon along anyway. This was probably as close to a field trial as they were going to be able to manage with any of the Survivors. Their Gifts made them too unpredictable to let out of their cells.

She glanced warily at Hancock, but the projective telepath was still in the Land of Nod, happily quiescent under the influence of the euphorics Beirkoff had given him. That was one good thing out of this whole mess. They didn't need any Monsters From The Id cluttering up the place.

She sighed, running a hand through her hair. An elf. She'd never believed she'd see one. She'd stopped believing in them years ago—forced herself to stop believing, because it just hurt too damned much. But looking into Aerune's fallen-angel eyes, skepticism was impossible. He'd been here. He was real. He burned at the touch of Cold Iron, just like all the books said.

And boy, was he mad. Madder than Jeanette had ever seen anyone get, in a serious career devoted to shining people on.

No, she had no problem believing in his reality. She had another problem entirely. Elves were supposed to be magic, and she'd certainly seen Aerune do magic, just now.

So what did an elf want with her retread junkies?

She blinked, blinded by the headlights of the big truck that pulled up, driving across the grass of the park. Robert jumped out of the passenger seat.

"Come on! We've got to get back to the lab—and hire some decent help," Robert added, his voice hoarse with disappointment. "These losers couldn't find a pig in a one-room schoolhouse. The target gave them all the slip." For the first time, he seemed to notice Moon. "What did she get? Did she read his mind?" he demanded eagerly.

"Yes, she got something," Jeanette answered, busy unlocking Hancock's handcuffs. "And no, you're not going to like it." She glanced up at the sky. It was already turning light. She glared back at Robert. "What do you want me to do, carry them? Get me some help here. And once we get back, you and I have got to talk."

"An elf. Jesus, Campbell, you been sampling your own stuff? Elves! Next you're going to be telling me the Smurfs are after us."

Robert paced back and forth in front of Jeanette's desk in her office down in Threshold's Black Labs. It was a little after six A.M. Saturday morning. The Talents—the four they'd managed to keep— were all back in their cells sleeping off the last of their T-Stroke, and everything was tidied away before the city was fairly awake. And now Robert was looking for someone to blame for tonight's fiasco.

"An elf," Jeanette repeated patiently. "That's what Vicky Moon said. That's what Aerune is." Somehow she thought it was very important to convince Robert of that fact. She'd read a lot about elves when she was a kid. They weren't the twee little Disneyfied things that Robert seemed to be thinking of. When mankind was still living in caves, they'd ruled the world, until Cold Iron had driven them Underhill. Even then, they were still formidable enemies.

"Or thinks he is," Robert said, still unconvinced. "Campbell, there's no such thing as elves, so this guy can't be one. Q.E.D." He smiled at her patronizingly. Jeanette sighed.

"Well, *he* thinks he is. You want to argue with him? What else fits the facts? You burned him. With your gun barrel, because it was steel. Didn't you see the smoke?"

"It was . . . it could be some kind of psychosomatic reaction. Or an allergy of some kind," Robert said, floundering just a little.

"The only thing with an allergy to iron is an elf," Jeanette repeated in a dull voice. "And besides, he vanished right in front of us. So either we've got ourselves an elf, or David Copperfield is looking for outside work."

"Yeah, okay, this Aerune's an elf," Robert said hastily, unwilling to bother continuing the argument. "If he's allergic to iron, that's good. It'll give us some way of handling him. The important thing is to get him back. He's obviously found some way to use his psi powers without burning out the way your test subjects keep doing. Do you think there are more of them? There has to be. If we can get our hands on them we could stop wasting our time with these trials and go right to the source."

Jeanette stared at him blankly. Did Robert actually think Threshold had the faintest chance of controlling someone like Aerune? His voice echoed again through her mind: *"I am the Lord Aerune mac Audelaine of the Dark Court—contest with me at your peril."*

The Lord of Death and Pain, Moon had said. *Oh, yeah, definitely somebody I want mad at ME.*

"And how are you planning to do that, Robert?" she asked, just to be asking.

"We'll set another trap for him tonight," Robert said in a crisp managerial style. "If he's after our Talents, you can shoot them up again so they'll attract him, and this time we'll be ready for him. No pointy-eared mutant is going to thumb his nose at me!"

Great. I'm now living in an X-Files *LARP. Mutants are so much more realistic than elves, right?* Jeanette thought. She made one more attempt to get through to him.

"But we've got something he wants, Robert—and he has something we want. We could summon him, yes, but then we could talk to him, strike a bargain. . . ." *Elves were always making bargains,* Jeanette remembered. It could work. And he could teach them so much. . . .

"We don't have to bargain. We hold all the high cards, and after tonight, we'll have this Aerune mac Whasis too. This *Highlander* reject won't be so high and mighty once he's got an iron collar around his neck. In fact, I think he'll tell me everything I want to know," Robert gloated.

"Uh-huh." Robert's refusal to negotiate frustrated her. Aerune was pure power—and Robert was talking like he was some kind of special effect that could be captured between commercial breaks. All Robert could see was what he *wanted* to see—not what was there.

This was not going to end well. It was time to cut her losses.

"Look, I've got to finish up some reports on our lab rats and tweak the T-Stroke mix before I go home and grab some Z's. What time should I meet you back here tonight?" she asked brightly.

Robert smiled, sure he'd won his point. "Be back here around nine. We'll set things up in the Park this time—after midnight there's nobody there but the muggers. We'll have plenty of elbow room and plenty of peace and quiet. And a few surprises for our mutie friend."

"Sounds good." Jeanette forced another smile. "See you then."

After Robert left, Jeanette spent a long time staring at her reflection in the black mirror of her office wall, making up her mind for sure. She'd always known that someday it would be time to leave this little party Robert was throwing, and actually, she'd been here longer than she thought she'd be. But she could smell disaster ahead, and with her own survivor instincts, Jeanette decided she didn't want to be here when it hit.

Aerune haunted her thoughts. Power. Promise. Danger. She felt the temptation to stay just to see him again beckon to her, and quashed it firmly. *It's time to go.*

She'd always known that someday it'd be time, and planned accordingly. Jeanette opened her guitar case and felt around in the lining until she found what she was looking for—a red plastic diskette with a smiley-face sticker on it. She loaded its contents to her computer and hesitated for a moment before pressing "Send."

Has to be done. She pressed the button. The virus began working its way through the system, erasing every hint of her presence—and her work.

Next she went through her desk, pulling all her paper files and shredding them. She took the bags to the incinerator herself—in her outlaw days, Jeanette had never relied on anyone else to cover her tracks: when you wanted something done right, you did it yourself.

When that was done, she took a last look around. The office where she'd spent so much of her time was completely sanitized. No trace of her presence remained, except for her guitar and sound system, a rack of CDs, and a few posters on the walls. She wasn't going to take anything but the guitar with her, but she couldn't leave the other stuff down here. This place wasn't supposed to exist.

Because it was Saturday, most of the day staff wouldn't be coming in at all. She commandeered a cart from the laundry and loaded the rest of her personal gear into it, and took it upstairs where it belonged.

Her "official" office cubicle looked strangely virginal, since she was almost never there. She took a few minutes to set up the stereo, scatter the personal things she was abandoning around it, and hang her posters on the walls. She took the cart back down to the laundry (details were important when you were planning to vanish) and came back up to the office to turn on her computer.

She tested her worm by logging in with her Black Projects user code, and was relieved to see the message "No Such User." She reset the time on her computer to a date last week and logged in under her rarely-used official, abovestairs account. Then she spent a few minutes writing memos that would "prove" she'd gone on vacation a week ago, and wouldn't be back for two more.

Let Robert start a war with Faerie. I hope Lord Aerune makes hash of him. And either way, I'm covered, and he's left holding the bag. Bye-bye, Lintel. I can't say it's been fun, because it hasn't.

When everything was arranged to her satisfaction, she took her guitar and went home. Her apartment had always been just a place to store her stuff, and Jeanette wasn't the kind of person who accumulated a lot of stuff she really cared about—she'd learned that lesson early and too well. She threw a couple of pairs of jeans and some T-shirts on the bed, and pulled her studded leather jacket and engineer boots out of the back of the closet. She took a moment to strip the vest with the Sinner Saints colors off the jacket—it'd been years since she'd worn her colors, and she didn't want to run into any old friends now—before diving back into the closet for her saddlebags. She packed quickly—clothes, music, and cash, lots of that—before putting on her boots and jacket.

Time to go. If that idiot wants to commit suicide, he can do it without me—and if he manages to survive, he'll still need me and maybe we'll do the dance. But I'm not taking any falls for him. Survival of the fittest. I'm sure Robert would agree.

Her Harley was waiting for her in the garage below—a cream and maroon touring beauty she'd named Mystery, on which she'd blown most of her first paychecks when she'd come to Threshold. She stripped off the protective cover and slung her saddlebags over Mystery's back, buckling them into place before lashing her guitar down to the pillion seat. It would make an awkward load, and she might have been willing to leave the instrument behind if she'd been sure she was coming back.

But she wasn't.

She wheeled slowly out of the underground garage, blinking owlishly at the winter sunlight even through the tinted face-shield of her full-coverage helmet. She debated where to go for a moment, but given her mode of transport, it was pretty much a no-brainer.

South. Somewhere warm, with no snow and fewer questions.

Campbell didn't show up at the lab at nine o'clock. At nine-thirty Robert checked her downstairs office, found it stripped, and called her house. At nine-forty-five he let himself into her apartment with a passkey he didn't think she knew he had, and looked around. The place looked like a hotel room that had been trashed by gypsies.

God, how can anyone live like this? You can take the girl off the street, but you can't take the street out of the girl, he thought in disgust.

She wasn't here either. He looked around. There were signs of hasty packing, and the ice-cream carton in the back of the fridge where Campbell kept her stash of ready cash was empty. He felt a wave of smug disdain. *So she's bolted. Da widdle girly got scared and ran. Jesus, isn't that just like a woman?*

But did this really change anything? Robert thought about that for a moment, making up his mind. It wasn't like she'd be going to the police, not with what he had on her. Actually, Campbell's bailout wasn't entirely a bad thing. Ever since the drug trials had started panning out, Campbell had been acting pretty skittish, and that mutant-guy from last night showing up had obviously been more than she could handle. *After all,* Robert Lintel thought sagely, *it's one thing to read about psychic powers in a fiction book and another altogether to see them in front of your face.*

He'd probably scared her into running by talking about setting a trap for the guy tonight. Women just weren't any good in military situations. Oh, she faked it better than most, but Robert had seen the flash of fear in her eyes when the guy in the cloak had showed up. She'd just lost her head and panicked. How typical. Women were all like that.

But I don't need her anymore. I've got more than enough T-Stroke to turn a sample over to a good research chemist and find out the proportions—and more than enough to finish the trials without her.

And once he'd done that, he could write his own ticket anywhere in the world and kiss Threshold good-bye.

In fact, maybe it's better to wait a day or two before trying to trap this Aerune again. He'll be sweating, and I'll have time to rope in a few more pieces of bait.

Pleased with his conclusions, Robert Lintel left the apartment.

Everything's going to work out just fine. . . .

NINE:
A GAME OF CHESS

Though his dreams were only dreams, they were haunted by the Unseleighe taint Eric had felt in Central Park and the nagging sense that there was something he was missing. He woke up late on Sunday morning, rumpled and disgruntled and aware that somehow he'd blown most of the weekend without getting his coursework done. His mind felt fuzzy—the mental equivalent of indigestion—and he badly wanted someone to talk it out with. But Greystone wasn't available—when he looked, the gargoyle wasn't even on its perch outside his window—and Toni and Jimmie had both made it pretty clear last night that the Guardians wouldn't welcome his involvement in the situation.

But the more he thought about it, the more Eric was convinced there was something back there in the Park that they'd all missed. Something important.

Well, if they won't talk to me about it, I know someone who'll at least listen.

Even the most avaricious capitalists took Sundays off, and Ria

215

Llewellyn knew from long experience that you got better work out of people if you didn't ask them to give 110 percent all the time. She'd been on everybody's back most of the week, getting a feel for her New York companies and finishing up with dinner with Eric last night—which, while fun, could not by any stretch of the imagination be called restful—and today Ria was looking forward to a leisurely day of shopping and sightseeing. Maybe she'd even succumb to the impulse to go down and see the giant Christmas tree at Rockefeller Center. She'd forgotten how much she liked New York—it was such a human city, so un-elvish, that she actually found herself preferring it to L.A., where not even the special effects were real, let alone the people. Too many bad associations there: tragedy and betrayal and her long painful climb back to life.

Besides, Eric will be here for at least another year. . . .

That was certainly one of the attractions. They'd made a good start last night. He wasn't as indifferent to her as he'd tried to pretend. And he wasn't out to kill her, either on his own behalf or someone else's. In Ria's opinion, both of those things made a good start to a relationship.

The windows of her sitting room at the top of the Sherry gave her a magnificent view over the Park, an unexpected oasis of green in the steel and concrete forest of the City. The trees were winter-bare, the grass a faded brown-green, but at night the lights shining down into the park gave it an air of mystery—a man-made fairyland, in sharp contrast to the inhuman beauty of Underhill. Ria preferred it.

She was lingering over a last cup of coffee, a legal pad on her lap, when her phone rang. Few enough people knew where she was that she had no hesitation about picking up the phone instead of letting the front desk take the call.

"Hello?"

"Ria? It's Eric!"

Eric! She allowed herself a small smile of triumph. The first one to pick up the phone lost. *And your loss is my gain.*

"Eric," she purred. "How wonderful to hear from you so soon. Did you sleep well?" she asked, layering a double meaning into the innocent phrase.

She heard a rueful chuckle on the other end of the line. "Not really. I'd like to talk to you."

And do more than talk, I'll wager. Should she lead him on for awhile to demonstrate her power? Or would immediately giving him what he wanted be more effective? *Decisions, decisions.*

"Of course. Why don't you come over here? I'm at the Sherry-Netherland. The view of the Park is spectacular. I'll order a fresh pot of coffee. Or would you prefer tea?"

"Central Park?" For a moment Eric sounded completely nonplussed. Then: "Sure. Give me about forty minutes."

"I'll be waiting." *And to hell with the coffee.*

Eric hung up the phone, staring at it as if it were about to do something strange and unusual. He didn't know what he'd expected when he decided to call Ria, but it wasn't this, well, *blatant* an invitation. What was she up to this time? *Other than the obvious, and if there's one thing you can say about Ria, it's that she isn't.* Anyway, he was committed now. And there couldn't be any harm in going up to her place to talk, now, could there? Besides, if he went there, he wouldn't have to risk stirring up the Guardians by poking his nose into their business. He thought the best thing might be to stay out of their way if they'd stay out of his.

Time to get dressed, but in something a little less warlike than what he'd worn to their last encounter.

He pulled out a chunky oatmeal-colored fisherman's sweater, and hesitated for a moment between slacks and jeans. Ria wasn't a jeans kind of person, he decided, and went for a pair of dark grey slacks. He grabbed the leather jacket he'd worn last night, and dumped the contents of his messenger bag out on his bed to make room for the flute. He gave the books and notebooks a resigned glance. Rector wouldn't cut him any slack; he'd better get his paper— or at least, *some* kind of paper—done before 2 P.M. tomorrow.

Somehow.

He'd been past the Sherry-Netherland a few times in his rambles, but he'd never been inside. It was an imposing structure, like something out of an Edith Wharton novel: very repressed, very Old New York. He almost expected the gaudily uniformed doorman to refuse to let him in.

He made his way across the lobby to the elevators, found the one that serviced Ria's floor, and got in. The elevator was an express, and took off with a *swoosh!* that left Eric's stomach far behind, though it mercifully released him a few moments later. The corridor outside its doors was painted a tasteful rose-beige that reminded Eric of something you might find at a mortician's. Ria's penthouse suite was at the end of the hallway, and as he approached it, Ria opened the door.

She was wearing a man-tailored blouse of heavy white silk that she'd wrapped, kimono-style, instead of buttoning, and it was pretty obvious that there was nothing under it. It was tucked into the waistband of a pair of wide-legged cuffed and pleated pants of bronze hammered silk, and on her feet she wore a pair of high-heeled gold mules. Eric could see that her toenails were painted Jungle Red. With her blond hair hanging loose in a Veronica Lake sweep, Ria looked like the Bad Girl from every film noir ever made.

"Nice to see you again," she said briskly. Spoiling the illusion? Or breaking a deliberate spell? With any other woman, he'd know. "Come on in."

Eric followed her into the main room of the suite. Her perfume hung in the air, the same subtle understated floral she'd worn last night at dinner. He tried to ignore it. He'd come here to talk over a problem, not be a slave to his raging hormones.

There was a coffee service set out on a low table bordered on three sides by loveseats in a pale shadow stripe. As Ria had said, there was also a splendid view of Central Park. Eric tried to locate the spot where he'd stood last night and failed. It wouldn't be hard to find again, though.

"Coffee?" Ria asked, and when Eric nodded she poured. He still found something deliciously perverse about drinking coffee, since what was harmless to him was so deadly to Kory and his other elven friends.

"I didn't mean to interrupt your day," Eric began, "but something pretty weird happened last night, and, well, I wanted to talk about it to someone who'd understand. You see—well, to begin with, the place I live isn't an ordinary apartment building." *Lame, Banyon, really lame!*

But Ria didn't zing him on it, the way Beth or some of the Sidhe would have.

"So I gathered, after I met your stony friend," she commented, sipping her own coffee. She regarded him over the rim of the cup with steady emerald-green eyes, their vivid color one of the many legacies of her mixed blood.

"Well, Greystone's just the tip of the iceberg," Eric said glumly, belatedly realizing how much he'd have to explain before he got to the Unseleighe Nexus, and how little Ria was probably going to like any of it. "You see, there are these folks called Guardians. . . ."

Quickly he sketched out as much as he knew of the Guardians and their mission to protect the average run of humankind from the Dark Powers. He told her about Dharinel and Kory's warning of Unseleighe activity in the city, and of his own strange, possibly prophetic, dream about the goblin tower overshadowing Central Park amid the ruins of Manhattan.

"I told Jimmie about it, but with the Sidhe you never know *when*. Right now? Next year? Next century? But last night after you left, Toni came to see me because the Guardians had run into something funky out in the Park that they wanted my opinion on. When I took a look, I found that the whole place is lousy with Unseleighe magic—and something else I couldn't quite put my finger on—and it looked to me like somebody was trying to open a Nexus."

"In Central Park?" Ria's voice was rich with disbelief. "Using what for a Bard? And leaving aside the question of what kind of Sidhe maniac would want to open up a Nexus in the middle of one of the biggest cities in the world? Sidhe magic would be almost worthless with all the iron and steel—and man-made electro-magnetic fields—around, even if they lived long enough to use it. Even a human sorcerer has trouble in a big city, with all those minds around clogging up the Etherial Plane."

"Seleighe magic wouldn't work here," Eric admitted. "At least not consistently. But Unseleighe power runs a little differently, doesn't it?" He knew Perenor had been acting pretty much as a lone wolf in his vendetta against Terenil, but someone that ruthless must have made overtures to the Dark Court at some point.

Ria considered, worrying at her lower lip with her teeth as she thought. "I don't know that much about the Dark Court, but I'd have to say that most of the power they use isn't that different. Not in kind, anyway, or ultimate source. But in degree, yes—the Dark Court isn't squeamish about feeding off other peoples' life-force. And in a city this size, I'd have to say there'd be enough prey available to take the edge off any discomfort Cold Iron would give them. Enough deaths would allow them to punch through any kind of interference, at least for a short time. But whoever it is that's trying to put up a Nexus here, he'd have to know he couldn't just maraud around and not expect to be stopped—by your Guardians, or the police at the very least. And for all that either of us knows, there's some alphabet agency out there like the Men In Black to save the world from the scum of Faerie. This isn't the Stone Age!"

Eric grinned slightly, savoring the mental image of a posse of sunglasses-wearing Feds in Lincoln Green Armani suits armed with high-tech wizard's staves and magnetized steel sword-phones. *It's almost weird enough to happen. . . .* Then he turned serious again.

"Maybe whoever it is doesn't realize what he's actually up against. If you're Sidhe—and practically immortal—and living Underhill anyway—you might not really have noticed the last two or three centuries go by, even though it's made a helluva lot of difference here in the world. Meanwhile, you can't deny he could do a lot of damage before someone stopped him—and what would happen if the Feds got real, concrete proof that the Sidhe existed? I tried to warn Jimmie and the others, but those Guardians are way in over their heads—and they won't even consider the possibility that this is something they can't handle. Quietly, I mean." *Or at all. Guardians die as easily as anyone else, and the Dark Court can put a lot of resources into the field.*

But Ria's attitude had changed while he was making his point. She looked almost disapproving, now.

"I'm flattered that you'd want to use me as a sounding board," Ria said, sitting back in her seat and regarding him with an unreadable expression. "But frankly, Eric, I don't see what this has to do with you or me, other than meaning we ought to get out of here before the fireworks start."

Eric stared at Ria in disbelief. He'd just naturally assumed that once he'd told her what the problem was, she'd immediately have some suggestions for what to do next to take care of it.

"If a Sidhe Great Lord starts a war with the United States, we're going to be drawn into it no matter what," he finally pointed out. "This is entirely leaving out the people who'll get killed, or hurt, or sucked dry before he's stopped."

"The Guardians think they can handle it. You said yourself they'll probably stop him eventually. And you're the one who's living here, not me," Ria said. "Besides, there's a faint possibility you've misread the situation. Maybe a few disappointments will change your Nexus-builder's mind about moving here before he throws down for a full-scale war. So why not let these Guardians do what they're here for? You said it was their full-time job. They probably have lots of experience."

"Not with this," Eric said stubbornly. "They don't get many Sidhe here in the city. They've never seen this kind of magic before. You have, and so have I. You know what kind of damage a situation like this can do." He leaned forward, willing her to understand how important this was. But even before she spoke, he knew he'd failed.

"Eric, people are dying horribly every day, all over the world. Even if I devoted my every waking moment to making things better for them, it'd be a drop in the bucket compared to what they're doing to themselves. I have responsibilities closer to home—to my employees, to my staff, to the people who depend on me personally to be there, and not go haring off on some kind of damnfool idealistic crusade designed to get someone close to me out of a midterm exam."

"Is *that* what you think this is about?" Eric demanded, recoiling in hurt. Ria of all people knew how much trouble a Nexus in the wrong hands could be. He'd been sure that the moment he explained things to her she'd be ready to help.

Ria smiled gently. "No, Eric, not entirely. But I think it is part of the reason you're trying so hard to push yourself into someplace you're obviously not wanted. Dharinel told you to stay out of it. These Guardians told you the same thing. Why not listen to somebody for a change?"

I've already been doing too much of that! Eric felt a stubborn anger rising inside him, and tried to push it aside. He'd been open and honest with Ria, and she seemed to be treating this as if it were all some sort of meaningless game!

"Okay. All right. I guess I deserve some of that. But at least come and look at the place in the Park with me. Make up your own mind about how bad this could be. And if you don't want to get involved then, I'll respect that."

He leaned forward, willing her to say yes. To that much, at least.

Ria sighed. "Okay, Eric, you've won me over. I'll come and look. But I can't do it today, and Monday's looking pretty full, too. I have companies to run; give me a few days. I'll clear a space in my schedule."

A few days could be too late! Eric took a deep breath and regained control of himself with an effort. He felt oddly disappointed—in Ria, in himself—as if a door that might lead to something wonderful had just been unexpectedly slammed in his face. He'd thought—well, maybe he hadn't actually *thought.* He'd been upset about what happened at the Park last night, he'd wanted to see Ria again, and he guessed he'd let his hormones do at least some of the thinking.

"Okay," he said grudgingly, hating how hurt, how *betrayed* he felt. "I guess that's fair. Why don't you give me a call when you've got some free time?" He got to his feet. "I won't bother you any more. I'm sure we've both got a lot of things to do."

Ria rose gracefully, her face a cool social mask of politeness. Bard or not, Truth-sense or not, he couldn't get a peek at anything behind her shields to judge her feelings. "I'll see you later, then, Eric."

With as much dignity as he felt he could muster under the circumstances, Eric left.

✠ ✠ ✠

Out on the street again, Eric took a few moments to catch his mental breath. Those mis-cues just now had been at least partly his fault—and more than partly, if he were being totally honest with himself. He realized that he'd been thinking of Ria as a sort of natural ally against the Guardians who'd fall in with anything he proposed—well, she'd disabused him of that notion pretty quick.

Then I'll do it myself, said the Little Red Hen.

He managed a smile. It would have been nice to have company and a little backup, but he was a Bard, after all. He could do his own investigating. *And I'm right here, and the Park is pretty safe during the day. All the muggers are probably out Christmas shopping, too.*

And it wasn't really going against Dharinel's advice. Not yet. Whoever'd put up the Nexus didn't seem to be around during the day, and Eric would be sure not to leave any trail that could lead an Unfriendly back to his doorstep. The guy was after Talents, and Eric didn't fool himself about the fact that his own power made him a pretty enticing mouthful. And he wasn't interested in being anybody's lunch, thank you ma'am.

But a little looking around wouldn't hurt. And Ria was right about one thing. With a quick glance in the dark and a bunch of other people around, he *might* have misjudged how serious the situation was. He waited for a break in the traffic and crossed the street, heading into the Park.

From the window high above, Ria watched him go. She felt an irritated mixture of anger and regret over what had just happened.

Just who the hell did Eric Banyon think he was, anyway? The Lone Ranger?

Not the old Eric Banyon, that's for sure. The old Eric, the one she'd kept as an intriguing pet, wouldn't have thrown himself into things this way. That Eric had waited to be led, or told what to do. This one made his own choices, and his own rules.

But I'm not going to play by them. He can be the Lone Ranger if he wants, but he'll have to find another faithful Indian companion!

She respected him enough to send him away today, rather than teasing him into bed. It would have been a sweet sort of triumph to distract him that thoroughly—Eric had always been a generous lover, and this new maturity made him even more interesting as a potential bed partner—but she wanted him as an equal, not a conquest. And that meant equality on both sides. If she didn't want Eric as a submissive follower, then he was going to have to learn that he wasn't automatically the leader, either. Living in the real world meant negotiating for what you wanted—and if Eric wanted her as much as she wanted him, he was going to have to learn that little lesson. *And hope it doesn't kill either of us.*

That didn't mean she was going to hang him out to dry, either. He'd been right about one thing: she knew this enemy better than he did. She hesitated a moment, coming to a decision, and then picked up the phone.

"Jonathan? Ria. Look, I've run into a little something out here that needs looking into, and I'm going to need some backup. Yes. Armed and *very* discreet. Who do we use in New York? Call me back when you have the number. I want to make the call myself."

About an hour later there was a knock on her door. She checked through the peephole, and then opened the door.

"Gotham Security," the man said, holding open a photo ID for her to look at. *Raine Logan,* read the name below the photo.

He was only a few inches taller than she was, but he carried himself as if he were six feet tall. He wore a dark blue nylon bomber jacket and jeans, with an army surplus duffle slung over his shoulder. His black hair was brushed straight back from a deep widow's peak, there was a day's worth of black stubble on his jaw, and beneath his bulky clothing, he had the trim, sculpted body of someone who worked out with weights for more than show. When she'd called the service, she'd specified needing someone who could keep her safe anywhere in New York—and blend in on the street. The man they'd sent more than fit the bill. You wouldn't give him a second glance anywhere from Spanish Harlem to Crown Point.

"Come in, Mr. Logan," she said, closing the door behind him.

"Just Logan. And you're Ria," he said. "These are for you." He held out the bag. "The service has your size and your profile; you've used our West Coast service in the past."

She opened the duffle and pulled out the contents. Worn jeans with the extra gusset at the crotch that would give them as much flexibility as a pair of dance tights, a tight black T-shirt, and a jacket. It looked like a cheap vinyl imitation of a black leather jacket, but when she lifted it, it was heavier than she expected. She checked the lining, and found it was lined in Kevlar—enough to stop anything up to a Black Talon cop-killer.

"The dispatcher said you'd be going into some rough neighborhoods. You don't want to go looking like money," Logan said.

"Thanks," Ria said, meaning it. Gotham Security was the best. They turned down more clients than they accepted, and the reason they still accepted her commissions was because she never argued with their decisions once she'd set the parameters. Ria respected competence in any field. When you hired an expert to keep you safe, there was no point in telling him how to do his job.

"Help yourself to some coffee. I'll go change."

She'd worn running shoes on the plane, but they weren't some expensive brand someone would try to kill her for. She stripped off the seduction outfit she'd worn for Eric and changed into the street clothes the bodyguard had brought, then braided her hair severely back and pinned it into a tight bun. She looked in the mirror, frowned, and then went into the bathroom to scrub off every trace of makeup. There were thin gloves in the pocket of the jacket, and she put them on. Satisfied at last, she came back into the sitting room of the suite.

Logan was standing where he could watch both the doors and the windows, a cup of coffee in his hand. He regarded her impassively, and then gave a short nod of approval.

"Let's go." He held out a black watch cap. "Wear this. Blondes aren't that common in some parts of town."

Eric hadn't told Ria exactly where the unfinished Nexus was, but once she got into the Park, the trail of Unseleighe taint was fairly obvious. Logan followed her like a silent shadow as she cast around, working her way into the center of the magic.

Here.

The partial Nexus shimmered in the dry winter air, invisible unless you were Gifted *and* knew what you were looking for. Its twisted magic made even Ria shudder inwardly. This was Unseleighe work, fuelled by death, *human* death. She could still see the faint smudges of levin bolts on the grass where the Sidhe Lord had destroyed the bodies of his victims.

The surrounding trees looked faintly haunted. If the Nexus came fully into being, this would become a bonewood, the trees taking on a malicious life of their own in imitation of their dark master.

So he—whoever he is—was here. But where did he come from, and where did he go? In and out of Underhill, of course. She wouldn't be able to track his movements Underhill from here, and even if she'd had the power to force an entry into Underhill from a standing start, she knew too little about her foe to make it a good idea. She turned her attention to another part of the problem. Eric had been here as well, and recently. Had he seen what she saw, she wondered? And if he had, where was he now?

Not chasing the Unseleighe, that's for sure. There's nothing to track.

She circled the area, frowning faintly. This wasn't Unseleighe Sidhe work alone. There was something else here as well.

Her hands wove small patterns through the air as she called upon her magic—not the Gift that was the birthright of the Sidhe, but sorcery that she'd learned painstakingly over the years. She worked slowly and carefully, and at last she had banished everything that was wholly of Underhill from her perceptions.

But something remained, the human taint she had noticed at first.

And *that* left a trail she could follow.

An hour before Ria left her hotel room with Logan, Eric headed into Central Park. He stopped just inside the grounds to dig his flute out of his bag and put it together. He blew a soft note into the mouthpiece to warm the cold silver, and seemed to feel the trees around him shiver in response. More proof, not that he needed it, that someone had been using major magic here—enough magic to wake the trees, let alone the dead.

Carrying his flute in his hand, Eric walked deeper into the park, back to the place Toni had brought him to last night. The scorch marks were still there, and in the daylight he saw something he'd missed the night before—the deep cuts of horses' hooves in the frozen turf.

And sure, there are bridle paths through the park, but they're clearly marked and the riders stick to them. And these tracks sure weren't made by any New York Rent-a-Nag. Where were you going, Mister Dark Lord of the Sidhe? And who were you after?

Let's see just how you've been spending your time. . . .

He lifted his flute to his lips and began to play. A few trills and runs first, just to warm up, and then he segued into "Sidhe Beg, Sidhe Mor," letting the plaintive demand of the music speak for him.

The light seemed to shift, some colors growing brighter, others vanishing entirely. The hard brightness of the afternoon sun became muted, fading almost into the unchanging silvery light of Underhill, while the latticework of the unfinished Nexus burned bright and clear, like a sculpture of purest purple-black neon. The constant background noise of New York—sirens, traffic, and the hum of a thousand conversations all taking place at once—faded to silence. Now Eric could see the magic plainly, yet he himself was as invisible to mortal eyes as magic normally was. Cloaked in his music, Eric could pass through the city unseen, even by his quarry. He turned, casting about.

The whole park was dotted with hoofprints that glowed with a deep scarlet light—the Unseleighe Lord, whoever he was, had been making himself right at home, him and his elvensteed. The creature's glowing scarlet trail crisscrossed the grass from a dozen directions, giving the dry winter grass a spuriously festive look.

I can't follow all of these! Eric shifted his bag higher on his shoulder. He had to pick one—but which?

At last he saw one set of hoofprints of a slightly different color than the rest—almost maroon, instead of the bright vermillion of the others. As he stepped into them, he caught a faint whiff of something . . . something almost raw and primitive next to the ancient malice of the Unseleighe Sidhe.

As good a way to make a choice as any, Eric decided, and began to follow the dark track.

The track quickly took him across town and out of the high-priced spread. He could see splashes of magic along the way—as if someone had been carrying it in a bucket that kept slopping over, staining the sidewalks and buildings. When he got further downtown, a fine red mist seemed to hang in the air like a fog of magic—too thin to really have any effect, but more evidence that its source—or even many sources—had passed through here, all leaking magic like a sieve.

What is this? A mage's convention? And if so, why wasn't I invited? he thought whimsically.

The odd thing was, the "splashes"—for lack of a better word—seemed to be concentrated around the street people. None of them seemed to be the source, but somehow they'd been *near* the source, and not very long ago. Eric guessed the Nexus point in the Park hadn't been started more than a day or so—the timing of its building coincided perfectly with his dream—and the traces he was following would fade away completely in another day or so.

Cold weather to be on the streets, Eric thought, watching an old man pushing along a grocery cart full of bits and pieces of unnameable junk. *A Sidhe Lord down here. Now THAT's culture clash.*

The contrast between the busy, purposeful shoppers—all of whom had homes to go to—and the shabby homeless that cowered back from them like hungry ghosts was jarring. He didn't remember there being so many street people the last time he'd been in New York—hell, he didn't remember there being any, but the Upper East Side tended to run them out of the area pretty rigorously. He'd gotten used to seeing them in the last few weeks—as used as you could get, anyway—but as he headed east, he realized that the ones in his neighborhood were just the tip of the iceberg. As he left Yuppieland

and entered the area of clinics, flophouses, and SROs[6] the tribe of the disenfranchised seemed to multiply, and for the first time Eric realized how very many people in this city had no other home than the streets. Not hundreds. *Thousands.*

And not just people living in slums or in welfare housing, but people who didn't have any place to go at night at all. He walked past a man in a tattered overcoat who might have been any age from forty to seventy and was carrying on an angry, animated conversation with the empty air. His hands were covered with small unhealed sores, and there were flecks of spittle on his cheeks. Greyish stubble covered his cheeks, and even in the cold he stank of urine, unwashed body, and illness.

Isn't anybody helping these people? That guy shouldn't be out on the street. But even as he wondered, Eric knew the answer. These were the "borderline" people, the ones who'd been dumped out onto the streets from the institutions where many of them had spent their entire lives to make their way as best they could in the world. The idea was that they'd have caseworkers and live in supervised housing, but there weren't enough beds or caseworkers to go around, and so most of these walking wounded ended up alone on the streets. Add to that the junkies who stayed away from social services for fear they'd be jailed, the street kids damaged by predators or the homes they'd run from, and you had thousands and tens of thousands of people living on the streets—the population of an entire shadow city living invisibly in the cracks of the city most people saw.

A bright flare caught his attention out of the corner of his eye. Magic—the same magic he'd been following. It ended at a brick wall, the glare of it so bright it nearly hurt his eyes. He touched the flaking brickwork, and recoiled when his fingers came away sticky and dark. He rubbed his fingers together. It was blood. Old, but not that old.

This wasn't Unseleighe magic he'd been following, but human magic. Eric blinked, bringing up the image of the human city to overlay his mage-sight, and bent over to inspect the wall and the

---

[6]Single-Room Occupancies, aka welfare hotels

sidewalk. Now he could see that there were bloody handprints on the concrete. The wall itself was covered with blood, great arcing gouts of blood, as if somebody had tried to batter his way through the bricks with his body.

And I'm betting that's exactly what happened, Eric thought grimly, straightening up. He felt nauseated. Echoing through his mind, preserved in the stone, were ghostly screams of fury, as if the raging spirit were still trapped here. He scrubbed his hand on his jeans and raised the flute to his lips, playing the first tune that came to mind, an old folk tune called "She Moved Through The Fair," the sweet wistful lament seemed to soothe the energies here, sending the spirit on its way in peace, washing away the death-fury that had happened here.

"Mister? Hey, mister?"

Eric lowered his flute. He'd put so much of himself into the music that he'd lost his cloak of magic, and with it, his invisibility. He turned in the direction of the voice. There was a man watching him, a man only a few years older than Eric with haunted, lost eyes. *That could be me,* Eric realized in pitying horror. *A little more bad luck, a few more missed chances . . . not meeting Beth, or Kory. Missing out on the Faire-circuit. That could be me.*

"That's pretty music," the man said, when he had Eric's attention. "I'm Gary."

"Hello, Gary," Eric said quietly, so as not to startle his new friend. Though his body was full grown, it was clear that the mind behind the eyes was much younger. "Do you know what happened here?"

Gary's face turned sad, as transparently as a child's. "Fury died. We always used to call him that. He got sick and yelled at everybody, and then he started to fight with the wall." Easy tears glinted in Gary's eyes. "Nobody fights a wall," he said sadly.

Not with any chance of winning, Eric thought, glancing at the bloodstains. He was tempted to slip back into his magic and leave, but he'd already seen enough to know that he had a lot of urgent questions without answers. Maybe Gary had some of the answers.

"Have a lot of people died lately? In just the last couple days? People like Fury?"

Gary stared at him blankly, a sudden sourceless fear growing in his haunted eyes. "The angels take them—the night angels. I have to go," he said suddenly.

"Hey—wait! I didn't mean to—"

Gary turned away and scuttled quickly down an alleyway, vanishing from sight.

"—scare you," Eric finished, gazing at the empty street.

He could run after the homeless man, but he didn't think Gary had any more to tell him. Fury's death hadn't fed the Nexus—those deaths had occurred back in the Park. And what were the night angels? Unseleighe Sidhe? If the Dark Court was using Manhattan as a hunting ground, there should be unadulterated traces of their magic all over, but the only thing he'd found here was the magic he'd followed.

Nothing was adding up. It was as if he had all the puzzle pieces—and they all turned out to be from different puzzles. He sighed and looked around. At the end of the block a blue neon cross shone into the night. Eric raised his flute to his lips again, gathering his cloak of invisibility around him once more. The light at the wall was gone now, thanks to Eric's music, but somehow the neon cross shone even brighter in his Shifted sight. It was a sign for a mission, one of the places that tried to feed and shelter New York's rising tide of homeless. Reluctantly, Eric turned toward it. He didn't want to see any more horrors, any more forgotten men and women, but he needed to find out why Sidhe magic was tangled up with the homeless here.

The inside of the mission was warm and welcoming. Tables were set up where men—and women, some with children—sat spooning up soup. At the kitchen in the back, volunteer workers doled out more soup, sandwiches, and chunks of bread to a long line of those patiently waiting. They were talking among themselves in low voices where the diners couldn't hear. Eric crept closer.

"Not a lot of people here tonight," a woman said. Her companion sighed, rolling his shoulders to take the kinks out.

"There's something bad out there on the streets. A lot of our regulars are afraid to come in. I heard Johnnie Rags talking to Lindy earlier. They think we might be poisoning them."

"*Poisoning* them?" The woman recoiled in shock.

The man shook his head grimly. "I've heard from some of the other soup kitchens and flops. A lot of people are dead. And more have just . . . vanished. All in the last seventy-two hours. I thought at first that a shipment of bad drugs might have reached the street—but where would our guys get the money for drugs? They can't even afford beds, most of them."

"Unless the dealers have started handing out free samples like the tobacco companies." The two of them laughed together in disbelief, sharing the bitter joke.

"And what are the cops going to do? A lot of people die down here every day," the woman went on.

"Not like this," the man said grimly, shaking his head. "Not like this."

Eric turned away. The answers he wanted weren't here, but he couldn't escape the feeling that he'd just been handed another clue . . . if he could only understand it.

Even Shielded as he was, Eric was reluctant to leave the light and warmth of the mission for the cold gloom outside, but he knew he had to move on, see if he could follow this trail to where it began . . . or ended.

As he turned to go, a young woman sitting at one of the tables got to her feet, heading for the door. She was skeleton-thin, but she'd made some attempt at looking pretty. She wore a down jacket a dozen seasons out of date and a thin bright summery dress. Her legs were bare.

"Where you going, Annie?" the man behind the soup cauldron called.

"Got me a date," Annie said belligerently. Eric could see they wanted to stop her, to call her back, but before they could do anything she was outside, hurrying up the street.

Eric followed her. She didn't go far. There was an alleyway a few doors down from the mission. Annie ducked into it with an ease borne of long familiarity. There was a crude shelter there, made of flattened cardboard boxes, and Annie scuttled inside, squatting down and digging into her jacket.

"Got me a free sample, got me a free sample," she sing-songed under her breath. Eric could see the glitter of a small packet of white powder in her hands. It radiated a kind of non-magical malignity that made Eric blink.

"Hey—don't do that," he protested, making himself visible again. He dug in his pocket for his wallet. "Don't take that. Here— I'll buy it from you. Okay?"

Seeing him, Annie crouched back with a feral cry of alarm. Before Eric could react, she'd torn open the packet and poured the contents into her mouth.

Its effect was immediate and drastic. Her eyes rolled up in her head and she slumped down, unconscious.

Oh . . . God. Eric stared at her, sure for a moment that she was dead. *I've got to help her.*

He pulled out his flute. The people at the mission knew her. They'd know what to do. But their help wouldn't be any good to Annie if she was dead.

He let the magic flow down into him, reaching out to the flicker of magic—Eric experienced it as music—that every living thing had. Her song was faint, the contents of the envelope poisoning her nearly to death. It was as if two songs were playing at once, creating a jangling discord. Imposing a third one wouldn't help much.

He listened as hard as he could for the original tune, there in the cold alleyway, and slowly began improvising a counterpoint around it, strengthening it without overwhelming it. The music became stronger—he could almost identify the tune—when suddenly he was knocked off balance by a blast of . . . music?

It reverberated through his head, soundless yet loud enough to make his teeth ache, overwhelming all other sounds. The music wanted him to follow—it was a call, a command, dark and powerful and magical. Resisting it was like trying to stand still in the path of a cyclone. Annie still needed help, but Eric couldn't "hear" his own magic against the howl of the magestorm. He ran toward the mission. He could at least summon worldly aid. The pull of the Summoning grew stronger by the moment; he pushed open the door to the mission and half staggered, half fell inside.

"Hey," Eric croaked, half-deafened by the buffeting he was receiving. "Annie's out there in the alley. She's sick."

The woman who'd been talking as she served the soup ran over to him. Dizzy and battered by the dark undertow of the magical Summoning, Eric clung to her for support.

"Are you hurt? Can you tell me your name? Come over here. Sit down—"

"No," Eric gasped. "I've got to—I've got to go. Help her. She's in an alley up the street, in a box. She took something. Something bad." It was hard to get any words out against the call of the Unseleighe magic, and finally Eric abandoned the effort. He pushed the woman away and thrust himself out into the night once more, turning in the direction of the summons.

As soon as he was moving with the pull of the magic, his head cleared enough for him to throw up some stronger shields. The power of the assault had taken him off-guard, but he had his bearings now. It would be a simple thing to isolate himself from its pull entirely, but Eric wasn't sure he wanted to do that. He'd come down here looking for the source of the magic that had befouled the city—and now, it seemed, the magic was looking for *him*.

Sorry, Master Dharinel. I know you wanted me to stay out of this one, but a Bard's gotta do what a Bard's gotta do. I just hope I'm around afterward to get yelled at for it.

And I think I'm glad after all that I didn't get Ria to come with me. . . .

The only way Ria could follow the magical trail was on foot, and that was a slow process. The trace was faint, and easily confused, but Ria always managed to find it again. It led her south and east, down into some of the worst neighborhoods in New York. She was glad more than once to have Logan at her back. Most folks who saw him just tended to veer off from whatever mischief they were contemplating.

Night came early in the winter, and by the time they finally crossed Houston Street it was already getting dark. Ria was footsore and hungry, but unwilling to give up the hunt just yet. She felt more alive than she had any time yet since her recovery. Ria was a born hunter, and if more of her stalks were in the world of finance than on the city streets, well, the instinct was the same.

On the Lower East Side a lot of the buildings were red brick dating back a century and more. New York had moved slowly uptown from the foot of the island since its founding, leaving behind outgrown neighborhoods to fall into decay. With taxes rising astronomically, many landlords found it more economical to let buildings rot where they stood rather than invest the money to make them livable again. The ever-growing population of those who had slipped between the cracks of what had once been touted as the Great Society had taken over the abandoned buildings, forming new tribes outside of the protection of society. As Ria and her shadow had moved downtown, out of the affluent neighborhoods, the number of homeless had increased. They huddled in doorways or crouched on the steam vents that led down into the subways, watching Ria's progress with empty eyes.

With Logan behind her, Ria headed eastward, across the Bowery. More than a hundred years ago, this had been the northernmost boundary of Manhattan, its then-cobbled streets filled with gracious ladies, fine gentlemen, and horse-drawn carriages. Of that era, only a few landmarked buildings still remained.

The trail she followed was stronger here, but her puzzlement was growing. What would a mage, human or Sidhe, be doing here, in the middle of such poverty and despair? There was nothing down here but crack houses, squats, and a few brave homesteading yuppies. Soon enough urban development would sweep through here, just as it had elsewhere, leaving a litter of Starbucks and Barnes & Nobles in its wake, but for now, the area looked like a bombed-out city in the aftermath of a war it had lost.

Yet here was where the trail began—or ended. Ria stopped in front of the old building her stalk had led her to. It didn't look particularly promising. Even in the cold, she could smell the pervasive fug of rotting garbage and old urine. She cast around, looking for some hint that the trail continued, but there was nothing. She would have been more reassured to find a Nexus here than what she *had* found. A blank wall.

What the hell is this? Some kind of magical roach motel? "Mages check in, but they don't check out?"

It was impossible.

It was the truth.

"Lady. Hey, lady. Gimme dollar?"

A man—a boy, really, younger than Eric—came shuffling out of the alleyway to her left. He had the look so many of the homeless had, as if he'd been sucked dry of some vital component; prematurely haggard, but no less dangerous for that. There were two more behind him, obviously there to follow his lead and share in any bounty he acquired.

She held her ground. To back away would only encourage them. Most predators—including the human predator—would chase anything that ran.

"You one a' them angels. You come down here, you gotta gimme dollar. Whaddya say, angel? Gimme dollar?"

He was close enough for her to smell him now. His hands were stuck in his pockets, clutching a knife, a club, or even a gun. She knew he didn't plan to hurt her, only to take what she had, but when did life ever go according to plan?

And why had he called her an angel? The incongruity of it made her smile. Almost.

"You don't want to do that." Logan appeared between her and the would-be predator like a drift of smoke. She couldn't see his face, but he held his hands out, open-palmed, defusing the situation with his presence and his will. The man stopped.

"She come down here, she gotta give me money," he whined, focussing on Logan. But he was hesitating now, uncertain. "She an angel. Angels take, they gotta give."

"No." Logan's voice was gentle and final. "You need to get on and take care of business somewhere else. Go on."

"Bitch. Uptown bitch." His companions had already melted back into the alleyway, discovering that Ria wasn't an easy mark. Their leader glared at Ria in frustrated disappointment. "Bitch! Angel bitch!"

"Go on," Logan said, still in the same calm voice. *As if he were dealing with a child or a lunatic,* Ria thought. *And I suppose these people qualify on both counts.* He dropped one hand to his side and flicked his fingers at her. Obedient to his signal, Ria backed away, stepping off the curb into the street. She crossed to the other side, turning her back on them reluctantly. Behind her, Ria heard a faint scuffle, and a cry, and when she turned back, the man was lying on his back on the sidewalk, and Logan was turning away.

"Let's go," he said when he reached her. "Unless you need me to take him all the way down."

"No. I'm finished here. Let's go find a cab."

A few blocks took them back to Broadway. It was like crossing into another world. Broadway was one of the city's main arteries, running all the way from the Battery at the southernmost tip of the city, all the way into Upstate New York. It was fairly safe even at midnight, lined with boutiques, shops, and all-"nite" delis. Ria did a small Summoning magic, and a few moments later, a cruising cab turned the corner and stopped.

The ride uptown covered in minutes the blocks it had taken her hours to walk. On Sixth the trees were strung with fairy lights. The bright shops and well-dressed shoppers were a universe away from the war zone she'd just left.

And Ria had more questions than she had answers to.

A human drug addict doesn't just suddenly turn into a magician without a cause. And an Unseleighe lord doesn't just start building a Nexus in the middle of one of the most densely populated human cities on Earth without some expectation of being able to finish it. There's a connection there, somewhere.

So . . . find it. Find the root cause.

I think I need to do some more research.

Aerune had been patient, and now his patience was to be rewarded. After his last defeat, he realized he had violated the first rule of war. Always make the enemy come to you. No longer would he follow the human cattle into their puny traps to gain what he needed. His prey would come to him. And so he had woven a dark spell, a calling-on, that would bring every creature with the wit to hear it to a place of his own choosing. The Crowned Ones would hear it . . . and so, he had no doubt, would those who sought to keep his rightful prey from him.

And then he had waited with Sidhe patience, his dark piper playing, until the prey should walk into his snare. At last he'd caught the scent he sought—the scent of raw untrained Power bleeding flagrantly into the air. This one was more powerful than any he had taken before, and Aerune needed that power to build his Gate.

And if the mortals should think to set a trap for me, then I will lesson these human upstarts well in the ways of Hunting. . . .

Drawing his horn, Aerune blew a long, deep note. It blended with the Calling-on Song, making that melody a part of itself, grew and reverberated against the buildings of the city streets, taking on a power and a life of its own, growing until it filled the world.

Come, my children! Come to your master!

The hounds came first, and then his hunters on night-black steeds of their own—the lesser Unseleighe lords who did him homage, the Lesser Sidhe to whom his magic was life itself.

Aerune lowered the horn from his lips, but its call continued to sound, filling the air. He drew his elvensilver sword and swung it in a circle over his head. "We ride!" he roared, spurring his mount.

Behind him the Hunt followed.

They'd had to work damned hard to do it in less than a day, but this time his men had prepared the perfect trap, and Robert had the perfect bait. There was no reason to wait any longer. He'd instructed the men thoroughly about what they were to do, and sent Beirkoff and Hancock out with them. When everything was in place, Beirkoff was to give Hancock a second dose of T-Stroke—a bigger dose this time. This Aerune would come after Hancock again as soon as he smelled him. Robert was sure of it. Whatever the guy was, he wanted these Talents as much as Robert did, and Robert was making sure he had a tight grip on the only source. He'd pulled in his field-test operation. There wasn't any more T-Stroke out on the streets, so little chance of any other random

Talents appearing for Aerune to poach. If he wanted what Robert had, Hancock would be his only source.

Let the games begin. . . .

"What're we doing out here?" Angel asked Elkanah.

"Waiting," Elkanah answered, out of the boundless well of patience that was (in Angel's opinion) the senior Threshold operative's single most irritating quality.

"Yeah, I know we're waiting," Angel echoed sarcastically. "Waiting for some nutcase on a horse to come kidnap our geek. But what's with the chain mail? The spears? Just because this guy thinks he's King Arthur doesn't mean we have to go along with it."

Angel twirled the six-foot spear with the steel head back and forth between his fingers as if it were a quarterstaff. When he shifted position, his chain mail jingled slightly. God only knew where the boss had come up with this stuff on such short notice. But he'd worn weirder things in his time.

"We've got orders. This guy shows up, we throw a net over him and switch on the generators," Elkanah answered. Like Angel, he wore a silvery shirt of chain mail beneath a dark sweater. Even if they were seen, there wasn't anything to ring warning bells in any civilian mind. And this deep in the Park, this late at night, there was little chance of them being seen at all.

"Like he's going to back off because of a steel and copper net and a little electricity," Angel grumbled, but fell silent.

There were twenty-four men—all of Threshold's Black-level security operatives—gathered here, though only eight of them had chain mail shirts. Four of the others were carrying longbows with quivers full of steel-tipped arrows. Most of the men and the trucks they'd come in on were concealed now by heavy camouflage netting. They'd been in place for hours, waiting, told to stay out of sight in case any stray tourists wandered past.

The bait had come in an hour ago in an unmarked car. The technician with him had shackled him to an iron stake driven deep into the frozen ground. The bait was wearing a straitjacket and a gag, and heavily sedated besides, but he didn't look like he could be much trouble. A catheter port had been inserted into his neck, and Angel watched as the lab geek stuck a needle full of something into it and rammed the plunger home. Angel was glad he wasn't the bait.

A few moments later the night began to shimmer, and Angel looked away from the bait, resting his eyes. Your eyes played funny tricks on you at night, and because of the searchlights mounted on the trucks, they hadn't been issued night goggles. There'd be plenty of light to see by once the balloon went up. They'd be as visible as a frog on a birthday cake, but Mr. Lintel had been very clear on the fact that this operation wasn't supposed to take long. They were going after the guy who'd made trouble for Mr. Lintel before, and this time he, whoever he was, was going to be way outgunned. Angel smiled. The hard men were the most fun to crack.

"Move up! Get into position!" Elkanah whispered urgently.

"Why? I don't—" Angel said.

And chaos came.

One moment the clearing was empty. The next, it was filled with men on horseback, men with dogs, shouting and screaming and blowing horns. Angel didn't waste any effort wondering how they'd gotten here. He rushed forward, his spear raised, looking for a target. If they wanted to come in like the U.S. Cavalry, he'd make sure they went out like General Custer.

A dog leapt at him, and Angel smashed it down with a Kevlar-reinforced glove. It backed off with a yelp and he hefted his spear, looking for a target. There. One of the horses.

He thrust his spear into its flank, pushing hard. There was a scream—horses screamed just like people—a flash of light, and the horse was rearing and dancing away uncontrollably, its rider shouting and flailing as he fought for control. Angel grinned, and thrust again, no longer caring who these people were or why they were here. He got to hurt them. That was all that mattered. Another rider tried to rush him. He got his spear into the horse's belly, twisted, and jerked back. Its guts spilled out onto the grass and it screamed and thrashed, adding to the noise of the battle.

Suddenly the searchlights came up, flooding the clearing with harsh white light. He could see his opponents clearly—men in fantastic armor, carrying shields and wearing swords.

The man on the horse he'd killed jumped free, dragging at his sword. He was wearing an ornate helmet, like something out of a Conan movie, and beneath it, his eyes glowed red in a bone-white face. So what? All the fancy makeup and special effects in the world wouldn't save him once Angel got close enough. All around him there were cries and screams, flashes of light when the steel drove home, and a smell in the air like ozone. Angel stepped back, momentarily worried. A heavy sword could slice his spear-haft in two, and it would take him moments he didn't have to get to his Uzi. But just then there was a hiss, and three arrows appeared in the attacker's chest. Angel had thought that archers were a dumb idea, but now, seeing the smoke billowing from the screaming man's chest, he changed his mind. Mr. Lintel had been right as usual. Iron turned these guys into wimps.

Something struck him full in the chest, burning away his shirt, but the steel mail beneath glittered unharmed. Angel laughed, and moved forward, searching for fresh targets.

As swiftly as they'd attacked, the riders pulled back. Now he and the other pikemen were between the bait and the horsemen, and the backup troops in the trucks were moving up. In the blinding light of the headlights, Angel could see fantastic armored shapes on horseback, like something out of a bad movie, and around them the turf seemed to flow like water. A mist was rising, making it difficult to see clearly. There was a scream from behind him—one of theirs— and he turned to see someone go down beneath the jaws of a dog the size of a small pony. There was another volley from the archers, and more screams. Hefting his spear, Angel ran to help.

Elkanah saw Angel run past him, shirt still smoking from one of the lightning-blasts the Bad Guys were using. As the Boss had promised, their chain mail protected them, but God help them the moment these guys figured out how few mail shirts they had. A couple of the men were already down, and there were *things* out there he didn't even want to look at. He'd seen the briefing tapes about what Hancock could do. The Boss had said he'd be on their side. Elkanah wasn't sure about that.

A dog leapt at him, taking Elkanah's spear full in the chest. It howled, smoking like it had just scarfed a doggy-treat full of napalm, no longer a threat. But the force of its attack knocked him to the ground, and its death-agonies jerked the spear out of his hands. He rolled away, fighting to clear his street-sweeper from its harness. Still supine, he yanked it up and fired. It caught one of the armored warriors full in the chest, blowing away armor and flesh with impossible force. For a moment, Elkanah could see the heart beating in the enemy's chest before he burst into flame, burning with a pale blue light. In the momentary breathing space Elkanah rolled to his feet, looking for his own lines.

"No order of battle ever survives first contact with the enemy." Got to hand it to old Clausewitz. *The man knew what he was talking about.*

Aerune roared his disapproval, his injured mount dancing and shying beneath him, half-blinded by the harsh white light. Try as he might, the Unseleighe Lord could not break through the ring of steel that surrounded his prey, and his magic seemed to have little effect on the humans who sought to protect it. He'd already lost too many men. There were archers at their back, their death-metal arrows taking a fearsome toll of his Hunt—and worse, the human Mage who had been the bait in the trap was summoning creatures of madness, creatures who preyed on mortal and Sidhe alike. But his attackers were few, and there were other ways to win this battle. He could make the mortals pay for their impertinence.

And he would.

"Flank them!" he shouted over the roar of battle. "Let none escape!" *In the name of Aerete the Golden, kill them all!*

TEN:
FOR ALL THE MARBLES

❖❖

"Well, what do you know?" Eric muttered under his breath.

The summons was coming from within the Park.

He'd had the brainstorm to summon Lady Day as he jogged uptown, and so had managed the rest of the trip quickly. At the edge of the park he'd dismounted.

"Go home," Eric said firmly.

The elvensteed quivered, her lights flashing in disapproval. She wanted to go with him. "Home!" Eric repeated firmly. "I'll call you when I need you."

It had taken a moment to force his will on the elvensteed, but at last she'd submitted, turning in the direction of home. The good thing about elvensteeds was that they followed orders, most of the time. And at least he wouldn't have to worry about anything happening to her.

Hostages to fortune. . . . Something Jimmie had said, about keeping innocents off the fire-line, came back to him now, and he smiled grimly. Now more than ever, he understood what she meant. He was prepared to risk his own life, but not anyone else's.

He turned back to the park. It was fully dark now, and the street-lights in the park cast faint cones of illumination around themselves. He wasn't sure what time it was, but the streets had fewer people on them than before, and the park itself was deserted.

And something was waiting for him there.

Eric thought again about turning back, catching a cab and just going home, but sheer stubbornness egged him on. The Guardians didn't want his help. Ria didn't want to help him. Underhill didn't want to get into a fight. Dharinel had told him to stay clear. But Annie's face was fresh in his mind. Whatever it was that was out there on the streets, he had to stop it.

So I'll do it myself, said the Little Red Hen.

Inside the low stone wall that bordered the Park the call was stronger, and Eric was willing to bet that it was coming from somewhere near the unfinished Nexus point. He headed toward it, more slowly now, wary of ambush from something else that might have answered this Call.

Suddenly there was a flash of light ahead of him, bright continuous light, and a sudden blast of sound as though someone had suddenly turned the volume on a television all the way up. Eric ran toward it.

:Man. Mortal man . . . :

The voice in his head stopped him halfway to the clearing. It sounded like World War Three was going on there, but Eric didn't dare go on leaving this at his back. He turned toward it.

A pool of shadow at the base of one of the trees rose up. Eric had the fleeting impression that it wanted to be a woman but didn't quite know how. It reached out for him yearningly, and Eric felt his teeth begin to chatter at the sudden sub-arctic cold as the creature sucked the last mote of warmth out of the winter air. He raised his flute to his lips, blowing a long steady low note. He let the magic flow up into the sound, caging the creature's power and letting it drain away.

She—it—vanished with a thin despairing cry. But there were more like it, heading toward him. Half-finished things that crawled and slithered and flopped along the ground, radiating fear and pain and a kind of magic he'd never sensed before. The woods were alive with them, just like the woods in his vision—filled with gibbering shadowy shapes that were all red eyes and hunger seeking his magic, his soul, and his blood. They weren't Nightflyers—thank all the odd gods for small favors—but there were more of them than he could count.

And they all wanted *him*. Eric summoned his shields, just in time as something like a wolf but six times bigger slung into the clearing, growling. The creature crouched on its haunches, unwilling to attack alone, but still far from foiled. Eric raised his flute to his lips again and blew a quick waterfall of notes. The wolf-thing sprang up onto its hind legs, twisting and howling as the magic tore it into fragments that drifted away on the air like a skirl of autumn leaves.

But there were more to take its place, an army of darkness seeping up like water out of the ground of this suddenly accursed place.

I need something to get rid of all of them at once. What? The magic creating them had a source; he could feel it, like cold and deadly sunlight. Slowly Eric began backing toward it, dropping his shields enough to lure them in. He had to stop whoever was making these things, and hope it stopped the creatures as well. They might be a part of whatever fight was going on, but plainly they had no interest in it.

Inspiration struck. He began playing the slow opening notes of a Bach cantata as the monsters gathered in a ring around him. *Come to papa, babies. It's lunchtime!* Bach was cerebral, mathematical, human—the antithesis of the nightmare Unseleighe power that he faced. Eric focused on the music, letting it fill him completely. He had time for one last coherent thought—*if any of these gets past me into the City, there's going to be a bloodbath even the Guardians can't stop*—before he let the music take him, shutting out everything but the battle before him.

As Aerune's Hunt eddied about the edges of the human warriors seeking an opening, the Unseleighe Lord suddenly heard a bright waterfall of music—Human magic, Bard magic, a thousand times more powerful than the pitiful flickering about the Crowned One before him. He turned toward the source and saw . . . a Bard.

The man walked slowly toward the tangle of human and elven warriors as if he saw neither, destroying the nightmares that had taken a heavy toll this night on mortals and Hunt alike. Here in full measure was the power Aerune sought, power to build a thousand Gates. Not crippled and half-complete like the others he'd harvested— no, here was power enough to play all of Aerune's dark dreams into reality.

The crazed Crowned One he'd sought was only an annoyance in the face of this greater prize. Raising his hand, Aerune slew him with a gesture. The levin bolt sparked and crackled through the iron the Crowned One wore, arcing and spitting in great wasteful fountains as it seared his flesh into bubbling ruin, consuming him utterly.

"Take him!" Aerune roared, gesturing toward the Bard. He blew his horn, summoning back his Hounds and lesser creatures.

The monsters he'd been fighting melted away like ice in a blast furnace and Eric stopped playing, feeling the magic he'd been following simply . . . stop. For the first time he became aware of his surroundings.

Searchlights. Gunfire. Elves on horses. Men with guns.

What the hell have I stumbled into?

The bait went up like a roman candle, dead in an instant. When Aerune turned, Elkanah took the break in the stalemate as an opportunity to move his men back toward the trucks. Their iron bodies should provide some cover, and he was still holding in mind the Eleventh Commandment: Don't Get Caught. They'd lost the bait, they'd lost half a dozen men, but if they could get the net over the guy on the horse, they still might be able to salvage something out of this mess.

The horsemen were ignoring his guys for the moment, and Elkanah was thankful for small favors. He yanked the net out of the back of one of the trucks, gesturing for those still on their feet to help him. The net hissed along the grass behind him like a metal serpent.

Then he saw what it was that had made Aerune pull back. An

ordinary guy wearing street clothes, with what looked like a flute in his hand. The searchlights made the silver radiate like a chunk of burning phosphorus, but even in the brightness, the guy *glowed*, a bright blue as deep as the October sky. Instantly, Elkanah made up his mind.

If Aerune wants this guy, then so do we.

"Get him!" Elkanah shouted, gesturing toward the flute-player.

Eric heard sounds behind him and risked looking away from the Unseleighe Lord on the horse. Behind him were half a dozen guys in commando suits. Some of them were wearing chain mail and carrying spears. All of them had guns.

"Sir? Step this way, please. You're going to have to come with us," their leader said with surreal politeness.

Eric backed away again, trying to keep both sides in sight. He couldn't imagine why the commandos hadn't run screaming—he'd never seen elves like these, but he knew what he was seeing—a Wild Hunt.

"Choose quickly, Bard!" the leader of the Hunt called to him, holding out his hand. "You will have no second chance, and I think your shields will not hold against their weaponry! Choose! Them—or us!"

The hell I will!

He had to get out of here, and knew he'd only have one shot at escape. He reached inside himself, to where the music ran like a deep underground river, and pulled up a melody for which there were no earthly terms. As it filled him, he reached out for the half-created Nexus, twisting it around him as a stage magician might swirl a cape.

And he vanished.

The Bard was gone! Aerune snarled his displeasure, his breath coming in a serpent's hiss. So close! And yet the Bard had dared to defy him! He would have liked to slay all those witnesses to his humiliation, but without a Nexus to draw from, he dared not waste the power. His vengeance must wait, and be all the sweeter for being so long denied. He wheeled his steed, slashing a Portal to Underhill open in the very air. His mount staggered beneath him, energy bled from every pore—he could hold this gate for seconds only, but it would have to be enough. Wielding his sword as if it were a whip, he drove the Hunt through the Portal ahead of him, letting it seal itself behind him.

Angel stared at Elkanah for a long moment in the sudden, surreal silence. The guy with the flute, the guys on horses, had all gone pop like a soap bubble. The Threshold operatives were alone in Central Park, and in the distance Angel could hear the sound of sirens. Their little excursion here hadn't quite gone unnoticed.

"Does anyone have an explanation for what just happened here?" he finally asked.

"We can worry about that later," Elkanah said. There was a livid burn along the side of his face, and he looked like he'd been through the wringer. "Right now we've got to sanitize this place and get out of here before the cops show up. Get out the flamethrowers—and get the wounded into the trucks!"

Those still on their feet hurried to obey, hosing down the dry grass to eliminate bloodstains, grabbing dropped equipment as fast as they could. Someone scattered a carefully prepared litter of expended fire-crackers and beer cans to dress the site for the police. In less than five minutes they were on their way, running dark through the Park to one of its northern exits.

He was not looking forward to the report he was going to have to make.

At six o'clock this evening, Robert Lintel had been a man well-pleased with himself and the world. It was midnight now.

Things had changed.

His men had vacated Central Park moments ahead of an army of cops. They'd lost Hancock. Beirkoff was a gibbering wreck. They hadn't caught Aerune. And when another wild card had turned up—someone Aerune wanted more than he'd wanted Hancock, by all reports—they'd lost him, too. Half his men were dead—burned by lasers or hacked to death by swords—and all the survivors could tell him were a lot of confused tales about armored men on horseback, giant wolves, and monsters.

Monsters. He'd thought better of them than that. They were supposed to be elite troops, the best soldiers of fortune that money could buy. And they ran away like a pack of frightened schoolgirls.

Robert shook his head, pacing the expensive carpet of his top-floor office. He knew they were good. They'd never failed him before. So what had *really* happened out there?

Before Campbell took off, she'd been babbling about elves and the hordes of faerie, but those things that had been in the park tonight certainly didn't act like anything Robert had ever seen in a cartoon. Still, maybe she and her stupid telepath hadn't been as crazy as he'd thought. Maybe there *was* something in what she'd been saying—maybe there were some kind of space aliens living here on earth, space aliens that had been the source for a bunch of legends about gods and elves and things, like that von Daniken guy said.

Robert relaxed, pleased to have thought his way through to the truth. That had to be it. Not elves. Space aliens. He'd have Dr. Ram turn Vickie Moon inside out to find out what else she knew.

Because whoever they are, they're poking their pointy noses in where they're not wanted, and if they can appear and disappear the way they've been doing, it won't be long before they come here.

He sat down in the cushioned leather chair behind his desk and pushed a button. "Find Beirkoff and get him up here. Bring Moon. I don't care what time it is. That's what I pay you for."

He sat back, thinking furiously. He was on the right track with T-Stroke, he knew it. That young guy who'd wandered into the middle of things—Elkanah said that this Aerune had spoken to him. If Aerune wanted him that badly, then so did Bob Lintel. The guy could obviously do everything the Survivors could do, and he didn't seem to be in any danger of shrivelling up and dying either.

If I get him and can find out how he does it, I can make more. And then I can write my own ticket. I don't know where he's gone, but he's got to come back some time. And when I've got a stable of psychic assassins who can kill with a thought, I'm not going to have to worry about the Justice Department or the SEC anymore. I'll be able to write my own ticket anywhere on the planet . . . and I think the U.S. Government would be more than interested in getting in on the bidding.

But why wait? Nobody ever made a profit sitting on their hands. It was time to take the war to the enemy. . . .

Fortunately Logan was still with Ria when all hell broke loose. She'd ordered up dinner from room service for both of them while she'd made some calls to the Coast. If junkies were turning into mages, somebody, somewhere was making the drugs that were turning them. And Ria wanted to find out who. It wasn't impossible that this was some Unseleighe plot. Some of them positively doted on working through human pawns, using long convoluted plots like something out of a James Bond novel when a simple bullet to the head would be a lot more cost-effective.

She was standing by the window, looking out over the city, when she saw the flash of light deep in the park. Seconds later the riptide of unexpected magic washed over her—Bardic, Unseleighe, and every shading in between. Ria staggered back, caught off balance by the sudden assault on her shields, and went down.

She woke up as Logan was lifting her onto a couch. His dark face was impassive and wary. "Are you all right?"

"Yes." She didn't elaborate. Her shields had gone to full strength in the second after the assault, but she could already tell that whatever it had been was gone now.

Waving Logan away, she got to her feet again and walked carefully back to the window. There were four police cars pulled up on the street outside the park, lights flashing.

"My," Ria said coolly, eyebrows raised.

Logan was already on the phone, calling his office. She heard him give his location and ask for a weather report. He listened for a moment, then hung up.

"There's been a report of shots fired inside the park and a lot of bright lights," he said tersely.

And more than shots, Ria thought. "I want to go down there. But I don't want to get involved with the police."

He glanced at her, and she saw him think the problem over.

"Let's give it a while. I'll check back with my office in a few minutes and see what the cops are reporting," Logan said.

Fifteen minutes later the police cars were gone. According to the frequencies Gotham Security monitored, the NYPD figured the disturbance was caused by some kids setting off fireworks. Ria knew better. The only question remaining was: what exactly *had* it been?

She entered the park cautiously, Logan taking point. He was wonderfully incurious about what was going on . . . but then Ria was paying good money for that. She only hoped his perfect manners weren't going to get either of them killed.

By the time they reached the spot Ria had marked from her window, there was nobody in sight. She wasn't particularly surprised to find it was the place Eric had been so interested in, but now the half-built Nexus was gone as if it had never been.

Suddenly there was a shadow above her—something big coming in for a landing. A pistol appeared in Logan's hand—a Desert Eagle .60, capable of taking down a moose with one shot or punching right through a car's engine-block.

"Wait," Ria said, raising her hand.

The creature landed, and bounded toward her, talking all the way. It was Greystone, the talking gargoyle from Eric's apartment.

"Blondie, we got trouble, big trouble—Eric just went 'poof' on us, and somebody was holding a real brawl here when he went!"

Running up behind him were a fortyish Latina woman and an exotic dark-skinned woman in a patrolman's uniform. Neither of them looked surprised to see Greystone. *So these must be the Guardians Eric told me about, showing up a day late and a dollar short. So much for the safety of the Free World.* Ria glanced toward Logan, but his Desert Eagle had vanished as if it'd never been there. His face was impassive. Like a good bodyguard, he faded back behind her, where he could watch what happened without intruding.

"Greystone, who is this? What's she doing here?" the Latina asked.

"She's Eric's ladyfriend, Ms. Hernandez," Greystone answered. "She's okay. Her name's Ria."

"What's happening? Where's Eric?" Ria demanded.

"Gone," Greystone repeated, sounding as rattled as a gargoyle ever got.

"We're friends of Eric's, too," Hernandez said. "We, um, heard he was having trouble up here, but when we got here it was all over. And what brings you here?"

"My hotel room overlooks the Park," Ria said. It didn't count as an answer, but at least it was a response. She knew what Eric had told her about the Guardians, and wondered what he'd told them about her. And, of course, how much of it they believed. . . .

"I'm going to take another sweep around," the patrolwoman said. "Nobody's done a real search of the area. Maybe there's a clue."

You certainly look like you could use one, Ria thought, but didn't say anything out loud. If this was Toni Hernandez, then her friend the cop must be Jimmie Youngblood, another of the Guardians. But even if Youngblood was no ordinary cop, it never paid to antagonize the police. When Youngblood walked away, Ria returned her attention to Hernandez. It wouldn't hurt to be sociable, especially since she wanted something from them.

"Hello," she said, holding out her hand, and smiling. "I'm Ria. Eric's told me so much about you."

"I'm Toni," the other woman said, smiling faintly at the inane exchange of social pleasantries. Ria took the proffered hand. Toni's grip was dry and warm. "Jimmie and I are trying to figure out what happened here. And just now, we wouldn't turn down any help." She studied Ria consideringly.

"I'll do what I can," Ria said, looking around. *Whether I'll tell you about it remains to be seen.* "Maybe you could start by telling me what you *do* know? I know that Eric was very interested in this . . . location."

Toni sighed. "We asked him to take a look at it last night. Let's just say there's been some weird stuff happening, and this spot seems to be the eye of the hurricane. Eric said there were Dark Elves involved, building some kind of doorway . . . would you know anything about that?"

From the look on her face, it was clear that Toni Hernandez would rather have cut off her hand than asked, but it was equally clear that she knew she was in over her head.

"Less than you'd think, but some," Ria said. "I *can* tell you right now that the doorway you're worrying about is no longer a problem. It's gone." *And Eric's gone with it, damn the man.* "Let me look around a little, okay?"

"Sure," Toni said, taking a step back. "But you won't mind if Greystone keeps an eye on you, will you?"

"As long as he doesn't step on my feet," Ria said, composing her face into another pleasant but totally unmeant smile. She turned away from Toni and began walking in a slow circle around the area where the Nexus had been, frowning in concentration. Both the other women had brought flashlights, but Ria could see clearly in dimmer light than this.

The ground was cut up and torn in a wide area, almost as if someone had been trying to plow it, or to dig something up, and there were wide burn-scars defacing the grass that remained. Ria blinked, summoning up her mage-sight. Now she could see that a lot of magic had been thrown around here. There were the scars of levin bolts on the grass and the trees, and the entire place reeked of Unseleighe magics and human death.

And as if that weren't trouble enough, the Wild Hunt had been here as well. Perenor had sometimes spoken of the Unseleighe *rade*— he'd had the right to call one, but had never done so, dismissing the Hunt as too flashy and undisciplined for his needs. More to the point, Ria thought now, it would have motivated the drowsing Court of Elfhame Sun-Descending as nothing else could have, creating an opposition that Perenor hadn't wanted to face. Every Elfhame within a thousand miles must know about this one—she was only surprised that the park wasn't crawling with Highborn.

But Central Park is in the middle of New York City. No elf would come here without a damned good reason. And you walked right into the middle of it, didn't you, Eric?

The Wild Magic she'd followed down into the slums was everywhere, stronger than she'd ever seen it before. Someone with Power had died here, in addition to humans and Sidhe. Ria could still see the dead wizard's ghost, hovering like a plume of red smoke in the air. Dead, and recently, and slain by the levin bolt whose backlash she'd been hit with.

But it wasn't Eric, which was some small relief.

Once she'd sorted out the Wild Talent and the Hunt, the remaining traces were easy to read. The lingering effects of very neatly done magic, all wrapped up with no loose ends, spelled Eric as plainly to her Second Sight as if it were a neon sign twelve feet high. He'd been throwing Bard-magic around as if he'd been trying to put out a fire, but even in the middle of a fight, his work was neat, disciplined, careful, the work of a fully trained Bard, confident in his skill. He hadn't killed the Wild Talent—that wasn't his style—so it had to have been the Unseleighe *rade*. But from what she'd seen before, the Wild Talent and the Unseleighe were allies of some kind.

She glanced over her shoulder. Both Toni and Logan were giving her a lot of elbow room.

Someone else wasn't.

"You gonna do a spell, Blondie?" Greystone asked hopefully.

Ria shot him a deadly look. "I haven't seen everything that's here to see, yet—something else was here besides your Dark Lord and Eric, but it wasn't magical, so it isn't leaving traces."

"Does this help?" On its stony palm, the gargoyle held out an expended shell casing. "I found it on the ground."

Ria took it from him with a gratitude she was unwilling to show. "It might." She held it in the palm of her hand, gazing intently down at the small piece of brass. :*Speak to me, smith-wrought forging. Who has touched you? Where have you been?*:

The shell casing was too small to retain much information, but Ria gained a blurry impression of men with guns— many guns—all holding shells like this one.

"There were soldiers here," she said slowly for Greystone's benefit.

"Some kind of paramilitary group, anyway." She handed the casing back to Greystone.

She frowned, trying to piece the puzzle together. Eric, the Hunt, and a wild Talent had been here. So had a team of purely human mercenaries. Since she couldn't imagine Eric allying himself with either group, the best guess was that Eric had been caught between the two and needed to get out of the way fast. The half-built Nexus would have been the weakest point in local reality, so he must have used it to escape to Underhill, which would explain why it had vanished so neatly. . . .

Ria relaxed slightly. He was alive. Eric had a lot of allies in Underhill, and even enemies would treat a Bard with respect and probably be willing to ransom him back to his own people. So if he was in trouble at the moment, it wasn't urgent trouble, and she could call in a few favors to make things easier for him if it wasn't possible for her to track him down herself.

She walked back over to where Hernandez stood. She wasn't interested in the situation here any further, but she supposed she owed Toni a hint of what the Guardians were dealing with.

"Do you know what a Wild Hunt is?" Ria asked.

Toni blinked, as if she were taken off-guard by the question. "Some kind of a . . . it's when the dead ride out to hunt down the living, isn't it?"

"Close enough," Ria answered. "Except that it's usually the Unseleighe Sidhe riding, not human dead. Bottom line: a Hunt has ridden through here recently. It looks to me like they clashed with some men with guns—the police had a report of gunfire here in the park about half an hour ago, didn't they?"

"Yeah. They checked it out and didn't find anything. Decided it was kids with cherry bombs. But why would elves be fighting humans here? Or maybe that question should be asked the other way around: how did the men know the elves would be here?"

That's your problem, not mine, Ria thought. *You're the ones who didn't want Eric's help when he offered it, and I'm not a public utility.* "I don't know. But apparently Eric didn't think you were taking his warning seriously enough and decided to look into things for himself. I know he came back here today around noon, but I wasn't with him so I don't know where he went from here." *Not that I can't find out if I have to.*

Toni Hernandez looked as though she were going to press Ria for more details, and Ria was debating how much more to give her, when the other woman—Jimmie—came running back.

"Look!" she said with excited self-mockery, "a genuine clue. Somebody's been moving trucks—big trucks, heavy enough to leave tracks even with the ground being frozen—through the park. I found this near one of the sets of tracks. Someone must have dropped it while they were bailing." She held it out to Toni. Toni took it, and held it up so Ria could see it.

"It looks like one of those magnetic hotel-room keys," Toni said, turning it over in her fingers. "But there's no name on it. Just a logo."

"May I see it?" Ria said, keeping her voice even with an effort.

She schooled her face to blankness, inspecting the card. It was grey, easy to miss in the dark on a quick inspection, and anyway, the police that'd been here earlier had been looking for perpetrators, not evidence. The card had a gold logo stamped on it . . . a logo Ria had become very familiar with over the past few days.

Threshold Labs. That's a LlewellCo subsidiary!

Someone is going to pay for this. Dearly.

"No, I'm sorry," she said, smiling sweetly as she handed the key-card back to Toni. "I travel a lot on business, and I thought I might recognize it, but I don't. Sorry." And with her shields at full strength, not even a telepathic gargoyle could get through them to see that she was lying through her teeth.

"Oh." Toni sounded disappointed. "Can't you tell anything else? You're one of them, aren't you? An elf?"

Ria winced slightly. "No, sorry." *Just a mongrel that neither side wants to claim.* "I'm sorry I can't be of more help, but I'm afraid I'm not on the Unseleighe Sidhe's Christmas card list, and this isn't really something I've got much experience with." She tried to keep her impatience from showing. Threshold was *her* problem, *her* responsibility. She intended to deal with it without any kind of New Age Occult Police help.

"You've been a lot of help already," Toni said meditatively. "I just wish we knew where Eric was."

Ria raised her eyebrows in surprise. "I thought I'd explained that. He took the Gate into Underhill with him. But I'm sure he'll be back as soon as he can."

"I guess you're right." Toni looked as if she had more questions to ask, so Ria spoke quickly to forestall them.

"If there's anything else you need, Eric has my number." She turned and walked quickly away, leaving the two Guardians and Greystone staring after her.

All of a sudden, everything was quiet.

Eric straightened out of his half-crouch, lowering the flute to his side and blinking in the deafening silence. The elves and the soldiers were gone, it was "day" instead of night, and it was warm enough that he was perspiring in his sweater and leather jacket. Eric was alone, somewhere Underhill. He looked around cautiously.

He stood in the middle of a primeval forest, one lit by the sourceless silvery light of Underhill. Trees that had grown unmolested since the beginning of Time rose high into the sky, and the ground beneath his feet was carpeted with a thick pale moss filled with tiny glowing blue flowers, making it look as if the earth beneath his feet were carpeted with stars. Despite its beauty, the forest had the faintly unloved air of a theater between performances; a stage without actors. None of the High Elves were in residence here, then—only the Lesser Sidhe, the Low Court, those which could not survive except in Underhill or near a Nexus grove. The low elves were scatterbrained at best; he could expect no help there.

As if the thought had summoned them back, he began to hear faint far-off birdcalls, and slowly, the forest filled with sound once more. An enormous purple butterfly, silver crescent moons upon its wings, wafted regally past, and at Eric's feet, something small and grey and furry exploded into action, zipping into hiding before Eric could quite see it. He grinned in spite of himself.

He was better off than he'd been a moment before, and even if the terrain was unfamiliar, there was plenty of magic here to play with. Unless he ran into a High Magus in a real bad mood, Eric could handle anything this stretch of Underhill had to throw at him.

But since I'm not going to be staying, the situation isn't going to come up.

He could open a Gate right here and step back into the mortal world, but without a Nexus to anchor him—and with no idea of where "here" was—he might find himself appearing on Earth centuries in the past—or the future, or thousands of miles from where he went in. It would be better to have an experienced conductor for this little trip, and Eric knew just where to find one. Elvensteeds were created for situations like this.

But first, he had to change his clothes before he fried.

That was a lot easier here than it would have been back in New York. Here there was so much magic in the air that it was like breathing pure oxygen. Eric concentrated for a moment, considering what he should wear, and settled on just getting rid of the heavy sweater and turning his wool slacks into a pair of jeans that wouldn't get ruined so easily by a walk through the woods. He might need the jacket if he Gated to someplace colder, and besides, he was more attached to it than he was to either sweater or slacks. There was no guarantee that having once banished them, he'd ever get them back; magic was funny that way.

Having switched to cooler clothes, Eric breathed a deep sigh of relief. He rolled his shoulders, easing out the kinks.

Now to get out of here. *Maestro, a little traveling music. . . .*

He raised his flute to his lips and began to play. First a few trills to reassure the forest that he meant it no harm, then he segued into his Calling. The forest around him shivered, half-wakened by Eric's magic, and, as if from far in the distance, he heard Lady Day's faint acknowledgement inside his head. The elvensteed would find him wherever he was, and reach him as soon as she could.

Now all he had left to do was wait—which was just as well, as he had a lot of thinking to do about recent events. Eric looked around, walking through the forest a bit until he found a comfortable place to sit. One of the great trees had fallen (or more likely, a fallen tree had been created by one of the Sidhe at just this spot the way the

Victorians used to build "ancient ruins" in their gardens), and its trunk provided a pleasant seat from which to think matters over—and if he got hungry waiting, he could just conjure up whatever he wanted to eat or drink from the magic in the air. While Eric hadn't mastered *kenning*, the ability to create exact duplicates of anything he knew well out of pure magic, he could certainly summon up anything within a reasonable distance to come to him.

So it's a great place to visit, but I don't think I'd actually want to live here. All things considered, Eric preferred the "real world," even though New York didn't seem to be a healthy place to be at the moment, at least for elven-trained Bards.

He'd blundered into something big and nasty back there in the Park—something even worse than Dharinel's gloomy warnings about conquest-mad Unseleighe—and if he didn't want to have his head handed to him the next time he ran into the Guys With Guns, he'd better stop and think things through now, while he had a breathing space. Dharinel always said that a moment of thought could save a year on the battlefield.

The Guardians said there was trouble in Central Park, and I found out that the Dark Sidhe was trying to put up a Nexus about where I dreamed of the goblin tower, but when I followed the trail of the magic he was using, it seemed to be all tangled up with the homeless folks downtown. At the Park, I think there was some kind of a mage with the soldiers that the Wild Hunt was trying to get at, but when the Unseleighe Lord saw me, he killed the mage, and that got rid of the monsters I was trying to take out. And I beat it out of there, but the Sidhe's already seen me. And EVERYBODY loves a Bard.

So . . . could things be any more of a mess? Maybe, Eric decided with a sigh. *But not easily. Guns and Sidhe don't mix.* He kicked at the moss beneath his sneakers. Tiny beetles glowing in a rainbow of colors scurried out of sight, and Eric watched them for a moment, fascinated. The air was filled with birdsong now, making his fingers itch for a notebook so he could try to get some of it down on paper. Whatever he wrote would be a poor copy of the original, though. Still, it might be fun to try.

At least his responsibilities in this mess were clear. He had to get back to his own time and place, and once he did, he needed to contact Elfhame Everforest and tell them about the Wild Hunt showing up in Central Park. That should be enough reason for the Seleighe Sidhe to break the truce and settle this particular Unseleighe's hash, but that wasn't the only problem. There was still the matter of all those guys playing soldier . . . the ones with the now-dead mage.

Back in San Francisco, the Feds who were chasing him and Bethie had been tangled up with a project that was trying to tap into natural psi powers. But most people didn't have much in the way of either easily tapped psi or innate Power: the Gift usually ran deep in humans, most of the time needing magic or training to bring it to the fore.

He flashed back to the packet of white powder he'd seen in Annie's hand in the alley outside the soup kitchen downtown. What if somebody had figured out a way around needing magic or years of training to make a wizard? What if they'd come up with some kind of drug that forced Talent to the surface? That would explain the twisted mage he'd been fighting, and if the bad guys had been testing their stuff on the streets, it might also explain all those deaths that the Guardians—and the people at the kitchen—had been talking about. *Magery while you wait. No wonder that nut on the horse was so interested. If that stuff can crank up a human into a mage, just imagine what it would do for an elf?*

Eric shuddered. That was something he'd just as soon not find out about. But if the soldier-boys meant that the Feds were mixed up in things again, he was in even more trouble than he'd thought. Because if they were looking for Bethie, they were looking for him as well . . . and his cover would be blown the moment anyone looked really closely.

Well, this is another fine mess you've gotten us into, Banyon. Master Dharinel was right, not that his being right would have kept me from meddling. But it doesn't really look like I've improved the situation once, and now both sides are after ME. Gee, Brain, what do we do now? Well, Pinky . . .

He needed help and advice, and from someone who was as

comfortable with high-level human politics as Eric was with Bardic magic. The trouble was, he didn't know anyone who fit that particular bill but Ria. After what he could tell her about today, he was pretty sure she'd help him if she could, but that help might come at a higher price than he was comfortable with paying.

Well, we can burn that bridge when we come to it, as Mason said to Dixon.

All of a sudden the forest fell silent. The birds stopped singing, and the creatures scuttling through the fallen leaves froze where they were. Eric looked around quickly.

Trouble.

Nothing in sight, but his shoulders crawled. There was someone behind him. He could feel it. Eric got to his feet, turning around slowly, shields at full, to see what had startled the forest.

He stared. It looked like a giant lawn gnome brought to hideous life. Upright, it would probably stand almost four feet high, but it was bent over so far it was hard for Eric to judge its size, balancing on grimy bare feet and the knuckles of its long, apelike arms. It was wearing human clothes centuries out of date—calf-length leather pants and a long grimy smock that might have been white once but was now soiled to a grimy brown. Its face was a caricature of a human face—almost noseless, with tiny piggy eyes. On its head it wore a crusty brownish-red cap that it had dipped in some thick liquid that was flaking away now as it dried. The creature stank of undefinable things.

When it saw Eric's face, it smiled, the grin splitting its nightmare face impossibly wide. Its mouth was filled with long yellow teeth.

Sharp yellow teeth.

ELEVEN:
LORD OF THE HOLLOW HILLS

Robert Lintel regarded his temporary headquarters with disgust. Even in December, the smell was incredible. It was filthy beyond anything he'd imagined possible—interior walls torn down, some covered in graffiti, whole rooms used as toilets, people sleeping anywhere, on torn mattresses or just piles of rags. This abandoned building was a haven for runaways. That was why he'd picked it.

He stared at the terrified band of feral children huddled together in the middle of the room. He was doing these kids a favor, he realized. They should be grateful to him for putting an end to their whole trivial sordid existence. For once in their useless lives, they'd get the chance to do something that mattered, something that would benefit people more important than they could ever be.

As far as he had been able to tell from Jeanette's notes and what he'd gotten from the Survivors back at Threshold before he'd used them up, the younger you were, the higher the initial dose, the better chance you had of surviving exposure to T-Stroke and developing the Talents that Robert Lintel needed. He didn't have any more time to mess around handing out free samples to dozens of people to get one or two Survivors. He needed broad-based success—and fast.

"Okay, you! Sabatini! Is this everyone?" he barked.

"Everyone in the building, sir," Sabatini said. Robert had brought the cream of his surviving security troops here with him. The eight of them were loyal—and smart enough to know that they were implicated in everything Threshold had done so far. They needed Robert's protection—and Robert needed what these children could provide.

"We've got all the exits sealed. Nobody goes in or out," Sabatini said.

"Good." Street hookers and runaways were no match for trained professionals. His men had taken the place over before half of them realized they were being invaded, and within minutes his operatives had searched the whole building and rounded all of the squatters up and brought them here.

The funny thing was, not one of them had fought back. Robert had seen this kind of behavior before. Most people took a certain amount of time to work themselves up to physical resistance in a traumatic situation. Often the difference between the amateur and the professional was their quickness off the starting blocks, not their martial arts skill. The amateur might be just as proficient as the professional, but it took him longer to make up his mind that the situation required violence. And that was the difference between success and failure. So to keep any would-be heroes off balance, Robert'd had his prisoners slapped around a little once he'd gained control of the squat, just to drive home who was boss now. The children huddled together like a pack of orphaned kittens, wearing lace and leather, lipstick and sequins, the tawdry finery of a pack of Lost Boys and Girls who would never live to reach Neverland. They'd seen the uniforms and the guns, collected a few bruises, and now not one of them was willing to do so much as complain, no matter what he did to them.

They might get their spunk back in a few hours, but by then it would be far too late. In fact, it was too late right about . . .

"Now. Start dosing them."

Angel and Sabatini shouldered through the circle of huddled children. Of the twenty-four men who'd been in Central Park last night, only these eight remained, but that was more than enough for his purposes. In fact, when he got what he wanted here, they'd be disposable, too.

Robert had brought one of those pressure injectors with him from the lab, and all the T-6/157 he could find. Even after the random doses they'd put out on the streets over the last two days, there were several kilos left—more than enough to build an army with. As Angel held a gun to their heads, Sabatini injected the street kids one by one with a double dose of T-Stroke. Most of them didn't even make it into a sitting position before passing out.

Robert smiled his approval as the last of the street kids dropped unconscious to the ground.

"Sir?" Elkanah asked. "What do we do with the ones that go crazy? If we put them out on the street, they might lead someone back here."

"Put them down in the basement." On his earlier reconnoiter of the building, Robert had seen that the steps to the cellar were gone. Anyone thrown down there—assuming they survived the eighteen-foot drop—would have no way of getting back out again. "Put the dead ones down there, too. They might as well have some company."

Sabatini was sorting the limp bodies now. Two thirds of the kids were still alive. *So I was right about younger subjects surviving better. All to the good. There'll be no lack of subjects. Thousands of kids vanish every year,* Robert thought.

Almost as soon as the dead bodies were cleared away, the Screamers started to awaken. They were harder to dispose of than he'd expected; supernatural strength seemed to go hand-in-hand with violent psychosis, and his operatives had to play rough. Fortunately only five of the surviving subjects needed that treatment, and with the doors between the kitchen and the front room shut, he couldn't even hear them screaming once they'd been dumped in the basement.

And if their presence lured that pointy-eared claim-jumper

Aerune back again, that was all to the good. A steel knife through the gut should settle him down and make him see reason.

Soon, the Survivors started to rouse, staring around themselves with wide, disbelieving eyes. There was a skinny blonde brat who seemed to be their leader. She glared at Lintel in terrified defiance, her mascara running down her painted cheeks in thick black streaks.

It doesn't get any better than this, Robert thought gloatingly. This was always the best part, watching someone who was too terrified of him to run away. Campbell had been an exemplary employee in many respects, but she'd never been properly afraid of him. Maybe he'd look her up and change that, once he had this situation squared away to his liking. He looked around for some place to sit, found nothing, and resigned himself to standing. He wouldn't be here for more than a few hours, anyway.

After that, he'd be taking the war to the enemy.

"Now—" he said, smiling predatorially at the Survivors. "This is what I want you to do. . . ."

Ria hadn't slept all night, and neither had a lot of people in the West Coast offices. She'd dragged Jonathan out of bed with her midnight phone call, but Ria was too angry about her discovery to care: she wanted action and she wanted it now.

Jonathan delivered, gods bless him. It hadn't taken him long to get the first of the answers she wanted, and the more she found out about Threshold Labs, the worse things sounded. The company had been draining even more money from LlewellCo than she'd realized at first glance, its depredations carefully camouflaged by the bright boys and girls in Oversight and Accounting.

And as for what Threshold had done with all that LlewellCo cash . . .

"Since when does a pharmaceutical company need a private army?" she demanded into the telephone. "These invoices are ludicrous! We've been shovelling money at them for *five years* and all we've gotten have been glowing promises—I want to know *exactly* what Threshold's been doing with its time and my money and I want to know *yesterday.*"

Baker and Hardesty were behind this. Only someone high up in LlewellCo could have covered things up for this long. Well, the two of them were going to be looking for new jobs by the time the sun set in California, Ria vowed.

As for Threshold's CEO, Robert Lintel . . .

Jonathan's people in Computer Security had gotten into the Threshold computers without trouble—no surprise, as most of them were former outlaw hackers, working for LlewellCo as an alternative to jail. According to what they'd pulled out of the files so far—the data would take weeks to sift thoroughly—Lintel had been running a black books research program for almost as long as he'd been running Threshold, something about triggering psychic powers in humans through the use of psychotropic drug cocktails.

And it looks like he got far enough with it to go to field trials. I am going to crucify him for this—and anyone else I can get my hands on!

She paced furiously, but she knew there was no point in coming down on Threshold until she had absolute proof. It would be too easy for them to start dumping records at the first sign of discovery— although, to Ria's fury, someone seemed to have anticipated her there as well.

Lintel certainly hadn't been doing the research himself—not with nothing more than a Harvard MBA—but whoever the production-end brains of the outfit had been, he or she seemed to have jumped ship, because there was no evidence of him or his research notes anywhere in the Threshold mainframe. If Mr. X had gone to that much trouble to remove all trace of his former employment, it was probably because he was on the run. Which meant that he was out of the picture for the moment, and out of reach.

But I'll find you, wherever you are. And when I do, you'll wish you'd gone down with Threshold!

She glanced at her watch, then over at the man sitting silently on the couch. Logan looked like some kind of hyperrealistic sculpture of a sleeping man, not that he was asleep. From time to time she surprised him watching her, as if he were quietly assessing the situation. She wasn't sure why she'd kept him with her, but now she was glad she had.

"I'm going downtown to break into a lab," she said. "I own it, but that probably won't count for much just at the moment. I'll need some serious backup."

"How serious?" Logan asked. He got to his feet and stretched, working out the kinks of a long sleepless night.

"They won't have tanks," she thought, thinking back to the scene in the Park. "Aside from that, assume the worst."

While the team was assembled, Ria went off to change. This assault would require armor of a different sort.

They arrived at Threshold just after the morning shift. The Guardians still had the key-card someone had dropped in Central Park, but Ria didn't need it. She went in through the front door.

"Good morning. I'm Ria Llewellyn. I own this company. If you want to have a job by tonight, you'll keep your hands off that phone and buzz us through," she said, her voice dangerous.

The receptionist took one look at Ria and the five men with her and pressed the button. Ria went directly to the top floor, and forced her way past a second receptionist and Lintel's private secretary.

But all for nothing. Lintel wasn't there. And from the look of the place, he wasn't coming back.

Ria swore feelingly. She'd been sure she'd get here in time to nail the slimy bastard. Lintel had too much invested in Threshold to just go slinking off leaving his turf undefended!

"Ma'am?"

The bodyguard she'd posted outside the door to watch the secretary came inside, dragging someone by the scruff of the neck. The victim was wearing a white lab coat, and looked absolutely terrified.

"I caught him coming out of the elevator, heading for Lintel's office. When he saw me he tried to bolt."

"Bring him over here," Ria said, leaning back against Lintel's desk. Because she thought she'd be facing a corporate raider this morning, she'd dressed to match: a dark green Dior skirted suit with matching pumps. Dagger optional.

It didn't take much in the way of Talent to read the man's mind.

His name was Beirkoff, and he'd been one of the group in Central Park last night. He'd also been Lintel's inside man on the black budget op that Lintel had been running, and now that he realized Lintel was gone, Beirkoff knew he'd been cut off and left to twist in the wind. He'd be willing to do anything to save his skin.

"Lose something?" Ria asked mockingly. "Your safety net, perhaps?" Beirkoff's face went grey, and for a moment, the bodyguard's fist in his collar was the only thing holding him up. The details of the project flashed through his mind—an underground testing lab, some cells, too many people dead. . . .

"Mr. Beirkoff, you have exactly one chance to save your life and your freedom," Ria said, getting to her feet and leaning toward him. "Take me down to the Black Labs and tell me everything you know about T-6/157."

There was a slot for a key-card on the inside wall of the Executive Elevator, and three unmarked buttons below it. Ria'd found the card in Lintel's desk, once she'd broken the lock. Beirkoff slid it into place and pressed the third button.

Beirkoff hadn't been good at forming coherent sentences, but Ria'd had no trouble getting most of the story by skimming the surface of his thoughts. Unfortunately, he had no idea what had happened after Eric had vanished from the Park, nor what Lintel might be up to right now. Lintel had sent him home for the night, and when he'd come back this morning, he'd walked straight into Ria.

The level the elevator opened onto showed every sign of having been hastily vacated. Doors stood open, files lay on the floor.

"Search it," Ria said crisply. Sorcerous telepathy wasn't admissible in court, and even direct testimony wouldn't really hold up well against a high-priced lawyer. She needed hard evidence to hang Lintel with.

She got it when Beirkoff took her down to the holding cells. A man in a white lab coat—Beirkoff's thoughts identified him as Dr. Ramchandra, the only other on-the-books Threshold employee with Black Level clearance—lay dead in the hallway, shot neatly through the chest. Beirkoff was horrified, and Ria suspected that he'd never seen anyone freshly dead before. Like so many yuppies, his only encounters with death were via the media, or perhaps the sanitized and beautified body of a friend or relative after the mortuary professionals had made it acceptable. Ria thought back to the battle in Griffith Park. She'd seen violent death in every possible aspect. Bored with his horror, she moved on.

All of the cells were full, and all of the occupants were dead as well. They looked like the mummies from the Egyptian wing of the Metropolitan Museum of Art. It was hard to believe they'd ever been human.

"They were the ones who survived," Beirkoff said from behind her in a shaken voice. "If the stuff didn't kill them on the first shot and you gave them a second dose, it was like they just . . . burned out."

"There's no one here," Logan said, coming back down the hall. He glanced at Ramchandra's body and then back at Ria, his expression unchanging. "But there's a lab back there that looks like somebody used it to cook up a major batch of something that isn't there now."

"Campbell did the cooking," Beirkoff said, recovering more by the minute. "She got the stuff as far as field trials and then she took off. But Mr. Lintel made sure she made up a big batch before she split."

And Campbell was the only one who knew the recipe, though any competent chemist could probably reconstruct it from a large enough sample, Ria read in his mind. *Campbell. Jeanette Campbell. I'll remember that name. Someday soon, Jeanette Campbell, you and I are going to have a short but interesting talk.*

It was time to call the cops and bust this situation wide open. A part of her couldn't help noting that this whole thing was going to be a media bonus for LlewellCo—valiant chairwoman discovers illegal research going on in one of her subsidiaries, does a Bernstein and Woodward, and turns the results over to the cops. She'd be a Movie of the Week for sure. She'd also be tied up in red tape and meetings for the next year, and Ria had other things to do just at the moment. She turned to Lintel's flunky.

"Listen to me, Beirkoff. You'd like to stay out of prison, right?"

Beirkoff nodded, obviously more terrified right now of Ria than of the dead body lying on the floor or the wrath of the absent Robert Lintel.

"You have exactly one hope of doing that. You are going to call the cops and report what you found here, and tell them the following story: You came to me with your suspicions. I sent you down here with a security team and orders to notify the authorities if you found anything. I wasn't here today. In fact, I've never been here at all. There will be a lawyer here in an hour to handle LlewellCo's involvement, but you won't wait for him. You're going to give the police full cooperation.

"Play it this way and you come out smelling like a rose. Cross me, and I guarantee that LlewellCo—and I personally—will do everything in our power to make the brief remainder of your sordid existence a living hell."

"Yes, sir! Yes, ma'am! I mean—yes. I can do that," Beirkoff babbled.

"Good. I'm out of here. The rest of you, stay here and keep Mr. Beirkoff honest."

When she stepped out on the street again, the contrast was as great as if she'd stepped through a Portal into Underhill. It was one of those bright winter days that sometimes came in December, the kind that made you think that New York was a nice place to be after all.

But right now it wasn't a nice place for somebody. Because somewhere out there right now, Robert Lintel was trying to turn ordinary humans into mages using a drug that had a one hundred percent net fatality rate.

And he and Eric were on a collision course.

Eric drew himself up and did his level best to channel Dharinel in a bad mood. The elven mage didn't suffer fools gladly at the best of times, and that damn-your-eyes arrogance was the only thing that would save Eric now.

"It took you long enough to get here!" he snarled at the gnomish Unseleighe lackey in his best imitation of a pissed-off elven noble, leaking a little magic past his shields to reinforce the effect. "Take me to your Lord—at once, do you hear!"

And they said spending all that time at RenFaires would never be good for anything. . . .

"Yes, High Lord. Urla hears and obeys. At once, High Lord!" The creature knelt, pulling the cap from its head and kneading it between enormous gnarled hands. Its wetness left brownish smears on Urla's skin. Eric had a sick feeling that he knew what it had been soaked with. Blood.

Not one of the good guys. That's for sure.

But for once Faire shtick wasn't just a way of amusing travelers and filling his pockets. This time he was playing for his life. His bluff had worked so far—it was a safe bet that any of the Lesser creatures he encountered would owe fealty to some High Lord or another, and even the Unseleighe Lords followed certain rules—which was more than Eric could say for this Urla. He knew that Lady Day would find him eventually, no matter where he went in Underhill. But until she did, Eric was more or less trapped here, though rather less than more.

"Get up—get up!" he said haughtily, waving the hand that didn't hold his flute. "I don't have time for this nonsense!"

The redcap crawled backward submissively before springing to its feet. Bowing and gesturing, it began to lead Eric through the forest. He took the time to take his flute apart and put it back in its case in his messenger bag before following. He didn't know what he might encounter along the way, and he didn't want to lose the instrument.

Urla led him onward through the empty forest until they came to an enormous tree. Its trunk was easily thirty feet around, and like many trees this old and large, its lower trunk was hollow. Eric followed Urla through the gap in the trunk, and when they came out the other side, the forest was gone.

The place Eric found himself in now wasn't nearly as nice. For one thing, it stank. He and Urla were standing on a hummock of grass in what seemed to be the center of a large swamp. Between the hummocks, the swamp water glowed a faint toxic green, simmering languidly as bubbles of gas worked their way to the surface and popped with an evil smacking sound. The illumination here was dimmer than the light of the forest and had a reddish cast. Thick mist hung from trees festooned with fleshy pale blossoms that gave off a nauseatingly sweet scent, as if they were rotting instead of blooming. Eric's skin crawled; he was in Unseleighe territory now, and no mistake about it. He could see large bat-winged things flying slowly through the distance, and as he stood gazing around himself, a terrible scream split the air—whether of predator or prey, he didn't know.

Urla looked up at him to see his reaction, beady eyes glittering. Eric glared back as arrogantly as he could manage, and the bluff seemed to work. The redcap hurried off, bounding from island to island of dry land. The islands were yards apart, distances Eric couldn't jump, and he'd have to be crazy to step down into the water. This was obviously some kind of test.

He summoned his power—he didn't need his flute here, or even music, but unbidden, a few bars of an old Simon and Garfunkel song skirled through his brain as he wove the magic. *Like a bridge over VERY troubled waters. . . .*

Silvery mist rose out of the swamp and coalesced, following the redcap's trail. Eric stepped out onto it cautiously. It gave slightly beneath his feet, like the surface of a waterbed, but it held him comfortingly far above the surface of the swamp. He stepped out onto the bridge and followed Urla dry-footed across the bog.

The exit Portal here was in a bank of mist. Eric knew enough about Underhill geography to know that the shortest distance between two points wasn't necessarily in a straight line. Navigating Underhill was more like solving a maze, one where every turn could take you half a dozen different places. The Unseleighe were a paranoid lot, defending their territories by making them hard to find, and even harder to enter.

Urla walked into the mist and Eric followed cautiously. He didn't trust the redcap at all, and Urla would certainly think it was a great joke to lead Eric into danger, but he didn't think the creature was trying to lead him into a trap. Not yet, anyway.

This time Eric found himself in utter darkness on the far side of the Portal, and quickly summoned a ball of elf-light. By its pale bluish illumination he could see that there was grass beneath his feet, short and trampled as if herds of animals had been running across it. A chill monotonous wind blew steadily, making him shudder more than shiver as he looked around. He was in the middle of a broad and featureless plain that seemed to stretch a thousand miles in every direction. When he looked up, there were no stars.

"I'm losing patience," Eric warned, in what he hoped was the approved Unseleighe style. It seemed to be what Urla expected, because the redcap grovelled again, swearing to the Great Lord that they were almost there, indeed, their destination was mere instants away. The redcap turned away and began to trot across the plain, picking up speed until Eric was hard-pressed to keep up with it. Without the elf-light he'd summoned, he would have been unable to follow at all.

A couple of times the ground shook silently as if something huge and heavy were running across it—though Eric saw nothing—and a couple of times he almost thought he'd heard something over the droning of the ceaseless wind, but he didn't dare stop to listen for fear of losing his guide. Bard or not, he had a notion that it would not be a good idea to be lost in this particular realm at the mercy of whatever it was that lived here. The swamp had been bad, but there was something almost honest about its malignity. This was a lot creepier.

At last they came to a henge: two black rough-hewn standing stones supporting a third laid across their tops. The three stones were the size of Greyhound buses, and seemed to be made out of some fine-grained stone. *Basalt,* Eric dredged up from a dark corner of memory. *Like in H. P. Lovecraft. I just hope whoever lives here isn't a fan of the classics.*

Urla trotted between the menhirs and vanished. Having no other real choice, Eric followed. As he'd expected, the landscape changed again. Now there was light. He stopped, blinking as his eyes adjusted.

Wait. I know this place.

He stood now in the wood that he'd dreamed of before—the black and silver wood where the winter-bare trees looked as if they were made of black and polished bone, and the ground was covered with a thick treacherous white mist. Urla was obviously on familiar ground now, for he moved more slowly than before—as if he didn't relish getting to his destination. Neither did Eric. Such a direct route to his destination indicated that whoever lived here felt he had little to fear from invaders, and that much confidence meant something old, powerful . . . and dangerous.

Dangerous enough to think invading New York would be a cake-walk. Oh, boy, Banyon. You sure know how to pick your enemies. . . .

In the distance, shining through the trees like a baleful moth-green moon, was the goblin tower of Eric's vision, but oddly, instead of worrying him further, he found himself with a treacherous desire to laugh.

Whoa! Who does the decorating here? Skeletor? That place looks more like Castle Greyskull than any place has a right to. This place was beyond over-the-top: it was just *too* grim and *too* gothic for him to be able to take it seriously—as if a Hollywood set designer had done a makeover on Hell.

You'd better take it seriously, Banyon. Because THEY sure are, and I bet Unseleighe Sidhe don't have much of a sense of humor. . . .

As they approached, Eric saw that the front gate of the castle was guarded by a pair of armed knights in full ornate elvish armor that glowed like tarnished silver. Both of them were holding long and wickedly barbed pikes, in addition to wearing swords. Their eyes glowed red in the cavern of their helmets, but it was plain to see that Eric's arrival—at least on his own two feet—was unexpected enough to disconcert them. More bad news: that meant they were Sidhe, not some kind of created servitors, things little better than those white-armored guys in Star Wars. If this lord could compel actual Sidhe to do gruntwork like this, well . . .

Let's just say I've got a bad feeling about this.

Urla hesitated, obviously expecting some kind of formal challenge from the guards, but Eric was pretty sure it wouldn't be a good idea to stop for one. He pushed past the redcap and strode through the castle gates as if he had every right to be there. He passed beneath the portcullis into the outer bailey. There was a second set of guards standing before the inner doors, as silent and rigid as the first.

The inner door swung open as he approached, and Eric strode through, Urla scurrying along behind him. Now he was in the outermost interior room, a space as vast as a performance hall. It was bare and empty, its black stone walls polished to mirror brightness and long narrow windows high upon the walls. An open gateway beckoned Eric onward.

If he hadn't already spent so much time in various parts of Underhill, he would have been lost immediately. But by now he knew enough of the interior layout of Sidhe castles—and castles in general—to have a good idea of where the throne room was. He moved quickly through the maze of corridors and chambers, working his way upward. He saw several guards, all armored the way the first sets had been, but no one challenged him. *They probably think that if I've gotten this far, I have a right to be here. One good thing about a really evil overlord is that his underlings don't tend to do a lot of thinking for themselves. . . .*

Urla seemed to have deserted him somewhere along the way, and Eric wasn't sure whether this was a good omen or not. At last he arrived at the outer chamber of the throne room, and unlike the other rooms, this one was inhabited. Fops in jewelled armor meant strictly for display lounged languidly, most holding leashes that led to doglike and less nameable things. Ladies of the court whispered and smiled, inspecting him over spread fans or beneath embroidered veils. One of them looked more like a leopardess than anything on two legs had a right to—she caught Eric staring and laughed, exposing a mouth filled with sharp carnivore fangs. Beautiful they might be, but no one who'd ever seen one of the Sidhe would mistake a member of the Dark Court for one of the Bright.

Word of his arrival had preceded him—he could tell by the whispers and glances exchanged by the elegantly dressed lords and ladies who filled the outer hall. He thought someone might try to stop him—to curry favor with their liege-lord, if nothing else—but no one did. Eric skirted the edge of the silent group, carefully keeping his back to the wall. At the far end of the outer hall, three steps led up to another set of massive doors of enamelled silver that depicted a battle between two groups of mounted elves. The red enamel drops of blood in the picture glinted as if they were backlit, as if somehow light was shining *through* the doors. It was a startling effect. *Whoever this Unseleighe Lord is,* Eric thought, *he had a helluva special effects budget.*

He skipped up the three wide steps—turning his back on the courtiers reluctantly—and gestured at the door, summoning up a simple knock-spell. For a moment he was afraid it wouldn't open, but like the first, it yielded to his power. A collective gasp went up from the watching Unseleighe Sidhe, and Eric heard the babble of conversation begin behind him as he stepped through the doors. As soon as he'd passed through them, the doors to the throne room closed behind him with the soft finality of the doors of a bank vault. Not a good sign. He bet they wouldn't open again as easily.

Still, he'd come too far to back out now. He looked around.

The throne room was enormous—far too big to have fit into the castle Eric had seen as he approached. For a moment he thought he was back outside in the bonewood, but then he realized that the walls were only carved in the semblance of a forest. The carven tree limbs spread to form a canopy far above, making the vault of the ceiling look like a blackened crown of thorns.

Nice image, Banyon.

The floor looked as if it had been poured from a single drop of liquid mercury, but Eric didn't dare break his momentum or show a moment's indecision, and to his relief, it was solid beneath his feet. At the far end of the chamber stood the same high throne he had seen in his dream. Only this time it was facing him, and occupied by the Unseleighe Eric had seen leading the Wild Hunt in Central Park. Refusing to think about what might happen next, Eric strode boldly toward the foot of the black throne and its darkling occupant.

Like his guard knights, the Unseleighe Lord wore full ornate field plate armor of a silver so dark it seemed black. On his head was a black crown set with cabochon rubies that glowed as brightly as the blood drops in the door had. Eric stopped at the foot of the throne and stared up at its occupant. He forced himself to smile nonchalantly.

"Hi. We need to talk. Now."

When Ria got back from Threshold, the package she'd asked Jonathan to send was waiting for her at the hotel desk. She was just as glad she'd left Logan with the others back at Threshold. What she had in mind now wasn't something a bodyguard could help her with, no matter how good a bodyguard he was.

She signed for the package, and carried it upstairs to her suite to open it. Bless Jonathan! Her own personal .38 snubnose revolver and a lightweight chain mail vest—steel rings as supple and flexible as heavy silk—lay inside. There was a box of steel-jacketed hollow points beside the gun, a load that would bring serious grief to anyone—Sidhe or mortal—that it hit.

There were two speed-loaders in the package with the gun. She loaded them both as well as loading the gun, but left the rest of the box where it was—any problem that eighteen bullets couldn't solve, magic probably couldn't solve either.

A distant part of her mind was amused by her preparations. Who would ever have thought that there would come a day when she'd come riding to Eric's rescue Underhill? He knew more about the Sidhe than she did, but it was equally true that he had no idea of what people like Robert Lintel were capable of in their sublime self-obsession. Lintel wouldn't give up now that he'd seen the kind of power Eric had and thought he saw a way to get it for himself. And if Lintel caught up with him, Eric would be as helpless as a child, no matter how gifted a Bard he was. Down deep, Eric was a nice guy, and that would always put him at a disadvantage when dealing with people like Lintel—or the Dark Court.

Fortunately, Ria thought, she wasn't nice.

She stripped off her executive power suit and dressed again in the outfit Logan had brought her to go slum-crawling in. She pulled on her tightest T-shirt and slid the vest over it before slipping on the

Kevlar-lined jacket and zipping it up to her throat. The combination should stop anything she might have to face, Sidhe or human. She slid the gun into her pocket and inspected herself in the mirror. Neither gun nor vest showed.

She was ready to go to war. Now all she had to do was find the battlefield.

Guardian House looked serene and untouched by recent events. In order to track Eric, Ria needed something that was his—something attuned to his personal energy that she could use as a link to him, and his apartment was the best place to look. Ria wasn't sure it'd let her in without a fight, but fortunately she didn't have to try. As she stood in the little courtyard of the apartment building, she heard the frantic racing of a motorcycle engine coming from behind the building, and over it Greystone's gravel voice pleading with someone.

"Aw, c'mon, sweetheart! Just—could you wait a minute here! Hey! Here now, *mo chidr*—"

She ran around to the tiny private parking lot in the back of the building and found Greystone standing in front of Eric's bike. The elvensteed was making frantic dashes at the gate—all by itself—but Greystone kept blocking them, wings outstretched. The bike flashed its—*her*—lights in frustration, and her attempts to get around the gargoyle grew more frantic.

"Hey! Blondie!" Greystone called when he saw Ria. "This thing can talk. Why ain't she talkin' to me, then?"

"It's an elvensteed," Ria answered. "She won't listen to you or let anyone ride her but Eric. But elvensteeds can travel anywhere without Gates or Portals, and if he's called for her—"

"We can follow?" Greystone said, brightening.

"Exactly. Just get out of her way before she decides to bite you."

Greystone stepped aside and folded back his wings. Lady Day zipped around him like a bull avoiding the matador's cape. By the time she was halfway up the block, she was gone from sight.

But if I can follow Eric, I can certainly follow you, my dear.

"She's gone! Hey, Blondie! What do we do now?"

"We follow. And Greystone . . . ?"

The gargoyle looked at her hopefully.

"Don't call me 'Blondie.'"

Aerune stared down at the bold interloper. It had never occurred to him that the mortal Bard might dare to beard him in his stronghold.

"Kneel to me, mortal," he thundered, mantling himself with Power and stretching out his hand. A massive ring gleamed, blood-red, on his outstretched forefinger.

"I don't think so," the Bard said. "We don't do much kneeling in the World Above these days. Or hadn't you noticed? Things have changed since the last time you led a Wild Hunt there. More iron, for one thing—but that's just the tip of the iceberg. Magic's really impressive, but Cold Iron will stop it dead, and we've got a lot of that in the World Above. We've also got machines that can do things you've never even dreamed of, machines that magic can't stop. If you want a bunch of mortals to pay homage to you, you're going to have to have a lot more in your bag of tricks than a little flashy magic and some big dogs. And I don't think you do."

Infuriated by the Bard's arrogance as he was, Aerune was an honest enough tactician to see that there was much merit in what the mortal stripling had to say. The mortal *Robertlintel* had been quick to defend himself with Cold Iron when Aerune had attacked him, nor had his servants cowered at the sight of the Wild Hunt as Aerune had expected. Fear and magic were the Unseleighe's two main weapons against the mortal kind, and if those proved ineffective . . .

"And the fact that you can't take us over isn't the worst of what I've got to tell you. Those guys in the park? The ones with the chain mail and the iron spears? They're playing you, Dark Lord. I don't know who sent them after you, but I do know the kind of person he is. I've met people like him before. He's got hundreds of 'warriors' at his command, and he wants your magic. He's already killed I-don't-know-how-many innocent people to get a handle on it, and he's getting closer to figuring you out every minute.

"And once he does, he's going to be coming after you—here. If humans figure out a way into Underhill, your intramural feuds won't matter anymore. Dark Court and Light—you'll both be history."

Such audacity and ruthlessness as the Bard described was worthy of Aerune himself, but the notion of a mortal having the temerity—and the weapons—to conquer Elven Lands was a sickening thought. Aerune considered the mad wizard he'd faced in the Park, the crude-but-effective weapons that had accounted for the lives of so many of his Hunt.

No. It is not possible. They were lucky, nothing more, he decided. *Now that I have taken their measure, I will cow them utterly. For Aerete.*

But the Bard was still talking, impervious to his own immediate peril.

"So you're going to have to choose. Work with me to take this guy out and bury what he knows. Or end up serving him with an iron collar around your neck."

"You have gone too far, Bard!" Aerune shouted, rising to his feet in a swirl of black cloak. "I am the Great Lord Aerune mac Audelaine of the Unseleighe Sidhe, and before I am done with you, you will beg me for death, as will any of your kindred who dare to raise their banners against me. *Guards!* Attend me!"

He would blast this mortal where he stood, hang his body on the castle gates as a warning to other impertinent trespassers! Aerune drew back his hand, preparing to strike.

And the throne room . . . *rippled* . . . as the fabric of Aerune's realm twisted sideways with a sickening and disorienting lurch. Mage-quake! Aerune staggered, fighting for balance in the aftermath of the disruption, as his tiny kingdom was destroyed and remade itself again in obedience to his will and his magics. But the Bard who taunted him here could not claim such power. . . .

"Told you so," said the Bard sadly.

Six of Aerune's guardsmen now stood within the doorway, obedient to his summons, but they were not the only ones within Aerune's throne room, nor was the Bard now the only human interloper.

A human man wearing the ugly grey clothing Aerune had seen in the World Above stood in the middle of his throne room, staring about himself with undisguised greed. With him were four human warriors wearing black and bearing weapons of Cold Iron that glowed and smoked in the magic of Aerune's Underhill realm. At their feet lay half a dozen dead humans, their bodies withered in the fashion of those Crowned Ones who had given up their power to Aerune's needs before.

"I will deal with you after I destroy them," Aerune growled to the Bard. He gestured to his guardsmen. "Take them!"

This is not good, Eric thought, hoping his shields would hold against stray bullets as well as spells, knowing that if the bullets were steel-jacketed they probably wouldn't after the first one or two. He'd been right, not that he was very happy about it at the moment. With humans and their Cold Iron weapons down here in Underhill, Seleighe and Unseleighe kingdoms alike would go under like wheat under a harvester. And with elven magery running wild in the World Above, the outlook for humanity wasn't very good either.

The Unseleighe guardsmen started forward, seeing only spears raised to stop them. One of the black-clad goons the Suit had brought with him raised a pistol and fired, and one of Aerune's guards staggered and fell to the ground, screaming. In moments elven-fire had consumed his entire body as the steel-jacketed bullet did its work.

Unfortunately, the Dark Lord Aerune didn't seem to be sufficiently impressed by this display to call off his men. More guardsmen poured into the room, swords drawn, red eyes gleaming. The human mercenaries turned outward, putting a ring of steel around the Suit. There was a chatter of machine-pistol fire, the bright flare of disrupted shielding, and the guardsmen moved in for close-quarters work. The mercenaries lowered their spears, obviously ready for them. There was a sudden clatter of engagement.

Eric wasn't sure what elvish swords were made of, but whatever it was, in the magic-charged air of Underhill, it sizzled like an ice cube tossed into hot grease when it met the iron blades of the spears the humans were carrying. After the first time a parry sliced one of the elven swords clear through, the guardsmen were more cautious about rushing their prey. A couple of the Suit's henchmen kept firing, covering the spearmen and choosing their targets with care. The throne room echoed with the sound of gunfire, and the faint acrid scent of gunsmoke filled the air. Elves fell beneath the onslaught of Cold Iron until the silvery mirror floor of the throne room was littered with elvish bodies, and the Suit and his hardboys were still standing. Aerune sat watching the carnage as if it were a play staged for his amusement.

Because soon enough they're going to run out of bullets, and I don't think they've got any way out of here now that they've used up their "batteries." Aerune hasn't even called up the heavy artillery yet, and he's not a very happy camper at the moment.... Eric didn't want to be here when Aerune decided to take out his frustrations on the interlopers—and he wasn't sure he could stop the Unseleighe Lord either. He could issue a formal Challenge—that might slow Aerune down—but the Dark Lord was on his home ground here, and magical duels had not been a major part of Eric's education.

He'd let his mind wander for a fatal instant. Suddenly there was a lull in the fighting, and Eric found himself staring down the barrel of a pistol.

"Work with me, big man, or the hippie gets it right here!" the man in the suit called cheerfully. "You've seen what our weapons can do to your people, so back off before it happens to you!"

Aerune waved a hand, and his guardsmen pulled back, forming a ring around the interlopers. The room had grown darker in just the last few moments: Eric could no longer see the walls of the throne room clearly, and it seemed to him that there were *things* lurking in the shadows outside the ring of Unseleighe knights. But despite that, the Suit was smiling, as if things were going just the way he'd planned.

"Allow me to introduce myself, Mr. mac Audelaine. My name's Bob Lintel, Threshold Labs. You've got something I want, and I believe we can work together to our mutual advantage. I have no problem with dividing territory. You help me back home, I'll help you here. If it's psi you want, I can provide you with a permanent supply. Let's pool our forces."

Whatever else Aerune mac Audelaine was, he was a realist. He leaned forward on his dark throne, fixing Lintel with a burning gaze.

"You have an odd way of asking for favors, mortal man," Aerune rumbled, "but your arguments are . . . compelling. Come here to me, and I will hear your petition. Perhaps you are right." Aerune gestured in welcome, smiling chillingly. The man in the suit smiled back, but didn't move from the safety of his mercenaries.

Aerune and Lintel stood frozen, each testing the other's resolve in a high-stakes game of "chicken" as Eric watched in unconcealed horror. This was the last thing he wanted—two killer sharks dividing up Underhill and the World Above like an extra-large pizza, no anchovies. *What am I going to do now?*

The Unseleighe guardsmen and the human commandos watched each other intently, neither side moving. For a moment, the room was utterly silent. And in the distance, Eric heard a faint sound that had no place in Underhill.

The sound of an engine.

A motorcycle engine.

Lady Day barreled through the open doorway to the throne room, vaulting the dead and scattering the living as she headed for Eric. Here in Underhill the elvensteed seemed to flicker back and forth between bike and horse, the strobe effect making Eric's eyes hurt. Headache or not, she was the most welcome sight he'd seen in a long time. Eric started toward her—

And Aerune froze her in place with a gesture, trapping her within a cage of flickering blue light. The elvensteed, fully in horse-form now, stamped her foot, eyes flashing dangerously as she tossed her head in frustration.

"Move, hippie, and I drill you right now!" Lintel barked, oblivious to the byplay. "You aren't getting away this easily. Aerune wants you, and so do I."

"Too bad neither of you gets him," a new voice said coolly. "I'd put that down if I were you, Mr. Lintel."

Eric felt like cheering. Ria Llewellyn strode through the door, followed by Greystone. If Ria experienced any surprise at her surroundings—or the bodies all over the floor—she didn't show it. She was wearing black leather and blue jeans, and looked deadly and confident.

And she had a gun.

Almost before she'd finished speaking, Lintel swept his pistol around and rapped off three shots directly at her chest.

"Ria!" Eric shouted, aghast.

But she didn't fall. She staggered back against Greystone, and steadied herself against the gargoyle's outspread wing, but she obviously wasn't hurt. She smiled a small wintery smile at Lintel.

"I've done plenty of corporate dueling in my time, but this is a little extreme," she said. "Oh, by the way. I'm sure we haven't met. I'm Ria Llewellyn. Your boss."

Then she shot Robert Lintel neatly in the knee.

He went down screaming, dropping his gun and scattering his men in confusion. Aerune's elven guards surged forward and stopped, uncertain of whether they should try to take advantage of the moment. One of Lintel's men knelt to try to help him. Eric ran down the steps and made it across the throne room to Ria's side in the confusion.

"Glad you could make it," he gasped.

"Wouldn't miss it for worlds," Ria answered. "Get back."

Greystone lifted him out of the way just as a levin bolt flung by an enraged Aerune struck Ria full in the chest. It popped and sizzled, running all over her body like St. Elmo's fire before sinking into the floor, but Ria stood her ground, as unharmed by elven magic as by mortal bullets.

"Stainless-steel chain mail," Ria called toward Aerune. "The least of mortal defenses. Very easy to make in the World Above—I'm sure Lintel's men are wearing it."

To Eric she said: "I'm going to distract him. Can you get your steed free? We're going to need her."

"I think so," Eric answered, his voice equally low. He reached out, feeling at the edges of the spell that had trapped Lady Day. It was a simple one, the Sidhe equivalent of a locked door. *Now let's see if I can find the key.*

As he concentrated, Ria stepped forward, away from Greystone's protection, and bowed her head, a conciliating, coaxing note entering her voice.

"My Lord, your power is vast and mine is very small. I am no match for you alone, even with weapons and armor of deathmetal from the World Above. But the Bard and I together can hold you off indefinitely. He has powerful patrons among the Seleighe Court who would much resent any harm you might do to him, nor is the gargoyle entirely friendless. I pray you, of your great mercy, allow us three—four—to depart your kingdom unmolested. We wish no quarrel with you."

Aerune looked at her measuringly, resuming his seat and regarding her with bleak expressionless eyes.

"Ria!" Eric hissed. She couldn't be suggesting what he thought she was—just *abandoning* those five guys and Lintel to Aerune's mercy? He looked behind him, through the open doors, but the rest of the Unseleighe Court seemed to have vanished; the outer room was empty. "What about Lintel and the others? We can't just leave them here!"

Lintel's agonized groans seemed to fill the room, setting his teeth on edge. A shattered kneecap was just about the most painful and crippling single wound possible to inflict.

"True," Ria answered, her voice low. "I can't afford to leave Lintel to strike a bargain of his own. Saddle up as soon as you can, Eric. We may be leaving quickly. Greystone, you too."

"Check, boss lady," the gargoyle said.

Aerune spoke again, a faint admiring smile upon his face.

"Very well, halfbreed. You, the Bard and his mount, and this . . . creature . . . which accompanies you, all have my leave to depart. But the others remain. Do these terms suit you?"

The magic around Lady Day dissolved, and the elvensteed bounded toward the doorway and Eric, changing form back into a motorbike as she did so. Aerune paid no attention. Reluctantly, Eric swung his leg over Lady Day's saddle. The elvensteed thrummed her engine, impatient to be away.

"They do, My Lord, and many thanks to you for your mercy,"

Ria said. She raised her gun once more and fired, placing a bullet squarely between Lintel's eyes. The corporate raider slumped to the floor, silent in death, and the commando squatting beside him reached for his gun.

"No!" Eric was half off Lady Day's back—though what he could do, he wasn't sure—when the elvensteed decided she'd had enough of this part of Underhill. With a banshee scream she took off, Greystone close behind. Nothing Eric could do could slow or turn her, and at the speed she was going, he didn't dare just jump off. Eric looked back wildly over his shoulder, catching a last glimpse of the throne room before it vanished in the distance.

Ria stood alone before Lord Aerune.

"You are properly ruthless, halfling," Aerune said, getting to his feet. Though irritated by his loss, he looked intrigued as well. She'd counted more than a little on that. Elves were suckers for a grand gesture.

Not that Aerune was a sucker in any sense of the word.

He stepped down from his throne, and stood facing her across a tangle of bodies, Sidhe and human. With a wave of his hand, he banished them all to another part of his domain. No trace of the battle—or Lintel's men—remained to mar the chilly perfection of his presence chamber. The doors of the throne room closed in the same moment, sealing Ria in with him.

Aerune held out his hand to her. The black mail gauntlet gleamed in the unchanging radiance of Underhill.

"It has been too long since I encountered anyone with such beauty who had yet the spirit to defy me. I do not think you have been properly valued by your kin, halfling, nor by the World Above. Matters could be otherwise. Have you considered—"

"And rejected, Great Lord," Ria answered steadily. This powerful Unseleighe Sidhe was offering her a seductive prize—his patronage, and with it, a place in Underhill. Once she could have asked for no greater reward.

Once.

"I want no bargain with you beyond that which I have already struck, Great Lord, though I prize your honorable offer for the tribute it is. I will go now, by your leave, and molest your realm no more. Lintel was my vassal, and he is well rewarded for his treachery. I leave you his men as my gift, to do with as you choose."

Taking a calculated risk, she turned her back on Lord Aerune and walked away. The doors of the throne room opened before her, and she walked out into the deserted castle. No one tried to stop her, but Ria didn't breathe completely easily until she'd reached the nearest Portal and taken herself beyond Aerune's reach—or at least, his immediate reach.

I know this isn't over. Now that he knows there's something of value in the World Above, Aerune won't stop until he figures out a way to get at it. But that's a problem for another day. Thank God for small favors.

TWELVE:
TO END WHERE
WE BEGAN

As soon as Ria reached the World Above, everything that had happened in Aerune's court began to take on a vague air of unreality. After passing through several Portals and nearly exhausting her store of Power, she'd come out in Sterling Forest, near the Nexus of Elfhame Everforest, and had to hike more than a mile before she found a phone she could use to call a car to take her back to the city. It was late Monday evening by the time she arrived back in New York—time ran differently in the World Above, sometimes to the World Above's benefit.

The drive back to the City gave her a lot of time to think, mostly about the look of horror on Eric's face as she shot Robert Lintel. There'd been no other choice, though. Aerune probably wouldn't have let her take Lintel without a fight anyway, and if she *had* managed to bring him back to the World Above to face charges, the New York courts would probably have let him off on a technicality. That was the way the legal system worked when you had money and influence.

Ria had always preferred justice to law, and she'd spoken no more than the truth to the Unseleighe lord. What Lintel had done was in some sense her responsibility. Threshold was a LlewellCo company. Lintel had worked for her. Ultimately, she was responsible for what he'd done. Now he'd paid the dead for their loss in the only way possible, with his own life, and that simplified matters. He'd never have the chance to use the information he'd gained at the cost of so many innocent lives.

And if she had to lose Eric's respect—and love—because of it, Ria was willing to pay that price, though it would hurt more than she liked to think.

I might as well find out now how it's going to be as soon as possible, she thought grimly. There was no point in waiting to get bad news.

"I've changed my mind," she told the driver. "I'm not going to the Sherry. There's a stop I want you to make first."

The ride from Aerune's castle to New York passed in a dizzying blur. After the first few seconds, he'd just closed his eyes and held on tight, and finally the elvensteed had stopped.

When he opened his eyes, the world spun giddily. Eric slid sideways off Lady Day's saddle and into Greystone's arms.

"Steady there, laddybuck. Strewth, that was the wildest ride I've been on since I was a gleam in the stonecarver's eye!" the gargoyle said cheerfully.

"Yeah," Eric said weakly. After a moment the world steadied, and he could stand on his own two feet.

He looked around warily. He was back in New York, behind Guardian House. It seemed strange that everything looked normal. It was dark. Eric had no idea what day it was, though from the powdered-sugar snow that fell lightly all around him, it was still December.

But what year? Not that I care right now.

"Let's get you inside," Greystone said. "If ever a man could do with a stiff drink, boyo, it's you."

"No," Eric said, feeling a little better. "Not a drink. But I wouldn't turn down a strong cup of coffee. Meet you upstairs."

Greystone bounded skyward with surprising grace, settling back into his place with a flourish and a bow.

A shower and a change of clothes helped. He was still trying to sort everything out in his mind, trying to fit the events into some kind of order. Eventually he was going to have to figure out something to tell Toni and the other Guardians. They deserved to know how the story ended.

Greystone had joined him inside, his cheerfully ugly face contorted into an expression of worry as he watched Eric move around the apartment. Finally, coffee and sandwich in hand, Eric sat down on the couch.

"I can't believe she did that," he said, sighing. As much as he tried to avoid it, Eric's thoughts kept returning to that one image of the bullet hole in the middle of Lintel's forehead, stopping him from thinking past it. He set his sandwich down on the table untasted. She'd just shot him. No hesitation, no remorse. Bam!

Greystone shook his head in sympathy. "I can't either. Man, talk about *cold . . . !*"

"No," Eric said, grudgingly fair. Somehow Greystone's putting his own thoughts into words made Eric see Ria's side of things. "As much as I hate what she did, I think she was telling the truth. She didn't have a choice. She couldn't leave Lintel there in Underhill alive. Believe me, he and Aerune were *this* close to making a deal. Cold Iron in Underhill—humans knowing about elves—magic in the World Above—it would have been . . ."

It would have been just like my dream: New York a wasteland. Thousands—millions—dead. And Underhill . . . gone. Humans and Sidhe need each other. Our lives are too intertwined. One can't really survive without the other. But that doesn't mean most people need to know about Underhill, or magic, or the Nexuses, any more than they need to know how to build a nuclear warhead. Ria knew that. She did what had to be done. But that doesn't mean I have to like it. . . .

"She could have brought him back here!" Greystone protested. "I could'a carried him. Easy!"

Eric shook his head reluctantly and drank his coffee. The bitter warmth helped clarify his thoughts. "Then he'd be back here, alive, still knowing what he knows, with his cache of designer poison still out there somewhere. Sure, there'd be a trial, but he'd probably be out on bail while he was waiting for his court date, and that means he could escape back Underhill, strike a bargain with Aerune, or come up with something else horrible I haven't even thought of yet. And Ria would be stuck in the middle of it—if she did anything to stop him here, she'd be the one who went to prison, not him."

"Maybe," the gargoyle said grudgingly. "But I still think we should'a brought him back here and let Jimmie and the gang sort him out."

"I don't know," Eric said unhappily. Maybe that would have worked. But with the stakes so high, was it worth taking the chance? The worst of it was, he probably wasn't going to see Ria again. He still wasn't sure how she'd found him, but she had. She'd rescued him, given him all the help he'd asked her for, and he'd thrown it back in her face—and deserted her, even if that hadn't exactly been his idea. He didn't even know if she'd gotten out of Aerune's realm alive.

Good going, Banyon. So much for your vaunted leadership abilities.

"I don't even know where she is now, or if she even got out alive. Greystone, can you—"

"Well," Greystone said abruptly, "guess I'd better get back to work. No rest for the wicked, and all that. See you around, boyo. I'm going back on duty before anyone notices I'm AWOL."

"Hey," Eric said, getting to his feet as Greystone climbed out the window. Maybe Greystone hadn't wanted to be asked if he and the Guardians could find Ria, but that didn't mean he had to just run off like that!

There was a knock at the door.

He stared after the gargoyle. The knocking continued. Thinking it was Toni, knowing that Guardian House would never allow in anything that could do its inhabitants any harm, Eric opened the door.

Ria was standing there, still dressed in battered denim and

leather. A few snowflakes lay on her hair and shoulders, melting slowly. She looked tired, uncertain of her reception.

A vast relief filled Eric, as if he were finally able to set down a heavy load he'd been carrying, and he smiled.

"Glad you could make it," he said simply.

Her face relaxed into a smile of sheer relief, as if she'd gotten good news she'd hoped for but hadn't expected. Eric stepped back, gesturing for her to enter.

"Wouldn't miss it for worlds," Ria answered.

Later—much later—there was time to talk it all out. Ria explained the whole story from the beginning as she'd managed to piece it together, about Threshold's black-budget project to come up with a drug that turned ordinary people into Wild Talents. How she'd tracked the project back to Threshold, found Lintel gone, and then followed Lady Day to find Eric, knowing that wherever Lintel was, he, too, would be hot on Eric's trail.

"I still don't like what you did," Eric said. "It wasn't the only solution. We could have taken him to the Seleighe Sidhe, made him *their* problem. . . ."

Ria shrugged. "I don't know that I trust them with Lintel anymore than I did Aerune. He was too much of a wild card. This was more expedient."

Eric already knew he wanted Ria to stay a part of his life. But if he let her set the terms for their relationship, they'd still be in the same situation they'd been back in L.A., and that wouldn't work for him.

"If we're going to stay together, you're going to have to promise me that if we get into any more situations, you won't do the expedient thing anymore," he said firmly, but inside he was holding his breath, waiting for her answer.

She regarded him with a raised eyebrow, for a frozen moment looking more elvish than she did human. At last she smiled faintly.

"I'll offer you a compromise, m'love. I won't do the expedient thing without consulting you and letting you have a chance to convince me otherwise. Have we a bargain, O great Sidhe Bard?"

Eric thought about it for a moment. Things had changed between them, he realized. He wasn't her pet. She wasn't his lackey. They were equal partners. He found he liked the idea very much.

"That'll work. I'll be your conscience," he answered.

"Just like Jiminy Cricket," Ria said mockingly. She kissed him lightly on the forehead and got to her feet. "Don't forget the cricket spent most of the movie as a ghost."

"I'm not worried," Eric said contentedly.

Ria smiled, looking younger and softer—and somehow hopeful, as if she'd been offered a new beginning.

"And now, the police are probably looking for me—and I'll bet you need to come up with an explanation for playing hooky from school today. I'll probably be out of touch for a while, but don't worry. Watch for me on the news. Then give me a call and we'll have dinner. We've still got a lot of loose ends to chase down."

"It's a date," Eric answered. He knew he was grinning like a fool, but he didn't care. He walked her to the door and stood in the doorway, watching her walk down the hall, still smiling.

I can't wait to tell Kory and Beth about all this, he thought to himself. *I wonder what they'll say.*

He heard the elevator cage rattle closed, and heard the elevator start down. *Louis, something tells me this is the start of a beautiful friendship. . . .*

SPIRITS WHITE AS LIGHTNING

DEDICATION

This one's for Mrs. Johnson and Mrs. Anderson,
my high school English teachers,
without whom I wouldn't be doing this for a living.

—Rosemary Edghill

The Spirits White as Lightning
    Would on my travels guide me
The stars would shake and the moon would quake
    Whenever they espied me
    —*Tom O' Bedlam (traditional)*

ONE:
THE SIMPLE GIFTS

❖❖❖

Sir Eric Banyon, the Queen's Knight, known as Silverflute wherever soldiers of fortune gathered together, strode manfully through the thronging crowd, determined to leave the memory of his disgrace at the hands of the foul Frenchman Black Levoisier behind him as surely as he had left the dastardly minions of his Great Enemy in his dust. . . .

Eric dodged around a bicycle messenger just dismounting on the sidewalk, then grinned, startling the bike messenger into an answering smile. *Heh. Banyon, m'lad, you ought to go in for writing Hysterical Historicals in your off-hours.* He actually *was* striding—though not exactly "manfully"—through the noontime crowd, heading for the subway and home. His classes at Juilliard were over for the day and no rehearsals (for once!) were scheduled for this afternoon. He could practice as well, or better, at home than in one of the practice rooms, anyway. And he *was* determined not to sour a perfectly good day with the memory of one jealous teacher trying to make a fool out of him in front of the entire class. Well, all right— maybe not the entire class. Just most of it. And anyway, Levoisier hadn't succeeded, though he'd certainly done his best.

Missing his midterm last winter (he'd been off saving the world, necessary though it had been) had given Professor Rector the chance he had been hoping for all term. He'd failed Eric, banishing him from Introduction to Music Theory with unprofessional glee. Fortunately, Eric's work in his other classes and in ensemble had been good enough that he had been given the opportunity to make up the lost Music Theory credit during summer term, and he had taken the chance to add a few more courses in order to lighten next fall's course-load. Still, this hadn't quite been the way he'd envisioned spending his July and August, which was out on Fire Island with a pitcher of virgin margaritas by his side. And Levoisier made Ethan Rector look like a prince of transpersonal fairness by comparison.

Parisians. Feh. Paris would be such a lovely place without all the Parisians in it, Eric thought grumpily. And the man had certainly been on form today, baiting Eric unmercifully in hopes he'd lose his temper. Once he'd lost it, the professor would have taken him apart in a cool and scientific dissection rendered without benefit of anesthetic.

Levoisier had begun with sarcastic comments about Eric's depth of experience—on the RenFaire circuit. (Why did they always obsess about that? It couldn't be jealousy.) *Not* exactly a concert-hall environment, as the professor had repeatedly pointed out. Nor were the customers who so praised his playing sober . . . or necessarily bright . . . or able to distinguish Bach from Bacharach . . . or a flute from a clarinet. Certainly even an idiot with three tunes in his repertoire could win acclaim on the RenFaire circuit—which only proved, to Eric's mind, how little Levoisier knew about the RenFaire circuit.

As the professor had expounded on each and every way in which he felt that Eric resembled half-drunk Fairegoers—at exhaustive length—Eric stood there silently. Every single word was calculated to get Eric to explode with temper.

And that would have worked, once, but Eric was a far different person now than anyone that the professor had ever encountered before, at least within the hallowed halls of academe. He had waited, quietly and calmly, until the professor grew frustrated by Eric's lack of agitation, embarrassment, or any other identifiable emotion.

When Levoisier finally ran out of insults, Eric had simply said, "The Review Committee and the Entrance Committee were satisfied with my performances, Professor, as are the rest of my teachers," and sat down again. And at that blessed moment, the change-of-class bell sounded, and he was free.

Not as satisfying, perhaps, as telling the professor off would have been. Not *nearly* as satisfying as pointing out the professor's own deficiencies as both a musician and a teacher—many of which Eric had already heard for himself during faculty recitals. Yehudi Menuhin, the professor was not.

Yahoo Menudo, maybe.

But the point wasn't to get the better of the arrogant Frenchman. The point, in fact, was not to even *bother* with making a point. The point was to take what was good, leave what was bad, and pass through all the name-calling and innuendo like the wind through the grass.

Be Teflon. That's the only way to handle guys like this. He's insecure, ignorant, and arrogant. Just let everything slide right off until he gets tired of not getting a rise out of me. By then he'll probably have gone far enough to expose himself as the trivial goon that he is. That might take the full eight-week summer session, but Eric didn't mind—while Levoisier was heckling *him,* he wasn't picking on the younger and more inexperienced students, who were not equipped to deal with him. The bastard had already reduced Midori to silent tears before he'd turned on Eric.

Well, let him wear himself out on me. Levoisier doesn't know half of what he thinks there is to know about me. I have a black belt in Verbal Aikido, you arrogant Frog.

Levoisier's appointment wasn't an insoluble mystery. Eric knew *why* Juilliard had such a miserable excuse for a teacher on its staff this year. Levoisier was no great shakes as an interpreter of music, but he was a brilliant technician. Even Eric was willing to admit there was a lot he could learn from the man, if he ever decided to stop humiliating the students and elected to teach. And even at his worst, he *was* teaching valuable things to his students.

Though he knows it not. Though he intends *it not.*

It was a cruel, cold world out there, a world singularly lacking in first-chair jobs in fine symphony orchestras and prestigious traveling ensembles, recording contracts, solo tours, and praise—and full of cruel critics and low-end positions teaching in schools or playing in little city orchestras under conductors who themselves had failed to make the cut for a high-end professional musical career. Trial-by-Parisian might harden some of them to the slings and arrows of outrageous fortune. The students at Juilliard were fairly well equipped to deal with professional rivalry and even sabotage from other students, but they weren't ready for the real world of real people and the fact that most of them were doomed to eke out a living playing in the Tacoma Sousa Band.

Or playing harps in hotel lobbies, pianos in cocktail bars, clarinets at weddings, and yes, flutes at RenFaires. Anything that Levoisier can throw at them isn't half of the abuse they'll get out there. Or, in the dark of the night, what they'll give themselves.

What had triggered today's attack, he suspected—given that Levoisier had first gone after Midori, then him—was the results of the placement auditions for the summer-session orchestra. Eric (and Midori) had been placed in *second* chair.

Now, Eric hadn't heard Midori's audition, but there was something that no one, including the Audition Committee, knew about Eric's. He would *never* get first chair, because all during his audition, he had been sending out a thread of Bardic magic.

No matter how good I am, you won't give me first chair, the magic had whispered, carried along on the wings of Debussy. *I don't need the experience, and you should give it to someone else.*

In fact, at the end of the audition, one of the committee had taken him aside, apologetically, and had said, "Banyon, you deserved first chair, but frankly, we can't give it to you. *You* don't need—"

"—the experience," Eric finished, with a grin and a toss of his long chestnut hair. "No worries, Doctor Selkirk. Frankly, what I need is a lot *more* experience in backing and supporting another flautist. They also serve, and all that."

Doctor Selkirk had sighed with relief and shook Eric's hand. "I knew we hadn't made any mistakes in readmitting you, Banyon. If running around in tights and floppy shirts on weekends would give our students that kind of maturity, I'd assign it as a course."

Eric grinned to himself again. *It's not as if I need experience in front of an audience. I rather doubt that I'm ever going to face a more hostile audience than a flock of Nightflyers, or a pickier one than an Elven Bard and Magus Major. And it's not fair to the kids to make them compete with me for something I don't need or want.*

The New York streets simmered with summer heat, and the kind of glare found when the only thing to take the sun's rays is stone, and glass, and more stone. His local friends told him that August would be even worse—if they got a really hot spell, even the blacktopped streets would go soft underfoot. He hadn't believed it at the time, but now Eric was just as glad that he'd spent the time last winter setting up bomb-proof spells on all his apartment windows: now, when he opened them into muggy July heat, he got arid January cold. It was a more elegant solution than nursing a power hog a/c along with Guardian House's cranky electrical system. His computer and stereo systems were already major power hogs, not to mention his pet microwave; he'd learned he had to shut down every other appliance in the place when he vacuumed. An air conditioner would have been the final straw. When Guardian House had been built back in the first decade of the 20th century, all those appliances hadn't even been distant dreams.

He was looking forward to getting home, opening all the windows, and maybe coaxing Greystone down into joining him for a glass of something cold. It wasn't likely anybody would miss the gargoyle if he deserted his post—not in a sweltering afternoon in July.

All he had to do was make it through the subway alive. Though most of the cars were air-conditioned to pneumonia levels, only some of the stations had any pretense to climate-control at all. Fortunately, the Lincoln Center stop was one of them. *Can't let the aesthetes and yuppies fry, after all.*

Eric joined the stream of humanity descending the steps into the subway, whistling a Bach gigue to purge his brain of any remaining taint of irritation with Professor Levoisier. There was nothing like Bach to rev up the old right brain and let logic take over from emotion.

He let the flow of traffic take him along towards the turnstiles. *Hey, it's Friday. I've got a whole weekend in front of me, the sun is shining, nobody wants to kill me, and there's not a single crisis Underhill or Overhill that needs sorting out.* That thought put a bounce in his step. Maeve had been born and Kory and Beth were planning to bring her for a visit. If the weather held, maybe they could make a run up Long Island and see how the other half lived. And if it didn't, well, if you couldn't find *something* to do in New York on a weekend, you were in pretty sad shape.

And when they go back Underhill, if Ria isn't up to her sculpted eyebrows in Bizness, I might even get her to go out with me to some New-York-Magazine-*Approved event. So maybe I ought to have a look for something she might not ordinarily go to. Not that Ria's actually a party animal at the best of times. How could someone who looks like she looks be such a grind? It's one of Life's Great Mysteries.*

He turned his mind back to the question of finding something fun he could tease her into attending. Anything musical was a good bet, but it would have to be both competent and something she wouldn't have thought of for her—

Something teased his ears as he passed the turnstile. A string instrument—

Banjo?

And a very, very familiar tune.

'Tis a gift to be simple, 'tis a gift to be free, 'tis a gift to come 'round where we ought to be—

Someone was playing a banjo in the subway.

That wasn't all that unusual. Eric had heard everything from bagpipes to string quartets to old-fashioned One Man Bands playing on subway platforms throughout the city. Busking was permitted in the New York subway system and on the city streets as well, but it was a peculiar form of busking. You had to have a license, and you only got the license by passing an audition.

It was a pretty good system, actually. The ears of the public weren't assaulted by talentless musicians, licensing kept down the territory wars for the best spot, and the beat and transit cops weren't put on the spot by having to bust a player who was doing the public a favor by being there. Eric didn't know *all* of the licensed buskers—New York was a bit bigger than any Faire pitch he'd ever worked—but he thought he was familiar with most of the ones who set up near Lincoln Center on a regular basis and he was sure that none of them played a banjo. The pleasantly jangling notes ricocheted off the echoing tile walls of the subway, the echoes providing a depth and richness to the music that was the reason so many musicians—including Eric—liked to play here. Something else teased his inner ear as well, as he approached the platform.

Magic.

Nothing overwhelming, just a gentle little lilt, a *Bardic* lilt to the tune, something to tease a little money from the pockets of the passers-by, but only by those who had it to spare. More of a reminder, really, to be courteous.

If you like what you hear, and can spare the money, drop a coin or two—if not, pass on, pass on. . . .

And *no one* with a New York City busking license was a Bard. Except, of course, him.

A sense of urgency hit Eric in the gut: not only did he want to catch this unknown Bard and find out who he was, he wanted to get to him before he was busted! He hurried towards the platform. The transit cops, who were supposed to enforce the busking licenses, could be along at any moment. Some of them were inclined to turn a blind eye towards the occasional violator, *if* he was good, *if* the cop in question liked that particular kind of music. *So how many of them like bluegrass?*

Eric shoved his way towards the cluster of people around the source of the music, and shouldered his way into the magic circle, ignoring the indignant looks of the two he squeezed in between. *"When true simplicity is gained, to bow and to bend we shall not be ashamed—"* his mind supplied the words to the tune.

The busker was a tall young man, built like a linebacker. Eric took it all in with a single glance. Blond. Longish hair, jeans, faded blue work shirt—and that indefinable something that said "not from around here" to city-trained eyes. He had an open, friendly face and piercing blue eyes, which held a promise of friendship out to the entire world, if only the world was wise enough to accept it. His banjo case was open at his feet, money in it, as he ran leisurely fingers through the intricate patterns of the old song. An old Army surplus duffle bag rested at his heels.

And the banjo— The banjo—*glowed*. Not that anyone other than Eric or an elf would have seen the glow. The strings were a network of silver-fire, and blue afterimages danced along the pattern of the busker's darting fingers.

An enchanted banjo?

There were legends of enchanted instruments in the ancient days. The traditional songs were full of examples. Flutes made from a Bard's bones. A harp strung with the hair of a murdered girl—

No, that's a bit too grisly. Nothing like that here. More like . . . an enchanted sword, forged for a paladin. I didn't know there was anyone left Overhill who could do work like that.

Not that he knew, yet, that the banjo had been made here. But if it were elvenwork, he would have sensed that, and Eric's Bard-trained senses caught no trace of Otherworldly craftsmanship here, just innate human magic.

A stir caught his attention—the glimpse of a uniform hat down by the turnstile. The transit cops.

The busker finished his song and coins and a couple of bills dropped into his banjo case, accompanying a spatter of applause. And in the pause, Eric pulled out his busking license and propped it in the side of the banjo case, *very* visibly, then got out his flute. He opened the flute case and put it behind the banjo case, and began fitting his instrument together as he stepped to the side of the very surprised banjo player.

"You need a license to play down here, friend—I've got one, and you just became my partner," Eric muttered under his breath just as the transit cops reached them. "So, 'Unquiet Grave'?" he said, louder, as if he and the stranger had been duetting for some time.

The stranger nodded, and they both began—quite as if they *had* been duetting for some time.

Mind, "Unquiet Grave" wasn't Eric's tune of choice, but it was the only Appalachian piece he had been able to think of on the spur of the moment. Plaintive and just a little on the spooky side, it wasn't one calculated to haul in the cash. But that was all right; it made some of the audience clear off, giving the transit cops a good look at the two buskers—and Eric's license.

And giving Eric a good look at them, just as he nodded to the banjo player to wrap it up. He sighed with relief; they were people he knew, who weren't going to quibble that his license was for himself alone and not with a partner.

"Top o' the marnin' t'ye, constable," he said in his best "Faire-Irish" accent. Officer Zielazinski laughed.

"More like afternoon, isn't it, O'Banyon?" the transit cop jibed good-naturedly. "Who's your partner?"

The banjo player answered before Eric could fumble. "Hosea Songmaker, sir, at your service," he said in slow syllables sweetened with the honey accent of the hills and deep with respect. Eric could sense the touch of Bard-magic here, too: *I am no threat to you; I will cause no trouble. . . .* He supposed a man as big and physically intimidating as Hosea Songmaker'd had plenty of use for that particular charm more than a few times in his life, and it made him like his new partner all the more.

Zee laughed, responding unconsciously to the touch of the benevolent magic. "Not from around here, are you! Well, you stick with Banyon; he'll show you the ropes. He's pretty street-smart."

The two transit cops moved on, back to business; there were more important matters to claim their attention in the subway than a couple of licensed buskers.

When they'd gone, Hosea gave Eric a sidelong glance, followed by a slow smile. "Reckon I owe you one," he said. Eric laughed.

"Just want to keep a good musician out of trouble," he replied easily. "How were you to know you need a license? Listen, let's collect a take while the collecting's good, and I'll tell you all about what you need to know afterwards."

Hosea nodded, and combed back the long blond hair that flopped down into his eyes back with a set of strong, brown fingers. "Old standard?" he suggested, and played the first few notes of "Foggy Mountain Breakdown."

Eric nodded. Everybody knew that one—the Lester Flat and Earl Scruggs classic had been the theme song to the movie *Bonnie and Clyde*. And while it was written for banjo and fiddle, there was no reason he couldn't take the fiddle part.

"Then—how about we follow straight into 'Devil Went Down to Georgia' and 'Mama Tried'?" Eric countered. *There. I'm not just a Celtic purist, you know.*

"Right." Hosea's eyes lit up slyly, and Eric suspected he was about to be given a run for his money. Hosea surged into the opening bars of the "Breakdown," his fingers blurring on the strings. Eric barely made his entrance in time to take the melody away from the banjo and carry it.

Hosea, like many an Irish player at the Faires, had a wicked sense of humor and liked to accelerate the pace of an already fast piece with each successive pass. But Eric was ready for him—not that it was all that difficult for a Bard to figure out what another Bard was going to do next. By the time they segued into "Devil Went Down to Georgia," they'd hit lightspeed. The crowd around them was thicker than before, and people were grinning and tapping their toes to the Charlie Daniels standard.

He'd had the joy of working with another Bard only Underhill, with his mentor Dharniel. That was always fun—if you could really use that word for anything to do with Master Dharniel—but it was nothing, *nothing* like working with another human Bard! There was a level of spontaneity and creative spark here that just wasn't present when he made music with the elves, and it made all the difference. Eric closed his eyes and gave himself over to the purest pleasure he'd ever felt outside of sex—and it certainly lasted a whole lot longer than even the most athletic sexual adventure he'd ever had!

It wasn't until he opened his eyes as he played the last flourish of "Mama Tried" that he realized they were surrounded six-deep by a gaping, grinning, toe-tapping human audience of people who *should* have been getting back to their jobs (or on to their lunches). The very moment they finished, money actually began to snow, rain, and hail into the banjo case, a veritable Hurricane Andrew of coins and small bills. Money that missed the case was scooped up and dumped into it by helpful hands, which was a small miracle in and of itself, as applause followed on the monetary accolade.

"Got enough to hold you for the next day or so?" Eric muttered *sotto voce* with a nod at the case.

Hosea grinned and nodded, his hair flopping into his eyes again. "That'll get me vittles and a bunk at the Y for a couple days, while I study on what I've got to do next," he replied. "Let's give these nice folk something to play 'em out on." His fingers began to move on the strings again.

Of all the tunes that Eric would have suspected Hosea would chose, this would not have been one. He listened as the banjo-Bard's clever fingers picked out the deceptively lazy little "pink-a pink-a pink-a pink-a pink (pause) pink-a pink-a pink-a pink-a pink (pause)."

Eric recognized it immediately, and knew the tune so well that his flute was at his lips and the soft notes spilling out at exactly the right moment after that second pause. "The Rainbow Connection" from the very first Muppet movie—how had Hosea known how much he liked that tune? And where had an Appalachian mountain boy learned it?

I guess that only proves that we live in a globally connected world, when an Appalachian mountain boy and a Juilliard student can recognize the same tune and play it like a couple of old buddies.

Simple tunes are deceptive things; superficially easy to play, they are the very devil to play *well*. But in the hands of not one, but two Bards, the very simplicity allows the heart and soul to shine.

When they finished, this time the reward was smiles as well as applause. Eric bowed with a flourish, Hosea with a kind of foot-shuffling modesty. Eric was pretty sure that though Hosea was a practiced musician, he hadn't been playing for money for very long—at least not as a street musician.

"Ladies and gents, *you* need to get back to your jobs, I'm sure—"

Eric announced with practiced Faire-patter. Groans, and a chorus of "aaawwww!"—surely the greatest music to a musician's ears—greeted this announcement.

"—so in the interest of making sure you don't get in trouble, my friend Hosea and I will be taking a break now for a few hours. Thank you all, and we'll be here off and on for the rest of the week!"

With no display of hurry, but with the efficiency of any busker who has sometimes seen his "take" vanish along with the rear end of a petty thief, Eric shoved the banjo case over behind Hosea's legs with his foot while he scooped up his flute case and began taking his instrument apart and cleaning it. The crowd dispersed—with a few generous souls lobbing a couple more handfuls of change at the case for good measure as they left.

"This is half yours," Hosea said, from a bent-over position, preparatory to doing something about the "take."

"Oh, just pull out enough for some lunch for both of us and I'll call it quits," Eric replied absently. "Fifteen bucks should do it; that'll leave you enough for bus fare to get to the Y and a street and subway map."

Hosea looked up at him doubtfully, but seemed to sense that Eric was in earnest. He just shoved most of the "take" into the duffle he'd had behind him, keeping out a handful of bills that he crammed into his pocket. He placed the banjo lovingly into his case, and handed Eric his busking license back.

He moved very gracefully for such a big fellow; shortly he stood up with duffle and case slung over opposite shoulders, looking very much at ease and entirely out of place.

"So—your name's Banyon," he said, giving Eric a slow and considering once-over with those piercing blue eyes. "Is that a first name or a last?"

"Last. Eric Banyon, former RenFaire player, current Juilliard student, at your service," Eric replied, making a little bow that mocked his status as "Juilliard student."

But Hosea's slow smile wouldn't accept the mocking attitude. "Figured you had to be from around there," he said. "Some feller told me it was up that-a-way"—he waved vaguely at the ceiling—"and I reckoned anybody could play like you was probably from there. Well, Eric Banyon, the cop said I was to stick by you, so where do we find lunch?"

Central Park on a July day was as good a substitute for country-side as you were likely to find within fifty miles, and a lot cooler under the trees than the city streets were. The park was a *lot* bigger, and had more secluded places, than anyone but a native New Yorker would be likely to guess—a lot of them avoided the Park anyway, fearing gangs and muggers. There had been a suggestion, a couple of years back, that wolves should be reintroduced—a suggestion that wasn't entirely a silly idea. Wolves would do very well here if they could be kept in isolation, but it was inevitable that they'd cross-breed with feral dogs, which in a few generations would only mean that there would be a resident pack of slightly-more-lupine feral dogs in the remoter parts of the place. Probably not the best idea in the world, given the unpredictable nature of lupine-canine crossbreeds. It was bad enough that coyotes had made their way here and had a thriving pack up by the Reservoir: no garbage can—or stray poodle—was safe.

Eric and Hosea gathered hot dogs and drinks from one of the Sabrett's carts outside the Park, and Eric led his fellow Bard into one of those quieter spots more familiar to the bird watchers than to the Frisbee throwers. There was, in fact, one of the bird feeders that the bird watchers maintained in this little bit of half-tame wilderness, and when they finished their food, Eric watched some sort of tiny birds flitting to and from it.

Hosea had clearly not eaten today, but he hadn't wolfed down the four (!) hot dogs he'd gotten for himself from the vendor. He'd eaten neatly and precisely, with not a crumb wasted or a bit of mustard smeared. He finished his soda, folded up all the paper neatly, and stuck it and the can into his duffle with the rest of his gear. No littering for this lad, evidently.

"So," Hosea said at last, breaking the silence. "Where do I get me one of them licenses so I can play for the folks without getting myself in trouble with the law?"

Eric explained the whole process while Hosea listened carefully. "The next audition isn't for another three weeks, though," Eric concluded, and as Hosea's face began to fall, he added quickly, "But don't worry—you can busk in the Park without one, and you can busk with me in the subway."

"Ain't you got classes?" Hosea asked doubtfully.

"I can work around them," Eric replied, then chuckled. "Besides, look what we did in half an hour together! There's probably about a hundred bucks there—figure we hit the lunch crowd and the commuters going home, we'll take in more than enough to cover your expenses until you can get a license for yourself. And you will," he added, with certainty.

Of course you will. You're a Bard, how can you not, if you put your mind and magic to it?

Hosea's earnest gaze met his steadfastly. "You've been helping me because . . ." There was a long pause, and for the first time Eric saw Hosea hesitate, as if he weren't quite sure how to put the thought into words. "Because of the music-magic. You've got the shine, too. Right?"

Eric hadn't expected him to put it quite so bluntly, though after the first few notes he'd been pretty sure that Hosea knew his own gift, and recognized Eric for a kindred soul.

"Well—yeah," Eric admitted a little sheepishly. "Where I come from, we're called Bards."

"Bards." Hosea rolled the flavor of the word over in his mouth and thoughts. "Like—back in the Druid times?" He grinned at Eric's raised eyebrows. "You reckon I'm right out of the hills, but we got libraries there, too. And the Internet."

Eric laughed, a little ashamed of himself for assuming Hosea was as simple as he looked. It wasn't precisely an act, Eric was coming to realize, but more of another defense against frightening people. Hosea was almost painfully courteous. "No offense meant," he said.

"None taken. So, I ain't never met another *Bard* before, except my Grandma. She had the shine, right enough. Guess I got it from her. I'm right glad you came to my rescue, Eric Banyon." Hosea's friendliness was as infectious as his grin.

"Right glad I did, too—" How could he *not* respond? There was something about Hosea that not only exuded trustfulness, but trustworthiness. He could no more have walked away from the guy than kicked a puppy in the face.

Besides, it isn't as if I need the money. Eric's needs were met— and more—by Elven magic. He'd gotten his busking license as much to help out some of the kids at Guardian House as to line his own pockets—or, admittedly, for the joy of playing for a live and mostly uncritical audience. His last assist had been to one of the dancers who lived on his floor—Amity was between dancing jobs and desperate to find something to pay her bills besides waitressing or cleaning houses. Eric had suggested that she bring a small square of "floor" with her down to the subway with him. He'd played, she'd danced, and together they made enough to pay her bills until the next job came along.

"Well, reckon you can find me the YMCA?" Hosea continued. "Friend of mine back home told me that was the place to stay when I got here; told me the rooms was cheap—at least, cheap as anything is here in the big city—and pretty safe. Not that I've got too much to worry about. Folks just take a look at me and just naturally think twice about making trouble, I guess."

Eric grinned. Most people would leave a Bard alone, even if they weren't sure why. And a Bard who was six-four and looked like he juggled pianos in his spare time was even less likely to attract undesirable attention.

He quickly thought about all the things he'd most needed when he first moved to New York. Bonnie and Kit had been there to get him settled in, but he'd still spent most of the first month getting lost every time he ventured out of his own neighborhood.

"First, we get you a street map, a bus-route map, and a subway map," Eric decided. "That'll help you find your way around. Come on."

A quick stop at a newsstand took care of those immediate needs, and for good measure, Eric picked up a guidebook that would give Hosea a lot of reference points—not just the tourist attractions, but the important buildings, the schools and libraries and other major landmarks. After that, it was no great effort to get Hosea planted firmly in front of the nearest YMCA. Once inside, and only then, Hosea dug the day's haul out of the duffle and counted it—he might not be street-smart, but he had a lot more common sense than a lot of people Eric knew.

They'd done better than Eric had thought. There was almost $200 there, even if half of it was in quarters and dollar coins, and a lot of subway tokens.

"I'm good for a week—" Hosea said, tentatively. He raised his eyebrows questioningly, offering Eric his share again as he paid for his room and took the key. Hosea didn't have a credit card—no ID of any kind but a driver's license and a library card, both from someplace in West Virginia—so the room clerk had asked for cash in advance. Hosea had paid for three days, after being assured he could extend his stay if he wished.

"No worries," Eric assured him. "Look—here's my phone number and address, but I'll come and meet you back here—Sunday night, say. That's day after tomorrow. We can run through some numbers and set up a playlist. Then at noon break on Monday, wait for me at the main entrance to the school and we'll do a lunch gig." He coughed, a little embarrassed. "I'd gig with you the rest of this weekend, but I've got friends coming in—"

"Reckon friends got to come before strangers," Hosea countered, with a grin. "You said that it's okay to play in the Park, right? So I'll play in the Park. I'll do all right. Don't you worry none about me, Eric Banyon. I'm a big boy and I can take care of myself. You go on and be with your friends."

Relieved, Eric clapped him on the back—and had to reach a bit to do it. "One of these days—and soon—they'll be *your* friends too, if I don't miss my guess. Okay, Hosea, I'll be out here Sunday night—about six. We'll get something delivered for dinner, talk some music, and see what happens."

"I'll be looking forward to it," Hosea said genially, then hauled his duffle up onto his back again as if it weighed nothing and headed for the elevator, his room key jingling in his hand.

Eric just shook his head, watching Hosea go. He tried to imagine all the trouble this guileless country boy could have gotten himself into within thirty seconds of arriving in the city, and couldn't even calculate it. If he wasn't a Bard . . .

Well, he is a Bard, and he'll be fine. And I need to get home and start cleaning before Bethie gets there and has a fit!

TWO:
THE TREES THEY DO GROW HIGH

By turning himself into a cleaning tornado for a couple of hours—and by recruiting Greystone for things like moving furniture while he vacuumed and then used the steam cleaner he'd borrowed from one of his neighbors—Eric got the apartment up to Beth's standards of hygiene, with all the windows wide open to let in blasts of borrowed winter cold. He even sucked all the crumbs out of the crevices of the couch and chairs—something he hadn't done since before the last party. Ordinarily he wouldn't have bothered doing the Martha Stewart thing. The floor and most of the surfaces were clear, and what was the good of being a Bard if you couldn't set a spell around your home to chase out cockroaches, insects, and rodents, after all?—but Beth was going to be a lot fussier about cleanliness with the baby around.

A baby. Bethie had a daughter. Eric could barely imagine it. And the thought that he might have had any part in the deed seemed to be the rankest fantasy.

"Have I ever told you about the time that Kory discovered microwave popcorn?" Eric called over his shoulder as he shook out a match. Just to be sure that Beth's nose didn't twitch suspiciously, he was lighting vanilla-scented candles on top of the bookshelves, while Greystone popped the Chinese he'd ordered into the oven to stay warm.

"No. What'd he do? Pop every bag in the cupboard?" the gargoyle asked with a snigger. Greystone was an actual, genuine, medieval gargoyle. He had a fanged doglike face and curling horns, long apelike arms, and hindquarters like a satyr's, right down to the cloven hooves. Great bat wings lay against his back like furled umbrellas. Except for his big dark eyes, he was a uniform, textured gray all over, right down to the soot smudges and patches of lichen. And despite the fact that he lived and moved and talked, he seemed to be made of solid stone. He'd been Eric's first friend in Guardian House, coming that first night to Eric's tentative request for a friend. And Greystone had been a good one ever since.

"And then some," Eric said. "Gulls ate well that day. You should have seen Bethie's face." It had been a sight, for certain-sure; they'd eaten the stuff for breakfast as if it was cereal, with Beth standing over both of them (as if *he'd* had anything to do with it!) brandishing a wooden spoon to make sure they finished every bite. Even stuffing themselves with popcorn three meals a day, there was too much to eat before it got stale.

But to see the dumbfounded expression on Beth's face when she'd come into the kitchen that morning and found it full of popcorn had been worth it. Eric smiled reminiscently.

The gargoyle (who normally spent most of the day on the cornice ledge just outside Eric's apartment) strolled into the living room, still chuckling. Though as much a creature of magic as any Sidhe, Greystone had been anything but isolated from progress during *his* long life. He'd been a constant eavesdropper on and observer of life in the big city from the time that the building was erected during the late 1800s, and often (if the occupant of "his" apartment was a Guardian or other user of magic) a participant in the ordinary life of a New Yorker—insofar as anyone Greystone would be hanging out with ever *had* an "ordinary" life, that was. Greystone knew as much about appliances and the amenities of a modern apartment as Eric did.

More, actually. We'd been on the run for so long by the time we went Underhill that I'd gotten out of the habit of being a techno-junkie, and Elfhame Misthold isn't exactly your local Circuit City.

Greystone had been delighted to discover that Eric wasn't the type to freak out when a stone gargoyle came to life and tapped on the window. The gargoyle often spent the long hours of late nights watching television in Eric's living room—but he never, ever imposed. Having him around was rather like having a congenial roommate with none of the disadvantages roommates often brought with them.

And he's alphabetized my CDs and DVDs. How cool is that?

Greystone cocked his head to the side. "They're on the way up," he announced, though Eric heard nothing. "Can I stick around?"

"With Bethie dying to show off Maeve to the world? No question!" Eric said. He was surprised at how relieved he felt.

Beth and Kory already knew about Greystone—they knew about Guardian House as well, at least what Eric knew; that the House had been built to shelter the Guardians of New York, a kind of magical police force set up to protect ordinary humans from those who would use magic against them—or from inadvertently stumbling into the path of the supernormal entities who shared their world. There were never fewer than two and seldom more than four Guardians living here at the same time—Eric wasn't yet quite sure how one became a Guardian, as that was a subject upon which the Guardians themselves were rather reticent—and the House itself selected those other "normal" people who would live here. If Guardian House wanted you, you saw a "Vacancy" sign in the super's window. If it didn't, you didn't. It was all as simple as that.

Most of the "regular" tenants were artists, dancers, and musicians. Most of them were quietly, but devoutly, religious, although the House didn't care *what* their religion was. Most of them had no idea that the Guardians were the sole reason for the House's existence, that the Guardians even existed, or that they supplied a positive and energetic "atmosphere" for the Guardians to live in.

But a few of the House's civilian tenants, like Eric, were true magicians, and *they* knew. They served as a kind of unofficial auxiliary force to be called on in an emergency.

But though the Guardians were powerful and far more knowledgeable than the average human, Eric had found that they didn't know everything. They hadn't known, for instance, that there were such things as Bards—or that elves, the real Sidhe of legend, actually existed. Hadn't, that is, until Eric moved in.

Then they'd found out in spades.

A light tap on the door told Eric that Greystone, as usual, had been right. He flung it open for two figures in motorcycle leathers and helmets, the tall one in blue and the short one in red, with a tiny baby in a matching red leather carry-sack slung across her chest.

Beth pulled off her helmet and shook out her long hair with a sigh of pleasure. She was still keeping the auburn tresses Kory had engineered for her when the Feds had been on their tail—her original hair color had been black, but the auburn suited her. Her skin still glowed with the hormones of her recent pregnancy, and her brown eyes no longer showed that peculiar "haunted" look that had been in them for so long. Instead, there was a softer, more contented expression on her face, especially when she glanced down at baby Maeve.

"Well, Banyon, are you going to keep us standing in the hall all day?" she asked, handing him her helmet. Eric grinned, stepping back to allow them to enter the apartment.

There was the usual moment of kissing and hugging and congestion in the doorway, while Greystone stood aside and grinned. Kory, as usual, looked every inch the Elven Knight, even though he had a motorcycle helmet under his arm instead of a helm, and leathers instead of armor. Tall, muscular, blond as a child of the sun, if any fashion photographer in the world had gotten a look at him, he could have named his price—except, of course, for the pointed ears and green eyes, with their vertical-slit pupils like a cat's. All elves had those eyes and ears; their natural hair color was blond as well, but not all of them stuck to the natural color. After all, just about anything was possible for an elf, even shape-shifting. Eric had seen elves with heads of pink, blue, and purple hair that would make a punker or raver drool with envy; he'd even seen elves sporting hairdos of feathers, leaves, or tiger stripes. He'd seen them with the gauzy wings of Victorian fairies, or batwings, or feathers—all functional, if not actually capable of supporting flight. Tails, horns, hooves—nothing was impossible, which might account for the sightings of so many kinds of creatures in myth and legend. Kory, however, preferred to keep to the "natural" form—blond hair, slitted green eyes, pointed ears, and otherwise looking human.

Eric carried an armful of leathers and helmets into the bedroom while Beth unpacked Maeve and made sure the baby had survived the trip unscathed. When everyone had settled in the living room, Eric made his introductions.

"Greystone, this is Beth Kentraine and Sieur Korendil, Elven Knight and Magus Minor of Elfhame Sun-Descending. Beth and Kory, meet Greystone."

"I've heard so much about you," Beth said, smiling. "And this is Maeve." She held up the baby in her arms, and then, to his horror, offered her to Eric. He had no choice but to take her—it was that or run, and Beth would have slain him on the spot.

Maeve's flushed face, surrounded papoose-like by a fleecy wrap, didn't excite much in Eric but apprehension.

"She looks like Winston Churchill," he said dubiously, looking down at a face with eyes screwed tightly shut and contorted into a disagreeable grimace. A faint whiff of baby powder and milk came up to his nose as she opened her mouth in a silent (for the moment) protest.

"*Eric!*" Beth exclaimed indignantly, while Kory looked puzzled, tucking his blond hair behind his sharply pointed ears. Elves loved children.

The baby scowled at Eric. Beth had said she was beautiful, but to Eric she was looking more every minute like a wizened old man in a temper. She mewed. It sounded as if she was thinking about howling.

Now what do I do? he wondered, just a hint of panic arising. She seemed to be all knees and elbows, writhing muscularly in his arms as if she very much did not want to be there.

"Don't be daft, Bard, she's lovely," Greystone scolded. "And you're holding her all wrong. Give her here." He held out his hands summarily, and Eric, not at all loathe, handed the baby quickly to the gargoyle. Maeve might be his—or rather, he was Maeve's biological father—but there was no feeling of parental bonding there so far as *he* was concerned. He'd never been around babies when he was growing up, and they were almost as scarce on the RenFaire circuit as they were Underhill.

With relief he saw Greystone cuddle the tiny creature in sturdy arms that seemed to understand instinctively how to make the baby comfortable.

"There's a lovely little lady," the gargoyle crooned, wiggling one finger in front of Maeve's nose. "Boojie, boojie, boojie wooooo." The baby looked up at him with blank, blue eyes, but lost that disapproving expression and even made a tentative gurgling sound.

"I think she likes you, Greystone," Eric said, a little surprised.

"Of course she likes me, ye gurt idiot," Greystone retorted with fond indignation. "Never saw a baby that didn't, and I've been nanny to every Guardian's child here since the House was built."

Eric took the opportunity to beat a tactical retreat, heading into the kitchen to gather plates, cutlery, and the cartons of Chinese food Greystone had left in the oven. He arranged them on a tray and added drinks—designer water for Kory and Greystone, tea for Beth—before carrying the meal out into the living room on a tray. Greystone and Beth were both bent over Maeve, clucking and cooing at her while Kory looked on proudly. The domestic tableau left Eric feeling a little unsettled, as if he were being shut out of something he really didn't want to be a part of. It was a peculiar feeling.

"Luncheon is served," he intoned, deliberately breaking the mood. He set the tray down on the coffee table and began setting out the plates.

"Not much Chinese carryout Underhill, huh?" Eric teased, watching Beth and Kory inhale his offerings with a fine appetite while Greystone amused Maeve, holding her in one massive arm while scarfing egg rolls with his free hand.

"They still haven't got the knack of making or even *kenning* and creating it, and when it comes to carryout, the Fairegoers would rather have pizza anyway," Beth replied around a forkful of moo shu chicken, "And for some reason I didn't want anything like this until *after* the munchkin came. Then I thought I would kill for lo mein."

Eric and Kory exchanged a wordless masculine look of complete incomprehension. Kory mouthed a single sentence—just a few words, really.

Honey-nut bread and cabbage soup.

Ah, so *that* was what Beth had craved during her pregnancy! Eric nodded with sympathy, though he privately thought that Kory'd had it easy. Maybe the meals he'd shared with Beth were monotonous, but at least the ingredients were easily obtained Underhill. What if she'd wanted sushi—or bird's nest soup—or some other weird delicacy?

On the other hand, cabbage soup, while being—ah—*fragrant*, wasn't exactly the aroma-of-choice that Eric would have picked for dinnertime. And it did tend to linger.

Finally, the hunger aroused by a long ride from the Everforest Gate to New York City assuaged, Kory and Beth declared themselves sated and Eric cleaned away the plates.

"Bethie, ye can count on me for babysitting any time you're Overhill," Greystone announced, handing Maeve back to her mother. He looked up now, and raised an eyebrow like a cliff cornice at her as she beamed at him. "How are ye feeding her, then? Just breast?"

Somehow, Eric had noticed, whenever the gargoyle was around Kory and Beth, his Irish—or pseudo-Irish—accent got thicker. Why a gargoyle should have an Irish accent, and not a French one, he couldn't fathom. It was just one of those New York mysteries, he guessed. Or maybe the apartment's first tenant had been Irish. Greystone had to have learned his English somewhere.

Beth blushed. "Well—not entirely. I'm not exactly—well—a Holstein. The healers concocted a formula that Maeve likes; Kory can magic it up for us when we need it."

Elves, even minor mages like Kory, could always *ken* an object or substance and conjure more of it up later. That was why Eric himself was, for as long as he was in school, financially solvent— Dharniel and Kory had supplied him with enough gold Krugerrands (which, conveniently enough, completely lacked any identifying serial numbers) to give him a fat and very golden nest egg.

Eric wasn't surprised that Kory was helping to supplement Maeve's feeding magically, since as was vividly obvious in the tight motorcycle leathers, Beth's figure was back to her pre- pregnancy slimness, probably in no small part due to a little help from elven healers Underhill.

And we could make a fortune out here in the mortal world if we could just bottle that! No need for the Jane Fonda Pregnancy Workout if you've got the Sidhe on your side.

"Well, good." The gargoyle grinned. "You can just be leavin' the little angel with me tonight while ye have some fun out in the city, an' I'll be givin' her the bottle while ye're gone."

"Oh, would you?" Beth exclaimed delightedly, and then blushed again. "Oh, that sounds awful, but—"

"But what's the harm in you havin' an evenin' out for a movie or summat?" Greystone countered quickly. "'Tis time for a little holiday, I'm thinkin', and the wee one will be fine here. 'Tis many a nappie I've changed in me time—" he chuckled, a sound like rocks grating together "—and it's a fine thing for me that I've no sense of smell to speak of."

Better you than me, Eric thought, but didn't say out loud. He'd been worried that their evening plans might have to be adjusted to include a baby—or worse, that Beth wouldn't want to go out at all. Before she could change her mind, he went straight for the computer and logged on to the net, pulling up the *New York Times* entertainment web pages.

"Here're your choices," he called over his shoulder, while Beth was still protesting that Greystone didn't have to be a babysitter and Greystone was insisting it would be a fine treat to have a baby in his arms again. Kory got up to peer over Eric's shoulder with interest— computer technology had changed a lot since the last time Kory'd seen a computer—while Beth paused in mid-sentence, then shrugged and laughed, acknowledging defeat.

"Okay, Banyon. I'm sold. What've you got for us this evening, then?"

After some discussion, they decided on *The Lion King*—it was finally possible to get tickets after months of nothing but sold-out performances, and it was the show Eric thought Kory would enjoy the most.

Movies they could always see later; with help from Elfhame Fairgrove in Savannah, the most technologically sophisticated of the hames, a limited amount of human technology had been brought Underhill for the benefit of Beth and other humans who had sought shelter there. One of those bits of technology was a DVD player—which worked better than the VCR they'd originally had down there did, for some reason. They were still trying to work out how to bring in satellite TV, according to Kory—right now when anyone from Fairgrove wanted to see NASA Channel, Headline News, or (most especially) Speedvision, they had to retire to one of the Fairgrove buildings Overhill.

Eric booked their seats through Ticketron Online—one of the perks of carrying an AmEx Platinum card—and for the first time in a long time, the three of them went out onto the streets of a city, to spend an evening together, as they once used to.

"That was great," Beth sighed, much later, after peeking into the portable crib set up in the bedroom to make sure Maeve was all right. Babies, Eric had discovered, needed about as much support gear as the average astronaut, but fortunately Beth, unlike most mortal moms, had a portable hole to carry it in. The amount of stuff she'd unpacked from it before she'd been willing to leave Maeve with Greystone had been purely mind-boggling.

"That was fantastic, in fact."

They'd made the curtain without any trouble, walking most of the way so that Beth and Kory could get a taste of New York. After the show they'd stopped at Luchow's for dessert, and were home by midnight.

Kory nodded, his green eyes still shining—literally!—with pleasure. "I forget, sometimes, just what a marvel mortal creativity is," he said, clearly without thinking who he was with. "Imagine creating something that has never *been* before, just with the power of the mind!"

Eric laughed. "So what am I, chopped liver?" he asked mockingly, and Kory flushed.

"Nay, Bard, I didn't—" the elf faltered.

"I know you didn't! I'm just teasing you!" Eric laughed—but behind the laughter was an inescapable thought. *When it was the three of us alone together, he wouldn't even have put that into a thought, much less words—he'd have wondered, maybe, when I would create something that would be on a stage. Now I'm "Bard," not "Eric"—and he forgets what I am. As if our life together never happened.*

"Listen, something really fantastic happened today," he said quickly, to drive away uncomfortable thoughts. "I met another Bard!"

The other three settled down to hear the story—though Greystone, being telepathic by nature, already probably knew at least some of it. But like the tactful guest he was, he never flaunted that very useful ability, and in fact, Eric wasn't really sure how much of his regular thoughts Greystone actually heard.

He told them all about meeting Hosea, about realizing what Hosea was, and about the two of them playing together in the subway. Then he told them about his plans to get Hosea on his feet. He realized he didn't know why Hosea had come to New York—he was becoming enough of a New Yorker himself to just kind of take it for granted that of course everyone who could would want to come to New York, the center of the world for so many things.

He couldn't help but get excited about the prospect of playing with the banjo-Bard again. Gigging with another good musician was one of the things he liked to do best, but gigging with another Bard had been an experience so enchanting that he couldn't wait to do it again. Kory nodded his understanding, and the more enthusiastic Eric got, the more pleased Kory looked—but Beth was frowning.

"I don't know, Banyon," she said slowly, her brows furrowing with unease. "This could all be a setup. I don't like it—I mean, you don't know anything about this guy—not really! Isn't it just a little too convenient that he's busking at your subway station just as you get out of class?" She put down her tea and shifted uneasily in her seat on the couch.

It was hard, now, to remember what Beth had been like when he first met her—hard to remember what *he'd* been like, come to that—but he knew she hadn't been this suspicious, jumping-at-shadows paranoid. Since Griffith Park, and everything that followed after, every year Beth seemed to be darker, more intense, more focused—and not entirely in a good way, either. It was as if the person she might have become had been destroyed by this other self—and equally true that she had always held the potential to become either one. He supposed it bothered him more because he'd been counting on Maeve to erase all the scars and make Beth the person she'd been at twenty. But that wasn't ever going to happen. Done was done, and living things changed.

But some changes weren't for the better.

"Bethie, this guy couldn't be a Fed," Eric answered firmly. "I've been here almost a year—if anyone were looking for me, they'd have found me already. Besides, no Fed I ever saw looked or acted like Hosea, or *could*. They're just not good enough actors."

"He doesn't have to be a Fed," she argued, leaning forward, her face intent. "What about those people that were using LlewellCo as a front to make mages on crack or whatever it was? What about the guys with the pet Nightflyers that were after us in San Francisco?"

"Not a chance. Trust me, those kind of guys stink of bad juju a mile away," he insisted. "I'd know. Believe me, I'd know." *I'm a Bard, Bethie. This is what being a Bard is. I'd know.*

But Beth still wasn't willing to drop the subject. "Maybe," she said grudgingly. "But you have to admit that the story is just—awfully pat. In fact, this sounds like a classic con job to me!"

Oh, Bethie, when did you become so stubborn, so blind? You used to be able to see what was right in front of your nose better than most people!

"He's a Bard, Bethie," Eric said patiently, throttling his irritation. After all, she had every reason to be paranoid; she wasn't Underhill ninety percent of her time because she *wanted* to be, she was there because "They" *were* after her. He'd never understood why it was Bethie they wanted, and not him or Kory, but there was no arguing with the facts.

"I'm telling you. I couldn't make a mistake about this. Trust me. I *know* he's a Bard; you can't fake that. I know he's one of the good guys—it's in his music. A Bard can't hide what he is—at least, not from another Bard. And anyway, a Bard isn't going to try to con another Bard! What would the point be? Anything he can get from me he can get for himself a lot easier just by using his magic!"

"Not if what he wants is *you*," Beth said, her jaw set in a stubborn line of temper.

"A Bard would not betray another Bard, *acushla*," Kory said, coming to Eric's defense. He put a hand on Beth's knee soothingly. "I know this. And our Eric is no fool; he can weigh the human heart as easily as I could weigh an egg."

Beth looked from Kory's face to Eric and back again, and finally shrugged and sat back. "I suppose," she said grudgingly, then smiled with a visible effort. "Well, you've done all right so far. I guess"— now it was her turn to falter—"I guess you don't need us to shepherd you anymore."

Eric forced a grin, though he'd rarely felt less like smiling. "Like you ever did—or at least, any more than I did the same for *you* two!" Eric scoffed, and the other two looked a little shamefaced and ill-at-ease.

They were all so uncertain with each other! This wasn't the easy seamless reunion he'd imagined. It was as if they'd never been friends and lovers, as if they were meeting now for the first time, none of them knowing the others any too well.

And that would never have happened in the past, either.

Greystone got to his feet, stretching his wings. "Well, I'll thank ye now for a foigne evening, but it's going I have to be. Can't be spending all me time away from me duties, y'know." He clumped across the room to the windowsill and ducked out onto the fire escape. "But any time ye need a sitter for the wee one, just gi' me a shout, eh?" In moments, he was back in his post on the cornice above.

Once he was gone, a silence descended that was just a bit too uncomfortable, and Eric hastened to break it.

"So is there anything planned for Maeve?" he asked, figuring that the baby was the subject least likely to cause any more awkwardness. "I mean, like a christening or a baby shower or something?"

"Oh, aye!" Kory brightened up again, his delight in Maeve transparently obvious. "There's the Naming ceremony—you'll be coming, of course—"

"Of course," Eric assured them quickly, and was rewarded by smiles.

"She will be brought up to the Court for it—you've never seen the Court, Eric—it is a sight beyond compare—and there'll be the godparents speaking for her, and a *ceileighe,* of course—"

Kory went on at great length, using a number of words Eric didn't know, but he did manage to gather that the real reason for the Naming was to have the biggest party Underhill had seen for a long, long time. Guests from every Elfhame known would be invited, and the ceremony itself would serve to confirm Beth's place as a member of the Underhill community. In one way Underhill was like a family—or the extended family of Rennies—in that it functioned as much as a web of kinships and relationships as after the fashion of a true feudal society. To be *known,* and to know people in turn, was the very foundation of Sidhe life. As the old saying went: it wasn't *what* you knew, but *who* you knew. . . .

All of this made Eric feel acutely aware of how very much he was no longer really a part of their lives, though he tried very hard not to show it. After all, that was the point of his being here, wasn't it? He had a different sort of life to lead, now, and it was nothing like theirs. It didn't even take place in the same world. Literally.

It's done. The break's a fact. He'd known that, he really had—but here it was in front of him, undeniable, and Eric's throat suddenly knotted with a surge of loneliness that took him entirely by surprise.

He was so lost for a moment in his own thoughts that he missed the change in conversation.

"—think you're going to ask Ria?" Beth was saying hesitantly.

Eric stared at her blankly. *To the Naming? You're asking me that?* Beth obviously mistook his blank incomprehension for something else, because she flushed and added hastily, "If it hasn't been a good idea to bring up her father and how *she* was born, I understand, but Kory and I haven't had much luck in finding out anything for ourselves. And I thought . . ."

He shook off his melancholy with a start, and frantically tried to put the bits of conversation together into a coherent whole. *Ria—Perenor—oh, of course! Not the Naming. About Sidhe/human crossbreeding.*

"I *have* asked her, actually," he said, hoping he hadn't looked too blank. "I even told her why—well, I had to, she came out and asked me," he added, in response to Beth's sudden scowl.

"Oh, I'm sure she was only too pleased with that—" Beth snapped.

"She's not your enemy," was all Eric said, not defensively, but determined that the feud between Beth and Ria—if there was one—was *not* going to go on. *Maybe bringing Ria to the Naming would be a good idea after all. Beth can't throw a fit in the middle of a big party, and Ria needs to get on good terms with her relatives. Half her heritage is Sidhe. You can't just ignore something like that.*

"She risked her life to save the Sun-Descending Nexus—and paid a heavy price for her help," Eric said firmly. "Elizabet and Kayla both say she's okay. Whatever happened in the past is over with, and if she could have told me anything that would help, she would have.

"Unfortunately, she says—and I believe her—that what Perenor did in order to father a child on her mortal mother was not something we'd want to repeat." He shook his head, and sighed. He hated to disappoint them—Beth and Kory wanted a child of their *own* so badly—but Ria's information had been pretty grim.

"You remember how we found out that Perenor drained all those young kids that *would* have been Bards if they'd had a chance to grow into their power?" he asked.

"And left them sad, empty husks, aye," Kory said, slowly, the horror of it dawning on him. "Do you mean—*that* was what he used to make the woman conceive?" The Sidhe knight drew back in horror, his green eyes wide.

"In a nutshell, yeah. He *kept* draining them for other reasons and other magics later, but that was the first thing he used them for." Eric shuddered. He'd seen a couple of the kids—Elizabet, their human Healer-friend, had gotten some of them as patients once she'd known they were there to look for—and in Eric's personal opinion, they'd have been better off dead. Actually, most of them *had* died, especially at first, and to Eric's mind, they'd been the lucky ones.

If anyone had taken the music, the life, the dreams I'd had out of my world and left it gray and drained and empty, I wouldn't have wanted to live.

Ria had told him that the actual spell Perenor had used had been a bit more complicated than simple draining. Perenor had forced two of the incipient Bards—one of them Ria's uncle, her mother's twin—into a kind of mind-bond; they'd hated and feared him and each other, and when they realized what he was doing, it had driven them crazy before it killed them. The backlash had damaged Ria's hippie mother's mind, leaving her with so many mental kinks her psyche resembled a ball of steel wool, and an insatiable craving for drugs that could not be explained by normal addictions—if you could call an "addiction" normal. Eric got the feeling she hadn't lasted long after Ria ran away and took refuge with her loving father, either. Perenor probably protected her from herself only so long as she and her friends were useful, literally "minding the baby."

"You're right," Beth said flatly, as Eric's explanation faltered to a stop. "That's not something we'd want to repeat. So it's a dead end. Another dead end." She seemed to fold in upon herself, as if the disappointment were a palpable weight.

There didn't seem to be much else Eric could say, and the conversation stumbled awkwardly into another subject. Eventually, around about three in the morning, Eric smothered a yawn and Greystone poked his head in the window.

"Streets are quiet as a nun's funeral," he said. "Are ye plannin' on stayin' the night, then?"

Beth and Kory looked at each other, a quick sort of "married people" glance.

"You can have the bedroom," Eric offered quickly. "Just like always. *You* know the couch makes up into a good bed—you picked it out, remember?—and it won't be the first time I've fallen asleep on it."

But Kory and Beth exchanged another one of those looks that excluded Eric, and Beth chuckled.

"I don't think so, Banyon," she said, not unkindly. "Maeve is as good as gold *except* for first thing in the morning. And she may not have anything else of yours, but there's no doubt she's got your lungs. She'd have the whole building up here, thinking we're murdering a cat."

Eric blushed, but laughed along with the other three, for Greystone seemed to find this observation hilariously funny. "Okay, then—I was thinking you'd spend the weekend, but—"

"What, and get in the way of you making a date with Ms. Llewellyn?" Beth asked, with just a hint of bitterness that she tried hard to conceal. "We'll send you word of when the Naming is—you *are* coming?" she asked again.

"If I didn't, you'd kill me," he pointed out.

"Well—unless you were in a hospital bed, yeah, I probably would," Beth admitted. Kory went to fetch Maeve from the bedroom, while Beth stood up and gave him a hug and a kiss that was, for one moment, like the old Beth's. "I'll try not to be so jealous, Banyon," she whispered in his ear. "As long as the bitch makes you happy. But if she ever hurts you—"

"That'll be between her and me," he replied, breathing it into her ear. "Don't interfere, Bethie. Not even out of love. I'm a big boy now. You can't always be trying to protect me."

She pushed him away, and looked into his eyes for a moment; hers were suspiciously damp. "You've grown," was all she said, but the smile she gave him wavered just a little.

Kory came back with Maeve. He handed Beth the baby to tuck into her carrier, then put an arm around Eric's shoulders.

"The Bard's a warrior now, *acushla*, well-trained and proven in dire battle. He doesn't need us for *protection* anymore." The elf smiled, that kind of smile that just melted the heart. "But I know he will always need us as friends."

"Always," Eric said, drawing both of them into a fierce embrace.

Maeve was a warm weight between them—between them, Eric now realized, in more ways than the physical. Beth and Kory were parents now, and he wasn't. "*Always*. Never doubt it," he repeated. *But it's a different kind of "always" than I'd planned for. . . .*

It was just as well that Beth and Kory left that Friday night, because Saturday turned out to be a day of running around on a hundred little errands that ate up all of Eric's time from the moment he got up around noon. Light bulbs blew, he ran out of toilet paper, then out of ink for his printer (at which time he discovered that he was out of paper as well). He went down to the basement to do laundry, and discovered he was out of detergent.

If it weren't for the party this evening, I'd be really bummed.

It wasn't anything major in the way of parties, but over the past several months those who were in the "know" about the true function of Guardian House—the four Guardians and a few others—had fallen into the pleasant habit of getting together once or twice a month to just kick back and socialize. These gatherings were usually held at Eric's place—Eric was a Bard, not a Mage, and, as Paul had been happy to inform him, Bards were legendary for their hospitality.

And practically speaking, Mages were solitary types who didn't much like getting their personal space invaded at the best of times, even if Paul's computers and reference library, José's birds, and Toni's kids weren't taking up all the available entertaining space in their various apartments. And Jemima, being a New York City cop, was particularly possessive about her space, which was her sanctuary from the horrors a patrol cop saw on a daily basis.

Eric had been invited in a couple of times; Jemima had a small one-bedroom decorated mostly in blues and greens, its walls hung with her collection of nature photographs, including an original Ansel Adams. It was a serene yet somehow impersonal space, reflecting its owner's personal reserve. Especially if you never got to see the sword hanging on the bedroom wall, its blade glowing with Runes of Intent. . . .

Eric shook himself free of the reverie with a smile. So what it all boiled down to was that his apartment had become the *de facto*

Mage Community Center for Guardian House. Fortunately, all he had to do was place his standing order with the corner pizza place and look forward to an evening of good talk and good people.

Tatiana and Alex were the first two to arrive. Tat was a book designer; Alex did indexing and research, as well as teaching part-time at the New School. Tatiana was tall and flamboyant, with pre-Raphaelite blonde hair and a gypsy taste in clothes. Alex was dark and saturnine, with a neatly-trimmed black beard and a positive addiction to sober suits. His hobby was stage illusionism, and on occasion Eric had seen him pull off feats of sleight of hand that he wasn't sure he could duplicate even with the help of Bardic magic. Both were what Alex called "research magicians," devoting more time to the history of the Art than to actual practice. They were members of one of the more close-mouthed magical lodges, New Age by courtesy, though unlike a lot of the New Agers Eric had met over the years, they weren't "in-your-face" about it. They spoke appreciatively about Eric's "air-conditioning," and Tat poked her head out the window to say "hi" to Greystone while Alex got them drinks—Vernor's with lime for himself, Schweppes' Bitter Lemon with ice for Tatiana.

One thing I've got to say for magicians—they certainly make cheap dates. Nobody I've ever met who had the Gift—and knew what they had—really drinks much. Or smokes, or, well, much of anything in that line. I guess once you've plugged into magic, the other stuff all seems second best.

The others began to appear fairly quickly after that, arriving from their various day jobs. Toni Hernandez was the building's manager, a pretty, no-nonsense Latina in her early forties, a single mother with two kids. As much as such an anarchic group as the Guardians had a leader—and Eric had gotten the feeling that they were a lot more like the Texas Rangers, or four Lone Rangers, than any organized Occult Police—the Guardians of Guardian House looked to Toni.

Jimmie—short for Jemima, and she'd kill you if you used it— was fashion-model tall and slim, with thick, lustrous, straight black hair, very dark eyes, a bronzy complexion under a good, even tan, and high cheekbones in a face too strong to be called "pretty." She was manic about keeping civilians off the fire line; back when she'd just been starting out as a Guardian, her partner had been killed because she'd been unable to keep him out of a paranormal investigation. Now she was adamant about protecting the innocent.

Paul Kern was a tall elegant black man with a hint of Islands British in his voice, who carried himself with the grace of a dancer. Paul made his living doing something esoteric with computers, and used the same valuable skills to find information about whatever problems the Guardians might face. Though his abilities had come up dry when the Guardians had faced down an Unseleighe Lord last year, Eric had no doubt that by now Paul had managed to corner the world market in elven lore.

Paul entered along with the fourth of the House's Guardians, José Ramirez. José was the building's super, handling the House's rare mechanical breakdowns, and a breeder of African Grey parrots. He was short and stocky, with the build of someone who lifted weights for use, not show, and the dark craggy features of an *Indio* Charles Bronson. Of the four Guardians, it was hardest for Eric to imagine how José had wound up as a mystical champion of the Light: he seemed so incredibly pragmatic and down-to-earth, not to mention fully involved in both day job and avocation. Eric had visited his apartment a few times—it was almost entirely given over to the birds. To Eric they looked like budgies on steroids, but there was no doubt that José loved them—or that his love was returned.

The last of the stragglers had arrived by eight, and the apartment was filled with eddies of talk and laughter. Earlier in the day Eric had filled his CD player with an eclectic mix calculated to appeal to everyone—some old favorites, some new finds—and more than once he caught people paging through the stack of jewel cases, trying to identify the music that was playing. The pizzas had vanished early, but Margot had brought cookies—someone usually did—and Eric had laid in a more than sufficient supply of sodas to fuel conversations far into the wee small hours.

Jimmie had looked pretty beat when she'd walked in tonight.

Eric had put that down to the stress of her job—in addition to everything else, the NYPD rotated shifts on a six-week basis, which meant she was always having to get used to new hours—but as the evening passed, the lines of stress in her striking face became more pronounced, not less. Something worse than usual was eating at her, something good friends and conversation couldn't touch.

"Want to talk about it?" Eric asked.

He'd followed her into the kitchen when she'd gone to get a refill on her tea. Eric had found that a Mr. Coffee did a good job of keeping a pot of herbal tea hot for hours—and after six or seven hours of steeping, even chamomile would get as dark as Lipton's.

Jimmie sighed, not turning around. "Is it that obvious?"

"Only to someone who knows you," Eric answered. "I'm surprised the others haven't been on your case about it already."

"What makes you think they haven't?" she asked, turning around, cup in hand, and leaning against the sink. "The only trouble is, none of us can figure this out. I was just about desperate enough to ask *you* for advice," she finished, with a faint ironic smile.

Eric smiled back, although he was now a lot more worried than he had been before. The Guardians were good folks, but they tended to be . . . insular. Jimmie's flat refusal to put civilians on the firing line was only the more extreme manifestation of the Guardians' general desire not to involve outsiders—no matter how magical—in their business. Either you were already in it up to your neck, so their reasoning ran, or you should take the chance to go live a peaceful, normal life and run with it. The fact that Jimmie was willing to consult him was proof that the Guardians were at the end of their considerable resources.

"Consider the doctor in," he said, doing his best to cloak his unease with lightness.

Jimmie took a deep breath, obviously organizing her thoughts. Eric glanced over his shoulder, but no one had followed them into the kitchen, and the hum of talk and music was still at an even level. They wouldn't be disturbed.

"Okay. For about the past . . . six months, maybe a little longer, I've been having nightmares. They sort of come with the territory, I know, but these have been something special. Fires, open graves, things . . . chasing me. Pretty grim.

"We tried to figure out a reason for them, sure, but it's been pretty quiet magically since Aerune tried his little stunt last winter. They can't really be coming from outside, not with my shields and the House's. And besides, Greystone doesn't pick up a thing—at least, not until I wake up screaming. As for work . . . well, the job is the job, and it never changes. But the dreams have. They've gotten more frequent, and they've gotten worse." She shrugged, glancing up momentarily to meet Eric's eyes. "I'm starting to think maybe I ought to take some personal leave."

These nightmares must be something pretty bad, Eric thought. He frowned. While he could certainly use his magic—with her help and consent—to give her sweet dreams in place of the nightmares, it would only be a temporary solution. The real question was what could break through a Guardian's shields and leave no trace for the House—or Greystone—to sense?

"And you don't think they're coming from outside."

Jimmie shook her head.

"But they could be." Eric cudgeled his brains to remember all Master Dharniel's lessons on magic, but the Sidhe Magus hadn't been big on lectures. Dharniel had been more the "learn by doing" type. "You've pretty much settled that this isn't something coming from within—if it were, it would probably have resolved itself by now. And I know that the House's shields would stop pretty much everything, but if you have blood-kin, they can almost always get through any shields you can raise. . . ." His voice trailed off. As far as he knew, Jimmie didn't have any living relatives.

"Mom's dead. Dad's dead. But . . ." Jimmie stopped with a heavy sigh. "There's still someone. He's as good as dead, though."

"Someone close to you?" Eric asked, feeling uncomfortably that he was prying into things that weren't any of his business.

Jimmie Youngblood smiled bitterly. "Once upon a time I had an older brother. I went into the Academy because of him—he was a cop, like Dad and Grampa. I wanted to be just like him. Only it turned out that he *wasn't* a cop just like Dad and Grampa. He . . . cut corners. Did things that no cop can do and stay clean. Dad found out about five minutes before Internal Affairs did. He turned El— my brother—in. He left the Force, and that was that."

"Do you know where he is now?"

"Eric, I don't even know if he's *alive*," Jimmie said in frustrated exasperation.

"My advice? Better find him," Eric said. "I can play you a charm to give you temporary relief, so you can get some rest, but all it will be is a stopgap. It won't make the dreams go away. And from the kind of dreams you've been having, I'd say it's a possibility that this guy might be in trouble."

Serious trouble.

THREE:
A DARK HORN BLOWING

In this forest it was always night. A red moon hung eternally overhead, its scarlet light turning the landscape below to ebony and blood, hiding the brambles and pitfalls that could trap a running man. The damp air resounded to the call of hunting horns and the howls of the pack. Whatever mortal encountered them was doomed, for they were the hounds of the Wild Hunt, and once set upon a scent, they never failed to take their prey.

He had seen them succeed four times before. He was the fifth and last, and sometime in this eternal night his end would come in the same way as that of all the others.

He did not know how long any of them had been here, suffering the tender mercies of their tormentor. Weeks or months—or maybe even years. The old stories said that time ran differently under the Hollow Hills than it did on Earth. But the time of year was the least of his worries.

Staying alive as long as he could—and dying well—was what mattered now. Was all that mattered now.

He stopped for a moment, his back to the trunk of a tree of no

338

earthly species, alert for the sound of the Hunt. If he could survive until dawn, he was free. That was what they'd told Hauman, and for a while all of them had hoped to escape—until they realized that in this world, dawn never came.

His antlers caught in the tree's branches. He shook his head irritably as he freed them. They were another part of the trap. There was no way to remove them. Once Aerune had strapped the gleaming silver antlers to your head, only death would release you. That was one of his tricks, and the Sidhe lord had a lot of them. Elkanah Youngblood had sampled them in plenty during his captivity.

Had the blonde bitch known what Aerune would do to them when she'd abandoned them here? Elkanah hoped so. It made Ria Llewellyn easier to hate, and hate was the only thing that gave him the strength to go on. There was no point in hating Lord Aerune— it would be like hating a mountain, or the sea, or the night itself. Aerune was too inhuman to hate, but Elkanah could fear him, and he did.

Too late now to wish he'd never followed Lintel's orders back in the day, nor followed the path that had brought him to the outlaw life of a hired gun. Too late to wish he'd died before Robert Lintel had magicked them all into Aerune's court with his captive espers. Too late to wish he'd turned his own gun on himself while he still could, before he'd become Aerune's prisoner. All that mattered now was surviving as long as he could without going mad. Or maybe going mad was better. Elkanah didn't know.

The one thing he did know was that it was marginally better to be ripped apart by the hellhounds pursuing him than to fall into the hands of the huntsmen. Liverakos had made that mistake. He'd held off the dogs until the Hunt had joined them. He'd hoped for clemency, or for a clean death. Instead, it had taken him hours to die, flayed alive slowly by creatures who fed on human pain.

And all of them—the surviving Threshold mercs—had been forced to watch.

Elkanah didn't know how often Aerune held these hunts. Time had no meaning here. There was being asleep, and being awake, and sometimes it was hard to tell the difference between the two. When

Aerune got tired of his petty torments, then it was time for another hunt. They'd never known who'd be chosen next to wear the silver antlers. Elkanah had that small advantage over those who had gone before him. When the last of the others had died in the hounds' jaws, he'd known he'd be next. Maybe that was why Aerune had played him as long as he did, tormenting him with the hope it wouldn't end for him the way it had for all the others. But this morning—it was impossible not to use the word, even though it was meaningless in this world—Aerune had summoned him to the throne room, and Elkanah had known his time had come.

And now he was here in the bone-wood.

The bone-wood was filled with bare, leafless trees like nothing on Earth. Even when there was no wind, the branches moved, rubbing against each other to produce a sound eerily like human whispering. Maybe if you listened long enough, you could understand what the trees said. Elkanah hoped he'd be dead before then.

Though he suspected spring and autumn never came to this place, the forest floor was covered with dead and rotting leaves. Thickets of leafless bramble grew between the trees, a trap for unwary prey, and somewhere beyond the bone-wood itself was a meadow—covered with sere dry grass that had never been green—and a river. He'd used every moment of the other Hunts to try to make a map of the territory in his mind, hoping it would serve him when his own time came.

Except for the silver antlers upon his head, Elkanah was as naked as any other hunted animal. They'd given him a head start before they released the hellhounds—the Unseleighe Sidhe had a warped notion of fair play—and he'd had a long time to plan for this day.

There was no way out of the forest, and no point in waiting for a dawn that would never come. The only hope he had—and all it amounted to was a choice of deaths—was to make the hunt last as long as possible, so that the *rade* got bored and didn't follow the pack very closely. Then he could be sure that the pack would tear him to bits before the hunters reached him. Until that time, he needed to confuse them, lay a maze of false trails, and use every way there was to throw them off the scent. The times he'd ridden with the Hunt to watch the others die would help him there. He could almost say he knew this forest.

The horns sounded again, closer this time, and he could hear the baying of the hounds. They were huge, monsters, like a wolf in a nightmare: four feet at the shoulder, with ivory fangs as long as his thumb and pupilless red eyes that glowed with the light of hellfire. His daddy'd been a jackleg preacher when he wasn't hard at work at his real job, and in his youth Elkanah had heard all about Hell and its creatures. He could say he knew the territory. If this wasn't Hell, it was the next best thing.

He turned, and began moving away from the pack at a slow, ground-eating lope. The river was near here. He could wade along it for a few hundred yards, then cross over and double back on his tracks. That should confuse them for a while. Later he'd find a tree to climb, move from branch to branch. Anything to throw them off the scent. He could even pretend that he hoped he could make it to the edge of the forest—assuming it had an edge. Hope could keep you alive, or it could kill you. Right now, hope and determination were the only things he had.

He heard the river long before he reached it. He had to force his way through a thicket of thorns to reach it, and he was bleeding from a hundred scratches by the time he made his way to the water. The surface of the water shone balefully red in the moonlight, and for a moment he worried about what might lay beneath its surface. The river was wider than he remembered, but the far bank was an easy slope. But Agel had made it across before he died, and Aerune's Hunt had forded it without difficulty. He had to try.

When he stepped into the water, it was as cold as liquid ice. The scratches on his body burned, a silver tracery of fire, before the cold numbed them. Gritting his teeth, Elkanah forced himself deeper, striking out with powerful strokes for the center. The current would be faster there, and do some of his work for him. Always providing the Hunt wasn't awaiting him downstream, knowing he would do precisely this.

Indecision is your worst enemy. On the battlefield, even a bad decision is better than none, he told himself grimly. *You've made your plan, now stick to it.*

The cold sapped his strength and made his heart hammer madly. He let the current carry him downstream as long as he dared before striking out for the far bank, knowing he had to save some of his strength to battle his way there. He didn't dare try to drown, though surrendering to the water's chill kiss was tempting. Aerune's healers were too skilled for him to risk it. He'd seen them work on the others, bringing a man back from the edge of death to be tortured again. The death that was his only way of winning this game had to be certain . . . and final.

But it was almost a greater effort than he was capable of to drag himself out of the water, and for long moments Elkanah crouched in the thick grass of the bank, gasping and shuddering with the cold. Only terror and determination forced him to his feet to stagger onward through the wood again. All around him the trees seemed to whisper to themselves as he passed, and he no longer cared if what he saw and heard was real or imaginary. Anything might be true here. The only thing he had going for him was the fact that the Unseleighe Sidhe didn't like to have their games spoiled. Nothing in this forest would hinder him as he ran, or do anything to cheat the Wild Hunt of its sport.

At least, they never had yet. He'd seen some of the other things that lived here—black horses with cloven hooves and ram's horns, small silvery fox-things that sobbed and cried like children, glowing women as insubstantial as mist. Creatures of nightmare, only here the nightmares didn't end with waking.

Each time he stopped to rest it seemed like only moments before he heard the hounds again, baying close behind as they followed his trail. He crossed a second, shallower stream, and Elkanah spent several minutes circling back and forth through it, making a tangled scent for the hounds to follow, before forging onward. The ground began to rise, and he realized that the trees were becoming smaller and farther apart.

This was a part of the Night Lands he'd never seen before on any of the Hunts. Perhaps if he reached the top of the ridge ahead, he might find sanctuary. A cave to hide in. Something. He had to hope, had to fool himself that he wouldn't die tonight. It was the only way he could manage to get through this, and put himself at last beyond Aerune's reach.

His entire body trembled with exhaustion, and his throat and lungs burned with each rasping breath he took. He didn't know how far he had run—miles, maybe—and he knew that he couldn't fool himself much longer. He was at the end of his strength, and the hounds were closer now. He could hear them. For the last few minutes he'd just been running flat-out, too stupefied with fatigue to turn and dodge and confuse the trail. This was open country, anyway. Backtracking wouldn't do any good. The hounds could see him, and unlike other hunted animals, he had no convenient burrow to hide in.

He risked a look back, and to his horror, he saw that the hounds were not alone. He could see the torches of the Hunt, the glow of the riders' bodies. Against all hope, this time the *rade* hadn't lost interest in the chase, had followed the pack closely.

Of course. Aerune would want to be in at this last kill. He might even deny the hounds their pleasure, saving Elkanah for some new torment.

Behind him, he heard the horn blow victory, the prey in sight. From a view, to a kill.

At that thought, Elkanah's last shred of control snapped. He could not—*would* not—die as Liverakos had. He ran, heedless of the stones that cut his feet, up the sloping ground toward the ridge.

There was a path cut into the hillside, leading up to the top of the ridge. Earlier he would have avoided it as a matter of course. Now it seemed to provide some haven, and he followed it unthinkingly. Twice he fell to his knees as his strength failed him, and twice he forced himself to stagger onward as the pack howled eagerly behind him. He could hear the riders now, shouting and laughing as they closed in, their horses scrabbling and slipping as they were forced up the steep narrow track. He grabbed one of the loose rocks as he ran. It was a poor weapon, but all he had. He would not give up without a fight.

The trail flattened out as he reached the top of the ridge. The wind was colder here, blowing steadily. He looked around, trying to see where the trail led now. There was a cave ahead. No—he paused to claw the sweat from his eyes—not a cave, just two rocks, leaning against each other to form the shape of a crude doorway. He should have been able to see through the opening to what lay beyond, but all he could see was blackness, blackness that shimmered and twisted like an oil slick on water. A Gate—he'd learned about them in his captivity. But to where?

But he had hesitated too long. The first of the hounds reached him, springing silently to the attack.

He went down beneath its weight, fighting to keep its jaws from his throat. He lowered his head and swung it fiercely back and forth, using the antlers as another weapon. The hound snapped at them, snarling, and that was enough to allow him to bring up the rock he still clutched in his hand, smashing it into the beast's head.

It yelped at the pain, sounding almost doglike in its surprise. He hit it again, and heard the crunch of bone. It squealed and scrabbled back, glaring at him with those mad red eyes. But it didn't attack again. It didn't need to. The pack was only moments behind it. He scuttled backward frantically with hands and feet, not daring to take the moment to stand or to turn his back on the hound. He heard the riders behind them, and fury banished his weakness. He'd been so close, so *close*. . . .

He felt rough stone at his back, and something more. Something like dark sunlight, a raw electrical tingling that made his bones vibrate. The Gate. With the last of his strength he thrust himself sideways, kicking out to propel his body through to whatever lay beyond.

It didn't matter what was on the other side.

The Hunt reached the Portal seconds later. The hounds milled about the stones, whining and yelping their displeasure and confusion at their quarry's sudden disappearance. The huntsmen dismounted and waded into the animals, driving them back with whips.

Aerune rode slowly forward, through the confusion of hounds

and huntsmen. Behind him, his courtiers waited in silence for the explosion of his wrath. No one had expected this. Never in a thousand Great Hunts had the prey ever made it this far, nor should the Gate have opened for them if they had.

But Aerune did nothing. He gazed at the Portal for a long moment in silence, and then turned back to his men.

He was smiling. It was a sight more terrifying than his anger.

"Now," Aerune said with quiet satisfaction. "Now, the hunt can begin. Now I have set my hunter upon the scent."

When Eric woke up on Sunday morning, he was clear-headed and full of energy—and it occurred to him that although he had made the plan to meet Hosea at the Y for a rehearsal session tonight, the Y might not be the best place to hold it. The walls of those little rooms were notoriously thin, and a flute tended to have a certain piercing quality. The neighbors might not appreciate their playing— or worse, might like it too much.

On the other hand, he had a perfectly good apartment here, with thick walls and unflappable neighbors. Why not bring Hosea here? They could play as long as they liked in peace and comfort, and Eric could run the Appalachian Bard past the House, just to be able to reassure Bethie that he wasn't going off half-cocked here. So, once again he cleaned like a mad thing—polishing away the remains of last night's party and taking several bags of paper plates and cups down to the trash cans. He realized he wanted to make a good impression on Hosea, and the thought made him smile. There was a time when he would have dismissed a concern like that as sheerest hypocrisy. *You've come a loo-o-o-ng way, bay-bee,* he sang lustily and off-key inside his head. Though he didn't have Greystone to help him tidy, at least there wasn't nearly as much to do.

Two cleaning sessions in two days. Am I turning into Mr. Mom *or what?*

When he stepped out onto the street around four, the day's stored-up heat hit him like a hammer. He'd been luxuriating all day in his Bard-crafted winter weather (a lot more appealing in July than in February), and the reality of a New York City summer was brutal.

The streets outside his Riverside apartment were the next best thing to deserted; in summer New Yorkers tended to retreat into their air-conditioned shells—those who had them, at any rate.

It took him a little over an hour to make it crosstown to the Y— not one, but two trains died the death and had to be taken out of service—and he was hot and sweaty when he got there. But if he'd been looking for relief, he didn't find it in the lobby of the YMCA. It was only marginally cooler.

Maybe going back to my place was a better idea than I thought.

He didn't bother to check in at the desk, since he already knew Hosea's room number. The elevator was slow and creaky, with absolutely no air circulation. He was glad to get out.

The hallway had the smells of long occupation and illegal hot plates. Several of the doors were open, and as Eric walked by, he could see that some of the windows were open as well, filling the hall with the smell of burnt asphalt and baking brick. Hosea's door was closed. Eric stopped before it, but as he raised his hand to knock, Hosea opened the door.

"I heard you coming up the hall," he said, stepping back to usher Eric inside.

The room was smaller than most of the dorm rooms Eric had seen lately. There was a twin bed and a battered dresser, a wooden chair and a fold-down shelf that served as a desk. The window opened onto an enchanting view of the airshaft, and the battered air conditioner in the window was doing its noisy best, but not making a lot of difference to the temperature. Despite his surroundings, Hosea looked as if he'd just stepped out of a bandbox: he was wearing a white T-shirt and neatly-pressed jeans. His banjo lay in its open case on the bed, which was made to Marine Corps standards of neatness. Hosea held out his hand and Eric shook it, but despite the fact that Eric's hand disappeared into Hosea's, the larger man's grip was firmly gentle. Here was a Bard who knew a great deal about control; Eric had the feeling that Dharniel wouldn't have much to teach him there.

"Glad you could make it," Hosea added. "Would you care for something cold to drink?"

"You've got something?" Eric asked in surprise. He hadn't seen any sign of a refrigerator.

In answer, Hosea reached under the bed and pulled out a large plastic sack. He opened it, revealing a selection of containers—Cokes, bottled water, and a carton of milk—nested in a couple of pounds of slowly-melting ice. "Easier than running down to the corner store every couple of minutes." He pulled out a bottle of water and handed it to Eric, who accepted it gratefully. "Cheaper when you buy them at the supermarket, too."

Eric twisted off the cap and chugged the water gratefully. It was as cold as the ice that had surrounded it, like drinking winter. He wondered if Hosea might have used a little Bardcraft on it, but he wasn't sure of how skilled in magic Hosea might be. Playing on people's emotions was a lot easier than affecting the physical world.

"You haven't brought your flute with you," Hosea observed, when Eric set down the empty bottle. Hosea picked it up and placed it fastidiously into the battered plastic trash can.

"There's been a change of plans. I think we'd be better off practicing at my place."

"Ay-ah, the walls do seem to be a mite thin here," Hosea said, echoing Eric's earlier thought. "Though I haven't noticed anyone ever going to bed at all," he added ruefully.

"The city never sleeps," Eric agreed, quoting an old advertising slogan.

"I've noticed that. Can't imagine how you folks get on."

"You get used to it, I guess." As he said the words, Eric realized that in fact he'd done just that. When he'd moved here a year ago, he'd thought that the noise and constant bustle would drive him crazy. Now he hardly noticed it.

Hosea greeted this remark with a silent—though eloquent—expression of disbelief. "Well, if we're going back to your place, just let me get my traps together. No point in putting temptation into the path of some poor weak-willed critter, is there?"

"No point at all," Eric agreed readily, since this was fitting in very nicely with a nebulous half-plan of his own. It took Hosea only seconds to return all of his possessions to the worn duffle bag and lock his banjo into its case, and only slightly longer to pour the ice-melt out the window and tie the bag full of ice up neatly. On the way out he knocked on a closed door, seemingly at random, and thrust the bag into the hands of its surprised occupant.

"Here you go, Leroy," Hosea said. "You share that with your friends, you hear?"

Leroy smiled, and said something quick in soft Spanish. Hosea smiled and continued down the hall.

"You speak Spanish?" Eric asked. Somehow it wasn't an accomplishment that seemed to go with his picture of a banjo-playing hillbilly Bard.

"Nope," Hosea answered easily. "But it ain't too hard to figure out what most folks mean, no matter how they put themselves."

They hit the street and headed for the subway. At Hosea's urging, rather than wait to get back to the apartment and phone for pizza, they stopped and picked up dinner on the way.

"Save a little that way," Hosea pointed out practically, and it did mean that once they reached the apartment, they wouldn't have to wait around for food to arrive. They stopped at the same place Eric had ordered the pizzas from for the party last night—*ought to just open a charge account here*—and ordered. The heat had pretty much killed Eric's appetite, but Hosea studied the menu for a moment and ordered three super deluxe sausage calzones, a kind of Moebius pizza with the crust on the outside and the topping on the inside.

"If I ate like that, I'd look like a city bus," Eric said ruefully, all too aware that a relatively sedentary lifestyle and a few more years had stepped his metabolism down a notch from his freewheeling RenFaire days. Hosea just grinned as he picked up the bag from the counterman.

"I'm a tad bit bigger than you are," he pointed out. "Reckon it comes from having to wrestle bears before breakfast," he added, grinning even wider.

"Yeah, right." Eric snorted. "Pull the other one." Hosea worked his country-cousin veneer like a wolf with a designer sheepskin. It was protective coloration, but not exactly the whole truth. They continued up the block, and turned the corner onto Eric's street.

Hosea's eyebrows rose when they stopped in front of Guardian House.

"Being a subway minstrel must pay better than I thought," Hosea drawled, gazing at the impeccable Art Nouveau exterior.

"I get by," Eric said, leading him inside. After this long, he could enter the ten-digit security code almost as a matter of reflex.

Hosea regarded the fragile-seeming brass elevator cage. "I reckon I'd rather take the stairs, if it's all right with you."

Eric grinned. "It's stronger than it looks, but it takes forever. That's why I usually take the stairs."

One more ten-digit code later, the two men were inside Eric's apartment. Hosea sighed appreciatively at the cool—he probably attributed the lack of a window a/c to central air—while Eric got napkins and plates, and a couple of bottles of ice water.

"I'm gonna have to let her set for half-an-hour or so before we do any playing," Hosea said, indicating his banjo. "This weather purely plays hob with her tuning."

"Banjos are kittle cattle," Eric agreed, setting down his burden on the coffee table. Hosea opened the sack from the pizza place and began tucking into his calzones.

"Listen, I've been doing some research, and did you know that the whole banjo modality and a lot of the tunes are derived from bagpipe music?" Eric asked. "Apparently it was hard to manufacture bagpipes and reeds and whatnot in the Appalachians when the Scots and the Irish immigrated there, so musicians borrowed an African instrument—the ancestor of the banjo—and set it up for the kind of music they were used to."

Hosea stopped chewing. "Seriously? Didn't know *that*."

Eric grinned. "Well, flute and bagpipe aren't exactly what I'd call natural duetting material, but that means we can probably pull off a lot of the Celtic and folk stuff *I* know, since that's Celtic modality."

Hosea nodded. "You play a tune a couple times, I can pick it up, Mister Bard."

"Same here." Eric chuckled. "As if you didn't know. *Mister Bard.* Ready to give it a shot? As soon as your lady is tunable, I mean."

"Suits me." They cleaned away the debris of the meal and spent a happy half hour going through Eric's CD collection, then got out their instruments and put them in mutual tune. It took Hosea quite a while to get his lady tuned—no professional kept tension on the strings when the instrument wasn't in use—and Eric remembered the old joke about the instruments' notorious temperament. *Q: How do you know when a banjo's in tune? A: It never is.* Having silver strings rather than catgut helped a lot, though, and after a little doodling around, they began working out a playlist.

There wasn't any magic involved in what they were doing, or not overt magic, at any rate, but there certainly was a level of "enchantment" that Eric hadn't felt since he played with Bethie's old group, Spiral Dance. In fact, when he compared that experience to this one, it was like predawn and glorious sunrise—which in itself was kind of odd, since according to Dharniel, in the old days, Bards had been, well, *tetchy* was the word the Elven Magus had used. Easily irritated, and subject to extremes of professional jealousy that would make a modern pop diva turn green with envy.

But in the old days they were regarded as the equivalent of kings, Eric reflected, as he played "Smash the Windows" for Hosea, while the latter listened with a concentration that would have been intimidating to someone who wasn't accustomed to that sort of reaction at Juilliard. *They were treated like nobility, so they acted like brats. Guess having to busk on the sidewalk for their dinners might have cured them of a little of that 'tude.* Certainly there was nothing like professional antagonism between him and Hosea—and the way the country boy had pitched right in and helped with the cleanup after dinner without being asked spoke well for Eric's other embryonic plan.

But it wasn't until well after dark, when both of them were satisfied that they had a solid list of audience-pleasing pieces—including one of Eric's favorites, almost a personal anthem, Billy Joel's "The Entertainer," which had a killer banjo part built right in—that Eric put the last test in motion. Greystone, of course, had been skimming his thoughts, and only waiting for his signal.

"Well," Hosea sighed, detuning the banjo and placing it with great care back in the case, "This's been more fun than I've had in a long time, Eric, but I reckon I'd best be getting back."

Eric nodded slightly at the window. "Would you mind meeting a friend of mine before you go?"

With a quizzical look, Hosea turned around to look behind himself, and froze.

"Y'all pick a pretty neat banjo, theah, boyo," Greystone drawled, with a wink to Eric. The gargoyle climbed in through the window and stood in front of Hosea.

Hosea thawed a trifle. "Thank you kindly," he said, punctiliously polite, then cocked his head to one side. Eric sensed little feelers of Bardic magic creeping cautiously towards the gargoyle. Greystone grinned, and opened his wings, just a trifle. "Reckon you may look more than a bit like Old Nick, but you ain't nothing unchancy—so what *are* you?" Hosea asked, with more composure than Eric had expected. "Besides Eric's friend, that is?"

"Oh, now *that* is a long story," Greystone replied, dropping the drawl. "Could take a couple of hours at least to tell it." Greystone turned to Eric. "The House likes him," was all he said, but that was all Eric needed to know.

"Listen, Hosea," Eric said, waving a hand to get Hosea's attention away from the talking gargoyle. "You just passed a couple of—well, tests. You need a better place to stay than that steam bath, I've got a perfectly good couch here that won't cost you anything, and you've already got all of your stuff *here*. Want to stay the night and hear what Greystone has to say? If you'd rather go back to the Y after that, no problem, but I've got this big old place with only me rattling around in it, and there's no reason why you can't move in for a little bit until you've got a stake for a decent place of your own. If you're planning on staying around New York, of course."

Hosea looked from Eric to Greystone and back. "Huh," he said, finally, clearly making up his mind. "Well, I came up here looking for new things; reckon I'd be pretty dumb to run off when what I was looking for shakes my hand and says howdy."

"Good enough," Greystone said, genially, and lowered his bulk onto the bench Eric had bought just for him. "Well, the story starts like this. . . ."

❖❖ ❖❖ ❖❖

She had spent the last six months looking for a place to hide, and here in the mountains of West Virginia she'd found it. She'd lucked into Morton's Fork while cruising the Appalachian Chain on Lady Mystery. Hillfolk, as a rule, were even more suspicious of the government than she was, and as closemouthed as the dead. Somewhere in these hills she'd hoped for a bolt-hole, and she'd found it here. No one would be looking for her in Morton's Fork. The town was barely a wide spot in the road. The last excitement in Lyonesse County had been the 1924 WPA project that had left a string of cabins behind. The nearest library was twelve miles away, the nearest supermarket, twenty. There wasn't even television or radio here—the guy down at the general store said there was something about the area that made it impossible for the signals to get through.

That suited Jeanette Campbell just fine. She'd set up housekeeping in one of the old WPA cabins, and for the last several weeks she'd been here, considering her next move. She'd cached her bike and most of her supplies under a tarp in the ruins of an old building about a mile up the hill—she'd found it by following one of the winding deer tracks that crisscrossed the mountain. She didn't like having Lady Mystery so far away, but the old sanitarium was the closest thing to a bolt-hole and a back door she could manage. And Lady Mystery would attract attention wherever she went—a big flashy cream-and-maroon Harley touring bike with all the extras, Jeanette's one extravagance from her time at Threshold. She didn't want to lose her.

When she'd bailed out on Robert last December, she hadn't known whether or not it was for keeps. Robert had been the one who'd found her as an outlaw chemist and rescued her from the Feds to head up a secret R&D project at his pharmaceutical company. She'd been chasing a dream—a drug that would unlock the psychic powers inherent in the human brain. Robert's dreams had been grander and darker, of a secret army of psychic ninja, loyal to him alone.

They'd both gotten more than they'd bargained for. The one hundred fifty-seventh compound of the sixth year of trials— T-6/157—had actually worked. You gave it to people and they manifested psychic powers: psychokinesis, telepathy, thought projection, teleportation, healing. . . .

Of course, it also killed them within hours, but neither she nor Robert had been too worried about that at the time. Neither had Aerune mac Audelaine, when he'd come riding out of Elfland to claim the drug—and the Talents—for his own.

And Robert, like the idiot he was, had decided to declare war on the kingdoms of Faerie.

Jeanette hadn't stuck around to see how that turned out. Everything she'd ever read told her that starting a fight with the Sidhe was all kinds of a bad idea. She'd taken a stash of the experimental drug, her guitar, some money, and her Harley and taken off before she got caught in the cross-fire. A copy of *Time* magazine she saw a few weeks later confirmed that she'd made the right decision.

There'd been a blonde woman on the cover, executive chic. She'd been wearing an expression indicating she was bucking for Pope, and the banner on the cover had said something about New Corporate Ethics. The caption identified the woman as Ria Llewellyn, owner of Threshold Labs. That had been bad enough. The story inside had been worse.

Threshold had gone down big time. Robert's black project was the lead story, along with Llewellyn finding out about it and taking full responsibility (and credit) for stopping it. There was even a photo of Jeanette's former lab assistant Beirkoff, "Llewellyn's man on the inside." Now *there* was a laugh. Beirkoff had been Robert's creature first and last, but apparently Robert wasn't on the game board any more. The article listed him as "missing." She only hoped Aerune had gotten him: it would serve Robert right. This was all his fault.

It listed her as "missing"—and wanted—as well. Jeanette Campbell, the science behind Robert's ambition, wanted for questioning in connection with several hundred deaths last winter. There wasn't a photo, but thanks to Beirkoff there was a pretty good police artist sketch. She'd cut her hair immediately and dyed it black, but that wouldn't help if anyone took a close look—and with rich-bitch Llewellyn and all her money and power screaming for Jeanette's head, people would look and keep looking until someone found her. Jeanette's only hope was to lie low and keep moving, but for that she needed cash money, and her emergency stash was almost gone.

She could have headed south, into Mexico, or made a run into Canada and hooked up with some of her contacts from the old desperado days. There was always work for a good outlaw chemist, and after her years at Threshold, Jeanette had gone from merely good to the best of the best. But leaving the U.S. would make her visible in a way she wasn't now, and she didn't want to take the risk if she didn't absolutely have to. She wasn't sure how long LlewellCo's reach was, or how personal Ria Llewellyn meant to get, and Jeanette still had a lot left to lose.

Her choices were few. On the one hand, she could turn herself in to the authorities and cut some kind of deal. On the up side, if Robert was missing-presumed-dead, he wouldn't be able to say much to contradict whatever story she had to tell. On the downside, with Robert missing, the authorities would need a scapegoat. Jeanette didn't have a lot of interest in spending the rest of her life in a Federal pen.

On the other hand, she could turn herself over to Aerune, if she could manage to find him. Aerune. A genuine, impossible-but-real Lord of the Sidhe. He had a use for the Talents Jeanette created with T-6/157—T-Stroke—and whatever had happened to Robert, Jeanette was pretty sure Aerune hadn't given up his plans. Once upon a time she could have asked for nothing more out of life than to meet a real live elf, but now the thought of ever running into Aerune again gave her nightmares. She'd used one of Threshold's Talents to tap his mind, and Vicky Moon had called Aerune "the Lord of Death and Pain." Jeanette had seen him up close. She believed it.

But though the idea made her shudder in revulsion, it had marginally more going for it than the first one did. Aerune would have a use for her, and from all she'd seen, he wouldn't care how many people her drugs had killed, so long as he got what he wanted. The only problem there was that she wasn't entirely sure what it was he wanted, and if she couldn't give it to him, the penalties were apt to be a lot more severe than a long life in a small cage.

The third choice, which had a certain horrible fascination to it, was to try the T-Stroke on herself and see what happened. That was why she'd wanted to create it in the first place, wasn't it? To give herself the powers she'd always dreamed of, the powers that would pay back everyone who'd ever teased and tormented her? She'd had a long time to go over her notes on her human test cases, and she thought she might have solved the sudden-death problem. T-Stroke didn't seem to create these powers, only develop the latent ones that were there. Her subjects had died because they burned themselves out, like an electrical circuit when you put a penny in the fuse box. It was as if they only got halfway through some kind of transformation—the body needed to tap into some outside source of power to use the Talents instead of cannibalizing its own resources, but it couldn't manage that before the initial dose of the drug wore off.

But if she used massive megadoses of T-Stroke over a period of days or even weeks, would that give the subjects the ability to control their newly awakened abilities and use them without burning out?

Maybe. And the only thing that was stopping Jeanette from testing her theory was the fact that only one in ten people seemed to have any innate Talent at all. It would be the blackest joke of all if she, who'd always thought of herself as so special, was a member of that humdrum ninety percent. And if you didn't have Talent for the drug to work on, it killed you outright.

It was like a game of Russian roulette with five of the revolver's chambers loaded.

Decisions, decisions. But a little long green makes them all easier. . . .

Jeanette looked around the little one-room cabin. The walls were papered with yellowing sheets of what passed for the local newspaper: *The Pharaoh Call and Record, Published Weekly for Lyonesse County, including the townships of Pharaoh, Morton's Fork, La Gouloue, Bishopville, and Maskelyne.* Heat was a wood-burning stove; water came in bottles from the general store. Her cot was in one corner, along with a folding chair she'd bought from the store and an end table made out of a wooden crate. She had a table, courtesy of the previous tenant, and her provisions were stacked around the walls in battered cardboard boxes. It wasn't a lot, considering what she'd started with.

But she could still make a living if she dared. She could go back to what she knew best—dealing. She'd always been on the production end before, not the street end, but she supposed she could manage. Only that would make her more visible, and probably put her on a collision course with whoever already had a corner on the local action. So that was her very last resort, when every other option had been exhausted.

This is the scene where the heroine pages through her address book and decides to look up some old friends. Only I guess I'm not the heroine of the story, and I sure don't have any old friends, Jeanette thought grimly. She'd cut all her ties to people and places long ago— not that she'd ever had many—and now she was alone, her back to the wall. She could turn herself in to the Feds, turn herself over to Aerune, or take the T-Stroke and see what happened. Maybe under its influence she'd be able to see a way out of her problems, or at least a way to fix the formula.

Maybe.

Jeanette sighed, and went over to pick up her guitar. Music was the only thing that had never failed her, the only thing she could love unconditionally. She brushed her fingers across the silver strings, listening to the whispery chords. She'd play for a while. Nobody would hear her, and maybe she could figure out what to do.

All I have to do is figure out which is the lesser of three evils. . . .

Greystone had told his story, all the while managing to entirely sidestep the subject of the Guardians, a feat of verbal terpsichore that Eric could only admire. If Hosea got the notion that the House had been built, and Greystone carved, to assist a group of protectors that no longer existed, Greystone had certainly never said so explicitly. And he'd certainly filled his narrative with a number of amusing anecdotes he'd never mentioned to Eric—like the night the Statue of Liberty had decided to go for a walk, why construction on the Second Avenue subway had been stopped, and the *real* reason the dirigible mooring tower on the top of the Empire State Building was never used. The gargoyle was a born storyteller, and he'd rarely had as appreciative an audience as Hosea.

"Well, laddybuck," the gargoyle said, sitting back with a sigh of satisfaction around midnight, "that's my story, and I'm sure our Eric will tell you his, if he hasn't already. But what about you, Hosea Songmaker? How is it you come by your gift—and that banjo? And what brings you to the wicked city?"

Hosea smiled and shook his head. "Reckon I owe you the round tale, but I guess it ain't gonna be all tied up as pretty as yours." He sat back and stretched ostentatiously, obviously settling himself to tell his story.

"I was born and raised in a little place in the hills called Morton's Fork. I hear tell it's been a kind of a special place for as long as folks've lived there, but with everybody moving to the big city, the countryfolk are pretty much gone by now. My folks died when I was little, and I was drug up by my grandpappy and mammy. Grandpappy Jeb came by his shine honestly—got it from his daddy, and on back to where the first white folks came up into the Fork and settled down with the local folks. After he came back from the War—that'd be dubya-dubya-two—he settled down with my grand-mammy Dora. They used to say she could play the devil up out of the ground with her fiddle; she was on the radio when she was a girl and everything. But she took one look at Grandpappy Jeb and said she hadn't any mind to making records and touring and suchlike, and Grandpappy, he said he'd seen enough working for Department 23—that's the OSS—to make him glad to settle himself in the place he belonged. Grandmammy said she'd got the banjo from her mammy, but she said it was just to hold it in trust, like. It's pretty old, and I guess just about every part of it's been replaced some time or another. She told me to always keep it strung with silver, and never to play it for any reason that was mean or unkindly."

The OSS! Eric sat up a little straighter. Dharniel had always hinted that WWII had been fought on magical turf as well as the mundane, and this seemed to confirm some of the Elven Bard's cryptic hints.

"So I'd guess you'd say I come by the music-magic naturally, but there wasn't no one in the Fork that could lesson me how to use it," Hosea continued. "Grandmammy had the music, and Grandpappy had the shine, but it'd take someone with the two of them together, he said, to really light me up, more than I could study out on my own account. So when I was growed, I went down to the flatlands to get me some more book-learning, but flatland folks don't know much about shining," Hosea said with a grin. "So I went back home to help out on my granddaddy's farm, as he and grandma was getting on in years. When she passed on last year, I knowed it weren't gonna be long afore he followed her, and so it wasn't. So I sold up for burying money, took me her banjo like she'd said to, and decided to follow my feet. I reckon somewhere in the world there's gonna be someone with the music-magic that can lesson me in what I need to know."

"Well," Greystone said in his gravelly voice, "it looks like you've come to the right place." The gargoyle got to his feet and stretched, his wings nearly touching the living-room walls on both sides. "I think you're going to find living here an interesting experience, Hosea Songmaker."

"Just about everything's interesting, if you come at it right," Hosea said. He stood, and offered his hand to the gargoyle. "It's been a fine evening of yarning, Mister Greystone."

The gargoyle chuckled and shook Hosea's hand. "Just 'Greystone,' boyo. And now, if you'll excuse me, I'd better get back to me post before someone counts gargoyles and comes up one short." He waddled over to the window and stepped out onto the fire escape. Hosea watched him climb up the side of the building to his perch before turning back to Eric.

"Well, now, it's been a long day and you look plumb tuckered out, Eric. If you want to show me where to sleep, we'll call it a day, and maybe make us some music tomorrow," Hosea said.

"Count on it," Eric said. A warm glow of contentment welled up in him. Things were working out so well! He had another Bard to gig with, and Greystone and the house both liked him. He wondered if Hosea might see a "Rooms to Let" sign in Toni's window sometime soon.

As for him, there was a call he had to make, first thing Monday morning. . . .

FOUR:
THE GLASS CASTLE

The carpenters hadn't quite finished, and the power still tended to flutter unpredictably at times, but it was a pretty impressive job of world-building for five months flat. Ria Llewellyn looked around her domain—corner office, executive suite, barricaded on the umpteenth floor of one of those soulless glass boxes that was taking over Midtown Manhattan. Her new home, and she had to admit that it was a better fit than L.A. had ever been. New Yorkers lived to work, and so did Ria.

She hadn't meant to move LlewellCo's corporate headquarters to New York. That had been the last thing on her mind when she'd come out here last December chasing Eric Banyon. But after the Threshold debacle, there'd been no one else to put out the fires that sprang up all over LlewellCo East, and as the days stretched into weeks and started looking like months, the problem seemed to get worse, not better.

It was bad enough that a couple of her subordinates had thought that buying Threshold was a good idea—she didn't know how far Baker and Hardesty had been in Robert Lintel's confidence, but they'd certainly known something was rotten there—and had kept on funding it. It was worse that Lintel had come up with the notion of whipping himself up a bunch of ninja-wizard super-soldiers with the help of a chemist who'd used to cook meth for a biker gang, and had decided to conduct field trials for his pet drug on most of the city's homeless population. But as she'd laboriously unwound the paper labyrinth that tied Threshold to LlewellCo, she discovered that wasn't, after all, as bad as things got.

What was the worst thing was that buying companies like Threshold and letting them do whatever they wanted had become the sort of thing LlewellCo did.

In a way, it was only to be expected. Ria's father, the power-mad elf-lord Perenor, had built the company to strike out at his enemies in a way that wouldn't draw attention from the other elves until it was too late. In its deepest essence, LlewellCo was fundamentally flawed: designed as a weapon, it carried destruction in the bones of its corporate culture.

Not that anyone saw that but her. Ten years ago, she wouldn't have seen it either—or if she had, she wouldn't have cared. She was dazzled by Perenor's profane charisma in those days, still dancing to his piping. But all things—good and bad—come to an end. Hers had come courtesy of a blow from a Fender guitar that had put her into a coma for a very long time, followed by an even longer period of recovery with the help of some very good—in all senses of the word, for a change—people. And while she'd been gone, LlewellCo had continued on its corrupted way.

She didn't blame Jonathan, her second in command, for what the company had done. Jonathan Sterling was principled and fiercely loyal. He'd done nothing she wouldn't have done if she'd been there. No one at LlewellCo's highest levels had really known what Threshold was up to, though maybe a more suspicious sort of person would have called them to account a little earlier. But returning after her long absence—and the wake-up call from Threshold—had made her see things in a different way than she ever had before. It made her see that LlewellCo needed to do more than simply clean up after Threshold. It needed to be reborn. And that meant giving everything—all their holdings, all their policies, all their plans—a very close look, and then changing the way they did things. Everything. Acquisitions, mergers, hirings, firings, R&D fundings, and venture capital outlay.

It would have been easier to sack everyone, divest the company of all holdings, dissolve it, and start over, but Ria had never been a fan of the easy way of doing things. That way, the innocent would suffer along with the guilty, and besides, LlewellCo was *hers*. She would not abandon it.

But—as someone once said about Hell—the paperwork went on forever.

Ria set the report she was reading down on the leather top of her rosewood desk and sighed, pinching the bridge of her nose. Monday morning—and she'd spent the weekend here as well, just as she had for the last six months. The Threshold debacle—the lawsuits, civil and criminal, the investigations that unfortunately seemed to lead right back to government at the Federal level—showed no signs of being over any time soon. If not for Eric, she'd be mired in the middle of it, guilty by association. As it was, she was the media's darling, the valiant corporate whistle-blower who'd stepped in the moment she'd suspected trouble and brought Lintel's evil empire crashing down.

That particular urban fairy tale was pretty close to the truth for once, and if nobody knew she'd chased Lintel to Underhill and executed him there, it was just as well. There were plenty of other villains to chase. The government clients who'd bought Lintel's voodoo pharmaceuticals, for one.

Jeanette Campbell, for another. The chemist who'd given Lintel the power to do so much harm.

You can run, but you can't hide. I'll find you. And when I do—

The intercom buzzed.

"Claire MacLaren," Anita said. "Your two o'clock, Ms. Llewellyn?"

"Sure. Send her in," Ria said with a sigh. "And send in some coffee, too, would you?"

"Sure thing, boss," Anita said. Ria could almost hear the phantom popping of gum: Anita liked to project a persona straight out of vintage film noir, but Ria wouldn't have hired her if she hadn't been formidably competent. Anita Drake was Ria's personal assistant, watchdog, and gopher (as in "go fer this, go fer that . . ."). She wasn't a secretary. Secretaries worked for *her.* She'd come from someplace like St. Louis, and said she wanted to try a job where everyone wasn't out to kill you and suck your blood. *Just wait till you know this world better,* Ria thought. Corporate dueling made the kind done with swords or pistols look bloodless.

The door opened, and Claire MacLaren walked in. She was a private investigator—Jonathan had found her and used her to locate Eric for Ria last year, and Ria had been impressed enough with her work to add her name to the little black book of utterly dependable specialists—some with quite exotic specialties—that she kept. Ria'd tried to hire her to come to work for LlewellCo full-time, but Claire preferred to keep her independence—"It's to your advantage, dear, especially considering the sort of thing you're sending me after."

"Come in, Clairy," Ria said, rising to meet her guest.

"Ria. Thanks for seeing me on such short notice. I know how busy you are."

Ria grimaced. "*That* never changes. But come, sit down. I hope the news is good."

Claire sighed. She was an uncompromising woman in her fifties, who made no effort to hide either her age or the fact that her figure had long since lost, if it had ever possessed it, the whippet-slenderness of youth. She resembled the Miss Marple sort of detective, gray-haired and kindly, but in spirit she was more akin to the Borderers who had made the wild lands of the Scots borders such a constant trouble to the English. Like her ancestors, Claire MacLaren never gave up.

"It all depends on your notion of 'good,' I suppose. But it's all in my report," she answered, gesturing with the slim portfolio under her arm. She settled onto the couch with a sigh. "You won't like it."

"You haven't found her," Ria said, sitting down in a chair opposite the detective.

"Our Miss Campbell is either dead, or very good at disappearing. She hasn't been arrested, used a credit card, or taken her motorcycle into an authorized dealer for servicing, and there's been no activity on any of her accounts. No one matching the description I've been given has left the country in the last six months—no one who didn't check out, at least. She hasn't contacted any of her old associates among the Road Hogs. No unclaimed bodies matching her description have turned up in any morgue in the United States, nor has the gun registered to her turned up. I can keep looking, but I'm afraid it's a waste of your money. If we're to find her, she'll have to make a mistake."

"She will," Ria vowed. "She has to." If Threshold hadn't sanitized Campbell's apartment so thoroughly in its own attempt to find her, there might have been something left behind that would have let Ria find her magically, but by the time she'd been able to start looking, the trail was both cold and muddled beyond repair.

"Oh, aye," Claire answered. "Eventually. But good as I am, as well funded as I am, I can hardly match the FBI's resources. Why not leave the police to do their job?"

"You know why I can't," Ria said.

The office door opened again. Anita entered, pushing a trolley with a silver coffee service on it. She laid out the cups and saucers— fine bone china with the LlewellCo red dragon logo—on the table between the two women, and added a plate of pastries. She poured both cups full, and set the pot, creamer, and sugar down before wheeling the trolley out again.

"The service here is lovely," Claire remarked.

"I pay for service," Ria said. She rubbed her forehead again.

"But there are some things that money can't buy," Claire pointed out. She added sugar to her coffee and took a pastry. "My dear, if you'll forgive a presumptuous observation, you look as if you're worn right out. You need to take a break from all this."

"And have it fall all to pieces the moment I turn my back?" Ria demanded sharply. She sighed. The headache was making her irritable. "I'm sorry, Clairy. It's not you. It's everything. If I don't find that little bi—find Campbell, we'll never know everything that Lintel was up to. Most of the people involved in Threshold's Black Lab operations are dead. Lintel's records have been destroyed.

Beirkoff wasn't involved with anything beyond the manufacturing of T-Stroke. He can't tell me what I need to know."

"You feel responsible." It wasn't a question. "But Ria, you've done as much as anyone could to repair the damage that brash young gentleman caused. The commitment LlewellCo's made to the homeless—spin-doctoring or not, it's doing real good here in the city."

"'The corporate crusader with a heart.' 'The avenging angel of Wall Street,'" Ria quoted mockingly. She held up an adminatory hand. "I know, I know. No one person can do it all. But I have to do what I can. I want you to keep looking, Clairy. I know the police and the Feds will keep looking, too, but they have other things to do. They can't spend all their time looking for one woman. But I can. And I want her." Determination turned Ria's voice harsh. She pulled back from her emotions with an effort and took a sip of her coffee.

"Ah, we'll," Claire said philosophically. "If you won't be told, you won't. I'll keep looking, but you're going to need a miracle."

"If you can tell me where to buy one, I'll get it," Ria said, forcing herself to smile. "If there's anything you need . . . ?"

"I'll ask for it, never fear," Claire said. She got to her feet. "Shall we say lunch next time? It'll do you good to get out from behind that desk."

"Lunch, then," Ria said, getting to her feet. "And maybe by then I'll have figured out how to broker a miracle."

After Claire left, Ria took her cup and stood looking out her window for a while. The streets below were yellow with taxi-cabs, the sidewalks filled with late-lunching pedestrians.

Claire's news was only what she'd expected, but she still wasn't happy with it. Though she'd done her best to conceal the fact, she was afraid Claire knew that Ria's hunt for Jeanette Campbell was something of a vendetta. Claire wouldn't go along with something like that. She'd made it clear from the first that any information she found about Campbell's whereabouts would be shared with the police as well as with her employer, and Ria respected her for it. But she had more reason to want Campbell found than simple vengeance.

Wherever she is, she knows how to make the drug that turns ordinary people into mages. And that's information I don't trust anybody to use wisely. Especially Lintel's former clients. They're probably looking for her as hard as I am, and if she disappears into somebody else's think tank, there will be hell to pay. Literally, in fact. Aerune's still out there, and if I know my Sidhe, he isn't even close to giving up.

And the Sidhe, as befit a near-immortal race, were accustomed to taking the long view. Aerune would be willing to wait years, even decades, for his plans to fall into place. Despite her half-Sidhe heritage, Ria was mortal. She didn't have the time to outwait him. Campbell had to be found. And neutralized.

The phone rang.

Ria glanced back at her desk. She'd told Anita to hold all calls unless it was a certified emergency, but the light for her private line was flashing. Very few people had that number.

She picked up the phone.

"Llewellyn."

"Have I called at a bad time?" a familiar voice asked.

"Eric!" Ria felt herself smile—a genuine smile this time. Her relationship with Eric was the one authentic bright spot in her life, stormy as it sometimes was. "How are you?"

"Not as busy as you seem to be. You sound tired."

"So they tell me," Ria said shortly. Eric ignored the warning note in her voice, though she knew he'd heard it. Eric was a fully-trained Bard. He was a lot smarter about people now than he'd been when she'd first met him.

"It seems like things should be quieting down, though," he went on, with that guileless note of teasing in his voice. "I haven't seen a story about you in the news for, oh . . . a week or so."

"Not so much quieting down as reaching a series of dead ends," Ria said wearily. "Look, I—"

"So I figured you could use a break," Eric said, interrupting. "So I wanted to invite you to a party."

"What kind of a party?" Ria asked, a note of suspicion in her voice. The one thing that hadn't changed about Eric Banyon in all the time she'd known him was his puckish sense of humor, and it hadn't been blunted in the least by all the time he'd spent Underhill learning his craft.

"A Naming kind of party. Maeve's been born, and Beth and Kory want me to come to Elfhame Misthold to see her Named. We can use the Everforest Gate, and be back before we've left, or almost. I even promise to talk Lady Day into turning into something with doors and a roof."

Ria stared at the phone. Maeve was Eric's daughter by Beth Kentraine, the woman whose Fender guitar had done such a thorough job of rearranging Ria's life. Eric had ceded his rights in Maeve to Kentraine and the Elven Knight Korendil, since he wasn't ready for the ties and obligations of parenthood, but apparently Kentraine intended for Eric to play some part in his daughter's life.

"Either you've gone mad, or I have," Ria said bluntly. "You're inviting me to come Underhill? To the Sidhe? To a Naming? To a party that *Beth Kentraine* is throwing?"

"Well . . . yes." Eric's voice lost its bantering note as he realized this would take some persuasion. "It'll be fun. You've never been Underhill—well, not socially anyway. And I'm allowed to bring a date."

"'Fun,'" Ria echoed. "You want to invite me to one of the Sidhe's High Holy Days—*me*—and you think it'll be 'fun'?"

The Sidhe loved children. Though Ria was a half-breed, raised in the mortal world, even she knew how seriously the elves took anything to do with children. Though Maeve was of fully human parentage, she was the daughter of a Bard and a witch, and in some sense Korendil's daughter as well. Elven children were an exceedingly rare occurrence and cherished accordingly. The Sidhe would consider her one of their own, and would take her Naming Day very seriously.

It was hardly the sort of thing to which they'd welcome the daughter of a renegade and a traitor, let alone a half-breed, the circumstances of whose conception were, to the Seleighe Sidhe, the vilest sort of sacrilege. Children born to a Sidhe/mortal pairing were even rarer than full-blooded Sidhe children, and Perenor had used the foulest sort of blood-magic to father Ria on her mortal mother—not to mention the fact that he'd tried to use Ria to destroy the Sidhe of Elfhame Sun-Descending. For years she'd lived in fear that the Sidhe would seek revenge for what she'd done, and once upon a time she'd thought that Eric had been sent back into the World Above to lure her to their vengeance.

And while he'd said that most of them really didn't care about what she'd done—considering how high a price she'd paid to thwart her late father's plans—that didn't mean they'd be happy to see her. . . .

"Okay, maybe not fun," Eric said as the silence stretched. "But I have a right to bring anyone I want as a guest and witness, and I think it would be good for you to meet some of the Underhill folk. You can't spend the rest of your life looking over your shoulder. If you come to the Naming, everyone will see that the Seleighe Sidhe have no quarrel with you, and that starting up with you will be the same thing as starting up with Elfhame Misthold."

"When did you suddenly become so savvy at politics?" Ria asked, and Eric chuckled.

"Live with the elves for a while, it's the equivalent of a master class. What else do a bunch of near-immortal wizards have to do with their time? The point is, they owe you for what you did against Aerune, and they need to know that. You do, too."

"I didn't do it for them." It didn't matter to Ria what feuds the Sidhe conducted among themselves. But Aerune had been after Eric, and that mattered to her a great deal.

"Yeah, well, elves are very results-oriented. It's what you did that counts."

"So you want me to come to the party."

"Yeah. I do. Besides . . . it'd be nice to have someone from *this* side of the Hill to keep me company. And I think it's time you and Bethie settled things between you."

So THAT's what's behind all this!

"So you want me to come and help her bury the hatchet?" Ria asked. The notion had a certain perverse appeal—and Eric was right that it could only do her good to form relationships and alliances

Underhill. She lived in the human world, but like it or not, she was part Sidhe, and that heritage couldn't be ignored. "So long as it won't be buried between my shoulder blades." She took a deep breath. "All right. When? And what shall I wear? I've never been to one of these."

"Oh, just wear whatever you'd wear to your average Royal wedding," Eric said breezily. "I'll pick you up Saturday. That'll give you a week to shop."

"In a car," Ria reminded him. "With seats. And doors. And a roof."

"I'll talk to Lady Day. And Ria? Don't worry. I won't let anything bad happen to you."

Ria made a rude noise of mock outrage, but found her smile staying with her as she hung up the phone. She and Eric made an unlikely romantic pair—not that Ria was entirely sure, sometimes, whether what they had going could be contained by any term so mundane as "romance." There'd been a bond between them from the first moment they'd met as adversaries, she as Perenor's pawn and he as the Sidhe's last hope. Both of them had cut the strings that bound them to the purposes of others, but the tie between them was not so easily broken.

A half-elven sorceress with a Fortune 500 company and a human Bard who prefers busking to playing at the courts of kings. We're a fine pair.

And if there's to be more to it than this, it's going to have to wait until neither of us is quite so busy with our own lives. Whenever that might be . . .

Still smiling faintly to herself, Ria picked up the report on her desk and began to read.

He was home. Or if not home, exactly—for it had been many years since he'd been able to call any particular place "home"— then at least he was back on Earth only a few months after he left.

No one had followed him.

Elkanah Youngblood found himself standing in the middle of a country road. It was night, and it had been raining. He could smell the summery scent of wet earth and growing things. He got to his feet, still aching and bleeding from the injuries he'd taken during his run from the Great Hunt. The antlers were gone, a kind of proof that Lord Aerune's spell didn't run here. He took that as a sign that his luck had finally changed. He was free.

He didn't waste time wondering how it had happened or worrying about what happened next. He had two items on his agenda.

Survive until morning.

And find Jeanette Campbell and wring the bitch's neck.

Survival was easy. Less than a mile away a hay barn provided shelter while he stole a nap to shake off the worst of his exhaustion. When dawn gave him enough light to see by, he followed power lines to the nearest house. It was an old farmhouse, with nothing around it but fields. He guessed he must be somewhere in the South or Midwest, and smiled grimly. Being in the wrong place with the wrong skin color was the least of his worries right now. He was pleased to see a fine cash crop of mary jane ripening in the field out back of the house: whoever lived here would be less likely to run to the cops than an honest citizen, but just to be sure, he cut the phone lines with a set of shears he'd found in the barn before venturing inside. The back door wasn't locked, but it wouldn't have slowed him down much if it had been.

The householders were still in their beds. By the time he woke them he'd found a shotgun. The sight of a naked, six-foot bronze-skinned man holding a shotgun had quieted them both down a good deal. They hadn't made much trouble when he tied them up and put them down in the cellar. If they kept their heads, they could work themselves free of the torn-up sheets in a few hours. He intended to be gone by then.

When he saw himself in a mirror, he was surprised at how normal he looked. A little thinner, a little banged up. Hair a lot longer. The beginnings of a beard. But no horns or scales or staring red eyes. He'd almost expected something like that, some kind of visible evidence of everything he'd been through. But there wasn't anything.

If I were dumb and stupid, I could convince myself it was all some kind of bad dream. But I don't have dreams like that.

Fortunately, none of his wounds was deep enough to need stitches. He washed off the dried blood, and after a shower and coffee, Elkanah made a thorough search of the house. As he'd expected, he found a small recreational stash of goodies, a lot of cash, and some very nice guns. He took the .45 and the .357, and left the shotgun and the rifles where they were. He scattered the drugs around the living room. They'd have to clean the place up before they called in the law, and that would buy him even more of a head start.

The man's clothes were all much too small for him, but he found a T-shirt and a pair of sweat pants that would stretch to fit and a gimme cap with a movie logo on it. He forced his feet into a pair of the guy's Nikes. His first stop would have to be for better clothes— if you looked like you belonged, you didn't attract attention. That was the first lesson of infiltration.

He'd found car keys in the kitchen, so he knew there had to be a ride around somewhere. He stuffed the guns and the money into an old backpack he'd turned up and went to look for it.

Stupid, stupid, stupid . . . Elkanah shook his head. The house and the outbuildings were falling apart, and those idiots had a Lincoln Navigator stuck in the cowshed: about 50K of luxury 4x4. Just the thing for driving to the local 7-11 inconspicuously! As well they lost it then. It probably wasn't even insured. He was almost doing them a favor.

The engine started on the first try.

By the time he hit the main road, he was pretty sure he was somewhere in Pennsylvania in August. He got directions to the nearest town at the first place he stopped for gas, picked up the local paper, and got the date. It was only about six months since he'd left.

Good. The bitch wouldn't have had time to run far.

He picked up clothes, a razor, and some basic medical supplies. He changed clothes in the men's room and slipped out the back, leaving the stained sweats in the dumpster. While he was in the parking lot he took the opportunity to swap the Navigator's plates for a set on another car. The unsuspecting donor probably wouldn't even notice. The trouble with people these days was that they just weren't detail oriented. God was in the details. His pappy'd always told him that.

He still didn't have a driver's license, or any kind of ID, but he didn't think it would matter. From the shopping mall he headed east, not questioning why he chose that direction. From the interstate he switched to the local roads, where he stopped and picked up a couple of bags of groceries, then hit the back roads, driving several hours before finding the place he wanted, an old beat-up no-tell motel, the kind of place that came with hot and cold running roaches, and where the sheets were changed once a month if you were lucky.

It would suit him just fine. He parked the Navigator out of sight of the office and walked back. A few minutes later he had a room for the week under the name Valentine Michael Smith, and he hadn't had to provide either a driver's license or a vehicle registration number.

He went in the room, locked the door, moved the dresser over to block the door, stretched out on the bed, and slept for two days.

When he awoke on the evening of the second day, his body was stiff from disuse, and he was lightheaded as though he'd just broken a high fever. But he was still here, and the room was still here, and his sleep had been without dreams.

Find the bitch. That was Job Number One. But before he did that, he should scope out the lay of the land a little. Find out how things stood with Threshold. Pick up one of his spare identities from one of his drops and find out if it was safe to come out. Housekeeping chores, really.

On the other hand, maybe they could wait. If he went straight for the bitch, he'd have a bargaining chip. He knew right where she'd be. He thought she'd told him about it once, this little bolt-hole she had squirreled away somewhere in Godlost, West Virginia. A good place to hide, she'd said, if anything happened she didn't like. She'd probably run straight to it when the balloon went up and been hiding under the bed ever since.

Morton's Fork, that was it. She'd said it just like he wouldn't know where it was, but he'd grown up in Pharoah, about twenty miles from Morton's Fork, West Virginia.

He shook his head and frowned, a headache starting to build behind his eyes. Hadn't he . . . ? His daddy had been a New York City cop. He'd never been anywhere near West Virginia. What was wrong with him? He found the bottle of aspirin he'd bought and shook half a dozen into his mouth, washing them down with a bottle of warm beer. The headache faded, and with it the sense of confusion and unease. Of course he'd grown up in West Virginia. He'd been a lot of strange places since, but you didn't forget the place where you were born. He'd go to Morton's Fork and find the bitch. That was Job Number One.

And wouldn't she be surprised when her worst nightmare came calling?

The gigging on Sunday had been great. They'd hit up half a dozen of Eric's favorite spots, and even without workday crowds to play for, the take had been more than ample. Hosea had insisted they split it right down the middle, and wouldn't take "no" for an answer.

"You're giving me a roof over my head, Eric, and I'm not one to take charity. If you're worrying about me getting together a stake for a place of my own, I'll be keeping what I make playing in the Park while you're hitting the books, and I guess I'll do all right."

There was no budging Hosea once he'd made up his mind, Eric had already realized—and in the same situation, he too would have been reluctant to take a handout. So he'd agreed to the split—but he'd stipulated that he'd be the one buying the groceries. *And with the way he packs it away, I think we'll manage to make this a more reasonable split on the take.*

He'd meant to call Ria before he left for Juilliard on Monday, but then he and Hosea had stayed up late talking, and a couple of friends had dropped over, so by the time he remembered Ria, he was nowhere near a phone. But Hosea had been out when he got back— Monday was a half day—and he'd been able to call Ria then. Hosea was good companionship, and fastidiously neat—the couch had been folded up, the sheets neatly folded and tucked away, and as far as Eric could tell, the duffle *still* hadn't been unpacked—but he'd been just as glad Hosea wasn't around to hear *that* conversation, as it would bring up things Eric wasn't really ready to discuss with him.

Elves, for one thing. Hosea had been pretty cool about Greystone, but there was something about elves that seemed to trip people's circuits. Half the time they started babbling about Disney and *Elfquest* and the Smurfs until you never could get them to settle down again. He didn't want to go there with Hosea.

But at the back of his mind, even when he'd been talking to Ria, was his Saturday night conversation with Hosea. Hosea was looking for someone to teach him the music-magic, and Eric knew some pretty good teachers. Magic was a peculiar force, and Talents were stubborn things. Once the magic had made up its mind to manifest one way, it was almost impossible to train it into a new path. If Hosea said he needed to be taught by a music-mage, he was probably right. Eric wondered how Master Dharniel would take to another human student. At any rate, he'd be seeing Dharniel at the Naming, and Eric could bring the matter up to him there.

It got dark early here in the hills. Jeanette sat at her worktable, measuring white powder into gelatin capsules by the light of a kerosene lamp. A cup of cold instant coffee sat by her elbow.

It was sweltering in the little shack, but she'd closed all the doors and windows and tacked up sheets over them to keep out any breath of air. There was a storm on the way, and all she needed was for a gust of wind to give her a face full of T-Stroke. That'd kill her for sure.

All drugs were poisons. In small doses they cured, but enough of anything, even aspirin, was toxic. Only T-Stroke was different. With T-Stroke, the more you took, the better chance you had of surviving.

Maybe. If she'd guessed right. There was no way to tell without a test.

And the only person around to test it on was her.

Russian roulette, with five bullets in the chamber instead of one.

She kept filling capsules—a thousand empty gel-caps bought from the health-food store in Pharoah when she made her weekly run for supplies. She wasn't sure what she was going to do with them, but they were a lot more portable than a bottle and a needle. Easier to move, easier to take.

If she decided to take them.

She sighed. It kept coming back to that.

She stopped what she was doing and listened intently. She thought she'd heard an engine. Watchman's Gap Trace ran past the cabin, and people did still use the old road—moonshiners, mostly—but there shouldn't be anybody out at this time of night. She checked her watch. Two-thirty in the morning.

Maybe it'd just been the wind.

Or maybe the Feds've gotten lucky, you spineless git.

She hesitated, and then got to her feet. Her .45 was lying on the bed—Road Hog had always said there wasn't any point to a little gun, when you wanted to show you were serious—and she picked it up. The oiled weight of it in her hand was reassuring.

She picked up the lantern and moved it to the far corner of the room. She lifted the edge of the sheet spread over her worktable and draped it over the mound of white powder. Then, swallowing hard, she catfooted it over to the door, pushed aside the blanket, and lifted the latch.

The air outside seemed stiflingly cold after the stuffy heat of the cabin. Wet wind dashed droplets of rain against her skin, mingling with the sweat. She could hear the Little Heller creek running hard, and hear the wind tossing the trees.

Nothing else. She stepped outside, letting the door close behind her. There was no light. Even after her eyes adjusted, and she could see the faint shapes of trees against the sky, there was nothing. No lights, no engines.

You've come too far to screw yourself over with an attack of nerves, girl. She waited a moment longer—*of all the things I've lost, I miss my air conditioning the most*—then backed inside and closed the door again.

It was a relief to put the gun down. Jeanette actually hated guns.

If you were waving one around, that meant things were already out of control and heading from bad to worse.

She took a deep breath, rolling her shoulders to get the tension out. There was still some ice from this morning. She'd crack a Coke and relax for a few minutes before getting back to work. She didn't like leaving all that powder out loose. It was too dangerous—this shack was a far cry from Threshold's pristine sterile laboratory conditions.

She opened the ice chest and stood for a moment, rubbing a handful of cubes across her face and throat. She'd thought a thousand times about dumping all the T-Stroke in the creek, but she'd given up so much to get it that she couldn't bear to, and sometimes now it was hard to remember why she'd wanted it so much.

There was a knock at the door.

Jeanette froze, the ice cubes dripping down her arm. Her mind was scrubbed white with shock and sudden terror—they were hunting for her, and now they'd found her, whoever they were. The knocking came again, hard and slow, as if Death himself were outside.

She dropped the ice cubes and lunged for the gun that lay on the cot. There was a thud at the door, and a creak as the wood gave. Cold air filled the room.

The gun was slippery and heavy in her hands. She scrabbled to get her finger on the trigger, falling to her knees.

Something landed on her. The gun went off and was torn from her hand. It was all over so fast. She lay on the floor, half under her cot, staring down at the soft splintery white pine floorboards of the cabin. She would not look. Whoever it was could kill her, but they could not make her look.

"Is that any way to greet an old friend, Ms. Campbell?"

The voice was familiar. Jeanette bit down hard on her lower lip to keep from bursting into tears. She was furious and terrified, and the game was over, but she would not let him see her cry. After a moment she got her breathing under control and sat up.

Elkanah—she'd never known if he had another name—stood in the doorway, her gun in his hand. He was wearing black jeans and a black T-shirt. She'd never seen him in anything but his Threshold Security uniform. She'd thought he looked scary then. He looked terrifying now. The door hung inward, and she could see the white splinters where the bolt had broken in half. The blanket she'd nailed over the door billowed in the wind.

"Elkanah." Her voice came out in a hoarse croak, but steady. She knew her hands were shaking. With an effort of will she got to her feet, hating the fact that he was seeing her barefoot, in a grubby sweat-soaked T-shirt and cut-off jeans. Hating the fact that she was helpless. "What are you doing here?"

"A lot has happened since you left us, Ms. Campbell," Elkanah answered in that maddeningly slow soft drawl of his. He glanced at her chopped-off hair. "Black isn't a good color on you. Maybe you ought to sit down. You don't look well."

"Neither do you," Jeanette shot back. Even in the dim light of the cabin she could see that. He'd lost weight. His skin was stretched tight over his bones, and there was a look in his eyes—a glittery, crazy kind of look—that told her he was capable of anything.

Of all the people she'd expected to come looking for her, he was the last on the list. Her legs trembled. She sat down slowly on the edge of the cot, feeling it creak under her.

"Okay. Now what?" she asked.

"Why don't you just sit there while I have a look around?" It wasn't a suggestion. She sat, careful to give him no reason to shoot her.

He closed the door, kicking it into place with his heel and letting the blanket drop. She watched as he looked carefully around the room before he moved. First he tucked her gun in the waistband of his pants, then went over to pick up the lantern. He set it back on the table and peeled back the sheet.

"My, my, my. What have we here?"

Jeanette didn't answer.

"You can tell me, or you can eat them." Elkanah's voice was mild, as disinterested as if he were commenting upon the weather.

"It's T-Stroke. All I have left," she added, for no other reason than that anything she knew and he didn't gave her a little power.

"That got us all into a lot of trouble," Elkanah said. "Mr. Lintel dead, the company gone. A lot of trouble. And that leaves me at loose ends, you might say."

Jeanette stared at him. She'd thought Elkanah was dead. If he wasn't, the Feds were looking for him as much as they were looking for her. But that didn't do her a lot of good while he was standing here with a gun. She had no idea what he wanted, and that worried her. If he'd meant to turn her in to plea-bargain his way out of things, why weren't the Feds right behind him?

And how had he found her?

"Lintel's dead?" she asked, just to keep the conversation going. "How did that happen?"

"You know the answer to that." Elkanah moved away from the table and the glistening pile of white powder. He rubbed his forehead as if it hurt. "It's your fault."

"I worked for him the same way you did." It was suicidal to argue with him, but she couldn't help herself. "What he did with what I gave him was his business." *But you didn't have to give it to him, did you, Jeanette? You didn't have to go to work for him. If Robert killed people, he did it with the weapon you made for him.*

"Business. That's what it all comes down to, doesn't it, Ms. Campbell? We're all just doing business. And that's why I'm here."

He'd moved back in front of the door again, just as if there were any real possibility she would try to run. Jeanette braced herself to hear bad news.

"That T-Stroke. You can make more of it, can't you?"

"Yes." There was no point in lying about that. It was the only thing that might keep her alive, the only thing of value she still possessed. "I'd need a setup and some supplies. But I can make more."

"That's good. In that case, I think we can do business. Get your things. We're leaving."

Jeanette got to her feet. "Where are we going?"

Elkanah smiled. It wasn't a nice smile. "I think that's on a need-to-know basis, don't you?"

I think I'm about to take a bullet, Jeanette thought, but oddly, she wasn't afraid. The worst thing she could imagine happening had just happened. She didn't have to be afraid of it any more, and that freedom brought clarity in its wake. *Boy, I really made a mess of my life, didn't I?* She moved over to her worktable.

If she were an action-movie heroine, she could blow the loose powder into Elkanah's face, blind him, and escape. But she wasn't. She was just another loser with very sharp teeth—she'd spent her whole life being taught that particular lesson. Life wasn't a movie, and even if it was, Elkanah wasn't working off the same script she was. He was at the other side of the room, out of reach.

She scooped the loose powder carefully back into its plastic jar and screwed the lid on tight. All the filled capsules were already in their jar. She put the lid on that one, too.

The Harley's saddlebags with her clothes were in the corner, and for a panicked moment Jeanette thought Elkanah might ask what had happened to her bike. She pulled jeans and a clean T-shirt out and turned her back to him to put them on.

"Afraid I'm going to lust after your lily-white body, Ms. Campbell?"

Jeanette set her jaw. She knew she wasn't any man's idea of arm candy, but she was glad Elkanah had spoken. It made it so much easier to hate him. *If at all possible, I'll see to it you die screaming, you Neolithic slab of rent-muscle.* She buckled the jeans and slid her feet into her engineer boots. Her leather jacket was way too warm for the weather, but she picked it up anyway. She'd need it later, if there was a later.

Carrying the saddlebags and her jacket, she turned back to the table and picked up the two jars of T-Stroke, glancing at Elkanah to see if that was okay. He didn't seem to object, so she stuffed the jars into one of the bags and buckled it shut, then slung them over her shoulder. Her guitar, her Walkman, and her tapes she left where they were. Music had always been her vulnerable spot, and she didn't have any time for vulnerability now.

"Okay," she said. "I've got my things. Now?"

"Now we go, Ms. Campbell." He stepped away from the door. "After you."

She went to the door and pulled it open. The top hinge had torn loose when he broke in and she had to drag it. She walked out into the night. It had started raining in earnest, and the rain plastered her short dyed hair to her scalp. She set down the saddlebags and pulled on her jacket.

Elkanah came out behind her. He was holding a flashlight in his hand. There was a red gel over the lens. A faint red beam illuminated the trees and turned the rain into a shower of blood.

"This way," he said, gesturing with the beam. "You first."

She stumbled through the rain, hearing him move more gracefully behind her. They were heading in the direction of Watchman's Gap Trace. His ride was probably parked there. If only she'd bolted the first time she'd heard an engine . . .

Too late for regrets, Campbell. By about a lifetime, I'd say.

She slid on last year's leaves and stumbled over rocks and branches. He did nothing to help her, but she didn't expect it. Occasionally he corrected her path, herding her uphill. About the time she thought they'd managed to miss the road entirely, Elkanah's light shone on the side of a panel van. It was painted primer gray—a totally nondescript vehicle. The Sinner Saints had used something like it to make bulk deliveries. It was the kind of ride you could park anywhere and have it go unnoticed.

"Stand still." She stopped. Elkanah walked up close and pulled the saddlebags off her shoulder. He walked past her to the van and opened the passenger side door. He threw the saddlebags in the back. Jeanette winced at the sound of the impact. *Lucky everything comes in plastic these days.*

The rocker panel on the passenger side door had been removed. There was a length of glittering chain welded to the steel beneath, with a handcuff on the end.

This would be a good time to run, Jeanette thought, knowing she couldn't do it. There was no place to go. And she was tired of running without a destination. In fact, she was just tired. Tired enough to sleep forever.

"Come here. Hold out your wrist. And be a good girl."

Sullenly, Jeanette did as she was told. Elkanah closed the cuff around her right wrist. It felt cold and heavy.

"Now get in."

She climbed onto the seat and pulled the door closed behind her. The inside of the van was shabby and well-used, but scrupulously clean. Sanitized. The rain made a faint tattoo on the roof. Elkanah opened the other door and climbed in. He fitted the key into the ignition. The motor roared to life, and a moment later the headlights flared into brightness, throwing the road and the trees into sharp relief.

The road was so narrow that Elkanah had to drive almost up to the ruins to find a place to turn around, and for a moment Jeanette thought he knew she'd lied and was going after the rest of her stuff. But he just turned around and headed back down the Trace, out of Morton's Fork.

How did you find me? she wondered again, but she didn't ask. There'd be time enough to ask questions later.

Or there wouldn't.

She had to find someplace to get in out of the weather. Damn all well-meaning fools—her last ride had told her she could pick up the main road just over the hill, and now she was wandering around in the rain, no sign of a road, and about as lost as a body could get and still be in West Virginia. Without her flashlight, she'd probably have broken her neck already.

Got to keep going, she told herself stubbornly. At least she was on some kind of a road. Roads had to lead somewhere, didn't they? *Just not always where you were planning on going.*

She wished she had something to eat. She wished she had a home where she could feel like somebody's daughter, instead of like another employee.

But that's over with, now, isn't it? You've picked yourself up and gone to Canaan, and if Lord Jesus wants you back the way Daddy's always saying He does, then He can come tell you so Himself.

Her name was Heavenly Grace Fairchild—though she preferred "Ace," and if she had her way, nobody was ever going to call her by her birth name again. Heavenly Grace, Inc. was her father's ministry, carried for an hour three times a week on several thousand

Christian networks coast-to-coast. Her earliest memories were of riding in the ministry's bus from one tent revival to the next, of singing hymns at the head of the Heavenly Grace Choir, but that had only been the start of things for Billy Fairchild. He'd had plans—first, for the Cathedral of Heavenly Grace, now a 25-story office building in Tulsa, Oklahoma, and then for a worldwide empire.

But she didn't want to be a part of that. It seemed that the more houses and cars and thousand-dollar suits her daddy got, the more he and Mama argued. And no matter how righteously her daddy pitched the Gospel, it always seemed to stop the minute the cameras stopped rolling. Jesus had been a poor man, hadn't he, bringing words of comfort and love to poor people? The older she got, the less she could see how what her daddy was doing had anything to do with Jesus. She'd begged him to let her stop performing, whipping up the audiences with hallelujah hymns in the studio, but he wouldn't hear of it. And when he'd hired that secretary of his, Gabriel Horn, she'd known that she'd never be allowed to stop. The plans for her going off to college that her mama had talked about so proudly had been set aside. There was plenty of money—there'd always been plenty of money, for as long as Ace could remember—but she wasn't going to be allowed to leave. Not if Daddy and Gabriel had their way.

So she'd run. She didn't know where she'd end up, but anywhere had to be better than Tulsa. And maybe they wouldn't want her back, now that she'd rebelled. Lucifer had rebelled, and been cast down out of Heaven for doubting God's word, but Billy Fairchild wasn't God, and Ace thought that sometimes you had to take matters into your own hands.

A flash of lightning turned the sky white, and in the brief illumination she could see a set of iron gates up ahead. That meant a house. Maybe they'd take her in for the night, or maybe at least there was a garage there she could hide out in until it stopped raining.

But when she got to the gates, she saw they were old and rusted, and the building beyond was only an old ruin, charred by fire. Still she kept on, hoping for shelter. The rain had stopped as she walked, and the clouds rolled back, leaving a full moon riding high in the sky. It gave her enough light to see by, but now the temperature was dropping—even in summer, wandering around at night in wet clothes was a good way to catch your death. She had dry clothes in her pack. Maybe there'd be someplace here she could change into them.

But when she got inside, she found that the years and the fire had left nothing behind but the house's shell. The upper stories had caved in and burnt to ashes, and where there had been cellars, those too stood exposed. Tears of disappointment filled her eyes, but she scrubbed them angrily away.

As her eyes adjusted to the gloom, she saw a bundle off to one side, something under a tarp. She set her pack down in the doorway and went over to look.

Somebody's left a bike here! She pulled the tarp all the way off, staring at it in wonder. A gleaming Harley-Davidson motorcycle, looking just like it had wheeled off the showroom floor. The keys were even still in the ignition.

I won't take it, she told herself, even if Johnnie had taught her to ride his old Indian before Daddy'd canned him for looking too familiarly at his only daughter. *But whoever left it here has got to live around here. I could just take it and ride it down to the road and leave it for them.* She hugged herself, shivering, but need won out over scrupulous honesty. She slipped her backpack on again and swung her leg over the saddle.

The bike started on the first try. She wheeled it down the steps and back onto the road.

When she saw the lights off to the side of the road, Ace couldn't keep her conscience quiet any more. This wasn't borrowing. This was *stealing,* and if she did that, she'd be just as bad as Daddy, taking things from people and saying it was okay because he needed them more than the other people did. She sighed, and turned the bike off the road, toward the light. At least she could tell the bike's owner that it wasn't a good idea to leave your ride out in the middle of nowhere with the keys in the ignition.

But when she got there, nobody was in the cabin. She knew the bike belonged here—there was a helmet in the corner, maroon and cream just like the bike. It looked like they'd left in a hurry, too— there was a glass of Coke sitting on the table, still cold and fizzy. The light was coming from a kerosene lantern, and it wasn't a good idea to just go off and leave something like that burning. When she went back to shut the door, she saw it'd been torn off its hinges, and the bolt was snapped clean through.

Somebody in a mean mood broke in here, Ace thought to herself with a shudder. She knew she ought to leave right now, but she was cold and wet and hungry—and worse than any of these, she was tired and lonely. *I'll just stay for a little while, until I dry off and warm up. Maybe I can figure out the right thing to do, something that'll help me and won't hurt anyone else. Or maybe they'll settle their problems and come back.*

But she had a cold feeling down in her bones, like whoever'd been here wasn't going to be coming back any time soon.

I'll just stay for a little while. Until I can figure out what to do.

FIVE:
THROUGH DARKEST ELFLAND WITH GUN AND CAMERA

Saturday morning dawned bright and clear. Eric had told Hosea that he was going to be away for the weekend and so wouldn't be available for busking, but Hosea took it in good part. He'd discovered the New York Public Library's reading room, and was spending a lot of his time there. During the week, Eric'd had a spare set of keys to the apartment made, and given Hosea the security codes, so Hosea could pretty much make his own hours. He was an early riser, often gone for the day before Eric awoke. For a man his size—or anyone, for that matter—Hosea was quiet as a cat, and never disturbed Eric on his early-morning exits.

Eric dressed with particular care in his flashiest RenFaire clothes. He buckled on his sword belt, and took his sword down from the top shelf in the closet. He hadn't worn it since he'd been living in Underhill, but the elves would expect him to wear it, as a symbol of his rank. He didn't put it on, though. Swords and modern cars were an awkward combination.

Last of all, he took his flute and slipped it into his embroidered gig bag, slinging it over his shoulder. He couldn't match the Naming Gifts Maeve would be receiving from everyone in Underhill, so he hadn't bothered to try. He'd gone to FAO Schwartz and bought the biggest stuffed pink bunny he could find, and for the rest, had composed a piece in her honor. Beth would like that—it was a variation on the piece Spiral Dance had always ended their sets with, called "The Huntsman's Reel"—and what better gift for a Bard to give?

Sword and flute in hand, bunny under one arm, he went down to the parking lot, where a gleaming candy-apple-red Lotus Elan awaited him. It had taken a certain amount of negotiation to get Lady Day to surrender her motorcycle form even for one day; elvensteeds could sometimes be stubborn. As a concession, he'd allowed her to pick the form, and this was what she'd chosen. It took a little work to cram the sword and the bunny into the microscopic space behind the seats, but he managed it and levered himself into the driver's seat. He almost wished she'd chosen something less conspicuous, but it ought to amuse Ria.

"Okay. Let's go," he said, and the elvensteed roared to life with the deep-throated hum of a racing engine.

Ria had offered to pick Eric up, but he elected to meet her up at the Nexus north of Manhattan instead. It was a great day for riding, and besides, on the whole, he didn't want to get into a habit of depending on her. He was still twitchy about that; the time he had spent in her father's Underhill domain as her private boy-toy was not among the moments he was particularly proud of. He headed directly for his destination, and only a few minutes after they started, Lady Day was heading over the bridge toward Sterling Forest.

It was surprising the amount of half-wild land there was so close to the city. If he hadn't known that NYC was 90 minutes away, Eric wouldn't have been able to guess from the surroundings. Sterling Forest State Park was nestled in the gently-rolling Ramapo Mountains—known for centuries to be filled with haunted places and strange creatures, and for good reason. The Nexus lay in a copse of trees accessible only from a long-disused farm road, the farmhouse itself long abandoned, nothing left but the foundation and chimney.

Behind the house, down a gentle slope, a deer trail led into woods, deep within which lay one special grove of trees that didn't look as if they'd ever been touched by anything but wind and weather. Where there was a Nexus—a power source that tied Underhill and the mortal world together—there was either a Gate already there, or Eric could make one easily. In this case, there was one already, a Portal that hung as a hazy curtain between two oak trees, visible only to those who had the eyes to see it. He was early; Lady Day had shut down the faux-engine noise she made as soon as they were off the main road, and they rolled up to the Gate surrounded by nothing more intrusive than the cracking of twigs under her wheels. He got out of the Lotus, looking around for Ria.

Eric didn't have long enough to wait even to wonder when Ria would get there; shortly after he and Lady Day rolled to stop, unshod hooves thudding on the turf warned him that someone was coming. Somehow he didn't think it was Ranger Rick.

Ria rode into the pocket clearing on a coal-black elvensteed with hooves and eyes of silver, dressed to the absolute nines in something silky and flowing and midnight blue. Eric didn't pay a lot of attention to high fashion, but this didn't look like anything he'd seen during glimpses of shows on the news during Fashion Week. It also wasn't High Elven as he knew it. As always, Ria was setting her own style, it seemed.

"I didn't know you had a 'steed," he said, as Lady Day shivered all over and made a transformation herself—into a blue-eyed white horse, who stared down her long nose at Ria's mount in friendly defiance.

Ria glanced at the giant pink bunny and raised an eyebrow. "It's more appropriate to say the 'steed has me," she replied with good humor. "This is Prince Adroviel's way of keeping track of me. Oh, he's very gracious about it, but there wasn't much question—if I want to enter Elfhame Melusine, I'd better be either in your company or Etienne's, and preferably both."

"Oh." There wasn't much that Eric could gracefully say to that, so he didn't say anything at all. Ria didn't seem put out—and she certainly looked fantastic, sitting up there sidesaddle on the magnificent 'steed.

"I hate being fashionably late," she said pointedly, as he got himself into Lady Day's saddle with a minimum of awkwardness. After more than a year Underhill, riding still wasn't second nature to him, but at least he wasn't as clumsy about it as he'd been when he first arrived there.

"So do I, and this should be a good party," he replied. "Do you want to key the Gate, or shall I?"

She waved her hand languidly at the shimmer of power between the trees, and he took that as answer that he should open it. It occurred to him a second later, as he whistled the little trill of music that fitted his magic into the Gate and gave it the place it should take them to, that the Prince might not have entrusted her with a key. The elvensteed could take her there, of course, but she and Eric wouldn't arrive together if it did. . . .

The shimmer brightened, then pulled aside, exactly like a curtain, revealing—nothing. Not blackness, *nothing*. Emptier than the space between the stars, the path of a Gate had scared the whey out of him the first time he'd seen it; now he just let Lady Day take up her place beside Etienne, and the two of them passed through together.

There was a moment of cold, a faint brush against his face and hands of something like threads spun of liquid hydrogen, and they were through.

They passed instantly from broad daylight into twilight; from the wild and overgrown, untidy forest covert into truly *ancient* forest, the kind that must have stood in North America before Columbus, that never knew the touch of an axe. Huge trees that would have been dwarfed only by the sequoias and redwoods of California rose all around them. The ground beneath the trees, regardless of the fact that there couldn't possibly be enough light under the thick branches to support much vegetation, was covered with lush and fragrant flowers in palest pink, faintest blue, and purest white. All except for the path, of course, which was literally carpeted in emerald moss as deep and soft as any high-quality plush number in a Fifth Avenue condo.

The fact was that there would never be any light under these trees; Elfhame Melusine lay in a perpetual twilight. Eric remembered from Dharniel's few "geography" lessons that Elfhame Melusine was one of the Old World hames, whose members had chosen to withdraw from the World of Men rather than cross to the New World.

"Well," Ria said, looking around, as the 'steeds paused to allow them to get their bearings. "Not very much like my father's domain, is it?"

"What, Elfhame 90210?" Eric asked, and was rewarded by her peal of laughter.

In fact, she laughed hard enough that she had to clutch the pommel of her saddle, and even her 'steed gave out a noise that sounded like a snicker. "Elfhame 90210! Oh lord—" she gasped. "90210! That's gorgeous!"

"Thenkew, thenkew," he responded, bowing at the waist slightly, and a bit tickled at his own cleverness. "Thenkew verrymuch, I'll be here all week, leddies and gennelmun."

"Oh lord—" She straightened up and carefully wiped the corners of her eyes with a fingertip. "It was, wasn't it? Poor Father! Even *he* couldn't keep from copying the mortals he despised."

"Well, I can't say that I hadn't seen places just like it in the Beverly Hills version of Find-A-Home, because I had," Eric responded truthfully. "And just about every room in one issue or another of *Architectural Digest*. No two rooms out of the *same* house, mind, but still . . ."

"Still," she agreed. "So, what's all this? It's not like Misthold or Sun-Descending, is it?"

The 'steeds paced forward onto the carpet of moss, making no sound at all.

"I met a guy from Savannah that calls this Elven Classic," Eric replied. "He says that over in Outremer they say this is how Elfhames looked for centuries—the ones tied to Groves and Nexuses in the Old World, that is. Some of the Seleighe Sidhe wanted things to look like the way they'd been at home when they moved over here to escape Cold Iron, and some, like Adroviel, want their homes to stay that way. There're variations, and these days there are even some who've remodeled their Elfhames to look like the way we— mortals that is—have described them in literature."

Ria's hand flew to her mouth to smother a laugh. "You *don't* mean that somewhere Underhill there's a Last Homely House?"

He grinned. "And a Hobbiton, and Galadriel's Forest. And, sadly, there's also places that role-playing gamers would feel right at home in, and a spot that looks like Ridley Scott just left it behind after filming *Legend*, complete with enough crap permanently floating in the air to give an allergist nightmares." *And every one of them the One True Elfland, for the ones who find it.*

She bent over again, laughing so hard that she wheezed. "I guess—that Father's taste—wasn't quite as bad—as I thought," she managed to get out.

Eric shrugged. "He had good taste, *really* good taste," he pointed out, as the 'steeds picked their way across a meadow full of swaying lilies of the kind normally seen woven into the hair of the maidens in Alphonse Mucha posters. "He only imitated the high-quality stuff. That's their failing, you know, their one big lack—they can imitate like nobody's business, but they can't *create*. That's what they need us for, or they'd fade away into Dreaming out of sheer boredom." *Maybe sleep and creativity are more closely linked than people think. Elves don't sleep, either—not normally.*

She sobered immediately. "I never thought of that. Why didn't I ever think of that?" She shook her head. "Father *never* did anything much with LlewellCo except use it as a way to launder *kenned* gold until I was old enough to be interested in business—"

Eric raised an eyebrow—a Spock-like gesture he'd practiced secretly for years just on the chance that one day he'd get to use it to maximum effect. "I rest my case," he said pointedly. "And, need I add, *that* was probably the major reason why he sired you in the first place. Using you as a spare battery pack was just lagniappe."

She didn't look stunned— she looked angry, but only for a moment before letting the anger go abruptly. "It makes perfect sense," she replied bitterly. "He wouldn't have to keep taming and training mortals every few decades—he'd figure to get at least a couple of centuries out of a half-breed like me. Though—he couldn't have known I'd have a head for business, could he?"

Eric shrugged, but she was already answering her own question. "Of course he could; he probably cast all sorts of spells when I was born to bend me in that direction—"

Let's not go there, shall we? "He *probably* counted on the natural cussedness of kids to do it for him," Eric pointed out. "Your mom was a classic hippie, you said—and *how* many hippie kids turned around and grew up to be yuppies? I think he figured it was pretty well in the bag that you'd run off to be as unlike your mom as possible. All he had to do was leave you with her long enough for you to get tired of living life *á la* commune, and as soon as you got a chance, you'd bolt for business school." He cocked his head to one side. "I mean, look at me—my parents wanted a little James Galway of their very own, and first shot I got, I bolted and turned into a busker."

That turned the trick; she smiled, albeit weakly. "You're probably right," she said, and left it at that.

At just that moment, the 'steeds came out of the forest altogether, and paused.

Probably so we get a chance to take in the full effect and are awestruck, Eric thought cynically. He looked down the hill they were on anyway, and so did Ria.

"My god," she said, not at all in the tone the Sidhe were probably hoping for. "It looks like a matte painting."

"I don't think that's the effect they had in mind, but you're right," he said, because the twilight vista stretching out in front of them *did* look like a special effect. Everything was *too*—too big, too much, too perfect.

The path stretched down the hill and across perfect fields, just irregular enough to be charming, divided one from another by old-fashioned English hedgerows. Some were full of peacefully grazing sheep, some of red cattle as graceful as deer, some of crops. No one tended them, of course; they were dealt with by magic, and looked as if they'd come out of the dreams of a Pre-Raphaelite landscape artist. Overhead the pale-violet "sky" was studded with "stars" that didn't move. The road led through the fields to a distant castle, but not like anything ever actually built in the mortal world. If Disney'd had an unlimited budget and could have revoked some of the laws of physics, he might have constructed something of the sort; a confection of tall thin gleaming turrets that should have collapsed under their own weight, of porcelain battlements and ivory crenellations, with shining walls encrusted with carvings; balconies, waterspouts, bridges leading from tower to alabaster tower; gold-embroidered awnings to shade against a nonexistent sun. The whole was surrounded by gardens that even at this distance looked lush. There was even a drawbridge over a moat upon which white swans glided—purely for effect, of course, since not even a military genius could defend a castle that looked like this one.

"Elven Classic," Eric pointed out. "Possibly modeled on the ideas of some of the changeling kids they took Underhill to protect them."

Ria smiled again, this time with real warmth. "Now *that* is something I can get behind," she said fervently.

"Remind me to connect you up with Keighvin Silverhair," Eric replied, and smiled himself. Elfhame Fairgrove in Savannah had what you might call an "active outreach" program for troubled youth.

Having given them enough time to be suitably impressed, the black 'steed now led the way down the hill towards the castle, Lady Day hurrying a little to catch up. As they drew closer, the road widened, and soon they weren't the only creatures heading for what was clearly going to be a bigger deal than Eric had imagined.

Not everyone on the road was elven, either, though they all had to be Seleighe, or they wouldn't be here. Some of them were downright odd-looking; creatures right out of a Brian Froud illustration. There was a group just ahead of them, with long, spindly arms and legs all gnarled like branches and hair seemingly made of twigs. There was another behind, armored knights riding black horses with flame-red eyes.

They caught up with a band of human-seeming folk who wore fur capes, and whose hems were soaking wet although the road was dry; they left little bits of seaweed behind them at every other step. Selkies, Eric guessed.

A band of fat little ponies overtook and passed them. The beasts wore neither saddle nor bridle, and carried creatures with elven features, but as small as children and with—yes—gauzy butterfly and dragonfly wings attached to their shoulders. *If this is Elfhame Classic, I guess those guys must be Sidhe Lite.*

"This is going to be some party," Ria murmured, as the last group passed them.

"I had no idea," Eric responded, more than a bit dumbfounded. "I really didn't."

"Hmm," was all she said, but she gave him a sidelong glance that he couldn't read.

He was glad enough to see, when they reached the castle proper, that there were young (at least he thought they were young) guards stationed at the gates to direct the crowds. One of them recognized Eric (or maybe Ria's steed) immediately and herded them off as expertly as any celebrity handler. Before you could say "VIP suite" he and Ria were being ushered into the castle and a lavishly appointed reception room, where a tall, crowned elven man and woman were chatting with selected guests. At his side, Eric spotted Kory with relief—then Beth with the opposite emotion. Bethie was not exactly on the membership list of the Ria Llewellyn Fan Club, to say the least, and while she knew he was bringing Ria, he'd wanted a chance to warn her so she could get her game face on before the two of them met. . . .

But it was too late now. Eric and Ria were being ushered politely but efficiently up to their hosts by a pair of majordomo types. Eric had just enough time to catch a glimpse of Beth's incredulous expression before he went into a full court bow, while Ria dropped into an exquisite High Elven curtsey, her skirts spreading around her in a perfect pool of star-spangled midnight.

Oh, I am going to be in such trouble. . . .

Prince Adroviel gestured for them to rise. "My lady Arresacl, I present to you Sieur Eric, Knight and Bard of Elfhame Misthold, and his lady, Mistress Arianrhod, daughter of Perenor the Destroyer."

Eric froze in the act of straightening up. Of course everyone in the room had heard Adroviel's words—the prince had pitched his voice to carry. He glanced at Ria from the corner of his eye. Her face was impassive, but he could almost feel the shock radiating from her like cold off ice.

"All who share our blood are doubly welcome here," Arresael said to Ria. She was tall and slender, with cat-green eyes and silver hair: Elfhame Classic. On her head she wore a diadem that on first glance looked like exotic flowers—and on second glance, revealed itself to be crafted of enamel, moonstones, and wrought gold. "And we have heard much of your valiant aid to our kindred of Sun-Descending." She leaned forward to kiss Ria on the cheek; a formal salute of welcome.

Eric relaxed, realizing what the Sidhe Prince had done. Adroviel had made it perfectly clear that he knew exactly who Ria was and welcomed her nonetheless. There'd be no trouble now, even if anyone would consider making trouble at a Naming.

"Thank you, my lady. You are as gracious as you are beautiful," Ria answered. She turned to Beth. "Thank you for allowing me to share this special day. I am honored."

Beth looked as if she'd swallowed a live mouse. "Thank you for coming. I never did get a chance to thank you for saving our . . . bacon . . . back there in L.A."

Ria opened her mouth to reply, but just then a chime sounded.

"That's our cue," Beth said. "See you later." The look she gave Eric promised him she'd make sure of it.

And she hasn't even seen the bunny yet.

Another elven courtier appeared at their side. "If you would accompany me . . . ?" he said.

Eric held out his arm to Ria, who placed her fingertips delicately upon his sleeve. They followed the courtier through the door he indicated. A small tingle of magic as they crossed the threshold warned them that wherever they were going, it wasn't physically connected to the chamber they were leaving.

Eric blinked, looking around. If you'd taken Chartres Cathedral and crossed it with the Roman Coliseum, it might look something like this. There was a semicircle of tiered seats rising into the distance, most of them already full. A gilded rail separated them from a row of more elaborate seats, and to either side of the dais were private boxes like the ones in an opera house. Banners hung from the ceiling, their bright silks swaying slightly in the air, and the sounds of music and conversation filled the hall with a susurrus of white noise. They'd come out on the floor below the tiers, and just ahead was a dais large enough to hold a full orchestra, covered in flawless scarlet velvet that was probably deep enough to hide in. It held two thrones, plus a number of lesser chairs.

Their guide ushered them to one of the boxes and opened the low door. "Does this meet with your approval, my lord?"

"Uh . . . fine," Eric said. No matter how many etiquette lessons Dharniel had dinned into him, he just didn't "get" courtly. It always made him nervous.

"Thank you," Ria said graciously, preceding Eric into the box. It contained two chairs only barely less ornate than the ones on the dais, and was obviously a place of honor.

Eric followed her in. The courtier closed the door behind them and turned away to guide others to their places.

"Well," Ria said.

"Look, I'm sorry about that—"

Ria waved his words away, sinking into her chair. "Never mind. It was good politics, and good theater. Now everyone knows where the Prince stands; they'd look pretty silly starting something after that. I just wish I'd brought my opera glasses."

"It's quite a show, isn't it?" Eric asked, seating himself beside her. They had a good view of the dais, and their position let them watch the guests without gawking.

A few minutes later, the last of the guests found their seats, and the babble of voices died down a little. There was a flourish of horns, and the hall became absolutely silent. A herald strode out onto the dais.

"All honor to Prince Adroviel of Elfhame Melusine and the Princess Arresael!"

Adroviel appeared behind the herald—*must be a Portal back*

there, Eric thought—leading Arresael by the hand. They took their seats—but not on the two thrones. As the herald called out more names, others appeared to take their seats on the dais, but the thrones remained empty.

"Korendil, Knight of Elfhame Sun-Descending, squire of the High Court, Magus Minor and Child of Danu—!"

Kory appeared, looking regal and knightly. He took a few steps away from the Portal and stopped.

"Mistress Bethany Margaret Kentraine, bringer of new life!"

Beth appeared, holding Maeve in her arms. The baby was wearing what—if they were anywhere but here—Eric would have identified as a christening gown. It was white lace, sewn with small sparkling brilliants, and its end brushed the ground. Beth was dressed in red and gold, a gown that would make any Rennie turn pale with envy. She wore a simple gold circlet on her red hair—a symbol of rank, Eric knew that much. The Sidhe were very picky about things like that: they were doing her great honor here today.

When she appeared, the hall went wild with cheers. She must have been told what to expect; she turned toward the audience, smiling, waiting for the cheering to die down. When it did, Kory held out his hand and escorted her to one of the two thrones, seating himself in the other. Today an elven knight and his mortal consort were ranked above princes.

Elves take children very *seriously.* If Eric had ever doubted it, here was the proof.

The herald stepped back, and Adroviel rose to his feet.

"People of Underhill. We gather here today in this holy place to welcome new life into the land. In the name of our Holy Mother, Danu, whose children we are, let it be so!"

Elves had some kind of religion, Eric knew, but they didn't talk about it much, and in all the time he'd spent Underhill he'd never seen anything remotely resembling church on Sunday, or even one of Bethie's Wiccan Circles. But that he was seeing it now, he had no doubt. The expectant silence was thick enough to cut with a sword.

"She comes among us small and helpless, yet may she grow great with help and love. And to that end, her mother has chosen wise counselors for her, who will guard and guide her as bone of their own, blood of their own, flesh of their own." He gestured, and a tall stately woman, seated in one of the lesser chairs on the dais, rose to her feet.

"The Lady Coinemance, Lady of Elfhame Misthold and of the High Court, Magus Major and Child of Danu."

"I do accept this task, this burden and this joy," Coinemance said. "I vow to teach this child all my arts, to bestow upon her all knowledge of magecraft and sorcery, bone of my own, blood of my own, flesh of my own."

"And I accept your oath for the child's sake. May all your arts turn against you should you fail of your vow."

One by one Adroviel called out names and titles, until four Sidhe stood beside him. Maeve's godparents, and heavy hitters all. As they stood, each accepted guardianship of Maeve, and vowed to teach her their skills of war, of sorcery, of healing, and of Bardcraft.

Then Arresael rose to her feet.

"Now do I call forth a Protector for this child. As it is written in the Great Book, she shall guard this child until she is grown, putting her safety before any other thing, even the defense of her home and her own honor. May she never be asked to take up her sword! Come forth, Lady Montraille!"

Eric had been expecting another Sidhe, but to his surprise, the woman who came to stand beside Arresael was human—or looked so. Unlike the others, she wore full armor save for her helm. Her red hair was cropped short, her face seamed with age and hard living. She regarded the assembly grimly.

"I come," she said in a thick French accent. "And I do swear, in accordance with your ancient ways, that I am a bachelor unwed, with neither kin nor mate nor child." She drew her sword, and held it high for all to see. "From this moment I vow, by this blade and my own heart's blood, that the demoiselle shall be dearer to me than honor or breath, that her safety shall be more to me than the defense of the hame, that I shall turn away from battle or challenge for her sake." The warrior sheathed her sword.

"I accept your oath," Arresael answered gravely. "May your

blade and every hand, here and in the World Above, turn against you should you fail of your vow."

The hall was absolutely still.

"Who names this child?" the Prince asked.

"Her parents name her," Kory said. He got to his feet and took Maeve from Beth as she, too, stood, then returned the baby to her. Side by side, they walked to where Adroviel stood.

"Her name is Maeve," Beth said firmly. "Know her name."

"Her name is Maeve," Kory answered. "Know her name."

"Welcome, Maeve," Adroviel said to the baby. "I give her a second name, a Name of power."

Arresael stood back. Maeve's sponsors and protectors clustered around as Adroviel bent down to whisper in the baby's ear. No one but they would know this Name. For a moment a bright glow surrounded them, fading slowly.

The others returned to their places. Kory, Beth (holding the baby), and Adroviel stood alone together in the center of the dais.

"Now let joy reign unconfined!" the Prince said. "Let there be feasting, and music, and dance—all in Maeve's honor. Let us welcome her as she deserves! Let the *ceileighe* begin!"

Once more the horns sounded. The hall erupted in wild cheering, drowning out the sound. Kory was grinning fit to crack his face—Beth looked a bit more uncertain, but still mightily pleased. They stepped forward to the edge of the dais, and Beth raised Maeve higher in her arms. From Eric's vantage point, he could see the baby yawn and stretch, unimpressed by all the noise, her eyes squinched tightly shut. After a moment, Kory led Beth back to her throne. The shouting diminished, replaced by a hubbub of conversation as people began to leave their seats.

"Pretty impressive," Ria said, leaning toward Eric so he could hear her.

"I'll say," Eric said. *Does she wish Perenor had done this for her? Does she miss the chances she should have had—would have had if her father had been anyone else?*

There was a discreet knock at the back of the box, and a door opened in the wall. The courtier who had escorted them to their seats was waiting.

"Sieur Eric? Mistress Arianrhod? If you will come this way . . . ?"

A *ceileighe* meant music and dancing, as well as the presentation of gifts to the new arrival. The presentations were less formal than the Naming had been, but that didn't mean everyone wasn't watching. Beth and Kory sat in thrones of honor on a small platform. The gifts were piled high beside them, and as each of the presenters advanced to present his gifts in person (something only a few of them were doing, Eric was relieved to note), a page put his gift into his hand. The gifts were as eclectic as the givers: everything from a golden harp, to a shiny red tricycle, to a tiny but perfect elvensteed with elaborate saddle and bridle.

Eric advanced and was handed the bunny.

"I thought she'd like this," he said, offering it to Beth.

She grinned. "You're one in a million, Banyon. And a good thing, too."

"Aw, c'mon, Bethie," Eric teased. "Every kid should have a few stuffed animals. I've got something else for her, too. I wrote a song for her. I'll play it later."

"Glad you're sticking around. This is going to be some party."

"Wouldn't miss it for the world," Eric answered. He stepped aside.

Ria was next in line. The page handed her a small drawstring bag. She opened it. There was a gold ring inside. She held it out to Beth.

"This isn't magic, but it does have my private cell-phone number engraved on it. If Maeve ever needs help in the World Above, she can call me from anywhere. I'll come."

"This is a princely gift indeed," Kory said.

"Yeah," Beth said. "Thanks. I mean it."

Ria smiled and stepped aside to make way for the next giver.

"Pretty cool," Eric said. "Makes my bunny look all no-how."

"She'll probably have more use for the bunny," Ria answered. "I can't imagine that kid'll ever need anything I can give her, but I thought it was a nice gesture."

"It was," Eric said simply. "C'mon. Let's go find something to drink. This is going to go on for a while."

The *ceileighe* filled several huge rooms. Servants passed among the revelers carrying everything from pitchers to wineskins to silver trays covered with champagne glasses. Ria snagged a glass and sipped it. "Cristalle. Very nice. What about you, Eric?"

"I think I'll stick to fruit juice. I'm driving."

A servant appeared at his elbow holding a large silver cup. He bowed and offered it to Eric. "Your cider, my lord."

Eric took the cup. The servant vanished from sight. He sipped. Pear cider. One of his favorites, and hard to come by even in as big a city as New York.

"Sometimes I wonder why you left," Ria said. "This kind of service would be very easy to get used to."

"Maybe," Eric said. "But I'm not tempted, and neither are you. We belong in the World Above. Down here we'd just wither away and die. There's no challenge to life here. That's why most of the changelings go back eventually. To a better life than they left, of course."

"I guess that's why the Elfhames never really severed their connection with our world," Ria said slowly. "And you're right. Rough as real life is sometimes, I do like a good scrap. If you can have anything you want with a wave of the hand, there's no savor to it."

In the next room, musicians were tuning up. The dancers stood waiting impatiently for the music to begin.

Sidhe danced. All the mortal accounts of them agreed on that much, and Underhill Eric had gotten a chance to see how good a dancer you could become if you had centuries to do nothing but practice. The formal dances tended to be elaborate, complicated, and very long: Master Dharniel had told Eric tales of elves so caught up in their dancing that whole Courts had dwindled away into the Dreaming, still dancing.

But while no mortal could live long enough to learn the steps of the Court dances, there were others far less complicated. He and Ria skirted the first set of dancers, following other music already playing, and found themselves in the midst of an Irish jig. The musicians were all wearing plaids—the Great Plaid, twelve yards of fabric and nothing more—and the dancers looked as if they'd just stepped out of *Riverdance*. The music was like a double shot of *uisighe*, going straight to the blood.

"C'mon," Eric said, grabbing Ria by the hand.

He'd expected her to refuse and need to be coaxed, but instead she grinned, as caught by the music as he was, and dragged *him* onto the dance floor. The other dancers quickly made room for them, pulling them into the dance.

They danced until they were glowing with exertion and the musicians—fiddler, bodhran, and pipes—stopped to refresh themselves from a keg of beer placed nearby. The dancers broke apart, into groups of twos and threes.

All of them were looking at him. They began to chant, clapping their hands rhythmically.

"Bard—Bard—Bard—"

"Oh, *hey*," Eric said, raising his hands in protest.

The chanting continued, and now Ria had joined it, eyes sparkling.

Finally Eric gave in and walked toward the stage. He took his flute out of his gig bag and fitted it together as they watched him expectantly.

"Lords—ladies—good gentles all," he said in his best Faire brogue, "I am but a mere traveling player, not fit to play for such a grand company—"

Happy catcalls, whistles, and hoots greeted these remarks, and Ria was shouting as loudly as any of them.

"—but since you're so insistent, it's an exception I'll be making for your foigne selves." He bowed deeply, and then raised the flute to his lips.

Nothing sad or solemn today, no reminders of ancient battles or beloved dead. He blew an introductory trill and swung directly into "Susan Brown," one of the pieces he and Hosea had worked up together. *Fiddle in the middle and I can't dance, Josie/Fiddle in the middle and I can't get around/Fiddle in the middle and I can't dance,*

Josie/Hello, Susan Brown! The dancers whooped and flung themselves into the music. He followed the tune immediately with another—"Turkey In The Straw," a fine old dance tune—and then another. After the first few, the musicians joined him, their instruments blending seamlessly with his own.

At last, fearing he'd be here all night, Eric played a last song, Mason Williams' "Cinderella Rockefeller." It was slow and sweet, and very silly, even without the lyrics, and by the time he was done, the dancers had all stopped to listen.

"Thank you, ladies and gentles all," Eric said. "It's been a great honor to play for such fine folk, but too much honor can kill a man with thirst. And so I leave you in good hands!" He bowed to the dancers, who cheered him lustily, and quickly made his escape to where Ria stood on the sidelines.

She handed him his cup, and Eric drank deeply. The pear cider was still cold, and the cup was still full, but he was used to that. The rules for normal were different in Underhill.

"Juilliard doesn't do you justice," Ria said. "You're at your best in a situation like this, playing for an audience who feels the music."

"I didn't go back to school to learn to perform for a crowd," Eric said. "I wanted to learn what I *don't* know, not what I do. C'mon, let's go find the food. I'm starved."

They passed other groups of dancers and other musicians—wild Cajun fiddles playing for an enthusiastic band of selkies; another fiddler and a caller playing for a group of centaurs whose square dancing more resembled polo; a small chamber orchestra playing a minuet for Sidhe in stately Georgian dress. Every form and period of music was represented—every form of acoustic, that was. While many of the Sidhe were passionate rockers, rock didn't mix well with unamplified venues and would be off in a separate space of its own.

Eventually they were forced to ask one of the servants where the dining hall was. He pointed to a Portal; once Eric had seen it, he could see others hanging in the air as well. They passed through. Here the musicians played for listeners, not dancers, and the air was filled with savory smells.

Soon they were sitting in what looked like a garden. It was night here, but the trees were filled with golden fireflies, and glowing will-o'-the-wisps floated gently through the air, shedding multicolored pastel light. Just inside the doorway stood the original Groaning Board where they'd filled their plates. Elsewhere in Adroviel's castle tonight there was everything from a formal sit-down banquet to world-class sushi chefs preparing food to order, but this was the first place they'd found.

"If I eat this, will I be trapped in Underhill forever?" Ria asked, holding up a cluster of Underhill grapes. They glowed with a soft violet light.

"That's just an old tale," Eric told her, biting into a hot roll. He'd loaded his plate with prime rib—all that playing and dancing had given him an appetite, and the evening was far from over. "It only works if the food's bespelled, and nothing here tonight is. Try them. They're good."

They weren't alone in the garden. Around them were other guests taking the opportunity to rest and refuel. Between the trees, the ground rose up in couch-shaped hummocks carpeted in green moss. They were just as soft as they looked. Eric saw a woman with green hair and skin who wore a garment of shining leaves. Her plate was piled high with bread and fruit—a little cannibalistic, considering that she was probably a dryad, but who was Eric to judge? Her dinner companion was a satyr. His small horns were wound with ribbons, and his hooves were polished and gilded. *The Sidhe can look like anything humanity can imagine, and a number of things they can't.*

It was peaceful here. "We'd better go find Beth and Kory after this, or we never will. They should be done with opening baby presents by now."

"It'd be easy to miss them in this mob," Ria said. "Fortunately, no matter how long we're here, Etienne can get me back to nine o'clock Saturday night. I've got a lot of work to get through tomorrow."

"You should take a day off once in a while," Eric said.

"I'm here, aren't I?" Ria answered. She tossed a grape at him; he grabbed for it, but a flying critter snagged it out of the air before he did. "You're so easy to tease, Eric. Always worrying about everyone but yourself. Who's going to worry about you, eh?" She reached out to brush a lock of hair back from his forehead.

"You are," Eric answered. He leaned forward, into the kiss.

There was scattered applause.

Both of them recoiled in opposite directions. They had an audience of tiny Sidhe, naked and sexless as kewpie dolls. The creatures had bright butterfly wings, and each wore a different full-sized flower as a hat.

"Scat!" Eric yelped, swinging at them with his flute. They scattered and ran, giggling in high squeaky voices. He glanced at Ria, who was at least *trying* not to laugh.

"Why don't we go find your friends?" Ria said after a long pause.

Beth and Kory were dancing—one of the simpler Sidhe dances. Five rings of dancers, each rotating in a different direction, jumped and spun and twirled to the music. At intervals, the rings would break into sets for a measure or two, as dancers worked their way into the inner circle of dancers and back out again. The two of them were completely intent upon the dance—it wasn't as simple as it looked, as the pairs bowed and curtseyed and flung themselves into the air.

Kory saw them and waved, and in a few minutes they worked their way to the outermost ring and freed themselves from the dance. There were others more than ready to take their place; the music itself seemed to have no end.

"Master Dharniel's looking for you," Beth said, only slightly out of breath from her exertions. "He's in charge of the playing order for the Bards."

Eric winced. Not even the sanctity of a Naming could squelch the dueling egos of most Bards, a circumstance not calculated to improve Master Dharniel's temper. No matter what order they went on in, someone wouldn't like it.

"I'd better go find him," Eric said. And do what he could to soothe matters. He glanced at Ria.

"Oh, I'll stay here," she said with fulsome sweetness. "I'm sure Kory and Beth will take very good care of me."

He had no choice but to leave her there, and of the two women, he wasn't sure which one he was worried about.

"So," Beth said. "Are you enjoying the party?"

"It's lovely," Ria said. "And you?"

"Oh . . . hell," Beth said, grimacing. "We could go on billing and cooing until the end of the world. I'd rather get real. Eric vouches for you, and the Prince and his lady accept you. I don't know whether I like you or not—I never had much in common with corporate types."

"Like me," Ria said. "And I don't know that I care much for elves, myself." She gave Kory a mocking glance.

"But you're . . . oh." Beth said. "Yeah, I guess I can see that. But all the Sidhe aren't like . . . your father."

"'Perenor the Destroyer.' How pleased he'd be to know he was so fondly remembered. Still, done is done: he's dead, and Sun-Descending is still there, keeping the wells of imagination flowing in southern California. Isn't it odd that the Sidhe, who aren't creative themselves, seem to inspire so much of it? Ireland . . . Canada . . . California . . . New York . . . wherever there's a hill, it seems to bring out the best in humans."

"Or the worst," Kory suggested. "Just as humans do, we cherish most what we lack. Mortals create. The Sidhe live nearly forever. You would not trade your imagination for our long lives, if you truly knew what it would entail."

"I, on the other hand, have the best of both worlds," Ria said lightly. "Human creativity, and at least a little of the Sidhe longevity." She looked at Beth. "Just as any children you and Kory produce will have," she said pointedly.

"Why don't we go somewhere more quiet?" Beth said. "Eric will find us."

Kory gestured, and a Portal opened in the air. The three of them walked through.

"This is the day nursery," Beth said. "Maeve's through there.

Don't worry. We won't wake Maeve. Once she's asleep, she's dead to the world."

"Do you want to see her?" Kory asked.

"Yes," said Ria honestly. "I'd like that very much."

They went through the doorway into the night nursery. In the middle of the room stood an elaborate bassinet, covered with ribbons and lace. Lady Montraille sat watching over Maeve, unlikely though it was that anything might happen here. With her were more ordinary nursemaids—in this case, three gleaming balls of light, one pink, one blue, one green—hovering above the bassinet. If Ria squinted, she could see a tiny figure at the center of each light.

She approached the cradle and looked down. Maeve no longer wore the elaborate christening gown, just a simple pink T-shirt and Pampers.

"I grew up in a commune until I was four," Ria said, speaking softly, looking down at the baby. "I hated it. There was never enough to eat, never anything good to eat—I slept in the same room with all the other kids. The older ones used to scare the littlest ones to make them cry, creeping around the floor growling like bears. I never cried. I already knew there were worse things than bears."

Beth sighed. "The more I see of other people's childhoods, the more I appreciate my own."

For some reason, that felt more real to Ria than expressions of sympathy or horror would have been, and she acknowledged it with a nod. "I didn't see much of my mother. She spent most of her time getting high any way she could. She didn't have much time for me. I suppose I don't blame her. She was just doing her best to stay alive after my father's magic fried her mind and killed her twin. She used to have terrible nightmares, waking up screaming about drowning in blood. I guess the others thought it was just acid flash. I don't know what I thought."

"What could you think?" Kory asked. "You were only a child. I suppose you accepted it; young things are like that, they accept whatever form the world takes, however cruel or strange."

That, too, was more sincere than Ria had expected. Now the words she had so much difficulty in forming flowed from her. "Then one day my father came for me. Perenor always liked to leave the dirty work to others. Now I was old enough to follow orders and be an asset." She shook her head, plunging back into a memory that had seemed golden at the time.

"I thought he was the most wonderful thing I'd ever seen. He came driving up in a big black limousine. He brought me candy. It was the first time I'd ever had chocolate. I suppose he gave it to me to see if it would kill me, if I'd inherited more from the Sidhe side than the human." And now, she recalled the calculating look on his face as she devoured the treat, the satisfaction when she asked for more. "He took me back to the commune and started to leave, and I ran after him, ran after the car. I'm sure he was waiting for that. Basically, he abducted me, not that anyone there ever cared. At the time, all I knew was that it was wonderful. He took me to a toy store and let me buy anything I wanted. I had pretty dresses, my own room, a governess who let me do anything I chose—it was paradise. But it came at a price. A few days later, when I started asking whether my mother was going to join us, he told me she'd killed herself. When I was old enough, I checked that out for myself, and he hadn't lied. She'd lost the battle. The commune was on the coast; she just swam out into the ocean and didn't swim back."

Beth and Kory both nodded, saying nothing, and she was grateful for that. Oddly, or perhaps not so oddly, that particular memory gave no pain. Her mother had never been more than one of the "chicks" who cooked, tended the kids, and did the housework when they weren't stoned. In fact, she'd seen less of her mother than any of the others because her mother had been stoned more often, trying to escape.

"He never stopped telling me how fortunate I was to be alive; how he'd wanted me so much he'd used special magic to sire me on a mortal woman. The only way that can happen is for the human partner to somehow become equally a . . . oh, I don't know, 'creature of magic' sums it all up. So either the Sidhe partner has to be weak and close to death, or the human partner has to become a temporary mage. Of course, that was the method Perenor chose. He found some potential mages—about ten percent of humanity has that potential, or so I'm told—and stole their power: their joy, their hope, their creativity—all of it—and fed it to my mother. One of them was her twin brother—that was one of the reasons he picked her, because her brother was a nascent Bard, and Power ran in her Line. Of course, along with the power of everyone Perenor sucked dry, she got their dreams, their memories, and their deaths. No wonder she went mad. Later, of course, he found other uses for that power."

"That much, we know," Kory said, stern and sad, though neither of those emotions was aimed at her.

Of all the ways this particular encounter could have gone, this was not one of the ones Ria would have put high on the list of "likely." She felt a catharsis, finally telling someone just what kind of burden her father had laid on her young shoulders in an effort to make her as hard as he was. She'd never dared say these things to Eric. Eric cared too deeply, felt too much. It would have hurt him. "Perenor made certain I would know exactly how much my life had cost. I don't suppose it ever occurred to him that having a dozen teenagers—and my mother, in the end—die so I could be born would bother me. After all, why should the strong care about the weak?"

"But that can't be the only way," Beth said despairingly. "There have to be others!"

"Crossbreeds are rarer than elven children," Ria said bleakly. Suddenly, she had to give them hope. Beth's naked anguish, although she didn't exactly understand it, had to be answered. "Perenor chose the most convenient method, but he knew most of the others. They all have the same basis: parity between the energy states of the two partners. Either find some way to turn yourself temporarily into a Sidhe without killing anyone—or turn your elf-friend here temporarily human." Kory and Beth looked at each other with an unreadable expression. "He did find some hints that Sidhe who'd slipped into Dreaming were more fertile with humans than normal Sidhe, but I don't imagine that's an experiment you wish to try?"

Kory shuddered, and Beth took his arm protectively. "There has to be some other way."

Ria looked at Beth's woebegone expression, and again offered a breath of hope. "It isn't impossible to find a way, you know, even if Misthold or Sun-Descending or even Melusine doesn't know how to get its hands on enough life-force. There's more to the World Underhill than the parts of it the Sidhe live in, and creatures out there old and powerful enough to make the Emperor Oberon look like a wet firecracker in comparison. Do what you'd do faced with a problem like this in the World Above. Find an information specialist and consult him. There have to be trade fairs of some kind here—the inhabitants may not be human, but they're not that different."

"I know of one." Kory spoke up. "I do not think it is precisely the sort of place you mean, but we may begin there."

"Do," Ria suggested. "And let me know what you find out, okay? Who knows? The day may come when I need to know myself."

One of the will-o'-the-wisp servants guided Eric through the labyrinth of interconnecting castle rooms all filled with revelers, finally arriving at the castle's equivalent of the RenFaire's Main Stage. Here only the most elite performers would present their work for the entertainment of the high-ranking nobles and their own coteries.

When Eric got there, Dharniel was talking to the Lady Harawain, one of Maeve's sponsors and a famous Bard. He'd played her work many times while under Dharniel's tutelage. Her instrument was the harp, and she carried it with her now, slung over her shoulder in a velvet bag. She was one of those Sidhe who had chosen to modify her natural form: her hair and skin and eyes were all in shades of gold, until she looked like a statue of living amber.

"—the young Bard must go last," she was saying in firm tones. "He's the one everybody will want to hear today, being Maeve's father as well as a great hero."

Me? Eric thought. *They can't be serious.*

"My dear Lady Harawain, your own natural humility keeps you from seeing what is truly the proper place for so honored a guest. He must go first, of course." The speaker was an elegant and very dandified Sidhe, with waxed moustaches and a goatee. He held a lute festooned with trailing ribbons by its ivory neck.

"If first is such a desirable place, Pirolt, by all means, it should go to none but yourself," Harawain shot back silkily. "Don't you agree, Lord Dharniel?"

"Oh, but I regret that I cannot accept. My lute, she is a temperamental mistress, and I could hardly be ready in time. I will, of course, be more than willing to perform last," Pirolt said hastily.

From his days on the RenFaire Circuit, Eric knew that the end position was the one most coveted by performers. It assured that yours would be the piece the audience remembered best because they'd heard it last, gave you plenty of time to warm up (and the audience to assemble and warm up for you), and meant you didn't have to spend the day waiting around for your turn or rushing to fill in if something happened to someone else. First was also good, for a lot of reasons, but the star attraction always went on last.

And Dharniel was saving that slot for *him*?

"Eric goes last," Dharniel said. "I am Master of the Revels and that is my decision. Pirolt, your concern for my protégé does not go unremarked. You will play first, so I suggest you begin tuning now."

The foppish elf drew himself up to his full height. His eyes flashed dangerously.

"You will find in me an implacable enemy, Master Dharniel."

"And you will find in me your last one, Master Pirolt. But do take your complaint to Prince Adroviel, by all means. I'm sure the prince would relish the chance to settle your dispute."

Pirolt looked as if he might say more, but settled for spinning on his heel and stalking off.

"Harawain, dearest lady, I place you just before Eric," Dharniel said.

Good lord—is Dharniel smiling? I thought his face would crack if he ever did that.

"The best of the Old Ways followed by the best of the New," she said without ego. "It is a pretty conceit, Master Dharniel. And here is the young Bard now."

Dharniel turned to Eric as Lady Harawain gracefully made her exit. "I suppose you, too, have some complaint of your position in the order of play?"

"None," Eric said hastily. "But there was actually something else I wanted to talk to you about. But if this isn't a good time . . . ?"

"So long as it is not a matter of artistic temperament," Dharniel said. "But stay. You will need your keeper so that you can attend upon the music in good time."

He plucked a knot of glowing ribbons out of the air and touched it to Eric's shoulder. Eric heard a faint chime, like the ringing of crystal bells.

"It will sound when it is time for you to come to the stage. Do not fail to heed it."

"I won't," Eric promised. As if he'd stand up the biggest audience he was ever likely to have, or miss the chance to hear the cream of Underhill Bard-dom play!

Dharniel regarded him, and Eric realized the elven mage was waiting for him to speak.

"I've found another Bard, Master Dharniel. A human Bard, in New York—"

Quickly he told the story of meeting Hosea Songmaker in the subway, of sensing his Talent, and related the bits of personal history Hosea had confided in him.

"And he's got a lot of natural talent, but he's looking for a teacher, so I thought . . ."

He stopped. Dharniel was smiling again. Mockingly.

"Congratulations, young Bard. You have just acquired your first apprentice."

"I—Me—? But I thought . . . *I* don't know how to train anyone, Master Dharniel!" Eric sputtered.

"So—as I thought—you slept through all my lectures. Well, no matter. As you are so fond of saying, you can always 'wing it.'"

"But I can't—" Eric said in panic.

Dharniel's face took on an expression of sternness. "Eric, for every Bard comes the time when their first apprentice is sent to them. None of the good ones think they are ready for such a responsibility. But you have learned everything I have to teach you, and learned more in your own life. Who better than a human Bard to train another? I shall look forward to meeting him when he is ready to present his masterwork."

And that seemed to settle that. Eric gulped. "I— Um, thanks, Master Dharniel. I think."

Maybe Hosea won't want me for a teacher, Eric thought hopefully, then banished the matter from his mind to think about later. Right now he had more immediate things to worry about.

All too soon it was time for him to go on. He'd switched from pear cider to plain water awhile back, and was glad he had—there was enough magic floating around in the air to make him dizzy.

The magic had another effect as well. Music—good music, no matter the style—was always about real things: hope and heartbreak, people and places long gone or yet to be.

Here, music made them real.

Music and magic went hand in hand; Bardcraft had always been about magic as well, about the controlling or the unleashing of power. But now he was seeing what that actually meant.

When the Bards performed, what their music spoke of became real for everyone to see. It was like stepping into virtual reality, bringing the audience with you.

Some of the Bards went for simple flashy effects—fireworks, showers of flowers. Others worked more subtle and more powerful magics. For her last piece—each Bard was restricted to three— Harawain had played a Homecoming Song that had left the audience weeping tears of joy—and Eric, too, even though he wasn't quite sure why. But at that moment, it had all been real: the cry of the gulls, the salt smell of the ocean, even the deck rocking gently beneath his feet.

A tough act to follow.

He knew better than to try to beat the Sidhe at their own game. For this performance, he was going to give them human music, ending up with "The Huntsman's Reel," the piece he'd composed for Maeve.

He started with "Bouree," a bouncy flute piece he'd found on an old Jethro Tull album and liked instantly. A touch of magic, and he was playing all four parts of the contrapuntal melody in perfect harmony with himself—a neat trick, and one he'd worked hard on. The music spun shapes of pure geometry in the air, sparkling and changing with each note. As the last note died, delighted applause washed over him. He could see Kory grinning— he, Beth, and Ria were seated beside the Prince and Princess in seats of honor—and Beth shot him a thumbs-up of approval.

For his second piece, he'd used Mozart's *The Magic Flute* as his inspiration. No magic this time beyond what the music itself produced, but that was enough. He lowered his flute at the end of the piece, and there was a moment of hushed silence before the applause began. When it had died down, he stepped to the edge of the stage.

"Your Highnesses, ladies and gentlemen, for my last piece I would like to play a new composition, dedicated to the Lady Maeve and written in her honor."

Suddenly there was a new quality to the respectful silence. An electric anticipation, almost hunger, that he had never felt before. After a moment, he realized why.

A new piece. New. I spent all day explaining to Ria that elves never create anything because they can't, and never stopped to think what an effect something like this would have. Even the Sidhe Bards don't create new music—they just adapt the old. What have I set myself up for?

There was no choice now but to go on with it.

He raised his flute and played.

The inspiration for the piece was a dancing tune, and the dance was still in its heart—but this was the mortal dance through life, growing and learning. Each time he returned to the original melody it was more complex, deeper, as the child became a woman, then a mother, then a wise counselor to her children's children. Then he stripped away all the ornament and reprised the motif as the woman stood alone, wise and full of years, looking back on all she had done.

When he stopped, there was a long silence from his audience, and for a moment, Eric was sure he'd mortally offended them. These were the Sidhe—firstborn of Danu, Folk of the Air, eternal and unchanging. What had ever possessed him to play something that was nothing less than a celebration of human mortality for them?

Then the cheering began. One by one, the audience stood, clapping and cheering. The Prince wept unashamedly. Beth was alternately hugging Kory and bouncing up and down. Ria, standing behind them, spoke silently, but he could read her lips:

"Only you, Eric."

He guessed he'd better get off stage while they were still applauding. Master Dharniel was waiting in the wings, most of the other Bards clustered behind him. The cheering could still be heard, though more faintly than it would be in a World Above venue.

"You're more than ready for an apprentice," Dharniel said curtly, turning away abruptly.

"As I said, the best of the New," Harawain said. She reached out to touch him gently upon the shoulder. "Won't you stay here with us, in Underhill? Your own kind will never value you as we do," she said wistfully.

"I'm sorry." Eric smiled regretfully.

Just then the first of the well-wishers arrived, the Prince among them. His presence kept things from turning into a mob scene, but Eric was still glad to make his escape. Fortunately, on this particular night, Beth could have anything she wanted, even the Bard that everyone wanted.

"Oh, Eric, you rock! That was so . . ." She stopped.

Eric grinned. "Just so you know there's more to me than bunnies, m'lady."

"You could have given us no richer gift," Kory said. "Truly this will be a night long remembered."

"'And gentlemen in England now a-bed/Shall think themselves accursed they were not here/And hold their manhoods cheap whiles any speaks/That fought with us upon St. Crispin's Day,'" Ria said lightly, quoting Shakespeare to good purpose. Beth shot her a wicked grin—it looked as if they'd settled whatever issues still remained between them, Eric noted with relief.

"So what do we do now?" Eric asked.

"What else?" Beth answered. "Party like there's no tomorrow."

SIX:
TO RIDE THE NIGHT-MARE

�֍

You could get used to anything, even fear. After a while, Jeanette Campbell stopped worrying about a bullet to the head.

There were worse things than death.

Being a madman's captive, for one.

There was something not *right* about Elkanah. She hadn't noticed it at first, of course. She'd been trying to get used to the idea of being dead. But after a while it'd become clear to her that he didn't mean to kill her—not immediately at least—and her mind had turned, with inevitable self-preservation, to what would happen next. Escape. Survival.

They drove all through that first night and well into the next day. He stuck to the back roads, so she still couldn't tell where they were going. She had the growing feeling that *he* wasn't sure either, and that was the first thing that worried her. The second was his driving. She'd stayed mouse-quiet, hoping to convince him she was no threat, but when the van began to weave from side to side on a road that was only a car-and-a-half wide—if that—fear of immediate death made her bold.

"Either find a place to pull over or let me drive. I don't want to end up dead at the bottom of a ditch."

Elkanah slowly turned to look at her, letting the van drift to a stop. His eyes were almost yellow, she noted with clinical detachment, and the skin beneath them looked bruised and puffy with sleeplessness and something more.

"Let you drive?" he said, in slow echo of her words. "And where would you go, Ms. Campbell?"

"How should *I* know? This was your idea," she snapped. "I don't even know where we are!"

He chuckled, an almost-soundless rasping that came from deep in his chest. "Don't you? I think you're funning me, Ms. Campbell. I think you know exactly where we are. You shouldn't've been so talkative back in the day, Ms. Campbell. I knew just where to find you."

There was no answer she could give to that because she'd never talked to him at length at all, and so she just stared at him, scared and defiant. After a moment, he put the van into gear and began driving again. But an hour later they'd reached a more traveled road, and he followed a weathered billboard advertising "Lester's Country Rest."

It wasn't much of a rest, but it was certainly country. He left her in the car alone—shackled to the door, of course—while he went to talk to the owner, and came back a few moments later with a room key in his hand.

"I guess you won't mind sharing a room."

He drove the van around to the back of the little row of battered cabins, got out, and came around to her door to open it. Mutely, Jeanette held out her wrist, and he unlocked the shackle. She rubbed her wrist, still able to feel the weight and coldness. She climbed down out of the seat, feeling stiff and unsteady on her feet.

"Come on." He put a hand on her arm and led her to the end cabin. The cabin door stuck, and he shoved it open. A wave of musty hot air rolled out. She walked inside, and when she turned, Elkanah was pulling another set of cuffs out of his pocket.

"Now, Ms. Campbell, I figure we can do this the easy way, or the hard way."

Jeanette swallowed hard. "What's the easy way?"

He smiled then, an expression more frightening than his bland disinterest had been. "I cuff your hands behind your back. And you stay put."

She nodded agreement, unable to trust her voice. As he approached her she turned her back, holding her wrists out behind her. As soon as the cold metal settled over her wrists, she realized she should have asked to take off her jacket first. It was hot in here, and would only get hotter as the day progressed. But something inside told her to stay as quiet as she could, not make him think about her too much.

She sat down on a corner of the bed as Elkanah went back outside to the van. She knew it was a test. Elkanah was armed, and somehow she didn't think that Lester would call the cops if he heard a shot. She'd been shot before, once a long time ago when she'd gotten careless. It was an experience she had no desire to repeat.

Elkanah returned carrying a small backpack. He shut the door, and then picked up the end of the bed and dragged it over in front of the door. Jeanette, caught unawares, fell to the floor. With her hands cuffed behind her it was an awkward fall, but she didn't complain. She thought that for just a moment Elkanah had forgotten she was there, and that was another disturbing thought to add to all the others.

He continued to ignore her, opening the pack and pulling out a can of beer and a small bottle. It was labelled "aspirin," and she only hoped it was, watching him shake the tablets directly into his mouth and wash them down with a long slug of warm beer. The situation was grim enough without adding drugs to it.

And drugs were what got you into this, weren't they, Campbell? And to think, this all started out with you wanting to be an elf. She rolled to her knees and sat cross-legged on the floor, watching him carefully.

Elkanah rubbed his forehead and sighed, and seemed to notice her again. "Would you care for a drink, Ms. Campbell?"

"I . . . sure," she said, realizing only then how thirsty she was. He walked over to her and held the can to her lips. She gulped awkwardly, spilling it down her T-shirt—it was warm, and she'd never cared for beer particularly, but at least it was wet.

"Now, I'm going to get some sleep. You just behave yourself," Elkanah said when the can was empty. "Or we can do this the hard way."

"No," Jeanette said. She had absolutely no desire to find out what "the hard way" might be. Her answer seemed to satisfy him, because he turned away and lay down on the bed. Within moments he was asleep.

She squirmed around until she got her jacket down off her shoulders. It cushioned the cuffs and she stretched out, half on her side. There was no rug, only bare and crumbling linoleum, and she had a fine view of the dust bunnies under the bed, but it was a better place than she'd thought she'd be in when he'd broken down her door a few hours earlier.

Sleep wasn't possible, and she had plenty of time to think. Her thoughts weren't good. Back in the van, he'd said it was easy to find her, talked like she'd told him something once that'd let him find her.

But even if she had ever had any conversations with Elkanah back at Threshold—and she hadn't—she'd wandered into to Morton's Fork completely at random. She couldn't have told anyone where she was going, because she hadn't known herself.

So how had *he* known? And why was he lying about it?

Who's he working for? He's hired muscle. He has to be working for someone.

Nothing about this felt right. It didn't match any way of doing business she knew of, legit, criminal, or any of the shades of clandestine in-between. Elkanah had been Robert Lintel's right-hand thug, a hired frightener. If Robert was gone, Elkanah should be too.

Unless Robert *wasn't* gone. Unless somehow he'd survived, and was putting the Black Ops program back together again. She shook her head in frustration, stifling a sneeze. At least Elkanah meant to keep her alive for now. At least she knew that much.

She just wished she knew why.

She must have slept, because she was startled out of confused dreams by Elkanah hauling her unceremoniously to her feet. It was dark outside, and the room was lit by one bare 40-watt bulb.

"What time is it?" she asked groggily.

"Time to go," Elkanah said, turning her around to unlock the cuffs. He gave her a push toward the bathroom. "You go wash up. We've got miles to go."

"Miles to go before I sleep." A scrap of an old poem she'd had to learn in high school surfaced in her mind. Mr. Johnson had said it was about death. She wished she hadn't remembered it now.

The bathroom was small and grimy, its tiny window painted shut. She ran water in the sink until it ran clear, then scooped up several tepid handfuls, gulping thirstily and rubbing it over her face and hair. There was a mirror over the sink. Her face looked blotched and puffy, her eyes big and scared. The dyed black hair looked unconvincing and dull—he'd been right, it looked awful, and with her hellbound for death or slavery, why should she care?

I don't care, she told herself. *I don't care what anyone thinks of me, or how I look. I don't.* She wished she could stay in there forever, but he'd only come in after her. She slicked her hair down as best she could and washed the beer out of her T-shirt and opened the door. Elkanah was waiting for her. He handed her a warm can of Coke and a granola bar.

"Breakfast."

She didn't argue.

The next day followed the pattern of the first. Elkanah drove, almost aimlessly, and Jeanette sat, chained to the door, and tried to make sense out of what was happening to her. She supposed she ought to be putting her soul in order and repenting her misspent life, but it didn't seem to her that any of this was her fault. She'd never told Robert to kill all those people. When she'd been an outlaw chemist, she'd never forced her drugs on anyone who didn't want to buy.

But they couldn't have done it without you, a remorseless inner voice said. She tried to shut it out, but there was nothing to do but listen to it, and finally she gave in. *Okay. If the Sinner Saints hadn't had me, they'd've found someone else to cook for them, but that's no*

*excuse. If Robert hadn't found me, he'd have found someone else, but
that's no excuse either. I didn't have to do those things. I'm responsible
for what I did.*

*But how could I have not done them? Once I got started all the
way back in high school, how could I have done anything different
than what I did?*

"Pretty good, you tracking me down like that," she finally said.
It was crazy of her to bait him that way, but the only other choice
was to listen to that accusing voice inside her head. Anything to shut
up her inner Jiminy Cricket.

Her only answer was a grunt.

"I thought I'd gotten away clean. It was more than six months.
I read about Threshold in the papers. I thought they'd got everyone
else."

Another grunt.

"I guess you must've given them the slip."

Now he glanced toward her. "I'm here," was all he said.

"Pretty good going," Jeanette offered, but Elkanah said nothing
more. But now that she'd started, she didn't seem to be able to stop
talking.

"You must have high-level backing. Robert did. All I do is make
the stuff."

Now he looked directly at her. "That's enough. That's what *he*
wants."

"Who? Robert?" But Robert was dead, wasn't he? Elkanah had
said so, back in the cabin.

For a moment she thought she'd pushed him too far. Elkanah
cut the van sharply over to the side of the road, stopped, and got out.
But he wasn't coming for her. He opened the door into the back. She
heard the rattle of the aspirin bottle, and craned over the back of the
seat to see. He was standing in the doorway—no, *hanging* in the
doorway, looking like Death on roller skates, slugging back dry
aspirins as if they were jelly beans. He looked up as she moved, and
for a moment she saw a silvery flash, like the reflection of light in a
mirror, but it passed too soon for her to be sure of what she saw.

"You talk too much," Elkanah said.

"I want to know what's going to happen."

He laughed. The sound came as if forced, ending in a wracking cough. "No you don't. You don't want to know what's going to happen."

"What?" she asked, fear breaking through her forced calm. "What's going to happen? What are you going to do with me? Where are we going? Who are you working for? What does he want?"

"Who said I was working for someone?" He glared at her in sullen anger.

You did. Just now. You said he *wants me.* "All I want to know is—"

"Shut up."

She did.

They stopped again soon after that at a convenience store. Elkanah bought sandwiches and coffee for both of them, a pair of dark glasses, and all the aspirin the store had. She watched him chase another half bottle of pills with scalding coffee.

He didn't have headaches like that when he was working at Threshold. If there'd been anything wrong with him then, that Healer we killed would have spotted it. She didn't like Elkanah, didn't care about him, but suddenly it seemed terribly important to her that he be well and whole.

"Caffeine helps," she said hesitantly. "You should get some No-Doz. It's got more caffeine than coffee does."

For a moment she almost thought he'd hit her, but instead he got out of the van again and went back into the store. She could see him talking to the clerk.

I should get out of here. I could scream. Make a fuss. Jump out of the van.

But if she did, she was still chained to the door. And the man she was with was entirely capable of taking off and dragging her. Her jacket would protect her from the road, but not for long. She sipped her coffee, hating herself for her cowardice. It wouldn't be an easy death, but it might be better than what Elkanah was taking her to. She shivered, suddenly cold. *"You don't want to know what's going to happen."*

He came back with a handful of bottles, tossing them onto the dash. Something called "Truckers' Pick Me Up." Watching him carefully for signs of displeasure, she reached for one of the bottles. Caffeine pills. He'd taken her advice. That was something.

They drove through the night without stopping except for gas. Near dawn he began to talk—to keep himself awake, she suspected—but it was information, all the same.

"Never did think about all the people you hurt, did you? Never thought about everybody you *left*. Little blonde bitch, left us all there. Didn't think I'd be back, did you? Didn't think I'd find you. Too smart for you. Miss Ria Llewellyn. Blonde bitch. Thought you could throw me off with a haircut. Too smart. Gonna take you back. Make you run. Fix everything. Teach you to leave us there."

Did he think she was Ria Llewellyn? He couldn't. He'd known who she was when he'd come for her. He'd talked about a partnership, made sure to take her stock.

"I didn't leave you," she said softly, not knowing what else to say.

Her voice seemed to rouse him. He glanced at her.

"I ran out on you—on Threshold, on Robert—but you were free to do the same."

"I guess you think we ought to stop," he said, as if they'd been having some other—more normal—conversation.

"That'd be good. I guess we still have a long way to go?"

He didn't answer, but a few hours later, as the sun was coming up, they stopped again.

She'd been too tired to really notice when it happened, but at some point during the night they'd gone from winding local roads to the main state roads. They were heading east. Toward New York. She was sure of it now.

Main roads meant a better class of hotel, too. This time the room had two double beds. They were bolted to the floor, so this time Elkanah took the pillows and blankets and made himself a bed in front of the door. He unplugged the phone and took it with him, falling asleep at once and leaving her to her own devices.

This time he didn't even bother to cuff her hands. Confidence that she couldn't escape—or was he getting sloppy?

It didn't really matter. The windows didn't open, and they were on the second floor. She could throw a chair through the window or set fire to the curtains with the lighter in her jacket pocket, but that was about all. She didn't think he'd sleep through either activity. She wouldn't escape, and she'd be in a worse situation than she was in now.

She could break one of the bathroom glasses and cut her throat, but aside from that, her options were limited.

She honestly considered doing that, staring into the mirror, but she couldn't quite bring herself to do it. Down deep in her heart, Jeanette was afraid that death wasn't a final end, and she was afraid of what lay on the other side—balance and payment exacted for the crimes and weaknesses of a lifetime. Her hands shook, and tears prickled at the back of her eyes, but she couldn't even cry. Something horrible was going to happen to her, and she knew she deserved it, but she couldn't help shrieking inside that it wasn't *fair*, that she hadn't known what would happen back when she could still change things, back while it would have done any good. And now, nothing she could do could ever make up for what she'd done. She didn't think she could do good if she tried.

So life isn't fair. You always knew that. But I just wish . . .

She shook her head. Might as well wish she'd never been born. Where had her life gone twisted? When she'd started selling drugs? In high school, when she'd dreamed of revenge on her tormentors and vowed she'd pay any price to get it? In kindergarten, when everyone had laughed at her for some reason she'd never understood and she'd hated them for it? How far back did you look for reasons, for the first failure of nerve or spirit that led to all the rest? Should she blame her parents, and their unspoken agreement that she deserved whatever happened to her, no matter what it was? If they'd been one of those happy loving TV families that stuck up for each other, would she have turned out quite the same?

Who knows?

Wearily, going through the motions of living that almost—but not quite—didn't matter any more, she stripped and showered. At least she could be clean when she died, even if she had nothing to wear but the clothes she'd been living in for days. Afterward she sat in a chair, watching the sun rise, watching Elkanah sleep, waiting for him to wake up and deliver her to her fate.

He woke in the late afternoon and took her back to the van. This time he didn't chain her to the door. He headed for Interstate 80, confirming her guess that they were heading for New York.

"Maybe it's time for you to fill me in," she said, trying again for information because it was the only thing she could do. They were on a high-speed road now, one filled with big trucks and drivers who all thought they were James Bond. He'd have to pay more attention to the road. Maybe he'd get careless. Maybe they'd crash and the Smokeys would come and arrest them both. Somehow a lifetime spent in prison didn't seem so bad any more.

"Back in Morton's Fork, you asked if I could make more T-Stroke. You said we could do business."

"What?" Elkanah glanced quickly toward her, his face blank with surprise, then quickly back to the road.

"What do you want me for?"

"I don't," he said flatly. Then: "It's dark." And it was, but there were headlights all around them, and somehow she didn't think that was the kind of darkness he was talking about.

"Just you wait until we get to New York, Ria Llewellyn . . ." His voice trailed off. And though she repeated her questions over and over again at prudent intervals, she never got any clearer answer. It was almost as if he didn't know she was in the van any more.

She'd made up her mind to run for it and damn the consequences when they stopped at the toll gate on the George Washington Bridge, but to her dismay they didn't head for the bridge. Elkanah went around the city, switching from the New Jersey Turnpike to the Garden State Parkway, and then to Route 17, a two-lane road that twisted through dark countryside.

"Where are we going?" she asked desperately.

"To New York," he said, in a terrifyingly reasonable voice. "We'll be there soon."

But they'd passed New York an hour before.

He was crazy. She knew it with a sick certainty. She'd counted on his sanity more than she'd known until the last hope of it was gone. He'd never been looking for her. He must have found her by accident—it was possible—and all the rest: about business, an employer, his accusations of something Ria Llewellyn had done, were all a smoke screen over his madness. Maybe *he'd* killed Robert Lintel. Maybe he'd killed all of them. And now he was going to kill her. Fear of capture had paralyzed her thinking until it was too late.

"We're going to need to stop for gas," she said, glancing at the fuel gauge. Anything, anything, to make him take her where lights and people were! She wasn't chained up now, and now, knowing what she knew, she'd do anything to keep him from chaining her up again.

"No need. We're almost there," he said, turning off the road onto a one-lane track. A sign flashed by almost before she could read it: Sterling Forest Park.

"Look. Could we stop and get something to drink? I'm really thirsty," she said.

"There's stuff in the back," he said, his eyes on the road. Though it was bumpy and narrow, he hadn't slowed at all. She would have jumped from the van if he had. But this was a chance, at least. She climbed around the seat, into the back of the van, and turned on the light.

Her saddlebags were still there, next to Elkanah's duffle. She scrabbled through her bags, hoping he'd brought her gun, but there was nothing in them but clothes, the jar of T-Stroke powder, and the two bottles full of filled capsules. She reached for Elkanah's duffle.

Aspirin. Caffeine pills. Bundles of cash. Half a six-pack of Coke, and one of those big plastic cups with a straw built into the lid that you got at highway rest stops, the kind that held 64 ounces. No weapon.

But she had a weapon, if she wasn't afraid to use it.

With shaking hands, praying he wouldn't turn and look, she unscrewed the lid of the brown plastic jar and dumped several ounces of powdered T-Stroke into the cup. *A low dose kills, a higher dose delays death.* She held it between her knees and ripped back the tab on a can of Coke, pouring it in over the powder. It foamed up the sides and she swirled it around. The powder melted away, leaving a murky brown liquid. She added a second can of Coke and clamped the lid on. Her hands were freezing. New York in August, and she was cold.

Cold as death.

Revenge is always an option. She used to think the phrase was cool, glamorous, a creed to live by. Now all she felt was despair.

The van was starting to slow down. Stopping. She stuffed the jar into her pocket and grabbed for the two bottles of capsules. *A low dose kills. A higher dose might let you live.*

He turned off the engine but left the headlights on as he climbed out of the van. A moment later he pulled open the sliding door of the van. In the wan light his skin was stretched tight, gray and shiny. Oily beads of sweat stood out on his face like sequins, gleaming in the light. He looked like a dying man.

"What's that you got there, Ms. Campbell?"

"Coke." Her voice was hoarse but steady, a tiny triumph to set against the sins of a lifetime. "Want some?"

"You first," he said, unsmiling.

She put the straw to her lips and sucked hard, tasting brackish warm sweetness, a faint tang of carbonation, and nothing more. She gulped hard, forcing herself to swallow the contents of the cup. Forcing herself not to know she was drinking poison.

"Here," she said, holding out what was left.

He took it and drank deeply, and as he did, his expression changed. Realization. Terror.

But not of her. Not of what was in the cup.

Bright pale spots appeared on his forehead. She watched in horror as something glittery burst through his skin, shooting out, branching, shining bright as chrome.

Horns. Antlers. Silver antlers.

He screamed, dropping the empty cup.

Then he reached for her, fast as a striking snake, yanking her out of the van and onto her knees on the summer-damp ground.

"Run, girl! As you love Jesus—*run!*"

She scrabbled away from him, moaning low in her throat with pure terror. Elkanah was clutching at the antlers, trying to tear them from his head, oblivious to her now. She managed to make it to her feet, staggering into the glare of the van's headlights, unable to make sense of what she was seeing. He swung his head from side to side, striking the antlers against the side of the van in his frenzy to remove them. The sound they made was a chiming like struck crystal, a high sweet ringing that grew louder instead of softer, growing and changing until the air was filled with deafening music.

Hearing it, Elkanah turned and ran, crashing off into the night. The horns he wore glowed as if they were made of starlight.

The music stopped. The grass crackled as it froze, turning from green to silver.

Oh, please, no.

Jeanette clutched at the hood of the van for support, then turned, clumsy with terror, to put her back against it.

An armored figure on horseback stood silhouetted in the glare. His black horse gleamed like polished stone. His armor was like something out of a medieval fever dream, fantastically ornate, the gleam of pure silver sparkling beneath a coat of night-black enamel. Long black hair flowed down over his shoulders, framing a face of inhuman beauty, such beauty that she wanted to run to him, throw herself beneath his horse's hooves, weeping, and beg his forgiveness for her ugliness. Behind him the night rippled, as if it had been shattered into a thousand pieces and re-formed once again. He was death and ruin, despair and pain, the end of all hope, all light.

She knew him.

"Aerune," she whimpered, sliding to her knees. Her heart hammered, flushing the T-Stroke through her system, promising her death or transformation, but neither soon enough to save her.

Aerune mac Audelaine, Dark Lord of the Sidhe, Prince of Air and Darkness.

Lord of Death and Pain.

Nothing could save her.

She closed her eyes, hearing the soft chiming as Lord Aerune walked his horse slowly forward.

"They said my hunt had failed." His voice was like ruined music, making her ache with sorrow. "But my hound has brought me the quarry I sought. *Look at me, human girl.*"

Her eyes snapped open as if he had shouted, and she stared up into his eyes, wanting to look away, unable to do anything but obey. She felt herself lost, felt as if she were falling into a deep pit lined with the sharpest of knives.

He leaned down from his horse and took her chin between his fingers. His touch was so cold it burned, as if his touch alone could wither her flesh and turn her skin to ash.

"You are the mortal alchemist who crowns men with fire?" he asked.

She didn't understand what he meant, but something inside her must have. Without conscious volition Jeanette felt her throat move, felt lips part and tongue move to form a single word.

"Yes."

Aerune straightened in his saddle, releasing her. Warmth and weakness flowed into her as he released her; she fell forward into the dirt, catching herself on her hands.

"And now the same unnatural fire flows through your veins." He sounded lightly amused. "No matter. Now you will be the hound to my hunting, mortal child. Now you are mine. *Get up.*"

Once more his voice acted upon her as if it were a physical force. Jeanette lurched to her feet, swaying unsteadily before him. He held out his hand, and his eyes gleamed cold and black. "Mount up and ride with me, Child of Earth. We have far to go, you and I."

Numbly, helplessly, incapable of doing anything else, Jeanette reached for his hand. All her questions were answered now: Elkanah had found her because he was Aerune's hound, given the magic to seek her out in the World of Iron. Aerune had given Elkanah another gift as well: forgetfulness, so that he did not understand why he hunted her or how he succeeded. His bruised and tormented mind had woven fantasies to cloak the workings of Aerune's magic, while all along Elkanah worked to bring Jeanette to Aerune, not knowing what he did.

Aerune pulled Jeanette up behind him on the horse, and

wheeled his mount in the direction of the shimmering black rainbow. A moment later they were gone, leaving the park to slow darkness as the van's lights dimmed and faded.

SEVEN:
WHEN THE GOING GETS TOUGH, THE TOUGH GO SHOPPING

It took her a few days to recover from the *ceileighe*—when the Sidhe threw a party, they threw a *real* party—but Beth spent that time planning her quest. Meeting Ria had not been particularly enjoyable, but Beth was honest enough with herself to admit that a lot of her current reasons for her feelings toward Ria were rooted in envy.

Back in her television days, Beth had always hated the game-playing necessary to get the job done. Working in television was as much a matter of playing political games as having the needed skill set to do the job, and she'd always resisted following the unspoken codes of flattery and expediency that allowed you to get and keep an assignment.

Hell, she'd even hated it in the RenFaires. But Ria Llewellyn seemed to swim through that treacherous sea with ease. Partly it was the power that came from being majority stockholder in a multibillion dollar company, Beth was sure—no groveling and scraping for jobs or funding there—but mostly it was Ria herself. Take everything away from her, and she'd build it back up with ease.

Beth wished she could be that kind of person. But everything she'd ever had—the glamour job in TV, the music gigs with Spiral Dance, the busking at RenFaires, even her place Underhill—she'd had to work hard to claim in an arena where ability counted no more, and sometimes far less, than networks of favors and friendships. As a small child, her battle cry had always been: *But that's not fair!* and she'd always been willing to do battle with the world as it was in the name of Fairness. It was one of the things that had drawn her to Wicca. The Craft placed a great premium on taking responsibility for your own life, working to ensure fair-dealing and justice for all, not just its own members.

Even going Underhill with Kory had seemed to her to be a defeat sometimes. The people chasing her had no right to do what they did. But while they didn't have Right on their side, they did have superior force. And so the three of them had gone: she to exile, Kory back to a home that sometimes chafed, as home did.

But Eric . . . for him Underhill had only been a way-station, not a final destination or a goal. He'd learned and grown, and gone back to take his place in Ria's world. To put it most unfairly, he'd succeeded where Beth had failed. Even having Kory's love wasn't enough to make up for that sometimes.

But having Maeve had changed everything. Through all the long months of her pregnancy, impatiently awaiting the birth of her daughter, Beth had thought she was ready for motherhood, willing to take up the responsibility, eager to protect and guide a new life.

She'd had *no* clue.

The moment she held her daughter in her arms, felt her weight and smelled her baby scent, looked into her kitten-blue eyes, the whole world had changed. Beth became the second most important person in her own life. All the old stupid clichés were true: she no longer cared about things because *Beth* wanted them, but because Beth-and-Maeve were important. Beth looked into a future that had to be put in order because *Maeve* would live there; she had to think and plan and prepare for the future because *Maeve* would be the one to grasp the opportunities there, this utterly beloved one who wrapped Beth in a gossamer web of *responsibility* for every detail of her existence.

It wasn't crushing. It was liberating and ecstatic and joyful all at once. Maeve didn't diminish her. Maeve gave her a strength and power she had never imagined possible—and suddenly so many things she hadn't thought about were vitally important. She wanted Kory's children for the joy they would bring to both of them, but now she also wanted those children for Maeve—brothers and sisters to tie her human daughter firmly into the web of kinship that linked all Underhill, friends and allies and protectors to share Maeve's grief and happiness as no one else—even her mother—ever could.

Suddenly all the things her friends with kids had said made perfect sense. Maeve completed her, changed her, made her stronger. Made her whole.

Made her worry every moment, even when she knew that at least some of those worries were irrational.

Beth grinned, leaning over the bassinet. No meteor was hurtling toward the Earth. No war was about to break out to ravage the halls of Elfhame Misthold. It didn't even rain. *"And there's a legal limit to the snow here. . . ."* Maeve had her very own Protector. And the Seleighe Sidhe adored children—*all* children—with a single-mindedness that was almost enough to satisfy a new mother's fierce protective instincts. It wouldn't be easy to leave Maeve behind, but Beth had no fear that she'd return to find anything other than a *very* pampered Elven-American Princess. It was for Maeve, for the future, for her daughter's unborn siblings, that she was going. And if she didn't come back . . . well, she was doing what mothers did, and she felt a peace in her soul that hadn't been there for a very long time.

Yep. It's a whole new Beth Kentraine . . . and ain't that a kick in the head?

Kory had taken care of the practical preparations for their trip. This was the first time Beth would be going outside the boundaries of one of the Elfhames, but to find what they needed would take them out into the Lands Underhill, and that world was far wider than the territory claimed by either Sidhe Court.

"If you need information, find an information specialist," Ria had said. This was the first step. Kory had consulted one of Prince Arvindel's advisors, the Lady Vivalant (who was also the librarian of his *very* eclectic collection of books) for information about a place called the Goblin Market. He'd told Beth that it was said that all roads Underhill led eventually to that place, and there you could find anything you sought. It was the closest thing to a trade fair that Underhill held.

There were dark rumors about the Goblin Market as well. It was said that you could buy nothing you did not already possess, nor sell that save what you wished to keep. But both Kory and Vivalant—and Master Dharniel as well, when she'd nerved herself to ask him—had thought it was still worth trying.

There was no day or night in a hame, but it still felt like early morning when they left. The elvensteeds stood ready, their saddle-bags packed with the necessities of the journey, as well as some trade goods from the World Above: coffee, chocolate, and even a couple of six-packs of Classic Coke.

Beth had been mildly shocked—all three contained caffeine, a deadly drug to all the Children of Danu—but Kory had assured her that not everything living Underhill shared the Sidhe's liability, and that such items were often eagerly sought.

"Figures. Next thing you know, McDonald's will be opening a branch down here."

Kory grinned at her, tightening his mount's girth. "Ah," he said wistfully. "Chicken McNuggets. Thick creamy shakes. And ketchup."

He was dressed in his full knightly regalia: elvensilver armor and sword, and looked every inch the faerie knight. Somehow the wistful look at the mention of Mickey D's didn't seem to go with the rest. Cognitive dissonance, that was what they called it.

"Don't," Beth begged, grinning. She'd lost her taste for junk food while she was pregnant and had never regained it, but ketchup was something she still missed.

"And Chinese food, no MSG. And pizza," Kory continued teasingly. "'Tis a pity we could not bring any of *that* with us. We could gain empires."

"You're right at that, kiddo. I guess when we get back I'm going to have to set up a kitchen and see about satisfying some of your . . . cravings." She winked at him, camping up her saucy Faire-wench persona—though her costume would certainly never have passed muster with any of the Authenticity Nazis. Beth was wearing woven leggings—embroidered down the outside of each thigh with a pattern of fruits and vines in glittering thread—tucked into high soft boots of green and gold. Above that she wore a cowled tunic in a green to match her boots, its hood, now lying over her shoulders, lined in a gold satin that matched her leggings, and around her neck a glowing pendant, warning any who could read it—and that was practically everyone they would meet—that Beth Kentraine was under the protection of Elfhame Misthold: mess with her, and you messed with them. Her tunic was gathered in with a wide belt of tooled leather, from which hung a very businesslike dagger. Under her tunic was a chain mail shirt of elvensilver worn over a linen shift, and beneath that, in a protective silk pouch embroidered with spells and hung from a thong about her neck, was her old flip-knife. Its blade was Cold Iron, anathema everywhere Underhill, carried only to be used as a last resort if things turned really bad.

She'd thought about asking to wear armor, but elven armor was as much for display as for protection. Kory's armor proclaimed him a Seleighe knight, and Beth, he'd insisted, should dress to reflect what she was as well. She'd drawn the line at the idea of wearing a long dress, though. She'd always been more of a blue-jeans person— and besides, neither she nor Bredana really cared for the sidesaddle that went with the dress.

Kory patted Mach Five on the shoulder—named long ago out of a *Speed Racer* cartoon, he'd once explained blushingly. The elvensteed whuffled and stamped his foot, and Kory turned to inspect Bredana. Finding everything there to his satisfaction (it was amazing, Beth reflected, how much of Pony Club stayed with you through the years), he held out his hand to Beth.

"All is in readiness, my lady. Shall we away?"

"You've been reading Howard Pyle again," Beth said, giving his shoulder a playful shove. He knelt and made a stirrup of his hand—elven armor was far lighter and more flexible than its World Above counterpart—and Beth stepped up, swinging her leg carefully across the saddle. The cantle was higher than a modern saddle; though Bredana could have created saddle and tack to look like anything, for this trip it was best that everything be Sidhe Classic. In a lot of places Underhill, it was safest to look like exactly what you were.

Kory mounted Mach Five and took up the reins. Grooms rushed to open the stable doors, and the two of them rode out.

The park was lit with the silvery unchanging light of Underhill. The air smelled of roses and apricots, and the world was filled with the singing of birds. In the middle distance, Beth could see another party, much larger than their own, lords and ladies out for a morning of hunting.

Beth had never been to the edge of the parklands that made up Elfhame Misthold—or rather, she had, but the magic had simply brought her back to the far side of the park, as if the whole place were somehow built on a Moebius strip, which for all she knew, it was. But today they were going through a Gate that would lead them into the world beyond.

Every Gate was essentially the same, Kory had told her, just as the essential magic of all the Lands Underhill was the same. Most Gates could be set to take their user to any of six "pre-set" destinations. Some could be set to open only to the proper code, others operated by anyone. You had to travel overland, hopscotching among friendly or neutral Gates, until you got to where you were going. Most of them led in and out of neutral or unclaimed territory; you couldn't just ride through a Gate and find yourself in the middle of somebody's living room. The Gate that led into someone's personal domain was usually well-guarded or well-defended—or both—and whoever was behind it would have a lot of warning that you were coming.

The Gate that led out of Elfhame Misthold was a golden archway—some long ago elfmage's pun on the Golden Gate, since Misthold's anchoring Nexus was in the San Francisco Bay Area—with an ornate design covering every inch of its surface. The space in the center of the archway shimmered faintly, like a curtain of gold chains. Two Sidhe in full armor stood before it. Once upon a time Beth had been surprised that with magic available for the asking, the Folk performed so many mundane tasks for themselves, like guarding doors and sweeping out stables, but at heart the Sidhe were warriors who knew that someday they might be called upon to fight. There were hames as decadent and luxurious as she could possibly imagine, and even hames where all the work was done by human changelings, but Misthold wasn't one of them.

Age and power seemed to radiate from the Misthold Gate. One of the knights saluted as they drew near.

"Fair morrow, Lord Korendil, Mistress Beth," he greeted them formally.

"Fair morrow, Sir Vinimene. My lady and I ride upon quest, at my lord Arvindel's good pleasure," Kory answered, equally formally.

"Quest well and come home safe," Vinimene answered. He stepped back, and Beth and Kory rode through.

She'd gone through Gates a lot of times, traveling between Earth and Underhill, but they'd always seemed to go from outdoors to indoors, or the other way around, and her mind had accepted the change. Here, it was as if the whole world vanished in an eyeblink. The flare of bright sunlight—sunlight?—caught her by surprise, and she swayed in the saddle just a little.

"Beth?"

"I'm okay. Just wasn't ready for it. Kind of weird, isn't it?"

"I remember being just as surprised the first time I saw a movie," Kory said fondly.

"But what's with the sun?" Beth asked, squinting up at it. "We aren't back on Earth, are we?"

The landscape resembled the park they'd just left—a little raggeder around the edges, the colors less bright, but still beautiful. She glanced over her shoulder. The Gate on this side was also golden, but smaller and plainer. It, too, was guarded by a set of armored knights.

"Perhaps in a land much closer to it than Underhill," Kory said, considering. "Or perhaps it is merely there for decoration. Either way, we will not be here long."

"Lead on, Kemosabe."

After riding for several hours, through a succession of Gates that led through some eye-poppingly strange places, Kory called a halt.

"We are here." He pointed.

It's the Faire! The old Faire—the one they bulldozed!

For a moment Beth's heart leapt with a pang that was not only homesickness, but nostalgia. The best parts of her young life had been spent at the Faire.

But when she looked again, she realized it wasn't *her* Faire. There was a scatter of brightly-colored tents and garlanded booths, and banners belled in the soft noontime breeze. But the longer she stared, the less it looked like the SoCal Faire, until she couldn't figure out how she'd ever confused the two.

"It's magic, isn't it?" she asked. "I mean, even more than usual."

"Yes." Kory didn't seem completely happy about it. "But we will take no harm here. Should a warrior meet his worst enemy at the Goblin Market, he must smile and pass him by. No weapon may be drawn in anger here, no power summoned to bind or harm a foe. Here is the place where all worlds meet. Even yours."

"I guess that's why it all looks so familiar," Beth joked, trying to conceal her unease.

"Do not trust it," Kory said. "The Goblin Market is . . ." He seemed to be at a loss for words. "It is a *neutral* place. In the human expression, 'proceed at your own risk.' If you come here, they feel you have accepted the risk."

"Gotcha," Beth said. "Lead on." She forced a smile, feigning a confidence she did not feel.

They entered the Market between two black-and-white striped posts—about eighteen feet tall and slender and straight as teenaged telephone poles. Kory turned Mach Five sharply left, riding along the edge of the fair until he reached what was obviously a parking lot of sorts. There were lines of hitching posts right out of the Old West, but the things hitched to them were anything but ordinary.

There were horses, both in the usual range of colors and in all the colors of the rainbow. Some she recognized as elvensteeds, others were ordinary horses, and some of them were neither one, but something else entirely in a horse's shape. But that wasn't the extent of the livestock. There were giant ostriches. Bridled lizards that hissed and snapped as the two of them passed. Even a hippogriff—half horse, half eagle.

Motorcycles. Bicycles. Hovercraft that looked like they'd been assembled by a mad Victorian inventor. A genuine antique Model A flivver painted a glaring yellow. A classic VW Beetle with an iridescent paint job. It flashed its headlights at them, but Beth was already staring past it, at a brass bed with ornate bed-knobs, complete down to the patchwork quilt and lace-trimmed pillows, that hovered several inches off the ground.

"I guess people come here from all over," Beth said in a strained voice. Next to the brass bed was a carousel horse that turned its head to watch them as they passed. Beyond it was a green tiger with purple stripes wearing a saddle and a glittering rhinestone collar.

"From everywhere there is," Kory answered. Beth was cheered to realize that he was staring just as hard as she was. "And from some places there aren't."

They found an empty post a safe distance from some of the more irritable mounts, and dismounted. The elvensteeds would stay unless summoned, and were more than capable of defending themselves.

"Hi, there. Need a guide?"

Beth stared. She was looking at a fox. A talking, five-foot-tall, cartoon-style fox. It was wearing a red James Dean jacket. Around its neck was a gold collar with a gold tag dangling from it. Engraved on the tag were the letters "FX."

"Special effect"? Oh, yeah. . . .

It swished its tail, and Beth blinked again. Not tail. *Tails.* Three of them, in fact.

"Allow me to introduce myself," the creature said, with a deep sweeping bow. *"I* am Foxtrot-X-ray. But you can call me Fox. Or you can call me handsome. Or you can call me adorable. Just call me, beautiful lady!"

"Uh, hi," Beth said, smiling in spite of herself. "Come here often?"

Kory had come to her side and was regarding Fox warily. Fox grinned, exposing a mouthful of gleaming teeth. "Hey, pretty lady, are you doubting my expertise?"

"No," Kory answered bluntly. "Only your sincerity."

"I'm hurt," Fox said, though he didn't sound it. "But if you'll pardon me for mentioning it, Sieur Sidhe, it's plain to see that this is your first time at our lovely fair, and I thought you might like a little help. No offense."

"And you would offer us this help freely?" Kory asked.

"Naw-w-w . . . but I figure, high-class folks like you, you might have a little something to make it worth my while. And I know where *everything* is. You could spend days wandering around here by yourselves."

"We don't—" Kory began. Beth put a hand on his arm. Hadn't Ria said to consult experts? If this creature was on the level, he could save them from spending a lot of time here, and Beth had the feeling that the less time they spent at the Fair, the better.

"I suppose you have references?" Beth asked.

"Absolutely!" Out of nowhere Fox produced a large parchment scroll tied with a bright red ribbon. He yanked the ribbon free, and the scroll unrolled.

And unrolled . . .

And unrolled. . . .

Beth walked over and peered down at it. It was covered in writing from many different hands, some of them even in English.

"Much have I travel'd in the realms of gold/And many goodly states and kingdoms seen;/Round many western islands have I been/Which bards in fealty to Apollo hold.—J. Keats." She read. *"He's the best there is at what he does, even if what he does sometimes isn't very nice.—W. Logan." "Down these mean streets a man must go who is not himself mean.—R. Chandler."*

"Ri-i-i-ight," Beth said, sighing. "C'mon, Kory."

"No, wait!" Fox yelped, jumping in front of them. The scroll vanished. "I'm one of the good guys! And you—you're those folks that saved the Sun-Descending Nexus, aren't you?"

There was a hiss as Kory's sword cleared its scabbard.

"Who asks?" the elven knight demanded in a low dangerous voice. Beth stared at him. Hadn't he said it was dangerous to draw steel at the fair?

Fox jumped back in terror or a good imitation, ears flat and eyes wide. "I've got friends—in the World Above. Friends of yours, too." He held his hands wide in a gesture of harmlessness.

"Names," Kory said, his blade still pointed at Fox's throat.

"Keighvin Silverhair—well, he's not really a friend of mine, but I do know somebody who knows him. Tannim. You know—he races cars at Elfhame Fairgrove?"

The names meant nothing to Beth, but they seemed to mean something to Kory. He sheathed his sword again and held out his hand. "The references again."

This time, Fox produced, not a scroll, but a perfectly mundane envelope, with the logo of a Holiday Inn on it. Kory opened the envelope and withdrew a single sheet of paper. Beth read over his shoulder.

"To whom it may concern: Fox is okay. —Tannim."

The words flared bright with magic, and slowly vanished from the page. Kory handed the paper and the envelope back to Fox.

"Very well. But I know your kind, kitsune. The fox kin are tricksters all," Kory said sternly.

"Yeah, but me, I got a soft spot in my heart for suckers," Fox snickered. "And you did say you'd pay."

Kitsune were Japanese fox-spirits, tricksters like Coyote or Raven. But the pranks they played were often harmless, and there were legends of them helping people in need, or so Beth had read.

"I said no such—" Kory stopped himself. "What do you want?"

Fox drew himself up with an elaborate display of unconcern. "Well, I couldn't help noticing when you rode in that you've got some fine trade items with you. Like . . . chocolate?" The kitsune licked its chops with a long pink tongue. "There's this girl I know. She's just crazy about chocolate, and I kind of thought . . ." He looked hopeful and abashed all at once, black-tipped ears swiveling out to the side. Beth wondered if that fur was as soft as it looked.

"If we give you chocolate, will you take us where we need— where we *want* to go?" Beth asked, catching herself just in time. One lesson that had stuck with her from all her fairy-tale reading was that the Fair Folk could be as literal-minded as any computer, and positively reveled in the chance to lead you into disaster by doing exactly what you said.

"Hey, pretty lady, I told you: I'm on the side of the angels. Give me chocolate, and I'm yours to command!" Fox said eagerly.

Beth turned back to Bredana and fumbled with the buckle on the saddlebag, reaching inside and pulling out one of the big Hershey bars. They'd brought smaller ones, but it didn't pay to be stingy. She tossed it to Fox, who examined it carefully, held it under his nose as if it were a fine cigar, and then tucked it away inside his jacket, regarding her brightly.

"We need to find an information specialist," she said carefully. "Someone with a lot of access and resources, who can do research on a project of ours and come up with answers. Trustworthy and reliable a plus."

"Woo-*hoo!*" Fox said. "You don't want much, do you? A research geek who stays bought. I might—might!—know someone like that."

"We don't care what you know," Kory interrupted. "You offered to guide us through the fair to where information about such a person can be found."

"O-kay, Mister Spock—meaning no offense, milord—" How Fox could grovel and look impudent at the same time was a mystery to Beth, but somehow the kitsune managed it. "If that's what you want, that's what you get." He bowed elaborately again, hand over his heart, tails lashing. "Follow me."

They followed Fox into the Fair, past a large sign that read "No Violence Beyond This Point." That explained why Kory had been able to get away with drawing his sword in the parking lot, at least.

The Market was a swirl of distraction and color. Beth held tight to Kory's hand, fearing to lose him in the crowds. This wasn't like

Elfland, where, weird as it was, everything seemed to be drawn from the same basic set of givens. The Sidhe were fond of experimenting with their forms, changing shape and size and color to suit a momentary whim, but here, a thousand totally-different realities rubbed shoulders. She saw men in medieval armor as elaborate as Kory's, and others in what she could only think of as space-armor, with blasters at their sides. There were anthropomorphic animals, things that looked like they'd walked right out of the Cantina scene of *Star Wars*, creatures whose bodies had the bright flatness of two-dimensional cartoons, and others that seemed to be humans (dressed in everything from feathers to blue jeans), or robots, and some who were both, like the woman whose body seemed to be made of golden rings, the featureless face dominated by a glowing turquoise bar where the eyes should have been. She moved with the grace of a dancer, and Beth craned her head to watch until she disappeared from sight.

But the fair-goers, exotic as they were, paled to normalcy beside the stalls of the vendors and the wares they sold. Half the stuff was so weird she couldn't even imagine what it was, other wares were so prosaic it was somehow an even greater shock—like the bookstall displaying a collection of paperbacks that wouldn't have been out of place on the shelves of any Barnes & Noble. The air was filled with smells—cooking food, fresh fruit, perfume, incense, wood smoke— and she heard scraps of music ranging from medieval to heavy metal.

Meanwhile, Fox led them on a twisting trail among the booths. To call their progress labyrinthine would be a grave insult to labyrinths everywhere. She lost all sense of direction after the first few turns, and could no longer tell where they were in relation to where they'd left the elvensteeds.

It was all too much. Beth clutched tighter at Kory's hand, feeling a familiar sense of vertigo and panic begin to overwhelm her. Everything was closing in, crushing her. . . .

No! Beth Kentraine, you are stronger than that! You've shopped at Macy's during the Christmas rush, by the Gods. You are not going to be gotten the better of by one lousy interdimensional Bazaar of the Bizarre!

She took a deep breath and held it, willing the panic to fade. Fox appeared at her side, looking worried.

"You okay?" he asked anxiously.

Kory stopped, looking at her questioningly. She could see fear in his eyes—whether for her, or of the Fair, or both, she wasn't sure. Beth let her held breath out slowly, willing calm.

"It's a little much," she said, and was pleased that her voice was steady.

"There's no place like this place anywhere near this place, so this place must be the place," Fox answered gaily. "Chin up, pretty lady. We're almost there. And you look like you could use a drink."

"A good stiff one," Beth muttered to herself.

They'd been moving in toward the center of the Fair, where tents replaced the booths and were mixed with more permanent structures.

"Up ahead," Fox said, pointing.

Surfeited with wonders, and used as she was to the Underhill habit of co-opting bits of the World Above and turning them to their own uses, she still wasn't prepared for what she saw when she looked where Fox was pointing. At the end of the lane was a large stucco building in a Moorish style. Its wooden double doors were studded with large square hobnails, and over the door was a blue neon sign that said "Rick's Cafe Americain."

It looked exactly like the Warner's set.

"Everybody goes to Rick's," she and Fox said in chorus. He looked hurt, as if she'd stepped on his punch-line.

"*Casablanca* used to be one of my favorite movies," Beth said darkly. *Humphrey Bogart, where are you when we need you?*

"Hey, *I* didn't design it," Fox protested. "But this is what you guys said you wanted."

"A place to find the specialist we need?" Kory asked suspiciously.

"Rick knows everything that happens at the Market, and a lot of other places, too," Fox said. "He'll know where you can find this researcher—or someone else there will."

Beth looked at Kory and shrugged. She guessed a bar was as good a place as any to start looking, especially when you weren't quite sure what you were looking for.

As they watched, the doors opened, and a large white rabbit stepped out, blinking at the daylight. He was wearing an elaborate waistcoat, with an ornate watch chain hooked across the front. He pulled a large gold watch from his pocket and gazed at it, then hurried off muttering to himself.

"Come on," Beth said.

"Uh-uh. This is where I leave you," Fox answered. "I'm not . . . well, let's say that Rick would prefer I didn't come inside after what happened the last time. You know how it is."

"The letters of transit are hidden in Sam's piano," Beth said cryptically.

"And Rosebud was his sled," Fox answered, mixing movies with gleeful relish. "Well, see you around."

"Be sure of that, if you've led us astray," Kory answered.

Fox vanished with a pop, like a soap bubble in a cartoon. A moment later, just his head reappeared, floating in midair like a fanciful balloon. "And don't say I didn't warn you," it said, and vanished.

"Although he didn't," Kory footnoted. "Though the Market itself is warning enough, I think."

"I thought I told you *not* to say that!" Fox reappeared, shaking a finger at them warningly and vanishing again instantly.

Beth shook her head, sighing. "Is everything here like him?" *I don't think I can deal with Life As Sitcom.*

"We'll see, won't we?" Kory answered. He took her hand once more, and the two of them walked up to the door.

It took a moment for Beth's eyes to adjust to the gloom, but once she did, they widened. The inside had no connection to the tumble-down exterior, nor to the movie *Casablanca*. It was several times larger than the outside, for one thing. For another, it looked like the unnatural liaison of an MGM musical and a Turkish bordello.

The central area directly ahead was filled with small round tables swathed in immaculate white linen, most of them occupied. Beyond them was a dance floor that looked as if it had been carved from one giant slab of blue goldstone. Its surface glittered like a starfield, and behind it stood a bandstand with an old-fashioned stand mike and a glistening white piano. To the right, the wall was lined with a series of curtained alcoves, their gold draperies shimmering. Some of the curtains were drawn back—Beth couldn't see the occupants very well, but she could see glowing eyes in a variety of colors—and arrangements—and pulled her gaze quickly away.

To her left was the bar—a long glowing sweep of something that looked like purple mahogany. Behind it stood the barkeep, in white dinner jacket and black bow tie, rubbing the surface with an immaculate polishing cloth. He looked just like Humphrey Bogart—if Humphrey Bogart had bright blue skin, long pointed ears and a ponytail.

"That must be Rick," Kory said. Beth nodded. *Okay, it's official. I've sprained my Sense of Wonder. . . .*

As they stood there, two men passed them, leaving. One was huge, muscled like Arnold Schwarzenegger. He had bright red hair and a beard, and was dressed in bearskins and a long red cloak. His companion barely came to his elbow, as small and slender as the other was huge, and dressed all in gray, down to his hooded cloak.

"I told you we shouldn't have come here, little man," Redbeard said.

"Ah, where's your sense of adventure? Even a barbarian like you—" the rest of Greycloak's rejoinder was lost as they exited.

Funny. Those guys look almost familiar. . . .

"Come on," Kory said. He led Beth to the bar, where they found seats between a red-headed woman carrying a sword and dressed in a bikini that seemed to be made entirely out of silver disks and a six-foot ferret wearing a gold collar and drinking tea in the Russian style.

"What'll you have?" Rick approached them.

"Water," Kory answered, pushing a gold coin across the gleaming wood.

"Lemonade," Beth said. "And information."

"Ah. Drink I've always got." The barkeep brought two tall glasses and a black bottle from beneath the bar, making the coins vanish at the same time. He poured both glasses full—but while Kory's glass was full of clear still water, Beth's was filled with lemonade, sliced lemons, and ice.

"Neat trick," she said.

"It passes the time," Rick said, smiling Bogie's crooked smile. His teeth were long and white and very pointed. "Oh, by the way. A friend left this for you. Said you'd be wanting it."

Beth stared at the blue ceramic ashtray for a minute before the penny dropped. She giggled. "Fox didn't lead us a-stray. He led us to an *ash*tray. . . ." *Incorrigible punster: do not incorrige.*

She missed the little critter already. Almost.

"And information?" Kory asked.

"Well, now, that depends," Rick drawled. "On who's asking, and what for. Don't believe everything you've heard about this place."

"What I heard is that here we might be able to find a research specialist. We are looking for information."

"If you can't find it in an Elfhame, that must be some information," Rick said. "Well, this is the Cafe Americain. You may find what you're looking for. 'Scuse me." He moved quickly down the bar toward a new customer.

Beth picked up her lemonade. Frost was forming on the glass. She sipped. Tart and sweet, not too much sugar, just the way she liked it. "I wonder what he'd have done if I asked for coffee?" she asked idly.

"Brought you a cup," Kory said. "Or if you had asked for Coca-Cola, or the Red Wine of Hengist, or ambrosia, or human blood. The laws of other realms do not apply here."

"Um," Beth said. An anarchist's paradise—no law but your own common sense. But freedom was a double-edged sword. If you could do anything you wanted, you could manage to get yourself into real trouble, too, with no one and nothing to get you out.

Several musicians had moved onto the stage and were setting up their instruments—a full-sized concert harp, a cello, violins, and a flute. They were all dressed in the height of 17th-century fashion, in lace, pink satin, and powdered wigs, but not one of them was human. There was a badger, a frog, something that looked more like an owl than not—although it had hands and fingers—a sheep, and some others whose species she couldn't place from what she saw. Once everything was arranged, they began to play. The music matched their garb, stately and baroque. Several couples got up from their tables and moved onto the dance floor.

Rick didn't look like he was coming back their way any time soon. "Why don't we go get one of the tables?" Beth suggested. "I'd kind of like to watch the floor show." She picked up her glass.

The entertainment at Rick's was certainly eclectic. The chamber-music group was followed by a black-leather-garbed crooner doing vintage rockabilly, but in a language Beth didn't know. His face was long and lupine—not quite a wolf, but not human either. More like a B-movie werewolf than anything else, Beth decided.

"You the folks lookin' for help?"

The speaker had slipped into a vacant chair while Beth was watching the stage. She looked—though by now Beth doubted anything here was exactly what it seemed—like a teenaged girl, and though it was hard to hear beneath the music, Beth thought she spoke English with a pronounced American accent. She had fire-engine-red hair with a silver streak in the front; it hung in an unkempt shoulder-length mop, and her eyes were the bright foil-green of Christmas paper. She was wearing a white T-shirt, a black vest, Levis, and motorcycle boots with spurs. Strapped to one leg was a battered and clangingly futuristic firearm.

"We're looking for information," Kory answered warily.

"Same dif." The girl signaled a waitress, who hurried over and set a drink in front of the girl. The drink was pink, with a paper parasol stuck in the top, and it smoked. The waitress hovered pointedly until Kory handed over another gold coin.

"So. Why don'cha tell me a little about yourselves?" The girl picked up her drink—she was wearing white leather driving gloves—and sipped daintily, wincing. "This stuff'll kill you."

"I am Sieur Korendil of Elfhame Misthold, and this is my lady, Beth Kentraine."

"Pleased ta. You can call me Cho-cho. What kind of information?"

"Can you help us find it?" Beth asked.

"Depends. You're Seleighe Court, right? I don't do business with the other guys."

"Would you believe us if we said we were? If we were of the Dark Court, we'd lie," Kory pointed out.

"You lie to me, buster, and you don't get a chance to do it twice," Cho-cho said. "I got connections." For a moment she seemed to shimmer, and Beth felt a flash of cold, as if someone had opened the door to a walk-in freezer. "But we'll take that as a 'yes.' Now. Here's the giggy. You tell me what you want, the more details the better, and I tell you if I can supply it. Then we argue about the price."

"Fair enough, Mistress Cho-cho," Kory answered. "Beth?"

Beth took a deep breath. Telling Ria her problem had been hard enough, but telling this total stranger was downright embarrassing.

"Kory and I want to have a baby together. More than one, actually."

"Mazel tov," Cho-cho said, sipping her drink. "There's more?"

"It takes magic. But the only methods we've been able to find are . . . Unseleighe," Beth said delicately. "We're looking for another way. So we need help. Research help."

"Huh. You wanna find something out, ask a librarian. Or somebody with a library." Cho-cho smiled, as if at a private joke.

"Do you know someone possessing such resources who would be willing to help us?" Kory asked.

"You need another drink," Cho-cho said. She signaled the waitress and turned away from them to watch the stage.

A waitress brought their drinks. The wolf-boy left the stage, to be replaced by a torch singer and her accompanist. The singer was wheeled out onto the stage in a large crystal fishbowl, her silvery tail glinting in the houselights. Her accompanist was a satyr—Chippendales dancer above, goat below. His horns were gilded, and his eyes were elaborately painted in the Egyptian style. The mermaid reached out of her bowl to grasp the mike and began to sing: "Stormy Weather."

Cho-cho sat through a medley of Cole Porter hits in silence. Finally she turned back to them.

"I got a line on a guy," she said. "If he don't know it, he can find it. Whether he'll help, that's between you and him, but he's got a kind of soft spot for humans with problems, and he's on the side of the angels, more or less. What you pay me don't cover what you'll owe him. I can tell you where to find him, that's all."

Beth glanced at Kory. His face was unreadable.

Was this a good idea? A stranger who could help, but might not? On the other hand, she didn't see anyone else lining up to help them. She nodded ever so slightly.

"And your price for this information—his name and his location both?" Kory asked.

"What've you got?" Cho-cho asked with interest.

"Gold?"

She snorted. "I can make that myself."

"Coffee?"

"I look like a wire-head to you, Mister Korendil?"

Kory shrugged. Neither of them knew what a "wire-head" might be, but it seemed to eliminate coffee as a bargaining chip. "I take it then that you would find neither chocolate nor Coca-Cola suitable either?"

For a moment she looked wistful, then shook her head firmly. "Can't use 'em."

"You must have something in mind," Beth said, playing a hunch.

"Sure. Depends on if your friend'll go for it, though."

Kory regarded the girl inquiringly.

"Safe passage through the elven lands."

So it all comes down to "Letters of Transit" in the end, Beth thought wryly. She wasn't sure how big a deal that was, and Kory's face gave nothing away, but Beth thought he'd twitched, just a little.

"And I to stand surety for whatever you do there," Kory said through gritted teeth.

"I don't want to do anything there," Cho-cho said. "All I want . . ." She stopped. "I just want to go home. They need me there."

"Wherever 'home' is, there are other avenues to reach it," Kory said. "From here, you can go anywhere."

Cho-cho shook her head. "You know how it is. 'You can't get there from here'? Believe me, I've tried, for longer than the two of you have been on this earth, kids. The only clear way is through the elven lands . . . and I'd rather not mess with the Dark Court. We got a history, y'see."

Everybody here seemed to have a history of one kind or another. "And where is home?" Beth asked.

Cho-cho grimaced. "You pay for that info, too, if you really want it, and I don't think you can afford it."

"You ask a high price for your help," Kory said.

"You don't have anything else I want," Cho-cho said simply. "Maybe someone else here wants what you got. And maybe they don't have anything *you* want. Your choice."

Impasse. The two parties stared across the table at each other, neither willing to give in.

"If I were to give you a letter of safe conduct—under guard—to my lord, Prince Arvindel of Elfhame Misthold, you might plead your case to him. More I will not do. Nor," Kory added, smiling a wolflike smile, "can I guarantee he will hear you, should he know more of you than I."

There was a long pause. Beth held her breath, afraid that Cho-cho would get up and walk away. "It isn't much," the girl grumbled.

"Nor is what you offer us. Only hope, no more."

"Okay," she said, putting both hands on the table. "We have a deal. You don't mind if I get the goods up front, do you?"

"I would expect nothing less," Kory answered.

Cho-cho snapped her fingers, and an iridescent lizard-maiden with improbable gauzy butterfly wings came over to the table. She had a tray slung around her neck, like the cigarette girls in old-time nightclubs. Beth couldn't see what it held.

"Pen, ink, paper, and seals," Cho-cho said.

It must have been an ordinary sort of request, because the lizard-woman produced the objects without hesitation from among the contents of her tray. Cho-cho pointed, and she set them in front of Kory. He dipped the pen into the inkwell and wrote: the letters sparkled and seemed to sink into the vellum as he inscribed them flourishingly. When he was done, he took off his seal-ring and picked up one of the disks of wax. He placed it on the paper and touched it with a finger. It softened and glistened, suddenly hot, and he pressed the ring into it until the wax began to harden.

Cho-cho reached for it. Kory didn't let go.

"Now you."

Cho-cho sighed. "Okay. This guy I know . . . you know anything about dealing with dragons?"

"Are you sure this is the right place?" Beth asked, quite a long time later.

They were standing in the middle of . . . nothing. Grey river mist surrounded them, thick and warm. It smelled like jasmine. The ground beneath the elvensteeds' hooves was covered with thick white sand. It sparkled whenever the sun broke through the mist above.

It was morning—again. They'd passed through so many different time zones that Beth wasn't completely sure how much time had passed. Elves didn't need sleep, of course, but she had the jet-laggy feeling that it was two million o'clock in the morning. If she fell asleep, Bredana would see to it that she didn't fall off, but Beth was hoping for a real bed. And soon.

Cho-cho had given them a name—Chinthliss—and drawn them a map. Or more precisely, she'd drawn an arrow on a map, but the arrow always pointed in the direction they needed to go. Ahead of them stood a Gate. Kory had examined it. It held only one destination, and Kory thought it led directly into the dragon's lair. Apparently this Chinthliss didn't mind being easy to find, and Beth knew enough about the Underhill way of doing things to know that meant he had power—power enough to deal with any enemies who might come calling.

He also seemed to have a sense of humor.

She looked at the sign that stood beside the Gate again. It was battered and weathered. Painted on it in English in big black letters were the words: "I'd turn back if I were you. Signed, the Management."

"Fair enough," Beth said aloud. "But we aren't going to."

The Gate itself was huge—two stories high, and wide enough to drive a matched team of semis through—and solid bronze. The decoration seemed to be more Oriental than anything else, flowers and birds and branching trees.

"But we *are* going to be very careful," Kory said seriously. "Dragons are very particular about matters of etiquette. It would not do to annoy him."

"Best behavior and company manners," Beth agreed. She yawned, unable to stifle it.

They dismounted, and led their horses forward past the sign. There was a large square red button at doorbell height at the edge of the frame. Beth was pretty sure it hadn't been there a moment ago. She looked closer. There was writing on it, one word: ENTER.

"Press 'Enter,' " Beth said. Something with this kind of a sense of humor couldn't be *all* bad, could it?

Kory pressed the button. With a shudder that seemed to shake the world, the great bronze doors swung inward, opening into mist. Kory reached out and took her hand, and slowly they walked forward, leading the horses.

They were in a hall. Its scale made the doors they'd just come through look petite. The walls were yellow, lined with enormous pillars painted Chinese red, and the floor was black. Burning torches in bronze baskets lined the walls, their glow almost lost in the chamber's vast dimensions. The air smelled of incense. Several football fields of distance away, a long flight of shallow stairs led to a curtained archway. On each step stood a large porcelain cache pot, each filled with a full-sized flowering tree. They were completely alone, and nobody seemed to be rushing to welcome them.

"Now what?" Beth asked in a whisper.

"Now we offer gifts and wait, most respectfully, for that is the first rule when dealing with dragons." Kory turned to Mach Five and opened his saddlebags. He began piling the trade goods they'd brought on the floor in front of them. Beth emptied her saddlebags as well. Four six-packs of Coke, twenty pounds of Hershey bars, and several large bags of whole-bean Jamaica Blue Mountain coffee. They looked very odd sitting in the middle of the floor of a dragon's temple.

"Great Chinthliss," Kory said after a few moments, "please grace us with your presence. We have traveled far to seek your wise counsel."

The curtains opened, and a slender man stepped out and slowly began to walk down the stairs. He was wearing an impeccable Armani business suit in a deep rich bronze, and instead of a regular necktie, a bolo tie around his neck, held closed with a bronze jewel at the throat.

Uh-oh. Looks like he's sending in the high-priced lawyers.

As the man came closer, Beth could see that he had skin the color of old ivory and brilliant amber eyes. His gleaming black hair was almost waist-length, brushed straight back from a high forehead and a deep widow's peak, and his topaz eyes gleamed from beneath heavy lids. He looked vaguely but not entirely Oriental. More like . . .

A brow like Shakespeare and eyes like a tiger . . . Holy Mother, we're having tea with Fu Manchu!

"Enchanté, madame," he said, bowing over her hand. His shirt was linen, with French cuffs, and the cuff links and the slide of the bolo tie both were in the same design: a curled bronze dragon with gleaming amber eyes. He smelled faintly of burning cinnamon. "How lovely to make the acquaintance of one so fair."

He turned to Korendil, who inclined his head respectfully. "Lord Chinthliss."

"*He's* the dragon?" Beth blurted, unable to stop herself.

Chinthliss regarded her, one eyebrow raised. Though his expression was bland, Beth could swear he was laughing at her.

"Does my appearance disappoint you, fair lady?" he asked mildly.

"I was expecting someone taller," Beth said, startled into bluntness by lack of sleep.

"Like this?"

The man was gone, his form dissolving like mist. In his place stood a dragon. A very big dragon. A gleaming bronze dragon big enough to fill the entire hall. His tail snaked up the stairs, its tip hidden behind the curtain, and his mantled wings brushed the walls. He lowered his head—it was the size of a bus—down to Beth's eye level, and regarded her with glowing yellow eyes. Tendrils of steam curled from his nostrils, and Beth could feel heat radiating from him as if from a stove.

"Um . . . yeah," she said weakly. "That'll do."

The dragon bared its teeth in a draconic grin.

"Excellent. I would hate to disappoint so fair a guest." The dragon was gone, and in his place stood the Oriental gentleman once more. "But you have come a long way and are weary from your journey. Please. Allow me to offer you the poor comforts of my little house. We can discuss your business after you have rested." He snapped his fingers. Two women appeared, dressed in full kimono. Except for the fact that they were slightly transparent, they looked as if they'd just stepped out of a Japanese scroll painting. "My servants will see to your animals."

The geisha took the elvensteeds' reins and led the horses toward the wall, vanishing before they reached it.

"Come." Chinthliss beckoned, smiling.

They followed him back up the long flight of stairs. Beyond the curtain was . . . a palace. High windows opened onto vistas of exquisite gardens that seemed to stretch into infinity. The walls were covered with painted murals done with such skill that it was hard to tell where the real garden ended and the painted one began. Beth tried not to gawk.

"I trust you will find these poor accommodations to your liking," Chinthliss said, stopping in front of another set of double doors. These were of sandalwood, carved and oiled until they gleamed like gold. They opened at a touch.

"Thank you," Beth said. "You're very kind."

The dragon smiled. "And now I will leave you. Do not hesitate to summon any of my servants to see to your needs." He bowed.

Beth stepped inside, Kory following. The suite was decorated with as much lavish ornamentation as the rest of the palace, but was obviously scaled to human size and needs. There were Western-style couches and chairs, a bookcase filled with books, and at the far end of the room stood an enormous canopy bed. Golden dragons twined about its ebony posts, and the hangings were all of scarlet silk embroidered in gold. In the center of the room stood a table filled with covered dishes. Whatever they contained smelled wonderful.

"My," Beth said.

"We are safe, for now," Kory said. His sword and armor had vanished, and he was dressed in more ordinary clothes. He approached the table and lifted one of the silver covers.

"Hey, look at this!" Beth had gone through the doorway to the right of the bed. She was standing in a bathroom that any Roman emperor would have killed for. A tub big enough to do laps in stood in the middle of the room. "Big enough for two," she said invitingly, when Kory joined her.

"Yes." Kory put an arm around her. "Why not? It would be churlish of us not to accept what is offered." He walked over to the tub and touched one of the taps—gold, in the shape of a leaping dolphin. Water immediately began jetting from it, filling the tub with hot water and perfumed bubbles. "And then you will eat and rest," he said firmly.

"And after that, business."

Beth couldn't remember the last time she'd slept so well and so deeply. She awoke in the morning—or at least, after long slumber—to the smell of bacon and eggs, and sat up in bed to see more of the semi-transparent servants laying the table for breakfast.

"Good morning," Kory said, sitting down on the bed beside her. "Did you sleep well?"

Elves didn't sleep—not under normal conditions, at any rate. More time for them to get into trouble, Beth had always thought, but lately she'd started to wonder what it was really like to have all that free time. It was almost as if Kory had a secret life, one she couldn't be any part of.

She yawned and stretched, banishing all such vague morning thoughts. "Did you have a good night?"

"The tea was hot, and the books were entertaining," Kory answered seriously. "And I had a great deal of time to think. Dragons are . . . experts at solving the problem we face. He can help us, I think, if he will."

"But what will he want for his help?" Beth said. Kory stood, and she swung her legs over the edge of the bed. "That's the real question, isn't it? Whether we can afford to pay?"

"For your happiness—for Maeve's—I will pay any price, but—"

"But some prices are too high," Beth finished firmly. Nothing that would endanger the elves, or anyone else for that matter. "Well, we'll see."

One of the nice things about magic was that the food was always hot, Beth reflected. They were just finishing—bacon and eggs, blueberry pancakes with real maple syrup, fresh-squeezed orange juice, herb tea—when there was a knock at the door. It opened, and instead of one of the little flowerlike geisha, the travelers were presented with the awesome sight of a Real English Butler in full formal livery.

"Good morning, Lord Korendil, Mistress Bethany. May I trust that you have found everything to your satisfaction?" His accent was as English as the BBC.

"Of course," Kory said graciously. "And we are looking forward to speaking with your master at his earliest convenience."

The butler bowed. "I believe Lord Chinthliss is in the conservatory at this hour. If you would care to accompany me to his receiving room, I shall inform him that you are awake."

Chinthliss's receiving room bore a strong resemblance to the library of an English country gentleman. There was an Oriental rug on the floor, and the oak-paneled walls were lined in books. A massive desk with a top carved from a single slab of green malachite dominated the area before the windows, which gave a magnificent view of a formal garden. If the view didn't match that available from the other windows, Beth didn't mind. This was magic, after all.

As they had been left to their own devices, she wandered around the room. There were some surprises: the elaborate stereo system tucked into one corner—

Nakamichi. Nice. I wonder how he runs it down here without electricity?

The silver-framed photos on the walls were another thing that didn't quite fit in with Beth's notions of a feudal draconic sorcerer: most of them were of race-car drivers, and signed.

Tannim Drake . . . Brian Simo . . . Doc Bundy . . . Fox mentioned someone named Tannim was a friend of Chinthliss . . . can't see Fox driving a race car, somehow.

She looked again at the black-haired young man, caught in the act of giving a grinning thumbs-up in front of his car. The words "Fairgrove Test Driver" could be seen on his coveralls. She'd heard of Elfhame Fairgrove. *I guess Eric and I aren't the only ones who've fallen in with elvish companions.*

Hanging near the picture of Tannim was a carved rosewood shrine, its doors standing open. Inside, on a small purple velvet pillow, stood another incongruous item: a Ford key, with a Mustang logo key chain. Obviously this was an item the dragon cherished. *I don't suppose I'll ever find out the story behind all this.*

The door of the study opened, and Chinthliss entered. He was dressed as he had been before, in the height of Western fashion, and this morning had added a set of lightly-mirrored designer shades to his ensemble. You could have dropped him anywhere in Hollywood and not raised a single eyebrow.

"My young friends. I trust you are now refreshed from your journey?" He crossed the room and seated himself behind the vast desk. "And now, what is it that I can do for you? Please, be frank."

How can I be Frank when I'm already Beth? she thought, but while she would certainly have answered Fox that way, Chinthliss seemed far too dignified to descend to the level of a punning contest. She and Kory sat on the chairs arranged in front of the desk.

"I— I'm not sure where to begin," Beth said hesitantly. She glanced at Kory. He shrugged minutely.

"I always find it is best to begin at the beginning," Chinthliss told her.

Begin at the beginning, go on till you get to the end, then stop. Humpty-Dumpty's advice to Alice echoed through her mind.

C'mon, Kentraine. You've made harder speeches. Beth took a deep breath and began.

Haltingly, she explained the whole story—about meeting Kory for the first time, her desire to start a family with him, about Maeve, and wanting her to grow up with brothers and sisters around her. It seemed to take a long time to tell, and Beth found herself rambling. Finally she stopped.

"And you, Sieur Korendil?" the dragon asked. "Do you concur?"

"All that she says is true," Kory said. A look of wistfulness crossed his face. "To have children—children of our own . . . that would be a blessing such as I had never hoped for, before I met Beth. Yet some prices are too high to pay."

"Perenor didn't think so," the dragon observed.

"Perenor was wrong," Kory said flatly. "To create new life, yes. But not at the expense of the suffering and death of others."

"Agreed," the dragon said. "And I'm delighted to tell you that my library *does* contain the information you seek."

"So all we have to do is get inside," Beth said.

Chinthliss raised his eyebrows, and said nothing.

He's waiting for us to offer him something.

Beth thought hard. What could she possibly offer someone of Chinthliss' resources? He didn't need money, that was for sure, and she doubted there was anything the elves could do for him that he couldn't do for himself.

She had an idea.

"That's a pretty nice music system you've got there."

Chinthliss preened. "A gift from a friend."

"Kind of hard to get CDs here, though, isn't it?" she asked idly. "Oh, well, I guess Amazon can ship just about anywhere, these days. And there's always MP3s."

"Alas." Chinthliss looked regretful. "I regret to say that even with all my arts, it has so far been impossible for me to get Internet access here. Computers, you see . . ." He shrugged.

Gotcha! Beth crowed silently.

The horse trading began in earnest.

Chinthliss insisted they remain his guests for the rest of the day, but the following morning saw Beth and Kory on the road once more, headed back for Elfhame Misthold. Without the need to make the side trip to the Goblin Market, the trip home should be relatively short and uneventful.

"This is great!" Beth said. "Chinthliss' library contains everything ever written about cross-species reproduction—and he'll let us spend as much time there as we need."

"Once we have met his price," Kory reminded her. "A computer that works Underhill—how are you ever going to deliver such a thing?"

"If his Nakamichi works there, a computer will, too. Computers are mostly plastic these days, and the newest models don't need a phone line to hook up to the net." Beth grinned, sensing victory within her grasp. "All I need to know is where to shop and what to buy. As for finding that out . . . I'm going to consult another expert."

EIGHT:
IT'S A SATURDAY NIGHT
AT THE WORLD

Just as promised, the elvensteeds returned Eric and Ria to the World Above the same day they'd left—or, rather, very late that same night. Eric had never been so grateful for Lady Day's autopilot abilities: he'd done a lot more playing—and dancing—after the Bardic competition. And it *had* been a competition as much as a performance, he'd found to his chagrin. Adroviel had led all the performers back out onto the stage to take their bows before the company—and then presented Eric with the golden laurel crown.

After that, the evening had been pretty much a blur, though alcohol wasn't to blame for that this time. But, as Eric had discovered, ambient magic could have much the same effect. . . .

He barely remembered saying good night to Ria at the door to her Park Avenue apartment, and remembered nothing at all after that until he awoke in his own bed with Sunday morning sun shining down on him.

Jumbled unreal memories of leaving Lady Day in the parking lot behind the building, of tiptoeing in past the sleeping Hosea and somehow getting his boots off before he flung himself in bed, surfaced as he lay looking at the ceiling. He was still wearing his Court clothes, and investigation proved that he'd gone to bed with both sword and flute.

But it'd been a heckuva party.

Just so long as there isn't another one any time soon, he thought, stretching. *Visits to Underhill are fine, so long as they're just that . . . visits.*

He checked the bedside clock as he rolled out of bed: 11:30. Not too bad for the morning after a late night. He could hear Hosea moving around the apartment. He'd better pull himself together so they could hit up a few of the better gigging sites. There'd be another audition soon, so Hosea could get a performer's license of his own, but not until the middle of August, still a couple of weeks away.

And August means the Sterling Forest Faire will be opening. I wonder if I should make arrangements to play up there for a couple of weekends? It would be fun to introduce Hosea to the Rennie world, and with a little Bardic magic, some of Eric's outfits would fit the Appalachian Bard.

Thinking about Bards made Eric remember Dharniel's comments last night. He wondered how Hosea would take to the idea of being taught by Eric—there was a lot more about his past he'd have to come clean with Hosea about, if he did. He wasn't sure how he felt about that.

I can think about it later.

He stripped off his Court clothes, flinging them into the back of the closet, grabbed his robe, and headed for the shower. When he came out a few minutes later, wet and dripping, he felt a lot more "grounded on the Earth plane," as Beth's friend Kit always used to say.

"Morning," Hosea said, as Eric wandered into the kitchen. "Must've been a pretty fine party last night." He held out Eric's laurel garland.

"Um . . . thanks." Eric took it. The leaves were made of pure gold, twined with a silver ribbon on which elvish letters burned with blue fire. Not your ordinary sort of party favor.

How do I explain this? How do I explain any of this? Suppose Hosea doesn't want me for a teacher?

He tucked the crown under one arm awkwardly.

"There's coffee brewing. Looks like you could use a cup. Oh, and someone named Margot came by and dropped off something for you. Looks like a letter."

Although with Margot one can never be sure. Eric cracked wise, if only to himself. He'd been Overhill long enough now to have gotten back his coffee habits—and had already needed the caffeine more than once. "I'll look at it after I get dressed," he said, and made a less-than-graceful exit from the conversation.

Dressed, caffeinated, and with the last evidence of his Underhill sojourn tucked safely out of sight, Eric adjourned to the living room, where Hosea was reading a book. He set his cup down on the coffee table and picked up the envelope.

It said "Eric" on it in bright purple calligraphic ink, and the envelope was liberally dusted with spray-on glitter. Definitely a Margot touch. It wasn't sealed. He opened it and pulled out a glittery violently purple sheet of paper.

"Calling the Usual Suspects: Lammas Party Next Saturday! 7:00 till Sanity intercedes! Bring yourself, bring a friend, bring munchies! Venue: the Basement!"

Every few weeks most of the building's tenants got together for a sort of informal mixer down in the building's basement. While only a minority of Guardian House's tenants were Wiccan, the eight festivals of the Wiccan year fell approximately 45 days apart, making a convenient schedule for parties.

Eric passed the flyer to Hosea. "You're certainly welcome to come—the building is mostly artists, so we tend to show off our latest work, play a little music, unwind a bit."

"Sure," Hosea said, passing it back. "Be mighty nice to meet a few more of the neighbors."

Hard to believe I was in Elfland just a week ago today, Ria thought, staring down at the mound of work on her desk. All the glamour—in the oldest sense of the word—seemed pretty far away when she was staring at the latest pile of paperwork on her desk. And she'd cross-her-heart promised to show up at a party Eric's friends were having at Guardian House later tonight.

Not her usual sort of entertainment; Ria's tastes ran more to the thoroughly civilized, such as ballet and opera. But there was no denying that Eric's friends were likely to be an engaging crowd . . . and that Eric was the main attraction.

Their relationship was an interesting one . . . doomed, you might say. Eric was a thoroughgoing do-gooder and idealist, believing, like Spider-Man, that with great power came great responsibility. Ria was more of a pragmatist: stone-cold dead cuts recidivism by 100%.

And they were opposites in so many other ways, too. She thought Eric was too trusting. He thought she was paranoid. She liked a mannered, organized life. Eric Banyon was the original free spirit. She thought that discipline was the most important thing about making your way through life. Eric thought that Love conquered all. LlewellCo—a billion-dollar multinational—was her entire life. Eric had no idea what he was going to do with his life once he got out of Juilliard. Ria hobnobbed with presidents and kings. Eric hung out with elves and street musicians.

Insurmountable. But somehow they were making it work—so long as each of them took care not to step too far into the other's life. But how long could they keep up this balancing act? Eventually Eric would be done with his schooling, and she'd be done with her work on the East Coast. What then?

You're daydreaming like a schoolgirl, Ria. She sighed, shaking her head, and reached for the file in front of her.

The phone rang. Ria reached for her desk phone before she realized her cellular was ringing. She'd set it to roll over calls from the apartment. But who could be calling?

"Ria Llewellyn."

"Ria? It's Elizabet."

Elizabet Winters was the Healer who had saved Ria's life. In mundane life, Elizabet was a psych therapist with the LAPD, dealing with crime victims and other trauma cases. She and her apprentice and adopted daughter, Kayla Smith, had brought Ria back from coma and insanity in the wake of the battle for Elfhame Sun-Descending.

"Elizabet!" she said warmly. "How wonderful to hear from you. Are you in town?"

The other woman chuckled. "No such luck. I'm stuck behind my desk with an ever burgeoning caseload. No, I'm calling about Kayla. I wanted to let you know that she's decided to take you up on your offer. I think its fair to warn you that the child still has champagne tastes."

Ria laughed. "So she's decided on a college and a major? Where?"

"Columbia," Elizabet said. "She got the acceptance letter last week. They've got a good computer school. She's thought the matter over carefully and decided she wants to train to be a Web designer."

"Well, she'll never lack for employment," Ria answered. More to the point, Web designer was a solitary profession with odd hours. Though Kayla's great Gift was Healing, you couldn't set yourself up as a free-lance medic without running into legal trouble, and even if Kayla'd had the patience, taking a medical degree to legitimate her skills would have been nothing more than a quick trip to early burnout or even death. A Healer and Empath needed a lot of time alone to process the pain from those she touched. There were going to be a lot of times when she'd really need to get away from people altogether, and Web designer would be a career where she could tailor both her hours and her interactions with others.

"And certainly I can cover her tuition. Just have the billing office get in touch with me. Which dorm will she be in?"

"Well, that's another thing I wanted to talk to you about." Elizabet sounded hesitant. "Columbia doesn't really have a lot of student housing, and I'm not really sure I'd be all that comfortable with Kayla around a couple of hundred other teenagers. She's a great kid, and of course she wrote the book on street smarts, but I think sometimes that we just tend to forget that she *is* a kid. I was hoping more for a situation where she'd have some adult supervision."

I think I know where this is going. Of course Elizabet was right—dropping an Empath into a cauldron of teenaged angst would be like dropping a firecracker into a tank of gas, personality issues aside. And Ria owed both Kayla and Elizabet so much that anything she could do in return would never be enough.

"I'll be happy to keep an eye on her," Ria said. "I've got a huge apartment that I hardly ever see. I'll be glad to have her stay with me."

Elizabet let out a sigh of relief. "I was hoping you'd say that," she said. "I know that babysitting a teenager is nobody's idea of fun . . ."

"Kayla's hardly your typical teen. And street-smart or not, she's never seen anything like New York before. Here, I'll give you my home address. Just crate her stuff up and ship it when you're ready. I'll be sure to meet her plane."

"You're a doll, Ria!"

They chatted for a few minutes more about various things, and Ria gave Elizabet the address of her Park Avenue apartment—*and be damned to the co-op board if they don't like it; I can always buy the building!*—and several emergency phone numbers. She also made a promise that they both knew was empty: that she'd do her best to keep Elizabet's young apprentice out of trouble. Kayla was drawn to trouble as the moth to the flame.

What am I getting myself into? Ria wondered as she hung up the phone.

What am I getting myself into? Eric wondered, not for the first time that week. He still hadn't been able to bring himself to mention the idea of becoming Hosea's mentor to Hosea; every time he rehearsed the words in his head they ended up sounding arrogant and stupid. But the longer he delayed, the guiltier he felt. *Tonight. At the party or after. For sure.*

They'd made the rounds of the usual spots this afternoon. The take was a little lower than usual—it was August, and a lot of Gothamites were fleeing the city for cooler climes—but still respectable. Hosea had insisted on knocking off early; he had a recipe he wanted to try for the party tonight. He'd called it "pocket dumplings," but when he described them, Eric recognized the recipe for Cornish pasties. *Makes sense. Just about everyone from that neck of the woods hailed*

*from the British Isles originally. In fact, I wouldn't be surprised if
there wasn't a Grove tucked away somewhere in those hills . . .*

So they'd gone shopping, and then Hosea had firmly shooed
Eric out of the kitchen. "I've seen what a kitchen looks like once
you're done with it, Mister Bard. You just do your part and eat what
I cook."

Eric had wandered around the living room for a while, unable
to settle. He thought about going for a walk, but the idea held little
charm—Manhattan in August was hazy, hot, and humid, and he
hated the thought of leaving his spell-driven air conditioning.

I wonder how Jimmie's doing? He hadn't seen her in the last
couple of weeks; she'd been working on Friday when they'd had their
get-together. But Paul had told him her schedule, and she should be
home now. He decided to go see her, maybe cadge a cup of tea.

A few minutes later he was standing in front of her door. He
knocked gently, and after a few minutes heard her walking down the
hall. She opened the door.

"Eric. How are you?" She tried for a smile and missed. Eric tried
to keep from looking as shocked as he felt. Jimmie looked like something the cat had dragged in—deep puffy black circles under her
golden eyes, and lines in her face that hadn't been there a month
earlier.

"I've come at a bad time," he said.

"No." She opened the door wider. "Come on in. Really."

He stepped past her, into the hall. It was lined with shelves full
of books on every conceivable subject—Jimmie Youngblood was a
voracious reader.

In the living room window, an elderly a/c wheezed and thundered,
working hard to cool the room. Eric walked over to it and touched
it lightly. He reached out with his power, asking it to remember the
days when it was new. It instantly began to purr quietly, and the
temperature dropped appreciably.

Jimmie sighed in relief. "Thanks. You could make real money
doing that."

"If I ever need a second job," Eric said. "But are you sure this
isn't a bad time? 'Cause frankly, Scarlett, you look like hell."

Jimmie shrugged. "Going from days to nights is always hard, and I haven't been sleeping well. It's not the nightmares. That charm you did for me worked fine, and they haven't come back. I've just got this feeling of impending doom. Every morning I wake up expecting to go into the bathroom and see a banshee doing laundry in my sink."

Eric smiled at the feeble joke. Legend held that those who saw a banshee washing her bloody garments were doomed to die within the fortnight. "But neither Greystone or the House has noticed anything?"

"Nothing," Jimmie answered tiredly. "I'm starting to wonder if I'm turning into one of those cranky old ladies who goes around prophesying the end of the world."

"Not you," Eric said gallantly. "Are you sure there isn't anything I can do to help? I mean, I know I'm not a Guardian—"

"You wouldn't want to be," Jimmie interrupted, cutting him off. "Once you get the Call, your life doesn't belong to you any more. You never know where you're going to be sent, or what you'll have to do. And it's not like there's an instruction manual for being a free-lance occult do-gooder. Sometimes I wish there was." She walked into the kitchen and came back a few moments later with two tall glasses clinking with ice. "Tea. Or as Grandma used to say, 'sweet tea.'"

Eric took his glass and sipped. It was sweet—sweet and cold and delicious, tasting faintly of mint.

"The secret, so she told me, was to put the sugar into the hot tea, so it dissolves completely. Then add the mint, wait for it to cool on its lonesome, and chill. I sure do miss her. She came up North to take care of us kids after Mama died, and never stopped complaining about Yankee ways until the day she died."

"You've never said much about your family before," Eric said.

"That's because I don't have one anymore—well, outside of Toni and the guys. And you, Eric. You've been a real friend. I'm glad the House chose you," she said, sitting down on the couch beside Eric.

"Me, too," Eric said. He sipped his tea. "Hosea's cooking for the party tonight, and suggested I could be of the most use by making myself absent." He hesitated, wondering if he should mention that he might be taking Hosea on as an apprentice. "When a Guardian trains their successor . . ." he began.

He was interrupted by a healthy snort of laughter from Jimmie. "Oh, my! I just wish we did! But that's not the way it works for us. If we're lucky, we get to *meet* our successor and pass on the Call in person, but that's about it. Usually it arrives like a bolt out of the blue, and then it's sink or swim time."

"Doesn't sound really efficient," Eric said, probing gently.

Jimmie grinned, savoring a private joke. "Who are we to argue with the Powers that Be's way of doing business? But seriously. There's no way to train for this job. You can either handle it, or someone else comes along pretty quick to replace you, on account of you taking a quick trip on the hurry-up wagon. Of course, you can spend a long time fooling yourself. I was pretty stubborn when my Call came. Thought I was losing my mind. It's different for everyone. Paul stepped right up like he was born to it when his Call came—but then, he'd been involved in the occult for years. I was just a dumb street cop." She drained her glass in several long swallows and set it down on the floor beside the couch. "And I sure wish I could shake this case of the blue-devils. I even took your advice . . . I did something I swore I'd never do."

Eric raised his eyebrows inquisitively. Jimmie sighed.

"I tried to get ahold of my brother. All I had was a P.O. box address from about a dozen years back. I wrote to it. But he never wrote back. I could use my contacts on the Force, maybe; see if he's Inside somewhere. But I don't really want to rake up old bones at the Job. Y'know, sometimes it doesn't seem like it when the *Post* gets going, but there's nothing a good cop hates more than a bad one."

Eric waited, sensing there was more to say. But if there was, Jimmie drew back from it.

"He didn't even resign. Just disappeared when Internal Affairs came calling. Damn near broke Dad's heart."

And yours, Eric thought, but didn't say so.

"So what's the deal, Eric? You look like somebody with something on his mind besides my little problems."

"Yuh got me, podnuh," Eric said. "It's not really a problem. It's just . . . Hosea came to New York looking for someone to train him as a Bard. And I've got an awful feeling I'm it."

"Can you?" Jimmie asked, cutting to the chase.

"Yeah, well, technically . . . yes. My teacher thinks so, anyway."

They sat in silence for a few moments. Eric could almost hear Jimmie thinking it over.

"So, don't you like him?" she asked.

"Sure I do," Eric said quickly, leaping to Hosea's defense. "He's a great guy. It's just that . . . what if I screw up?"

He'd never been *responsible* for anyone but himself, not even Maeve. That was what it came down to. She was Kory and Beth's. Not his. Saving the world was one thing (though he wasn't over-confident about his abilities there, either, if truth be told), but crises tended to boil up and blow over pretty quickly. Taking on an apprentice was a long-term commitment to another person—and at Juilliard, he'd had ample chance to see the harm that a bad teacher could do.

"What if you don't—screw up, I mean?" Jimmie asked reasonably. "Spend all your time worrying about what *might* happen, and you'll never get anything done. Good advice. I ought to take it sometime," she said broodingly.

"I'm sure you'll figure this out eventually," Eric said. It sounded like hollow comfort, even to him. "Maybe it's all blown over and this is just the aftershocks. Meanwhile, why not come to the party this evening? Shake off that gloom'n'doom feeling?"

"I should," Jimmie said. "I will. Wouldn't miss the chance to sample your friend's masterwork."

She forced a smile, and the talk turned to other things.

The basement was already full when Eric and Hosea came down, balancing two large cookie sheets covered with warm, golden-brown pasties. Alex was there, talking computers with Paul, and Margot and Caity were spreading a paper tablecloth over the top of the washing machines, converting them to a makeshift buffet for the evening.

The basement of Guardian House ran the entire length of the building. Part of it was walled off, forming the "magical bunker" that Toni had told Eric about in his first days in the building, and there was even an apartment down here—a small studio, its only access to the outside world a high narrow strip of windows along one wall. No one lived there; it'd been vacant since her predecessor's time, Toni had told him once, and was now used for storage.

Eric introduced Hosea to the others. Tatiana—in full war paint and more trailing shawls than Isadora Duncan—camped and vamped at him, cooing about "big, strong men" until Hosea actually blushed. Seeing that, she relented, and went off to get them drinks from the bar-by-courtesy, though aside from a couple of bottles of wine, there was nothing stronger than fruit punch there.

By the time Ria arrived, the party was in full swing. Someone had brought down a boombox, and a World Music sampler—mostly ignored—vied for attention with the fragmented sounds of various musicians trading licks. The live music usually came later in the evening, when everyone had mellowed out and finished exchanging gossip and news. Hosea's pasties had vanished early on, but Toni had brought empañadas—a Puerto Rican specialty—and Paul had brought a couple gallons of the Famous Punch (a mixture of exotic tropical fruit juices, savory and non-alcoholic). Eric had a glass of it in his hand when he "felt" Ria arrive, and went upstairs to guide her down.

"Cozy," she said, looking around the basement. "Done in early catacomb?"

She was wearing a pale gray silk business suit and looked like the well-tailored heroine of an Alfred Hitchcock movie. She had on a pair of green jade earrings that played up the green of her eyes, and her ice-blonde hair was held back by a wide clip of the same material.

"Think of it as a trendy after-hours club," Eric said cheerfully. "C'mon. I'll get you a drink."

"I brought my own," Ria said, brandishing a large bottle of white wine. "After the day I've had, I could use a drink."

"Trouble?" Eric said, leading her over toward the buffet.

"More in the line of chickens coming home to roost. You remember Kayla, Elizabet's student?"

"How is she?" Eric asked.

"Starting school at Columbia this fall. And living with me while she does."

Eric was startled into laughter. "The punkette and the Uptown Lady—how'd you get rooked into that one?"

Ria looked faintly cross. "Elizabet asked me, as a favor. She doesn't want Kayla living in the dorm, and wants somebody local keeping an eye on her. L.A.'s a long way from New York."

"And you're elected," Eric said.

"I volunteered," Ria corrected him. "But as for what I'm going to do with her when I get her here . . ." She sighed, shrugging. "How bad can it be? But I've got to say, what I know about teenagers you could engrave on the head of a *very* small pin."

"Well, she's not exactly your ordinary teenager," Eric said, imagining Kayla in Ria's posh uptown apartment. *Let's just hope she doesn't decide to redecorate.* "Kayla's a good kid. And like you said: how bad can it be?"

"I'm sure I'll find out," Ria said darkly. "And pretty soon, too: Elizabet's going to send her out here as soon as she can get a cheap flight so she can settle in and get her shields up to speed."

Though Los Angeles was a major city, it was far more sprawling than New York was. Manhattan's population density would pose special problems for an Empath and Healer.

"You know you can count on me for help. Babysitting, and so forth." He expertly peeled the wrapper off the neck of the bottle and twisted the cork out, pouring a plastic cup half-full for Ria.

"I'll remember that," Ria said. "And if you're good, I won't tell Kayla that's what you said."

"Truce!" Eric cried, throwing up his hands in mock surrender. "The last thing I want is to have Punky Brewster mad at me. C'mon, I'll introduce you around."

The tenants were mostly cool—there were only a couple of remarks of the "you're *that* Ria Llewellyn?" sort—and finally Eric steered her over to where Hosea was.

He was leaning against the wall, his banjo slung across his chest, intently trading riffs with Bill, a guitarist and sometime member of various Soho bands.

The two of them waited politely until the musicians had finished, then Eric caught Hosea's eye. "Hosea, Bill—I'd like you to meet Ria Llewellyn. She's a friend of mine."

There was a moment as Hosea and Ria sized each other up, each recognizing the power in the other. Then Hosea held out his hand.

"How do you do, Miss Llewellyn. Eric's said a bit about you, all good."

"Pleased to meet you," Ria said. "Are you still looking for an apartment?"

"Yes, ma'am," Hosea said. "But at the prices you cityfolk are charging, you'd think I wanted to buy the place, not just live there."

Even the most run-down studio apartment in a bad Manhattan neighborhood rented for $600–800 a month, and some Gothamites were paying a couple thousand a month for a place smaller than Eric's living room.

"I may have a solution, at least a temporary one. LlewellCo is going to be putting up some new low-cost housing on the Lower East Side as an anchor point for redevelopment of some pretty grungy neighborhoods. We're relocating the current tenants, of course, but it's going to be November or so before the building's actually condemned. Meanwhile, the place is standing half empty. I'd been going to put in a security guard—idle real estate being the devil's workshop—but if you'd like to move in and keep an eye on the place until we raze it, you'd have a place to stay—free—and I wouldn't have to worry about squatters moving in and making trouble for the remaining tenants." She smiled hopefully at Hosea.

Wow. She sure played that one right, Eric thought in admiration. He knew Hosea wouldn't even consider taking charity, but Ria'd figured out a way to offer him a free apartment that he'd still be paying for, in a sense—and she wasn't lying when she said she'd need someone looking after the place.

He watched Hosea carefully turning the offer over in his mind, considering it from all angles. Finally he smiled. "That'd be a kindness, Miss Llewellyn. I've been taking up Eric's couch for too long already. I expect he'd like his living room back."

"It's no problem," Eric protested. A guilty twinge reminded him he still hadn't suggested to Hosea that he take him on as a pupil, and part of him realized that Hosea having his own place would make that easier. Emotions between teacher and student could sometimes run high, and it was better not to add that dynamic to the fact of living under the same roof.

"Why don't you come down to the office on Monday?" Ria said, fishing a business card out of her jacket. "I'll make sure Anita has the keys; she can run you over there and get you settled in. There should be enough cast-off furniture there to take care of you, otherwise we can just rent some for a few months. You don't want to be sleeping on the floor. I've been there—some of the roaches are big enough to saddle and ride."

Hosea grinned, tucking the card into his shirt pocket. Unwanted insect life was no problem for a Bard—a few tunes, and the critters tended to go elsewhere. But he only thanked her again for her kindness.

The party broke up around two. Ria had left earlier, pleading a heavy workday on the morrow. Eric and Hosea stayed to help with clean-up—despite her promise to attend, Eric hadn't seen Jimmie Youngblood anywhere tonight—and then headed upstairs.

"Y'know," Eric said tentatively, once they'd gotten into the apartment, "there's something I've been meaning to bring up with you, but I didn't know just what to say."

Hosea stopped and regarded him placidly. "Ayah, you've been looking as broody as a hen with one chick for nigh on a week. Guess it'll be easier now that I'm moving on."

"It's not that," Eric said quickly. "It's . . . when I went to that party the other week, I got a chance to talk to my old teacher. I knew you were looking for somebody to train you as a Bard, and I thought he might be able to recommend somebody."

Hosea waited, listening intently.

"He did. Me."

He saw Hosea wait for the punch line, realize there wasn't one, and consider the matter. "Would you be willing to do that?" he asked in his slow mountain drawl. " 'Cause I don't think you could pass me the shining without you was willing, and I can't think of any way I could pay you back, leastways not for a long while."

"Don't even think about paying me," Eric said firmly. "You don't pay this back. You pay it forward. The question is, do you *want* me to teach you, if I can? I've never done anything like this before."

The anxiety with which he waited for Hosea to answer surprised Eric. Somewhere between here and Maeve's Naming Day, it had come to matter to him very much that Hosea think Eric worthy of being his teacher. He valued his new friend's opinion that much.

Hosea grinned. "Then I guess we've got a lot to learn together, Mister Bard." He stuck out his hand. "Let's shake on it."

Eric took his new student's hand. "Done deal. I'll teach you everything I know, however much that turns out to be. And I guess I'll be learning a lot of things, too."

Patience is the first lesson a teacher learns. A memory of Dharniel's voice echoed in his mind. "We can start as soon as you're settled into your new digs."

On Monday mornings Eric didn't have any classes until after noon, and he usually took advantage of that fact by sleeping late. "Morning person" was *not* in his job description, and even busking with Hosea, they generally skipped the morning rush-hour crowds.

This morning was different.

Screams woke him—no, not screams. *Scream.* The House itself was screaming, a soundless air-raid-siren wail of protest. And beyond that, audible to his ears and not his mind, the sound of a door slamming, over and over.

:Scramble! All units scramble!: he heard Greystone shout in his mind. He lunged out of bed and flung himself into the living room, clawing his hair out of his eyes.

Hosea wasn't there. The front door was slamming itself rhythmically and springing open again.

:Greystone!: Eric mind-shouted. There was no answer.

He couldn't stop the House's alarms, but he could shut them out with a spell of his own. He did so automatically, and as it faded to a thin wail of protest, he apported the first clothes that came to mind—the jeans and T-shirt he'd been wearing last night—and ran for the door. It banged open and stayed that way as he passed through it.

Several of his fellow tenants were standing in the hall in various states of dress from business suits to nudity, all talking agitatedly at once. Most of them seemed to feel there'd been either an explosion or an earthquake, unlikely though the latter was for New York. Someone—he didn't stop to see who—was holding a broadsword, its blade glowing a deep black-light purple.

Eric lunged down the stairs, barefoot, taking them three at a time. He was heading for the lobby. Whatever the source of the disturbance was, it was there. He could feel it.

But when he reached the ground floor, all he saw was Hosea, standing there in bewilderment. He had his duffle bag and his banjo with him.

Of course. He was going to pick up the keys from Ria today.

The wailing was louder here, loud enough to pierce his hush-spell. As Eric reached the lobby, Toni came charging out of her apartment. She was wearing an apron and carrying a baseball bat.

"Get back in there!" she shouted behind her at her two boys. The door slammed shut the way Eric's had.

"What?" she demanded, staring around wildly, looking for the threat.

"All I did—" Hosea began.

Footsteps on the stairs behind Eric told him that the other Guardians were coming. Paul had obviously been in the shower when the alarm came—his hair was still full of shampoo and he wore nothing other than a terry-cloth bathrobe. José had been asleep—he was wearing a pair of striped pajamas and looked as confused as Eric felt. As for Jimmie, she arrived with gun drawn, looking as if she hadn't slept yet.

"All I did—" Hosea began again. He took another step back from the door.

"Enough. Quiet," Toni said, though not to them. Eric breathed a sigh of relief as the wailing ceased.

:*I dunno, Boss. It's quiet as church on Sunday out here. Gotta be something inside:* Greystone said, cutting Eric in on his side of the conversation.

"What's going on?" Jimmie demanded. The four Guardians seemed to commune silently for a moment.

José ran a hand through his disordered hair. "I've never heard anything like that in my life. It even woke the little ones," he said, speaking of his beloved parrots.

"As well as everyone else in the building, Sensitive or no," Paul said tensely. "You might have a little explaining to do, Toni."

"What *was*—or is—it?" Toni demanded, more sharply this time.

Jimmie slowly lowered her gun. Eric heard the *click*, loud in the stillness, as she put the safety on.

By now several of the tenants had reached the first floor. Without seeming even to notice the gathering in the lobby, they hurried past them and out the front door, to cluster in a tight knot on the sidewalk staring anxiously back at the building.

"Well, if that don't beat all," Hosea said, gazing at the door with surprise. "It was locked when I tried it just a moment ago."

"Locked?" Jimmie said. "It's never locked from the inside."

The exodus of tenants had ceased and the door had swung closed again. Jimmie walked over to the door and grasped the handle. It opened easily. She stared at the others in confusion.

"Try it again," she said to Hosea, stepping back from the door.

He glanced back at Eric, who nodded.

As Hosea approached the door, they all felt the House tense, as if preparing to give voice again.

"Wait," Toni said. Hosea stopped, his hand inches from the door. "*You* try it," she said to Eric.

Shrugging, Eric walked over to the door. He hesitated for a moment, steeling himself for the psychic equivalent of an electric shock, but there was nothing. The door opened silently and easily. He opened and closed it several times. Nothing.

"No one else had any problem; neither Bard, Guardian, nor civilian. Only this young man," Paul said.

"I think we'd better find out why," Toni answered grimly. She glanced out at the cluster of people on the sidewalk.

"You figure out what to tell them, and with Eric's permission, we'll convene a council of war at his place—in, say, about fifteen minutes?" Paul said.

"Sure. No problem. I'll put up some coffee." *And maybe get my heart started again.* "C'mon, Hosea. No point trying to leave now."

The hallway outside the apartment was empty when Eric and Hosea reached it. Eric's door swung open peremptorily as soon as they reached the top of the stairs, but, to his relief, stayed still and allowed him to close it himself. He didn't bother to lock it. He'd just had a taste of how very efficient the House's security systems were.

"Just the way I'd want to start a Monday morning," he said, sighing. He looked at Hosea with what he hoped was a reassuring smile. "I know you're going to have to go over it again when the others get here, but . . . what did you do?"

Hosea looked troubled, and when he spoke his Appalachian drawl was thicker than Eric had ever heard it. "Nothing I ain't done most every other morning. I figured I'd just take my traps with me when I went down to Miss Llewellyn's office, and that way I wouldn't have to double back to get them. So I locked up, same as I always do, an when I got to the front door, it was locked. And all of a sudden, something started hollering in my head." He shook his head ruefully. "I hope Miss Hernandez ain't too put out with me. That woman's got a temper on her when she's bothered, and that's the certain truth."

Eric regarded Hosea, puzzled. He knew the other man was telling the truth—and the whole truth, as he knew it, at that. Unfortunately, it didn't answer any of Eric's questions.

"Why should everyone else be able to leave and not you? Why this time and none of the others?"

❖❖ ❖❖ ❖❖

It was a question still unanswered half an hour later, as Eric, Hosea, and the four Guardians—with Greystone listening in from his perch outside the window—gathered in Eric's living room. Toni had given the other tenants the cover story that there'd been an explosion in the boiler that provided the building's steam heat, but that it was all taken care of now and the building was perfectly safe. The explanation would do as long as nobody thought too closely about it, though of course, those who had sensed the House's alarm for more or less what it was would have to be told something more. And the six of them were no closer to the truth than they had been downstairs.

"So what was different about this time?" Jimmie asked Hosea.

The country Bard shook his head in bafflement. "Nothing I know of. I was going to go and get settled in to my new place, and then come back here to pick up Eric—you know, so we could go busking in the subway?"

"Wait a minute," Jimmie said slowly. "What 'new place'?"

"I'm moving out. Miss Ria, Eric's ladyfriend, she offered me a place to hang my hat for a few months, an—"

"That's it," Paul said, interrupting him. "It's got to be. It's the only thing that's changed. This time you weren't just going out for a few hours. You were *leaving*."

The six of them looked at each other.

"Well, now we know *that* much," Toni said sourly. "Not that we know anything at all."

"We know that the House doesn't want Hosea to leave," Jimmie said slowly. The four Guardians looked at each other. "And we know what that means."

"No we don't," Eric said. "At least, the two of us don't."

Jimmie and Toni looked at each other, and again Eric had that sense of unspoken communication. After a long moment, Jimmie answered him.

"You know that the House picks its tenants for its own inscrutable reasons. If it wants you, you can stay. When it doesn't want you, you go—you *have* to. But sometimes, it *really* wants somebody. And when it does, it encourages them—strongly!—to stay. My guess is that your friend here wasn't taking the hint. So it stopped hinting—and yelled."

"But there are four of us," José said, as if continuing a different conversation. "There've never been more than four. Why him? Why now?"

The House wants Hosea? As a Guardian? Eric thought blankly. José couldn't mean anything else.

"It's not as if there's a hard-and-fast set of rules about this sort of thing," Paul offered, looking thoughtful. "There are four of us, and as we know, that's a lot of Guardians to gather in one place. Why *not* five?"

"No vacancies?" Toni suggested. "The place is full, Paul. Every apartment's rented, and they're all good people. Who am I supposed to evict?"

"There's that studio in the basement," Eric said. "You could clean that out. We'd help."

"Just a doggone minute, here," Hosea said. "What's this all about?"

"I think," Eric said slowly, "that it's about you joining the Occult Police. Becoming a Guardian."

"I can't do that!" Hosea protested. "I ain't a—a—" He groped for the word. "A *root doctor* like you folks. I got me a little shine, sure, but I'm a Bard—leastways, I'm gonna be one as soon as Eric here gets to training me. Right now I don't know much of anything."

The four Guardians looked at each other again.

"Well," Paul said, "it does look like you're going to have the time to learn whatever it is you're here to learn, my young friend. Because no matter for what purpose the House wants you, I truly don't believe you'll be allowed to leave until you agree to stay."

"As much sense as that makes," Jimmie offered.

"The basement apartment's not much, but I can get it cleaned out and painted by the end of the week," Toni said. "Then it's yours."

"I don't want no charity," Hosea said, looking stubborn. "I've got a place to go to, all ready and waiting for me. I don't have to stay here."

Oh, brother! Eric thought. No wonder the House'd had to shout, if that was how Hosea had been responding to its gentler suggestions.

"You may be stubborn as a pig in mud, but I guarantee, this place is stubborner," Jimmie said. "Don't pick a fight you can't win, Hosea."

"*Por favor,*" José begged. "For the sake of my little ones. And to spare me another awakening like this one."

Toni was looking at Hosea critically. "Well, maybe you're wrong, Jimmie. As far as I can tell, he hasn't been Called." The others nodded agreement, seeing something Eric couldn't. "But the House wants him to stay. Mr. Songmaker, would you consider doing us all a very great favor and staying on until we can get this sorted out? The rent won't be much for that small a studio, and I've got a certain amount of latitude in what I charge, anyway. Eric tells me you'll be getting your busking license soon, and I can wait for the rent until then. Besides, if you *do* stay, I won't have to wake José up any time I need some heavy lifting done," she added with a grin.

Hosea still hesitated.

"Do it," Eric said firmly. "I don't want another wake-up call like that one, either. We need the time to figure this out."

"I hate to disappoint Miss Ria that way," Hosea said tentatively.

"She'll survive," Eric said. "You aren't irreplaceable there. But it looks like you are here."

"Well . . . okay," Hosea said. "I accept your kind offer, Miss Hernandez. And I'd just like to say that I'm sorry for putting you good folks to all this trouble on my account."

"Don't mention it," Jimmie said, smiling crookedly. "Battle, murder, and sudden death our specialty. And I'm just as glad to know that we aren't going to have to find out what kind of crisis requires *five* Guardians on tap."

"It's settled, then," Toni said briskly. "C'mon, Hosea. You can help me empty that place out and figure out where to stow all that junk." She got to her feet.

"I guess I'll go knock on a few doors and reassure our Sensitives that the Last Trump hasn't blown," Paul said, also getting to his feet.

Toni and Hosea left, and in a few moments the others followed.

"Hey, Jimmie? A word?" Eric said, as she prepared to follow them out.

Jemima Youngblood stopped and turned back to Eric, closing the door.

"What's *really* going on here?" he asked. "Is Hosea a Guardian now, or what?"

"I wish I knew," Jimmie said, sounding as puzzled as Eric felt. "I've *never* heard the House alarms go off like that for anything else—not even the time it suckered that child molester into the basement so we could deal with him quietly, or the time one of our other tenant's guests found his ritual tools and decided it'd be fun to conjure up a demon. But . . . you recognized Hosea as—what? a fellow Bard?—the first time you laid eyes on him. Well, it's the same for us. One Guardian always knows another. And as far as that recognition factor goes, Hosea isn't a Guardian. I just wish I knew what the House knows that we don't."

Yeah. Me, too, Eric thought. "Oh, well. At least he'll be close by for his Bardic training."

"Look on the bright side," Jimmie agreed. She glanced at her watch. "Nine-thirty. And I'm working four to midnight this month. If I don't get my head down soon I'm not going to be worth much at all."

"You'd better go on and get some sleep, then," Eric said. He opened the door for her. "Sleep well."

"Thanks," Jimmie said. "And thanks for convincing your stubborn friend to take the path of least resistance. I'm not surprised the House had to yell to get his attention."

"We'll try to avoid that in the future," Eric agreed.

But how? he wondered, long after Jimmie had left.

NINE:
PUT YOUR HAND INSIDE
THE PUPPETHEAD

Bonnie Wing and Kit Duquesne were friends of Beth's from the old days back in L.A.—Bonnie was a scriptwriter for animated series, and Kit had been a show runner until deciding that the Hollyweird pressure cooker wasn't for her. By a flukey stroke of luck, a spec script of Kit's had been auctioned about the time she was deciding to get out, and she'd used the money to put a down payment on a down-at-heels New York apartment building that faced Inwood Hill Park. With her lover Bonnie, Kit had moved back East and started fixing the place up.

Beth, Kory, and Eric had stayed with the two of them last year when Beth and Kory were getting Eric settled in to his new digs, and Beth had welcomed the opportunity to renew her friendship with the two women. Beth and Kit—a tall regal blonde, equally adept with ritual blade and rattan sword—had been in the same coven back in Los Angeles, and Kit had started another one when she'd moved back East; Kit was the closest thing to a real-life Rupert Giles of *Buffy the Vampire Slayer* fame that Beth knew. If anybody could solve the problem that Chinthliss had set them, it was Kit Duquesne.

"Beth—and Studly!" Kit stared at them in surprise through the crack in the door. There was a rattle of chains and deadbolts, and then she opened it all the way. "Come in—when did you get back?"

"We're just in town for a day or so. We left Maeve with Kory's family, but we did bring pictures," Beth answered. "Sorry to just drop in like this. . . ."

"No! It's great to see you both! I'll put on the tea. Bonnie's on a deadline, for *BattleMages* or *Teddybear Bikers from Hell* or some damn thing. She'll be out in about an hour."

Kit walked off to the kitchen, leaving them in the large sunny living room for a moment. Two futon couches were angled to take full advantage of the high windows, and a large air conditioner wheezed and rattled as it did battle with the August heat. Hallow, a very large gray tabby, slept atop it, oblivious to the noise. Two more—a tiny black kitten (new since Beth's last visit) and a regal long-haired white cat (Mistwraith)—drifted over to inspect the newcomers. Kory knelt down, and the kitten, taking this for an invitation, promptly swarmed up his arm and settled itself on his shoulder, purring noisily.

"Do you really think she can help us?" Kory asked quietly, straightening up and offering his fingers to the kitten on his shoulder, which promptly bit down with an expression of blissful contentment.

"I hope so. I don't know of any Sidhe with the kind of experience we need," Beth said.

"And how," Kory asked her, "will you phrase the question?"

"Talking secrets?" Kit asked, walking back in carrying a tray. "Bonnie's been baking—she always does when she's putting off work—and you reap the fruit of her procrastination. Ah, I see you've met Beltane. Don't let her bully you. Hallow is terrified of her," she added, indicating the sleeping tabby.

She set the tray down on the large handmade coffee table in the center of the room. Mistwraith instantly hopped up to investigate, and was set on the floor—several times—by Kit.

Maeve's baby pictures were brought out and admired, herb tea and orange muffins were served and consumed, and idle chitchat about the building, Bonnie's work (in addition to her various cartoon gigs, she also wrote a comic called *The Elite*, which was starting to gather a following), and various events mainly of interest to New Yorkers occupied several minutes.

"Now," Kit said, putting down her empty mug. "What's the deal? It can't be love of the Big Apple that brings you here twice in three months. Are you and Studly Do-Right here on the lam again?"

Beth smiled. "No, but we do have a problem we need some help with. It's kind of a long story."

Kit sat back on the futon couch. "We've got all day."

Beth looked helplessly at Kory. Coming here had seemed like such a great idea, right up until the time came to tell Kit why she was here. Kory was right. Figuring out what to say was going to be harder than she thought.

"We need to buy a computer system for a dragon," Kory said simply, "and we're not sure what kind will work in his kingdom. Beth thought you might be able to help."

Beth's jaw dropped.

"Uh-huh," Kit said, poker-faced. There was a long pause. "What does a dragon need with a computer?"

"Dragons prize novelty and innovation above all things. Also, he wishes to 'surf the net,'" Kory added, with the pride of one who has mastered an unfamiliar vocabulary.

Kit looked at Beth. Beth smiled weakly. Somehow, telling the simple truth had not been on her list of approaches to the problem of getting Kit to help them.

"Joke?" Kit asked, when it became apparent that Beth wasn't going to say anything.

"No joke." Beth sighed. *In for a penny, in for a pound. . . .* "Kory, it might help if you showed her."

Kory glanced at her, eyebrows raised, then dispelled the glamour that made him look like nothing more exotic than a very tall human. Beltane purred harder, and Mistwraith jumped up into his lap.

Kit stared at Kory and said nothing—very eloquently—for several minutes. "Bright Court or Dark?" she said at last.

"Bright," Kory said, sounding faintly miffed.

And that's a hell of a first question for someone who ought to never have seen an elf before, Beth thought.

"That's all right, then," Kit said. "And you aren't planning to start a War of the Oaks in Central Park, or anything like that?"

"Why does everyone ask that?" Kory wondered plaintively.

"It's a book," Beth explained. "Several books, actually. No, we're just passing through, Kit, honest. Most Sidhe don't want to have anything to do with New York. There's too much Cold Iron here for them."

"Uh-huh," Kit said again, still in that noncommittal tone. Whether she believed them or not, Beth still wasn't sure. "So, you want a computer that will work in Elfland? It won't be cheap, I can tell you that."

"No problem," Kory said.

The story of whatever experience it was that had made Kit so ready to believe in elves would be a tale for another time. Kit didn't go into it and Beth wasn't sure she wanted to ask right now; Kit simply accepted Kory and moved on to a series of questions about the computer. Beth wasn't sure whether she was disappointed or not. Over the years, she'd kind of gotten used to people being weirded out by the idea of Real Live Elves, and here Kit was taking it far more calmly than she'd taken the news that Beth was going to have a baby.

And if Beth had hoped for more dramatics from Bonnie, she was to be disappointed there as well. When Bonnie finally emerged from her office (looking rumpled and distant, most of her mind still obviously on her writing) and saw Kory—who had seen no reason to restore his human-seeming—she barely blinked. Bonnie was petite and dark, her classic Oriental beauty making her look fragile and innocent. This impression usually lingered with new acquaintances until they saw her fight.

"SFX?" Bonnie asked Kit in the shorthand of long partnership.

"Nope. True gen: Sidhe," Kit had replied. By now she was surrounded by reference books, in which she was looking up this and that esoteric factoid.

"*More* of them?" Bonnie asked in disbelief, as though she were talking about tourists or butterflies. Dearly as Beth would have loved to chase down *that* remark, she was not to be given the chance. Bonnie had her workout bag over her shoulder, and was obviously on her way to the dojo. "Grins. Bang-boom. Later?"

"Yeah. Gonna take 'em down to see Ray. Deep pockets for this one. Script done?"

"Bang. Boom," Bonnie said. "Kiss-kiss." She waved to Beth. "Late. Toodles." Explanation delivered, she left.

"'Ray'?" Beth asked, eyebrows raised.

"Friend of mine," Kit said. "Tenant, too. Knows *way* more about all this stuff than I do, but that's not the point here. I know enough spelltech and psionics to figure out that side of it, but I know jack about computers. Meanwhile, we can decide what to do about dinner. Bon eats out on class nights, so we don't have to wait for her."

Over dinner preparations, Kit told the two of them a little more. Ray—Azrael Arcane if you were being formal—lived on the floor below Kit and Bonnie and built special-needs computer systems—and if Beth's project wasn't a special-needs system, Kit said, she didn't know what was. She'd inherited him from the previous owner of the building, and as far as she knew, he never left his apartment. He wouldn't be available until a few hours after sundown, Kit explained, so they made spaghetti and garlic bread, in between bouts of rescuing Hallow from Beltane and insuring that Mistwraith remained a white cat and not a tomato-colored one.

Beth found herself relaxing, because now the big secret was out and nobody seemed to care—and Kory had the Sidhe knack of easy charm, which he exercised in full measure.

"Is that name for real?" Beth said, returning to the subject of their evening's appointment following a luxurious dessert of strawberries in crème fraiche. Kit had wanted to serve them tiramisu, but the coffee and chocolate it contained would have been deadly to Kory.

"It's on his rent checks. And you're a fine one to talk, Miss If-It's-Tuesday-I-Must-Have-A-New-Alias," Kit teased.

Kit was one of the few people who Beth had kept in touch with following the Griffith Park Massacre, and one of the few who knew anything about the real situation of Beth's life, though of course Beth had been careful about what she'd told her. Now, she wondered if she'd needed to bother. Kit obviously didn't boggle at elves. "That's different," Beth said defensively. "I didn't have a choice."

"Yeah, sometime you're going to have to tell me the whole story—the *whole* story—about that. It just seems a little too *X-Files* to believe—you know, the government being after witches?"

"Psychics, really. And you're a fine one to talk. You don't even blink at seeing Kory, and you think a government conspiracy is too weird?"

"Not too weird. Too done-to-death. You'd think even the government would be bored with conspiracies by now," Kit amplified, tossing strawberry hulls for the cats to chase. "If you want conspiracy theory, talk to Ray. He's up on all of them from Gemstone to Trapdoor."

"Is he Wiccan?" Beth asked, because Kit spoke as if she knew him well.

"He's . . . eccentric," Kit said measuringly. "But systems designers can afford to be. I think he can help you, and he owes me a favor. Beyond that, there are things that woman was not meant to know. It's late enough now. Let me go call and see if he's around."

"Curiouser and curiouser, as Alice said," Beth commented to Kory when Kit had left the room.

"I suppose it is presumptuous to ask sorcerers to be commonplace," Kory said musingly. "Like Bards, their lives are their art."

"Eric's normal," Beth said, stung by the implication.

"In Bards, such normalcy is eccentricity beyond compare," Kory pointed out inarguably. "I love and value him, but Eric strives for the commonplace as others quest for dreams and far enchantments—much as if I were to drive a taxi and live in Queens."

"I'd love to see that," Beth muttered under her breath.

"The doctor is in," Kit announced, returning from her call. "C'mon. I'll take you down."

After what both Kit and Kory had said, Beth thought she was

braced for every possible sort of Earth-plane weirdness—or at least, for the sort of theatrics and eccentricity she'd grown used to from her New Age acquaintanceship. But Azrael's *bizarrerie* was of an entirely different order.

There was a keypad lock affixed to his door in place of the usual sort of key and cylinder lock, and Kit tapped out a quick nine digits then pushed the door open into darkness. The hall lights illuminated a long hallway with floor, walls, and ceiling painted matte black. Kit ushered them in and closed the door behind her.

"Don't mind this. The light hurts his eyes, so he keeps the place pretty dark." She led them down the hall and into the living room, which was lit by a faint red glow.

It, too, was painted flat black, making Beth feel as if she were floating in a vast empty space. It was disorienting, but comforting, too—on a level far below consciousness, she was aware that nothing could harm her here. Despite its outré appearance, this was a safe place, a good place.

As her eyes adjusted, she could make out more details of her surroundings, and spared a pang of envy for Kory's natural advantages—elf-sight could see everything as plain as if it were broad day. There were several computers racked against the far wall, but all the screens were dark; the green and amber status lights giving the only sign that they were powered up. She could make out a sectional sofa—also black—that lined two walls, and the window was covered with heavy blackout drapes, drawn against the mild summer night. Despite this, the air was cool and fresh—somewhere a very quiet air conditioner and ozone generator must be running. The only illumination came from a strip of red neon that ran all the way around the ceiling.

"Hello, Kit. You must be Kory and Beth. Welcome."

And in all this, he wears dark glasses, Beth thought in disbelief, seeing their host at last. The self-styled Azrael Arcane got to his feet and came over to them, leaning heavily on a silver-headed cane. He was indeed wearing dark glasses: square-lensed, faintly antique-looking things, whose lenses appeared entirely black in the weird scarlet light. He had long straight hair, as pale as Kory's—though in the neon it looked candy-apple red— that fell straight down his back, and was wearing an open-collared Poet Shirt beneath a dark suit of the Earlier Victorian period. He was barefoot. The whole effect was exotic in the extreme.

He held out his hand for Beth to shake. Seeing the darkness of her skin against his, she realized what the eccentric lighting was designed to conceal—Azrael Arcane was an albino.

No wonder it's so dark in here. If his albinism is acute, he's practically blind in strong sunlight. Well, that explains a lot.

I think.

Maybe.

He shook hands with Kory as well, who had resumed his human disguise, and motioned them toward the couch. "Sit down, please. Kit tells me you need to consult about the specs for a special needs computer system. Environment or user?"

"Environment," Beth said, remembering that Chinthliss could look perfectly human when he chose, and so would not need something that could be operated by someone the size of a small aircraft. "What we really need is a top of the line, newer than tomorrow system that's totally self-contained. No outside power source, no hookup to phone lines—" let Chinthliss figure out his local ISP; that part wasn't her problem "—and it has to be stable in . . ." She faltered. Just how did you describe the physical conditions of Underhill without describing Underhill itself?

"In Between-the-Worlds conditions," Kit supplied smoothly.

"You want to run a computer in a Circle without interfering with the raised power?" Azrael asked. "Why not just do your computing after you take the Circle down?"

"We can't," Beth said quickly. "This is a sort of . . . permanent Circle." She looked at Kory, who nodded agreement.

Now why didn't I come up with that explanation earlier? Not that Kit would have bought it for a New York minute. Elves would have had to come into it somewhere.

But Azrael didn't seem inclined to pry, taking the explanation—and the parameters—at face value. "Well, it can be done, of course," he said, sounding puzzled. "But it will take a lot of space, and a *lot* of money, and it'll eat batteries like nobody's business. Your best bet might be a small gas-powered generator—"

"This must be done without Cold Iron," Kory said. "As much as possible."

Azrael glanced at Kit, and some unspoken communication passed between them. "You like a challenge," she reminded him.

"Hm. Well, some of the new Lithium-Ion batteries have a pretty long life, or you might want to run it off solar; the new ones run on what comes through on a cloudy day. If you use solar cells to charge your LION pack, you can recharge while you're not using the computer. Is iron-free your only restriction?"

Beth glanced at Kit, who seemed to know where Azrael was going with this and was able to translate. "That's all. We don't have to worry about planetary influences with the other metals."

"And price is no object?" Azrael asked. "We're talking thousands, here. Several thousands—possibly several *ten* thousands, even waiving my usual exorbitant fees."

Kit looked at them.

"None," Kory said firmly. "And we will be happy to pay your fees as well."

There was enough *kenned* gold on deposit in a special bank account that Elfhame Misthold used for its World Above purchases to cover almost any need, and when funds ran low the elves could always *ken* more gold. There was no fraud involved, for the gold was good—true metal, not faerie gold, to vanish when the spell dissolved.

"No, this is a favor to Kit. Okay. If you can give me a day or so to make some calls, I can give you a set of plans for the cage, and a shopping list for the computer. Your best bet is probably to hit up Comdex next month and pick up something there. You said top of the line?"

"The newest and most fancy," Beth said, on secure ground when it came to shopping. "But . . . what cage?"

"A Faraday Cage, of course," Azrael said. "Named for the magneto-optic effect in which the polarization plane of an electromagnetic wave is rotated under the influence of a magnetic field parallel to the direction of propagation."

Beth blinked, having gotten lost somewhere around "magneto-optic." Azrael smiled and took pity on her.

"Michael Faraday was a nineteenth-century inventor who discovered that an electrical discharge, such as lightning, would flow outside and around a metal cage to go to ground. This is the reason airplanes and cars can be struck by lightning without harm to the occupants: they're a type of Faraday Cage. But when you build one out of copper or some equivalent neutral conductor and run a current through it, it cancels out *all* electromagnetic field energy. Cages of this type are used to shield delicate electronic equipment from stray EMF fields, and when J. B. Rhine was doing his ESP experiments at Duke University back in the last century, he discovered that his subjects' accuracy tended to skyrocket when they were placed in a Faraday Cage, leading to the theory that psionics—and, by extension, *magic*—involves some kind of manipulation of electromagnetic or bioelectric fields. What this means for you is that the computer's magnetic field and sphere of influence will stay inside the cage, and the magical energy will stay outside the cage, and never the twain will meet."

"But won't that kind of insulation keep the computer from connecting with the Internet?" Kit asked.

"Possibly. I couldn't say for sure unless I saw it up and running in its host environment. The simplest solution is just to run a copper ground to your landline, but it might need to be tweaked with. You'll probably need to run a few tests to see how well your system connects—it will, however, run without disrupting the magical environment, so long as it's in the cage and the cage is powered up."

"Can it really be so simple?" Beth marveled.

"Only in the sense that it can be conceived and described. After that, you're talking money—large cartloads of it, and that's where you run into trouble. Most magicians have more interest in the Great Work than in getting rich. Governments commonly have large cartloads of money, but have trouble attracting competent magicians. Magic is anarchic by its very nature—Do What Thou Wilt Shall Be The Whole Of The Law doesn't get along very well with beancounters in suits. Any competent tyrant with any awareness of the Unseen World starts out by restricting access to it: Hitler didn't round up all the Adepts he could get his hands on in the 1930s—from astrologers to Freemasons and everything in between—just to be mean. He saw them as a threat to his power. Fortunately, these days nobody takes magic that seriously. Something to be thankful to the New Age fluffy bunnies for."

"Some people do," Beth said, repressing a shiver.

"Well, there's Sun Streak and Stargate and things like that, but those projects seem to be focusing more on psionicists, fortunately. So long as they're concentrating on natural Talents, and not on Adepts, they should lose interest eventually. And if they do decide we're a nuisance, probably all they'll do is make study of the Art illegal. We've been underground before. We'll survive."

"Except for the people who get caught," Beth said tightly.

"That's right," Azrael said levelly. "Except for those who get caught. But I'm sure Kit warned you both about my hobbyhorse, and I don't think I'm going to transgress the bounds of hospitality by riding it tonight. You'll forgive me, I know." He smiled at them engagingly, and Beth found herself liking him more and more.

"I think—in the long list of people the government is likely to build internment camps for—that occultists come way, way down the list," Kit said.

Beth and Azrael exchanged glances of wordless disagreement. Both of them thought that Adepts were much higher on that list than Kit seemed to—and when you came right down to it, it didn't matter if they were at the top of the list or the bottom, if they were on the list at all.

"Well, that's enough for tonight, ladies and gentleman. I've got places to surf and people to annoy. I should have that stuff you need by tomorrow night, and after that, it's up to you," Azrael said.

"That seems fair," Kory said.

"More than fair. You've been a great help. Are you sure there isn't anything we can do in return?" Beth asked.

Azrael smiled. "Sure there is. When you get it up and running, let me know how it works, okay?"

"We will," Beth promised.

✥✥ ✥✥ ✥✥

After Hosea left to go and clean out the basement room, Eric paced around the apartment, still edgy. There was no real point in trying to go back to sleep—not with the adrenaline surging through his system. He fielded a couple of calls from friends who lived in the building—mostly they wanted to compare notes on what *he* thought had happened. Finally he decided he might as well get his stuff together and go on over to the school. At least at Juilliard, he'd face a different kind of annoyance. And maybe he could shake his feeling that there was trouble on the horizon—distant still, but surely coming.

Must've picked that up from Jimmie. But the Guardians are supposed to have some kind of Distant Early Warning System, and it doesn't seem to have gone off. Every attack of the blue megrims doesn't have to herald the end of the world—I guess it's true what Freud said: sometimes a cigar is just a cigar.

He was on his way out the door when the phone rang again. At first he just looked at it, unwilling to answer it and field yet another set of vague yet apprehensive questions. All the psychics in the building knew perfectly well that there hadn't been trouble with the boiler this morning, but even if he wanted to tell them the whole truth, he wasn't sure what it was. So far, this morning was a story without an ending. None of the Guardians, or Eric for that matter, knew why the building wanted Hosea, or for what—and Eric wasn't sure if the discovery that Guardian House could act independently of the Guardians wasn't the creep-worthiest part of the whole thing.

After the fourth ring, though, he turned back to answer it. Might as well do his damage control now as later.

"Eric? I was afraid I'd missed you!"

"Bethie?" She wasn't quite the last person he'd expected to be calling him, but she was certainly in the bottom ten. "Where are you? Is everything all right?"

"We're at Kit and Bonnie's up in Inwood. Everything's fine, actually, for a change. Kory and I are off to Comdex tomorrow to buy a computer system for a dragon—we took Ria's advice, and it worked out great!"

She sounded happy and excited. Beth was in better spirits than Eric had seen her for quite a while—more like the old, pre-everything self, bubbly and effervescent.

"Wait—wait—wait—slow down. You're buying a dragon?"

"A computer *for* a dragon," Beth corrected, laughing. "His name's Chinthliss, and he can help us—Kory and me—figure out how to have kids. He's a friend of someone named Tannim, at Elfhame Fairgrove, he says—you know, with the race cars? All he wants is a computer system that will work Underhill, so he can surf the net, and Kit's friend Azrael figured out how to make it work— all you need is a Faraday Cage and some really big batteries—this is going to be great!"

Beth was burbling, and well she might, if this Chinthliss had solved the problem of her and Kory's future offspring. How had that been Ria's idea? He'd have to ask her.

Are you sure you can trust this Chinthliss? Eric wanted to ask, but kept himself from asking. She'd said Kory was with her, and Kory would cut his own throat before he let Beth wander into any perils Underhill. If the two of them had cut a deal with this dragon, Chinthliss must be all right.

"So where are you going to find this computer?" Eric asked, when Beth ran down a little.

"Comdex. That big trade show they hold in Las Vegas every September. Kory says he thinks there's a hame there—some of the Seleighe Sidhe took over an Unseleighe casino, if you can believe that, so we'll have a Gate right there. And then we bring the stuff back through to Chinthliss' place, and he'll give us the information we need! He said so! Oh, Goddess, I can't wait to get home and tell Maeve she's going to have a little brother or sister!"

Eric smiled, listening to her cheerful prattle. At least things were looking up for someone. He wasn't quite sure where that thought came from; *his* life was doing okay. This thing with Hosea would work out, he and Ria were doing fine, and nobody was even trying to kill him lately.

"Well, that's great," he said, a little lamely. Beth picked up on his tone at once.

"You sound a little down. Things working out okay at your end?"

"Oh, sure," Eric said hastily. "I just got up way too early this morning. It looks like Hosea's going to be living here—there's a studio apartment available in the basement, and he's getting it cleaned out now. He's okay with my teaching him, too. I'm the only one who's worried about that."

Beth laughed. "Banyon, sometimes you worry way too much! You'll be a great teacher. You wouldn't want to contradict Master Dharniel, now, would you?"

"Perish forfend," Eric said, smiling in spite of himself. He found that deep inside he was actually looking forward to the day he could introduce his new student to his old master. "Hey, I hate to cut this short, but I've got class and I don't want to be late. You guys going to be around this evening? We could get together, maybe."

"I wish we could, but Kory and I are going back to Everforest in an hour or so and then out to Lost Wages, and then from there to Chinthliss'. Come see us when we get back?"

"If I can," Eric promised.

"Gotta run," Beth said. "Love you!"

"Love you, too," Eric answered. He stared at the phone for a long minute after he hung up. Beth's good news ought to have made him feel better, but the strangely unsettled feeling he'd had all morning didn't want to go away. He hadn't wanted to burden Beth with his own problems, but ignoring them didn't make them go away, either.

Just what *did* the House want with Hosea . . . and why?

She'd thought she'd been afraid before, but it was nothing to the terror Jeanette felt now, clutching at Aerune as he rode through the shadows of this unearthly place. She could feel the T-Stroke burning through her veins, pulling her down into darkness. She fought its effect frantically. If she lost consciousness here and fell from Aerune's horse, she did not know what would happen to her.

They were no longer on Earth. Somehow she knew that, though there was little she could see. Aerune's cloak whipped back over her, blinding her, as the stallion moved from a trot to a canter, and the chill surrounding her fought with the fire in her blood. She could see a full moon above them, horribly distorted, and around the horse's legs shadowy pale things yelped and gibbered, leaping into the air to attack the riders and falling back in defeat.

Then the moon was gone in a blinding flash of light, and they rode across a sun-hammered desert of cracked clay beneath a dark brass-colored sky. Furnace heat struck like a blow, and in the sky above, black shapes wheeled and screamed.

Then darkness again, and on the horizon, torn by the black peaks of mountains, a distorted, blood-red sun filling half the sky. The air was thin here, and Jeanette found herself gasping for breath. Her lungs burned with the need for oxygen, and the sky above was black, filled with unwinking stars.

Then air and light—the foggy dimness of a swamp filled with giant trees festooned with corpse-pale moss. Aerune's stallion splashed and skidded through the slime, and with each step it filled the air with the stench of rot. She looked down, and saw that the black water was filled with writhing white worms, each longer than a man. She shut her eyes tightly then, and did not open them until a shock of cold told here that they were again elsewhere.

—An arctic plain, the snow only marginally whiter than the sky overhead. In the distance, a vast structure of black stone, and the sound of a strange high-pitched refrain: *Tekeli-li! Tekeli-li!*

—Darkness more absolute than blindness, the only sound the stallion's running hooves.

—Cold again, the stallion running faster, along a thin shining bridge only inches wide. Stars above and below, shining dimly through veils of violet haze. Ahead the bridge ended, and the stallion gathered itself to spring, leaping out into nothingness. She screamed then, the sound thin and flat as the world shifted once more.

The stallion slowed to a walk.

They were in a forest. It was dark, but this time the almost-comforting dark of night. Everything was lit by faint greenish moonlight, though she could see no moon. The trees were like nothing she'd ever seen: black and smooth and leafless, looking unpleasantly like polished bone. The ground was covered with a low white mist that reached to the horse's knees concealing everything beneath it. She felt flushed and nauseated as the drug worked through her, and Jeanette knew she had only a few minutes of consciousness left. The trees wheeled dizzyingly around her, and she could not tell whether that was an effect of the drug, or whether they really were moving.

When they finally left the forest, Jeanette could see the source of the light. Far in the distance, at the top of a peak that rose up out of the center of the bone-wood, stood a tall gothic castle, shining with a baleful moth-green light. Try as she might, she could not see it clearly; walls and towers seemed to meet at impossible angles, and it wavered in her sight like a heat mirage, though the night was damp and cool. The castle grew to fill the entire world, burning brighter and then blindingly bright.

And then there was nothing at all.

Consciousness returned in slow stages. For a long time she drifted back and forth, aware enough to know she was awake, but unable to remember why that might be odd. Finally, a single fact floated to the front of her mind, pulling awareness with it like a train of boxcars.

She'd taken T-Stroke.

Aerune had kidnapped her.

The T-Stroke hadn't killed her.

She was somewhere in Elfland.

Aerune's castle?

Jeanette opened her eyes, rolling over in the same movement and crashing to the floor as she fell off the narrow bed she had lain on. The pain completed the process of her awakening, and the last few hours settled back firmly into memory. She looked around.

She'd been lying on a narrow shelf cut into a wall. She was in a small room, much taller than it was wide. Twelve feet up there was a door set into the wall; a latticework of iron bars through which light spilled. The walls and floor were made up of large gray stone blocks, like every dungeon in every movie ever made. Torches burned in iron brackets on the walls, but the light was white and directionless, too steady to be coming from the flickering orange flames or the doorway above.

It's like a stage set.

She got to her feet and quickly sat down on the bed, her heart racing with excitement and fear. She'd gambled and won: by the very fact that she was alive, she knew she was one of the lucky 10%— she'd survived her dosing, and now, by rights, she should be able to manifest some sort of paranatural power.

But what? She felt no different. All the test subjects had used their powers instinctively, but she felt no instinctive pull to do anything out of the ordinary.

What was true was that she was dying. All the subjects who had received T-Stroke had died in a matter of days or hours. She felt a small thrill of triumph at cheating Aerune of his victory by dying, but quickly stifled it, unwilling to look beyond this moment to her own death. If Elfland existed, then so must Hell, in some form or another, and Jeanette knew that Hell was her destiny for what she'd done in life. To distract herself, she resumed her study of her cell and herself.

The clothes she had come here in—jeans, jacket, boots—were gone: she was barefoot, wearing a sleeveless grayish knee-length tunic of some coarse stiff fabric. There were chains and shackles set into the walls, and she walked over to inspect them, hefting the fetters in her hands. By rights they should have been black iron, and they *were* black, but the sheen and smoothness told her they were not iron. If anything she'd read about elves was true, cold iron would burn them like a red-hot poker, so the metal must not be either iron or steel. Pewter? Silver? More mysteries. It did explain the absence of her clothes, however. Everything but the T-shirt had iron in it—the studs on her jacket, the toe caps of her boots, the hooks and eyelets on her brassiere, even the snaps and rivets on her jeans. All steel, and thus taboo in this place—or should be. How much of what she'd read in old books could be trusted, and how much was sheer fabulation? Trusting anything she thought she knew could be fatal.

She did know one thing for sure and certain, however. Aerune had not brought her here just to lock her up and leave her to rot. And there was only one thing that made her valuable: her ability to manufacture T-Stroke.

But what did a faerie lord want with a drug that gave humans psionic powers? Jeanette frowned, puzzled. Elves had magic powers—she'd certainly seen enough hard evidence of that from Aerune—so she couldn't imagine why they'd need what T-Stroke could do for them. T-Stroke didn't give anyone magic powers, anyway; it gave them psionic powers—a fine distinction, but a real one. While magic could play cut and paste with the laws of physics, psionics were essentially bound by them: with psychic powers you might be able to read minds or see the future—or *heal*—but you couldn't turn lead into gold, raise the dead, or teach a pig to speak English. And while natural psychics might manifest several different psychic gifts in varying strengths, her T-Stroke-created Talents only seemed to be able to do one particular thing, which must make them doubly inferior to an elven magician—though it was also true that Aerune *had* wanted her test subjects, inferior or not. Back in December he'd been grabbing them before she or Robert could get to them, though presumably he could do everything they could do and more. She'd never found out why; she supposed she'd find out now.

She knew she should be more afraid than she was, but all Jeanette felt was numb. Shock, she thought—that and the certain knowledge that she would die soon whether Aerune tortured her or not. Death was such a final answer—and however much she feared it, she couldn't escape it—so why not embrace it as much as she could?

Because she was too afraid to, that was why.

Just then there was a rattling sound from the doorway above. She looked up, just in time to see the doorway sink majestically downward through the stone like a descending elevator cage, until the opening was level with the floor.

Two trolls—they couldn't be anything else—gazed through the bars at her.

Their smooth shiny skin was the greenish color of tarnished copper, and a wave of stench like rotting frogs rolled into the cell from their presence. They were about five and a half feet tall, alike as twins, and cartoonishly muscled, with shoulders nearly as wide as they were tall, and arms that dangled below their knees. Their faces were like a caricature of Early Man: flat noses, massive jaws, and heavy beetling brows from beneath which their eyes glowed with the silvery redness of beasts'. The long tips of pointed ears extended for an inch or two above their flat skulls, and dull lank hair the color of old moss began low on their foreheads and straggled down their backs. They were dressed in a parody of medieval costume: knee-length chain mail shirts beneath black tabards with a crimson blazon, bronze bracers laced onto their huge forearms, and shaggy boots that seemed to have been crudely made from imperfectly-emptied bears. Each of them held a seven-foot billhook in his hand.

One of them reached for something she could not see from inside the cell, and the portcullis rose with a rattle of chains.

"Come out, little girl," the other said, leering. His voice was low and hoarse, like granite boulders mating. His teeth were huge and yellow, like a horse's, but with long upper and lower fangs. Jeanette could smell his breath six feet away. It smelled like rotting meat.

"Bite me," Jeanette said sullenly. No matter how unnatural they looked, they were only another incarnation of big, stupid street muscle, the sort she'd dealt with when she ran with the Sinner Saints. They answered to a master—Aerune—and to show them either fear or deference would be a bad mistake.

The troll looked puzzled, trying to decide whether to be angry. He shifted uncertainly, gazing at his partner.

The other troll walked into the cell. He was not so much tall as massive—*must weigh close to a thousand pounds*—Jeanette estimated. He bowed, holding the billhook to one side and resting the knuckles of his free hand on the floor.

"Mortal lady. The great prince Aerune requires thy presence, and we are sent to escort thee into his presence." The words were subservient, but his manner wasn't.

The smart ones are always trouble. He made her feel like Elkanah always had—as if he knew something she didn't, as if all the knowledge and power she possessed would be useless against that secret wisdom. She got to her feet.

"Okay. Fine. Let's go."

She stepped past him, out into the corridor. The stone was rough beneath her bare feet, and cold. Torches lined the walls, but again the illumination was flat and directionless, as if the torches were only a sort of window dressing, and not the real source of the light. Barred doorways, such as the one she'd come through, lined the walls all the way to the ceiling. From some of the higher ones, liquid trickled down the wall, staining the gray stone to black. There was a faint whiff of latrine, perceptible beyond the ripe rankness of her guards. She felt queasy and ill, as if she were coming down with the flu, but put it down to a combination of emotional shock and T-Stroke. She steeled herself against showing how she felt; any show of weakness could be fatal, and she still had to face the main event—Aerune.

The dumb one led the way, and the smart one followed. They went up a winding staircase, the steps sized for trolls and not humans; Jeanette was aching and breathless by the time they reached the top. Here the workmanship on the stones of the corridor was finer, the doors of solid wood.

They walked for at least half an hour, seeing no one, as the corridors slowly changed, becoming more refined and upscale, until at last Jeanette was walking across smooth mosaic floors between walls of carved alabaster hung with tapestries. She felt less sick now, though all around her there was the same sort of waiting tension that heralded the storm. There were guards here and there along the way—elven knights, this time, not trolls, wearing elaborate jeweled armor and holding long silver pikes. At the end of one corridor, her captors stopped before a pair of them. The elves' faces were invisible within their helmets, but she could see the faint red spark of eyes deep within the shadows.

"Here is the woman whom Lord Aerune has summoned, lord," the smart troll said.

The elven knight bowed silently, and gestured for her to advance.

"Be good, human girl," the smart troll said. "Or the prince will give you back to me to do with as I choose." Despite the unspoken threat, Jeanette had the odd feeling the words were kindly meant.

"And if you can't be good, be careful," she said in return.

"Silence!" one of the elves snapped.

This time both members of her escort preceded her, obviously unable to imagine that she would run (they were right, but she still thought they were stupid). They walked only a short distance before stopping before a pair of gigantic doors that seemed to be carved of one giant sheet of black jade. As they approached, the doors swung open, and she followed her guards into Aerune's throne room. Once inside the doorway her escort stopped, and waited for her to go on alone.

The throne room was enormous—big as a sound stage or a church, and empty save for Aerune. The walls were carved in the semblance of a forest, copies of the same black trees she had seen upon her arrival, their carved branches rising to form a vault above the room.

The floor beneath her feet was the glassy dull silver of liquid mercury, treacherously smooth. In the center of the room, atop a round three-step dais of the same smooth black material as the doors, stood a throne. It was black, massive, and intricately figured, but somehow it was not quite *there*, as if parts of it curved off in directions the human eye was not equipped to perceive.

And on the throne sat Aerune.

This was the first time Jeanette had gotten a really good look at him, and once again her heart twisted at the sight of his beauty. Save for the helmet—for Aerune's head was bare—he wore the same full ornate field plate armor as his guards, but of a silver so dark it seemed black. On his head was a black crown set with cabochon rubies that glowed as brightly as if they were lit from behind, and on his black-gloved hand he wore a matching ruby ring.

All her life Jeanette had dreamed of a moment like this, when she could cast aside the bonds of Earth and walk the halls of Faerie. And now that the moment had arrived, she could think of only one thing.

He can't be serious.

Everything that she'd seen was just too overblown, too derivative, too much. It was all done with money to burn, but it still looked like an episode of *Dr. Who*. It had no *heart* to it. Actually, *Dr. Who* had heart; it didn't take itself seriously and it was on a bargain budget, so heart was all it had, but it had a lot of it. No, this looked as if some avaricious goon with all the money in the universe had decided to copy *Dr. Who* on an infinite budget without the least understanding of what made the BBC series live for its fans. This place was hollow— the exact opposite of *creative*.

So now you know why they call them The Hollow Hills. Good going, Girl Detective.

"So, mortal girl. At last you face your ultimate desire—for I am Death, and Pain, and the end of all things."

Jeanette wasn't sure whether to laugh, cry, or just stamp her foot in frustration. She'd ruined her life, killed hundreds, to get here . . . and this was all there was? This fanboy weenie from hell?

And worst of all, she was still terrified. And he was still beautiful as the morning.

As she stepped onto the floor, something lying at the foot of the throne raised its head. She hadn't seen it before because it was so black; it looked a little like a wolf crossed with a Doberman, if the result were the size of a small pony and had eyes that glowed a featureless red. It opened its mouth and yawned, exposing ivory teeth and a blood-red tongue, then put its head back down, joining the other creatures coiled at the foot of the throne in sleep.

"Lord Aerune," she said, reaching the foot of the shadow throne and looking up at him.

"Come, little alchemist. Kneel at my feet, and I will tell you how you may serve me."

Despite herself, Jeanette stumbled forward and up the steps of the dais to kneel at his feet. One of the hellhounds growled as she approached, and Aerune held out his hand to silence it.

"Know, first, that all your comrades are dead, including your former master. The slave Elkanah, whom I sent to retrieve you from the human world, is undoubtedly dead now, and by your hand."

Tell me something I don't know, Jeanette thought sullenly. She'd hated Elkanah, and feared him, but part of her was happy for him. He was dead. He was free. No one should have to live with the memory of being Aerune's pawn.

"Very well," Aerune answered, a hint of displeasure in his voice. "I shall tell you that I shall destroy your pestilent, arrogant race, and your work shall be a weapon in my arsenal. If it can kindle the power of the Starry Crown in such fleeting creatures of mud and stench, then what more may it do for the Children of Danu? Armed with its power, we will nevermore fear your Cold Iron, nor your foolish violence. And my Aerete shall be avenged."

There was genuine sorrow in his voice, and when Jeanette dared to look up, she could see that his face was set in lines of bitter grief.

"Once," Aerune said softly, "the world was ours. There was no Dark Court, no Bright—only the Immortal Sidhe, the firstborn of Danu. Your kind was less than the beasts—animals whom we raised up from the rest of the brute creation and taught to serve us. And for many years you understood your place and kept to it. But you became presumptuous—and to our eternal doom and sorrow, there were those among the Sidhe who helped you to rise from the dust where you belonged. Aerete the Golden was one such—guardian to your tribe, aid and protection against all who would harm you, though I offered her my heart and my crown. Yet even would I spare you for her sake, turn aside when you incurred my just wrath . . . yet you slew her with your deathmetal, and I will never rest until all your race has paid the price in full measure for slaying her whom I loved—my soul-twin, my mate, the only creature who could lift my being from the darkness and eternal night. . . .

"And you yourselves shall be the instrument of my vengeance— you and your endless inventiveness."

"I won't," Jeanette said. Tears were running down her face— fear for herself, grief for Aerune's loss. She knew what it was like to be denied the chance to *be* through a cruel trick of fate, and she felt his sorrow as if it were her own. But she could not help him kill again. "I won't make T-Stroke for you. I won't shoot up your guinea pigs."

Shockingly, Aerune laughed, and reached down to tousle her hair as he might pat the head of an unruly dog.

"Do you presume to know my mind, or to tell me the extent of my power? I do not need you to create more of your poison—I already have enough of your Crownfire to *ken* enough to drown the world. And as for proving its worth . . ."

He raised a hand and gestured. The doors to the throne room swung inward once more, and Jeanette blinked. This time they were gold and jeweled. This was what living in a world made with magic was, she realized: a universe in which there were no certainties, even those extending to the continuity of the world which surrounded you.

Two of Aerune's armored knights entered, dragging a third between them who struggled and snarled curses in some unknown language. The bright silks he had worn were in rags, and his body bore the marks of a world-class beating, but he was still defiant. As he approached Aerune's throne, the hounds raised their heads and growled, watching him intently. And somehow his speech turned to English, so that Jeanette could understand what he said.

"Kneel before your master: Prince Aerune, Lord of Death and Pain!" one of the knights said.

The stranger fought like a wet cat as they forced him to his knees. He spat at Aerune, and one of Aerune's guards backhanded him with a metal-clad fist. The impact of the blow was a sound like wood hitting wood, and blood sprayed across the mirrored floor. Jeanette felt pain shoot through her, leaving her weak and shaking, with a throbbing headache. But the stranger remained defiant.

"Prince of nothing! Oathbreaker and fool! Know that I am Aliagrant Tannoeth, Knight and Magus of Elfhame Thunders-mouth, herald and cupbearer to Prince Seithawg and the Lady Cyndrwin, traveling beneath a ward of truce across lands held by no lord! Release me at once—or risk my lord's terrible vengeance!"

"Such passion," Aerune murmured. "Such foolishness, here in the stronghold of your enemies, but I forget: you are but a boy. Do you truly think Aerune is bound by the treaties that bind the Dark Court to the Light, or that your people will know what fate has befallen you? Shall I fear Seithawg, whose father's father I slew, or the *lennan sidhe* who rules beside him? Or shall I fear Lady Aniause to whom you ride, and who will seek for you in vain once word reaches her that you have vanished? There is danger in the Chaos

Lands. All know that. But in your pride you would dare them, and so you have found . . . me."

From his expression, Aliagrant was not hearing anything he liked. It was as if Jeanette could feel his fear, like silent music. And Aerune was right—he *was* young. Even if the elves were immortal and eternal, Jeanette could tell that much about him.

"So. You see I speak no more than the truth. Bow down and swear fealty to me, boy, and perhaps I will allow you to live."

But afraid and in pain though he was, Aliagrant still would not submit. "Kill me, then!"

"Perhaps in time. Meanwhile, you *will* serve me—in one fashion or another."

Once more the doors opened, admitting two more . . . creatures.

One looked like The Old Witch from the cover of EC Comics: an ancient, ugly, hunchbacked woman, dressed in rags. Her nose and chin were hooked, her toothless mouth fallen in upon itself. One eye was white and bulging, the other a narrow slit. She carried a tray upon which stood two objects: a jeweled wine cup, and one of the brown plastic bottles of T-Stroke that Jeanette had in her jacket pocket back at the van.

The hag's companion was small, barely the size of a child, but with a distorted, misshapen form . . . and very long arms. It wore a laborer's smock and ragged pants, and upon its head there was a soft cap of bright scarlet, as bright as the blood of men. It looked like it had wandered out of the background of some Hildebrandt painting. It looked like a hobbit on crack.

"Don't do this," Jeanette whispered, cowering and shivering against the foot of the throne. She could feel Aliagrant's pain radiating from him like heat from an overstoked stove, and in the middle of everything else, she had a horrible intuition that the T-Stroke had worked—and what the Talent it had given her was.

Aerune stepped down past her and over to the hag. He picked up the brown bottle and poured a generous dose into the wine, then stirred the mixture with a long golden spoon. Then he picked up the cup and gestured to the redcapped hobgoblin.

It scampered over to where the two elven knights were still

holding the boy on his knees. The redcap crouched behind him, pulling his head back with one hand and forcing his jaw open with the other.

Then Aerune stood over him and poured the contents of the cup into his mouth. The boy choked and tried to struggle, but the redcap was far too strong for him. Wine ran down his chin and onto his chest, but he ended up swallowing more than half of the mixture.

"You see?" Aerune said, turning to Jeanette. "I have no need of your assistance." He gestured to the knights, who released their victim.

Aliagrant began to scream, joined half a beat later by Jeanette. She was burning, she was dying—she felt what Aliagrant felt, and the pain was hideous, it felt as if she was drinking Drano, and far worse than the pain was the terror of an immortal creature being sent down into death.

For Aliagrant was dying. She could feel it more surely than she could feel her own body—the flesh withering and dissolving as his body burned away to nothingness.

And then it stopped. Blessedly, it stopped.

Barely able to focus, she looked up fearfully, scrubbing her face dry on her bare forearm. All that was left of Aliagrant was a mess on the floor, as if a mummy were in the process of crumbling away into ash. As she watched, the body crumbled further, then dissolved altogether, leaving only a smear of dust that sank into the mirrored floor, leaving no trace behind.

"Interesting," Aerune said impassively. "What calls up magic in your race destroys it in mine—and that, you will have observed, my mortal alchemist, is fatal." Aerune sounded more interested than put out by that fact. "Still, its effects are entertaining—are they not, Urla? Far more so than elfbane or caffeine."

"Yes, Great Lord," the redcap answered. It had a high, hoarse voice, like that of an evil child.

"And it still works on humans—on precisely those humans who will have to be eliminated to ensure that my race may once more assume its rightful place as their overlords—the magic users, the Crowned Ones, whose ancestors mingled the blood of their race with my own. Why should they not be useful in death?"

He looked back at Jeanette, smiling gently. "I never needed you to make more of your wizard's potion. I needed to find out what you knew, and to keep you from falling into the hands of my enemies to become their weapon. And now I see that the sorcery you have worked has made you useful to me beyond that." His smile grew wider and more razored. "You think that this T-Stroke will save you from me, that it will grant you a quick and easy death beyond my mercy, but in truth, for all your arrogance, you know so little about my kind. How can the sands of your life run out if Time itself does not run Underhill? No, you will live as long as I choose, and serve me. But not in that unpleasant form . . ."

He reached for her, smiling, and when he touched her, Jeanette began to scream.

TEN:
(I'LL STOP THE WORLD AND)
MELT WITH YOU

The day that had started out so badly did not improve. Eric was inattentive in class, and Levoisier took a sadistic delight in gigging him for it. He was sloppy in rehearsal, fumbling around like a novice, unable to keep time with the other musicians or make his entrances on cue. Finally he gave up. The world wouldn't come to an end if he cut his last class. And besides, Eric wanted to see how Toni and Hosea were coming with the basement apartment.

The phone was ringing as he got into the apartment, and when he looked at the counter, it registered 27 previous messages.

"Eric," he said, picking it up.

"Eric!" Ria sounded absolutely frantic. "Where *were* you? I've been trying to reach you all afternoon!"

"Not everybody's cellular," Eric said irritably. "Sorry. Bad day. What's up?"

"Kayla's coming. Today." Ria made it sound as if Kayla was a combination of the Black Death, the Four Horsemen, and the IRS. "And I'm stuck in this damned meeting—in fact, I'm supposed to be in there right now—and I can't get away. I don't know how long I'll be. Her plane's coming in at three; I've sent a car for her, but I don't want her coming back to an empty apartment. Could I have the driver drop her at your place? I swear I'll be there as soon as I can."

Eric had never heard Ria sound so rattled. It struck him that she owed Kayla and Elizabet a great deal. Taking care of Kayla properly on Kayla's arrival in New York was probably as important to Ria as being a good teacher to Hosea was to him, and she was probably just as uncertain of her ability to do it right.

His black mood vanished. "Hey, Ria. Don't worry about it. Have the guy drop her off here. We'll order pizza and watch DVDs until you get here. Promise."

"Thanks." He heard Ria breathe a deep sigh of relief. "I hate to ask, but could you possibly call Anita for me and tell her? She'll phone the car. I have *got* to get back in there!"

"Sure," Eric said. "Knock 'em dead." The phone went dead before he'd finished speaking.

Well, that takes care of the rest of the day. He looked up the number and made the call to Anita, then went to look over his DVD collection, wondering what sort of movie Kayla would like. "Hey, Greystone," he said aloud. "Company for dinner."

Hosea came in about half an hour after that, looking very much like someone who'd spent a hot August day cleaning out a non-air-conditioned basement.

"Better hit the shower," Eric advised him. "A friend of mine's going to be here pretty soon. Name's Kayla. She's a Healer. Going to be going to school up at Columbia—but not living here," he added, noting Hosea's faint look of alarm. "I'm just taking care of her until Ria can pick her up."

"Ayah, a shower sounds good. I feel like I've been juggling pianos," Hosea said ruefully. "But I got all that lumber moved out of there, and after I scrub it down with lye soap, I can paint it up spicker than span." He shot a curious look at Eric. "A Healer, say you?"

"That's right," Eric said. "But I'll let her tell you about it herself. Wait till you meet her."

Hosea headed for the shower.

❖❖ ❖❖ ❖❖

:They're comin' 'round the far turn: Greystone told Eric about five minutes later.

"That was quick," Eric said. He thrust his feet into sandals and headed for the street.

The car was just pulling up as he reached the sidewalk, which felt very much like walking into an oven at this time of day, as the concrete gave back a day's worth of stored heat. Ria'd sent her personal car: a maroon vintage Rolls Royce limousine. The driver—in matching livery, right down to the archaic jodhpurs and riding boots—climbed out and walked back to open the passenger door.

Kayla wasn't waiting for him to get there. Eric saw the door swing open and a . . . vision . . . in glitter and Spandex stepped out of the car.

The last time Eric had seen Kayla, the sixteen-year-old had been heavy into punk, right down to the safety pins in place of earrings. But two years was an eternity in a teenager's life.

Things had changed.

She still had the black leather jacket—and was wearing it, in defiance of the weather—but now it seemed to glitter in places. She was wearing artistically-damaged fishnet stockings, and on her feet were spike-heeled pointed-toed ankle boots with more straps than a Bellevue special. Between the ankle boots and the leather jacket was a black lace tutu, the layers of black lace tulle glittering with purple and black sequins and standing almost straight out.

Kayla reached back into the car to grab her backpack, and blew the driver a kiss before striding across the street to Eric. As she approached, Eric could see that she'd carried out the glitter-Goth look in all aspects: her hair was dagged and shagged, dyed flat black with indigo and fuchsia streaks. Her face was powdered dead white, eyes heavily lined in kohl and mascara, and mouth painted a glistening red-black. Silver batwing earrings dangled from her ears. Under the jacket, she was wearing a very tight cropped tank top with a black velvet rose pinned to the neckline.

"Hiya, Eric," Kayla said. She held out a hand. She was wearing fingerless lace mitts—black, of course—and her nails, still cut back almost to the quick, were painted black with a dull silver glitter overlay.

"This is a new look for you," Eric said. A lot more high-maintenance than the old one, but he guessed Kayla'd finally gotten used to the fact that she had a home and a family, and didn't have to scrabble on the streets just to survive. He waved to the driver, who'd followed Kayla across the street.

"Are you Eric Banyon?" the man asked.

"That's right," Eric said.

"I just wanted to make sure the little lady got where she was going," the driver said. "I've got a daughter about her age." He smiled and went back to his car.

"Sheesh," Kayla muttered, embarrassed.

"Hey, you know Ria'd have his head if he let anything happen to you," Eric said. "C'mon, let's get upstairs. It's hot out here, and you must be about to fry."

"Nice place," Kayla said, looking around the apartment. She set her backpack down on the floor and peeled off her black leather jacket. Her shoulders glittered with a mix of makeup and sweat. "Nice air conditioning," she added a moment later. "Gotta say, Eric, you do know how to land jelly-side-up."

Hearing voices, Hosea came out into the living room. He was wearing jeans and a new white T-shirt, his shaggy blond hair still damp from a hasty shower.

"Hey," Kayla said appreciatively, "you didn't tell me Chippendales was in town."

"This is a friend of mine," Eric said. "He's staying with me until his place is ready. Hosea Songmaker, meet Kayla Smith."

Hosea stepped forward and held out his hand. After a moment's hesitation, Kayla took it. If he noticed her outlandish costume, he didn't indicate it by so much as an eye blink. Eric could see the look of concentration on her face as she made sure her shields were in place—any touch was intimate if you were an Empath—but then he saw her relax and give Hosea a genuine smile.

"Any friend of Eric's is a friend of mine," Hosea said firmly in his slow pleasant drawl. "Pleased to make your acquaintance, Healer Kayla."

"And yours . . . Bard," Kayla said after a short pause. "Hey, Eric, you didn't say you were collecting 'em."

"Just a happy accident," Eric said. "Hosea came to the city looking for someone to show him the ropes, and I guess I'm elected."

"I couldn't ask for a better teacher," Hosea said. "But you must be plumb tuckered out from all that traveling, Miss Kayla. Would you care for something cold to drink? There's lemonade, fresh-squeezed, and every kind of water you can imagine."

So that's *why we've got all those lemons.*

"Lemonade, please," Kayla said. She glanced toward the sound system. "Mind if I check out the tunes?"

"*Mi casa es su casa,*" Eric answered in bad Spanish. "Feel free. I don't know how long Ria's going to be—she said she'd get here as soon as she could, but—"

"But Ria's a busy girl, yadda," Kayla said. "Glad you kids are getting along," she added absently, drifting over to the wall of CDs.

"You know you look like Tinkerbell on drugs, don't you?" Eric said to her back.

Kayla turned and flashed him a smile. "Gotta blend in with the natives, right?"

Eric didn't really expect Ria any time soon, so after checking with Kayla about her preferences—he already knew Hosea's—Eric phoned down to the pizza place for three large pies with everything. The three of them sat and ate pizza while listening to Kayla's music selections. Her taste was more eclectic than Eric had anticipated, everything from salsa and classic rock to grand opera.

"I'll try anything once—twice if I like it," she said, in answer to his quizzical look. "So, Hosea, how'd you find out you were a Bard?"

"Eric told me," Hosea said, swallowing a mouthful of pizza. "I just thought I had a little shine, but I guess there's a name for everything. And you?"

"Oh, I brought somebody back from the dead, and things went on from there."

❖❖ ❖❖ ❖❖

As soon as the Portal closed, sanity returned. The *geas* that Aerune had placed upon him along with the silver antlers was gone; Elkanah's mind was clearer than it had been in weeks. He saw it all now. The Sidhe lord had used him as a Judas goat—let him think he'd escaped, let him think that searching out Campbell was his own idea, though it had been Aerune's magic that had led him to her and then led him back here, to a place Aerune could claim her easily.

He'd been a fool. A *pawn*.

And to top it all off, the bitch had poisoned him. Elkanah could feel the T-Stroke burning through his system. In a few hours, he'd be dead.

But there was something he had to do first. Not for Campbell's sake. But because there were innocents in the line of fire, and because those innocents had to be saved . . . or at least warned. He staggered toward the van, fighting the wave of drug-fuelled oblivion.

He did not reach it before he fell.

Another Monday night in Paradise, Jimmie Youngblood thought, piloting her blue-and-white through the traffic snarls of Lower Midtown. She felt better than she had in weeks—hell, *months*—as if the wave of Impending Doom had finally broken, or at least as if some part of her mind had finally reached an accommodation with whatever unspoken warning had disturbed her for so long. She felt released, but unsettled. Maybe Eric had been right: some problems just went away, and you never knew afterward exactly what they'd been.

Her radio woke to life, spitting out a jumble of ten-codes: someone had set a van on fire near the Lincoln Tunnel, local units please assist. She checked and confirmed she was the closest unit, turning her vehicle in that direction. The dispatcher would alert the fire department, but she'd get there first.

As soon as Jimmie saw the smoke, she could feel something tangled up with it, like an astral riptide undercutting reality. *Power.* Someone down here was using magic—bad magic. It brought all her uneasy feelings rushing back—and worst of all, there was something oddly *familiar* about the source.

Bomb? Phosphorus grenade? Salamander? Someone isn't having a lucky night.

She barely remembered to give her 10-20 when she arrived. Traffic was already snarled behind the charred wreckage—even at ten o'clock at night the Lincoln Tunnel was busy. She pulled her unit around to block the tunnel completely, hearing the wail of other sirens in the distance. Fire Department and Traffic Control, right on schedule. But she was the first on the scene.

She climbed out of her unit, staring at what was left of the van. It wasn't just burning. It had been torched—the tires were melted pools of rubber on the blacktop and the van itself was too charred for her to know what its original color had been. No need to worry about the gas tank exploding—from the looks of things, it already had.

Or else whatever brought it here didn't need gas to make the engine run. . . .

Worst of all, she knew that something had gotten out of it alive. She could see puddled footsteps where the blacktop had melted in the street, as though something very hot had just . . . walked away. Something that reeked with Power like a spill of fresh blood.

No time to call the others in on this. She had to find that thing before it hurt anyone else. That there were no casualties already was a minor miracle. She grabbed her nightstick and her vest and followed.

The blocks around the Tunnel were a wasteland of urban decay spawned by the new Conference Center, which was a mixed blessing. With the Javits Center empty, there were few pedestrians around to get in her way, but a lot of empty lots, parking garages, and derelict cars to provide cover for her wandering perp. The tracks stopped at the edge of the concrete pavement, but she could still see signs of his handiwork.

Here, a charred stump that had been a living tree. There, a half-melted basket full of trash, still burning. A smear of cinder on the side of a building, just where a tall man might rest his hand. And all around, the reek of baneful magic like a choking cloud—magic born of pain and death and suffering.

She stopped long enough to shrug into her Kevlar vest, though she doubted that something that would stop a bullet would stop whatever she followed. She had the sense that what she followed was wounded and in pain, but no less a danger for all that. She reached down to shut off the radio on her belt—no point in alerting her quarry, and no help she could summon in time would be able to face down what she followed. She'd made that mistake once. Never again.

Oh, Davey. You shouldn't have had to die for me to figure that out. She spared a brief thought for the other Guardians, but it would take too long to summon them as well. She had to contain what she followed before innocent civilians met the same fate as the charred van. She could smell the burning on the air.

Ahead of her was an alleyway, leading between two derelict buildings. Behind them was an empty lot, the building it had once contained gone to bricks and rubble—a favorite hangout for junkies and rent-boys. The alley was the only exit. Whoever it was—*what*ever it was, she had it cornered now.

There were no lights on the street. The only illumination came from the last dregs of summer twilight, and the sky glow from the city itself. She hesitated. *Stupid to go in without backup. That's why they call it Tombstone Courage. . . .* She forced herself to stop, to use her radio, tell them her position, tell them she was in hot pursuit of the arson suspect. It didn't matter now. By the time her backup got here, it would be over, one way or another. The dispatcher told her to wait, of course, but even as she heard that rational, sensible counsel, Jemima Youngblood knew she couldn't wait. Lives depended on her. She could already smell smoke.

She drew her gun and stepped into the alley, letting out her breath in a long sigh as she saw it was empty. But the fire glow painting the far end told her she was right. The empty lot was burning.

She hesitated, thinking again of warning Toni and the others that magic was afoot once more. She was reaching for her cell phone when the scream came, a scream of primal agony, of someone being burned alive.

She ran toward it, cursing her luck.

The screamer pirouetted like a top in the middle of the empty lot, wrapped in a shroud of flame, howling out his fear and pain to the night. He was burned past saving—she knew that already, from the black and ruined skin she could see through the flames that covered him—but she had to try. She knocked the shrieking dervish to the ground, beating at the flames with her bare hands while his skin flaked away like charcoal from a half-burnt log. His blood boiled on the surface of his skin, and before the flames were gone, the screaming stopped. He was dead.

"Jimmie."

A familiar voice, filled with pain and sorrow. A voice she had never expected to hear again. She looked up slowly, not wanting to see. Her searching hand closed over empty air—she'd dropped her weapon trying to put out the fire. She had a backup strapped to her ankle. Still kneeling, she reached for it, slowly, burned palms stinging and tearing.

"Jimmie. Little sister. What are you doing here?"

Her fingers touched the metal of the gunbutt.

"I'm a cop, Elk. Like you were, once." She held her voice steady by a great effort.

Elkanah Youngblood stood a few feet away. He was naked, his bronze skin covered with soot and fresh burns. Power radiated from him like light from the noonday sun, but he wasn't another victim. He was the source. All around him, everything that could burn was burning—weeds, garbage, wood.

Pyrokinesis. Without control, the fires that he set were burning him as well, eating him alive.

But that shows up early, in childhood, and Elk never—

"I have to tell you—" he said. "I have to tell—" He staggered toward her. His eyes were white, blind with heat. "You have to stop—" He moaned, a long sound of agony and despair.

"Don't come any closer!" She felt blisters break as her fingers closed over the gun. A .38 snubnose—useless at a distance, but not against a naked man at nearly point-blank range.

"*You have to stop him!*" Elkanah howled. "Jimmie—please Campbell—Aerune—Stop—"

He fell to his knees, reaching out to her as he died. Her scream melded with his own as the fire consuming him from within burst forth from mouth, eyes, ears . . . from his outstretched hand, still reaching toward her.

Burning everything he touched.

Burning the world.

The phone had rung about fifteen minutes ago. Ria was finally out of her meeting and on her way to Eric's. When it rang again, Eric thought it was Ria calling back, saying something else had delayed her.

"Banyon."

"Eric." Toni's voice, so hoarse and distorted that at first he didn't recognize it. "Is Hosea there?"

"Toni?" Something was horribly wrong—but what? He'd had no warning. He could hear the ragged sobs around the edges of her voice every time she inhaled. "Yeah, he's here, but—"

"Jimmie's . . . in Gotham General. It's bad. She's asking for him. How soon can he get here?"

"We're on our way."

The others were already on their feet, alerted by his face and voice.

"Jimmie's in the hospital. She's asking for you," Eric said to Hosea. Lady Day would get them there fastest. He sent a call to the elvensteed and felt her worried reply. "C'mon."

"I'm coming too," Kayla said. "I can help."

There was no time to argue. Eric headed for the door. Where was Greystone? Why hadn't he warned them that Jimmie had been hurt?

The three of them reached the front steps just as Ria was pulling up in the Rolls.

"What's wrong?" she demanded, seeing their faces. The elvensteed was waiting at the curb, quivering with urgency.

"Jimmie's hurt. We have to get to Gotham General as fast as we can," Eric told her. Lady Day was already sitting at the curb.

"We'll take the car," Ria said. "It'll be as fast as an elvensteed at this time of night."

"You go with Kayla. Hosea and I will meet you there," Eric said. The two men turned toward the bike. There was no time to bother with helmets, and Lady Day would keep them from harm if she had to jump through a Gate to do it. Hosea climbed on behind him without a word.

"Go fast," Eric whispered to his 'steed.

The world vanished in a gray blur of absolute speed. Eric felt Hosea clutch at him, but almost before he'd adjusted to the sensation of flying, the trip was over. Lady Day was standing at the front door of Gotham General, kickstand down.

"Hey! You can't park there!" someone said as Eric was climbing off. *:Go home:*, he Sent to the 'steed. *:Wait there.:* He turned to help Hosea off, steadying the big man as he staggered, ignoring the speaker.

"Hey . . . !" the voice trailed off weakly as the elvensteed drove off, eliminating the problem.

Eric turned to face the speaker—it was a man in surgical scrubs, obviously out for a quick smoke. "How do I get to the—"

:Burn Trauma Unit: Greystone's voice came in his head. *:Paul will take you. Brace yourself, laddybuck. It's bad.:*

Paul Kern was coming down the steps. He'd obviously been waiting for them. His face was haggard with grief.

"Eric—Hosea. Come with me. Hurry. I don't think there's much time."

"But what happened?" Eric asked, as soon as they were in the elevator. Gotham General covered several city blocks; getting where they were going couldn't be done quickly.

"Someone . . . burned Jimmie," Paul said starkly. "Maybe gasoline. The officers who brought her in didn't know. Thank God she listed Toni as next of kin—they aren't letting anyone else in to see her, and we didn't want to push without more information."

"You said she's asking for Hosea," Eric said.

"When she's conscious," Paul said tightly.

"Burn Trauma" . . . *he said something burned her.*

Eric looked at Hosea. The tall man's face was grim.

And she asked for Hosea.

José was waiting at the elevator. An expression of relief crossed his features when he saw them. "Hosea! Hurry!" he turned back to the floor. "She's this way."

"Won't they stop us?" Hosea said, following the others. The Burn Trauma floor was quiet, without the usual noise and bustle of a big city hospital. There were signs on the walls reminding nursing staff to follow sterile procedure and restricting visitors, and several of the doors had signs on them prohibiting entry without Clean Room protocols.

"They won't know we're here," Paul said. "Greystone and I are making sure of that."

And in fact no one did stop them. There was a nurse in the room as they entered, but she didn't even look up.

There were bags of saline and whole blood—and a morphine drip—hung around the head of the bed like a flock of toy balloons. A sheet concealed the body in the bed—Jimmie—tented up on a framework to keep any part of it from touching her. All Eric could see was her head, swathed in dressings, even the eyes bandaged. It was warm in the room—burn victims lost the ability to regulate their own body temperature, and a chill could be fatal.

The room was filled with the smell of cooked meat, which puzzled him. Finally Eric realized that what he was smelling was *Jimmie*, and had to fight hard to keep from gagging. He heard a strangled gasp from Hosea as his companion realized this as well.

Toni looked up. She was sitting on a chair beside the bed, bent toward Jimmie. "She was asking for you, before," she said to Hosea. "We don't know why." She got to her feet and came over to the others. "Would you sit with her awhile, Hosea? She might wake up."

Hosea nodded. His face was very white. But his steps were steady as he crossed to the bed and took Toni's place in the chair.

Eric had known it was bad before, when Toni called, but at the back of his mind there'd been the certainty that Jimmie would be getting better. Now, looking at Toni's face and the still figure in the floatation bed, he no longer thought so.

Jimmie Youngblood was dying. His *friend* was dying. And there was nothing he could do about it.

Bardic magic could work wonders. It could summon the power to allow creatures of magic—such as the Sidhe—to heal themselves. It could hasten the healing process for something that was going to heal anyway. But Jimmie wasn't going to heal. If he listened, Eric could hear the song of her life slowly slipping out of key, growing slower and more distorted by the minute, with nothing he could do to draw it back in tune. And if he could hear it, the Guardians certainly could, too.

But Kayla's a Healer! She can fix it! he thought desperately.

As if he'd summoned her with his thoughts, Eric heard a disturbance in the hall, and then felt a cold wash of Power soothing it ruthlessly away.

Ria.

The door opened, and Kayla walked in alone. Her black lace and glitter was even more jarringly out of place in the harsh dull light of the hospital room than it had been in his apartment.

"She's a Healer," Eric said, as the others turned toward this new intruder.

"Can you help her?" Toni asked Kayla. Eric heard the naked pleading in her voice, and knew what it cost Toni Hernandez to beg.

"I can try," Kayla said. Her face was pale and still beneath the mask of makeup, and the neon-bright streaks in her hair looked flat and unreal.

She walked over to the bed—slowly, as if moving through deep water. No matter how good her shields were, a hospital was no place for an Empath. She hesitated at the side of the bed, looking from Hosea to Toni.

"I have to touch her."

"I reckon you'd best do what you can." It was Hosea who answered. "You can't hurt her any worse than she's been hurt."

"What's her name? Jimmie?" If Kayla had other questions, she didn't ask them. Ultimately, they weren't important.

Jimmie. Dumb name for a girl. Go on, stupid. You can do it.

Kayla spoke loudly in her own head to cover her own fear and Jimmie's pain. She could feel it even without touching her, even through the morphine, agony radiating like waves of heat from the summer streets. Damage, slow and deep. Trauma that the body couldn't handle. Pain, whether emotional or physical, was a cry for help—always. Elizabet had taught her that.

Her hand was shaking in anticipation of pain to come. Kayla forced herself to reach out—slowly, gently, until her fingertips barely touched the bandages on Jimmie's forehead. Contact! Blue light crackled over her hand, like a spark jumping a gap. Like heat— lightning—fire.

Fire!

It filled Jimmie's body-memory: fire, its first chill wash, then pain, building on itself, melting Kevlar, searing her body as the metal she wore turned molten and sank into burning flesh, burning, *burning . . .*

Everywhere Kayla looked there was ruin—fluids seeping into tissues, running over bared muscle where the skin was cooked away, veins and arteries ripped open by boiling blood, tendons heated and shriveled, nerves blackened and twisted, or screaming endlessly for help that never came. Every time she fixed something, something somewhere else broke. There was no way she could be everywhere at once, no way she could give this ruined body what it needed, no matter how much of herself she spent. She felt herself sinking, dissolving into the fire, but somehow she was cold, so cold . . .

Suddenly the link dissolved. Kayla felt someone grab her, wrenching her away. She fought for a few seconds—desperate to help, to *heal*—

Hosea slapped her.

Not hard, but it made her open her eyes and draw a deep breath, safe behind her shields once more. She stared up at him, for a moment too stunned to realize what had just happened. Tears welled up in her eyes and spilled down her face, though she had no sense that she was crying, and she was shuddering with cold. Worse than any of that was the knowledge that she'd failed. There was nothing she could do to heal Jimmie—she could spend her entire life-force, drain herself to death, and she could not save Jimmie Youngblood. She stood in Hosea's arms, panting as if she'd run for miles.

"Kayla . . . ?" Eric asked.

She shook her head, closing her eyes. "It will take weeks," she mumbled, barely aware of what she was saying. "Weeks of pain. And she'll die anyway."

Think, you stupid cow! There's always something you can do. To comfort the dying . . .

"Then there's nothing you can do," Toni said, grief in her voice.

"No. There's something I can do." Kayla pushed herself away from Hosea and took a deep breath. She hesitated, as if to say what she would say next would make it more real than it already was, create a single defined future from a fan of other outcomes.

But there *was* no other outcome.

"There's something I can do," she repeated. "I can make it quick. I can block the pain. I can let her go now, while she's still Jimmie," Kayla said.

She was able to look at them now that the worst had been said. Eric looked shocked, still not quite able to believe that Jimmie was hurt. Hosea looked sad but determined. Of the other three, whose names she didn't even know, the woman looked angry, as if Death were something you could hit. The two men looked stunned, so closed off their auras were impossible for her to read.

"You can kill her, you mean," the woman said harshly.

"I can give her the choice. Hey, *chica*, it's more than you can do for her, isn't it?" Kayla snapped. She blinked, and felt more tears slide down her cheeks. *Ruined my makeup, dammit,* she thought distractedly.

The woman lunged for her, but Hosea stepped between them.

"No," was all he said.

"You said something about a choice, Kayla, is it? I'm Paul Kern, and these are my associates, Toni and José. I only wish we'd met under happier circumstances."

I wish we'd never met at all, Kayla thought mutinously. She gave

Paul points for not offering to shake hands, though. He must have met people like her before.

"And I think Jimmie would like to have the choice you're offering her. What would you have to do?"

"I need to block what she's feeling, so that she can wake up. I can't do something like this without her consent. That'd be murder." Kayla ran her hands through her hair. "Can any of you tell me anything that will help?" she asked, her voice quivering slightly. "Jimmie . . . she's not *normal*, is she?"

Of the three of them, it was Paul who understood the question Kayla asked.

"If she can do anything to aid you, she will; Jimmie is no stranger to magic. She is a formidable magician in her own right, A Guardian, as we are, so perhaps in that sense she is not 'normal.' She, like us, is sworn to defend ordinary humanity from magical assaults."

"Only this wasn't magical. This was just a stupid, random, *thing*—done by one of those people we're supposed to serve and protect! And all her power couldn't save her from it," Toni said bitterly. "It isn't fair!"

Hosea retreated to sit at Jimmie's side again. Paul put an arm around Toni's shoulders and Toni leaned her face into his neck. Kayla made a conscious effort to shut them out, block their grief and pain so she could concentrate on Jimmie. For a moment it seemed almost impossible to do, then she felt a calming touch at the very edge of her shields, felt new strength and certainty flow into her. She looked up and met Hosea's eyes across the bed.

Of course. Stands to reason I'd land in the middle of a bunch of Gifted. Banyon said Hosea was a Bard, but he's not quite the same thing as Eric. . . .

"What can I do to help?" Eric asked quietly from behind her.

She tried to smile at him, to look more confident than she felt. Kayla hadn't expected anything like this to happen quite this fast. Just this morning she'd been in Los Angeles, and all of a sudden she was at St. Elsewhere, playing for all the marbles. *Elizabet's gonna freak.*

"Just make sure I get back, okay?"

"You got it," Eric said soberly.

Kayla rubbed her hands over her arms, the lace mitts scratchy against her bare skin. She took a deep breath and turned back to Jimmie. This wasn't going to get any easier, and she owed it to Jimmie to do it as fast as possible. She focused her energy and her will, and let her fingers drift down to touch Jimmie once more. This time there was no crackle, no spark, just a cold blue glow, almost invisible in the harsh fluorescence that lit the room.

She worked quickly, deftly, with a control and precision she couldn't even have imagined a few years before. All the body's nerves led to the spine; Kayla climbed that column slowly, closing off the neural nexuses, keeping their messages from reaching Jimmie's brain.

It was more than dangerous. Close off the wrong nerves and she would stop Jimmie's heart, keep her lungs from drawing breath. Close down the neural pathways on a healthy person, and they'd lose all touch with their bodies, becoming capable of doing shattering damage without pain to warn them.

But Jimmie no longer needed warning.

Jimmie? Jimmie Youngblood? Where are you? Kayla Sent urgently.

:Here.:

A power as great as her own but far different swept through Kayla, and suddenly she was somewhere else.

A living room, its walls painted a cool blue. Packing boxes were everywhere, as if someone were moving.

Yeah. Moving out.

She turned around and saw Jimmie. The uniform was a surprise. They'd told her Jimmie was a magician. They hadn't told her Jimmie was a cop.

"Hi. I'm Kayla."

Jimmie smiled. "Nice to meet you, but the circumstances suck. Pardon the mess. I wasn't expecting visitors. You're not the new tenant, are you?"

It was hard to remember that all of this was an illusion, a

metaphor for dying constructed from both their memories, lent its reality by Jimmie's trained will. Kayla clung to that knowledge—if she believed in the reality of what she saw, she might die along with her hostess.

But Eric won't let that happen.

"Is Hosea here?" Jimmie asked suddenly. "He's the one I was expecting."

"Sort of. He's in the hospital room with you."

"Hospital?" Jimmie asked blankly. "Who's hurt?"

This was common enough; a sort of partial amnesia that made dying a little easier. It was a pity they couldn't afford to let her go on dreaming.

"You are," Kayla said bluntly. "Something bad happened to you tonight. You're dying."

"Oh, my God." Jimmie put a hand to her forehead trying to remember, and for a moment the light dimmed to red, and Kayla smelled smoke. Something was burning.

"I've got to talk to Hosea!" Jimmie's voice was frantic. "It's important. There's something I have to tell him."

"It's okay. You'll have time for that," Kayla said soothingly, willing Jimmie to trust her, to believe. "That's why I'm here. Are you ready to hear the rest?"

Jimmie composed herself with an effort. She wasn't wearing her uniform any more. Now she was wearing armor, armor the brilliant blue of the fire in the heart of a sapphire. There was a helmet on her head, and a sword belted at her side. She glanced past Kayla to the door, as if there was somewhere she had to go, and soon.

And there was, but it wasn't a journey Kayla wanted to accompany her on.

"Go on," Jimmie said steadily.

"You're going to die. I guess that's the door you see. I can help you get through it. Without my help, you'll still die, but it might take a week, maybe more, and you'll be in agony the whole time, I won't lie about that. But if you want, I can help you go now. Tonight. I'm a Healer, but that's all the help I can give you. You're too badly burned for anything more."

She watched as Jimmie accepted that, weighing it in her mind. This was beyond creepy, Kayla decided, like talking to a ghost . . . only Jimmie wasn't dead yet.

"Yes. That would be the best way. But can you wake me up first?" Jimmie asked, her voice crisp and decisive. "I have a few things to say to the living before I go." Her mouth quirked in an ironic smile, and Kayla felt a pang of grief. This was a woman she would never get the chance to know.

"Yes. But not for long, so if there's anything I can tell the others for you, you'd better pass it on now."

Jimmie hesitated. "I don't remember. I must have reported for shift and gone on patrol. But I don't remember what happened then."

"It doesn't matter," Kayla said soothingly. Whether it did or not, it would be pointless cruelty to say it did.

:*Kayla.*:

Eric's voice, a thin whisper of sound from her outward ears.

"I have to go."

"Sure," Jimmie said vaguely. "How did I ever get so much stuff? I'll never get it all packed in time."

"You will." *They always do.* Kayla closed her eyes—

—and opened them in the hospital room. She didn't know how long she'd been gone, or what happened while she was gone, but when she opened her eyes again Ria was there, standing close beside Eric, looking furious and worried.

Kayla felt cold and tired, and as if she was going to throw up. She had an absurd impulse to say, *I saw Jimmie. Don't worry about her; she's fine,* and stifled it. She wasn't finished yet.

"She's agreed to go. She wants to talk to you first, Hosea. She didn't say why. I think she thought she had. I've got to clean the morphine out of her system to wake her up, and it'd be nice if someone turned off that damned drip." Her voice came out in an angry rasp; she was stretched thinner than she thought.

"I've got it." Ria stepped forward and placed her fingers on the tubing. The plastic grew cloudy, and the morphine stopped running into Jimmie's veins. "Anything else?"

"This is going to have to be fast, so no long good-byes, okay?

She'll say what she has to, and then I'll help her go through the door. Ria, will you be my anchor?" Between them, she and Elizabet had practically rebuilt Ria from the ground up: Kayla knew Ria better than anyone else in the room, and that familiarity would help her to find her way back.

"I will," Ria said formally.

Kayla reached beneath the sheet and took Jimmie's bandage-swathed hand. No harm in that, now that Jimmie could no longer feel it. She summoned up her power and let the glow spill through Jimmie's body, sweeping the drug from her blood. Almost at once Jimmie's breathing changed, becoming deep and hoarse.

"Elkanah?" she whispered.

The others looked at each other. *Her brother,* Toni mouthed silently, for Kayla's benefit. "We're here, Jimmie," she said. "Paul and José, and I. We've brought Hosea for you."

"Hosea." Jimmie's voice was slurred and seared, a damaged croak. "Hey, Toni, you didn't have to clean out the basement after all. He can have my place." She tried to laugh and started to cough, liquid and retching.

Kayla put a hand on her chest, and Jimmie's breathing calmed, but Eric could see the effort it cost the young Healer to ease Jimmie. "Hurry up," Kayla said tightly.

"Hosea?" Jimmie whispered.

"I'm here."

"Take my hand."

He glanced at Kayla, who nodded, then slipped his hand beneath the sheet to clasp, very gently, the bandage covering what was left of Jimmie's other hand.

"Would've liked to know you better. Liked to explain. Never any time for that. Eric knows. Sorry. Your problem now. Sorry."

As Jimmie spoke, *something* happened. Kayla ignored it, but Eric and Ria stared at each other, neither quite sure what it was. There was the sense of Power in the room, just out of their reach.

"Only four," José said in a broken voice. "Always four."

"We should have known!" Toni said in fierce despair. Paul put a hand on her arm, quieting her.

What just happened? Eric wanted to ask, but he was afraid he knew. There was a Power surrounding Hosea now, something Eric's Bardic magic barely acknowledged. The same power that touched Toni and the others. Guardian power.

:I didn't want to tell you:, Greystone said sorrowfully, mind-speaking to Eric alone. *:It might have come out another way. But it never does. Your boy belongs to the House now. To the Guardians.:*

"Good-bye," Jimmie whispered. "Thank you, all."

"Okay, that's it," Kayla said fiercely. "She can't take any more." Kayla closed her eyes, willing herself to touch Jimmie's spirit as she had before.

This time the apartment was white, as if freshly painted. All the boxes were gone. The curtains—gray—were drawn across the windows, and the bare wood floor was gray as salt-bleached drift-wood. Jimmie's blue armor was the only color.

"I'm ready," Jimmie said.

Geez, did you have to just dump all that on him and leave? You couldn't have mentioned it while you were still walking around? "Okay," Kayla said aloud. She turned toward the door. It wasn't really a door. It was a symbol of what Kayla was about to do, severing Jimmie's spirit from her ruined body, setting her free.

Kayla opened the door.

And forgot. Forgot her life and everything that called her to it, forgot her responsibilities and her name, all for the sight of that Light which held within it everything that had ever been, and every-thing that might ever be. Jimmie walked past her, into the Light, and vanished. There was a moment of piercing brightness as her armor merged with the Light, and Kayla saw echoes of that brilliance, as if Jimmie had gone to join a great host of her kindred, welcomed by all who had gone before her.

Then she was gone, the body she had left behind starting to die, and Kayla was alone in the place that was a symbol of Jimmie's dying body. Kayla heard her mother's voice, calling for her from beyond the door, felt the love and the joy at their reunion. Her mother loved her, wanted her—everything else had all been a terri-ble mistake. She took a step toward the Light, following Jimmie—

—and felt Ria's fury, her implacable determination, dragging Kayla back into the world of the living.

No—no!

"No," Kayla whispered, but she was back now, and could not even remember what it was beyond the door, calling to her. She shook her head, took a deep breath, the images and memories fading from her mind.

"I'm okay."

One of the monitors started to keen. Ria silenced it with a chopping gesture, and all the equipment at Jimmie's bedside went dark.

"Good-bye, *querida*," José said softly. "We'll miss you."

Toni sobbed, a thick choked sound of fury and grief.

"We'd better leave," Paul said, his own voice far from steady. "I don't know how long Ria can hold her spell, but its better if the hospital doesn't have any unaccountable time lapses to explain. Come on, Toni. We have to leave. Jimmie's gone. She isn't here now."

The ride back to Guardian House in Ria's Rolls was a silent one. Eric was stunned, aching with grief and the abrupt senseless loss. Jimmie had been his friend. They'd been talking together, laughing together, only that morning.

Now she was gone. Dead. For nothing—no great battle, no great victory—just an accident of the kind that happened in New York a thousand times a day.

And she'd named Hosea her successor.

Eric glanced up at Hosea. The big man was withdrawn, contemplating something only he could see.

"Eric knows," Jimmie'd said back in the hospital room. The conversation they'd had a few weeks ago about the Guardians came back to him: *"Once you get the Call, your life doesn't belong to you any more. You never know where you're going to be sent, or what you'll have to do. There's no way to train for this job. You can either handle it, or someone else comes along pretty quick to replace you. If we're lucky, we get to meet our successor and pass on the Call in person, but that's about it."*

Does that make you one of the lucky ones, Jimmie? Eric wondered. *Did you feel lucky?* His eyes ached with unshed tears. Jimmie was gone. Everything they could have shared was gone. Over.

ELEVEN:
YOU WANT TO DRESS IN BLACK

The suite of rooms was an elaborate fantasia upon death; a medieval *memento mori* elaborated by a big-budget madman with a flair for detail. Paintings and statuary depicted every possible way a person could die, and a series of pictures painted upon the ceiling showed every stage in the dissolution of a corpse, a motif repeated on the mosaic floor, so that whether you looked up or down, you saw decaying bodies.

The bedposts were skeletons—elves might not sleep, as Jeanette Campbell knew now, but there were still some things they needed beds for—and the coverlet was jeweled and embroidered with more variations upon the gentle art of murder. Bed curtains of cobweb-fine black lace surrounded the bed, making it look even more like a catafalque. Imprisoned within this suite of rooms, Jeanette had nothing to do but contemplate the death, in all its forms, that was forever to be denied to her. And boredom was an additional torment.

Invisible servants hovered around her to fulfill her every whim—fill her bath, bring her food, play music for her, dim or light the lamps. But there were no books for her to read, and all the music sounded like it came out of the Middle Ages: weirdly atonal and military, like funeral marches played on bagpipes. She'd asked for a guitar, but that request hadn't been granted, and she thought the invisibles might not know what it was, because when she confused them, they simply ignored her orders: they wouldn't bring her coffee either. When she got tired of trying to order them around—it was like dealing with a balky computer—she could look out the window at the unchanging night and the eternally moonlit forest below. It had been a real shock when she discovered that she could see the same moon in the same position from windows on the opposite sides of the room.

Other than that, she could sleep, or pace the floor—trying to avoid catching sight of herself in any of the enormous mirrors—or (as much as she hated her confinement) pray that Aerune wouldn't come again to let her out. She could study the death images until she'd memorized every detail. And then, for a change, she could nerve herself up to try looking in the mirrors without flinching.

The mirrors were Aerune's other joke—funny, with all the time she'd spent imagining what elves would be like if they were real and she could meet them, she'd never imagined they could be so mind-numbingly petty. It was one thing for Aerune to still be in mourning for a girlfriend killed, as far as Jeanette could figure out, about five thousand years ago, and to be intending to wipe out the human race in revenge. That was almost dignified. Romantic, Byronic, all those things that she loved and hated at the same time. But at the same time, to have him invent this whole elaborate sniggering joke, not only on the way she looked now, but on her humanity as well. . . .

That was cheap and petty, a symptom of an arrogance so vast it didn't only not care how it appeared to outsiders, it couldn't even imagine any point of view but its own. And that amount of self-obsession sort of took the edge off the whole romantic lost-love thing.

She went over to the stained-glass windows and pushed them open wide, leaning out as far as she could. Damp smells of forest and water welled up out of the night, and in the distance she could hear the sound of a river. But aside from minor variations, the landscape was as unchanging as a photograph. The moon (or moons) never moved, the sun never rose—sometimes the place went to a foggy twilight, but on no particular schedule—and somewhere at the edge of the forest, the world stopped and turned back on itself, and the only way to get somewhere else was through a Gate that only a Sidhe could work.

She had only the vaguest idea of how long she'd been here— even when Aerune took her out to hunt, she couldn't get an accurate idea of the time, and the time where she went didn't seem to have any relation to the time here—but she'd learned a lot during her captivity. About the nature of the Sidhe, about Aerune's plans, about magic itself. Once she would have given up anything she had to see and do the things she'd done. Now, she only wished she'd been spared the disappointment of finding out what she knew. She hadn't wanted to know that elves were so petty, so mean, so . . . empty.

The whole place seemed as if it'd been assembled as a scrapbook of Gothic Evil Through the Centuries, with the emphasis on the High Medieval period. There was nothing new here, nothing exciting— nothing, in fact, that she couldn't have made up for herself. Sure the creatures were weird—but no weirder than she could see in the movies. Sure the landscape was alien—but no more alien than she could see in a painting. Sure her surroundings were opulent—but you could get awfully sick of gold and jewels. Everything was grand, but nothing was comfortable. It was like trying to live in a museum.

She should have turned herself in and gone to prison when she'd had the chance. At least they let you read in prison.

But Aerune would have found her there, too. And Aerune still scared her, terrified her, frightened her on levels she didn't know were in her. He was trite, but he was also monstrous. She forgot what he was like the moment she left his presence—a form of self-preservation, she suspected—but when he was near she resonated to him, like a crystal goblet that someone had struck. And that hurt, like a dentist's drill that never stopped.

That was what the T-Stroke had done to her—turned her into an Empath, and she resonated to the physical and psychic pain of anyone she was near. She had no control over it. And she was drawn to magic, to Talent, to what Aerune called Crownfire, most of all. That was what made her so useful to Aerune. She could no more *not* sense the presence of Talent than she could hold her breath forever, and try as she might, she couldn't hide her reaction. All Aerune had to do was drag her within range of someone with Talent and she vibrated like a tuning fork. Every time he took her out of here, it was to find people like that.

And then Aerune killed them. Sucked up their magic, their potential, their Talent, and killed them.

And there was nothing she could do about that, either. She'd tried to kill herself. It didn't work. It hurt a lot, and it scared her, and it didn't work. She'd given up trying.

She'd also tried to refuse to do what he wanted, but all it got her was pain—and if she still tried to refuse, he would begin to kill people. Surely it was better to give him what he wanted? That way, only a few people died. Fewer.

Funny how I can't seem to stop doing things like that. So much for good intentions.

Time to try the mirrors again—that or throw herself out the window. She kept covering them up and turning them to the wall, but the invisibles always put them back again the way they'd been. Maybe she'd get used to what she saw in them eventually. She turned away from the window and crossed the room, her long heavy skirts swishing. She was dressed in what she guessed was Elvish *haute couture*, and it made everything even worse. These weren't her kinds of clothes. They didn't suit her, and she didn't deserve to be wearing them. They made everything worse.

She approached the mirror, eyes closed—after this long, she knew every inch of her prison and all its accessories well enough to navigate it blindfolded—and stood before the mirror for a long moment before she could force herself to open her eyes. A stranger stared back, looking like a caricature of the self she knew. This was what Aerune had made of her.

Her eyes were now wide, the bright unnatural green of a child's crayon, fringed with thick black lashes. Her body had been fined down to asexual slimness, stretched and remade. Her hair was long and thick and moon-silver, cascading down over her shoulders and back, giving her the look of some exotic bird. This was her the way she'd always wished she was, and that was the cruelest joke of all—that Aerune had taken her secret dreams and dragged them out into the light of day, making them dirty with his touch. She hated it, hated him, and hated herself most of all.

As she watched, the elaborate silk gown she wore began to flow and change like melting wax, darkening and molding itself to her body until she was clad head to foot in a sheath of form-fitting black leather covered with matching silver studs along the shoulders, arms, and legs. Around her neck was a heavy leather collar with silver spikes, the kind a hunting dog might wear.

This was her hunting costume.

"No. Oh . . . no," she whispered, backing away from the mirror.

And then her image vanished as well, and Aerune stood within the ornate frame, holding out his hand.

"Come, my hound. It is time to hunt once more—and this time, I have a special treat for you."

She made a sound in the back of her throat—a groan of utter despair. Useless to fight him, impossible to try. Hating herself, she held out her hand to him in response. There was a jarring wrench of translocation, and they were . . . elsewhere. Now she had a leash upon her collar, and Aerune held the end.

"Do you like it?" Aerune asked her.

She looked around herself, wondering where he'd brought her this time. Back to Earth, somewhere in daylight, in some sort of office building.

No, not an office. The halls were filled with teenagers, wearing clothes that hadn't been in fashion in a very long time. A school of some sort, she supposed.

No one saw them. No one would see them unless Aerune wished them to. But Jeanette could see—and feel—everything. Emotions buffeted her naked senses like gusts of wind—despair, murderous anger, fear and pain and joy so intense it made her reel drunkenly, bathed in the emotional storms of adolescence.

This was high school. *Her* high school.

Recognition brought horror. James K. Polk High School, sometime in the late eighties. The same time she'd been going there.

"Why did you bring me here?" she demanded furiously.

"To hunt," Aerune answered. "Do you wish to see yourself as you were? There you are."

He pointed. A girl was walking down the hall. Her mouse-blonde hair was skinned back in an unflattering ponytail, and she wore no makeup. Her skin was blotched with acne. She was wearing a cheap leather jacket that didn't fit very well and carrying an armload of books. Her head was down and her shoulders hunched, as though she expected somebody to hit her.

Me. That's me. But why don't I stand up straight? Scuttling along like that, it's practically like wearing a "kick me" sign.

She stared at herself, feeling the faint recognition of Talent thrill over her skin. It was no surprise; the T-Stroke would have killed her outright if she didn't have it. But it was stifled, suppressed, ignored. Covered over with a sullen anger that didn't look outside itself, that poisoned everything it touched.

Stupid. I was so stupid.

Jeanette watched as her younger self stopped in front of her locker, awkwardly juggling books as she reached for the padlock. A boy in a cream and gold varsity jacket strode toward her, deliberately banging into her and spilling her books all over the floor.

Cary McCormack. Oh, god, I hated him!

As she bent to pick them up, one of the boys with Cary darted forward and slapped a sticker onto the back of her jacket. It was a promo sticker for a local rock band, and adult Jeanette thought it looked pretty cool. But she felt the flare of rage from her younger self like a spike in her guts as younger-Jeanette wheeled on her tormentor, hissing curses.

All of the boys laughed, even Cary, but she could see into them as well as she could see into her other self, and there was none of the gloating joy she expected to see—just worry and uncertainty, boys feeling their way into adulthood just as her younger self was. And stuffed into Cary's back pocket, a well-thumbed paperback novel, one that she had read and loved. He was watching her younger self anxiously, a little bit of him hoping for some other reaction than rejection and anger, an acknowledgement that he hadn't meant her any real harm.

He just wants to talk. But boy, is he going about it the wrong way!

But how could she expect more? They were children, all of them. They were still learning how to do all the things adults took for granted—make friends and alliances, fall in love, serve conflicting loyalties, react wisely to unfairness and cruelty, and all the rest of the things that were supposed to set adults apart from children. If she'd been willing to make an effort, she could have turned the whole situation around, made a joke, maybe even talked to Cary. . . .

But she hadn't. She'd pushed hard to make them enemies, because it was easier, because she was young, too. She'd made them into monsters and they'd done their best to be what she wanted.

But I could have wanted something else. I threw away my whole life and let them bring me to this just because I was stupid!

It was an epiphany, but she didn't like it very much. The best revenge wasn't revenge, it was living well, and she hadn't. She hadn't revenged herself on her childhood tormentors by turning into Aerune's hound—she'd finished their work for them.

The boys went on. Young Jeanette got her locker open and began picking up her books again. A clique of girls—the bright ones, the pretty ones—went by, pointing at her and sniggering, but inside each of them was the fear: am I like that? What makes me different? What if I'm not pretty any more? How do I *do everything right* when I don't know what I'm doing at all?

They could never have been her friends—their interests were too different—but they didn't have to have been her enemies. She hadn't had to notice them at all, one way or the other. That was the part that had been her choice.

"Can we go home now?" she asked in a hard voice.

"There is still the hunt. You know what I seek. Find it for me," Aerune answered implacably.

She looked at the kids still filling the halls. They all thought of themselves as fully adult—only she knew how much of their lives' journey was before them. Refuse to do what Aerune wanted, and those unfinished lives all ended here. She didn't remember a bloodbath happening in her high school years here, but that didn't mean Aerune couldn't arrange one now.

The few for the many, and no matter what she chose, Death would come to JKPHS today.

Defeated, she began the hunt, pacing through the halls at the end of Aerune's leash. For a while back in the beginning she'd used to hope that if she spent enough time back in the Real World the T-Stroke would catch up with her and burn her out, but Aerune had quickly destroyed that hope. While she hunted for him, his spells kept time from touching her, even here. There was no escape.

She had no way to block the pain radiating from the kids around her—this one was pregnant, that one's parents were divorcing, the other was trying drugs for the first time and was terrified he was going to hell—but if she forced herself, she could let it wash through her, sifting through it for what Aerune sought. Several times a pang of Talent made her stop and quiver, but a lot of kids had Talent that burned out within a few years at this age. That wasn't what Aerune was looking for, and God help everyone here if he didn't find something to make his Hunt worthwhile.

Then she felt it. Burning like the sun, heat and life enough to warm her cold bones, banish all the borrowed pain. Helpless, she turned toward it. Refuse to follow the trail, and the killing would begin.

One or two instead of a dozen. That's good, isn't it? Isn't it a better choice?

There were other wellsprings of Power here. She could feel them. But this one was the strongest, the closest, and so she could concentrate on it and not give warning of the others. It was all she could do.

It was lunchtime, so most of the classrooms were empty. She passed each one, seeing glimpses of a world as foreign and lost as ancient Atlantis inside. There were real tragedies here, and cutthroat social climbing more intense than anywhere outside of Hollywood, but at the same time, there was a certain innocence to all of it. That was why people always spoke of high school as the happiest time of their lives . . . if they managed to forget the pain.

She hadn't. She'd let it rule her. And this was the result. She'd become someone she didn't even *know.*

She followed the trail of Power to the school auditorium. No one was supposed to be in here, but it wasn't locked. James Polk had been a nice upper-middle-class school in a good district. Parents all congratulated each other about not having the problems with violence or vandalism found in other schools. She and Aerune went inside.

It was dark in here. The school had been built in the thirties, and the auditorium bore a more than passing resemblance to a theater, with balconies, stage, and thick red velvet curtains, now drawn back to reveal an empty stage. A few lines of Shakespeare were carved on the archway above:

All the world's a stage, And all the men and women merely players: They have their exits and their entrances; And one man in his time plays many parts . . . As You Like It, *Act 2, Scene 7.*

There was someone sitting at the foot of the stage, leaning against it; a small untidy boy with an ever-present spiral notebook in which he had constantly been doodling.

That's Strange Stan Chandler. He ran away from home his junior year and nobody ever found out what happened to him.

Now she knew. She could feel his power, his creativity, that wonderful gift that the Sidhe lacked. She could see the life he would have had as if a movie were unrolling in her mind: high school, then art school, then an apprenticeship at one of the major animation studios, then ground-breaking work in CGI and a series of brilliant movies that would bring a renewed sense of childhood wonder to all who saw them. . . .

And none of it was ever going to happen. Because Stan Chandler wasn't going to get a chance to grow up to be a wizard. Because Stan Chandler hadn't run away at all.

"So this is the one," Aerune said, as Jeanette died a little more inside. There was a ripple of Power, and she knew they were suddenly visible.

"Come with me, little one," Aerune said. "Come into my kingdom."

She saw Stan's face awaken with wonder, with hope, with incredulous disbelief and gleeful awe, saw him jump to his feet—a skinny kid with big ears and thick glasses, somebody that nobody would ever look at twice—staring at the elf-lord in amazement. And then saw suspicion replace wonder, saw the fear begin.

But by then it was too late. Aerune had reached him, taken his hand. And the world melted around the three of them like a disrupted reflection, to re-form as Aerune's throne room.

Jeanette backed away—he'd dropped her leash, now that his prize was in his hands—but she could not block out what came next. Somehow Aerune *reached* into Stan, finding the reservoir of his Talent and draining it away, into himself.

It hurt. She covered her ears, but that didn't block out the screams. Or the pain. She crawled up the steps of Aerune's throne and huddled against its coldness, begging and praying that the pain would soon be over.

For both of them.

A long time later she became aware that people were talking above her head—Aerune and someone else. This was rare, but not unheard of, and she tried not to listen. If Aerune noticed she was here—if Aerune noticed she was here and didn't *like* it, he would transport her to some other place. If she were lucky, she'd wind up back in her room. If she weren't, it would be some place like an open grave, or a swamp filled with maggots, or a bright place where *things* she could never remember clearly afterward did . . . something. Something horrible.

But she couldn't shut out the voices. Because while one of them was Aerune's, the other was human, from her own world and time.

"Oh, we're moving forward, Lord Aerune. People are willing enough to believe in you after Tunguska and Roswell and Grover's Mill. I'm sure you don't mind if they think you're space aliens—'elves' is a little hard for folks to swallow these days, but it doesn't matter what they call you, so long as it gets the job done. And psychic space aliens are even scarier than the other kind, if you get my drift—especially once they start encroaching on humanity."

Whoever he was, he wasn't afraid of Aerune. Jeanette listened in amazement. It was almost as if they were . . . allies.

"I believe I do, Mr. Wheatley. But I trust that your inner circle is quite aware that the invaders are not 'space aliens,' but the Sidhe?" Aerune asked.

"Indeed they are, Lord Aerune. The bodies you've provided have been quite helpful in that respect. But I have to ask—when are my boys going to have a live specimen to play around with? We can go just so far with sweeps and drills."

She didn't dare move, didn't dare look up or draw attention to herself in any way. Aerune was talking like Earth was being invaded by elves in all directions, but as far as she knew, the only one who wanted to invade Earth was Aerune, and he couldn't get any of the other Sidhe to play along.

So he'd gotten this human to help him present elves as a threat to humanity, so that elves would see *humans* as a threat. Couldn't this Wheatley see that if Aerune's plan worked, he'd be as dead as everyone else? How stupid could bureaucrats be?

Aerune was speaking once more.

"I am aware of your concerns, but I must counsel patience. You may continue to use the special equipment I have provided to search out those members of the Bright Court who live among you, passing as your own kind. Properly handled, even their discovery can bring about the war we seek. Meanwhile, I shall endeavor to provide you with captives who will be properly . . . unconcilliatory, but it will require time."

"Yeah. The last thing we want is to grab one of those Bright guys who'll go all reasonable and multicultural on us. We need a real fighter," Wheatley said cheerfully.

"All in time. And what of your plan to move against those of your own kind with Power?" There was a gloating note in Aerune's voice that made Jeanette shudder.

"Well, there we're seeing real progress," Wheatley said, gloating. "We've consolidated a number of those dumb-ass government psychic research programs under our agency umbrella—Anomaly, Trapdoor, Arclight, and so on—and we're massaging the results to make it look not only as if psionic powers are widespread and reliable, but that the Spookies present a real threat to the power structure. You'll have the screening programs and internment camps you want within five years, or my name isn't Parker Wheatley. When you come right down to it, the Psionicist Threat is the perfect social control: fear of a minority that's invisible, that you can't prove you don't belong to. We can put down anybody we need to by saying they're psychic once this gets rolling."

"I am glad you are pleased—" Aerune broke off suddenly, and Jeanette realized with a pang of sick despair that he'd noticed her after all. She scrambled back off the edge of his throne, hoping to beg for mercy. But the floor swallowed her up as if it were water, and then she was falling, falling down into the night.

By unspoken agreement, they all gathered back in Eric's apartment on their return from the hospital, huddled together like the survivors of a disaster. For a long time no one spoke. Finally Paul got up and left, returning a few minutes later with a bottle of Scotch and a large silver cup.

"I'd been saving this for a very special occasion. There's none more important than saying good-bye to a beloved comrade. We'll hope it's unique." He poured the *calleach* full—it took half the bottle—then set the bottle down on the floor, very gently.

"Here's to Jimmie Youngblood. Warrior and friend. I will miss her." He drank, and passed the cup to Toni.

"I loved her," Toni said, her voice stark in its grief. "*Waes hael*, girlfriend. Go with God."

The cup passed, each person saying their own good-byes.

"She gave me more than I ever gave her. I wish we'd had more time." Eric took only the barest sip, but his farewell was no less heartfelt for that.

Kayla was next. "I didn't know her. I wish I had. Death bites."

Ria followed, giving nothing but a simple toast and passing the cup. He ought to get up and make some coffee, Eric supposed, but it didn't seem worth the effort. He sat on the end of the couch, the smoky taste of the Scotch on his lips, and mourned the future that would never be. It was one thing to die fighting for something that mattered, giving up your life so that the innocent could live on in happy ignorance of their peril. But that wasn't how Jimmie had died. She'd died in an accident—a stupid, pointless, meaningless fluke, as random as if she'd stepped off the curb and been hit by a car. After all she'd done, all she'd suffered, all she'd given up to be a Guardian, her death should have had more meaning than that. It was as if God had just lost interest in her and blotted her out.

It wasn't fair. He bowed his head, not caring if the others saw his tears.

"If Jimmie had to die for me to become a Guardian, I don't want the job," Hosea said thickly. "She was a righteous lady, and I won't ever be able to fill her shoes." He drank deeply, passing the cup to José.

"Good-bye, my friend. You should not have had to die for so little."

Greystone had joined them, his wings held high and tight over his back as if he wished to shut out the events of the night.

"Farewell, *mo chidr*. We can't always choose our fights, but you never ran from yours. Fare you well." He accepted the cup from José and drained it.

There was a long moment of silence. "The first time I saw Jimmie," Paul said softly, "it was raining. She was standing outside of the House—no umbrella—looking like a wet cat, and about that mad. . . ."

But talking about Jimmie didn't make the loss of her easier to bear. It made it worse. They were whistling in the dark, choking on their own despair, each wondering when their own painful pointless death would come. Why live? Why do anything, when your death would be nothing more than a ripple, counting for nothing, quickly forgotten. If life meant so little, if death was so cruel, why not hasten the moment? If you could control nothing else, if there were no true choices in life, why not choose death and get it all over with? There was no way to win against it. Everybody died, and no death meant anything in the long run.

✤✤ ✤✤ ✤✤

"A test." Aerune's voice came out of nowhere, rousing Jeanette from her aching daze. She could see nothing, could barely feel the surface on which she lay. Everything hurt; her eyes burned and her throat was raw with screaming, but worse than that was the terrifying blankness in her mind. She could not remember where she'd been, or what had happened to her, since she had been in Aerune's throne room.

Worse, she felt as if the information lurked somewhere beneath the surface of her mind, and to recover it would drive her mad.

But it did not do to ignore Aerune when he was speaking. He was still angry with her. She could tell.

"What test, my lord?" she asked. She reached up and felt her face. Her eyes were open, but she still saw nothing. Blindness? Darkness? Or some kind of spell? Asking would only bring her more trouble.

"Of your abilities. I will bring you to a place where there are many of those whom I seek. You will find me the strongest concentration of them. And I will use their power to give Mr. Wheatley the proof he so ardently desires."

"Yes, lord." She staggered to her feet, groping for stability in the darkness. When would she stop caring about what he used her to do? When would she go numb, or mad, or just die? When would he be *done* with her?

"Come, then."

She felt a whisper of air, and then the tingle of magic as Aerune opened a Portal. She stepped through.

The assault on her unshielded senses was as if a million people were shouting at once in a language she didn't understand. She staggered, blinded now by the wash of physical and psychic pain, choking, gasping for breath. She fell against the side of Aerune's elvensteed, felt his armored leg against her back. He moved his mount away from her touch and she fought to stay on her feet. If she fell, he wouldn't let go of her leash.

She forced her eyes open. Night. Trees. City lights. Hot summer air, the smell of car exhaust and hot asphalt and the distant wail of sirens. Aerune usually chose less populated places for his hunts—Cold Iron was deadly to elves, as well as screwing up their magic, and big cities were full of it. He wouldn't have come to a place like this without good reason.

Her heart hammered faster, racing, and waves of chill and nausea swept over her. Something was different this time, but she couldn't take the time to puzzle it out right now. Aerune wanted results, but how could she find one trace of Power among so many false clues?

She was in a park, near the edge. As she peered at the buildings across the street, she realized she knew where she was. New York. Central Park.

Almost home.

New York must have some kind of connection to Aerune's home base, somehow—he'd first appeared here when Threshold was doing field tests, and she didn't think he'd have noticed the tests if he hadn't been here, in the same world at the same time. New York must interest him somehow, and she didn't think it was because it was the center of the global business economy, or a great cultural center, or the home town of American publishing, or one of the biggest and most advanced cities on Earth.

No. That must really be the reason. Aerune wanted to take humanity down *here,* because if he took out New York, no place else could be any harder to destroy. If she were a Sidhe looking to build a beachhead in the mortal world, she'd pick some place like Minneapolis or Toronto to start with—smaller cities with fewer people. Or maybe someplace with no people to speak of at all, like the Great Plains, or Russia, or Antarctica. But obviously Aerune felt differently.

Arrogant. Stupid. And powerful enough that it probably didn't matter, in the long run. Make a big Sidhe fuss here, in the Big Apple, and there'd be no way on earth the government could hush it up. He'd have all the panic he wanted—and the war he wanted, too.

But right now, Aerune wanted a Hunt.

Jeanette picked a direction at random and began walking, trying to get her bearings and cull information from the agonizing and bewildering wash of sensations that surrounded her. She needed to strike a trail, and fast. Aerune's patience was close to nonexistent at the best of times, and this was more than a test. Somehow, this was a trap.

Is what I overheard so important that I've got to die? That can't be it. He could kill me any time he wanted to. And who would I tell about Wheatley, anyway? Everyone in that place belongs to Aerune body and soul, even the High Elves. None of them would betray him. None of them would even care.

All the while, something had been trying to get her attention, like the high faint peal of a bell over the roar of a storming ocean, and she finally focused on it.

Power.

Enormous power. The thing Aerune sought—that he must have known was here, somewhere in New York, before he ever set her on its trail. She stopped in her tracks and turned this way and that, trying to get a bead on it.

North and west.

"That way." She pointed.

Aerune reached down and pulled her up behind him on the horse, riding in the direction she indicated. It drew her, swamping all other input. Not one Talent, but too many to count—an ocean of power, enough to drown in.

Enough to turn Aerune into a god.

And if she didn't help him find it, there were millions here for him to slaughter. He didn't even have to kill them one by one. All he had to do was take down the power grid, and thousands would die as the carefully-balanced machinery of the city ground to a halt.

And if she did help him find the Power he sought, how many more would die?

How could she make that kind of choice?

The elvensteed broke into a trot. They were near the river now, and Jeanette realized he was no longer waiting for her directions. Whatever the source, it was big enough—and close enough—that Aerune could sense it himself now.

They stopped on a darkened side street. She didn't know what time it was, but she knew it was late—there wasn't any traffic here, and most of the buildings around them were dark. On her left was a parking lot filled with motorcycles and an assortment of small cars—the lot itself unusual on the Upper West Side, where real estate space was at a premium.

And beyond the lot was the source of what had called her. An apartment building, with a few windows lit. Every apartment contained Talent of some sort, and behind one of those windows, a concentration of pure Power, and anguish so great that Jeanette tried to curl up where she sat, and only succeeded in sliding from the saddle to the ground, to huddle at the elvensteed's feet.

Aerune jerked on her leash. "Stop that." The Sidhe's voice was lazy; he sounded almost drunk on the pain that was killing her. "Do you not see? My other hound has done me one last service in his dying, striking a heart's blow against these petty mortals who would oppose my will. He has opened a path through their defenses; helpless in their grief, they will not sense me until it is far too late. In their destruction, the seeds of mortalkind's destruction will be sown as well."

He was gloating, Jeanette realized with numb indignation. But she could barely concentrate on his words, let alone react to them. The torment was too great, worse than ever before. It was as if . . .

She was dying.

In his impatience to tap into this concentration of Power—or perhaps because he needed all his own puissance to survive here— Aerune had loosed the spells that kept time from affecting her. The T-Stroke was working again, weakening her, burning her out.

If only the people in the building would keep Aerune distracted, keep him from noticing her again until it was too late. She hated herself for the thought, but she had no illusions left. She was a coward, a user, a destroyer. A victim, not a hero. Even if she dared to try to do something right, things only got worse.

All she could do—the only thing she could ever do—was try desperately not to be noticed. To escape, any way she could.

If only mortals knew what power lay in their despair.

Aerune could sense his hound's anguish—he fed upon it, increasing it as he did the pain of those who lay in the fortress beyond. It had been Jeanette's helpless rage and self-loathing that he had most loved about her. Her empathic power had only been an incidental thing, his use of it a way to pass the time and learn more of the mortal world while his long-range plans came to fruition. He had been surprised at her strength—no matter what he did, she did not surrender, did not come to fawn upon him with the helpless groveling love of his Court. With time enough, she would have realized what power her despair gave her, and that would be tiresome and inconvenient. Better to end it here, now, by allowing the poison she had taken to work its will upon her at last—or would it be more amusing to let her think she had escaped, then to snatch her back from the gates of Death?

Only a small part of Aerune's consciousness was occupied with that idle speculation. Most of it was engaged in siphoning off the rich banquet of power and grief that lay before him, slipping his subtle magics past the lax wards of the stronghold and turning the anguish of those inside back upon itself so that they could think of nothing else, and in their sorrow become utterly vulnerable to his attack.

For I am the Lord of Death and Pain, and all who sorrow and weep do me homage . . .

Aerune no longer felt the weakness brought on by the death-metal surrounding him. Once he had drained these enemies dry, destroyed the last of their defenses, all that set them apart from the ordinary run of humanity would be gone, to flow through his veins, allowing him to strike them down with impunity. Power to spare, power to waste, power to shield him from their monkey tricks and petty impediments . . .

Kayla's eyes ached with unshed tears. The power she'd expended tonight had left her exhausted, and there was nothing to show for it. *The operation was a success, but the patient died,* as the old joke went. Her head drooped, and she shivered, even though she'd reclaimed her leather jacket when they got back here and was huddled into it now. Everything in her urged her to give up, surrender, make an end to things now before life could hurt her any more than it already had. . . .

Wait . . . wait . . .

Her thoughts were groggy, as if she'd had a lot more to drink than just a sip of Scotch.

This isn't right.

It was hard to think. She was drowning in the others' grief, resonating to it like a water glass to a soprano.

Not just me . . .

Cautiously she lowered her shields, wincing at the uprush of grief that spilled past her barriers. Gritting her teeth, she reached past her immediate surroundings. The House itself was grieving—it, and everyone in it: the Sensitives who did not know the cause of their overwhelming sorrow; the magicians who set up wards against it in vain; even the other tenants, those who were only as sensitive as any artist. All of them mourned, turning inward, shutting out the world beyond their walls.

And something outside those walls was feeding on that pain, magnifying it and siphoning it off at the same time.

Kayla drew back inside herself, making her shields as tight as she could. But there was such a sweetness in surrendering to the pain, a dark joy in the knowledge that she could receive no greater hurt in life than that she had already received, that turning away from that submission was the hardest thing she had ever done.

"Hey . . ." Kayla said. Her voice came out in a croak. "Something's wrong."

Paul looked at her, his red-rimmed eyes bleak. "Everything's wrong. The good die and the innocent suffer, and there's nothing anyone can do about it," he said in a flat voice.

Kayla pulled herself to her feet, the dragging weakness—physical and emotional—making her stagger and reel. "No!" she said, louder now. "Something's *wrong!*"

The others ignored her as if she hadn't spoken. Sat, drained and grieving, emotional zombies.

I've gotta do something! Something to turn them out of themselves, away from Death, back toward Life. But Kayla was tapped out. She had barely enough energy to keep herself on her feet, and none to spare to heal them.

Music. Could that help?

I've got two Bards here, they oughtta be able to do something.

She looked at Eric. He was sitting with Ria's head on his shoulder, staring at nothing. His eyes were empty, swollen with unshed tears. Maybe if she put the flute in his hands . . .?

She staggered toward the bedroom. The floor tilted crazily with her exhaustion, and she could barely feel it beneath her feet. She clung to the wall, keeping herself upright by sheer bloody-mindedness.

There! The flute case lay on the bed, and beside it, Hosea's banjo. She tripped over the edge of the flokati rug and fell to her hands and knees. It would be so easy just to lie here, give in to her exhaustion, sleep and pray to never wake up again.

Wimp.

She pulled herself to her feet, clinging to the edge of the mattress, then grabbed the flute case and the banjo. They seemed to burn in her hands, weighing far more than they possibly could. It was only with an effort that she kept herself from using the banjo as a crutch as she reeled back into the living room.

She dropped the flute case in Eric's lap. "Play something— something happy," she demanded raggedly.

Eric looked up at her, moving as though underwater. "Not now," was all he said.

"Eric, we need this. Play." *Oh, please. Don't make me beg. I don't have the strength.*

He shook his head.

"It's too soon. Let the dead rest," Hosea said, dully.

Kayla rounded on him, holding the banjo like a club. She felt anger building inside her and fed it, welcoming the burn of fury. It was all that was keeping her going. And when it was gone, there would be nothing left.

"Oh, yeah. *That's* a great idea! Jimmie'd be real proud of you, farmboy—she goes through hell for you and this is how you pay her back? Lie down and die? So she's dead—play her out, then! Play for *her!*"

Hosea's eyes focused on her, and slowly he reached for the banjo. "Guess I can do that much," he said. He began to play, something slow and mournful—"John Barleycorn," she thought.

"Oh great—is *that* how you want to remember her? A dead loser? You want to lie down in that grave with her?"

Hosea stopped and looked at her. "That ain't fair, Kayla."

"*Do you think this is how she wants you to remember her?*" She spun around and glared at Eric and Ria, although the world was graying out around her. "Do you think she just wants you to give up and die? *Play!*"

Slowly Eric began to fumble with the flute case, plainly unable to understand why Kayla was so upset. Hosea began to play again: "Ashokan Farewell." Kayla groaned inwardly. Not much livelier than the other thing. But when she looked at him, she could see confusion in his eyes as he began to sense the wrongness here. By the time the melody came around again, Eric had joined him, the flute wailing like the wind in high lonely places. She could see he didn't get it, and she had no more to give. She sank down to the floor, sitting at Eric's feet.

But still the two Bards played, pulling themselves agonizingly from song to song, like travelers crossing a frozen river: from "Ashokan Farewell" to "Lorena" to "Bonnie Blue Flag" to "Dixie." It almost didn't matter what they played, not really. Music was life, and anything would help. Then faster: "Marching Through Georgia" and "Union Forever"—fighting songs, those—and "Susan Brown" and "Turkey in the Straw" with their catchy cheery rhythm, and she could see the power linking the two Bards like binary suns. Power—and life, that spilled over into the others, through the walls and the floor, filling the entire building with their defiance, filling Kayla until she twitched with it, all exhaustion banished.

The others roused, shaking off the seductive despair that had wrapped them like a burial shroud, breaking the cycle of grief and surrender. It seemed as if Kayla could feel the House itself taking a deep breath and shaking all over like a wet dog.

And then at last they could all sense the threat that came from without: the malignancy—and triumph.

❖❖ ❖❖ ❖❖

:Bogeys at six o'clock! Scramble!: Greystone Sent, panic in his mental voice. They could all feel it, that power like no other: the mark of the Dark Lords, the Unseleighe Sidhe. Eric ran to the window and stepped out onto the fire escape. Behind him he heard the apartment door slam as the Guardians ran to defend their turf. The front door of the building was "twelve o'clock," so the enemy was at the back, in the parking lot.

Aerune. A sickness twisted in Eric's gut as he recognized the rider on the black elvensteed. Aerune was the one who had been feeding on their anguish, turning their grief to despair. He vaulted over the railing, and let a touch of Power carry him lightly five stories to the ground. Outside the bespelled air conditioning of his apartment, the summer heat enveloped him like a glove, plastering his white dress shirt to his body as sweat sprang out of every pore.

The other three—no, *four*—Guardians reached the ground at the same time he did and fanned out, not seeing Aerune yet. Eric didn't see Ria—she was probably still inside, sitting on Kayla. That was a small mercy. The last time any of them had faced Aerune, he'd been kidnapping and draining Talent—and Kayla would be just the sort of morsel that would whet his appetite—if he weren't already glutted with the power he'd siphoned off from Guardian House and its inmates. Aerune glowed with Power in Eric's mage-sight—power enough to rock the city around their ears.

But tonight it seemed that Aerune had other plans.

"Greetings, mortal pests—and Bard." Aerune bowed with a flourish, leaning over his mount's saddle, hugely pleased with himself. When he spoke, the glamourie that surrounded him vanished, and the others could see him as well. "It is a lovely evening, is it not?"

"What does he want?" Toni whispered to Eric. "You're the expert on elves."

"Good evening, Lord Aerune."

Eric stepped forward, bowing in turn. Good manners, due form, these were vital in dealing with High Court Sidhe, whether Dark or Bright. Ignore the forms, and they could kill you out of hand, but if you played by the rules, they had to as well. "You are far from home."

"I ride over lands I intend to claim," Aerune said. "Had you fallen into my trap, I could have done so tonight without difficulty—but no matter. I am an apt pupil, Bard, and I have learned your lessons well. My allies daily grow stronger . . . and I can wait while you wither and die. Mortals die so easily—ah, but you have already discovered that this fine evening, have you not?"

He means Jimmie, Eric realized, and held onto his temper with a great effort. Fury was weakness. It would not help him.

"Yes, I can wait," Aerune continued, "while all you can do is age and die, pathetic mortal meat that you are. Perhaps I will save you from that, and grant each of you a hero's death."

Aerune drew back his hand. It glowed blackly with levin-fire. Eric barely had time to throw a shield over himself and the others, but they were not his target. Aerune struck at the House itself, balefire fountaining over bricks and mortar, until the walls of the building itself ran with cold fire.

Eric could hear screams coming from inside. The Sensitives of Guardian House would have nightmares for months, but he dared not look away from the Unseleighe Lord. He wasn't powerful enough to take on Aerune by himself, the Guardians had no experience with the Sidhe, and Hosea was untrained either as Guardian or Bard. And nightmares were better than body bags.

Seeing that none of them would attack, Aerune began to laugh. "But not tonight. No, tonight, in token of the great love I bear for you all, I bring you . . . a gift."

Something—someone—staggered forward, sprawling at their feet. It was a girl—a woman—dressed in a glove-tight suit of black leather studded in silver, that covered all of her but her face. Silver hair spilled down her back, glittering in the parking lot's merciless halogen lights.

She wore a collar and leash, and she was human.

Aerune's mount reared and vaulted through the Portal he had opened. The Portal vanished, but his laughter echoed in the air.

Eric ran forward to help the girl up, but she scrabbled backward on hands and knees, whimpering. The leash dragged along the ground. She was hemorrhaging Power, radiating like a beacon, and Eric could detect no hint of shielding.

"Hey, take it easy. We won't hurt you."

She shook her head—he still couldn't see her face—but she began to laugh breathlessly, a sound chilling in its hopelessness.

"What the *hell* is going on?" Ria demanded, arriving with Kayla. "What's that?"

"Aerune said she was a present," Eric said tightly.

The crouching figure looked up.

There was a frozen moment of silence.

"*You,*" Ria breathed, fury in her voice.

The woman scrabbled to her feet and tried to run, but Ria was faster. She lunged forward, grabbing a handful of silver hair and dealing a stinging open-handed slap with the other. She drew back her hand to slap the woman again, but Eric grabbed her.

"Ria! Stop it! What's going on?"

Ria glared at him, green eyes flaming, her hand still fisted in the woman's hair. She shook her victim. Ria's handprint stood out lividly against her skin.

"Don't you know who this is, even with the clever plastic disguise? Meet Jeanette Campbell: she invented T-Stroke, and I'm going to make her wish she'd never been born. Let go of me!" She struggled, trying to pull her arm free of Eric's grip. Jeanette cowered back, panting and whimpering.

"Now, Miss Llewellyn," Hosea said mildly. He picked up the trailing leash and looped it around his hand. "She isn't going anywhere. And I think we'd all like some answers."

"She's mine!" Ria snarled.

"No, she isn't," Eric said levelly. "Let go of her, Ria. We have to find out what she knows. And then the law can make her pay for her crimes."

"No," Jeanette said, her voice barely intelligible through sounds of pain. "No, it can't."

Ria let go of Jeanette's hair to try to break Eric's grip, but he refused to release her. Jeanette ran to the end of the leash Hosea still held and dragged helplessly at it, trying to get away. Hosea reached for her to try to calm her.

"*Oh, God, no!* Don't touch me!" Jeanette shrieked. The raw agony in her voice stopped all of them cold for an instant, but an instant was enough.

"She's an Empath," Kayla said, her voice flat with discovery.

"I don't care if she's Mother Teresa," Ria growled, yanking herself free of Eric.

"I think," Paul Kern said, "that we'd better take this inside if we possibly can." He pointed back at the House.

Eric looked up. It was well after midnight—nearly dawn, in fact—but all the windows on this side of the building were lit, and he could see people at most of them gazing down into the parking lot. In a few moments some of them would come downstairs, asking a lot of questions that the people standing in the parking lot wouldn't want to answer.

"Yes. Greystone, is this some kind of trap?" Eric asked.

:*Not that I can see, laddybuck. She's harmless:*, the gargoyle replied in mindspeech. :*Come on in.:*

"You guys go ahead," Eric said.

They went, Hosea dragging Jeanette by the leash. She shied away from all attempts to touch her. Ria stalked into the building without looking behind her, back stiff with fury.

But Ria's anger was a problem to solve later, if he could. For now, some damage control was needed. Eric stepped back from the building, lips pursed in a soundless whistle as he summoned Power. The simplest of the Bardic Gifts—a spell of sweet dreams and forgetfulness for all those who stood watching from their windows, and for everyone else within the House it could reach.

Safe. You're safe here, all is well. Nightmares belong to the night and fade with the sun. It was all a dream, an evil dream, and it's over. You're safe. All is well.

The magic sounded forlorn and lost, like a candle in the wind. But each time the tune circled round again the magic was stronger, more hopeful. Eric ran through the simple tune that worked the spell nine times—three to shape it, three to set it, and three to bind it well—before he was satisfied. And finally he could feel it reach out to the people inside the House, touching them, bringing them comfort and hope, drawing force and reality from their hesitant belief.

It wouldn't be enough to banish the effects of Aerune's levin-bolt, but it would do for tonight. Later he and the others would have to see what they could do to unweave the harm that Aerune had done here, but tonight they had a more immediate disaster.

When he got back upstairs, Ria was sitting in the corner, seething, with Hosea hovering over her like a prison guard. Jeanette cowered in the far corner of the living room, her back against the wall, hugging herself and moaning. Her too-beautiful face was haggard, etched with lines of suffering. She looked like a bad plastic surgery case. Kayla knelt in front of her, several feet away, talking softly.

"I don't care *what* Aerune's done to her—it isn't enough," Ria said angrily when Eric arrived.

"Maybe not. But right now, finding out what he's up to is more important than revenge," Eric said.

Ria growled wordlessly and looked away.

"Yeah, facts are always nice to have," Kayla said, "but you aren't gonna get anything out of her while she's like this. She's got no shields, Eric. None. How can somebody be an Empath, and her age, and alive, and not have shields?"

Eric shook his head. "Maybe we can give her some."

"Wait a minute." Ria surged to her feet and took a step toward Jeanette. "You're going to *help* her?" She glared furiously at the three of them. Kayla glared right back.

"I'm going to—" Eric began.

"Don't worry, Ria," Jeanette said painfully, her voice a whispery croak. "Just a little time . . . I'll be dead and it won't matter." She smiled with great effort, as if this were a good joke on someone.

"You took T-Stroke," Eric said in abrupt understanding. Suddenly it all made terrible sense. *That's why she has Gifts and no idea of how to deal with them.*

Jeanette flinched. To an unshielded Empath, strong emotion

was like salt in an open wound. He saw her meet his gaze with a grim struggle. "I thought Elkanah was going to kill me and T-Stroke was my only weapon. I wish he had," she added in a ragged whisper. "He killed someone here. Aerune said so."

Elkanah? Toni said that was Jimmie's brother's name! It made terrible sense—Jimmie's brother would have been able to get through her shields. If she had felt his pain, if he had led her to her death . . .

"Let me help you," Kayla repeated, reaching out.

"Don't touch me!" Jeanette gasped, shrinking back. "Whoever you are, you can't fix this. I've seen Healers die. I know. *Please.*"

Kayla drew back. "We've got to do something. We can't just let her die," she said pleadingly to Eric.

Eric looked at Ria. Of everyone there, she was the only one, aside from Jeanette, who knew anything about how T-Stroke worked. All Eric knew was that Jeanette Campbell had come up with a drug that turned ordinary people into Talents . . . and killed them.

"Yes, we can," Ria said. "That's what T-Stroke does. It kills people a few hours after someone gives it to them. Only your clock wasn't running while you were in Underhill, was it, Campbell? Too bad Aerune's hung you out to dry, isn't it? Maybe now you'll know what it's like to die the way all the people you killed died."

Jeanette met Ria's gaze, though Eric could see that for her it was as much of an effort as to thrust her hand into an open fire. And just as agonizing.

"I never hurt you, Ria. Just your pride. Others have a lot more right to my head than you do. Stand in line." Jeanette gasped and doubled over, hugging herself against sudden stabbing pain, coughing raggedly until she began to gag. Kayla winced, flinching back from Jeanette's distress. Hosea crossed the room and swooped Kayla up as if she were a doll, depositing her on the couch at the far side of the room.

"You have got to stop Lord Aerune," Jeanette got out through gritted teeth. "He's got help." She curled into a fetal ball on the floor, shaking and gasping.

"I think if you've got any rabbits, Eric, now's the time to pull 'em out of your hat," Hosea said quietly.

But what could he do? He couldn't send Jeanette back to Underhill—from the looks of things, she wouldn't survive long enough for Lady Day to make it to the Everforest Gate. And he couldn't heal her—she was right; whatever T-stroke did to the human body, it was beyond the ability of either Healer or Bard to undo. Her time was running out.

But if he could stop time *here* . . .

"I'm going to try something," Eric said to the others. He thought about asking Hosea to help him, but he wasn't sure how Guardian Magic layered over Bardic Gift worked, and this wasn't any time to go doing field tests. "It'll buy us the time to figure this out, I hope, but it might feel kind of weird. Don't fight me, okay?"

"Whatever help we can give is yours," Paul answered.

Eric looked at Ria. She had power that stemmed from her half-Sidhe heritage and a lifelong study of sorcery. She could help him—or make this impossible.

Ria took a deep breath and nodded. "You're right. *She's* right. Do what you can. I won't stop you."

The first of the two spells was easy: a simple warding, to build the shields for Jeanette that she couldn't build herself. Eric saw them settle into place around her, saw her uncoil from her fetal crouch, panting with relief.

The second part was harder: to stop time itself for all of them here in this room. He didn't know if he could do it at all, if the House would permit it, and if he could, it wouldn't be for long. But he had to try.

For Eric, for any Bard, magic was music. He took a deep breath, holding the finished tune—the finished spell—fully formed within his mind—then letting it uncoil, filling him with music as he filled it with power. *"Backward, turn backward, O 'Time in Thy flight . . .'"*

It was like rolling a giant boulder uphill. He gritted his teeth, focusing his will on that impossible task. He got through the first iteration, but there were eight more to go before the spell was truly complete.

Seven—six—five— And he had no more to give. For a moment he thought he would fail, that the spell would uncoil right then, then new strength came flowing into the working.

Ria.

:I said I'd support your decisions, remember?: her cool voice came in his mind.

*Four—three—two—one—*and the spell was set and began to run. The walls of the room grew pale and indistinct, the doors and windows vanished, leaving the eight of them suspended in a bubble of silvery timelessness.

"You must teach me that sometime," Paul said respectfully, looking only a little rattled. José and Toni were looking around at the transformed apartment, wary looks of wonder on their faces.

"Yeah," Eric said, sighing. He turned back to Jeanette. She was sitting up, breathing more easily. She looked at Eric.

"This is magic, but it isn't a cure," he told her. "I don't know how long I can hold this bubble, but when it pops . . . you're probably going to go with it," he finished reluctantly.

"Just as well," Jeanette answered. "I've killed a lot of people. It's time I paid for that."

"It isn't enough."

It was Hosea who spoke, coming to the center of the room and looking down at Jeanette with a stern expression on his face that Eric had never seen before. "I'm not sure who you are or what you've done, ma'am, but Miss Llewellyn seems to think it's something pretty bad. You can't wipe out something like that with one grand gesture and a quick death. It's gonna take a power of effort and time—a lifetime of doing good, and more."

"I don't *have* a lifetime," Jeanette said, looking at him. "And I suck at social work. If you can think of any way around that, I'm open to suggestions." She shook her head, looking away. "I did have, once. All the time in the world—a lifetime to use however I wanted. But I pissed it away and you don't get a second chance, so be happy, Ria, because I'm going to fry in Hell for a thousand years." She closed her eyes, gathering her resources. "Here's what you need to know. Aerune found where I was hiding. He sent Elkanah, one of Lintel's Threshold ops, to bring me to somewhere he could get his hands on me. He's got most of my stash of T-Stroke, but it doesn't work on elves."

"Elkanah? Elkanah *Youngblood?*" Toni demanded in amazement. "Jimmie's *brother?*"

Jeanette stared at her. "Maybe. How do I know? People in our line of work aren't that free with last names and home addresses, y'know?" She took a deep breath. "Elkanah didn't know he was working for Aerune until the end—neither of us did. I thought he was going to kill me, so I dosed both of us with T-Stroke. The higher the dose, the more time you have—maybe if you take enough, you get to live, I don't know. But Aerune came. He took me Underhill and left Elkanah behind. I don't know what happened to him, but he's dead now, for sure. At least I know he deserved it," she added quietly.

"Most of what happened then isn't important. But this is: Aerune has human help—a guy from this side of the Hill. Parker Wheatley. They're working together—planning to start a war between humans and elves so Aerune can get us to bomb ourselves back to the Stone Age. I get the idea Aerune found a bunch of government elfchasers and gave them a little help. Wheatley depends on him now. If you can't stop them, they're going to drag all your precious secrets onto the front page of *The New York Times,* and then what I've done is going to look like a wet firecracker next to a neutron bomb. They were talking about . . . internment camps for witches. Crazy stuff."

Even insulated as she was, Jeanette was still painfully weak, and delivering the message had cost her a lot. She hung her head, breathing hard. "There's a lot more to tell you, but I don't think I have time."

Eric knew she was right. His spell couldn't hold, even reinforced with Ria's power. In a few minutes, it would fade away, and time would run normally once more. And a few minutes after that, Jeanette would be dead.

"You could have." Hosea spoke again. "Time."

Jeanette looked up at him, hate and hope in her expression. "Yeah? And how do you figure that?"

"Your body has to die. You don't. Instead of going on, why don't you stick around and clean up some of your mess?" Hosea said, as if it were the simplest thing in the world.

"Become a voluntary ghost?" Paul said doubtfully. "That has certain drawbacks, you know. Once a spirit has chosen to tarry, for whatever reason, moving on becomes a rather ticklish proposition. And you'd need an anchor to hold the spirit in place."

"Like a building," Toni said. "But I don't want her haunting Guardian House."

"It could be a physical object, not a house," José said. "A sword, or a mirror, as the old tales say. Or a harp."

"We're a little short on any of those objects right now," Paul pointed out, looking around the room. "Even if the lady agreed."

"And we don't have a lot of time to discuss it," Eric said tightly.

"Hey, so you don't have a harp. You've got this," Kayla pointed out, holding up Hosea's banjo. "Will this work?"

Paul took the instrument from her hands and studied it carefully. "If Hosea consents, and Miss Campbell does as well, I think this will do nicely. But I warn both of you: though we can hold her here, we can't set the terms of her imprisonment, and I do know one thing— if the banjo is destroyed without Jeanette's spirit being released from it, she will be dead in this world and the next, with no reprieve possible."

"I'm game," Hosea said, and looked at Jeanette.

"A choice between Hell and bluegrass," Jeanette said. "I'll take bluegrass—if you'll have me, Hosea?"

"This isn't right," Kayla said. "I saw— When Jimmie— Shouldn't she go on and find what's waiting for her?"

"No, thanks," Jeanette said briefly, and shuddered. "I think I've seen it."

"Everybody deserves a chance to fix what they broke," Hosea agreed. "If you do right, Miss Jeanette, I'll do right by you."

"Folks—" Eric said urgently.

"Come here, Jeanette. Take the banjo. Eric, when I give the word, release your spell and let us cast ours," Paul said. "I warn you, Miss Campbell, this isn't going to be pleasant for you. Keeping a spirit from passing over is a terrible thing, painful for both the spirit and the enchanter, even when full consent is involved. You may wish we hadn't."

"Just do it, for God's sake." Jeanette crawled to the center of the room and sat, reaching out to take the banjo and cradling it in her arms. The Guardians formed a circle around her, even Hosea, who looked very unsure of himself.

"Call this your baptism of fire," Toni told him.

"I can't—" Eric said, just as Paul said: "Now."

With a pang of relief, Eric stopped feeding power to his spell and felt it uncoil and vanish. Time rushed back into the room like the incoming tide filling a sea cave. Jeanette gasped and fell over on her side, groaning and clutching the banjo tightly.

Light surrounded the five of them, like an egg of multicolored opal. Ria reached out for Eric's hand, and he took it.

Eric wasn't sure he believed what he saw happen next. He saw Jeanette—a ghostly, different-looking Jeanette—climb to her feet, stepping over the slumped body on the floor. She gazed around, frightened, shaking her head, obviously looking for a way out. But there was nowhere to go. She beat against the walls of the egg, crying out silently in frustration.

Kayla jerked forward.

"No, Kayla," Ria said. "Her choice, right or wrong." Ria coaxed Kayla to sit down again. The young Healer's face was a mask of frustration. "You don't *know*," she repeated.

"Jimmie went to what she deserved, after a lifetime of service and self-sacrifice. Do you think Jeanette wants to face what *she* deserves?" Ria asked.

"How can you be sure you're right?" Kayla demanded.

"I don't have to be," Ria said austerely. "All I have to do is let her make her own mistake."

Slowly, the egg of light shrank, keeping Jeanette imprisoned within it despite her struggles, dwindling until it surrounded the banjo alone, forcing her down with it.

Then the light was gone.

"Ladies and gentlemen, we have created the world's first

haunted banjo," Paul said wearily. "And I wish I felt better about doing it."

"You did what you had to, Paul. We all did," Toni answered.

Hosea picked up the banjo from where it lay against Jeanette's dead body. One of the strings promptly broke, and in the faint ringing Eric thought he could hear the echo of a human voice.

:Bluegrass . . . :

"Feels heavier," Hosea said, hefting the instrument. He began to detune the banjo, taking the tension off the remaining strings.

"Well, this has been a hell of a night," Ria said.

"Look," Kayla said. "The sun's coming up."

And it was. The sky outside the living room window was gray with dawn.

"What now?" Eric said.

"We need to make plans," Toni said, "but first things first. We all need sleep. And then . . . Hosea, I guess Jimmie's apartment is yours now." Her eyes filled with tears as the reality of Jimmie's death hit her anew.

"Eric, you should warn Misthold about Aerune's plans. I don't know much about Underhill politics, but maybe there's something they can do about him from their side," Ria said.

"Yeah." Weariness—healthy weariness this time, and not Aerune's spell of despair—overwhelmed Eric, and he dropped into the nearest empty chair. *But I doubt it. Aerune's too clever to give them an excuse to move against him, and by the time I convince them he's a real threat to Underhill and the World Above alike, it might be too late. Elves don't do anything in a hurry, and nothing much excites them. Kory's the real exception there, and he's young. The others just won't listen—or if they do, they won't do anything.*

"But that's a matter for another day," Ria went on, seeing his face. "Come on, Kayla. It's time to get you home and settled in."

"No way. I'm staying here." Kayla got to her feet and walked to the middle of the room, glaring at Hosea and the other Guardians. "You people need a keeper, you know that? If I hadn't blown the whistle on Aerune, he woulda slurped you all up like a Coffee Coolata—and where'd you be then? You're great at taking care of everyone else, but who's taking care of *you?* You need me, and I'm staying. End of discussion."

Her speech took the Guardians by surprise. "You?" Toni asked.

"You see anybody else applying for the job?" Kayla shot back.

The Guardians looked at each other, and back at Ria, who shrugged, looking almost as tired as Eric felt.

"I'm not her mother. And I think it would be okay with Elizabet if Kayla lived here, so long as someone was keeping an eye on her."

"I think we can arrange that," José said, with the ghost of a smile. "And I think I speak for all of us when I say that your offer is most welcome, *munequita.*"

"Well, good," Kayla said. She'd obviously been expecting more of an argument, but by now Eric was used to the speed with which the Guardians made decisions. And as for Ria, having seen Kayla's taste in clothes, he was pretty sure Ria was a little relieved not to have Kayla on hand to redecorate her Park Avenue apartment.

"Then it's settled. I guess you can have the basement apartment, now that . . ." Toni said. She took a deep breath and went on. "Why don't you go home with Ria tonight, and tomorrow we can see about getting you settled in. And there will be the . . . funeral arrangements for Jimmie. She died in the line of duty. There will be a Department funeral, I think. I'll have to check."

"That can wait," Paul said, putting an arm around her shoulders. "Now it is time to rest, and to gather our strength. There will be time enough to say our proper good-byes."

But how much time was Aerune—and his unknown allies—going to give them? Eric wondered.

TWELVE:
CELTIC HOTEL

"Welcome to Glitterhame Neversleeps—and the Tir-na-Og Resort Hotel and Casino! I'm your friendly neighborhood VIP greeter, and you two are certainly VIPs."

Beth blinked, looking around herself as the Portal dissolved behind her. She and Kory stood in the center of a pristine greenwood of towering oaks—a Node Grove—and beneath her feet, the ground was covered with thick emerald moss in which violets and tiny blue starflowers bloomed. But beyond the trees she could see neon in every shade of the rainbow, and the light overhead was filtered through the glass skylight of the casino atrium, ten stories above.

"I'm Geraint mac Merydydd, but you can call me Gerry— Meredith, as it were. Prince Arvindel told us you'd be coming. It's November, the temperature is a balmy 50 degrees Fahrenheit, and sunset is at 4:33 today to be followed by a waxing moon. Please adjust your calendars and watches and return all tray tables to an upright position before exiting the heartwood."

Though two days ago it had been August, Beth's time, in the world two months had passed, as she and Kory had used the Gates at Everforest and Neversleeps to arrive both when and where they wished to. In essence, it was time travel, though the elves rarely used the gates in that fashion, and Beth's mind had been boggled the first time she'd understood that it was possible.

"But why don't you use it? Go back in time and change things that went wrong? You could keep Perenor from buying the Node Grove, keep Susan from building the Poseidon machine—"

"The web of the world is woven as Danu wills," Kory had told her, "though we may affect some small threads of Her weaving, we dare not unravel the design. I am but a Magus Minor, with small gifts, and so I do not perfectly understand the why of these things. Our wisest Adepts could explain, though they might not choose to. But it has always been so."

"But how do you know when 'now' is?" Beth had asked, frustrated. "If there's no time in Underhill, and you can go back and forth in the time of the World Above as you please, how do you know?"

"And what else is a Node Grove for, but to anchor the hames into the 'now' of the World Above?" Kory had answered, smiling. "And that anchorage is vital if we are to come and go between the two worlds in safety and ease. There are worlds as real as your own, places in the World Above, where there are no Node Groves, no Portals, and no Elfhames. Such worlds are difficult to reach, and easy to become lost in forever, nor does magic work so well in such worlds as it does here. And so we accept time as the precious gift it is, and do not make light of it."

"After all, it does keep everything from happening at once," Beth had quipped, and let the subject drop. As far as she could figure, the Sidhe used time the way humans used magnetic north: as a useful aid to navigation, but something they could ignore if they chose. Still, they were in November now, and in a day or so they'd go back Underhill, and if she stayed there long enough, everything would sort itself out. So long as she didn't think any more about it, her head wouldn't hurt. And meanwhile, there was their host to consider.

Gerry Meredith looked as if the description "lounge lizard"

might have been invented just for him, and his glamourie made him look human—though far more handsome than any human had a right to be. He was wearing a white sharkskin suit with the casino's logo—a Celtic dragon coiled around a tower—embroidered in gold over the suit pocket, and a black satin shirt open to the waist. His short black hair was slicked straight back; he wore an ornate gold hoop in one ear, a host of gold chains around his neck, and jewel-studded rings on every finger.

"We're, uh, pleased to be here," Beth said, taking the proffered hand. Gerry's smile broadened into a conspiratorial grin.

"Quite a shock, isn't it? We like to think of our little casino as a teensy bit of home here in this great big desert—and where better to hide something than in plain sight? The tourists think that the Grove is just part of our lovely Celtic ambiance, and with the trees indoors instead of outside, we aren't disrupting the local ecology either—which is more than I can say about *some* people, with their seventy-five-thousand-gallons-a-day-lost-to-evaporation waterfalls. Well! No point in weeping over what can't be mended, is there, dear ones? Let me get someone to take your luggage, and we'll show you to your suite. If there's anything you've forgotten, you can probably find it in one of our tragically-trendy concourse-level shops. All on the house, of course. Nothing too good for our honored guests."

He snapped his fingers, and two bellhops dressed in tights and doublets arrived. Gerry pointed at the two small bags—Beth and Kory didn't plan to be here very long, but each had brought a few things just in case. "Those go to the Lady In The Lake Suite in Tower Four," he said. Each man picked up a bag and walked off through the wood, and Gerry turned back to Beth and Kory.

"Now if you'll come along with me, you can see a bit of the casino on the way up to your rooms," Gerry said. "I understand you'll be attending Comdex along with 250,000 other lovely people? A very busy time of year for us. We have your passes and badges all taken care of—we can pick them up along with your keys when we get to the desk—but of course you'll be wanting to take care of all the teensy details yourself—we don't pry. Discretion is our watchword here at Neversleeps—after all, if we told everyone simply everything, what *would* there be left to gossip about?" Still chattering, Gerry ushered the two of them through the little greenwood.

Beth could see that there were colored floodlights ringing the base of each tree—the place must look amazing at night—and in the distance she could hear the splashing of a small fountain.

Neat. They can use magic practically openly, and the mundanes'll think it's just another special effect. Nobody ever really expects to be told the magician's secrets, now, do they?

At the edge of the heartwood a red velvet theater rope marked off the trees from the rest of the casino floor and discouraged casual wanderers. *There must be five acres under this roof,* Beth marveled, looking around. When Kory had told her that elves were running a casino in Las Vegas she hadn't been sure what to expect, but she sure hadn't expected . . . this.

The motif here in the main casino was Celtic kitsch—as if Liberace'd had a heavy date with the cast of *Riverdance*, with a lot of *Camelot* and some *Robin of Sherwood* thrown in. The carpet beneath their feet was a multicolored Celtic knotwork pattern, dizzying to look at for very long. Half the wait staff wore kilts and poet shirts and looked like demented Highlanders, while the other half wore diaphanous—and very short—glittery togas with sequined Celtic motifs and sparkly "fairy" wings.

The air was filled with sound—piped-in Celtic music (rather good, to Beth's surprise, and not the potted Muzak one usually heard in public buildings), the *ching!* of slot machines and the clatter of jackpots being paid off, the low calls of the croupiers, the hum of a thousand conversations, and over it all, the ring of other bells and chimes she couldn't begin to guess the reason for. Despite the fact that it was broad day, there were plenty of customers, both at the banks of gleaming slot machines and clustered around the tables. Las Vegas was a true 24-hour town. *"Neversleeps" indeed. For once, that Sidhe quirk must come in really handy,* Beth thought.

While the table games were pretty standard—poker, blackjack, baccarat—even the slot machines carried out the theme of the casino, with leprechauns, pots of gold, rainbows, castles, and dragons prominently displayed on the faces. But the wackiest thing, in Beth's opinion, was the twelve-foot-high vertical roulette wheel that towered over the rest of the casino floor, prominently captioned "Arianrhod's Silver Wheel of Fortune." It promised a $100,000 payoff on double zero, and the most frequent payouts on the entire Strip.

"Oh, my," she murmured to Kory, pointing circumspectly. "Have they *no* shame?"

"None at all, my lady," Gerry said brightly. She'd forgotten how acute elves' hearing was. "We give the tourists what they come to see—and if we have a bit of fun with it, too, where's the harm? We run the quietest, safest, friendliest house on the Strip—only the people who need to lose do so here, and the people who need to win do that too. It all works out." He beamed at them happily.

"Friendly, perhaps. But how honest?" Beth wanted to know. This whole place was too big, too gaudy—and too good to be true. It made her suspicious. What were they *really* up to?

Gerry grinned at her conspiratorially, obviously aware of her reservations. "Devil a bit, m'lady, but does that matter? The good are rewarded, the wicked are punished—and as for those who are sick beyond our power to help them and wish to lose themselves in games of chance as others do in drink or Dreaming, why, somehow they never come in our doors—or if they do, it's for a quick drink, a pull of the slots, and then they're on their way. We harm no one here, nor allow anyone to come to harm. This is Tir-na-Og, the Land of Dreams, and all our dreams are pleasant!" Gerry swept his arms wide, indicating the casino floor with a proud flourish.

"But surely more need to win at your tables than need to lose," Kory pointed out. "If more money is paid out than taken in, how do you survive?"

"As to that, Prince Korendil, it's a fine old Vegas tradition to cook the books, and really, we don't even need to do much of that. More people need to lose money than you'd think—for one reason or another. We get a lot of convention traffic, and with two five-star restaurants and three shows nightly in Merlin's Enchanted Oak Room, we do quite well. And if there are any shortfalls . . . well, there's fairy gold aplenty here in Tir-na-Og!"

With enough *kenned* gold to back it, Beth supposed, any business could afford to run at a loss. And casinos had traditionally been used to launder funds . . . though somehow she suspected that Tir-na-Og was one of the few casinos in Clark County without a Mafia silent partner hovering in the background.

"I do hope you'll be able to make the time to stop in and see one of our shows. The prettiest girls, the most toothsome boys, and more. Magic. *Real* magic. Stage illusionism—prestidigitation in the grand tradition of Kellar, Maskelyne, Houdini—the very best in the business!"

"Real magic?" Kory said, delighted. He turned to Beth. "We must—we could see the show tonight!"

"Why not?" Beth said. It was strange, when even a Magus Minor like Kory could perform feats of magic that no human could hope to duplicate, that most of the elves she'd met were bonkers for stage illusionism, which involved no "real" magic at all, just misdirection and sleight of hand. It was just another aspect of their endless fascination with human creativity, she guessed, but it did seem odd. Like their obsession with microwaves. And their lust for pretzels.

Elves were pretty strange when you got to know them.

"Splendid! I'll get you tickets for the midnight show—and you can have dinner beforehand in the Merrie Greenwood. You'll see us at our best, I assure you!"

It seemed to Beth that they'd been walking for miles. It was hard to tell, with all the mirrors and flashing lights, and the casino floor was laid out in a labyrinthine path that required anyone passing through it to loop around and double back, passing the maximum possible number of temptations, to reach their destination. But at last they reached the hotel desk.

It was an imposing structure—the desk itself, nearly as wide as it was tall, was pure white Carrera marble with gilt accents—and was carved with fierce warriors and mythical beasts in an antique style, sort of *Xena Meets the Monks of Lindisfarne*. The space behind the desk was paneled in a good approximation of golden English oak, and all the informational signs were done in uncial script, with illuminated initial letters after the Book of Kells. But the staff behind the desk was courteous and professional, all wearing matching white Tir-na-Og blazers with nametags. Beth supposed that none of them were Sidhe; though she couldn't be sure. The Seleighe Sidhe had the weirdest notions of what was fun, sometimes.

Gerry stopped at the end of the desk, under a sign that said "VIP Services," and spoke to one of the staff.

"The Misthold party is here. Be a good little elf and fetch me their check-in package."

"Of course," the woman behind the counter said. She flashed Beth a dazzling smile. "Welcome to Tir-na-Og. We hope you'll enjoy your stay with us." Her name tag read: *Hi! My name is Galadriel* and her slitted pupils were narrowed against the dazzling lights.

Beth blinked. Gerry had spoken no more than the truth when he'd called her a "good little elf." She was probably Low Court, one of the host of Sidhe linked almost symbiotically to the anchoring Node Grove and its Gate. Low Court elves could not travel any great distance from the trees to which they were linked, either in Underhill or in the World Above, and would die if their parent grove was harmed. Unlike their High Court brethren, the Low Court elves were unable to completely disguise their Sidhe nature. They were also said to be more scatterbrained and mischievous than their High Court brethren, with less of an interest in the future—it was from encounters with members of the Low Court over the centuries that most of the tales of "mischievous spirits" had entered human myths, while the High Court figured predominantly as shining heroes and sometimes gods.

But that was a long time ago, Beth thought, watching the saucy Sidhe tuck envelopes, keys, maps, and coupons into a white leatherette folder with the hotel logo stamped prominently on it in gold. *From gods to resort owners. Wonder if they miss the olden days?* Galadriel handed the folder to Beth with a cheerful smile. Probably most of the people who stopped by her counter didn't even notice her eyes, or thought they were costume contacts.

"Will you be needing anything else, Ms. Kentraine, Mr. Korendil?" Galadriel asked.

"Uh . . . not right now," Beth said, taking the folder. This place was as strange and unworldly in its own way as the Goblin Market and Rick's, and at that, the Tir-na-Og wasn't that different from most of the other A-list casinos on the Strip. *I guess the guy who said that truth is stranger than fiction knew what he was talking about. . . .*

Galadriel wished them both a lovely day at the Tir-na-Og Resort Hotel and Casino, and Beth and Kory followed Gerry past a row of shops selling souvenirs and sundries—the high-priced designer boutiques were on the other side of the casino—and over to a bank of elevators. The doors were golden, showing the castle-and-dragon logo being dive-bombed by a number of scantily-clad fairies with jeweled wings. He led them to an elevator at the end that was marked "Penthouse Suites Only."

"You'll need your room key to access the elevator, and it only stops at the top two floors," Gerry explained. He took Beth's portfolio from her and extracted the room key, fitting it into a slot beneath the row of buttons. When he did, all the buttons lit up, and he pressed one of them. Beth immediately felt the sensation of weight that told her she was in a high-speed elevator.

"How many floors does this place have?" she asked.

"Twenty-five," Gerry answered promptly. "The top two floors are for Paladin-class guests such as yourselves—and most of our Underhill guests, of which we're seeing more every year, I'm delighted to say. You'll find *no* Cold Iron anywhere in our Paladin-class accommodations, and of course you'll have noticed there's very little deathmetal on the casino floor. Why, even the flatware in our restaurants is silver, not stainless."

"You must lose a lot of it," Beth said.

Gerry smiled. "Not really. Most of our guests think it's plate, not worth stealing. And it's enchanted to come back, anyway, if someone tries to take it out of the building. Much easier that way."

At that moment the doors opened.

The hall carpet was a deep rich purple, bordered in a subdued knotwork pattern in gold that was picked up in the wallpaper. Reproductions of some of the more whimsical Pre-Raphaelite paintings hung on the walls—not that Beth was sure they were reproductions. Some of the hames entertained themselves by collecting art and literature about the Fair Folk that was created by humans, and that would certainly be right in line with Glitterhame Neversleep's corporate culture.

"This way, dear ones."

They passed a few tastefully gold-leafed doors with various Celtic motifs done on them in low relief—serpents, claddaughs, Celtic crosses, triskelions—but not many. These were the kind of suites that every Vegas casino kept for its high rollers, and Beth had heard that they were enormous.

At last they arrived at their destination. Gerry opened the door with a flourish before handing the key card back to Beth.

"Welcome!" he said, stepping back so they could enter.

"Oh, my," Beth said.

They stood in the main room of the suite. The curtains were drawn back from one curving glass wall to show her the eastward-looking view of the late-afternoon Strip. The Superstition Mountains were a faint blue smear in the distance, and even with the dust and fuss of the city's building boom, the air seemed clear and impossibly crystalline. She could see the various casinos all the way down to the MGM Grand and Excalibur, looking tawdry and faintly apologetic without their nighttime neon.

"There's a balcony on the other side—and, of course, the Roof Terrace. And now, I'll leave the two of you to settle in. If you have any questions, or need anything at all, no matter how infinitesimal, don't hesitate to give me a jingle. My card is in your information packet, and as you already know, we never sleep here in the City of Sin." Gerry waved gaily and sauntered out, closing the door behind him.

"And I thought Underhill was weird," Beth said. Tearing her attention away from the view—it *was* mesmerizing, and would be more so come nightfall—she turned to inspect their lodgings.

It was obvious no marketing department or consumer focus group had been consulted in decorating the suite, because their suggestions would have run to the bland, the inoffensive, the middle of the road. And this wasn't that. It had a cheerful vulgarity, a no-holds-barred excess, a lurid exuberance that made Beth smile. *See?* the room almost seemed to say. *It's okay to play around with bright colors. No Fashion Police here! And remember: Glitter is Good.*

If she'd had to characterize the style, she'd have said Celtic-Egyptian, providing, of course, it'd come by way of the Sun King's court in France. There were several sectional seating groups in bright colors—red, blue, purple—stone-topped gilded tables in the shapes of fantastic beasts, paintings and a few statues and some knick-knacks and several vases filled with gaudy lilies scattered across the top of the bar and the entertainment armoire. The whole room fairly radiated self-confidence, the cheerful happiness of someone secure in their own style, no matter how far from the mainstream that might be.

On the coffee table was a large fruit basket, a jeroboam of champagne, and an equally enormous candy box with an unfamiliar logo, all gifts of the management. Beth went over and lifted the lid, puzzled. This couldn't be chocolate . . . ?

It wasn't. The box was filled with marzipan and divinity, candied apricots, caramels, sugar-glazed nutmeats: in short, everything *but* chocolate. *Oooh, Purina Elf Yummies. Cool.*

"I must say, we're certainly getting the VIP treatment. As advertised," she said to no one in particular. Kory was wandering around the room like a cat in a strange place, picking things up and setting them down. He went off into the bedroom. Beth followed, nibbling on an apricot.

The bedroom was decorated mostly in soothing blues and greens: there was a second bar, a second television, and enough closet space to get lost in. It had a bed bigger than anything Beth had seen outside of Underhill dominating the room, with a green velvet tufted headboard that went halfway up the wall, and a matching half-canopy jutting out above it, satin-lined drapes held back with tasseled gold ropes.

But the bathroom, so far as Beth was concerned, was the star attraction, filled with enough Eurogadgets that by rights it should have launched you into orbit, not just gotten you clean. There were heated vibrating massage beds, towel warmers, infrared lamps, a heated floor, an omnidirectional step-in shower, and a whirlpool Jacuzzi big enough to baptize an entire parish at one go. The counter was filled with bottles of complementary toiletries, everything from bath gel to toothpaste, and there were more fresh flowers in a silver bowl, filling the room with the scent of roses and oranges.

"Can we take this whole place with us when we go back to Underhill?" Beth asked, only half joking.

Kory smiled. "I think Maeve would like it. I think I would, too. I have never . . . seen any place quite like this in your human world."

"Just goes to show you what happens when you turn elves with money loose in Las Vegas," Beth quipped. "Now, we'd better go start making those phone calls and find out where those vendors Ray promised to hook us up with are going to be tomorrow."

Travis Booker already knew he was in over his head. His ID (should he need to produce it) said he was working for Greenwood Security Limited, one of the Paranormal Defense Initiative's screen organizations—and if that were really the case, he'd have no problems. Greenwood Security had a booth at Comdex; it was actually a legitimate business, providing on-site security services for vendors concerned about industrial espionage. The fact that its findings trickled upstairs to its governmental masters was something that very few people—its clients not among them—needed to know.

Until ten months ago, Travis had been a researcher. There wasn't much else you could do with a Ph.D. in folklore and anthropology— when he'd written his paper on urban myths, he'd had hopes of a bright publishing career, or at least a plum teaching job. Neither materialized—but the United States Government in its infinite wisdom had plenty of jobs for someone whose only real talent was hitting the books. He knew he was working for one of the alphabet agencies, but even Travis wasn't sure which one: his paycheck said General Services Administration, just like everyone else's; he'd been hired by the State Department (just like everyone else), and his time was occupied either in preparing briefing memos on whatever esoteric subject appeared in his in-box, or in boiling other such documents down into two-page memos.

It seemed to him sometimes that life would be simpler if they all just stuck to writing two-page memos in the first place, but the same governmental department that swore it was too busy to read the information it asked for also insisted on in-depth coverage of its subject.

Then one day a man had come to him and asked him if he'd like a new job. Travis had warmed up to Parker Wheatley immediately—the man was obviously a Washington insider, clearly going places. Wheatley had said that he was forming a special new department, and Travis's qualifications and clearances fit him admirably for work there.

For a while his new job was the same as the old—his paychecks still came from the GSA, and he even had the same office—but instead of putting together reports on the political history of Afghanistan, the subjects he was called upon to research were universally wacky. UFO sightings over major cities. Appearances of elves and fairies since 1900. A list of cryptozoological sightings organized by geographical area, with special reference to those grouped around sites of current nuclear power plants. He found it a nice change to be able to put his degree to some use, but wondered vaguely what his tax dollars were up to, if his new employers were investigating Bigfoot.

After a while, he began receiving what were obviously field agents' reports, with a request to match the descriptions in them to the closest known folklore motif. Curiosity was something discouraged in Travis's line of work, but he couldn't help beginning to piece things together. There actually was something out there. Something with *huge* implications for national and global defense. Something that had been here before, leaving legends in its wake, and was back again now. John Keel had called them "ultraterrestrials"; Keel's being a sort of Unified Weirdness Theory that whatever the source of this weird phenomena, it was Earthly and continuous, not extraplanetary and recent, in origin. Travis duly wrote a lengthy paper cross-referencing *The Field Guide to Extraterrestrials* with Arne-Thompsen and passed it up the chain of command.

Shortly after that, Parker Wheatley had called to invite him to lunch at the exclusive Cincinnatus Club, and Travis had leaped at the chance. Something was definitely up, and he suspected he was about to be given a chance to find out what.

What he didn't expect was to be offered the chance to be a field agent for the newly formed Paranormal Defense Initiative, successor in interest to Project Broad Church, for which he had been recruited. Mr. Wheatley had assured him that he could pick up the field skills he needed as he went along—with intensive coaching, of course— but that it was very important to the PDI to have field agents who had some idea of what they were dealing with.

"My doctorate is in folklore," Travis reminded him, trying not to be overawed by the vibrations of money and power that filled the Cincinnatus Club's dining room. It very much resembled an exclusive English men's club of the 19th century—it was meant to—and was the sort of place that people like Travis rarely saw. Parker Wheatley, on the other hand, was obviously a frequent guest.

"So it is," Mr. Wheatley had said. "And surely you've gained some idea of our mandate from all the work you've been doing for us?"

This was dangerous ground, for thinking was next door to prying into matters that didn't concern you, and a good way to lose your job, your clearances, and your government pension.

"Well, really, sir, I'm just doing my job. And I know I'm not seeing the full picture. After all, it isn't my job to speculate. Only to provide factual information."

"Let's just suppose for a moment that I were to ask you to speculate. Based solely on the material that crosses your desk in the line of duty, of course, and with the full understanding that you don't have all the pieces. I'd be interested to see what you'd come up with."

"Well . . ." Wheatley obviously wasn't going to let him off the hook. "I guess I'd have to say that you're interested in a class of phenomena whose manifestations explicitly predate 1947, and in fact have occurred in essentially the same form as far back as we have written records, though the interpretation of them has naturally changed over time."

"Neatly put," Wheatley said. "And what would you say those phenomenal manifestations *are*?"

"I can't say," Travis pointed out. "No one knows. I can say that at various times in history, these same phenomena have been classed as gods, demons, various forms of non-deific supernatural beings, and, most recently, as space aliens, of which the Alien Grey is the most commonly recognized, but certainly not the only type. Whether there's really anything there—and if there isn't, why people keep seeing them with such peculiar consistency—isn't something I can tell you."

"Well, then, Travis, let me put the question I asked you earlier in a different way: would you like to go and see for yourself?"

Put that way, it had been an offer he couldn't refuse, one which had led him, over the course of nearly a year, to standing around a Las Vegas airport in the ugliest green suit imaginable, looking for . . . what the rest of the PDI was looking for: Spookies.

Travis hated the green suit, but the stealth technology woven into the fabric didn't take dye very well, so Headquarters said, so the field teams were stuck with looking like a bunch of forest-green fashion plates. Fortunately, in a town like this, they didn't stand out, and Travis had to admit that the cut itself was stylish.

Las Vegas was far from PDI's usual beat, but Headquarters had gotten a tip that some Spookies might be showing up at Comdex, so he'd been tasked to keep an eye out at McCarran International to see if he spotted one coming in through the airport. Spookies could look like anything, but the black box on his wrist impersonating a watch didn't lie. It was designed to respond to the presence of parasympathetic energy, and PS waves always meant Spookies.

Nevertheless, he'd been as surprised as anyone to see his watch light up when the tall woman passed him. He would have stared at her regardless—she was well over six feet tall, even without the high-heeled black boots, and had long red-streaked black hair that hung straight to her waist. He slipped on his sunglasses to take a better look. Their special filtering technology was supposed to cut through

Spookie illusions as if they weren't there, and for the first time, Travis'd had a demonstration of what that meant. His quarry's business suit and porn queen boots vanished. Now she was wearing what looked like a black velvet riding habit, and she had *the ears*.

Gotcha, babe. You may run, but you can't hide. His heart raced with excitement—he knew the Spookies were dangerous, often savage, and totally unpredictable, but he was actually seeing one up close! He hurried to follow her as she headed out the front of the airport toward the waiting line of cabs.

The cab ride to the Strip was short, and he had no trouble keeping hers in view. She pulled up at one of the casinos; he stopped his cab at the next one and walked back, following her inside. His black box promptly lit up again, and this time the entire face went red, unable to give him a directional indicator. The whole place was loaded with PS energy!

He shook his head, suddenly dizzy. He had an urge to go back out onto the street, back to the airport, but a sense of duty stopped him. He'd tagged a Spookie, and he wasn't going to stop until he chased her down. PDI was always hoping for the pot of gold: a live Spookie capture, not just a bunch of glimpses and second-hand reports. If he was involved in a capture, it could mean promotion, maybe even a bonus.

Maybe I'd better report in, he thought, worried. The GPS locator all field agents wore would let the local office know where he was, but no more than that. Just then he spotted her again, over at the Reservations Desk.

And she was surrounded by Spookies. Half the people behind the desk looked just like the ID sketches he'd seen—the long pointed ears and brilliant overlarge hypnotic eyes. He swept a glance around the rest of the casino. More of them. The place was crawling with Spookies—a whole nest of them!

He started to panic, then controlled himself. They didn't know he was here, and they didn't know about the PDI. He was safe for the moment. And he needed to find out as much as he could about what they were up to before he made his report.

❖❖ ❖❖ ❖❖

Roderick Gallowglass—his name was Rhydderich, but Roderick was close enough—was a happy elf. He'd been security chief for the casino for the last three years, and he never tired of watching humans. They were so endlessly inventive, so passionate. A joy to work with, really—and with the whole place loaded to the gills with Trouble Begone spells, he rarely had to do anything more taxing than point out the bathrooms to bewildered tourists.

Today, however, might be different.

He'd spotted the Unseleighe the moment she walked in the door, of course—that "you are all peasants" arrogance would have been a dead giveaway, even if she weren't swaddled in glamouries that rendered her true seeming invisible to humans (though not to Roderick)—but the Tir-na-Og was a neutral zone, protected by truce. So long as they didn't make trouble, members of the Dark Court were as welcome here as were the Bright.

The man who'd followed her, however, was a different proposition. There was something odd about him—not quite magic, but odd nonetheless. Roderick could see the casino's wards swirl around him, unable to get a good grip, and felt an urge to rest his own eyes somewhere—anywhere—else. As he watched, Roderick saw the man hesitate, staggering a little as the magics did their best to push him out the door. But Tir-na-Og's gentle wardings were not designed to combat a determined will, only to turn aside those who could be encouraged to go elsewhere. Obviously the young man in the green business suit thought he had business here—and with the Unseleighe lady, at that.

The lady picked up her registration and headed for the elevators, and the nervous young man moved to follow.

Ah, laddie, the likes of her isn't for the likes of you. Time for me to save you from yourself.

Roderick moved forward to intercept the young man as he attempted to follow the lady into the elevator. He nearly didn't make it—for some reason, the green suit was particularly hard to see in the casino's misleading illumination.

"Excuse me, sir. Those elevators are for guests only. May I help you?"

The young man turned toward him, anonymous in his sunglasses, and Roderick saw his mouth gape with shock. "You're one of them too!" he gasped, reaching into his jacket.

He sees me as I truly am, Roderick realized, equally stunned. Not so stunned that he didn't take the young man's arm gently but firmly, keeping him from whatever he was reaching for—and hustled him through a door marked "Staff Only."

The nervous young man did his best to put up a fight, but Roderick's greater strength put paid to that airy notion, and by the time the lad thought of shouting, they were well away from public eyes. A small spell opened the door of one of the Quiet Rooms, and Roderick dragged his charge inside, plucking the object the lad had been reaching for from his pocket as he did. On the streets of Victorian London, Roderick had been an accomplished pickpocket, and he liked to keep up the old skills.

His fingers tingled and burned with the presence of Cold Iron— none of this new-fangled steel or alloy, but the pure deathmetal itself. The device resembled an old-fashioned zip gun, but instead of bullets or darts, it held a clip of inch-long iron spikes. It might annoy a human, but it would kill or cripple one of the Sidhe. He tossed it quickly into a containment bin for later examination, and rubbed his blistering fingers together. A nasty piece of work that, put together by someone who knew more about Roderick's kind than was strictly comforting.

"Now. What can we do for you?" he asked pleasantly. It was still difficult to keep an eye on his young guest—baffling, that, as Roderick could detect no magic, though the force acting upon him certainly wasn't physical. Still, whatever power the young man had of avoiding the eye, it would do him little good in a small locked room.

"You can let me go. I've done nothing wrong," the lad—little more than a boy, really, even by human standards—said sullenly.

"*Au contraire.* You were on the verge of annoying one of our guests, and you just tried to kill me, as well you know. Best make a clean breast of things, lad. If you're in trouble, we can help you."

"Help us? We've had more than enough of your kind of help!

I— I have nothing to say." The lad backed away, putting the table in the center of the room between them. His expression was hard to read through the mirrorshades, but he sounded terrified.

As well he might, did he have dealings with the Dark Court, Roderick thought philosophically. Still, that didn't mean he had to bring his vendetta here.

"Nothing to say? Let me help you," Roderick said. He cast a simple glamourie, one that would make the young man see him as a trusted friend.

Nothing happened.

Roderick frowned, moving toward the boy, who recoiled. "I'll call the police!"

"From here? A good trick, that. I rather think you ought to tell me who you are, first—and if you canna do that, then you'll have to show me."

He cornered the boy quickly, and plucked the glasses from his face. As Roderick touched them, he felt a tingle of not-quite-magic, from the glasses and the suit as well. It was they which held the interference to his spells, not the lad. *Possibly not a private vendetta, then.*

Ruthlessly—and with little cooperation—he searched the boy, removing all loose objects from his person. No other weapons, and not much in the way of the gadgetry and paperwork humans carried with them everywhere they went. He tossed the items to the table and looked through the wallet.

"Well, now, Travis Booker, what business is it that you have with the Sidhe?"

"The what?" Travis clung to one hope only—that the months of hypnotic conditioning he'd undergone would protect him from the Spookie's alien psionics. Without his special glasses, the Spookie looked like anyone else—a big blond bodybuilder type, well over six feet—but Travis knew better. It was one of *them*—the enemy—and now Travis was a prisoner in an undeclared war. He owed it to humanity to reveal as little as possible about who and what he was. Only the PS detector he was wearing could possibly implicate the

PDI, and its components would fuse if it were taken from him; it was designed to self-destruct within a few minutes if its ambient temperature dropped below 98.6. He pulled it off and tossed it to the table. "There. You've got everything. Now can I go? I'll leave—I won't make any trouble for you."

"You've already made a certain amount of trouble, young Travis. Why not spare us both the rest? You already seem to know a bit more about us than would ease my mind, but we've always been on good terms with your folk. What business do you have with that lady? I warn you, she's no one to be trifled with, but if she's done you harm, perhaps we can mend it."

"Is she your queen?" Travis asked, probing for information even though it did not look as if he'd ever be able to use it. They had so little hard information about the Spookies that any crumb was valuable. *He asked what business I had with the* Shi—*is that a personal name, or a tribal designation? Oh, Lord, if I could only sit him down and ask him some questions.* But Travis—and the other field agents—had seen the morgue photos of people who'd tried that, their bodies burned almost beyond recognition by a combination of hard radiation and corrosive poison. By nature and inclination, Spookies were merciless predators, using their mental power to trick and destroy their prey.

But weirdly, his question only made the Spookie laugh. "*My* queen? Not bloody likely, young Travis. Nay, she's nowt but trouble for your kind and mine, if she takes it into her head to make it. But she's here peacefully, and so should you be."

"I . . . all right. I won't make any trouble." Could escape be this easy? The briefing book said that Spookies didn't think like humans. Maybe a promise—even if one he had no intention of keeping— would be enough to get him out of here.

"Now how am I to believe you, when a moment ago you were so hot at hand?" the Spookie protested, smiling his inhuman smile. "Perhaps if you were to tell me all about yourself, we could come to some accommodation."

The Spookie looked into his eyes, and Travis found himself unable to look away. He felt a pressure in his head, as if the air had grown suddenly dense, holding his skull in a soft yet merciless grip. But the conditioning held, and he said nothing.

The Spookie sighed, pretending disappointment. "Ah, Travis, you're being less than forthcoming with me, aren't you, coming here as you have with armor and weapons? Still, we can settle this peaceably, can we not?"

"Kill me, you mean?" the young cockerel blustered, still full of fight.

Roderick sighed inwardly. Too much television, that's what it was. Everybody thought that violence settled things, as if it didn't just put off the trouble to a future time. And the lad seemed to be able to resist all Roderick's encouragements to confide in him—worrisome, but a certain percentage of humans were naturally resistant to mind-magic, and Travis might be one of that happy few.

Ah, weel, there's more ways to skin a cat than by buttering it with parsnips.

If the lad couldn't be induced to tell why he was here, surely making him forget all he'd seen would serve nearly as good a purpose? Let him hunt elsewhere—in vain—for his vengeance.

"Kill you?" Roderick asked. "Nay, you'll live out your years in quiet content. But you'll trouble us no more, Travis Booker."

It had taken a great deal of Power to set the spell, to wipe the lad's mind clean of the day's events and cast him into slumber, but in the end, Master Roderick was well satisfied with his work. When Travis lay asleep on the floor, he examined the items on the table, but found nothing odd about them, and tucked them back into Travis's pockets. As for the suit itself, perhaps he'd been mistaken, for the heavy cloth held no trace of magic or spellcraft that Roderick could sense—and in any event, he could hardly take it and leave young Travis to foot it home in socks and smallclothes, now, could he? But the strange glasses—and the lethal little weapon—would remain here. Roderick would show them to Prince Gelert, and see if his lord could make any more of them than he had. But young Travis would trouble them no more.

And the puir laddie had broken his wristwatch, as well, for it lay cold and dark and unresponsive in Roderick's hand. He shrugged, and buckled it back onto Travis's wrist. Now to put him in a cab, the slumber spell timed to lift as Travis reached the hotel whose key had been among his things. With any luck at all, he'd just think he'd fallen asleep on the way to his destination, and with a little time, the boy's own mind would create a plausible tale to fill in the missing hours.

Another crisis solved. But I do wish I knew what had set him on.

THIRTEEN:
YESTERDAY UPON
THE STAIR

The Las Vegas Convention Center was the largest single-level convention facility in the United States, containing 1.9 million square feet in its 102 meeting rooms and 12 exhibit halls—so the literature in the package she and Kory had received at check-in said—and after a morning spent trying to find the displays of the people she'd talked to last night, Beth Kentraine was inclined to believe it. This was the first day of Comdex, and the place was crammed with convention-goers.

It wasn't that she'd never been to a trade show before. When she'd still had a mundane job in television (though that time now seemed as if it belonged to someone else's life), Beth had attended ShoWest and a number of other conventions, some of them even held in this very place. But Comdex outstripped them all—there were hundreds of vendors, offering everything to do with computers that was even imaginable, including products that wouldn't reach the wider market for years, if ever. In just the short walk from the main entrance, Beth had seen wraparound computer monitors as wide as a Cinerama screen, 19-inch screens that you could hang on the wall like a picture, laptops that would fit in your purse but whose monitor and keyboard unfolded to the size of a desktop system. She'd seen servers the size of shoeboxes, computers so small the CPU was built into the keyboard, solar-powered computers, and computers on which you could surf the net from the heart of the Amazon jungle, no phone lines, electricity, or cables required.

It was dizzying.

Their first stop was Haram Technologies. Haram's business was shielding and buffering equipment, and they were picking up the Faraday Cage here. It had been Azrael who'd suggested they just order the stuff and pick it up at Comdex. For one thing, everyone they would want to deal with would be here. For another, if the components were shipped to Comdex as part of the trade show paraphernalia and then sold off the floor, there'd be no detailed paper trail leading back to who bought them. And that, Beth considered, was a very useful thing.

The sales rep at Haram had the slightly-unbelievable name of Mike Fright. He and Beth quickly checked over the component list for the cage (the directions said it was easily assembled; Beth personally doubted that), and Beth paid with a certified check drawn on the Elfhame Misthold account. The equipment would be shipped to the Tir-na-Og at the end of the show—just as well, as it came in a crate weighing several hundred pounds.

Their next stop was a small Seattle-based company called Orion Power and Light, where they took delivery of solar charging arrays and LION battery packs to run both the Faraday Cage and the computer system that would be set up inside it. The two booths were a serious distance apart, and Beth and Kory still had several more stops to make—computer, monitor, printer, software—before they'd have taken care of their shopping list. They could carry some of the smaller items with them, but the cage and the batteries were too heavy.

It was while they were looking for Hesperus Microsystems that Beth realized that the same guy had been behind them, just a few feet away, every time she'd looked for the last forty minutes. Even in a trade show full of eccentrics he was easy to spot—how many people wore business suits in that shade of green? He looked as if he'd mugged a sofa to get it.

"Kory," she said, stopping to nudge him. "See that man? Over there? The one in the green suit? Don't let him see you looking. I think he's following us."

Kory glanced carefully behind him, but saw nothing. Men in suits aplenty, of course, but none of them in any of the colors humans might call green. He glanced at Beth, worried.

"I see nothing," he said.

"Well, I know he's following us," she muttered crossly.

She looked worried, and Kory was worried as well. He'd had no idea this Comdex would be so *big*—and Beth hated crowds. No wonder she looked so drawn and fretful. He thought of suggesting that she go back to the hotel and leave him to complete their shopping, but he knew that Beth did not entirely trust him to be on his own in the World Above—and to be fair, Kory did not entirely trust himself either. Much as he loved the human world, it was an extraordinarily vast and complicated place, and the penalties for being revealed to be other than what one seemed were great.

But at the same time, he wasn't sure there was any present danger to concern himself with. It was true that there were still warrants out for Beth's arrest, but as Kory understood it, the hunters were not actively looking for her, and unless she ran afoul of one of their security databases, or returned to the San Francisco Bay Area, she should be safe from their hunt. The last time they had been captured, it had left Beth with a legacy of panic attacks, and it was possible that one had been triggered by the crowds surrounding them now. The press of people here even made Kory edgy—in comparison to human lands, Underhill was sparsely populated, and a quarter of a million of anything gathered together in one place was a sight one of the Seleighe Sidhe might expect never to see even in the course of his long life. In the World Above, of course, such gatherings were commonplace, but that didn't make Kory any more used to them.

"Do you see him now?" Beth demanded. "Look!"

Once more Kory looked where she pointed, and once more saw nothing.

"I see the booth where we are to pick up the computer," he offered, pointing in his turn.

"Good. The sooner we get this over with the better. I just wish he weren't following us. Whoever he is."

Kory looked again, hoping to see what she saw, and still saw nothing.

It could be worse. They could be wearing black. Sean Collins had heard all the MIB jokes he cared to since joining the PDI's field teams. At least the conspiracy nuts weren't looking for guys in green. Not yet, anyway.

The whole unit had been on alert since the incident with Booker yesterday. According to the tracking software, Travis'd left the airport, gone to one of the casinos on the Strip, and then gone back to his hotel. Unfortunately Booker couldn't explain why he'd done any of those things, because Booker didn't remember doing any of them. He didn't remember anything at all that had happened yesterday, or where he'd left his weapon and his optics. He had no idea why his PS detector had melted down. In short, Booker'd had a Close Encounter, and now they were all on alert. Sean had flown in from Washington last night, about the time the local shop reeled Booker in and found out what had happened. Now he and his team were looking for an answer the size of a needle in a countywide haystack, with precious little notion of where to start.

The others were checking out the casinos, but Sean had decided to cover the trade show almost on a whim—if Spookies were hitting Vegas now, it stood to reason that it might be linked with the other big event hitting town. He was wearing his PS detector, but not consulting it. The special optics would tag a Spookie just as fast— their special filtering technology cut through Spookie illusions as if they weren't there.

To his surprise, he hit paydirt almost immediately. A tall blond man with a redheaded woman, both dressed Corporate Casual. She was human, he wasn't. Sean wondered if she knew the truth about her companion. Best to bring them both in, just in case, but priority one, as always, was a live Spookie capture.

He phoned to bring the rest of his team in—the fact that they were in the neighborhood at all was the one lucky break they had from whatever had happened to Booker—and waited for them to get here. Meanwhile, he stuck close.

Beth was furious. Kory's air of gentle bewilderment was all too obvious: he *didn't* see the guy in the green suit with the green-tinted mirrorshades. He thought she was having visions, or some damn thing—but she wasn't, and she didn't dare point the guy out openly for fear of letting him know she knew he was there.

But *why* was he following them? There was no way for the government to know she and Kory were here, for one thing, even if they did know what ID they were traveling under. Sure, you had to show ID every time you boarded a plane, these days, but they'd used a Gate to get here.

And for another, he didn't really look like a Fed.

Maybe he thinks we're somebody else. The thought made her smile humorlessly. No matter who he thought they were, the moment he arrested them and ran their prints through VICAP, her outstanding warrants would show up—and she wasn't sure *what* Kory's fingerprints would look like. Elven glamouries and spells couldn't do a lot to fool machines, only the people who ran them.

But the green man wasn't going to arrest them. Not if Beth had anything to say to the matter. *:Bredana? Can you hear me?:*

There was a long wait—seconds—before she felt the elvensteed's faint reply. Bredana and Mach Five were at Elfhame Misthold, but they were stabled in the World Above precisely in case Beth or Kory needed to Call them. *:Come here—quietly—and bring Mach Five with you. I think we may need a quick exit.:*

She felt the faint tickle of the elvensteed's assent. San Francisco was at least eight hours away by car, and while the 'steeds could duck back Underhill to make their way here swiftly, she couldn't count on them to be here much inside of half an hour—twenty minutes if they really pushed things. She knew Kory would think she was just being paranoid to summon them—or, worse, that she was seeing little (or big) green men who weren't there. To be honest, she'd spent enough time jumping at shadows before they'd gone Underhill to live to give him good reason. But this time it was different.

He is there. I do see him.

Why can't Kory?

They reached the Hesperus Microsystems booth, and Beth pulled Kory past it. No sense in giving the Man In Green their whole itinerary. It was bad enough that their watchers would be able to find out everything they'd already bought—and while the information couldn't help them, nor could they trace the equipment once it had been taken Underhill—Beth resented giving up any information to her persecutors.

She stopped a few booths down from Hesperus, in front of a booth that seemed to be selling very large concave mirrors. She could see herself and Kory in them, weirdly distorted.

And she could see the green guy.

"Look," she said, in a teeth-gritted voice. "There. Look in the mirror. See him? Behind the booth with the yellow banner."

"I see him," Kory said.

Relief washed through her. *Oh, thank the Mother! I wasn't completely sure I wasn't losing my mind.* "He's the one that's been following us since we got here."

Kory turned slightly, pretending an interest in the booths on the opposite side of the aisle, and looked behind him. His hand closed over Beth's, and she could feel his shock.

"I don't see him."

He glanced back at the mirror. "Only here. In the mirror. Not there."

"What? That's not possible." Elves were immune to most broad-spectrum glamouries. If Beth could see him, there was no reason Kory shouldn't.

"It is true," Kory said. "I see him in the mirror. But when I look directly at him, he isn't there."

"Let's get out of here," Beth said in a low voice. "I called our rides, but I don't know when they'll get here."

"And they cannot enter the convention center in any case," Kory said practically. He began moving toward the exit, pulling Beth with him. "We must get back to the hotel. Prince Gelert will know what must be done."

"What about our stuff?" Beth asked in spite of herself. They couldn't just abandon it, not when it was their passkey into Chinthliss' library.

"We'll get it somehow. I was a fool to bring you here and expose you to such danger," Kory said bitterly.

"Hey—my choice," Beth said reassuringly. "I just wish I knew what the hell's going on."

Something had spooked the Spookie. Sean grinned mirthlessly at his own joke. He wasn't sure what—the stealthtech woven into his suit should keep the thing from reading his brainwaves, much less seeing him unless he directly approached it, but there was no point in trying to argue with the facts. The Spookie and the redhead had stopped wandering and were heading purposefully for the nearest exit.

"Caboose. All units, move up. On me," he said into his throat mike.

"There's another one," Beth exclaimed, alarmed. Same suit, same glasses. Proof, if she'd needed or wanted it, that something big and dangerous was after them both. Or . . . just after Kory? If he'd been here alone, he couldn't even have seen them until it was too late.

Someone hunting elves with magic they can't sense? Well, that makes my day complete.

"Where?" Kory demanded, his voice filled with exasperation and fear. Beth's heart sank. If Kory couldn't see them, how could they get away?

"Two o'clock. Moving toward the exit. Hold on to me, and don't let go."

"Always," Kory answered grimly.

They turned away from the exit, trying to keep the crowds

between them and the men in green. But Beth spotted a third one, and realized there was no point any longer in pretending not to look. *Please, oh, please, let them be trying to get us somewhere quiet before they try something.* She pulled Kory to a stop.

"This would be a good time to tell Bre and Mach to hurry," She said tightly. Three that she could see—and how many she couldn't spot?

"They say they're coming." Kory was better at communicating long-distance with the 'steeds than she was. "But can we get to them?"

"Bring 'em in here if we can't get out. Ten to one everybody'll think it's another floor show." She turned back toward the center of the hall, where the crowds were thicker. As she did, she caught the eye of the green-suited thug she'd first spotted. As she did he smiled and nodded, cocking thumb and forefinger in a make-believe gun and pointing it at her. *Gotcha,* he said silently.

"Oh, Sweet Mother," Beth groaned, looking sharply away. She felt panic well up inside her. They were after her—after them—and didn't care if they knew it. The exhibition hall reeled around her, and everything was suddenly too bright and too loud. She couldn't *breathe.*

No! Not here—not now—no matter how good a reason she had, she couldn't lose it and leave Kory helpless. She took a deep breath, half choking, fighting back the panic.

"I will not let them take you," Kory said. Comfort and calm flowed into her from their clasped hands.

"Funny," Beth said in a strangled voice, "but I don't think it's me they're after. If it was, how come I can see them but you can't?"

"Then leave me," Kory said promptly. "Get away while you still can."

He tried to pull away, but Beth wouldn't let him. "No! They've seen us together. They'll want me, too, now. And if you think I'm throwing you to the wolves, Mister, think again. If we can just get back to the hotel, we'll be safe. Gerry can glitter them to death."

"Good idea," Kory said, smiling tightly.

Trying to make headway through the crowds was like swimming

upstream through day-old Jell-O. Several exits loomed temptingly near, but if Beth was right in her guesses, to leave the main floor for any of the stairwells or walkways would play right into the hunters' hands. They had to stay in plain sight until the 'steeds were near, and *then* run like hell.

She'd never felt so exhausted. Tension, and the cat-and-mouse game they were playing, sapped her strength and will. The exhibit hall was a blur of sound and color around her, every display a place the enemy could hide. Kory had little strength to loan her—he needed to save his own in case they had to fight their way out. As the long minutes passed, she tried to keep herself from looking at her watch—Bredana and Mach Five would get here when they got here, and not a moment before. She concentrated on watching for telltale flashes of green clothing among the eclectically-costumed press of attendees—dressed in everything from three piece suits straight off Savile Row to Hawaiian shirts and Birkenstocks—that filled the convention space. She wasn't sure now whether there were dozens of them or she was seeing the same few over and over.

"They're here," Kory said, and a moment later Beth, too, could feel the elvensteeds' worried presence.

"Okay," she said. "Time to make a break." She was glad her voice sounded steady, because she felt about ready to burst into tears. At last they began slowly working their way toward the exit.

"Two more Spookies," Cat said over the radio link. "Outside on Paradise Road near the Visitor Information Center. You won't believe this one, Chief. They're horses that look like motorcycles."

"Nothing surprises me about Spookies," Sean answered, into his throat mike. "Okay, kids. Looks like our boy is trying to make a break for it. Move up. Cat, stay away from whatever those things are. We don't know what they can do."

"Gotcha, Chief. I've called up the Fantasticar, just in case."

"Good girl." No matter where the Spookies ran, the Special Ground Vehicle could catch them. It was packed with gadgets that made everything here look like a set of Legos, and its built-in AI was smarter than most of the field team. If only they had more than the one prototype, they could wrap up the Spookie threat over the weekend and all go for a nice six-week vacation in Aruba.

We do what we can with what we've got, Sean told himself philosophically. As Wheatley always said, there were better days ahead, providing you got through today alive.

"Let's catch ourselves a Spookie."

The exhibit halls were arranged on both sides of the Grand Concourse, which had a second floor that led to skywalks that connected both with the Hilton and one of the parking lots. Beth had been tempted to try for the hotel earlier, but had been afraid of what would happen once they left the safety of the convention crowds. With the elvensteeds waiting just outside, however . . .

She and Kory hurried out into the concourse and turned west. They'd have to go up a flight of stairs to get to the walkway. That would be the danger point—when they were away from the protection of the crowds, easy prey.

Hand in hand, the two of them hurried past a number of closed doors—meeting rooms, with programs going on inside—drawing curious glances from passersby still wandering the halls. She didn't see any of their pursuers, and for one sweet moment, Beth thought they were home free.

Then the original man she'd seen—their leader, Beth was morally certain—stepped out of the stairwell and walked toward them, hands open, smiling.

Beth glanced toward Kory. He was looking in the other direction, back the way they'd come. She squeezed his hand frantically. He looked where she was looking, and she saw sudden awareness in his eyes, as if he could at last see what she was seeing.

"Hi," the stranger said. "I wonder if you could—"

The air crackled as Kory let go of Beth's hand and flung a spell-bolt that would knock the stranger senseless and clear their way. It splashed against his shirtfront, going from invisible to visible, from violet to pale yellow.

And nothing happened.

"Not very friendly," the stranger said, reaching into his jacket. Beth could see now that he was wearing one of those Secret Service earplugs. "Zeppelin. All units converge." His hand came out of his jacket holding a small pistol-shaped object. "Stay where you are, both of you."

Kory stepped back, dropping the glamour that made him appear human and calling up his elven armor as well. There was a hissing sound as his sword cleared its scabbard.

Though the stranger apparently knew a great deal about elves, this move—and Kory's appearance—seemed to take him by surprise. Beth could not see his eyes behind the green sunglasses, but the rest of him was eloquent of disbelief. Kory swung the flat of his sword at the hand that held the pistol, but even in the face of a Sidhe warrior in full field plate, the stranger's reflexes remained good. He jerked his hand up and fired.

Beth expected a loud explosion, but the strange gun only made a short hiss, like a sneeze. Louder than the sound of its firing was the plinking sound made as its projectile struck Kory in the chest. Kory uttered a startled cry. There was a short, dull-gray dart sunk into the armor's elvensilver breastplate. The armor smoked and melted around it like dry ice around a red-hot coal, and magic flared and sparked unevenly.

"I can put the next one through your eye, if you move another inch. It's Cold Iron. I imagine it will hurt."

Kory froze, sword half-raised.

Beth flung herself at the stranger, terrified into bravery.

His gun went off. She felt a burning, cramping pain high on her left shoulder as the dart sank in, but she was no creature of magic to burn at the touch of iron. She scrabbled for the gun, trying to get her hands on it.

There was a sound of glass breaking in the stairwell, as thick, crack-resistant, shatterproof glass gave way beneath the assault of elvensteed hooves. Kory jerked her away from the stranger—Beth yelped in pain as his hands closed over her injured shoulder—and pointed his sword at the stranger's chest. The man froze, hands spread wide.

"I do not know what quarrel you think you have with us, but I will tell you plainly: leave us alone!" Kory said.

Beth ran past him, to the door to the walkway, and jerked it open. The elvensteeds—in equine form—floundered up the last of the stairs, clumsy in such close quarters, and trotted into the hall. Bredana nuzzled Beth anxiously, smelling the blood on her, and Beth pushed the 'steed's head away before she could be burned by the iron. She reached up and grasped the end of the dart, pulling it free. It looked like a golf pencil, or a child's crayon: harmless, not powerful enough to penetrate more than an inch or so.

But deadly to elves.

Her left arm felt numb and tingly, too weak to be of much use in mounting. Bredana shivered all over, and suddenly in place of the gleaming white mare stood an equally-gleaming motorcycle. Gratefully, Beth threw her leg across the seat and settled aboard.

Kory backed away from his downed foe and vaulted aboard his own 'steed, still in armor. Once in the saddle, he reached up to pluck the dart free of his armor and fling it away; the armor of his gauntlet sizzled and popped but protected his hand long enough to keep him from burning. Then he turned and sent Mach Five back down the steps, Beth and Bredana close behind.

For a moment, it looked like they might make their escape. There was no sign of pursuit when they hit the street, and even the sight of a knight on horseback didn't draw more than a few glances—this was Las Vegas, after all, and the Excalibur Hotel was just up the Strip. They headed for the Tir-na-Og at a gallop, planning to cut around back and go in through the service entrance, where they'd attract less attention. Once inside the casino's spellshields, they should be able to go to ground and figure out just what it was that had been chasing them.

In the parking lot, Kory morphed from armored Sidhe knight to Mundane in khakis and blazer, and Mach Five transformed from fiery charger to high-ticket bike as they accelerated toward the main road. No one was looking when he changed, and if they were, it wouldn't really matter. The two of them were already in enough trouble without worrying over whether or not they became an X-File.

But as they reached the Strip, a shadow appeared between them and the sun. Beth looked up, over her shoulder.

A large black limousine without any wheels was hovering over them, ready to follow them anywhere they went. As she watched, it shimmered and vanished, leaving behind nothing but a disturbance in the air like a heat mirage. It still cast a shadow, but that was a lot less noticeable than a flying bathtub cruising the noontide Strip.

Beth felt her mind slowly and carefully boggle, a sensation not unlike having a lounge chair languidly collapse under you. She could believe in elven knights, dragons, winged fairies, unicorns, and magic castles without a single blink. But this flying car thing chasing them was straight out of *Star Wars*. It didn't seem possible—let alone real—and it might be able to do anything.

We can't go back to the casino, she realized with a sinking feeling. *We'd just be leading them right into the middle of Glitterhame Neversleeps—and these guys probably aren't all that picky about which elves they kidnap.*

Glancing to her side, she saw that Kory had come to the same conclusion. He pointed south—down the Strip, out of town. Beth nodded, glad that her dark turtleneck and blazer concealed the amount she was bleeding. He knew she was hurt, but the last thing she needed was for Kory to be worrying about her when he ought to be worrying about himself. And it wasn't a bad injury. More of a puncture wound, painful and annoying and messy, as if someone had driven a tenpenny nail into the fleshy part of her shoulder.

The two elvensteeds accelerated down the road, weaving in and out of afternoon traffic with blithe disregard of local speed laws, but no matter how fast they went—and at the end of the first mile they were doing well over 100 mph—the flying car kept up with them (at least as far as Beth could judge from the coffin-shaped shadow that raced ahead along the ground). The two elvensteeds were invisible to ordinary traffic now—but no matter how they zigged and detoured, the vehicle paced them as though they were plainly visible. Beth very much wanted to talk to Kory, to ask him what he thought, but that would involve stopping, and the only thing that was keeping them even slightly safe at the moment was sheer speed.

We can't hide, and we can't run. What does that leave?

All they needed was a few seconds and a little privacy, and the elvensteeds could open a Portal that would take them back to the casino, but that assumed that the Men In Green couldn't follow *that* as well, and at the moment Beth thought that was too dangerous an assumption to make. The best thing to do—and undoubtedly Kory's plan—was to lose their pursuers entirely before doubling back.

If they could.

The airport flashed by in a blur of palm trees, and in a few seconds more they were on the open road. Even in November, the desert sun hammered down on blacktop and pale red rock, casting the harsh desert landscape into merciless relief.

And still the shadow over their heads paced them.

At the moment it began to seem that the contest would settle into one of sheer endurance, the hovercraft opened fire. Pale flashes of light wove a lattice in the air ahead of them, driving them off the road, herding them in a circle back the way they came—and undoubtedly into the arms of other pursuers. The elvensteeds exerted themselves to the utmost, reaching unimaginable speeds, but the hovercraft easily paced them, throwing up barriers of laser fire whenever the 'steeds tried to escape. That they wanted to capture, not kill, the two of them was clear—and frightening, especially since it seemed like only a matter of time until they got their wish. The elvensteeds were fast, and nimble, but doubly handicapped by having to care for their riders: sudden stops and changes of direction might fling Beth and Kory from their saddles, and Beth, injured as she was, couldn't hold on very well.

Suddenly Mach Five wheeled around and turned back the way he'd come. Beth waited a moment for Bredana to follow—and was filled with sudden stricken fury when she didn't. Everything she tried was useless; the elvensteed would not obey her.

"*Kory! Damn you!*"

Unable to make her mount heed her, Beth flung herself from Bredana's seat. The elvensteed, sensing her intention, had barely enough time to bring herself to a stop, but Beth still bit the dust hard, sending a lance of pain through her shoulder. She staggered to her feet, growling deep in her throat. Kory and Mach Five were only a faint speck upon the horizon, the invisible hovercar somewhere above them.

The elvensteed came up behind Beth timidly. Beth swung around and grabbed her by the handlebar with her good hand, shaking with rage. How *dare* Kory go off and sacrifice himself? How was she ever going to get him back once the MIGs had him? Didn't he understand that going off in this quixotic fashion didn't *help?*

"Find him," she told Bredana in a low dangerous voice. "Find him *now.*"

If he lived through this, he would certainly receive—and deserve—a severe scolding from Beth, Kory thought distractedly. A part of his mind was occupied with sorting the chaotic pictures Mach Five sent him of the terrain the elvensteed had covered on its run here; as much as possible, he wished to choose his ground for what he was about to try. Not for the first time, he wished he had more of his elders' skill in the Art, but Prince Korendil of the High Court of Elfhame Sun-Descending was only a Magus Minor; gifted with little more than the native skill in *geasa* and glamouries that were the birthright of all the Children of Danu. What he was minded to try now would tax the power of a great Adept, a Magus Major. But he could imagine no other solution to their problem. They must escape the flying car, and they could neither outrun it or hide from it. They dared not lead it back to the other elves, for he now realized that Beth had been right—the strange men in the green suits seemed to be hunting the Seleighe Sidhe, and doing it with tools that seemed near magical in effect, yet held nothing of the Art.

That any sufficiently advanced technology was indistinguishable from magic was a favorite saying of Beth's, and right now Kory hoped desperately that she was right, and that what they were facing was an advanced technology. Because if it wasn't, his plan wouldn't work. And if it didn't work, he and Beth would be prisoners within the hour.

He urged Mach Five to greater speed across the open desert, exulting inwardly when the flying car followed. Let them think he fled in blind panic, so long as they pursued him at the pace he set. And then he withdrew all his attention from his surroundings, to concentrate on the spell he must cast.

Node Groves held Gates, semipermanent Portals between Underhill and the World Above that anchored the elfhames both in time and in space, and most of the traffic between the worlds used such Gates. Elvensteeds could, by their very nature, open a Portal anywhere at very little cost to themselves, but only for themselves and their riders. The Sidhe could open Portals away from the vicinity of a Gate and pass anything through them, but to open such a Portal away from a Node and its anchoring Grove took both Art and Power—the more Cold Iron or inanimate mass involved, the more power it took.

Beth said modern computers contained very little metal because they were so advanced. Kory only hoped that an invisible car that flew was even more advanced than the computers he had seen today, or the backlash from his spell would guarantee he would not have to concern himself with Beth's scolding.

He closed his eyes and concentrated, making the shape of his intention clear in his mind. He drew on Mach Five's power as much as he dared, adding it to his own, though he well knew he could not take too much or his elvensteed would not be able to maintain the pace Kory had set. Desperation drove him—he would not think about the fact that his spells had been useless against the Man In Green before, he would not think about the fact that if he failed here he would be helpless, all his power spent. He concentrated, summoned up all his power, his will, his *need* . . .

And opened a Portal directly in the path of the onrushing aircar.

It hurtled through and vanished, the Portal closing behind it. Kory only had the strength to hold a Portal for seconds—he had needed to ensure that both he and his pursuer were going so fast that the aircar could neither stop nor turn aside. Mach Five staggered to a halt and stood, head hanging, sides heaving. Kory, drained and exhausted by that ultimate effort, slid from his 'steed's back to lie dazed and motionless beneath him in the desert sun.

Beth reached them a few moments later. She jumped from Bredana's saddle and staggered over to where Kory was groggily trying to sit up.

"What happened?" Beth demanded. "Where are those guys that were following you? Are you all right?"

"I don't know," Kory said, his voice blurry. "But I do not think they will be back for a while."

On the long—and considerably slower—return trip to Las Vegas, Kory explained what he had done. They were riding together on Bredana, leading the exhausted—but smug—Mach Five.

"Perhaps it was not the safest course to take, nor yet the wisest, for now they are somewhere in Underhill with their vehicle and their weapons, but it was the only one I could think of, Beth, and I did not want you near me when I tried. It was possible that the backlash would have . . . So I wanted you out of the way before I tried anything."

"If you *ever* scare me like that again, Kory, you'll wish they *had* gotten you," Beth promised feelingly. "But . . . how can we be sure you got all of them, or that they won't be back? Leaving aside the question of who they are in the first place."

"I can't," Kory said somberly. "But if they last saw us fleeing into the desert, that is where they will seek us—and our vanished pursuers—and we may gain the sanctuary of Glitterhame Neversleeps unmolested. I think it is time to lay this whole matter before Prince Gelert and cry his aid. It is a greater peril than I have wit to solve."

Upon their return to the Tir-na-Og Casino, Beth and Kory immediately sought out their host, glad to discover that there was stabling for Otherworldly steeds as well as more conventional parking beneath the casino.

Gerry Meredith was devastated to hear about the trouble they'd had at Comdex. "But lovely people, how hideous that something like this should have happened to you on your very first visit to our wonderful city! Certainly you must not stir a *step* from your rooms, and I assure you, we will all be *supernaturally* vigilant! Don't worry a hair on your pretty little heads about your shopping list—leave it entirely to me; I have oodles of entirely human employees just eating their heads off who would *jump* at the chance to go pick up some lovely computer equipment! We can have it brought here and transshipped to Misthold before you can say 'Owain Glyndower,' never fear. And no one at all will suspect the fair hand of the Fair Folk in the matter."

Their audience with Prince Gelert later that day was less encouraging.

"Green men upon whom the magic cannot take hold, say you? This makes for ill hearing. One such came here yester'een—but he was following an Unseleighe lady, and we thought he had some private quarrel with the Dark Court. We are not so great a secret among mortalkind as some among us might hope—many mortals know of our existence, and not all of them have had good of our kind."

"I don't think this is a private quarrel, Prince Gelert," Beth said carefully. "It seems more organized than that. What happened to the young man who came here?"

Looking around the Prince's rooms, Beth was pretty sure whose taste was reflected in the decor of her own suite and the rest of the casino—but here there was no need to even pretend that the suite's trappings were such items as might be found in the normal everyday human world, and the whole effect was like the inside of a jackdaw's jewelry box.

"Ah, my Rhydderich set a glamourie on him, casting from his mind all that had befallen him that day, and sent him back to his own place. At the time we thought no more of it."

Prince Gelert frowned, pondering the matter. The Seleighe lord was what Beth would have to call "thoroughly acculturated"; even here in his private penthouse suite, while discharging his princely duties, he wore Earthly garb—though the double-breasted suit in pale mauve silk (with matching tie) was a bit on the flamboyant side. Only his speech patterns betrayed any hint of his true age; fascinated as they were by novelty, the Sidhe were as prone as anyone else to gravitate naturally to the styles and fashions learned when they first became adults. And if your adulthood lasted several centuries, a certain amount of cultural jet lag was bound to set in. . . .

"Have we enemies, my Rhydderich? And of ourselves, or of the hame, or of the Sidhe in general?" Gelert asked.

The casino's security chief—and head of Gelert's personal guard—bowed his head. "I know not, my Prince—and the fault is mine for letting my prisoner go so lightly!"

"You acted under my orders," Gelert said kindly, excusing the fault. "We wish no trouble with mortalkind, no matter how they come to discover our true nature, and you had little reason to think he was not alone. You acted wisely—I do confess, I would like to know more of these enemies before I do face them."

"Maybe you could see if any of the other hames have been attacked," Beth suggested cautiously. "Or see if anyone looking suspicious and wearing green has been hanging around them."

Or if a lot of elves are all of a sudden going missing, she thought and did not say. What did they *want* with Kory and the other elves, anyway? She wished she knew—but not at the price of ever seeing those green-clad whackos again.

Gelert sighed heavily. "We must warn our Underhill guests of what it is that may stalk them while here in our city, and I fear that too many of them will regard it as a chance for great sport. Meanwhile, I shall send word to my brother princes of all that has befallen us here, and I am sure your lord will have his own questions for you when you return home, Prince Korendil. Be easy in your mind that we shall do all that we may to see that your mission here is accomplished as you would have it, and that your visit here is troubled no further."

He looked sorrowful and proud, a combination that clashed oddly with his dress and his surroundings, but after so much time among the Sidhe, Beth barely noticed the incongruity. Now that they had warned the Prince about the trouble in his own backyard, she was anxious to finish their business here and return to the safety of Underhill. Not even the prospect of delivering the computer system to Chinthliss and achieving the solution to her quest could comfort her at the thought of what had nearly happened today. Though the chase had come to naught, the terror had awakened old ghosts, and Beth dreaded the thought of sleeping tonight.

Three days later, Beth and Kory stood once more before the gates to Chinthliss' palace.

After a long night of unbroken nightmares, Kory had demanded that Beth return to Elfhame Misthold without him. He had followed the next day, driving a wagon drawn by two affronted elvensteeds that was piled high with the booty from Comdex. Computer, printer, monitor, software, batteries—and the Faraday Cage that would make it all run in Chinthliss' Underhill domain.

The Gate opened as they approached, and once more they found themselves within the dragon lord's great hall. Chinthliss was there to greet them himself, regarding the cart's contents with ill-concealed eagerness.

"We have brought all that you asked," Kory said, bowing.

"Excellent," Chinthliss purred, rubbing his hands together in glee.

"If you've got a room with an, um, skylight," Beth said, "that would be the best place for it. It's set up to run off batteries and solar cells, and it has a wireless connection for your Internet link." *Though where you're going to dial in to, and how, I'm not sure I want to know.*

Chinthliss snapped his fingers, and servants appeared to unload the cart and carry away the boxes. Unlike the flowerlike geisha Beth had seen on her last visit, these servants were burly, bald, and half-naked—picture-perfect dacoits from the pages of an old penny dreadful.

"All is in readiness. Perhaps you would like to see it assembled? I have asked my son to see to that trivial and insignificant detail."

Son? Beth wondered, as she and Kory followed the dragon.

The room Chinthliss had chosen for the computer looked as if it had started life as a Victorian greenhouse. The walls and ceiling were made up of hundreds of panes of leaded glass, and jasmine trees in colorful porcelain pots ringed the walls. A large mahogany table stood in the center of the room, awaiting the computer.

By the time Beth and Kory reached it, the servants had already gotten most of the equipment unpacked. A young man in jeans and a T-shirt stood surveying the mess; Beth was surprised to recognize the black-haired race-car driver from the photo in Chinthliss' study.

"My son, Tannim. Tannim, this is Prince Korendil and the lady Beth Kentraine. They have come to use my library."

"And paid handsomely for the privilege," the young man said, grinning. "Hi. I'm Tannim, from Fairgrove." He held out his hand. Fox had said Tannim was a friend of Chinthliss', but the dragon called the young man his son. *Which is true?* Beth wondered. *Both?*

"Hi," Beth said, taking his hand. His grip was strong and warm, the palm slightly rough in the way of those who work with their hands. "I'm Beth, and this is Kory. I sure hope you know more about this stuff than we do." *And if you're from Elfhame Fairgrove, I guess we'd better warn you about little green men with nail guns before you go.*

Tannim grinned engagingly. "Not really—but I read directions really well. Hey . . . what's this?"

Beth explained about the Faraday Cage, and to her relief, she didn't have to explain much.

"We use them sometimes at Fairgrove, too. Pretty cool."

With so many helping hands, the work went quickly. The Faraday Cage was unpacked and assembled—despite Tannim's protests of mechanical helplessness, he certainly seemed to know what to do with a toolbox—and soon the gleaming copper mesh, a cube twelve feet square and eight feet high—filled the room. Tannim and Kory unrolled rubber floor mats and covered them with an Oriental carpet before the servants moved the mahogany table back inside. It had to weigh as much as a small car, but Chinthliss' impassive servants handled it as if it weighed nothing at all.

Soon the computer itself was spread out upon the table, an Omnium processor—only one generation up from the Pentium, not two, but Intel had looked at its choices of names—Sexium, Septium,

Octium, Nonium—and wisely opted to skip them all—with a 27-inch flat screen, full-color laser printer, and wireless Internet connection. Cables ran to the solar array lying on the floor beside the table, an LED flashing slowly as it began to charge.

"I guess we better switch the cage on before we turn on the computer," Tannim said, "or there isn't going to have been much point to this, right?"

Just then Chinthliss' butler arrived, to announce that luncheon was served. He fixed his master with a militant gaze, as if daring him to mistreat his guests. Chinthliss nodded reluctantly, although Beth could see that he was as excited as a kid on Christmas morning, and just as eager to play with his new toys.

Over lunch, Kory told the others the tale of their flight and narrow escape from their pursuers in Las Vegas.

"And you mean that those guys are somewhere Underhill? Wild," Tannim said. He didn't sound particularly worried. "Hope they've got more with them than those dart guns. Not everything down here is allergic to iron."

"What is of greater concern to me—as it will be to Keighvin Silverhair—is the motive for their attack, as well as their methods," Chinthliss said. "You say they used no magic?"

"None that I could sense," Kory admitted. "Yet their artifice was such that they were invisible to me, though Beth could see them. And I do not understand how their vehicle could operate at all."

"Beats me," Tannim said, interested. "Fairgrove is pretty up-to-date when it comes to automotive technology, and offhand I can't think of anything that could do what you've described. Flying fast—and silently—and with some kind of cloaking device—there isn't anything out there, or in development, that could do that."

"Unless it did not come from your world at all," Chinthliss supplied helpfully. "Underhill is vast, and there are realms within it that rely as much upon technology as the Sidhe do upon magic. Yet why should they choose to trouble the elfhames upon Earth?"

"That's the sixty-four-thousand-dollar question," Beth agreed. "We've run into people before who wanted to treat Talents like lab rats, and there's all those psychic research programs the government runs, but . . . these people *knew* about elves. And were hunting them."

"It would be sad indeed were the ancient alliance between Sidhe and human to founder upon this rock of enmity," Chinthliss said. "I shall consider the matter, and see if any of my resources can provide an answer to this riddle. And now, let us return to our work."

By the time the four of them returned to the conservatory, the boxes had been tidied away and the solar panels were up and running. "Here goes nothing," Beth said, flipping the switch to power up the Faraday Cage.

She heard a faint whine that cycled quickly up past the edge of human hearing, and Kory winced. When the others moved to enter the enclosure, he stepped back.

"I believe I shall remain here."

Beth glanced at him curiously for a moment, then understanding dawned. If the cage worked as advertised, and sealed off everything inside from the currents of magic constantly wafting through Underhill, stepping inside would be like going into a soundproof room—or worse—for Kory. It was tempting to fall into the habit of thinking of the Sidhe as invulnerable, but the truth was, they had as many weaknesses as mortals did. They were just different ones.

Whatever the reason for Kory's distaste, it was plain that Chinthliss didn't share it. He led the other two into the cage and seated himself in the squamous leather chair behind the table. Beth felt a faint tingle—as if a storm were brewing—as she stepped inside, and smelled a faint tang of ozone, but nothing more.

"What do I do?" the dragon asked eagerly.

"Well, first you load the operating system," Beth said, leaning over his shoulder.

An hour later, the software they'd brought was installed and running, and there was a fat pile of manuals at Chinthliss' elbow. Even the internet was up and running, on a T1 line to a standard server with a cross-worlds energy link via tightbeam broadcast to Underhill through a Nexus. Chinthliss had not only gotten his e-mail up and running, he'd ordered several thousand dollars worth of CDs to be delivered to a P.O. box in Tulsa, Oklahoma.

Well, it's a good start. . . .

"It'll take you a while to get the hang of all these apps," Beth said, regarding the screensaver full of flying toasters that moved smoothly across. A bouncy march played over the computer's speaker suite in flawless high-fidelity concert hall sound. "But that's everything."

"Excellent. I am truly impressed," Chinthliss purred.

"And now, my lord?" Kory said from outside the cage. "We have fulfilled our side of the bargain."

Reluctantly Chinthliss shut down the computer, watching as the screen went inert and dark. Then he got to his feet and walked out of the Faraday Cage.

"Just as I promised you," he said, reaching into his suit jacket and placing a large gold key into Kory's hand. "Full access to my library and all that it contains. The information you seek is there. Tannim and I will be away on business for some days, but my house is yours. Charles will provide you with anything you desire."

"Charles" must be Chinthliss' formidably-correct butler. As if he had been summoned by the speaking of his name—and for all Beth knew, that was literally the case—the manservant appeared in the doorway.

"Prince Korendil, Lady Beth. May I show you to your rooms— or would you prefer to go directly to the library?"

"The library," Kory said decisively.

Beth turned to Chinthliss and Tannim. "Thanks so much for all your help."

"Hey, my pleasure," Tannim said. "I'll check out those guys you mentioned when I get back to Fairgrove. Haven't seen anybody like that hanging around, but you never know. There's some weird folks out there."

"That's the unvarnished truth," Beth agreed, and turned away to take Kory's hand. "See you around."

"Come down and visit," Tannim urged. He waved, and followed Chinthliss from the room.

"If you will be so good as to accompany me?" Charles said.

The entrance to the library was on a par with the rest of the palace's semi-Victorian sensibilities: a double set of coffered oak doors twelve feet high, surmounted by an elaborate plasterwork coat of arms. The golden doorknobs were in the shape of eagle claws grasping jade spheres, and there was a keyhole on the right-side panel just beneath the knob.

"If you require anything further, do not hesitate to ring," Charles said. He bowed stiffly and walked off, leaving the two of them standing before the library doors.

"Well," Beth said, suddenly nervous. "This is it."

"Yes," Kory said. "But somehow I fear ..." He shrugged, leaving the sentence unfinished, and inserted the key in the lock.

Both doors swung inward. Beth drew a deep breath, stifling a squeak.

The room was huge—four stories tall and as long as a football field. Books lined the walls, all the way to the ceiling. There were ornate gilded catwalks circling the room so that one could reach the higher volumes, and ladders on tracks were set on each level so that the top shelves could be reached. There were long tables running down the center of the room, and a number of comfy chairs that seemed to urge her to curl up in them with the nearest handy volume. The alabaster lamps that hung down from the ceiling bathed the entire room in a soft shadowless light. Beth took a few steps into the room, gazing around herself in wonder.

"There must be about a billion books here," she said in awe.

"Yes." Kory looked around, frowning. "A great number of books. But where is the catalogue?"

Beth wandered over to the nearest shelf and inspected the titles. A copy of *The Arabian Nights* stood next to a book on practical gardening for the weekend gardener. The book next to that had no title at all on its spine, and when she picked it up, she saw that the pages were covered in a strangely ornate script that she didn't recognize. She put it back. Next to it was a book in French—the title was something like *A Saraband for Lost Time,* but Beth wasn't confident enough of her French to be quite sure. Next to that was an Oz book, but not by Baum.

"They're not in order," she said, turning to Kory. "They're just . . . here."

"As the information we seek is here," Kory said gloomily. "Somewhere."

"But why would he do that to us?" Beth could think of nothing else to say.

Kory sighed. "I do not think he meant us harm. It may not have occurred to him that we could not find something here as easily as he could himself. Or perhaps it did—but this is what we asked for—access to his library. He has fulfilled the bargain we asked of him."

Beth walked over to the nearest chair and sat down numbly, staring at acre after acre of randomly shelved, uncatalogued, unindexed books. Even if they searched every volume—a task that could take years—they had no guarantee that they'd even recognize the information they wanted when they stumbled across it.

Dumb, Kentraine, dumb. You were so careful at the Goblin Market to ask for exactly what you wanted. Why couldn't you put your brain in gear when it really mattered?

"All is not lost, Beth," Kory said.

"Oh yeah?" she answered bitterly. "It sure looks like it from here."

FOURTEEN:
TOGETHER WE

❖❖

After the grief and exertion of the night before, Eric slept as if someone had hit him over the head with a blunt instrument. He awoke, still exhausted and disoriented, in the late afternoon, barely able to remember what day it was.

Tuesday. I think. And that means I missed class today, but somehow, I can't find it in my heart to care. Jimmie's unjust death was still too fresh, and everything surrounding it too unbelievable and tangled. Hosea a Guardian. Aerune back to make more trouble. And, unless he'd slept a *lot* harder than he thought, sometime last night the lot of them had infested Hosea's banjo with the soul of a thirtysomething underground chemist.

I need a shower. I need tea.

He staggered blearily out from behind the closed bedroom door, and was mildly surprised to see Hosea in the living room, his banjo across his knees. Hadn't Hosea . . . ? Oh. Memory smacked him on the brain once more, and Eric continued wordlessly on to the shower.

Ten minutes under a shower hot and cool by turns put what was left of Eric's brain into working order. He dressed and went into the kitchen to see about the tea.

As he was standing over the kettle waiting for it to boil—Eric was a firm believer in the adage that a watched pot needs the help—his mind registered the fact that Hosea was playing quietly. And more than that. There seemed to be a kind of whispering sound mixed in with the melody, like the sound of wind through leaves, but whenever he *tried* to hear it, it disappeared again. Curious enough to abandon his morning-transplanted-to-afternoon ritual, Eric went out into the living room. Hosea looked up as he entered.

"Afternoon, Eric. For a while there, I thought you were going to sleep the clock around."

"I still feel like I'm a few days short on sleep," Eric sighed, running a hand through his hair. He glanced at the banjo in curiosity.

"Oh, Jeanette and I was just getting caught up on a few things, and I was hearing all about that Dark Lord feller we run into last night. He sure is a piece of work."

"Yeah. Kind of 'Welcome to the Hollow Hills, now go home.' But you said you were *talking* to, um, Jeanette?"

"It's the darndest thing. When I'm playing, it's just like I was talking to her—only I'm thinking, and I guess she is, too."

"Can she hear me? I mean, right now?" Eric asked.

Once more Hosea ran his fingers over the strings, and again Eric caught the overlay of eldritch whispering. Hosea grinned.

"She says she's dead, not deaf. Seeing's not quite the same, but she can hear real fine."

"Um . . . great." Eric cudgeled his brains. "I guess we kind of need to know what Aerune's planning, and then figure out some way to stop him." *And good luck to that. I don't think the Guardians would stand much of a chance against a Magus Major, and Aerune's a lot more than that. It's not so much that the Unseleighe Sidhe are more powerful than the Bright Elves as it is that the Dark Court doesn't care what it has to do to gain its power and the Seleighe Sidhe do. Still . . .*

"Ayup. Miss Hernandez called while you was still sleeping and said she wanted to get together tonight and study on that with you and the rest of . . . us." Hosea looked a little discomfited at the renewed realization that he, too, was one of the Guardians, and quickly changed the subject. "And Kayla's been here for awhile. She took a look at that studio down there and went out to buy a couple of gallons of black paint."

Eric grinned faintly, thinking of Ria's reaction to Kayla redoing her Park Avenue pastels in basic black. It was nice to think that one thing in this mess had worked out for the best.

"Any word about the funeral?" Eric forced himself to ask.

"Day after tomorrow. I guess I'll have to go out and get myself a dark suit."

"Yeah. I'd like to help you out there, but I don't think the two of us wear the same size."

That got a grin from Hosea. "No, sir. I reckon we don't. Well, I expect I've been loafing long enough. Time to get back to work. I'm packing up Jimmie's things." Hosea laid the banjo aside.

"I'll help," Eric said, though it was about the last thing he wanted to say. Still, it was a brutal job, and Hosea shouldn't have to do it all by himself. And it was a last service Eric could perform for a fallen comrade.

"So we can't fight this Aerune, and we can't get the elves to fight him? That doesn't leave much," Toni said in disgust.

The four Guardians, Eric, and Kayla were gathered in Eric's apartment once more. For the last several hours the six of them—with advice from Jeanette via Hosea's banjo—had been trying to figure out what—if anything—they could do about the threat of Aerune mac Audelaine.

"It's not that we can't get the Sidhe to come in on our side," Eric explained patiently. "It's just that we can't get them to do it *fast*. By the time they're convinced Aerune is a real threat, and organize to stop him, a lot of damage will have been done."

"A good thing to prevent, if we can," Paul said. "And from what Jeanette has told Hosea, our Sidhe friend has learned some lessons from the last time you went up against him. He's got allies in *this* world working to sow distrust between human and Sidhe—a neat trick, since humans are largely ignorant of the Sidhe's existence and the Sidhe, from what you've said, are largely indifferent to the common run of humanity."

"That's about the size of it," Eric admitted. "And as usual, humans can manage to do a lot more damage in this world than any number of Sidhe. Aerune's more immediately dangerous, but it's his allies that worry me. Cut off Aerune's involvement with them, and that threat might disappear, though."

Eric spoke from experience. Aerune was undoubtedly giving the mysterious Parker Wheatley Jeanette had told them about the ammunition to put on a pretty good show for whoever was backing him in government circles. Remove that aid, and the whole conspiracy might collapse under its own weight.

"Well, isn't there some way you guys can just stop Aerune from coming around here? Nail his door shut, or something?" Kayla suggested.

"We can't exactly put a lord of the Sidhe under house arrest . . . even if we could get to him," Toni said dubiously. "Or can we?" She looked at Eric.

"I'm not completely sure on this," Eric said, "but I kind of think he could break through any barrier we set in place . . . and to keep him from being able to enter the World Above, we'd have to be able to seal *all* the Nexus points connecting Underhill with the World Above. And even if we could get all the Elfhames to agree to that, it'd have severe repercussions for humanity. From what Beth and I could see back when Elfhame Sun-Descending was in danger, humans and Sidhe are pretty closely intertwined. We're the ones with the creativity, but something about them feeds that creativity in us. Split us off from each other completely, and we'd lose something pretty important."

"Still . . . house arrest," Paul mused. "There has to be some way to trap Aerune Underhill and sever his connection with our Mr. Wheatley."

"Pop quiz," Kayla said. "How do you trap something bigger and stronger than you that can bust through any walls you put up?"

They sat and stared at each other in glum silence. Suddenly

there was a scraping at the window, and Greystone stepped through.

"Sure an' it's surprised at your lack of a classical education I am," he said in a broad stage brogue. "Hasn't a one of you ever heard of the Minotaur?" The gargoyle winked at Kayla, who grinned. She'd met him for the first time earlier today, and taken his arrival with a lot more sangfroid than Eric had exhibited.

"The Minotaur!" Paul exclaimed. "Of course! The solution has problems of its own, but—"

"Hey?" Kayla said, raising her hand. "For those of us playing along at home?"

Paul smiled at her. "There's an ancient Greek legend about a monster called the Minotaur, a beast with the body of a man and the head of a bull, enormously strong and powerful. It was said to be the son of King Minos of Crete, born to his queen, Pasiphae, as a punishment for disrespect to the gods. Unable to control it, Minos asked his court artificer, Daedalus, for a solution. Daedalus built the Labyrinth beneath Minos' palace, and installed the Minotaur at its center. The creature roamed the maze endlessly, unable to find a way out, and Crete was saved from its ravages."

"So we need to find this Daedalus and have him build us a maze?" Kayla said doubtfully. "And how do we get this Aerune guy into it?"

"But is this the best solution?" José asked. "Caged enemies can escape."

"It certainly seems like the most promising one we've come up with so far," Toni said. "And I don't like the idea of setting out to execute someone in cold blood. Assuming we *could*, which I wouldn't bet on, even if we got the drop on him. Eric?"

"It could work. And it would at least solve the Aerune part of the problem—better than killing him, which even if we could do it, might gain him some allies among the Sidhe, and end up starting that war after all. Decoying him into the cage would be easy—he's always looking for Talents to drain them, and we've got two Bards and a Healer to bait the trap with. But where do we find someone to build a maze that would keep him in?"

"You're the one who gets invited to parties Underhill," Hosea pointed out slowly. "Don't you know any wizards who owe you a favor?"

When all else fails, ask an expert. And hey, I can live without sleep.

It wasn't really much of a plan, not yet—more of an idea that needed more research, and as Eric was the one with the Underhill contacts, that part of the matter fell to Eric. Could a labyrinth be built that would keep Aerune inside it, cut off from the World Above? And, if so, who could build it?

At least it was a good excuse to take Lady Day for a run. Going Underhill in person would actually be faster than sending e-mail, and if you were asking for favors, it was always best to do it personally.

The ride to the Everforest Gate sped by with the quickness of familiarity, and once through, he left the route to Misthold up to the elvensteed. She shifted to horse form once she was Underhill—there weren't a lot of paved roads here, and four legs were better than two wheels for covering the ground safely—and Eric changed from his biking leathers to the silks and mail of a Bard. It wasn't long before they reached the golden gates of Elfhame Misthold. The guards recognized him, and let him through without difficulty.

He thought about going directly to Prince Arvindel, but realized that might play directly into Aerune's plans. Dharniel had warned him about Aerune before. It might be best to start there; scope out the territory before he put his foot in it. And Dharniel was Prince Arvindel's Master of War. Eric would be following protocol as well as using common sense to see Dharniel first.

You have learned wisdom, Grasshopper, Eric told himself with a wry smile. He went to Dharniel's suite of rooms, and asked his old master's chief man-at-arms for an audience. To his surprise and pleasure, his request was granted at once.

"So, young Eric, is your student proving too much for you already?" Dharniel asked, once they were seated in the Elven Bard's inner chamber.

The room was strewn with a working musician's litter—sheaves of music half-transcribed, bundles of strings looking like strange silvery pasta, a half-finished lute neck drying in a heavy padded clamp. A young girl—Dharniel's newest apprentice, Eric was willing to bet—had brought them spiced fruit juice and small sweet cakes, then withdrawn to leave them alone. Eric had waited as patiently as he could manage through these preliminaries, knowing that they were inevitable.

"I haven't really started working with him yet. Right now I've got another problem—you remember that Unseleighe Prince you talked to me about a few months back? The one with an interest in New York?"

To name someone in Underhill risked drawing that person's attention to you, even within the walls and wards of an Elfhame. As Dharniel had been cautious in giving his initial warning, so Eric was cautious now.

"Aye." Dharniel's face had gone still and watchful. "I remember."

"I've seen him recently. My friends and I think we need to take him out, but we haven't got a lot of good ideas."

"A moment, Sieur Eric," Dharniel said.

He got to his feet and went to a cabinet on the wall, from which he removed a surprisingly prosaic item. It looked like a fat white candle, set in a shallow dish of carved green stone. Dharniel cleared a space on his worktable and set it down, then called fire from the air to light it. And Eric got his first surprise.

The light was . . . thick. As the candle flame rose to its full height, the thick syrupy glow of its light seemed to roll outward slowly, like one of those enormously slowed down films of a big explosion. As the bubble of light reached him, Eric could feel it, like a fine warm mist breaking over his body.

"Whoa!" he said, startled. "What's that?"

Dharniel smiled, pleased with the reaction he had provoked. "You may call it 'hard magic,' young Eric, and think of it as a compression of the Power all around us into this tangible and highly-concentrated form. While it burns, we are as safe as we may be anywhere from prying ears and eyes. But I will not spend it without cause, so do not dawdle in this tale you have to tell me."

Accustomed to this sort of rebuke from his stint as Dharniel's pupil, Eric told his story as concisely as he could: Aerune's appearance last night, his taunting promise that he had discovered a way to destroy Eric and the Guardians, their discovery—through Jeanette—that Aerune had human allies, and intended to force the Sidhe into war with the World Above.

"And so we figured the best thing we could do was cut him off from his human allies and keep him from meddling any further in the World Above. Paul suggested a kind of maze-prison, but even if it would work, none of us has the faintest idea of how to build one."

"And so you came at once to me," Dharniel said sourly, for it was plain that Eric's news hadn't made very good hearing for the Sidhe Bard. He shook his head. " 'Tis a long time to mourn a lass, even one so fair as Aerete the Golden."

"You *know* her?" Eric asked, surprised. Hosea had told them what little Jeanette knew about Aerune's lost love, but Eric hadn't expected it to be common knowledge.

"She was a Lady of my Line—one still revered Underhill, for she gave her life to save her people from the scourge of war and slavery. That her sacrifice was all for naught when Aerune slew the folk she had taken under her protection does not make her deed any the less, and so we honor her, though her name is lost to Men."

Oh.

"Well, Aerune still seems to be in the slaying business, and if he's teamed up with a bunch of humans to broker a human/Sidhe war, you ought to be worried, too."

"If he can," Dharniel commented. "But mortalfolk are kittle cattle, as likely to betray him as aid him, even if he can forget his ancient feud with them for long enough not to strike out at them first."

"I think he can—and so do you, or else you wouldn't have warned me about him in the first place," Eric said boldly. "His allies won't get too far with their war without his help, though, so that brings us back to the original problem."

"To slay him, or to trap and imprison him," Dharniel said. "You cannot kill him, Sieur Eric—once your kind believed him a god, and worshipped him in terror, and he is not easily slain by such guile and power as you and your allies might command. And the Wild Lands are littered with the bones of those who cried Challenge against him, and sought to fight him in accordance with our ancient laws, so you would be well advised not to attempt such a course. But to imprison him in a labyrinth . . . such a course might well succeed, if it is crafted with sufficient power. And yes, I think it would be for the best, for he has long been a trouble to us, and should he turn his attentions to his fellows once more, no good would come of it." Dharniel sighed, as if the words had cost him something to say.

"I would suggest that you ask Lord Chinthliss to aid you in crafting your prison; he has certain ties to the Elfhames, and is well disposed to Sidhe and mortalkind alike. And it would be just as well that my lord Arvindel and the rest of the Folk were not consulted in this matter."

So he'd been right about the way the winds of Elvish politics blew, Eric thought to himself.

"Chinthliss?" It was the second time in two days Eric had heard the name—Chinthliss was the dragon that Beth and Kory were consulting.

"Who better to build a labyrinth than one of the kings of the earth?" Dharniel said, as if it were incredibly obvious. "Such a prison as he might craft could baffle the power of a god, let alone one of the Folk of the Air."

"I . . . er . . . well, do you think he'd do it?" Eric asked.

"If you put the question to him with as much wit and style as you have just put it to me, how can he not?" Dharniel asked waspishly. Eric grimaced. He was a Bard, not a diplomat!

"But as I have said, he bears your race a certain love, and if you bargain well with him and meet his price, I do not think it impossible," Dharniel said, relenting. He regarded Eric, obviously waiting for his former pupil to say something intelligent. Eric took a deep breath.

"Okay. How do I find him?"

Distances in Underhill were difficult to measure, as so much depended more on *how* you went than *where* you went. Time was a slippery concept Underhill, and Eric tried to think about it as little as possible. Fortunately, no matter how long he spent here, Lady Day could make sure he got back to New York the same day he left, so there was little possibility he'd miss Jimmie's funeral. Before dousing the spell-candle, Dharniel cautioned him again not to speak of his mission to anyone else in Misthold, and said that if asked about Eric's visit, he would put it about that Eric had come to consult with him about Eric's new student—a plausible enough excuse for the visit. Eric had no trouble agreeing to keep the real reason for his visit a secret. Aerune scared him, and he had no desire to bring the Dark Lord's vengeance down on his friends.

Even if that would wake them all up to the threat he presents. But there are prices too high to pay for being proved right.

Dharniel provided him with a guide to his destination—maps were as little use Underhill as clocks were—and a short time later, he and Lady Day stood before the gate to Chinthliss' domain. The glowing will-o'-the-wisp that Dharniel had given him in lieu of a map hovered in front of them, blinking impatiently.

"Okay," Eric said aloud, to quiet it. "I'm here, but how do I get in?"

The ornate bronze doors gave him no clue. He'd walked all the way around them once. They looked the same from the back as they did from the front, but if he could manage to pass through them, he knew he would be inside of Chinthliss' domain, a kingdom carved by the dragon's power and will out of the formless Unmanifest of the Chaos Lands.

The question was, how to get them to open? An ordinary Gate—one put up to allow travelers to shuttle from one domain to the next—would have keys for as many as six destinations, but this one didn't seem to have any key at all. Not even a door knocker. And him without his flute to play a tune and hope someone inside heard him.

Oh, crumbs. I must be short on brains along with sleep. That hardly needed to be a real problem right here, right now, did it? He always forgot how *strong* the magic was in Underhill. It didn't take any strength at all to summon up a flute out of thin air. The flute he summoned was a thing of solidified air, no more than a shimmer to the eyes, but real and solid beneath his fingers, smooth as glass. He didn't really need one to conjure the music, but Eric liked the feel of the instrument between his fingers, the interplay of body, breath, and power that shaped the Bardic magic.

He thought for a moment about the most suitable tune to play—he planned no more magic than a simple announcement of his presence—and then began a sprightly and very baroque version of "Break On Through," one that Jim Morrison would certainly never have recognized, though Ian Anderson might have enjoyed it.

The will-o'-the-wisp departed in a miff, its purpose completed, but *something* seemed to be listening. Emboldened by even that amount of success, Eric's playing grew more fanciful. He drew the melody to a close and waited expectantly.

Nothing seemed to happen, but now, when he looked at the ornate bronze door, he could see a door knocker, set just at human height. Had it been there before, and he'd just missed seeing it? Or had it appeared because of what he'd played?

No sense in breaking my brain about things that don't matter, Eric told himself, and stepped up to the door. The knocker was in the shape of the head of an Oriental dragon, and the scaled ring of the door knocker was cool in his hand. He brought it down against the door—once, twice, thrice—and heard unreal booming echoes, as if he knocked at the door of an abandoned church.

The doors swung inward. Eric walked inside, Lady Day following closely. The hall he was in was as big as an aircraft hangar, decorated in hues of red, yellow, and black. The place had the same vaguely Oriental look as the doors of the Gate he'd just walked through— Chinese dragons were supposed to be very wise, and concerned with the welfare of mankind. Eric hoped this was a good omen. Lady Day snorted and nosed him nervously.

"Welcome, Bard."

Eric blinked, though after all his time with the Sidhe, he ought to be used to surprises like this. The speaker didn't look much like a dragon—more like a really high-priced lawyer.

Appearances could be deceiving. Eric produced his best courtly bow.

"Thank you for allowing me into your home. I am Eric Banyon. I've come seeking the great Lord Chinthliss." A little sugar never hurt, especially when you were coming to ask a favor you weren't sure you were going to get.

The man in the bronze Armani suit bowed his head. "You have found him, Bard Eric. And he is entirely at your service."

Not bloody likely. Eric knew better than to take such courtesies at face value, but they were certainly nice to hear. He bowed again.

"Lord Chinthliss. My master, Lord Dharniel of Elfhame Misthold, sent me to you. I need help."

Chinthliss inclined his head graciously. "Surely you will receive it here. But come. We will go someplace more comfortable, and take tea. And you will tell me of your need."

A few moments later the two of them were sitting in an ornate and very English drawing room that wouldn't have been out of place on *Masterpiece Theater*, being served tea by a genuine English butler. Eric had attended weirder parties. He kept his face smooth and put on his best company manners. He'd never met a dragon before, but Bards were traditionally used as go-betweens in Underhill, and Dharniel had included a few lessons on diplomacy in his training. He'd never thought he'd need to use them, though.

"I'd hoped for a chance to meet you," Eric said, shading the truth only slightly. "My friend, Beth Kentraine, spoke very highly of you."

Chinthliss smiled. "Ah. The Lady Beth and her fair knight Korendil. Did you come seeking them? I regret to say they are not here at the moment. They are discharging a small commission for me in the World of Men. But if you would care to wait, I am certain they will return soon."

"No. That isn't really why I came. I need a maze. I think."

Chinthliss looked pleased. "A maze. It has been long since one of the Children of Men came to me to ask for a labyrinth." He regarded Eric with open curiosity. "But perhaps a maze would not serve your purposes best. Pray tell me everything. Leave out no detail, no matter how seemingly insignificant." He sat back in his chair and steepled his fingertips, waiting.

"I, um . . . no disrespect, sir, but is it safe to talk openly? The person I'm concerned with . . . I don't think it would be completely healthy to draw his attention by saying his name."

"Be of good heart, Bard Eric. I am not quite no one, and all who sojourn within my realm are under my protection."

Once again, Eric found himself explaining about Aerune. It turned out that Chinthliss did indeed want to know everything. Under the dragon's probing questions, Eric found himself back-tracking, clarifying, explaining everything he knew about the entire situation, from the trouble with Threshold that had drawn Aerune to New York in the first place, to as much as he knew about why the elf-lord had chosen to make it his home, and the death of his love, Aerete the Golden, which had driven him to his bitter hatred of mankind in the first place.

"And it's not like I *approve* of the Unseleighe Court, because they can be a real pain in the—well, they're evil, but it's not like they have the power to wipe out the human race, just to add a little more misery here and there. But if Aerune gets this government connection of his up and rolling, it could make real serious trouble for everybody. I'm not sure what to do about that, but if we can just separate Aerune from these guys, his conspiracy might curl up and die. So I guess that's where we want to start—putting Aerune somewhere that he can't meddle any more."

"It is always best to use as little force as possible, and allow your enemy to defeat himself. And such a prison as you describe would indeed be sufficient. He would be trapped within it forever, unable to extricate himself." Chinthliss sat forward and reached for his fragile Sevrés porcelain teacup, staring meditatively into its depths before replacing it on the table before him. "I can build such a structure as you require. But my help comes at a price."

"Fine." Eric set down his cup as well. "I'll pay it."

The dragon raised his eyebrows. "Without knowing what it is?" he asked.

Eric sighed, exhausted from answering the dragon's questions.

"I'm no good at bargaining," he said bluntly. "Dharniel says you're good people, and Beth and Kory wouldn't have anything to do with you if you weren't. I trust you to set a fair price. Whatever it is, I'll find a way to pay it. This is too important to haggle over. Aerune's about as cold-hearted a murderer as I've ever heard of. He's killed a personal friend of mine already. He'll kill everyone I know, and a lot of people I don't, if he isn't stopped."

"The trust of a Bard is no small gift," Chinthliss said gravely. "Wait here."

He got to his feet and left the room, leaving Eric to wait. Eric was too keyed up to stay seated. He got to his feet and began to pace the room, not seeing any of its contents. Even if Chinthliss could give him what they needed to trap Aerune, even if this turned out to be a good idea, they still had to get the Sidhe lord *into* it.

And what if they failed?

Well, then, at least I won't be around to see what happens next. Cold comfort, but all he had. *And if he kills me, at least that will get Misthold up off its duff. Not that I'm sure that's a good thing. I just know that things can't go on the way they're going now.*

Just when Eric didn't think he could wait any longer, Chinthliss returned carrying a small box. He held it out to Eric.

"This is what you seek."

Eric took the box. It looked awfully small for a labyrinth, but appearances could be deceiving. The box was about four inches square, made of a highly-polished close-grained golden wood. He opened it. Inside, nestled on a bed of blue velvet, was a small, wrinkled, silvery object about the size and shape of a walnut. He glanced at Chinthliss for permission before lifting it from its case. It was remarkably heavy, as if it were made of some substance denser than lead, and tingled coldly between his fingers as if a faint electric current were running through it.

"It is a seed," Chinthliss said. "Plant it anywhere in the Chaos Lands, and such a maze as you desire will instantly appear. It will work in the World Above as well, of course, but the maze that will grow there will be of a different sort—and I do not think it would serve your purposes as well."

"Thank you," Eric said, a little stunned. It almost seemed too easy, but having the maze to trap Aerune in was actually the least part of the problem he and the Guardians faced. "How can I repay you, Lord Chinthliss?"

The dragon smiled. "As I have said, the trust of a Bard is no small gift, and I would be sad to see the place from which comes so many beautiful things destroyed. Only think of me kindly, Bard Eric, and perhaps some day you can do me some trifling favor in return."

"Count on it," Eric said feelingly. "I . . . thank you again."

The dragon bowed. "No small thing, to render a Bard speechless," Chinthliss observed. "Fare you well, Bard—and good luck to you in the coming battle."

"We'll need it," Eric said bleakly.

It seemed unfair that the day on which they laid Jimmie Youngblood to rest should be so bright and sunny. It was one of those clear sparkling late August days—hot, but without the heat haze that cloaked New York through most of the weeks of summer.

The NYPD had turned out in force to salute their fallen comrade. Jimmie's coffin was draped with a flag, and the chapel where the funeral service was held was filled with officers in dress uniforms and detectives in plain dark suits and dresses. A number of Guardian House's tenants had come as well, and tonight there would be a wake in her honor at the apartment. Jimmie had been well-loved, though no one had known her very well.

Did I know her? If I'd known her better, could I have stopped all this from happening? Eric wondered desolately. He stood beside Hosea at the front of the chapel, both men dressed in dark navy suits with mourning bands on their left arms. Ria was there as well, looking severe and correct in a black Chanel suit. Even Kayla had been persuaded into something less flamboyant than her usual Goth garb. In a plain black dress, her face bare of all but the most minimal makeup, she looked very young. Far too young to expose to Aerune's danger.

If there's any way around it . . . Eric promised himself.

Toni stood close beside Paul, wearing dark glasses to conceal eyes red and swollen from grieving tears. She held a rosary in her gloved hands, her fingers moving over the smooth beads. Paul's face was cast in harsh and impassive lines, the mask of a man who felt deeply and knew the emotion must not be allowed to sway him.

The minister spoke of a life dedicated to duty and service— soothing words, meant to comfort those Jimmie had left behind. But there was no comfort for the Guardians, knowing she had been slain almost randomly by her own estranged brother in a bizarre side effect of Aerune's plotting.

The service and its aftermath passed in a blur, and Eric barely registered the names and faces of those who came up to him to offer their condolences and share their grief. Her co-workers were the men and women who knew Jimmie best, who knew that her death could have come for any of them.

After the service itself, the coffin was taken to a cemetery on Long Island for interment, at a second ceremony attended only by the departmental honor guard and Jimmie's closest friends. As the coffin was being lowered into the ground, the terrible finality of it all struck Eric like an unanticipated blow. This was real. This was forever. He stood, gazing down at the ground, until Kayla came and pulled him away toward the waiting Rolls.

Ria had volunteered her car to drive the Guardians and Eric to the cemetery, as New Yorkers rarely kept cars, Lady Day couldn't manage anything larger than her Lotus Elan shape, and Toni's venerable Toyota couldn't accommodate them all.

Why do we grow up thinking life should be fair? Who told us that it should be? Because it never is, and finding that out . . . hurts worse than a lie.

As the car passed through the gates on its way back to New York, its occupants were unusually quiet, constrained by the depressing occasion. Even Kayla had nothing to say.

Ria leaned forward in her seat and caught Eric's eye. "Whatever you're planning, I want to be a part of it."

Eric blinked, taken by surprise. Ria took the hesitation for disapproval.

"Oh, come on! Do you think I think you're going to just let this slide? You're planning something, and I can help."

"I, um . . ." He hadn't really thought about involving Ria. He'd gotten used to thinking of this as his fight, and the Guardians'. But Ria was a trained sorceress. And someone with her high-level Real World contacts could be a lot of help in unraveling the human end of Aerune's plot. "Are you sure? This isn't really your battle."

"As much mine as yours," Ria pointed out, with a certain justice. "Leaving aside the altruistic—that he's coming after everyone pretty much equally—let's descend to the selfish: if Aerune does what Banjo Girl says he wants to, I'm going to be persona non grata on either side of the Veil."

That much was true: Ria's mixed blood would make her as unwelcome with Aerune as it would make her a target for Aerune's human allies.

"I know," was all he said.

"And for that matter, I'm already involved. You know I've been chasing down the people Lintel was selling Threshold's black-ops drugs to. What do you want to bet that some of them are the same people Aerune's dealing with?"

"It's kind of you to wish to help . . ." Paul began.

Ria snorted. "I'm not kind. Ask Eric. But I'm not stupid, either. You have a better chance of success with my help than without it."

"We don't generally involve outsiders in what we do," Toni said, her voice neutral.

"I'm not an outsider, any more than Kayla and Eric are," Ria shot back. "You Guardians think you're special because you have abilities most people don't, and know more about the way the world really works than most people do. Well, surprise, so do I."

This had all the earmarks of degenerating into a nasty fight. Eric spoke up quickly.

"If this were just a problem like you've faced before, Toni, I'd be glad to stay out of it, and Ria too. But Aerune's my problem too, and Ria's. This involves both Underhill and the World Above, and you're understrength at the moment. Hosea's untrained, either as

Guardian or Bard, and from what I've found out, Aerune eats guys like you for breakfast, no offense."

"None taken," José said gravely, glancing toward Toni and Paul.

"So let's wait till we get back to my place and hash things out. I've got the maze-seed. It might take Aerune out, but it's going to take teamwork to use it."

"That?" Toni Hernandez said in disbelief an hour later. "That's our weapon? What next, a sack of magic beans?"

There had been no chance for Eric to talk with the others before the funeral, so this was the first opportunity they had to hear the tale of his visit to Chinthliss. He'd produced the box containing the maze-seed and passed it around for the others to examine.

"All the old fairy tales have their roots in truth, maybe more so than we imagine," Paul said musingly. "So . . . yes. Magic beans are not impossible." His eyes sparkled with the excitement of a scholar on the trail of hot new information. Toni passed the box to him, but Kayla grabbed it next.

"Hey," she said, holding the silvery seed in her closed fist. "It *tickles*. Weird."

Ria frowned at her firmly, and she passed the seed to Paul. José took possession of the box, examining its craftsmanship with pleasure.

"If this will not be needed afterward, may I have it to keep? It is a beautiful thing."

"Sure," Eric said. "I only hope we're going to be in a position to want souvenirs after this is over."

"Hear, hear," Ria drawled. "Okay, you've got your prison, and it shouldn't be hard to get the six of us into the Wild Lands to plant it. But how are you going to get the genie *into* the bottle?"

"Hey," Kayla said. "Can't you count? Seven—Hosea, the other three Guardians, you, me, and Eric." The others looked at her. Kayla glared back stubbornly. "*Oh*, no. You're not cutting me out of this deal, pat me on the head and leave the poor little girl on the sidelines to see if you come back. You *need* me! Who's going to put you back together when you come to pieces? Who's going to sucker this Aerune into coming after you in the first place?"

Eric shot Ria a guilty look. Involving Kayla would be an enormous help in bringing off the plan he didn't quite have yet. But it wasn't fair to involve a teenager in this. The danger was too great.

"No," Ria said flatly. "Elizabet would skin me with a dull knife."

"It might not be necessary," Eric began reluctantly. Kayla made a rude noise.

"Perhaps it would be simplest if you began by telling us what you had in mind," Paul said, handing the maze-seed to José. The other man placed it back into the box and handed the closed box back to Eric.

"The plan is to keep Aerune from being able to meddle in the World Above ever again," Eric said. "The method is to trap him inside a magical labyrinth—he won't be able to get out, and no one else will be able to get in. So we decoy him into the Wild Lands, and distract him while we plant the seed. When it grows up, he'll be inside, we'll be outside. Simple." *I hope.*

"Nothing in life is ever that simple," Ria commented.

José frowned. "I see two weak points in this plan. How do we get him to come to us in these Wild Lands—and how do we distract him until the labyrinth is complete?"

Hosea fingered the strings of the enchanted banjo, listening intently. "Jeanette says that Aerune's fief is carved out of the Wild Lands—would that be about right, Eric?"

Eric nodded. The borders of some Underhill domains actually touched, but more of them didn't.

"So if we raise up a great big magical fuss just outside his front door, he's bound to come and see who's out there," Hosea said.

"Then all we have to do is fight him to a standstill for long enough for your magic beans to grow." Ria looked at Eric. "Do you think it's possible?"

"If anybody has a better idea, I'm open to suggestions," Eric said grimly. "What we've got going for us is that the Guardians' powers are going to be as unfamiliar to Aerune as they were to me. And we don't have to defeat him. Just hold him for however long the maze takes to sprout."

"Then you definitely need me," Kayla said. "You've said that Aerune likes to eat Talent. Well, I've got Talent. He'll come after me."

Eric expected an immediate objection from Ria, but she actually appeared to be considering Kayla's suggestion. "You're right that we need bait to draw him out, someone chock-full of tasty Talent. We can't use Eric—Aerune's met him before, and Aerune might not want to antagonize the Elfhames by openly attacking a Bard. But he offered me an alliance, once. I could say I've changed my mind."

"But wouldn't he be suspicious? You turned him down once, and he's seen you with us now," Paul said.

"It doesn't matter if he's suspicious, so long as he comes," Ria said simply.

The talk went on—arguments, objections, attempts to plan for a situation that none of them could really predict. Ria pointed out that they would need armor and weapons of Cold Iron. The Guardians had swords, and Ria promised to provide them with chain mail shirts similar to her own, which would at least deflect any levin-bolts Aerune chose to throw. Kayla continued to argue for her inclusion in the mission, and Ria was just as firmly opposed.

"I think we're all forgetting something," Toni said at last. "The other night, when Aerune attacked Guardian House, Kayla was the only one who noticed. I think she needs to come."

Ria opened her mouth to protest. Toni raised a hand.

"I don't think she should be the bait. But I think she should be there. We've planned for the fight, but we need to plan for losing it, too. If we lose, what happens to Kayla?"

"Aerune will naturally return to Guardian House," José said, "seeking to complete his revenge. If Kayla is here alone—forgive me, *querida*—she will be easy prey."

"Whereas if she's with us, and things go bad, we can put her on a fast horse out of Dodge—Eric, is there somewhere you can send her that would be safe?" Toni finished.

"Lady Day could take her to Beth and Kory at Elfhame

Misthold," Eric said. "Quit glaring, Kayla. Somebody's going to need to tell them that things went wrong, and how, and who was responsible, and an elvensteed won't be able to."

"And, meanwhile, she might be able to keep Aerune from pulling the wool over our eyes," Paul said. "I'm afraid I'm in favor of including her. She's not so much younger than Toni was when Toni became a Guardian."

"And I've already been an elvish blue-plate special once," Kayla pointed out. "And if something happens to you, Ria, Elizabet will kill *me*. So it's settled. I'm going."

Ria sighed, recognizing defeat. "Maybe we'll be lucky and *all* be killed," she said sardonically.

"I guess it's settled, then," Hosea said. "We all go. And the Good Lord willing, we all come back. The only question left is . . . when?"

"Soon," Eric said. Aerune had boasted that he was in no hurry to implement his plans, but that didn't mean he would leave them alone. If they were going to attack at full strength, it had better be a preemptive strike. "How soon can everyone get things ready?"

FIFTEEN:
THE EAGLE AND
THE HAWK

❖❖❖

The funeral and war council had been on Wednesday, and Ria said it would take a few days for the armor to arrive, and for her to make arrangements to be away from her office for a few days. The others also had real-world commitments, and arrangements to make—fortunately, Caity had one of José's birds, and could be trusted to take care of the rest of his little ones for a few days. Toni would send Raoul and Paquito to her sister in Brooklyn for the weekend, and none of the others had any dependents to be harmed by a few days' absence.

Eric was particularly glad to have the extra time to prepare. Hosea needed to know everything Eric could teach him, and he needed to know it fast.

Eric remembered Prince Terenil, who had been the first to show him what magic *was*. Terenil had done it by loaning Eric his own memories—a quick-and-dirty form of training worlds apart from the slow, disciplined instruction he had suffered later under Lord Dharniel. But that had been a desperate time, with Perenor set to destroy all of Elfhame Sun-Descending and its inhabitants. And it had given Eric the first insight into using his power. If they were to face down Aerune in his own back yard a few days from now, Eric owed Hosea at least as much help as Terenil had given him.

Little good though it had done Terenil, in the end. He had died in the battle for the Sun-Descending Nexus, though at least he had taken Perenor with him. *And the rest of us are still here, and so are the elves, so I guess we have to count that as a victory, even if it doesn't feel much like one when I think about it.*

"I don't know if this is going to work," Eric said. The two Bards were sitting in Eric's apartment the morning after the funeral, Hosea with his banjo, Eric with his flute. "I'm not even sure I can do it."

"I reckon you can," Hosea said in his slow Appalachian drawl. "I reckon it's like quilting—if you trace out the pattern, and I follow it, I'll end up with something that's mine alone."

"I guess," Eric said dubiously. "I hope. This isn't the way I wanted things to work out."

"We can't always have what we want, Mister Bard," Hosea said with a smile. "And I guess, if I came all this way to have you kindle up my shine, I can't kick about how you do it."

"I . . . yeah. So let's get started."

The first thing Eric did was summon up some heavy duty shields to insulate them from the rest of the House. It had been a rough week for the psychics who lived there, and he didn't want to add to their troubles, especially if something went wrong.

The healing circle Kayla had organized at the wake last night was a good start to healing the damage Aerune had done to the psychic fabric of this place. The more Eric saw her work, the more impressed he was. Kayla had good instincts. And if her Gift wasn't as flashy as Bardcraft or as initially impressive as that of the Guardians, in the long run, it made a lot more difference to the quality of life for ordinary people.

I guess that's what Jimmie meant about the Guardians' job being to let other people get on with their lives. It's all that, and about making a safe space for people like Kayla to use their gifts. She'd make a great battlefield medic for the psychic wars, but the important thing is to make a world where she can do something else instead. And I'd better get on with my part in arranging that.

He didn't think he could do what Terenil had done—there were advantages to being as long-lived as the Sidhe, and having a thousand years to practice your craft—but he could try to do something that had the same effect. Raising his flute to his lips, Eric began to play: long slow tones, not yet a tune. No one would be able to hear it but Hosea, and as he played, Eric tried to will his experience into the music, letting his mind rove over every time he'd used his magic, over all his lessons with Dharniel. As he did, the slow notes slowly evolved into music, a slow wandering tune of nothing in particular.

He risked a glimpse at Hosea's face before closing his eyes to concentrate upon the tune that he wove. The other Bard's expression was one of wide-eyed concentration, as though he listened to more than the music.

Eric drew his consciousness inward, focusing entirely on the *Bard*-ness of the music. *Music is magic. The whole world is made out of music, if you can just hear it. Shape the tune, and you shape the thing . . . and yourself. Feel the music of the world. Hear it. Play it.*

Slowly, Hosea began to join in the music. At first only a note here and there, the *plink!* of the banjo's strings like pebbles thrown into a swiftly-running stream. Then more—scraps of music woven around the song of the flute, blending perfectly with the unplanned melody. The tune Eric played was faster now, more urgent, more insistent. *Hear this. Hear what I have to tell, hear what I have to teach.* He found he was playing the story of his life, all its disappointments, cowardice, and false starts. A part of him cringed at stripping himself so naked before another human being, showing himself so utterly open and defenseless. But another part was stronger. *That is what I was, not what I am. I am stronger now, wiser, but I do not hide from the mistakes I've made.*

And slowly, as Hosea's music joined his like two streams running together, Eric could see into the other man as well—every pettiness, every failure, every moment of cowardice . . . but love and courage and greatness as well. Then the music carried them onward, away from *self* and selfishness alike, carried them on into the bright world of Creation of which Underhill itself was a mere shadow, into the place where the wish and the deed were one. Both men were playing flat-out now, blending their power as they blended their music— Eric's with the power of a trained Bard, Hosea's full of promise and power yet to be, power that Eric could shape to his own ends, or twist, or destroy.

Those were easy traps to avoid, but there was a greater and more subtle one waiting. Eric could teach Hosea the way to call his magic. He could teach him that Eric's was the only right way, teach Hosea to do only as Eric had done and could do, and no more.

But that was not what it meant to be a teacher. Hosea must grow to be all that *Hosea* could be, not what Eric could foresee for him with the limitations of his human personality. And so, somehow, he found himself able to step aside now that he had shown Hosea the way into his power, to stand beside him as an equal and a friend in the face of that ultimate source of their shared magic, letting Hosea drink his fill from that wellspring and learn all that he could learn. Hosea had trusted Eric to lead him here, and now it was Eric's turn to trust—in Hosea's kindness, his goodness, his essential decency. If the pupil was worthy to be trained, there came a time when the master must allow the pupil to train himself, to use and become all that the master had seen in him, fulfilling his true potential.

Letting go like that was the hardest thing that Eric had ever done. Every instinct screamed that *he* was the one with the training, that his experience and wisdom must control all that Hosea learned. But that was a trap, one that every teacher must confront and defeat. If Eric gave only what he thought was best, Hosea would never be more than a pale reflection of him, touching the magic only through Eric's understanding of it, not forging his own. He played more softly now, supporting Hosea as his magic soared, as the Bardic fire within him kindled and flamed, letting him make his own choices, shape his own path.

I wonder if it was this hard for Dharniel? Eric mused. As the thought clothed itself in words, he tumbled down out of the moment, out of the realm of endless light, and the sharing was over.

The two of them were nothing more than two musicians, having an impromptu morning jam session in a New York apartment.

He opened his eyes.

Hosea played on alone, jamming with the melody Eric could no longer hear. He . . . glowed, bathed in a white radiance of power that flowered within. The banjo's strings burned like silver fire, the white doeskin of the soundbox glowing like the moon seen through clouds as Hosea's fingers flew, drawing music out of silver and bone, skin and wood. There were tears on the big man's face, and Eric was surprised to find that his own eyes were wet.

This was the power of the Bard, the power to sing things into creation, the power that caused the Sidhe to venerate them above all others.

Slowly, Hosea drew the melody to a close. It seemed to echo in the room long after he hushed the strings with one massive hand. He opened his eyes and looked at Eric.

"Is . . . that what I'm supposed to be? What I am?"

"That's right." For a moment Eric was able to forget the deaths that had brought them to this place, the deaths that might be yet to come. This was the most important thing he had ever been taught— that the magic wasn't *for* something, that it wasn't a means to an end. It simply *was*.

"It seems so easy," Hosea said.

"It is. We're the ones that make it hard," Eric said. He summoned a grin and drew a deep breath. "That doesn't mean I let you out of all the practice and drills, though. We'll start with an easy one. Call up a shield."

Hosea frowned, consulting his memories. "Like this?" he asked. He slowly strummed a minor chord, each note separate and distinct. A faint rippling light seemed to grow up around him.

Eric batted it down with a triumphant major. "Yeah, but make it stronger. Push back when I push you, or that shield isn't going to do much good."

Half an hour later, both men were panting and out of breath. Instinctively, Hosea used his magic in a much different way than

Eric did. Where Eric tended to confront an enemy and do his best to overawe it with a display of superior but (now at least) elegantly-crafted power, Hosea relied on seeming harmless and not being noticed—pretty much an extension of his real-world behavior. After a while, Eric's attacks on Hosea's shields just slid aside: it wasn't that the shields had a great deal of strength, something that would only come with more practice and skill, but more as if they were shaped to deflect the attack, rather than meet it. If Eric was a lance, then Hosea was the stubborn round stone in the middle of the road. The stone could break the lance, or the lance the stone, but it was likeliest of all that the lance would simply . . . slide away.

"Crane and turtle," Eric said, standing and stretching. *I guess Ria's style would be tiger. What does that leave for Kayla: monkey? She'd kill me if I ever suggested* that. "We ought to open a school of the Bardic martial arts."

"Too fancy for me," Hosea said, stretching until his muscles cracked. "I'm a simple country boy. Let's go find the young'un. I could eat a whole horse, raw or cooked."

"I won't tell Lady Day you said that," Eric said with a grin. After the morning's workout, he felt a peace and confidence that had been absent from his life for too long, as if he'd found the work he should do and was doing it. It was a good feeling.

The smell of fresh paint greeted them when they went downstairs. The door to the basement apartment was open, and some items of furniture—and the rest of Kayla's luggage, delivered from Ria's that morning—were waiting in the laundry room. There was a futon couch, a table and two chairs, some bookcases, and a couple of lamps, all contributed by the tenants of the house and customized by Kayla with fresh paint in shades of black, ultraviolet, poison green, and hot pink. The sound of hammering came from within.

Eric knocked loudly on the open door. "Kayla?"

"C'mon in! Ooh, is that the scent of Bardic power I smell? It smells like victory!"

Eric and Hosea walked cautiously into the main room. Kayla had been working hard, and it showed.

The walls had been painted an even velvety black, then stenciled with Celtic borders halfway up their height in a glittery dark purple. More of the glitter was painted on the walls themselves, so that they glistened in places like mica-studded granite.

The ceiling was the same deep purple as the Celtic border, painted with swirling clouds and a yellow crescent moon. A bead curtain of iridescent dark purple moons and stars had been set up to screen the studio's kitchen from the rest of the space, and a mirror wreathed in black silk vines and roses had been hung on the bathroom door. The battered linoleum floor had disappeared under several moth-eaten but still serviceable Oriental rugs. Kayla was standing on a short stepladder, hammering a curtain rod into place over the high narrow windows. Black lace curtains were piled on the floor waiting to be hung.

"You gonna help me with this, or just gawk?" she asked. Hosea moved forward to hold up the curtain rod—black iron, with twining leaves for finials—as Kayla finished sinking the last of the nails.

She jumped off the ladder and turned to face them, grinning. She wore black cigarette-leg jeans and a cropped black (and paint-spattered) "Anarchy" T-shirt. Her navel was pierced. Eric blinked.

Am I getting old, or just out of the loop? Fashion or not, that looks painful.

"Pretty neat, huh?" she asked.

"I'm sure Ria is blessing her narrow escape," Eric answered.

Kayla made a face. "Oh, sure, like I'd do this to somebody else's apartment! But this is mine, all mine—I can do anything I want! Toni said so."

"And you certainly have," Eric said. "How'd you get all this done in—what?—two days?"

"Oh, everybody helped. Margot gave me the bead curtains, and Caity did the stenciling, and Tat gave me the couch—all I had to do was go out and buy a new cover for it. Everybody's nice, and it's not like they're . . ." She searched for a word. "*Hurting* inside all the time. I like this place."

"And it likes you," Eric said, "or you wouldn't be here." *And maybe it needs you, too. The Guardians protect the city, but who protects the Guardians?* Aloud he said: "Hosea and I were going to go out and grab some lunch. Want to come?"

"Sure," Kayla said. "And then when we come back you can help me move the furniture in. I think it's all dry now."

If it wasn't now, it would be before he put his hands on it, Eric vowed. He had no desire to go through life wearing a coat of black enamel in interesting places.

Kayla studied Hosea critically. "You look taller. Did it hurt much?"

Hosea grinned at her amiably. "Not too much. You'd better do some growing on your own, Little Bit, or I'm liable to trip over you one of these days."

"Size elitist," Kayla grumbled, but she sounded pleased. "Just let me get my stuff, and I'm there."

The three of them walked a few blocks to a fried chicken place on Broadway, where Hosea ate most of a family-style dinner for four while Kayla nibbled on fries and an order of buffalo wings and Eric contented himself with a chicken sandwich and a Coke.

"So is he ready?" Kayla wanted to know. Eric had warned her about his morning's plans—for one thing, there'd been the possibility that Kayla'd be needed to do a patch job if something went wrong.

"That'd take a lot longer than one morning. But he's made a good start," Eric answered, grinning at Hosea.

"Shucks, ma'am, it wasn't nothing. I've got a magic banjo, you know," Hosea said, playing up his drawl.

"That's so dorky it's almost cool," Kayla said, brandishing a French fry as if it were a conductor's baton. "But really."

"We won't know until we get there," Eric said, his earlier good humor fading as he concentrated once more on the threat they faced. "But it's as good as I can do in the time we have." *And pray that it's enough. I don't think I can bear any more deaths on my conscience.*

All too soon, it seemed, Saturday came. Eric had continued with his summer classes—if he wanted to graduate from Juilliard, he couldn't let them slide—but had given very little attention to his studies, devoting all his concentration to the training sessions with Hosea. Fortunately his native skill could carry him through a little scholastic sluffing off, but he was really going to have to hit the books when he returned—*if* he returned—if he wanted to go into the Fall term with passing grades in his summer make-up courses.

Now there's a cheery choice: death or summer school.

At first he'd been surprised at how nervous he was over the upcoming battle, but then he realized why. All the other messes he'd gotten into had been last-minute, skin-of-his-teeth races against time. This was more like deciding to go clobber somebody in cold blood. Never mind that it was vitally necessary and they had more than enough cause to act. Aerune wasn't *here*, wasn't an immediate threat. If Eric wanted to go into the realm of serious denial, he could even tell himself that Aerune would lose interest in destroying humanity, that the elf-lord's real-world allies would fall into disorder and doubt and no longer be a threat. That he didn't really have to do anything at all.

I guess I'm starting to see the elves' side of things. When you live that long, most problems do *tend to go away if you ignore them. So how could they know that this one is going to be different?*

If it is. But waiting to find out isn't a chance I really want to take.

There was also the fundamental difference between Elvish psychology and that of humans. Terenil had explained it to him, when Eric was taking his first steps into the world of magic.

"We are virtually immortal, Bard. Our lives are measured in centuries, not decades. That can be as much curse as blessing. Firstly, we are few in number. Secondly, strong emotional ties bind for centuries, not mere decades. Your legends call us lightminded and frivolous in our affections—but think you for a moment. Suppose you have a love that turns to dislike. But you are tied to the place where that love dwells, and there are perhaps a few hundred inhabitants of that place. Try as you will, you must see that love every day. For the next thousand years. Unless one of you finds a way to leave. So do we avoid both love and hate, granting either only when there is no other choice."

Kory was an exception to Sidhe customs. Barely two hundred

years old—a very young man by Sidhe standards—he cared passionately about many things. It made him a sort of freak in the world of Underhill, and Korendil had always preferred the company of humans to that of his own kind. But Kory was comparatively lucky. He was a child of the High Court. He could leave his Grove and its Nexus, and go elsewhere if he chose, or if he needed to. And he had Beth.

But what if Beth . . . died? What would Kory do then? Would he hate whoever had caused her death? And over the course of a hundred centuries, would that hatred grow and fester until he became a monster like Aerune?

Eric hoped not, but he didn't *know.* Any more than he knew what Aerune had been like before he had loved Aerete the Golden and seen her die at the hands of humans. Just as Kory had, Aerune had broken the first commandment that governed the life of the Children of Danu. And as Terenil had warned Eric, so long ago, not knowing what he warned him against, it had destroyed Aerune.

It's no excuse for what he's done. No matter how badly you're hurt, that doesn't give you a free pass to hurt someone else. But I wish we could think of a better solution than just locking him up.

And maybe they could, if they had infinite time and resources. But they didn't have either. They had to stop Aerune *now,* and then see about undoing the damage he'd already caused in the World Above.

"No brooding," Kayla said with mock sternness, rousing him from his reverie.

"Sorry," Eric said sheepishly. "Just thinking about how to change the world."

Early Saturday morning—too early, by Eric's standards, though he hadn't slept well the night before—the seven of them gathered once more in Eric's apartment.

Toni, Paul, and José had brought their swords. Toni's and José's were conventional longswords, carried in long slender cases that looked like instrument cases, but Paul carried only an elegant sword cane, an antique, ebony with a silver ferrule and a large cairngorm set into the silver ball-handle. He was dressed as if for an afternoon's grouse hunting, with lace-up calf-high boots, khakis, and a Norfolk jacket in an understated tweed. The other two were wearing everyday clothes—Toni in jeans and a pink sweatshirt, José in a dark workshirt and twill pants.

Toni had suggested that Hosea take Jimmie's sword—like the rest of her magical paraphernalia, Hosea had inherited it along with her apartment—but the big man had declined.

"I guess I wouldn't hardly know what to do with a sword. I'll stick to my banjo, if it's all right with you all."

Toni had wanted to argue, but Paul convinced her that it would be better for Hosea to go into the field with no weapon at all rather than one he didn't trust. "And Eric has assured us that the young man is coming along quite well with his Bardic studies, so it is not as if he will be quite defenseless."

Ria was the last to arrive. She was dressed in a street-casual outfit Eric hadn't seen before—black jeans with the extra gusset at the crotch that would give them as much flexibility as a pair of dance tights, a long black linen duster, black dance boots that came up over the knee, and a long silvery mail coat, its links so fine that it shimmered like hammered silk.

"You look like an outtake from *Highlander*," Eric told her.

"Wait till you see my sword," she answered with a tight smile. She patted the pocket of her duster. It hung heavily, and Eric suspected she was carrying a gun and several extra clips or speedloaders. Steel-jacketed hollowpoints could cause serious damage to any of the iron-averse Underhill folk, even kill.

"I left the shirts in the car. Not only do they weigh about a hundred pounds, but you'll be a lot more comfortable on the ride up to the Gate without them. Eric, are you going to ride with us? I think we should take the 'steeds with us. Etienne's waiting for me up in the park with the rest of our gear. If anyone sees her, they'll just think they've seen a deer."

"If Eric's going up on his bike, I want to ride with him," Kayla said instantly. "Hey, this could be like, my last moments on Earth. They should be fun. Eric? Puh-*leeze*?"

"Fine with me," Eric said, grinning in spite of himself at Kayla's exuberance.

"Okay, let's go," Toni said.

Eric savored the ride up to the Everforest Gate. In another lifetime, he might have been on his way up to the Sterling Forest RenFaire, with nothing more on his mind than a feathered hat. Now he was riding into battle.

He could sense Lady Day's excitement. Unlike mortal horses, the elvensteeds were bred for battle, and relished a good fight. He tried to take comfort from her easy courage—Eric was no coward, though he'd spent the first half of his life running away from anything that looked even vaguely like a fight, but this was a different kind of fight than any he'd ever been in. It hadn't been forced on him. He'd had plenty of chances to back out. But he'd chosen to be here. If that was courage, then he guessed he was brave. But it seemed perilously close to desperation.

All too soon they arrived at their destination. The Faire would be running for a few more weeks, but the Everforest Nexus had been set on state park lands, away from the crowds.

He pulled the bike to a stop in the clearing that held the Gate, and he and Kayla dismounted. She looked around, turning in a circle. "Hey. Untouched nature. Who'd'a thunk there could be something like this so close to the city? Hey, what's that?"

She pointed. There were tire tracks sunk deep into the mud, and burn marks on the grass.

"Levin-bolts, or something similar, and probably a van. Jeanette said Aerune had Elkanah bring her here so he could take her Underhill easily."

"Creepy." Kayla hugged herself and shivered, though the day was warm. "He isn't coming back, is he?"

"I hope not. But this is the closest Nexus point to New York City, so most of the East Coast Underhill traffic comes through here."

Kayla didn't say anything, though Eric could tell she was thinking hard. Just then Lady Day shivered all over, and in place of the red-and-white touring bike stood a neat-footed black mare with golden eyes. Kayla goggled as if she'd never seen a horse before, and Lady Day minced delicately forward and nudged her with a soft black nose. Kayla reached up tentatively to stroke it.

"Hey, she's *soft!*" the young Healer exclaimed. "Am I going to get to ride her? I mean, like she is now?"

"Maybe. That's kind of between you and her," Eric answered. He knew Kayla had grown up on the street, abandoned by her parents when her Talent began to show, but somehow the experience hadn't hardened her. She pulled up a handful of grass from the turf at her feet and began to feed the elvensteed, who almost purred under the admiring attention.

A few minutes later, the Rolls pulled up, moving slowly over the narrow bumpy track. Ria was driving. She pulled the car to a rocking stop, and the venerable machine seemed almost to sigh with relief. Rolls-Royces were built like a bank vault, but by no stretch of the imagination were they off-road vehicles.

Ria got out, followed by the other four. She pulled a large suitcase off the driver's seat and began to unzip it.

"These are for you," she told the Guardians, opening the suitcase and hauling out the first of the shirts. "They're lined in Kevlar fabric, at least partly so they don't chafe, but you won't want to go jogging in them; they're heavy, and they don't breathe. Iron can kill the Sidhe-folk, and it also makes their magic run wild, one of the reasons Aerune is a lot less powerful here in the World Above than he's going to be when we go to meet him on his home turf. The steel part of these shirts will absorb some magic and deflect a lot in the way of levin-bolts, but some of it gets worn away each time."

"So if Aerune keeps hitting one of us, he'll eventually burn through the shirt?" Paul said, examining the shirt with interest.

"Try not to let that happen," Ria said, deadpan.

"Won't he know we're wearing these?" Toni asked, holding a shirt up to herself to check the fit. It was too small, and she passed it to Kayla. Each was slit up the sides and laced shut—with plastic-coated steel cording—to ensure a tighter fit.

"Sure. Think about it—if I were him, I'd be expecting it. There still isn't much he can do about it—if he touches you while you're wearing that, he risks getting his widdle fingies burned off," Ria said.

Kayla had pulled off her leather jacket and was slithering into the mail shirt. She wore her full elaborate Goth makeup and jewelry, but had elected to dress sensibly—jeans, Doc Martens, and a long-sleeved T-shirt that fit as if it were sprayed on. Hosea helped her lace the sides shut. "Ain't we gonna be a little conspicuous dressed like this?" she asked Ria.

"Not Underhill, so far as I know," Ria told her. "Unfortunately, it may be a long walk to reach the borders of Aerune's domain, but they're lighter to wear than to carry, I assure you."

Etienne appeared then, summoned by Ria, trotting out of the forest and greeting Lady Day with a whinny. The two elvensteeds nuzzled at each other, exchanging greetings in their own way. Whatever differences the two had once had seemed to have been dealt with.

"Eric?" Ria asked, holding out a shirt to him. He thought about it, and shook his head.

"I'll call up my armor once I'm on the other side of the Gate. Might as well go in all flags flying."

"And hope we don't go down with the ship." Ria walked over to Etienne and vaulted into the saddle with one easy motion. In her black duster, she looked like a vision straight out of the Old West.

Once they were all re-dressed, Toni and José opened their sword cases and removed their magical weapons. Toni's was long and elegant, with a cross set into the pommel and Hebrew letters running down the gleaming blade. José's sword was simpler—almost a short sword, with a browned-iron blade and a plain leather-wrapped hilt.

Hosea slung his banjo over his shoulder and looked at Eric.

"I guess this is your show now, Eric."

Eric nodded, touching his hip to assure himself that his gig bag was in place. He pursed his lips and whistled a soundless phrase.

A portion of the air in front of them seemed to darken, shimmering like a deep pool. As it faded into existence, the trees beyond it slowly disappeared.

"Is that it?" Paul said, hefting his sword stick.

"One gen-u-wine, accept no substitutes Sidhe Portal," Eric said, feigning a lightness he didn't really feel. He held out his hand, and Lady Day put her nose in it, her warm breath flowing over his hand.

"Let's go, then. I'm not getting any younger," Toni said. In the silvery mail armor, carrying her sword, she looked like a medieval warrior saint.

Eric mounted Lady Day, and reached a hand down for Kayla. She scrambled up behind him and settled snugly against him, her arms around his waist. With Ria leading, the small party passed through the Gate.

"It looks just the same," Paul said, sounding disappointed.

"No it doesn't," Toni said. "It looks the way everything did when I was a little girl—all bright and clean and new."

They were standing in the Underhill counterpart of the Sterling Forest glade. There was a theory that the Underworld places near Gates tended to grow to mirror the World Above they were connected to, and Everforest was an example of that. But if these were the Ramapo Mountains, they were those mountains as they had been before any humans at all had come to trouble the land: lush and wooded and green.

Eric could feel that they were being watched, but that was common enough. There were Low Court elves in the area, of course, and other creatures too numerous to name, any of whom might take an interest in visitors.

"Which way?" Hosea asked.

"You tell me," Eric said. "Jeanette's the one who's been this way."

Hosea played a few bars of "Foggy Mountain Breakdown," his head cocked as if listening. Here in the magic-rich air of Underhill, it seemed as if Eric could almost hear her too: complaining but resigned.

"She says it was dark when she came through here, and she was busy being poisoned. She also says you *don't* want to go the way Aerune took her, unless you've got a taste for dying young. But I think—ain't there something with shine over that-a-way?" He pointed.

Eric focused his senses on the direction Hosea indicated. It was *like* listening, but not really; human language was pretty inadequate when it came to describing what magic felt like. After a moment he nodded. "There's a Gate that way. Let's try it."

Before they started off, Eric transformed his garb into the flashy silks and gleaming armor of an Underhill Bard. The four Guardians frankly stared, and Ria applauded mockingly.

"I think I'm going to have major feelings of inferiority after this," Toni said a little breathlessly.

"Don't," Eric said. "There's no way I could do half of what you can—our magics are completely different—and you'll probably find that your abilities are increased here, too. Magic is as common in Underhill as, well, as cable TV in the World Above."

"A good thing to remember," Paul said. "Well, it's a lovely day for a walk. Shall we get started?"

Eric wished he'd been able to borrow elvensteeds for the others, but they weren't given out lightly, and to ask Prince Arvindel for some might have tipped Eric's hand. He wasn't sure how much he wanted Misthold to know about what he was doing until it was over—even if they disapproved of Aerune, having a bunch of humans come Underhill to take him out might have made some of the elves a little uneasy.

When they reached the Gate, Eric chose their direction from the available destinations already set into it. He and Ria had both been to Aerune's domain, and Jeanette had been in and out of Aerune's land several times. Locating the Goblin Tower wasn't going to be the problem. Getting to it safely was. Travel in Underhill was sort of a cross between cross-country hiking and code breaking.

The Gate led them through to a land considerably less lush and tended than the one they'd originally entered. It looked as if it might have belonged to someone once, and now was returning to the wilderness it had originally been. Depending on how much magic had been used to create it, it might go on this way until a new owner claimed it, or dissolve back into the mists of the Chaos Lands.

It's not knowing which until afterward that's so amusing, as Humpty-Dumpty said to Alice.

The maze-seed was a heavy weight at the bottom of his gig bag, and Eric couldn't keep his thoughts from fixating on the battle to come. *The real question is, am I sure that what I'm doing is right? And the answer is, I can't think of anything else to do. And something has to be done.*

The next Gate brought them to a tropical seashore, where a smooth white sand beach as fine as sugar formed a broad shining ribbon between pale clear water and a cliff of dark craggy rock. The light was sunset-ruddy, but there was no sun to be seen anywhere on the horizon. This was the first major discrepancy the Guardians and Hosea had experienced, and Eric could tell it unnerved them a little. But at least this realm was safe for them to pass through—friendly, or at least neutral. This was obviously the domain of some oceangoing branch of the Sidhe, such as the Selkies, or of another aquatic race, such as Undines or Nereids. The upside of this was that sea dwellers tended to be fairly indifferent to humanity, having no interest in them for good or ill. There might be a pretty long walk to the next Gate, but they were unlikely to encounter anything fiercer than a sand crab along the way.

But as they walked along the beach, Eric realized he had other things to worry about than their immediate danger. He'd never really thought about it before, but he'd spent so much time Underhill that he was, if not quite accustomed to its wonders, at least no longer dazzled into slack-jawed amazement by them. It was hard now to remember how astonished he and Beth had been when they'd first seen the halls of Elfhame Misthold, and how long it had taken either of them to get used to (or at least to be able to function around) the sheer beauty of Underhill. Magical, enchanting, and glamorous weren't just empty words to the Sidhe—and "stunning" was pretty relevant, too.

All of which became a problem when four people who'd never seen Underhill before, and who comprised most of your fighting force, were going there to pick a fight with a native on his own turf. While Kayla had been briefly Underhill once before, and Ria had spent half her life in Perenor's pocket domain, neither of them could be considered really experienced with Underhill, either. Even beauty had its dangers.

Eric glanced back over his shoulder. Kayla was openly gawking at the landscape, but she wasn't the one whose reactions really worried him. Paul, José, and Toni were staring around themselves like kids on their first trip to the big city. If their minds were blown by an empty stretch of beach—admittedly a pretty gorgeous beach, but still just a beach—how were they going to react when they got to a place where things got weird—children's-book-illustration, role-playing-game, sci-fi-movie weird?

He didn't know. And there wasn't anything he could do at this point but worry about it. Even drawing attention to his fears might simply make them worse.

"Oh . . . look!" Toni exclaimed in awe. Reaching down, she plucked up a seashell out of the sand. It was as big as her hand, and perfect: a gleaming pale golden color as luminous as a unicorn's horn. She held it up, and the ruddy light made its surface sparkle like an opal.

Paul and José stopped to examine it. All three of them looked . . . spellbound, somehow as if they'd never seen a seashell before and it was the most fascinating thing in the world. If something in Aerune's domain made them freeze up like that, distracted them . . .

We'll all be toast.

"It's beautiful, and wholly unfamiliar," Paul said. "What manner of creature inhabited it, or what its native environment is, are things we may never know. Suddenly the world becomes as vast and uncharted as if we lived a thousand years ago."

Reluctantly, Toni set her prize carefully back down on the sand. She looked around wistfully. "I only wish there were some way I could bring Raoul and Paquito here to see this. It is so beautiful. It seems as if nothing bad could ever happen here."

"When you know the Sidhe a little better, you'll realize that beauty is their greatest weapon. While you're being dazzled, they're sticking a knife in your back, or doing whatever else they damn please."

Though Ria's voice was lightly mocking, there was an undertone of real bitterness in it as well.

Toni looked up at Ria, her dark eyes as startled and hurt as if Ria had interrupted a lovely dream. "So you're saying this is all a sham? A trick?"

"I'm saying it's beside the point—it doesn't count much one way or the other, except to put you off your guard. The ancient Greeks might have thought that what was beautiful had to be good, and vice versa, but I think we've managed to learn a little better in the last 4,000 years. The Sidhe live in a world where magic flows freely and they can alter their appearance and surroundings almost at will. If you can do something like that, the way things look becomes just another tool. Or a weapon."

"I hadn't thought of that." Toni's voice was flat. Disappointed. "I suppose human nature isn't much different even when humans aren't involved. C'mon, folks, let's get a move on. No telling how far we're going to have to walk today." She settled her sword on her shoulder once more and strode off ahead.

Eric glanced across at Ria. Her face was expressionless, except for a coolly-raised eyebrow. *Yeah, I know this looks bad,* Eric told her in his thoughts. *But it was the only idea any of us had. And I'm not sure even a few test runs would have prepared folks for this—and it might have alerted Aerune to our plans.*

"So how come we're taking the scenic route instead of the express?" Kayla wanted to know, thumping Eric on the thigh to get his attention.

"Believe it or not, this *is* the fastest way, or at least the fastest safe way," Eric told her. "There aren't any straight lines through Underhill, not really. It's more like playing Connect The Dots. And based on some of the things Jeanette has told Hosea, one of the important things about finding our way to Aerune's involves not getting killed in the process."

"I'm behind that. But I'd kind of like not to starve to death before we get there."

"Don't worry," Ria called to her from Etienne's back. "I've packed a lunch. And if we choose our Gates carefully, Aerune's kingdom won't be too far from here."

This was one of the smaller domains—at least, the dry land part of it was—and a few minutes more brought them to the next Gate, the one that would take them further into Underhill and possibly to a destination one of them recognized. It lay in the depths of a sea cave hollowed out of the black rock by the unceasing caress of the ocean, the smooth black walls glowing greenly with phosphorescent algae and luminous starfish.

They waded inside through the shallow water, leading the elvensteeds. Kayla stood at the back beside Ria, holding Lady Day's reins. The keys for this Gate were in the form of small seashells embedded in the rock almost at random, but their aura of Power made them easily visible to Eric, and probably to the others as well. Eric and Hosea considered where the Gate might take them.

Hosea's hands fanned over the strings of the banjo, calling forth silvery whispers that echoed in the darkness.

"That one," Hosea said, pointing.

Eric touched it, feeding the Gate with his Bardic Power to activate it. The back wall of the sea cave dissolved as he keyed the Gate, and the seven adventurers could feel a cold wind blowing over them from whatever lay beyond it, but no light spilled through the opening.

Cautiously, Eric and Hosea stepped through into the darkness, followed quickly by the others. The Gate closed when the last of them had passed through, and Eric could feel winter-dry grass crunch beneath his feet. But no matter how hard he strained, he could still see nothing.

A chill monotonous wind blew steadily, making him shudder more than shiver as he looked around blindly, unable to keep from trying to see. If not for the evidence of the sound and feel of the wind, and the dry scent, like musty hay, that assailed his nostrils, he would have wondered if he'd wandered into some trap that had stolen his senses. But only sight was missing.

"Eric . . . ?" Hosea sounded—not frightened, exactly, but *concerned*. The kind of "concerned" where if you don't get answers in a hurry you might start screaming.

"Wait." *I know this place.*

Eric summoned a ball of elf-light, and saw what he had

expected to see: a broad and featureless plain that seemed to stretch a thousand miles in every direction, its short dry dun-colored grass trampled as if herds of animals had been running across it.

Urla had brought Eric here—to what Eric thought of as the Blind Lands—when he was bringing Eric to Aerune. There was a Gate directly into Aerune's domain from here.

Somewhere.

"I get the feeling it isn't a good idea to linger here," Ria said, summoning her own light. Etienne was fidgeting wildly under her, and Eric could tell that Lady Day was equally spooked. The black elvensteed pulled and fretted against Kayla's grip on her reins.

"Me neither," Eric said. "But I don't want to end up right in Aerune's lap, either. I've been here before. The Gate here leads directly into Aerune's domain."

"Does it lead anywhere else?" It was Toni who asked the question. Eric's eyes widened in surprise as he looked at her. The sword in her hand was glowing brighter than the elf-light, the blade as fiery as a bar of burning phosphorus.

"We'll have to find it to tell."

A tremor suddenly shook the ground, as if something heavy— many somethings—ran hard nearby, but even with the elf-light, Eric could see nothing. The two elvensteeds trembled like mad things, eyes rolling and coats dripping with foam, but stood their ground.

Turn back, look for another direction? They could wander Underhill for years and miles and come no closer to Aerune's domain than this—and Jeanette had said that most of the pathways to the Goblin Tower led through worse places.

"We need to get out of here," Paul said, his voice tight. He gestured at Kayla. The young Healer stood, staring around her with eyes wide and terrified. Her fists were clenched at her sides, and her whole body was rigid.

"Everything's *afraid*," she said in a small voice.

As if her words had shaped the thing itself, Eric could suddenly feel the fear pressing in around him, waiting only a kindling spark of their own terror to fill them all with panic. Urla must have had some sort of safe-conduct, to bring him through here unscathed before. The seven of them had nothing.

And Hosea began to play.

The banjo's notes sounded flat, almost muffled. For a moment Eric thought he'd stop, but the novice Bard persisted, playing grimly, almost doggedly. A moment later he began to sing. "*'You couldn't pack a Broadwood half a mile—You mustn't leave a fiddle in the damp—'*"

The sense of panic drew back, as if affronted.

When all else fails, try Kipling. It was "The Song of the Banjo," set to a tune of Hosea's own creation, one as impudent and saucy as its bragging words. Hosea strode forward, moving as easily and certainly as if he knew precisely where he was going. Only Eric saw the strain and concentration on the big man's face, the effort it took to keep his own fear out of his voice and the music.

The chorus came round, and now Ria joined in, her voice soaring bell-like over Hosea's rumbling baritone. Eric joined her, his clear tenor soaring and twining with the other two as though they'd rehearsed for months. Whether by accident, or good guess, Hosea was moving in the direction of the next Gate; Eric walked back to Lady Day and swung up into her saddle. The elvensteed was quieter now, though she still trembled.

Paul handed Kayla up to Eric. She held on tight, and he could feel the shudders that racked her body, but she took a deep breath and added her voice to the others. Eric dug the flute from his gig bag and began to play, the flute weaving its silvery counterpoint into the banjo's sparkling melody as the black mare trotted after Hosea. The music seemed to form a bubble of protection in which they could move safely through the mad blind terror that surrounded them.

They did not dare stop singing. It did not matter that between the light and the music they were attracting the attention of anything within ten miles. It was one of Kipling's longer poems, and Hosea knew every word, but he'd reach the end eventually, and the music they made was the only thing that would keep the Blind Lands' utter despair at bay long enough for them to cross it alive.

The song ended. It was Ria, surprisingly, who saved them then.

"Oh, what do you do with a drunken sailor—" The chantey had dozens of verses, and new ones were easy to make up on the fly. Eric sighed with relief. They could keep this one up for hours—and he had, on occasion.

And so they arrived singing at an enormous henge whose black stones were the size of city buses. Eric dismounted, handing Kayla Lady Day's reins, and advanced upon the Gate.

Only two destinations were coded, the other four left blank, their buttons dark and lifeless. As he touched each of them, an image of the place formed in Eric's mind. One led to Aerune's domain. The other probably led someplace worse—he jerked his fingers back with a gasp, heart hammering, with a confused impression of an arctic wasteland filling his mind. They wouldn't last ten minutes there. The weather alone would kill them.

One or the other, and both choices bad. But Eric was a Bard, and there were four unused destinations available. With skill, and luck, he could make the Gate take them where he chose.

Only he'd have to withdraw his magic from protecting the others to do it.

He had no choice.

He reached out and touched the Gate itself. The stone was as cold as dry ice beneath his fingertips, burning painfully. This must be what Kory, what any of the Sidhe, felt when they touched Cold Iron. He imagined blisters welling up, bursting, the blood freezing as it oozed over this cold burning.

He shut out the pain, reaching into the stone with his magic. Its music was dark, unsettling, sliding off-key in a jangle of minor chords before settling into a new mode for a few seconds. He could feel a dim slumbering mind deep within the stone, passive yet malevolent. An echo of the magic that had formed it. He fought to control the shifting chords he heard in his mind, to make sense of them.

Here.

Yes, here was Aerune's domain. The shape and sense of it filled his mind in a wordless knowing impossible to explain. But that wasn't where he wanted to go. Near it, yes, but outside. Just outside, into the unclaimed Chaos Lands where every stray thought could become real. Had he warned the others about that? Could any warning be enough?

He forced himself to concentrate. To shape the sense of his destination was like transposing music into a different key, adapting a known melody to the needs of an entirely different instrument. With the way into Aerune's domain to guide him, he changed, edited, added, and at last produced what he could only hope was a viable direction.

He opened his eyes, not remembering when he'd closed them, and saw that now three, not two, destinations were marked with a cool blue-green fire on the Gate's surface. How long had he been entranced? His Bard's silks were drenched in sweat, and every muscle ached. He withdrew his hand from the stone, feeling a pang of relief that the skin was whole and unburned. Had the pain been only an illusion? Or would the damage have become reality if he'd failed?

Ria's elf-light and the two Guardians' swords were their only source of light here in the Blind Lands. The singing sounded ragged—they'd moved on to a startlingly bawdy ballad, of which only Ria seemed to know all the words. Hosea's playing sparkled with metronomic precision, but Eric could sense the other Bard's weariness at the unfamiliar exertion.

Wonderful. We're all exhausted before we start. Great tactics, Banyon.

But there'd been no other way. They couldn't Gate directly to their destination, and they couldn't drive there either—or ride. This was the best they could do. Maybe they could win a breathing space before Aerune noticed them. *God, I sure hope so. He won't even break a sweat if he takes us on while we're in this condition.*

But to delay here a moment longer than they absolutely had to would be fatal, with only their magic to protect them from the baleful influence of this realm. Eric took a deep breath and keyed the Gate to the destination he'd chosen. The opening shivered and went white. The glare made his eyes water after so long in the Blind Lands. He waved the others forward.

SIXTEEN:
WELCOME TO MY NIGHTMARE

"So where are we now?" Toni wanted to know, resting her longsword point first against the ground and leaning upon its quillons. She took a deep breath of relief, seeming to regain more strength with each passing moment.

Everything around them was grayish-white and misty, with the flat even illumination of indirect lighting, or of sunlight on a very cloudy day. Even the ground beneath their feet was colorless and springy, as if it were made of modeling clay.

Hosea stopped playing, and the banjo's silver strings whispered to silence. He rubbed his fingers, grinning at Eric reassuringly.

Eric grinned back—it had worked! They were all here, all safe—or as safe as you could be in the Chaos Lands. And they could find another way home.

"We're . . . exactly nowhere," he said in answer to Toni's question. She made a face. "No, seriously. This is what Underhill looks like when nobody decides to impose their own reality on it. They call it the Chaos Lands."

"Which means that nobody here better think too hard," Ria

658

said, "because whatever you think about is likely to come walking out of that mist and bite you."

"We're shielded, of course," Paul said. "I'd say that being here is pretty similar to casting a spell—the magician had better keep a tight rein on his intention. But that may make it a little hard for Aerune to find us when the time is right."

"Oh, he'll find us," Ria said darkly.

"I don't think Aerune will notice us until we make him," Eric said hopefully. "Let's take a breather. Is everyone okay?"

The others nodded. The Guardians looked shaken, but not as worn down by their ordeal as Eric had feared. José was his usual imperturbable self, Paul looked like a cat with a new toy, and Hosea and Toni were looking better by the minute. Even Kayla managed a grin and an impudent thumbs-up when he looked at her. She reached down to pat Lady Day's neck, and the black elvensteed shook herself and tossed her head, making the silver bells on her tack jingle.

I wonder why she chose to be black for this trip? Eric thought. The question wasn't an idle one. Elvensteeds could look like anything they chose and Lady Day usually had a reason for choosing to be a particular color or shape.

"Everything's just ginger-peachy," Kayla said sardonically, swinging a leg over Lady Day's back and dropping to the ground. "Sheesh! And I thought L.A. had some bad neighborhoods."

"Jeanette says there're worse ones here. Much worse," Hosea said.

"I don't want to go there," Kayla answered simply.

Ria dismounted from Etienne, patting the elvensteed on the neck. The white mare was ghostly, almost insubstantial, in the formlessness of the Chaos Lands. It was good camouflage. She nuzzled her mistress as Ria reached into one of the saddlebags and pulled out a two-quart hiker's canteen.

"Water, anyone?" she asked, passing the canteen to Kayla.

The teenager twisted off the cap and drank thirstily, passing the canteen to Hosea. "Good job with the tunes, stud," she said.

Hosea actually blushed, pulling out a bandanna to wipe his face.

"It wasn't anything more than a bit of plinking. If I thought this Aerune'd answer to that kind of medicine, the rest of you could have stayed home."

"So what do we do now?" José asked, looking from Toni to Eric.

Eric reached into the bottom of his gig bag for the little wooden box. He opened it and took out the maze-seed. Its magic buzzed in his hand like a trapped honeybee, stronger now that it was back in the world it had been made for. All they had to do now was get Aerune here and trap him inside.

"We call him," Eric said grimly. "And then we lock him up forever."

Aerune mac Audelaine, born to the Bright Court, later called among mortalkind the Lord of Death and Pain, sat in his dark throne room in the heart of the Goblin Tower, contemplating his own thoughts.

The encounter with the upstart Bard should have been more satisfying. Certainly it had been an elegant insult to gift him with Aerune's mortal hellhound, knowing that her dying would wound the soft-hearted mortal far more than the loss of her would inconvenience Aerune. But there was something about the whole matter that left Aerune feeling vaguely unsettled, as if he had made some unfortunate mistake.

But there had been no mistake. The hound's death was meaningless and completely inevitable, once he had lifted the spell of timelessness that kept her alive in mortal lands. She had never been more than a diversion for Aerune, her real worth lying in his ability to withhold her skills from his foes. It was true that he had so far forgotten himself to boast of his plans to the mortals, but again, there was no loss to him in doing so. Though the conspiracy was small and inconsequential now, what he had set in motion in the World of Iron would thrive—with his help—until it had consumed humanity utterly. Aerune was an excellent judge of men, and he had chosen Parker Wheatley well. The man's ambition and self-hatred would lead him to follow Aerune's plans blindly, unable to see anything beyond his own immediate advantage. The simple toys with which Aerune had provided Wheatley had helped to befool him—artifacts from an Underhill realm where the memory of magic lost had caused the inhabitants to craft ever more subtle engines to counterfeit its actions. As the first small blemish upon the apple presages the destruction of the entire fruit, so did Wheatley's first faltering acts herald humanity's doom—a war against the Underhill realms which would cause the Sidhe, both Bright Court and Dark, to rise up and destroy the World Above.

No, all went forward as it should—but in that case, wherein lay his unease? No enemy raised its banners before his gates, nor sought to gain entry into his realm by treachery.

But there was something . . . something well-known to the point of invisibility, that teased his ethereal senses with its elusive familiarity.

From the magic that surrounded him, Aerune formed a familiar, a part of himself in the shape of a great black bird, and sent it forth to search. It soared over the bone-wood, finding nothing, and he sent it through his Gate to the Chaos Lands beyond, searching.

There!

The hound. *His* hound. His toy and victim, here—Underhill—and alive!

Infuriated by the insult, Aerune sought no further. He strode from his throne room in a black fury, shouting for his horse and his hounds. He would reclaim her, whip her to his kennels, and make her beg for the death he would forever deny her.

The first hint they had of disaster was when the landscape around them began to darken. The mist boiled away to emptiness at the touch of another's mind.

:Trouble . . . : whispered the banjo. *:He's coming.:*

There was no need to ask who.

The Guardians formed a circle around Kayla, facing outward. Ria and Eric stood outside it, preparing to take the first assault. Eric heard a crashing major chord—someone opening a Portal—and then Aerune was there, astride his black stallion. Giant black dogs crouched at his horse's feet, and behind him, changing and nebulous as fog, rode the hosts of the damned, called from nothingness by the power of Aerune's will.

"Fascinating," Paul said. There was a hiss as he pulled his blade free of the sword cane. "A classical Northern European Wild Hunt."

Aerune glanced at him, eyes blazing red, but Paul did not hold his interest. Toni did. The Latina Guardian held her sword in her left hand as she crossed herself, her lips moving in soundless prayer.

"So . . . you would use your iron nails to slay Faerie?" Aerune growled. "Die as all who have set the White Christ's magic against me have died!"

Eric was barely fast enough to shield Toni from Aerune's first attack—*crash of major chords, high skirl of a piccolo, deep booming of a chorus of horns*—but somehow he couldn't draw Aerune's attention to him no matter what he did. Something about Toni infuriated Aerune to the point of recklessness. He concentrated his fury upon her, and she barely held her own, though her blade glowed so brightly that Eric couldn't even look in her direction. He had problems of his own, though—the shadowy creatures that rode with Aerune—monsters and damned souls all, if the legends held any truth—were spreading out to encircle them. He moved forward, searching for an opening, his fingers clutched around the maze-seed, raising it up and—

—rubbing the smoothing stone gently along the shaft of the bone flute.

The afternoon sun was warm against his back as he squatted here in the clearing in the center of the crescent of turf huts that made up the village of his people, and from time to time he would stop, holding his work up to the light so he could judge his progress. Once he had scraped the bone smooth it would be time to drill the holes along its length with a sharp deer-horn drill, then polish it again with fine sand and deer hide until it was as smooth as river-tumbled stone, then rub it with beeswax until the bone turned a translucent gold. When he was but an apprentice Bard, his teacher had told him it was important to make the bone as thin as possible so that the sound would be pure, and he had always remembered that. Only the very best was worthy to be offered up to the Bright Lady Aerete, source of all Bardcraft and magic.

Eric frowned, his thoughts elsewhere. They would need their best if they were to win their next battle with the Eastmen, who had come to the Isle of the Blessed in their wooden boats to kill and enslave the Folk, armed with weapons of the gray metal that broke stone and bronze as if they were nothing more than rotted wood.

But they would win. Eric was a Bard of a Hundred Songs, blessed by the Lady herself, and his apprentice, whose instrument was the harp, had already learned his spells and genealogies, and had made a good start on learning the songs which contained all the wisdom of the Folk. In the doorway of their hut he could see Hosea putting fine new strings of deer gut upon his bride-harp, whose white body was carved from the shoulder of a black bull which had been slain at the start of the Dark Year. His songs could soothe the sick and ailing, ease a wounded soul's transition to the Summer Lands.

Reluctantly, Eric set aside his work, wrapping it tightly in a painted doeskin to keep it safe. He could not spend as much time as he wished here. It was time to go among the wounded once more, to add his magic to the Healers' craft. Too many of their village's warriors lay wounded, kissed by the deathmetal of the Eastmen despite all the protection spells Eric had laid upon them.

He got to his feet. Hosea looked up, willing to follow, but Eric gestured for him to stay. It was more important now that he finish restringing the harp, so he could play their warriors into good heart for the morrow. Meanwhile, Eric would see to their wounded.

Eric walked through the village, greeting his clan-fellows. His creature was the lark, as was fitting for a Bard, for birds were especially sacred to the Bright Lords. All bowed their heads in respect, for a Bard was second only to the Lady herself, and the equal of kings and the Chief of all the clans.

The High House was his destination. The great hall stood upon the earthen mound his ancestors had erected when they had first come to this land, beneath which, in vaults of dressed stone, their dead—too many dead, these days—were laid to rest to provide counsel and wisdom to their children. He walked up the hill, toward its carven gateway painted with the totem animals of each clan of the tribe, along the path bordered in white stones.

Ria, chief of the fighting women, approached him as he neared the door. She wore a loincloth of white doeskin, and gold at her throat and upon her arms, for she was a lady of high rank and a king's daughter. Her hair was braided into one long queue, wrapped with a red cord and studded with the raven feathers of her totem. The marks of warrior's magic still showed, pale azure against her fair skin. Tonight she and the other warriors would dance to his playing, singing the war-songs and painting themselves afresh for tomorrow's battle.

"I greet you, Bard," she said formally, though Eric could see that she seethed with impatience at being denied entry. Those whole in body, and not bound to the Bright Lords as Eric was, were not permitted to enter the High House when there were injured present, lest their war magic disturb the healing magic.

"I greet you, Ria of the warriors," he answered. "How may I serve you?" *I would serve you in all ways I have not pledged to the Lady, did you but allow it.*

"I would know how it will go with us upon the morrow," she answered, her voice as harsh as that of the battle-raven.

"Only the Bright Lords may know that," Eric said sharply, for in truth he was afraid to look into the future again for fear he would see another defeat. "Ask of the Lady, not of me."

He frowned, seeming for a moment to hear the echoes of battle in another place, but surely it was only the ghosts of the newly slain, hovering among their kinfolk to give what comfort they could before making their journey to the Summer Lands to dwell forever with Aerete in her shining palace.

Ria sighed, as if he had given her only the answer she expected. "Then tell me how my sword-sister, Toni, fares, of your courtesy, Bard. I would sorrow to go into battle without her to drive my chariot."

Eric smiled, glad to be able to give some good news. Toni had taken a blow from a deathmetal sword in the last battle, but had killed her attacker with her spear. The cut was healing nicely, without fever.

"You will have no cause for sorrow," he said, "for she will be at your side. The Lady wills it."

The Bright Lady Aerete had been tireless in employing her healing magics for the good of the tribe, and many more than had died in the battles would have been lost without her protection. But no one was all-powerful, not even the Bright Lords, and even her power could not save those whom deathmetal had wounded too deeply. Fortunately, Toni's cut had been shallow.

"That makes good hearing," Ria said. "I will leave you to your work."

She bowed to him formally and turned away, walking down the path to the village through the pale spring sunlight. Eric watched after her for a long time, before turning and ducking through the hanging hides that shielded the doorway to enter the High House.

Inside, a peat fire smoked fragrantly on the round stone hearth, giving heat to the injured. He could see Paul and José moving among them, bringing healing brews and changing the poultices upon wounded limbs. The Lady Aerete had taught them all that mortals could learn of her healing magics, and even Eric stood in awe of their power, that could trick Death when even his songs could not.

He went first to Toni, who was drinking soup from a wooden cup. She smiled when she saw him, though her dark eyes were shadowed by recent pain.

"Ria was asking after you, warrior," Eric told her, smiling as he knelt beside her. "I told her you would be with her soon."

"The healers say I may leave the High House at sunset," Toni told him proudly. "And I will stand with her at the war-fire tonight."

"And ride with her to victory on the morrow," Eric said, feigning a confidence he did not feel. Toni was Ria's charioteer, and such brave warriors, who rode into battle unprotected by bull's-hide shield, faced greater peril even than the foot spearmen.

Suddenly the air was filled with music, and Toni's face lit with pleasure. "Ah, Bard, see—the Lady comes!"

Eric got to his feet, turning toward the dais of limewashed stone that stood at the north end of the High House. A light as bright as the sun shone there, and as it faded, the form of Aerete the Golden was revealed.

She wore a white gown woven of Underhill magic, and her long golden hair was garlanded with blue flowers that shone as brightly as the stars in the night sky. Their perfume filled the High House, mingling with the scent of peat smoke and healing herbs. She was more beautiful than any woman of the Folk, tall and supernaturally fair, and her long graceful ears proclaimed her Otherworldly lineage plain for all to see. Since before Time began, Aerete had been their Lady, guarding and guiding them, protecting them from the dark spirits of glade and pool. She had taught them the arts of music and poetry, of healing and metalworking, protecting women in childbed and sending game to the hunters' nets. She was Aerete, and they were her people.

Eric knelt in reverence, as did Paul and José. Aerete moved slowly among the wounded, pausing to caress a bowed head or bring ease to a painful wound. At last She came to where Eric knelt, and he shuddered with pleasure at the touch of Her hand. All he asked from life was to serve Her, who was so wise and just.

Again that moment of discordant music. But when he looked up into Her sky-colored eyes, the pang of unease faded.

"Bard," She said, and Her voice was a melody. "Walk with Me, and tell Me how goes the day."

Jesus. Kayla made a rude noise of disgust. She didn't know who the blonde elf-bimbo was, but the way Eric was looking at her made Kayla want to puke. He was practically *drooling.*

She aimed a hearty kick at his backside, but though she felt it jar through her as she connected, he didn't react.

None of them reacted. Not Eric, not Ria, not José or Paul. Even Hosea hadn't noticed her, no matter what she did.

It was creepy. One moment they'd been in Hell's Own Kitchen, with Aerune about to eat them all for breakfast, and the next minute . . . here, in some kind of place that looked like a cross between a retro *Braveheart* and *Merlin: The Lost Years.* The whole *Quest For Fire* look had been amusing for about five minutes—who'd'a thought José was so buff under all those workshirts?—but the whole body paint and loincloths thing got old real fast. Everything looked real, felt real, smelled real—but her friends couldn't see or hear her. She wasn't even a ghost.

What had Aerune done to them? Was this real—whatever "real" meant, when used in the same sentence with "Underhill"? And if Aerune was behind this, shouldn't there be more dead people around? Shouldn't *they* be dead?

Helpless, angry, and far more frightened than she was willing to admit, Kayla trailed after Eric and the elf-lady. Everybody was talking like an episode of *Masterpiece Theater*—as if they'd forgotten all their usual words. Hosea'd even lost his homefolks accent, and Kayla would have been willing to bet good money this morning that wasn't possible.

And Eric . . . ! Eric didn't *grovel,* which was what his conversation with this "Aerete"-bimbo sounded like to Kayla. It was like they'd all been replaced by pod people. And if they had, why wasn't she included?

Were they dead? Was *she* dead? *And if not, could I just wake up and go home? Please?*

She trailed farther and farther behind Eric and Aerete, not having the stomach to listen to them. If Eric was groveling, then Aerete was talking to him like he was the family dog—kindly enough, but not as if she was particularly impressed by his intelligence.

Kayla passed the hut where she'd seen Hosea before, but he wasn't there. Probably off making daisy chains or something.

:Kayla . . . :

She stopped with a gasp. Someone was calling her from inside the hut—a faint voice, almost a whisper—but when she went in, there wasn't anyone there, just a bunch of bearskins and the harp Hosea'd been working on before, sitting on top of the pile.

:Kayla!:

It was the harp.

"Okay, the harp is talking to me."

:It's Jeanette.: The harp sounded impatient. *:Can you hear me? Kayla, this isn't real.:*

"News flash," the young Healer muttered, going over to pick up the harp. When she touched it, she almost dropped it—it was warm, and seemed to vibrate faintly in Kayla's hands. "So it isn't real. I got that. So what is it?"

:I don't know. I think Aerune's dreaming. They don't sleep, you know, but they dream sometimes while they're awake. And he's caught the others up in his dream.:

Elves dreamt awake, she meant. But somehow the humans had gotten caught in it.

"So why not you or me?" Kayla asked.

:I'm dead:, the harp whispered, and Kayla could swear the thing sounded smug about it. *:And I don't know. Maybe you can fix whatever he does to you before it affects you.:*

Wonderful. "What do I do? We have to get out of here," Kayla announced, hating the fear she heard in her own voice.

:Follow Aerete. Maybe she'll lead you to Aerune and you can find out what's going on. Maybe you can wake the others up . . . :

The harp's whispering speech stopped. Kayla stared at it for a long moment, then set it down gently and ran out of the hut, looking around wildly. Aerete and Eric were standing a few yards away, talking. She leaned down and kissed him on the forehead, the way a mother might kiss a small child. Then he turned back toward the village, and she walked on.

Kayla hesitated, unsure about which of the two to follow, then shrugged. Might as well take Jeanette's advice. How could she be in worse trouble than she was now? She sprinted after Aerete.

If she'd hoped Aerete would be able to see her, Kayla's hopes were quickly dashed. The woman walked on as if she were alone, though Kayla was beside her close enough to touch her dress. The elf-woman's destination seemed to be a ring of standing stones that stood on the crest of a low hill. They weren't all that impressive by Stonehenge standards—the tallest of them came up only to Kayla's shoulder—but if you had to find them, dig them up, and hump them up to the top of the hill with muscle power alone, she guessed they represented a considerable effort. The hill was taller than it looked, too. By the time they reached the top, Kayla was panting, though her companion showed no sign of strain.

Aerete walked into the ring of stones and vanished.

For a moment Kayla stood watching, unable to decide what to do; then, muttering curses, she followed.

There was the eye-blink transition she'd gotten used to going through the Gates. She was in a hall. It was like the one back in the village—round with a round firepit in the middle—but everything here was of finer construction, as though someone had taken the other and improved upon it. *Eric says the elves can't create things, only change them. So I guess if this is the Bronze Age, they've got to be Bronze Age elves.* The walls here were of polished golden oak, and the torches set in the walls in golden brackets burned with a clear smokeless flame. Where the dais had been back at the High House was a block of polished white marble draped with bright silks, and on it were two chairs—Roman, by the look of them—and a table with a goblet and decanter on it.

Aerune was sitting in one of the chairs.

Kayla shrank back with a hiss of dismay, but he didn't seem to see her. He was looking at Aerete. Kayla studied him. Aerune looked different than the dark monster she had faced twice before. He wore a golden crown around his forehead, and was dressed in tunic, leggings, and boots in shades of green and gray.

Aerete walked forward until she stood at the foot of the dais, and knelt. Aerune sprang to his feet to raise her up.

"Aerete, my heart—you must never kneel to me!"

"But I would ask for your help, Lord Aerune," Aerete said, and there was real pain in her voice for the first time.

Guess she can drop the Lady of the Manor act here.

"Anything—you know you have my heart, Aerete. What can you ask for that I would not give you?" Aerune told her passionately.

"Kindness for my people, Lord Aerune."

Kayla saw him wince, as if Aerete had touched on a sore point. "They are not worthy of your love, my heart. Creatures of mud who return to the mud in the wink of an eye. How can we, who are formed of the stuff of stars, care for such as they?" There was pleading in his voice, as though it was an old argument he knew he couldn't win.

"I had hoped your love for me had softened your heart, my lord Aerune," Aerete said softly. She settled into the chair he offered her, and Aerune hurried to pour her a cup of wine.

"Have I not avoided their villages at your request? No longer does my Hunt ride among them. I take neither their children nor their maidens for my sport, all because you have asked it of me. Tell me what troubles you," Aerune begged, leaning toward her.

He really loves her, Kayla realized, impressed. She knew that Aerune was old even as the Sidhe reckoned years, and that what she was seeing now had happened a long time ago, if it had ever happened at all, but right now Aerune seemed a lot like the bangers she'd known back in East L.A.—proud, touchy, desperately in love and afraid of looking stupid.

He seemed very young, somehow. Young, and vulnerable.

"They *die*," Aerete said sorrowfully. "They die and I can do nothing to save them. Strangers from across the water invade their lands, and harry them far worse than *you* ever did, Aerune. Many die, and I am powerless to save them. I have gone to the chief of the Eastmen and asked for peace. The Isle of the Blessed is wide, and surely there is room for all to live there in peace. But he does not know our kind, and there is a strangeness about these Eastmen. My magic has no power to soften his heart."

"Let me rip it from his chest, and you will find it soft enough, Bright Lady," Aerune said. Aerete sighed and turned her face away, bowing her head.

"They live so short a time—must we take even their brief span of years from them? I want peace, Aerune, not more death."

Aerune sighed and shook his head—unwilling to say anything that would hurt her, but certain he was right, Kayla could tell.

"The mortalkind are not like us, Aerete. Their lives burn as hot and bright—and brief—as the fires they kindle upon the hills in spring, and their hearts seethe with emotions so raw and ardent that to feel one tenth of their passion would destroy any of Danu's

Firstborn. Their lives are too short for them to value life; they spend their hatreds thoughtlessly, welcoming the death they have not the wit to understand. And so I tell you plainly—the only comfort your folk may find is in death. And the only peace you can find for your mortal pets is in the death of their enemies."

Aerete bowed her head. "I know you would never lie to me. But is it the only way to save them? I had hoped for another answer."

"Would you bring them Underhill and dare Oberon's wrath for your disobedience?" Aerune asked. "Or fly for sanctuary to the Dark and put yourself and them at the mercy of Queen Morrigan? The halls of the Dark Court are not for such as you, my love. I have walked them. I know."

"Then must they die?" Aerete asked, and Kayla saw tears glittering in her eyes. "Must they all die?"

"They must fight against the Eastmen, and live as best they may," Aerune answered. "Only with the death of their enemies can they live as you hope them to."

Aerete rose to her feet, her face sad. "I thank you for your wise counsel, Lord Aerune. I must go now. They face their enemy in battle on the morrow, and I would not deny them what comfort I may give them in the little time that remains."

"Will you come to me again?" Aerune asked her eagerly, reaching for her hand. She clung to him a moment, as if drawing strength from his touch, then pulled away.

"When the battle is done. When they are safe, Lord Aerune, I will come to you again."

This is bad, Kayla thought. For all Aerune's fancy talk about not having human feelings, she could tell he loved Aerete with all his heart. *I've got to warn him that she's gonna die tomorrow—*

But suddenly Aerune's hall was gone. Kayla stood upon a hillside overlooking a wide valley through which a shallow stream meandered. It was early morning, and she shivered with cold even with the protection of her mail tunic. Mist still covered the ground, and the sun hovered just above the horizon. Below her, on the hill, she could see the warriors of the village gathered in battle array—chariots at the front, pikemen behind. She saw Ria and Toni in one of the chariots, Eric standing beside them with a flute in his hand, his hair garlanded with flowers. Hosea, Paul, and José were at the back, among the spear carriers. There were too many people here to count, but less than a hundred, Kayla thought. *More like one of those SCA events Elizabet took me to in L.A. than a real army.*

And across the valley, five times their number. The enemy wore armor, not painted skins, and she could see strong wooden shields and spear tips glittering with metal.

They're gonna get creamed!

There was a shimmer and a flash of light, and suddenly Aerete was there beside Eric. She was mounted bareback upon a white elvensteed, dressed now in the fashion of her people, wearing nothing more than the white doeskin loincloth and short red-dyed leather cape that her lady warriors wore into battle. Painted runes gleamed on her skin, as blue and bright as neon, and her hair was braided and feathered as theirs was. She obviously meant to ride into battle with her warriors, to ensure their victory by fighting beside them. Was she that brave—or did she not know what the iron spears the enemy carried could do against elven magic?

"No! Don't do it!" Kayla shouted, running down the hill toward the war host.

But before she could reach them, a horn blew from somewhere in the ranks of the villagers, answered by a deeper horn from the other side of the valley. A cheer went up, and the chariots began to roll down the hill. As the enemy saw the host begin to move, they began to howl, beating their swords against their wooden shields with a sound like distant thunder, surging forward to meet their foes.

Kayla barely reached the bottom of the hill—too late to stop the charge—when the first bright agony lanced through her as one of the spears found its mark. She had one brief moment to realize that coming to a battle was probably a pretty stupid thing for a Healer to do.

She concentrated on her shields, gritting her teeth and forcing herself to stand where she was, willing herself not to feel. In moments the orderliness of both armies had dissolved, and there was only a mob of men and women armed with swords and spears trying to kill each other. Aerete was in the forefront of the charge, as visible as if God was shining his own spotlight on her, and even in the brightening day Kayla could see the flashes of blue fire as she struck at the enemy with her levin-bolts. Kayla felt every strike, every sword-blow, that either army landed, but distantly, as if the pain were being felt by someone else. *Shunt it aside,* Elizabet had told her. *Be the rock in the stream, unharmed by the water's flow.*

Kayla was glad to be so far away that she could not see what was happening clearly. What she could hear was bad enough—the screams of people and horses, the dull thick sound of metal hitting meat. She held her breath, crying without knowing it, digging her fingers into the palms of her hands. What could possibly be worth this much pain? Couldn't they see—couldn't they *feel*—what they were doing to each other?

For a while it seemed as if Aerete's presence would be enough to gain victory for her folk. Despite their superior weapons and numbers, the enemy had little taste for facing one of the Sidhe upon the battlefield, and stayed away from her as much as possible, allowing the spearhead of Aerete's warriors to plunge deep into the shield line. But Kayla knew how this story ended.

She didn't see who threw the spear. She only saw the moment when Aerete's white horse plunged sideways, the moment when its shining rider fell to earth. There were groans and cries of dismay from Aerete's folk; Kayla watched through tear-blurred eyes as they clustered around, trying to save her. But the blow delivered by the spearhead of Cold Iron was mortal.

Suddenly the sky darkened, as if there were about to be a thunderstorm, though a moment before the sky had been clear. Cold winds whipped up, driving black clouds before them, covering the sky. Aerune appeared, standing where Aerete had fallen. He knelt beside her and saw that she was dead, then rose to his feet with a howl of despair that could be heard above every other sound upon the battlefield.

And then he began to kill.

Kayla watched in horrified fascination, unable to look away. He must know now that the weapons the enemy carried could kill him, but it didn't seem to matter to him. None of them touched him or the creatures he summoned to aid him—black wolves the size of ponies, ravens bigger than the biggest eagle ever hatched. It was like watching something out of a horror movie, like watching a harvester move over a field of standing grain. Aerune moved across the field, his sword spinning in his hand, and every time it struck an enemy died.

The Eastmen would have fled or surrendered, but Aerune did not let them. His creatures harried them from behind, keeping them on the battlefield, herding the invaders toward Aerune's sword as the storm he had summoned gathered and finally broke, the rain turning the blood-soaked battlefield to a sea of red mud. In the end, the Eastmen were fighting one another to stay away from him, killing nearly as many of their own in their frantic attempts as Aerune did.

Aerete's people watched in stunned amazement, the survivors of their army standing huddled together about their fallen lady. At the bottom of the hill, Kayla watched it all, battered by their pain and grief, too numb to think about what she was seeing. It was so horrible it was unreal.

It's a dream, it's a dream, oh please please please *let it be a dream—*

At last no Eastmen were left alive. Aerune turned back in the direction of his fallen love, and saw her people gathered around her, weeping. For a moment he hesitated, and Kayla held her breath.

Then he slew them all, lashing out at them with levin-bolts until none stood, howling his anguish over the sound of the storm. Kayla screamed too—no shielding could withstand such agony. She fell to the wet grass, trying not to see what she could not help seeing. She saw the Guardians die, Eric and Ria and Hosea all cut down by Aerune's madness, and screamed until her throat was raw.

And then the storm and the screaming was gone, as if someone had changed the channel.

For long moments she was too stunned to care, huddling in a tight ball of misery, feeling the anguish of the dead vibrate along her nerves. She tried to breathe as Elizabet had taught her—slow deep breaths that drew strength from the earth and let the pain flow away— but it was hard. She choked and gasped, fighting against herself, until at last she found the rhythm. Slowly her muscles relaxed, and the memory of the pain eased. At last Kayla came back to herself enough to realize that her eyes were closed, and opened them warily.

The sun of an unblemished spring day shone down upon the small village. She was huddled beside the well, curled against its rough warm stone. In the doorway of a nearby hut, Eric and Hosea worked on their instruments. She pulled herself to her feet and leaned against the sun-warmed stone, dizzy with nausea and disorientation. The screams of the dying still echoed in her ears, but the battle had been wiped away as if it had never been.

Because it has *never been. It's still in the future, from here. This is the way it started when the Chaos Lands went away. This is where I was when it began. Oh, God, is it all going to happen again? I can't watch that happen again. I can't!*

Maybe she *was* dead, because living the same two days over and over again, with the same terrible ending, was a pretty good approximation of hell, in Kayla's opinion. She took a deep steadying breath, welcoming anger.

No. It ain't gonna work out that way. This time I'm gonna make them hear me if I hafta grab each one of them and wrestle 'em to the ground to do it!

"Jeanette!" she shouted at the top of her lungs, but the harp that was Jeanette Campbell's form in this world was in Hosea's hands. Unstrung. Voiceless.

Kayla wasn't in the mood to let something like that stop her. She wanted to talk to Jeanette, and concentrated with all her fear and frustration, all her Healer's power, on making that happen.

"What?"

Jeanette walked around the well and stopped in front of Kayla, hands on hips. She was hard to look at; her form kept shifting back and forth between the sleek leather-clad hellhound that Aerune had made of her, and a dumpy irritated woman in a leather jacket and jeans. Neither form seemed really real.

"Why are we back here?" Kayla asked hoarsely. "If this is Aerune's way of attacking us, he won. So why do we have to start over?"

"Oh, you aren't dead yet," Jeanette said airily. "Out there you're still fighting. None of you will stay dead here until he kills you there."

"That's comforting," Kayla muttered shakily. *Even if trying to think about it makes my head want to explode.*

"Of course, each time he kills the others here, he weakens them there. It's quite elegant, really. As for you, you might just go mad, seeing the same disaster happen over and over." Jeanette sounded wistful, as if death were something desirable.

Should'a thought of that before you decided to become a banjo until the end of time! "You are being so fabulously helpful," Kayla said through gritted teeth. "I thought you wanted to make up for killing all those people."

"I don't know *how!*" ghost-Jeanette cried in real exasperation. "I'm no good at being nice—only at knowing things and telling them to people if they want to listen. If you want to change things, you've got to make the others realize this is a dream. There's no point trying to wake up Aerete or any of the other villagers. Only Aerune or the people you came with can deviate from the script, because they're the only ones who are *real.* And if you wake them up *here*, it might distract them enough so he kills them *there.* And then he'll have you." Jeanette shuddered and bowed her head. "Don't let him. Die first."

"But you know what's going on in both places," Kayla said. Jeanette nodded reluctantly. "So tell Hosea *there*, so he can tell the others, while I try to wake them up *here*. Are you with me, Banjo Girl?"

"You say it like it's so easy," Jeanette said sullenly. "It might not *work*—don't you understand? If I try, if I do it wrong, I could kill them!"

"That's what you're here for," Kayla said grimly. "To try. Do it."

Jeanette turned away, and her jangling discordant image vanished. Kayla was alone again in Fantasyland.

What do I do? What do I do? She felt a panicky flutter in her chest. It wasn't as if she was a stranger to tough situations and sudden death, but this time she wasn't just fighting to keep herself or her friends alive in a place where she knew what the ground rules were. She was trapped in a dream world whose rules she didn't understand. It wasn't enough to get out—if she couldn't figure out the *right* way out, she and all her friends would be tortured to death, and then Aerune would start on everyone else. Everyone she'd ever met. Everyone she'd ever known. Just . . . everyone.

The pressure made her feel ill, made her want to go off somewhere and hide and pretend it wasn't happening. And if she did that for long enough, everything would come crashing down and she'd never have to try . . . and fail.

She wished with all her heart that she could believe she was going to do that.

She squared her shoulders and headed over to where Eric sat.

"Eric." She kicked at the squatting figure halfheartedly. He didn't move. *"Eric!"*

That didn't work either.

How did you wake someone up who was already awake? It was like trying to heal somebody who wasn't hurt.

Hurt . . . heal . . .

Eric wasn't hurt, but he certainly wasn't all right. Could she tap into the power she used to heal to rouse him to wakefulness? And if she did, would it doom him in whatever passed for the Real World here?

If it's a choice of dying quick or dying slow, I know which one Elizabet's favorite apprentice picks. . . .

She stepped up behind him, and hesitated. Healing someone was easy—or at least, it was natural to her. The injury itself was what called forth her power, and though she directed its use, its scope was defined by what it healed. Most of a Healer's training involved learning to *not* use her power: to shield, to disengage, to hold herself back in the face of a serious hurt, lest in trying to heal it, she spent all of her own life-force.

Now she was essentially trying to call up that power without that sort of stimulus, doing consciously what she normally left to instinct and reflex. It was like trying to figure out what you needed to do in order to walk. Biting her lip, Kayla touched her fingers to Eric's temples, trying to push the power out through her skin. For a moment nothing happened, then it welled up and rushed out of her as if she'd pulled the cork out of a bottle.

Eric, wake up! Eric, see me! And try not to get killed in the process, she added as an afterthought.

Eric jerked as if he'd been stung. He turned and looked up at her, his eyes foggy and unfocused. "Who are you?" he said blankly. He didn't know her, but at least he saw her. That was a start.

"I'm Kayla. You're Eric—Eric *Banyon*. None of this is real, Eric—it's some kind of a dream!"

"We're all dreaming," he told her kindly, getting to his feet. "Are you a spirit?"

Kayla ground her teeth. He could see her, but the rest didn't look promising. "I'm your friend. New York—the Guardians—Aerune—Hosea—remember?"

"Hosea is my apprentice," Eric told her, still with that maddening kindly smile, like he'd joined some kind of mind-control cult. "Have you come to bring him visions? I think he will be a very powerful Bard, when he is trained."

"I think you are all going to *die* tomorrow, if you don't get with the program! This is Aerune's nightmare, and it's only got one ending. You've got to change that!"

"Your words are strange," Eric said. "And your clothes are, too."

Look who's talking. "Eric, *please,* try to grow a brain! Remember Aerune, the psychopath on the big black horsie? This is his dream. He's cast some kind of spell on you to make you forget."

"I forget nothing!" Eric snapped, suddenly very haughty. "Spirit, I am a Bard of a Hundred Songs."

Kayla wanted to shake him. "Then be a Bard! Wake up! Try to remember—you, and Hosea, and Ria, and the other Guardians—Aerune's got you all playing roles in his dreams, but you've got to make the dream come out differently."

"Ah." Comprehension seemed to dawn, and for a moment

Kayla believed she'd reached him, until his next words made her heart sink. "You come to bring word of the future. Tell me, Spirit, what shall I do to save our folk?"

"Tomorrow the Eastmen are going to kill Aerete. You have to stop them."

"Aerete the Golden cannot die." Now Eric looked troubled, but he was worrying about the wrong thing. "She is one of the Bright Lords. No weapon made by men can harm her."

"Iron can. The Eastmen are carrying iron weapons. She's going to die."

"Master?" Hosea came over to Eric. "Master, you speak to the air."

"A spirit has come to foretell the battle," Eric said, turning to Hosea. Kayla tried not to look—it seemed as if wherever this was, it was strictly clothing optional.

"Do we win?" Hosea asked.

Kayla saw the sorrow in Eric's eyes, and knew he was going to lie.

"Yes. She promises us a great victory."

Hosea smiled with relief. "We should tell the others."

"Tell Aerete!" Kayla urged, knowing that warning her would do no good. Eric had his stubborn look on—*that* hadn't changed—and she could tell he'd made up his mind not to pay any attention to her. She turned to Hosea, grabbing his arm.

"Hey! Farmboy! *Look at me!*" The power flowed out of her more easily this time, as if it had learned what to do.

Hosea's eyes focused on her and alarm replaced relief. "*Kayla?*"

"Hosea—remember Jeanette! None of this is real! It's a dream that repeats over and over—you have to change the ending or we aren't going to be able to get out of here to fight Aerune!"

"Eric." The big man moved slowly, as if he were under water. "Eric, it's Kayla. Wake up. Jeanette says . . ."

For a moment the world shimmered, and Kayla caught a flash of the Chaos Lands. But before she could get her bearings, they were back in the village again, and both men were staring at her with identical looks of horrified comprehension.

"Jeanette. *Jeanette.* Kayla—what?" Eric stammered.

"Oh, thank God!" Kayla gasped, but the moment of relief made her lose her concentration. The village blinked out of existence, and she was back on the hillside, overlooking the field of battle.

No—no—no!

She closed her eyes, dropping to her knees where she stood. Once more she heard the cheers, the rumble as the two armies clashed.

The screams. She hugged herself, moaning, trying not to be there. She heard a howl of despair from the villagers, and knew that once more Aerete had died. Once again the storm came. Kayla opened her eyes, knowing she couldn't bear not to see, and Aerune moved through the enemy army, cutting them down with his sword of elvensilver. Once more they all lay dead, and Aerune turned upon the remnants of Aerete's army.

But this time Ria rode out to meet him, Eric at her side.

This isn't the way it went before! Kayla thought with a pang of hope.

Ria leaped down from her chariot, raising her spear. Aerune sliced it in half with a single blow, his sword so covered with blood that it sprinkled the Bard and the warrior who faced him with tiny drops of red.

Both knelt before him, offering their necks to his blow.

And Aerune stopped.

Turned away.

Left.

And Kayla stood once again beside the well in the sunlight, back in the village, staring at Eric, who was staring back at her, bewildered and appalled. Whatever had happened this time, he remembered it too.

It wasn't enough. It didn't work. Even if he spares the villagers, Aerune still blames humanity for Aerete's death.

"We have to get out of here," Eric said. He stared down at himself, frowned, and the loincloth and Celtic jewels vanished, to be replaced by elven Bardic silks.

"Get the others," Kayla said pleadingly. "Help me make them remember."

❖❖ ❖❖ ❖❖

"The real question is, how long is this taking? What are we doing out there while we're in here?" Paul asked.

The four Guardians, Eric, Ria, and Kayla, were all gathered in Eric's hut, while outside the afternoon of the dream played itself out. It had taken hours of subjective time to gather them together and break the others free of the dream-spell, but even that wasn't enough to free them from the larger dream. They were still here—though at least they all had their own clothes back. That helped.

"It's a dream, you said. If that's the case, it shouldn't be taking any time at all," Toni said.

"That's about right," Hosea said, stroking the neck of his banjo. "I can see it—what's going on there—kind of, through Jeanette here."

"We don't dare let him keep the advantage. We have to get out of this loop, or we're going to die—here *and* there," Eric said. "If I used magic—"

"Jeanette doesn't think that will work," Kayla said quickly. "She thinks trying that here will be enough of a shock to get you killed there."

"Maybe," Ria allowed grudgingly. "Maybe not. But I think we should save the heavy artillery for a last resort. If we're inside his mind, we're also inside most of his defenses. Maybe we can stop him here."

"How?" Eric asked. "I'm open to any and all suggestions." He looked at Kayla.

She took a deep breath. "We have to derail the dream, make it come out differently, break the cycle. Jeanette said that the only ones who can affect the outcome are us—or Aerune."

"He isn't likely to want to help us," Ria said.

"But he will!" Kayla said. "Or at least, the dream-Aerune will. He's not like the other one." *Although he's still a pain in the you-know-what.*

"But he will become the Aerune we know, when his lady dies," José said. "Her death, it is a terrible thing. She was so beautiful, and so kind."

And treated you all like pedigreed lap dogs! Kayla thought rebelliously.

"And we stop that—how?" Ria demanded.

"Tell him," Eric said. "Tell Aerune she'll die if she rides into battle."

The others slowly nodded, agreeing. The dream-Aerune was the vulnerable point of the Aerune who was trying to kill them now in the Chaos Lands. If they could change him, they might be able to affect the outcome of that battle as well.

"Kayla, can you take us to the Gate Aerete used to get to Aerune's Hall?" Eric asked. "I think we'd better all stay together. That way, if anyone starts to . . . forget . . . the rest of us will be here to yank them back."

"Sure." Kayla got to her feet. The next mad elflord's dream world she got trapped in, she vowed, was going to have chairs. "Come on."

She walked to the door of the hut, and stopped. "Uh-oh."

Eric shouldered past her. "This isn't good."

The rest of the village was gone. When they'd gone into Eric's hut to plan, a cluster of sod huts had stood around the base of the fairy howe and the High House erected upon its summit. Now the mound was empty, and only a few huts besides their own remained, and those looked fake and shadowy.

"Have we gone further back in time?" Toni asked, bewildered.

"No . . . the High House was here first. I think," Eric said. "C'mon, we have to see if the Gate is still there."

The village wasn't the only thing that was different, Kayla realized, as they hurried along the path that led to the ring of standing stones. Before, everything had been realer than real, down to the tiniest detail of flower and leaf. This time, it looked almost like a soundstage—things near them were still sharp and clear, but the farther away they got from the main road, the less detail everything had. It was creepy.

"I just thought of something," Ria said suddenly. "What if we win? What if we kill Aerune—out there?"

Nobody answered her. But if they killed Aerune, odds were they'd die with him, dying as his mind died.

Kayla did her very best not to imagine what that would feel like.

To her immense relief, the standing stones were still there. Kayla ran up the hill and stopped at the edge of the ring. "She just walked through. And then she was there."

"Let's try it," Eric said, taking her hand. "Everybody, stay close together. Kayla, think hard about what you saw on the other side."

Holding hands, the seven of them passed through the stones. Kayla closed her eyes tightly, thinking hard about Aerune's Great Hall.

And they were there. Aerune sat upon his chair, a pack of shaggy black hounds at his feet. One of them lifted its enormous head and growled, staring at the intruders with baleful red eyes.

"Can he see us?" Paul asked in a half whisper.

"I hope so," Eric whispered back. "And I hope he doesn't recognize us."

"Who enters my domain?" Aerune demanded, staring around the room. "Show yourselves!"

He gestured, and Kayla felt magic touch her skin like an icy spray of water. Aerune leapt to his feet, staring at them in shock.

"Great Lord," Eric said boldly, stepping forward, "we come to bring you a warning." He managed a courtly bow.

"Who are you?" the Sidhe lord demanded, staring at them in something very much like fear. "Mud-born? I can send you to realms of nightmare with but a single thought—and I shall!" He raised his hand, but hesitated, obviously bewildered by their outlandish appearance and clothing.

"Lord Aerune, how can it harm one of the immortal Sidhe to hear our . . . humble . . . petition?" Ria stepped out from behind Eric and bowed her head meekly.

"We beg this boon in the Lady Aerete's name," Paul added quickly.

"So you *are* her folk," Aerune said, sounding reassured. "You grow strong in your borrowed magic." He settled back into his chair, and reached down to stroke the head of the nearest hound. It stopped growling and licked his hand. "Speak, then. For my lady's sake, I will hear you."

So the dream-Aerune didn't recognize them as his enemies. That was a point in their favor.

Eric took a deep breath and stepped forward. "Tomorrow the village faces the army of the Eastmen, and Aerete will fight at—*our*—side. But the Eastmen carry deathmetal, which is proof against all magic, and death even to the immortal Sidhe. If she goes into battle, she will die."

"Die?" Aerune got to his feet again and strode from the dais to stand before Eric, glaring down at him. "That cannot be! Her magic arms her against all the weapons of the mud-born!"

"Deathmetal destroys all magic, and burns the flesh of the Bright Lords. She will die," Eric said.

Aerune raised his hand to strike Eric, and seemed confused when Eric didn't cringe away from the blow. He lowered his hand again.

"Great Lord, what does it matter if the Bard is right or not?" Ria said smoothly, diverting Aerune's attention. "Your course is plain. Fight in her stead, slay her enemies, and preserve her from harm. Is that not the duty of a lord to his sworn lady?"

"Am I to take counsel from mud-born animals?" Aerune growled. He looked more closely at Ria. "You are not as they. How can this be?"

"The blood of the Sidhe runs in my veins," Ria answered carefully, "and by that blood, you know what I say is true. You must save your lady from those who would harm her."

"I—" Aerune began, and for a moment he looked very young, and very frightened. "I— She *cannot* die!"

The world rippled around them. They were back on the hillside. By now Kayla was almost used to the jarring transition. Though she cringed inside at the thought of the slaughter to come, she tried to take comfort from the fact that this time they all stood together, watching the two armies prepare to fight.

"This has happened before," Eric said quietly. "I . . . remember it. I think. What happens now?"

"You fight, Aerete dies, Aerune kills everybody in sight," Kayla said tightly. She pointed, to where Aerete and her elvensteed stood beside the first line of chariots. "That hasn't changed."

"But we've warned him. And we're here, not there," Toni said.

"I've got an idea," Kayla began. Then the horn sounded, and the two armies rushed to converge.

But before they could meet, Aerune was there. This time he did not wait for Aerete to fall, but turned upon the enemy host, sword flashing.

Kayla closed her eyes and leaned against Hosea's shoulder, trying to shut it all out. Hosea put his arms around her and held her tightly, but she could still hear the shocked sounds of horror and dismay from the others as they watched. In a much shorter time than before, there was silence.

She turned in Hosea's arms and opened her eyes.

The enemy army lay dead—all of them. Aerete's people were untouched. Some knelt. Other lay full-length upon the ground in terror, prostrating themselves before one of the Bright Lords. Only Aerete stood tall, proud and angry, mounted upon her shining white mare.

Aerune walked slowly toward her, his sword dripping red and wet in his hand. But when he would have knelt at her feet, she stopped him with an imperious gesture.

"Stay back!" Aerete cried, and in the utter silence, her words carried clearly to the watchers upon the hill. "You disgust me. How could I ever have thought to love a monster who kills so easily? Go, and never come before me again till the end of your days, Aerune mac Audelaine!"

"This isn't working," Eric said wearily.

They were back in the hut. Kayla supposed that soldiers in battle must look the way they did now—shell-shocked and browbeaten. She felt like crying, but refused to give in to it.

"It seems we are doomed to replay the seminal event that formed Aerune's character forever, in every possible variation," Paul said slowly. "Once he loses Aerete's love, he begins to hate humanity."

"And even if we save her, that doesn't change," José said flatly. "She rejects him for them, and he turns to the Dark."

"And breaking out of here by magic still carries the same risk. Kayla. Back there, on the hill, you said you had an idea," Eric said. "I think we could all use a good idea right now."

"I think . . . Paul and José are right," Kayla said slowly, piecing the words together as she spoke. "Aerune's hurt. That's why we can't make this come out right. When Aerete died, something inside him broke, and everything that comes afterward comes because of that."

"So what are you suggesting?" Ria snapped. "Tea and sympathy? He's trying to kill us—and doing a damned good job of it!"

"We can't raise the dead," Eric said sadly, and Kayla knew he was thinking about Jimmie.

"No," Kayla said slowly. "But we can heal the hurt. If he never sees Aerete die, then all the rest won't happen."

"Kayla," Eric said gently, "we can't do that. We can't go back in time and change the past that way. What else would change? It's like that SF paradox: if you go back in time and shoot your grandfather, you're never born, so you never go back in time and shoot your grandfather."

"I'm not even sure that saving Aerete would be a good idea," Toni said musingly. "I—remember—what it was like to be one of Aerete's people. She was a loving mistress, but Aerune was right about one thing. We were *pets*. And I don't want to be somebody's pet, no matter how kind they are."

"We don't have to change the past," Kayla insisted. "Just change his mind, change the hate. Look, this is one of the things Healers do. Take the bad memories and make them stop hurting so much. Elizabet told me once that a Healer can even *erase* memories—make them go away for good. But it's dangerous—both to the Healer and the person they're working on. And it takes a lot of power. More power than I've got."

"Which brings us back to 'how,' " Eric said. "If we broke out of here—got ourselves back into real time somehow—"

"We'll be toast," Ria said succinctly.

"Sounds to me like the little 'un's right," Hosea said suddenly. "Can't we just make Aerune forget that his lady friend's dead? If we could, it wouldn't be in the past. We're in Aerune's mind *now*, not then."

"We can't make it so tomorrow never comes," Eric said. "But you're right. If we can make it so that Aerune doesn't *remember* that it ever did . . ."

The seven of them looked at each other.

"We'd better hurry," Kayla said, looking toward the door of the hut. "Because I think the sun is going out."

SEVENTEEN:
THE MAGNIFICENT SEVEN

Eric stood in the corner of Aerune's Great Hall, playing a soft tune upon his flute. Into it, he put all he knew of Aerete from this journey through Aerune's memories. The cloaking spell he had set in motion before they passed through the ring of standing stones kept Aerune from sensing their presence, and in a few moments, if this worked, it would no longer matter whether it held or not.

Behind him, the four Guardians stood in a ring around Kayla and Ria, their arms crossed, holding each other's hands to form a tightly-woven ring of protection around the two women. They were taking a mad gamble—that the source of their power was compatible with Kayla's healing ability—but it was their only chance. Undermine Aerune's power here, the power that fed on his rage at Aerete's murder—or break free of the dream by force and face him in the Chaos Lands, with Aerune at the height of his powers.

If this worked, Kayla would be able to reach into Aerune's mind to erase the memories that caused him such pain. They would be free of Aerune's dream, back in the Chaos Lands, and—if they were lucky—Aerune would be off-balance for the precious moments they needed to set the dragon labyrinth around him.

If Kayla could heal him. To do it, Kayla would have to go deeper into the elf-lord's mind than any of them were now. Even with Ria to act as her anchor, there was a real possibility that Kayla might lose herself. And without Kayla to bridge the two worlds—the real and the dream—the rest of them would fall back into Aerune's nightmare once more, this time for good.

And they'd die.

Eric concentrated on his playing, on creating the imago of Aerete. To remove the memories without Aerune noticing and fighting back, there had to be something both to call them to the surface and to go in their place. That was where Eric came in—to craft a dream of Aerete, alive and loving and whole, to set in the place of the memories of sorrow and loss.

It could be Kory up there, Eric thought fleetingly. *Kory, with Beth dead and no way to get her back.*

Then there was no time for such thoughts. He threw himself into the music and the spell.

Kayla clutched Ria's hands tightly, trying to think of nothing but the healing she was about to attempt. She and Elizabet had done this before—with Beth, with Ria, with others who came to Elizabet to heal wounds not of the body, but of the spirit. But what she was about to do now bore the same resemblance to that work as the Space Shuttle did to the Wright Brothers' first airplane. To do it, she would have to become both surgeon and scalpel, drawing upon the energy the Guardians sent her just as she normally drew on her own life-force. The attempt could kill them all.

But hey, who wants to live forever, especially on Aerune's terms?

Slowly, she reached out to the Guardians, touching their power. It spilled into her like sunshine, and she took a steadying breath. *Okay so far.* She didn't need to touch Aerune to do this—she was already inside his mind, inside his defenses, inside his dreams. That was the only reason this could possibly work. She closed her eyes, concentrating on Eric's music.

Aerete. Think of Aerete.

※ ※ ※

The Great Hall and her companions were gone—she was deep in Aerune's memories, seeing through his eyes. She could smell the blood, hear the moans of the dying. She—he—*they* held Aerete's body in their arms, felt her cooling blood upon their hands, and Aerune mac Audelaine knew that in this moment his world had ended. Men had done this, men had killed his love, and in his dead love's name, Aerune swore that their treachery would be repaid. He had shown them mercy for her sake, and now that they had slain her, they had slain all mercy and kindness as well. A cold fury welled up in him, destroying all other thoughts, all other purposes. For so long as Time itself endured, they would be his prey and his enemy, and he would not rest until he had slain them all—

Kayla felt his agony rip through her like a high wind. He had killed elves before, though Death was a rare visitor to the Sidhe. Among the mortalkind he had seen Death in all its guises, but no death had ever touched him until now. It was unendurable pain, and only hate could protect him from it. Never again would he love—he would hate, hate forever the worthless animals who had destroyed him and slain his love. In her name, he would hate forever, until the very sun grew cold. . . .

She reached out, taking his pain and letting it flow through her. Again and again she reached out, smoothing away the pain and loss until nothing of that terrible moment remained. Kayla gasped with effort, feeling her heart thunder in her distant body. The memory of Aerete's death was gone, but that wasn't enough. There was still too much pain. She had to take every memory of Aerete from his mind, leaving Aerune only the loving presence of the Aerete in Eric's music. She closed her eyes, and let the music lead her deeper into Aerune's mind.

The firelight flared, and Kayla opened her eyes. As she did, the world came real—the smell of fragrant wood smoke, the cold bite of the winter night, the sound of drums and piping. She was Aerune.

There was a bonfire ringed by dancers. The lines of men and women wove in and out, and every few moments one of the dancers would rush toward the center of the ring and leap the fire, to the accompaniment of much laughing and shouting. The firelight gleamed on their oiled skin, and Kayla saw the shadowy marks of tribal paint and tattoos.

And Aerete danced with them, her bright hair shining, her jewels gleaming with elvish fire. She leaped into the circle and over the fire, and all her people shouted with joy. Kayla felt Aerune's anger, his uncomprehending pain and sullen hurt. *How can she love them, who does not love me?*

She touched the memories with her power, soothing them away. Gone. It was easier this time. And Eric's music pulled her elsewhere.

The walls of Aerune's Great Hall gleamed golden in the light of torches. Banners of bright silk hung from the ceiling, waving softly in the updrafts of warm air from the fire in the firepit. The ivory dais was draped with rugs of jewel-bright weaving, and on it stood a gaming table, its surface covered with carven counters of gold and precious stones. Aerete leaned over the board, her pale hair a fall of shining silk, regarding its surface intently. Suddenly she saw a move and pounced, sweeping the enemy counters from the board. She clapped her hands and laughed, as happily as a child, and Aerune knew there was nothing in all the worlds as beautiful as her face, that without her there was no happiness anywhere—

Gone.

The air was filled with flowers and the scent of new green life. They rode through the early morning mist, he on his black stallion, she on her white mare, and all the time-bound Earthly world was their dominion. In her hair she wore a garland of his weaving—May flowers, as pale and perfect as her silken skin. Her arms were full of flowers, their petals showering down like warm soft snow. The air was filled with birdsong, and larks wheeled and darted about her head, teasing and calling. For her sake, he had forsworn the Hunt, and no longer took the Children of Earth as his rightful prey. She held out her hand, and the birds of the air came to her call. He prayed that this moment would last forever, that she would not turn again to the mortalfolk, those unworthy recipients of her precious love—

Gone.

He rode forth with the Hosts of Hell at his back—landless

knights cast out by their hames, Low Court spirits bound to him by magic—to hunt and harry where he would, for this time-bound world had long been his playground. Once this land had been green and silent, but then Men had come to it, hunting the red deer and the gray wolf, cutting down the great trees. Now he rode toward one of their villages of sticks and mud, intent upon their destruction.

But as he rode toward them, a lone rider blocked his way. He thought to run her down, but then recognized that she was of his blood, as fair as the undying lilies of an Elfhame. A woman, little more than a child, who gazed at him fearless and unafraid.

"Yield the road to me, child. I ride to the village beyond," Aerune said harshly.

"Not this day, nor yet any other, while I live," she answered boldly.

"Child, do you know me? I could slay you with a thought."

"All in this realm know you, to their sorrow, Aerune mac Audelaine, Lord of the Hunt. Too long have you harried the folk who cry out to me for protection. I would have you cease."

He gazed upon her shining form, he who had never bent to another's will, and something in her fearless gaze reached a part of him that he thought could never yield to the touch of another. Aerune hesitated.

"Tell me who you are, that I may tell your kinfolk who to mourn."

"I am Aerete, child of Melusine, and I will not let you harm my people."

He gazed once more into her face, and saw that she would not yield. He had slain others as he would slay her now, and forget her death before the sun set in this mortal world. And so he raised his hand—

He could not do it, and did not know why. And the Hunt turned aside—

Gone.

Gone. All gone. The flash of her eyes, the scent of her skin, the touch of her hand. Joy and sorrow, love and hate, gone. All gone, smoothed away from his mind as if they'd never been, Eric's spell set

in their place. All the memories, all the pain, gone, gone forever—
    :KAYLA!:

Ria's mental cry jolted Kayla from the healing trance. She staggered and fell, crying out with despair at the beauty she had destroyed—gone forever, all gone—

She fell to her knees on the misty ground of the Chaos Lands. Time ran normally once more, but Kayla hardly cared. She was sick, she was cold . . . and tired, so very tired—

"Get back—get back!" Toni shouted, sweeping her sword up to meet Aerune's blow. There was a ring of metal on metal, a hiss as elvensilver met Cold Iron. Someone grabbed Kayla by the scruff of her mail shirt and flung her away like a bag of dirty laundry. She hit hard and rolled, fetching up at Lady Day's feet. She clung to the stirrup of the elvensteed's saddle, dragging herself to her feet.

It seemed that only seconds had passed since Aerune's arrival, and the discord between that fact and what she remembered made Kayla lightheaded. She heard music, buffeting her as if she swam in an ocean of harmony, being pulled this way and that by clashing currents, and heard the flat boom of a big-bore handgun, its bark louder than the roaring of the hellhounds. Toni and José were circling Aerune, trying to draw his attack while Paul and Eric—and Hosea—shielded them with magic. Ria stood in a shooter's brace, both hands together, firing at the creatures that followed Aerune, and every shot found its mark. The Unseleighe creatures burned where the steel-jacketed slugs had hit them, collapsing inward around the lumps of deathmetal like ice thrown onto hot coals.

Was it only hope, or did Aerune's attack seem the least bit uncertain, as if he were no longer quite sure why he fought?

A thousand thoughts clamored for attention in Eric's mind, but he forced them back. There was no time to think, only to *be*, responding to each of Aerune's attacks with the swiftness Master Dharniel had drummed into him through long and painful lessons. He knew that they could not win this way. They had to stop fighting a purely defensive battle, knock Aerune back long enough to plant the dragon seed.

Then Aerune swept through Toni's guard, hammering her to the ground with one blow from his black mailed fist and catching José off-guard with a backswept blow from his longsword. He raised his sword to deliver the deathblow to the fallen Guardian—

And suddenly there was another warrior here, between Aerune and Toni. Her plate armor was the deep blue of the midnight sky, and her sword burned like starlight.

"Jimmie . . . ?" Eric whispered, unable to believe it.

Knowing it was somehow true.

Jimmie fought Aerune back with a flurry of sword-blows, forcing the elf-lord to give ground, moving him away from the downed Guardians. Each time their swords met they gave off a shower of sparks. Jimmie moved with superhuman grace, as though Death had burned away all that was gross and mortal, leaving behind only the beautiful spirit of the warrior-mage.

"Eric!" she shouted over the clang of metal. "Do it!"

This is the only chance. Eric ran forward, the labyrinth-seed clutched in his fist. Aerune was totally focused on this new opponent. He paid no attention as Eric raised his hand and dashed the seed to the ground. As he did, Jimmie slowly faded away, her last work done.

What happened next was over in an instant, and at the same time seemed to uncoil so slowly that he could see every detail. As the maze-seed struck the ground it began to sprout, unfolding layer after layer of labyrinth, with Aerune at its heart. Walls and passageways, chambers and blind turnings, twisting and twining and leading back into themselves with a mad geometrical complexity. And then— instantly, eventually—there was nothing there but a silvery latticework sphere hovering a few feet off the ground, its shining tracery winding all the way to its heart.

Silence, and the impossible memories came flooding back, making the Chaos Lands reel around him.

Eric stared around at the others. They were all here, all alive. José was helping Toni to her feet. Ria stood head bowed, her gun held out stiffly in front of her. The elvensteeds huddled together, and Kayla, green-faced, was clinging to Lady Day's stirrup, as if that were the only thing holding her upright. As he watched, she let go and sank to her knees, retching. He took a step toward her, but his knees buckled under him and he fell.

Ria ran past him, cradling the fallen Healer in her arms and wiping her face with a handkerchief. After a couple of tries, Eric managed to stagger over to join her.

"Kayla! Are you all right?"

She winced at the loudness of his voice. "Backlash," she whispered, and groaned as Ria lifted her in her arms. "What happened?"

"We won," Eric said.

"Good," Kayla muttered, and closed her eyes.

"Is she . . . ?" Toni asked. Eric looked around. Toni looked battered and drained by the fight, and the mail across her chest was charred and blackened where one of Aerune's levin-bolts had struck. A bruise was rising on her cheekbone where Aerune had struck her, but her eyes were clear.

"Sleeping," Eric said. He rubbed his eyes, realizing he still held his flute clenched in his right hand. He looked at it. The silver was twisted and fused, distorted beyond repair, but he could not remember when or how it had happened. Too many contradictory memories fought for possession of his mind—had they fought Aerune here, or in the shadowy corridors of the elf-lord's mind? Which had been the real fight?

"I thought I saw . . . Jimmie," Toni said slowly.

"I saw her too," Eric said, unsure now of what had been real and what had been a dream. "She saved us. She saved all of us."

Ria laid Kayla down and got to her feet. She put an arm around his shoulder. He could feel her muscles trembling with exhaustion. "Try not to think about it," she advised kindly. "Maybe it was her. If it wasn't, it was something that wanted us to win. These are the Chaos Lands. No one can really say what's possible here."

Eric glanced back at the dragon labyrinth. "But what did we *do?*" he demanded in frustration, looking around at the others.

"Healed him. Imprisoned him. Either way it's over," Paul said heavily. He wiped his blade with a silk scarf, and slid it back into the cane-sheath, then leaned upon it as if he needed its support.

"But if we did the one, we didn't have to do the other. Right?" Toni asked, sounding as bewildered as Eric felt. She reached out to touch José's shoulder, as if trying to convince herself he was there.

"But the village . . . Aerete . . . it all seemed so *real*," José said, sounding lost. "The beautiful lady, like the Virgin come to Earth—"

"It was. And it wasn't," Eric said. But it was real enough that he mourned its loss—the sense of security, of *home*. If they had won, it had been at a cost. Even if they had erased Aerune's memories and his pain, they would all now carry the scar of Aerete's death with them until the end of their days.

"I think we did heal him, or maybe gave him a chance to heal himself," Hosea said slowly, answering Toni. "And if we did, that labyrinth is the best place for him, now. Think about it." He ran his fingers across the face of the banjo, but the instrument was silent, its strings broken and twisted.

"Aerune made a lot of enemies in his life," Eric said, reasoning it out. He was so tired—every fiber of his being screamed for sleep, for rest—but the Chaos Lands weren't safe to linger in. "But—if it worked—he won't remember any of them. Us."

"He'd be helpless against them," Ria said. "But locked up in there, he'll be safe. And the cream of the jest is, he probably won't even notice he *is* locked up. He'll have Aerete—the Aerete you made for him with your music, Eric—and she'll never die. I suppose you'd call that a happy ending." She gave Eric's shoulder a last squeeze. "We'd better go."

Toni cried out, pointing. A dark shape banked through the mist heading toward them.

"Something's coming," Paul said grimly, as the shape moved toward them through the mist. It landed, folding its great wings. Hosea turned, picking Kayla up.

Eric tried to summon the strength to face this new foe, and knew with a sinking sense of despair that the battle had taken everything he had. Then he saw what they faced clearly, for the first time.

"Pretty," Chinthliss said, craning his long bronze-scaled neck to inspect the shining silvery ball. "One of my more elegant creations."

"Is that . . . a dragon?" Toni asked in a tiny voice.

"A friend," Eric said, his voice shaking with relief. *I hope.*

The dragon turned its enormous head to inspect all of them, amber eyes glowing. "And an exquisite battle, may I say, Bard? My compliments to you and your friends."

"Thank you," Eric said. He tried for a courtly bow and staggered. He would have fallen if Ria hadn't been there to catch him.

"I would welcome the opportunity to hear the story of your success in detail," Chinthliss said. "Perhaps I might extend the hospitality of my humble domain to you all until you have rested? I fear such prodigious magics as you have done here today will inevitably attract such persons as you will not wish to meet at this time."

Or ever. "Thank you, Lord Chinthliss. We would be—"

The dragon spread its great wings.

"—honored?" Eric finished weakly, boggling at the sudden smooth transition from *there* to *here.*

The Chaos Lands were gone. The seven of them—and the two elvensteeds—stood suddenly in the inner courtyard that Eric remembered from his last visit to the dragon's domain, and in place of the enormous bronze dragon stood an elegant Oriental man in a bronze silk suit.

"*Madre de Dios,*" José said, crossing himself fervently.

Blessed Lady, hear our call, we who are Your folk . . . Eric shook his head, wrenching himself out of the automatic prayer, too exhausted to think straight. There was no point in praying to the Bright Lady Aerete for her aid as his instincts and memories demanded. Aerete was gone, gone with the paradise she had created, leaving only them to mourn her.

"But come," Chinthliss said, clapping his hands to summon his servants, and drawing Eric's mind back to the here-and-now. "Rest, and awaken refreshed."

Eric didn't even remember making it to a bed. But he dreamed.

Aerune mac Audelaine, child of the Sidhe, walked the halls of his silver castle beyond the stars. He did not know how he had come to be here, and did not care. He walked in music, his heart filled with the gentle melody of his beloved, a shining presence that accompanied him always. Around him bloomed the undying gardens of Underhill, and the rooms of his dwelling were filled with beauty, harmony and light. He had no reason to venture forth, no interest in the world beyond his domain.

Aerune knew he was loved. He was content.

EIGHTEEN:
JOURNEY'S END

"Wake up, sleepyhead," Ria said. She sounded amused.

Eric opened his eyes and found himself staring up at an unfamiliar canopy of yellow silk. He tried to remember how he'd gotten here, but his mind felt . . . bruised, and all he could dredge up at the moment were confused memories of Maeve's *ceileighe,* of the enormous wonders of Underhill. He could hear birds singing, and morning sunlight was spilling in through the windows. He felt as if a long time had passed, but wasn't sure exactly how much. *It must have been one hell of a party. . . .*

"Where . . . ?" He sat up with a groan. Every muscle felt stiff, as if they had been strained to their limit, and that recently.

"Lord Chinthliss' palace, everyone's fine, you've been asleep for a day and a half, and some friends of yours are here, and very anxious to see you," Ria rattled off, as if reading the headlines.

Eric shoved the hair out of his eyes and blinked. Ria was sitting on the edge of the bed, dressed in an elaborate scarlet silk kimono, her hair swept up in a pair of ornate jade combs.

"Friends?" he asked groggily. Memories came jangling back in a confused indigestible lump. The Chaos Lands. The fight with Aerune. The village. Aerete. Jimmie.

Seeing from his face that Eric was finally awake, Ria got to her feet. "You might as well come in," she called. "He's just washed his brain, and he can't do a thing with it."

"Eric!" Beth bounced onto the huge bed in a flurry of motion, and snatched Eric into a bone-crushing hug. "Are you all right? What happened? What are you doing here? Chinthliss wouldn't let anybody wake you up, and— Are you *okay?*" she demanded in a rush, not giving Eric a chance to get a word in edgewise.

"He is alive," Kory said, settling at the edge of the bed and putting an arm around both of them. "And from what little young Kayla has told us, that alone is a great accomplishment. You should not have faced such a foe alone, Bard," he added sternly. "Not without your friends."

Great. I save the world and get scolded for it.

"I—" Eric began. His stomach rumbled loudly. "I'm *starving.*" The last meal he could remember was a hurried breakfast, and he was no longer sure how many days ago that had been.

"Then come and eat," Ria said. "There's enough food here to feed an army."

Breakfast was waiting in the outer room of the lavish suite. Eric wrapped himself in a robe—sky-blue silk embroidered with silver and gold cranes—and followed the other three out of the yellow silk bedroom. The Guardians and Kayla, Ria told him, had been up for almost a day already. "Everyone's doing pretty well—just minor bumps and bruises, even Kayla, but Chinthliss wanted to wait until he could see everyone at once before hearing the story of what he calls our adventure. Better brace yourself, O Bard of a Hundred Songs. I think he's going to want you to set it to music."

Eric winced. *Adventure, yeah. I guess that's what you call it when everybody comes back alive.*

Over breakfast—a smorgasbord of delicacies from bacon and eggs to lox and bagels, all kept hot beneath enchanted silver covers— Eric gave Kory and Beth an abbreviated story of what had happened since the last time he'd talked to Beth a few days ago. A lot of his recollection of the fight was still jumbled—human language wasn't very good for explaining what you'd been doing when you felt like you'd been in two places at once—but he managed to cover the important points.

"But why did you not ask for our aid in helping you defeat Aerune?" Kory demanded again. "In the face of such a threat, surely Elfhame Misthold, at least, would have sent allies to your cause."

Yeah, and if I'd known how powerful Aerune was going to turn out to be, I might have asked for them, no matter what Dharniel said. I'm not sure now that the labyrinth would have held Aerune if Kayla hadn't drawn his fangs.

"I didn't want to involve the Sidhe," Eric said, thinking it over. "After what Dharniel told me when I spoke to him, I wasn't sure they'd be too hipped on having a bunch of humans take out a Sidhe—and by the time I convinced them Aerune was a real threat to them, too, it could have been too late."

"Maybe it's already too late, if what we ran into in Las Vegas is any indication," Beth said unhappily. "Nuts in green suits with flying cars—that has to be Aerune's work, doesn't it? His human helpers?"

"Maybe," Eric said. "But without Aerune's backing, they won't find it as easy to swing government support for their elf-war any more."

"Especially after I make a few well-placed phone calls," Ria said contentedly, biting into a slice of crisp toast slathered with orange marmalade. "In the course of straightening out the Threshold mess from last year, I've met a lot of interesting people wandering around the corridors of power, and more than a few of them owe me favors. *Big* favors. I'll make some calls when I get back. It may not be fast, but we'll get everything fixed up eventually." Her eyes glittered. "There's one good thing about the black ops people so far as we're concerned. They're all so paranoid and so greedy about getting bigger slices of the black-budget pie that all you have to do is set one project off to discredit another one, and the next thing you know, you've got internecine warfare that makes the Blue and the Grey look like

Woodstock." She laughed—and to Eric's relief, there was actually some real humor in it. "You just leave that part of it to me. A hint here, a budget page carelessly left there—I just wish I could be a fly on the walls."

"But what about you?" Eric asked Beth and Kory. "You've heard my story, now what about you two? You went to Chinthliss for help—how did that work out?"

Beth's face fell, and her eyes filled with tears of angry frustration. "Not well," she said. "He gave us everything I asked him for . . ."

"And it was not enough," Kory said bleakly. He put an arm around Beth, and Eric saw her force herself to smile reassuringly.

This is not good. "But what did you ask for?" Eric asked.

"Oh, never mind that now," Beth said crossly, wiping at her eyes. "I screwed up. It happens. We can go into it later. Right now, I don't think you should keep Chinthliss or your other friends waiting—and I want to hear the rest of the story—the *real* story, including the parts you left out just now."

Eric wasn't sure where his own clothes had gotten to, but the ones the geisha servants had laid out for him when he returned to the bedroom were lavish enough to replace even the finery of an Underhill Bard—wide pants in heavy black silk that shimmered in the sunlight, a dark red *ghi* top woven in a geometric brocade and a long gray and maroon robe embroidered with birds and flowering trees to go over it, held in place with a long gold sash. For his feet, there were ankle boots of soft doeskin leather, held closed with a carved jade button at the outside of each ankle. *I've worn weirder stuff. But I feel like an extra in* Shogun.

When he was dressed, Ria rang for Charles, and Chinthliss' butler conducted the four of them to the very English drawing room that Eric had seen before.

Kayla and the four Guardians were there waiting for them, along with a fox-faced young human man with unkempt black hair, dressed in a T-shirt and jeans. The others were wearing opulent Oriental garb similar to Eric and Ria's—except for Kayla, who had somehow managed to convince Chinthliss or his servants to provide her with an approximation of her glitterpunk garb—tight silver-scaled leggings mostly covered with black thigh-high stiletto-heeled boots, and a brief tube top that looked as if it was made of marabou feathers. Her face was elaborately painted in geisha fashion—Kayla's notion of a concession to the prevailing dress code—and her silver batwing earrings flashed in her ears.

Eric was relieved to see that the others all appeared well and healthy—Toni's face wasn't even bruised—though Paul looked as if he were bursting with a thousand unasked questions. Even Hosea's banjo was restrung with shining silver strings.

Good as new, whatever that means in this situation. I hope Jeanette's all right. She did her best for us back in the Chaos Lands. Without her, we might never have made it out of Aerune's dream.

"My, my, my—you're looking good these days, Eric," Toni said with a grin and a nod toward his Oriental finery. She came over and enfolded him in a quick fierce hug. "For a while there we were wondering if you were ever going to wake up."

"Slugabed," Hosea said, with a broad smile. "Glad to see you back on your feet."

"Glad to have feet to be back on," Eric said. "Folks, I'd like you to meet two other friends of mine, Beth and Kory. Guys, you've already met Toni Hernandez from when I moved in, and you remember Kayla, but this is Paul—José—and Hosea, who in addition to being a Guardian, is also an apprentice Bard."

"An' this is Tannim," Kayla said, pulling the dark-haired man over to greet Eric. "He drives race-cars for a living. How cool is that?"

"She makes it sound more glamorous than it is," Tannim said, smiling. "I'm really more of a test driver, not a competition racer." He held out his hand, and Eric shook it, feeling the hard calluses of a mechanic's hands beneath his grip.

"You're with Elfhame Fairgrove, aren't you?" Eric asked. The Fairgrove elves took a far more active part in the world than the elves of Elfhame Misthold.

Tannim grinned wider. "What can I say? I've always had a taste for fast cars and low company, which is probably why I hang out with Chinthliss so much. But I never thought I'd meet another Guardian—let alone *four* of them."

"You've met Guardians before?" Eric asked, surprised.

"One, once. At my high school prom, if you can believe that, so don't ever let anyone tell you that Oklahoma is dull. But we'll have to save that story for another occasion, because I've got the feeling the show's about to start."

As if speaking his name aloud a few moments before had summoned him up—and in Underhill, such a thing wasn't as impossible as it seemed—the double doors at the far end of the salon opened and Chinthliss strode in.

"Ah, my young friends. I hope the day finds you well? Now that you are rested, I am eager to hear all that transpired."

The party seated themselves in comfortable chairs arrayed around a low table laden with cups and half a dozen carafes of wine and juice. Chinthliss waited until everyone had served him- or herself with their beverage of choice, then folded his hands and regarded them all expectantly.

"Well," Eric said hesitantly. Everyone was staring at him—even Ria—expecting him to start things off. "I guess it more-or-less started the night Aerune showed up at the apartment building, but maybe the real beginning was a few weeks ago when I was coming home from school and found Hosea busking in the subway. . . ."

The tale took longer to tell to Chinthliss' satisfaction than Eric had expected, with each of the others contributing their own version of the events they'd taken part in.

Beth and Kory added the full story of their meeting with the Men In Green at Glitterhame Neversleeps, which did seem to be tied up somehow with Aerune's plans, though "now" in the World Above for Eric and the others was still August, and Beth and Kory's "now" was November.

When I get out of this, no more trips to Underhill for a long time. Time travel—if that's what it is—makes my head hurt! One more paradox, and I think it'll melt completely.

At last they had finally answered all of Chinthliss' questions as well as they could. Telling the story over also helped them to sort it out in their own minds—if what they remembered wasn't exactly what had happened, it was close enough for folk music and government work, as the saying went.

"So . . . what now?" Toni asked, looking around the table.

"Now, my young friends, you return to your own worlds and your own lives," Chinthliss said. "Do your best to forget what transpired on your journey through the fair and treacherous realms of Underhill, remembering only what you must. It will be more . . . comfortable for you thus."

"I don't know," Toni said consideringly. "Comfort has never been really high on the Guardians' list of priorities. And I think this is going to put a whole new spin on the way we look at the world."

"Amen to that," Paul said. "Knowing about Underhill, that it exists—that elves exist, and dragons . . . it explains so much."

"And raises as many questions as it answers," Chinthliss said, not unkindly. "Or so you will find. But for now you will do as seems good to you, and perhaps I can offer you one last word of warning, before you return to your own place and time: to think too much about a thing is often to call it to you, for good or ill."

"I don't know that we've got much to worry about there," Paul said. "Any elf that shows up in New York City is more likely to get mugged than be able to make trouble."

"As you say," Chinthliss said, nodding gravely. "But now you will be anxious to return to your home and loved ones. The battle you have fought has been a greater boon to Underhill than you can easily guess, for if the Sidhe-Lord Aerune's plans had borne their intended fruit, it would have brought great disruption to this realm. And so in gratitude for all your labors, let me extend you one last small courtesy, and convey you swiftly and safely back to your own place—and time."

There was a moment of silent consultation, and Toni shrugged minutely, getting to her feet. "Sure. Thanks. I'm not sure how long we've been gone, but the kids are probably driving their aunt crazy by now."

"My little ones will miss me," José said, rising to his feet as well.

"And Columbia will miss Kayla," Ria said meaningfully, regarding Kayla.

"Eric?" Paul asked.

"You guys go on ahead. I've got a few things to take care of here—if that's alright with you, Lord Chinthliss?"

The dragon lord bowed his head in agreement. "Please accept my hospitality for as long as you care to enjoy it, Bard Eric. And now, my young friends, if you would care to accompany me . . . ?"

Chinthliss left the room, ushering the others before him.

"I think I've gotta go water some plants or something," Tannim said, grinning as he got to his feet. "You folks look like you've got serious stuff to discuss." He followed Chinthliss out, and they could hear him start to whistle before the doors to the salon closed again, shutting off the sound from the corridor.

Eric looked at Beth and Kory.

"Okay. I've been patient. Give."

"This is the library," Beth said, a few minutes later.

Eric stared at a room the approximate size of the Houston Astrodome, completely full of books.

"'Free access to his library, and all it contains,'" Kory quoted bitterly. "That is what we bargained for, and that is what we received. But there is no catalogue of these holdings, no order to them—and no way to find the information we seek."

"Ah, there you are," Chinthliss said, strolling into the room. "You will be pleased to know that your friends are all returned safely to their homes, the very day they left them—though Mistress Ria did say something about needing a tow truck for a Rolls Royce. Splendid vehicles," Chinthliss said musingly.

"You tricked them," Eric said hotly, unable to contain his anger. "You tricked my friends!"

Chinthliss gazed from Eric to Beth, his face blank with surprise. "But I did not. They asked for the use of my library, and bargained well for the privilege."

"Because they thought they could find what they needed here. You told them they could—you told them the information was here," Eric accused, unable to stop himself.

"And it is," Chinthliss said, sounding even more baffled at Eric's anger.

"Dragons are notorious packrats," Tannim said, coming out of the stacks, holding a book. "But nobody ever said they were *organized*. He didn't cheat your friends, Eric. The old lizard is used to just hunting through things until he finds what he's looking for— I told you that you needed a librarian for this pile, didn't I?" he said to Chinthliss.

"And refused to undertake the task yourself," Chinthliss said, sounding hurt. He looked hopefully at Beth. "Never would I have made a shoddy bargain with you, Lady Beth. The book you seek is indeed here."

"Somewhere," Kory muttered under his breath.

"All that remains is to call it forth," Chinthliss said.

"Which means calling in a little help," Tannim added.

"And that's where *I* come in," a familiar voice said out of nowhere.

Beth turned around. Eric stared.

There was a cartoon fox, standing in Chinthliss' library about twenty feet off the floor. It was wearing a red James Dean jacket and a gold pendant around its neck that said "FX," and instead of one tail, it had *three*. On its long vulpine nose were perched a pair of overlarge black horn-rimmed glasses giving the creature an unconvincing intellectual look.

"Do you know him?" Eric asked Beth.

"Know him!" Beth yelped. "He's— I— If I'd just *listened* to him back at the Goblin Market— That's Foxtrot-X-Ray," Beth finished weakly, disbelieving mirth bubbling in her voice. "He's a *kitsune*—a fox-spirit. Kory and I have met him before."

As they watched, Fox sank slowly toward the floor, walking in neat circles as though descending an invisible spiral staircase.

"Heya, cupcake, dry those tears. When you absolutely positively have to have something yesterday, just whistle. You know how to whistle, don't you? Just—"

"The book, Fox?" Tannim asked, trying to hide a smile of his own.

"Oh, that." Fox reached into his jacket, and produced a book approximately as large as he was. It had a red leather binding and gold clasps, and had several gold ribbons bound into it to serve as bookmarks. "Here it is. *Dixon's Guide to Interspecies Reproduction, Fifth Edition.* I've marked your place." He held the book out to Beth, smiling coaxingly.

Beth took the volume, staggering under its weight—it was heavier than Fox had made it look. With Kory to help her hold it, she opened it to the page the gold ribbon bookmark indicated.

"'To conceive a child of the Sidhe by lawful means—'" she read aloud, and skipped quickly through the entry. "It says the magic of two Bards working in harmony is needed to channel the power of Underhill to the mortal partner. Two Bards! You were at the *ceileighe*, Eric—getting two Bards to do *anything* together is like trying to herd cats!"

Eric grinned, and leaned across the book to kiss Beth on the nose. "Well, almost. But not always, as it turns out. Hosea isn't a full Bard yet, but he will be, soon, and we work together just fine. So I'd say that if this book is right, it looks like there won't be any problem with you giving Maeve a little brother or sister when the time comes."

Beth stared, and slowly dejected disbelief turned to radiant happiness, her eyes sparkling with tears of hope. "But will he—? Would he—?"

"He will, and he would," Eric said firmly, recklessly promising Hosea's aid as he closed the book. He already knew enough of the big man's character to feel safe in making such an offer. Kory handed the tome back to Fox, who staggered under its weight this time.

"And I think that calls for a little celebration."